TO THE ENDS OF THE EARTH

William Golding was born in 1911 and educated at his local grammar school and Brasenose College, Oxford. He published a volume of poems in 1934 and during the war served in the Royal Navy. Afterwards he returned to being a schoolmaster in Salisbury. *Lord of the Flies*, his first novel, was an immediate success, and was followed by a series of remarkable novels, including *The Inheritors, Pincher Martin* and *The Spire*. He won the Booker Prize for *Rites of Passage* in 1980, was awarded the Nobel Prize for Literature in 1983, and was knighted in 1988. He died in 1993.

Books by
Sir William Golding
1911–1993
Nobel Prize for Literature

Fiction
LORD OF THE FLIES
THE INHERITORS
PINCHER MARTIN
FREE FALL
THE SPIRE
THE PYRAMID
THE SCORPION GOD
DARKNESS VISIBLE
THE PAPER MEN
RITES OF PASSAGE
CLOSE QUARTERS
FIRE DOWN BELOW
TO THE ENDS OF THE EARTH
(comprising *Rites of Passage*,
Close Quarters and *Fire Down Below*
in a revised text; foreword by the author)
THE DOUBLE TONGUE

Essays
THE HOT GATES
A MOVING TARGET

Travel
AN EGYPTIAN JOURNAL

Plays
THE BRASS BUTTERFLY
LORD OF THE FLIES
adapted for the stage by
Nigel Williams

WILLIAM GOLDING
TO THE ENDS
OF THE EARTH

A SEA TRILOGY
comprising

Rites of Passage

Close Quarters

and

Fire Down Below

Published by
Faber and Faber

LONDON

First published in 1991
by Faber and Faber Limited
3 Queen Square London WC1N 3AU
This film tie-in edition first published in 2005

Photoset by RefineCatch Limited, Bungay, Suffolk
Printed in England by Mackays of Chatham, Kent

A CIP record for this book
is available from the British Library

ISBN 0–571–22541–1

2 4 6 8 10 9 7 5 3 1

CONTENTS

Foreword

Courteous historians will generally concede that since no one can describe events with perfect accuracy written history is a branch of fiction. Similarly the novelist who deals with "before now" must pay some attention, respectful or not, to history. He is faced with a spectrum. History lies at one end—infra-red perhaps—and what is thought of as fiction occupies the opposite end—the ultra-violet. If he fails to employ his utmost accuracy in terms of the succession of commonly known events—Declaration of Independence, Battle of Waterloo *et cetera*—he does violate some kind of civilized expectation. He must admit to writing history with the same good humour as a historian shows when admitting that he writes fiction. It is a question of degree. The novelist, more allied than the historian to rogues and vagabonds, gets away with what he can. Generally he will find research such a bore! If you have a story to tell why not go straight on and rely on what accumulated in your head? After all, the reader will pick up your book in hopeful anticipation. He will be very willing to suspend that celebrated disbelief and be on your side. Of course there is a limit. At the play he will accept Sartre's picture of Kean and the Prince Regent roystering together because the piece is a comedy. But who, having an average knowledge of European history, has ever felt easy at Schiller's scene between Queen Elizabeth and Mary Queen of Scots? We all know they never met and our principal awareness as we watch or read is that tragedy is not being deepened, but history trivialized. So let the novelist respect history where he can!

The present volume began as three separate books and

I have made tentative gestures towards turning them into a trilogy. But the truth is I did not foresee volumes two and three when I sat down to write volume one. Only after volume one was published did I come to realize that I had left Edmund Talbot, a ship and a whole ship's company, to say nothing of myself, lolloping about in the Atlantic with their voyage no more than half completed. I got them some way on with a second volume and home and dry with a third.

It is no part of my business to give descriptions of how I, or I suppose any writer, will work. But I have to admit that some of the experiences of the writing were odd to say the least. For one thing the scene of Talbot boarding the ship, the ship herself and her people, emigrants and passengers was extraordinary and more like a memory than an imagination: which perhaps is no more than to say that our memories become imaginations and our imaginations memories. But whatever the reason, the beginning of *Rites of Passage* provided me with much material which I had not known was concealed there. People casually mentioned had their own lives and future. Or as Edmund Talbot might declare from his simple faith in the classics, they were there *in posse* who were later there *in esse*. The old ship herself, a main character in the story, provided the Necessity which confined people and things to certain actions and events, not others.

Nevertheless, now that all three volumes are to appear under one cover, changes and corrections and additions—to say nothing of omissions—are necessary. *Rites of Passage* was first published in 1980 and *Close Quarters* in 1987. I did not refer back to the one book as I wrote the other, relying on my unaided memory which proved to be somewhat defective. I kept in mind certain examples of people who, when publishing several volumes under one cover, had made major alterations to the text and in my opinion seriously damaged their original work. I have corrected some errors of historical fact. In sheer carelessness I had reversed the position of poop and quarterdeck, a piece of botched carpentry which remarkably enough was adjusted by a stroke of the pen—see what a delicate, not to say ethereal fabric a fiction is! Other corrections encyst a tiny fragment of arcane knowledge with which a correspondent has delighted me. Some corrections are the result of severe remarks made by professional critics, those seldom welcomed teachers.

Sometimes I have gone my own way. I am aware that people of Talbot's social standing, let alone others among my characters, would have been affronted had a friend addressed them by their Christian name. To do so would have presumed an extraordinary degree of intimacy. Nor would such people customarily have made use of such contractions as "aren't" or "don't". But amusing pastiche as it might be for a few pages to reproduce that state of affairs throughout it would end by wearying the reader. I preferred to offer him a concocted language which only now and then reverted to an archaism as a reminder of "before now". There is one sort of critic with whom I will take what I will call *mild issue*. He or she believes apparently that a word only comes into being when it is printed in a dictionary. But a novelist, wading through that changing, coloured, glittering and stormy plenum in which he works will claim—*must* claim—that any word was likely to be in use for at least a generation before a lexicographer pinned it to his page. Of course there are many exceptions to that rule and to respect the authority of a dictionary is wise. But we must not be slavish, for that is the shortest way to a dull and sterile page. Thus, for example, "squeegee" appeared in print for the first time in 1844, so I was gently rebuked for using the word as if it had been in use in, say, 1813. Yet I should be very surprised if Nelson (died 1805) had not known of the "squeegee" and its use about the deck—and known too of "squeege" as a verb—since that appeared in print as early as 1782. This leads conveniently enough to a note about "Navalese" or what Mr Talbot called "Tarpaulin", a better word, I think, and hope to find one day in the third edition of the *Oxford English Dictionary*. I learnt this language first of all from books and later from service in the Royal Navy during the Second World War. The language was one of my few pleasures during that experience and I immersed myself in it to the extent that by the end of the war professionals sometimes had difficulty in knowing what I was talking about. I believe it was Kipling who declared that the Navy always had the right words for things. Certainly I have felt it was so, even in the bits which I invented myself.

Tarpaulin, then, pervades this book and so does class, or to use a word better understood by my characters, "rank". This is a difficult subject since we British are still so dunked from childhood in that hierarchy we become unaware of it. Even so, English readers will pick up the social nuances readily enough since in a book they are seen objectively. My American readers will have some difficulty in this, unless of course they live and have been brought up in New England where much the same system was alive and kicking in the sixties when I became acquainted with it.

I would like to say a word on the subject of the optimism which some readers have thought to detect increasingly throughout the three volumes. As far as Great Britain was concerned Edmund Talbot and his class had considerable cause for optimism. A coalition of nations led by Britain had defeated Napoleon and they, or the British at least, would rule the world for more or less the whole century. In any case, whether the reader agrees with that statement or not, the three volumes are thought to be the work of Edmund Talbot, an intelligent but brash and optimistic young man. I myself am commonly thought to be a pessimist, a diagnosis with which I heartily disagree. Perhaps then it was my own optimism which gained the upper hand in the daily toil of putting down words. So Edmund Talbot or perhaps I myself found myself, himself or ourselves less and less inclined to portray life as a hopeless affair in the face of *this* enormity, *that* infinity and *those* tragic circumstances, particularly the ones which plagued poor Robert James Colley. It is my conviction, intuition, or what you may if you please call only my personal opinion, that both comedy and tragedy outside books as well as in them are subsumed in an ultimate Dazzle. Neither is a Cosmic truth, only a vivid universal one. (The separation of the meanings of Cosmic and universal is my own and unsupported as yet by the dictionary.) That was my conclusion as I was writing. I was bored with thinking—which fact will be laid to my discredit as a blasphemy if not abdication. But there are higher languages than that of the toiling mind, deeper intuitions than can be overtaken by the microscope or telescope, even a space one. They require metaphors, and mixed ones at that. So let Edmund FitzHenry Talbot achieve the degree of happiness of which he is capable. Let Mr and Mrs Prettiman at once fail and succeed in their impossible quest, finding thereby a passion which Edmund could never know.

And now my poor old ship must set sail on her last voyage. I must apologize to her for one or two inadequacies, some inaccuracies, one appalling howler concerning her construction and here and there a bit of fudge. She is or was, I have to remember, a piece of imagination which had to confront an imaginary sea. But she came to have a kind of reality, had the weight of a ship and moved with sails as ships did and do. She even had a spark of life as sailors always come to feel whether they say so or no. I am sure Edmund allowed himself to be half-convinced, standing as he did halfway between the classic and the romantic. As men forget their war service at last he will have forgotten the stench and sodden bilges of the unnamed ship and remembered only those moonlit sails, that world of whiteness which smote and blinded the very apple of the eye. However, I did have a name for her. I found it in the admiralty lists of those years and meant to include it somewhere but got no further than references which owe a certain quality to my knowledge: but I have forgotten both the name and the references so those correspondents who want to know what it was must be content with my apologies. For my part I should be happy if she were to be known only as a *Good Read*.

WILLIAM GOLDING

June 1991

TO THE ENDS OF THE EARTH

Rites of Passage

(1)

Honoured godfather,

With those words I begin the journal I engaged myself to keep for you—no words could be more suitable!

Very well then. The place: on board the ship at last. The year: you know it. The date? Surely what matters is that it is the first day of my passage to the other side of the world; in token whereof I have this moment inscribed the number "one" at the top of this page. For what I am about to write must be a record of our *first day*. The month or day of the week can signify little since in our long passage from the south of Old England to the Antipodes we shall pass through the geometry of all four seasons!

This very morning before I left the hall I paid a visit to my young brothers, and they were such a trial to old Dobbie! Young Lionel performed what he conceived to be an Aborigine's war dance. Young Percy lay on his back and rubbed his belly, meanwhile venting horrid groans to convey the awful results of eating me! I cuffed them both into attitudes of decent dejection, then descended again to where my mother and father were waiting. My mother— contrived a tear or two? Oh no, it was the genuine article, for there was at that point a warmth in my own bosom which might not have been thought manly. Why, even my father—We have, I believe, paid more attention to sentimental Goldsmith and Richardson than lively old Fielding and Smollett! Your lordship would indeed have been convinced of my worth had you heard the invocations over me, as if I were a convict in irons rather than a young gentleman going to assist the governor in the

3

administration of one of His Majesty's colonies! I felt much the better for my parents' evident feelings—and I felt the better for my own feelings too! Your godson is a good enough fellow at bottom. Recovery took him all the way down the drive, past the lodge and as far as the first turning by the mill!

Well then, to resume, I am aboard. I climbed the bulging and tarry side of what once, in her young days, may have been one of Britain's formidable *wooden walls*. I stepped through a kind of low doorway into the darkness of some deck or other and gagged at my first breath. Good God, it was quite nauseous! There was much bustling and hustling about in an artificial twilight. A fellow who announced himself as my servant conducted me to a kind of hutch against the vessel's side, which he assured me was my cabin. He is a limping old fellow with a sharp face and a bunch of white hair on either side of it. These bunches are connected over his pate by a shining baldness.

"My good man," said I, "what is this stink?"

He stuck his sharp nose up and peered round as if he might see the stink in the darkness rather than nose it. "Stink, sir? What stink, sir?"

"The *stink*," said I, my hand over my nose and mouth as I gagged, "the fetor, the stench, call it what you will!"

He is a sunny fellow, this Wheeler. He smiled at me then as if the deck, close over our heads, had opened and let in some light.

"Lord, sir!" said he. "You'll soon get used to that!"

"I do not wish to get used to it! Where is the captain of this vessel?"

Wheeler dowsed the light of his countenance and opened the door of my hutch for me.

"There's nothing Captain Anderson could do either, sir," said he. "It's sand and gravel you see. The new ships has iron ballast but she's older than that. If she was

4

betwixt and between in age, as you might say, they'd have dug it out. But not her. She's too old you see. They wouldn't want to go stirring about down there, sir."

"It must be a graveyard then!"

Wheeler thought for a moment.

"As to that, I can't say, sir, not having been in her previous. Now you sit here for a bit and I'll bring a brandy."

With that, he was gone before I could bear to speak again and have to inhale more of the *'tween decks* air. So there I was and here I am.

Let me describe what will be my lodging until I can secure more fitting accommodation. The hutch contains a sleeping place like a trough laid along the ship's side with two drawers built under it. Wheeler informs me these standing bedplaces have been provided for the passengers as we go far south and such "bunks" are thought warmer than cots or hammocks. At one end of the hutch a flap lets down as a writing table and there is a canvas bowl with a bucket under it at the other. I must suppose the ship contains a more *commodious* area for the performance of our natural functions! There is room for a mirror above the bowl and two shelves for books at the foot of the bunk. A canvas chair is the movable furniture of this noble apartment. The door has a fairly big opening in it at eye-level through which some daylight filters, and the wall on either side of it is furnished with hooks. The floor, or deck as I must call it, is rutted deep enough to twist an ankle. I suppose these ruts were made by the iron wheels of her gun trolleys in the days when she was young and frisky enough to sport a full set of weapons! The hutch is new but the ceiling—the deckhead?—and the side of the ship beyond my bunk, old, worn and splintered and hugely patched. Imagine me, asked to live in such a coop, such a sty! However, I shall put up with it good-humouredly enough until I can see the captain. Already the act of breathing has moderated my awareness of our stench and the generous glass of brandy that Wheeler brought has gone near to reconciling me to it.

But what a noisy world this wooden one is! The south-west wind that keeps us at anchor booms and whistles in the rigging and thunders over her—over *our* (for I am determined to use this long voyage in becoming wholly master of the sea affair)—over our furled canvas. Flurries of rain beat a retreat of kettle-drums over every inch of her. If that were not enough, there comes from forward and on this very deck the baaing of sheep, lowing of cattle, shouts of men and yes, the shrieks of women! There is noise enough here too. My hutch, or sty, is only one on this side of the deck of a half-a-dozen such, faced by a like number on the other side. A stark lobby separates the two rows and this lobby is interrupted only by the ascending and enormous cylinder of our *mizzen mast*. Aft of the lobby, Wheeler assures me, is the dining saloon for the passengers with the offices of necessity on either side of it. In the lobby dim figures pass or stand in clusters. They— we—are the passengers I must suppose; and why an ancient ship of the line such as this one has been so transformed into a travelling store-ship and farm and passenger conveyance is only to be explained by the straits my lords of the Admiralty are in with more than six hundred warships in commission.

Bates, the saloon steward, has told me just this minute that we dine in an hour's time at four o'clock. On my remarking that I proposed to request more ample accommodation he paused for a moment's reflection, then replied it would be a matter of some difficulty and that he advised me to wait for a while. On my expressing some indignation that such a decrepit vessel should be used for such a voyage, he, standing in the door of the saloon with a napkin over his arm, lent me as much as he could of a

6

seaman's philosophy—as: Lord sir she'll float till she sinks, and Lord sir she was built to be sunk; with such a lecture on lying in ordinary with no one aboard but the boatswain and the carpenter, so much about the easiness of lying to a hawser *in the good old way* rather than to a nasty iron chain that rattles like a corpse on a gibbet, he has sunk my heart clear down to her filthy ballast! He had such a dismissiveness of copper bottoms! I find we are no more than *pitched within and without* like the oldest vessel of all and suppose her first commander was none other than Captain Noah! Bates's parting comfort to me was that he was sure she is "safer in a blow than many a stiffer vessel". *Safer!* "For," said he, "if we get into a bit of a blow she'll render like an old boot." To tell the truth he left me with much of the brandy's good work undone. After all that, I found it was positively required I should remove all articles that I should need on the voyage from my chests before they were *struck down below*! Such is the confusion aboard this vessel I can find no one who has the authority to countermand this singularly foolish order. I have resigned myself therefore, used Wheeler for some of this unpacking, set out my books myself, and seen my chests taken away. I should be angry if the situation were not so farcical. However, I had a certain delight in some of the talk between the fellows who took them off, the words were so perfectly nautical. I have laid Falconer's *Marine Dictionary* by my pillow; for I am determined to speak the tarry language as perfectly as any of these rolling fellows!

LATER

We have dined by the light of an ample stern window at two long tables in a great muddle. Nobody knew anything. There were no officers, the servants were harassed, the food poor, my fellow-passengers in a temper, and their ladies approaching the hysterics. But the sight of the other vessels at anchor outside the stern window was undeniably exciting. Wheeler, my staff and guide, says it is the remainder of the convoy. He assures me that the confusion aboard will diminish and that, as he phrases it, we shall *shake down*—presumably in the way the sand and gravel has shaken down, until—if I may judge by some of the passengers—we shall stink like the vessel. Your lordship may observe a certain pettishness in my words. Indeed, had it not been for a tolerable wine I should be downright angry. Our Noah, one Captain Anderson, has not chosen to appear. I shall make myself known to him at the first opportunity but now it is dark. Tomorrow morning I propose to examine the topography of the vessel and form an acquaintance with the better sort of officer if there be any. We have ladies, some young, some middling, some old. We have some oldish gentlemen, a youngish army officer and a younger parson. This last poor fellow tried to ask a blessing on our meal and fell to eating as bashful as a bride. I have not been able to see Mr Prettiman but suppose he is aboard.

Wheeler tells me the wind will *veer* during the night and we shall get a-weigh, make sail; be off, start on our vast journey when the tide turns. I have told him I am a good sailor and have observed that same peculiar light, which is not quite a smile but rather an involuntary expansiveness, flit across his face. I made an immediate resolution to teach the man a lesson in manners at the first opportunity—but as I write these very words the pattern of our wooden world changes. There is a volleying and thundering up there from what must be the loosened canvas. There is the shrilling of pipes. Good God, can human throats emit such noises? But *that* and *that* must be the signal guns! Outside my hutch a passenger has fallen with many oaths and the ladies are shrieking, the cattle are lowing and the sheep baaing. All is confusion. Perhaps then the cows are baaing, the sheep lowing and the ladies damning the ship and her timbers to all hell fire? The canvas bowl into which Wheeler poured water for me has shifted in its *gimbals* and now lies at a slight angle.

Our anchor has been plucked out of the sand and gravel of Old England. I shall have no connection with my native soil for three, or it may be four or five, years. I own that even with the prospect of interesting and advantageous employment before me it is a solemn thought.

How else, since we are being solemn, should I conclude the account of my first day at sea than with an expression of my profound gratitude? You have set my foot on the ladder and however high I climb—for I must warn your lordship that my ambition is boundless!—I shall never forget whose kindly hand first helped me upwards. That he may never be found unworthy of that hand, nor *do* anything unworthy of it—is the prayer—the *intention*—of your lordship's grateful godson.

EDMUND TALBOT

(2)

I have placed the number "2" at the beginning of this entry though I do not know how much I shall set down today. Circumstances are all against careful composition. There has been so little strength in my limbs—the prive-house, the loo—I beg its pardon, I do not know what it should be called since in strict sea-language the *heads* are at the forward end of the vessel, the young gentlemen should have a *roundhouse* and the lieutenants should have—I do not know what the lieutenants should have. The constant movement of the vessel and the need constantly to adjust my body to it—

Your lordship was pleased to recommend that I should conceal nothing. Do you not remember conducting me from the library with a friendly arm across my shoulder, ejaculating in your jovial way, "Tell all, my boy! Hold nothing back! Let me live again through you!" The devil is in it, then, I have been most confoundedly seasick and kept my bunk. After all, Seneca off Naples was in my predicament was he not—but you will remember—and if even a stoic philosopher is reduced by a few miles of lumpy water, what will become of all us poor fellows on higher seas? I must own to have been reduced already to salt tears by exhaustion and to have been discovered in such a womanish state by Wheeler! However, he is a worthy fellow. I explained my tears by my exhaustion and he agreed cheerfully.

"You, sir," said he, "would hunt all day and dance all night at the end of it. Now if you was to put me, or most seamen, on a horse, our kidneys would be shook clear down to our knees."

I groaned some sort of answer, and heard Wheeler extract the cork from a bottle.

"Consider, sir," said he, "it is but learning to ride a ship. You will do that soon enough."

The thought comforted me; but not as much as the most delectable odour which *came o'er my spirits like the warm south*. I opened my eyes and lo, what had Wheeler done but produce a huge dose of paregoric? The comfortable taste took me straight back to the nursery and *this* time with none of the melancholy attendant on memories of childhood and home! I sent Wheeler away, dozed for a while then slept. Truly, the poppy would have done more for old Seneca than his philosophy!

I woke from strange dreams and in such thick darkness that I knew not where I was but recollected all too soon and found our motion sensibly increased. I shouted at once for Wheeler. At the third shout—accompanied I admit with more oaths than I generally consider consistent with either common sense or gentlemanly conduct—he opened the door of my hutch.

"Help me out of here, Wheeler! I must get some air!"

"Now you lie still for a while, sir, and in a bit you'll be right as a trivet! I'll set out a bowl."

Is there, can there be, anything sillier, less comforting than the prospect of imitating a trivet? I saw them in my mind's eye as smug and self-righteous as a convocation of Methodists. I cursed the fellow to his face. However, in the upshot he was being reasonable enough. He explained that we were having a *blow*. He thought my greatcoat with the triple capes too fine a garment to risk in flying salt spray. He added, mysteriously, that he did not wish me to look like a chaplain! He himself, however, had in his possession an unused suit of yellow oilskin. Ruefully enough, he said he had bought it for a gentleman who in the event had never embarked. It was just my size and I should have it for no more than he had given for it. Then at the end of the voyage I might sell it back to him at second hand if I chose. I closed there and then with this very advantageous offer, for the air was stifling me and I longed for the open. He eased and tied me into the suit, thrust India rubber boots on my feet and adjusted an oilskin hat on my head. I wish your lordship could have seen me for I must have looked a proper sailor, no matter how unsteady I felt! Wheeler assisted me into the lobby, which was running with water. He kept up his prattle as, for example, that we should learn to have one leg shorter than the other like mountain sheep. I told him testily that since I visited France during the late peace, I knew when a deck was atilt, since I had not walked across on the water. I got out into the waist and leaned against the bulwarks on the larboard, that is the downward, side of the deck. The main chains and the huge spread of the ratlines—oh Falconer, Falconer!—extended above my head, and above that a quantity of nameless ropes hummed and thrummed and whistled. There was an eye of light showing still, but spray flew over from the high, starboard side and clouds that raced past us seemed no higher than the masts. We had company, of course, the rest of the convoy being on our larboard hand and already showing lights, though spray and a smoky mist mixed with rain obscured them. I breathed with exquisite ease after the fetor of my hutch and could not but hope that this extreme, even violent, weather would blow some of the stench out of her. Somewhat restored I gazed about me, and found for the first time since the anchor was raised my intellect and interest reviving. Staring up and back, I could see two helmsmen at the wheel, black, tarpaulined figures, their faces lighted from below as they glanced alternately into the illuminated compass, then up at the set of the sails. We had few of these spread to the wind and I supposed it was due to

the inclemency of the weather but learnt later from
Wheeler—that walking Falconer—that it was so we
should not run clear away from the rest of the convoy
since we "have the legs" of all but a few. How he knows, if
indeed he knows, is a mystery, but he declares we shall
speak the squadron off Ushant, detach our other ship of
the line to them, take over one of theirs, be convoyed by
her to the latitude of Gibraltar after which we proceed
alone, secured from capture by nothing but the few guns
we have left and our intimidating appearance! Is this fair
or just? Do their lordships not realize what a future Secretary of State they have cast so casually on the waters? Let
us hope that like the Biblical bread they get me back
again! However, the die is cast and I must take my chance.
I stayed there, then, my back to the bulwark, and drank
the wind and rain. I concluded that most of my extraordinary weakness had been due more to the fetor of the *hutch*
than to the motion of the vessel.

There were now the veriest dregs of daylight but I was
rewarded for my vigil by sight of the sickness I had
escaped. There emerged from our lobby into the wind
and rain of the waist, a parson! I supposed he was the
same fellow who had tried to ask a blessing on our first
dinner and been heard by no one but the Almighty. He
wore knee-breeches, a long coat and bands that beat in the
wind at his throat like a trapped bird at a window! He
held his hat and wig crushed on with both hands and he
staggered first one way, then the other, like a drunken
crab. (Of *course* your lordship has seen a drunken crab!)
This parson turned, like all people unaccustomed to a
tilted deck, and tried to claw his way up it rather than
down. He was, I saw, about to vomit, for his complexion
was the mixed pallor and greenness of mouldy cheese.
Before I could shout a warning he did indeed vomit, then
slid down to the deck. He got on his knees—not, I think,

for the purpose of devotion!—then stood at the very moment when a *heave* from the ship gave the movement an additional impetus. The result was he came, half-running, half-flying down the deck and might well have gone clean through the larboard ratlines had I not grabbed him by the collar! I had a glimpse of a wet, green face, then the servant who performs for the starboard passengers the offices that our Wheeler performs for the larboard ones rushed out of the lobby, seized the little man under the arms, begged my pardon and lugged him back out of sight. I was damning the parson for befouling my oilskins when a heave, shudder and convenient spout of mixed rain and sea water cleaned him off me. For some reason, though the water stung my face it put me in a good humour. Philosophy and religion—what are they when the wind blows and the water gets up in lumps? I stood there, holding on with one hand, and began positively to enjoy all this confusion, lit as it was by the last lees of light. Our huge old ship with her few and shortened sails from which the rain cascaded was beating into this sea and therefore shouldering the waves at an angle, like a bully forcing his way through a dense crowd. And as the bully might encounter here and there a like spirit, so she (our ship) was hindered now and then, or dropped or lifted or, it may be, struck a blow in the face that made all her forepart, then the waist and the afterdeck to foam and wash with white water. I began, as Wheeler had put it, to *ride a ship*. Her masts leaned a little. The shrouds to windward were taut, those to leeward slack, or very near it. The huge cable of her *mainbrace* swung out to leeward between the masts; and now here is a point which I would wish to make. Comprehension of this vast engine is not to be come at gradually nor by poring over diagrams in Marine Dictionaries! It comes, when it comes, at a bound. In that semi-darkness between one wave and the next I found the ship and the sea comprehensible not merely in terms of her mechanical ingenuity but as a—a what? As a steed, a conveyance, a means working to an end. This was a pleasure that I had not anticipated. It was, I thought with perhaps a touch of complacency, quite an addition to my understanding! A single sheet, a rope attached to the lower and leeward corner of a sail, was vibrating some yards above my head, wildly indeed, but understandably! As if to reinforce the comprehension, at the moment when I was examining the rope and its function there came a huge thud from forward, an explosion of water and spray, and the rope's vibration changed—was halved at the mid-point so that for a while its length traced out two narrow ellipses laid end to end—illustrated, in fact, the *first harmonic*, like that point on a violin string which if touched accurately enough will give the player the note an octave above the open one.

But this ship has more strings than a violin, more than a lute, more I think than a harp, and under the wind's tuition she makes a ferocious music. I will own that after a while I could have done with human company, but the Church has succumbed and the Army too. No lady can possibly be anywhere but in her bunk. As for the Navy— well, it is literally in its element. Its members stand here and there encased in tarpaulin, black with faces pale only by contrast. At a little distance they resemble nothing so much as rocks with the tide washing over them.

When the light had quite faded I felt my way back to my hutch and shouted for Wheeler, who came at once, got me out of my oilskins, hung the suit on the hook where it at once took up a drunken angle. I told him to bring me a lamp but he told me it was not possible. This put me in a temper but he explained the reason well enough. Lamps are dangerous to us all since once overset there is no controlling them. But I might have a candle if I cared to pay for it since a candle dowses itself when it falls, and in any case I must take a few safety measures in the management of it. Wheeler himself had a supply of candles. I replied that I had thought such articles were commonly obtained from the purser. After a short pause Wheeler agreed. He had not thought I would wish to deal directly with the purser who lived apart and was seldom seen. Gentlemen used not to have any traffic with him but employed their servants who ensured that the transaction was honest and above board. "For," said he, "you know what pursers are!" I agreed with an air of simplicity which in an instant—you observe, sir, that I was coming to myself—concealed a revised estimate of Mr Wheeler, his fatherly concern and his willingness to serve me! I made a mental note that I was determined always to see round and through him farther than he supposed that he saw round and through me. So by eleven o'clock at night—*six bells* according to the book—behold me seated at my table-flap with this journal open before me. But what pages of trivia! Here are none of the interesting events, acute observations and the, dare I say, sparks of wit with which it is my first ambition to entertain your lordship! However, our passage is but begun.

(3)

The third day has passed with even worse weather than the others. The state of our ship, or that portion of it which falls under my notice, is inexpressibly sordid. The deck, even in our lobby, streams with sea water, rain, and other fouler liquids, which find their way inexorably under the batten on which the bottom of the hutch door is supposed to close. Nothing, of course, fits. For if it did, what would happen in the next minute when this confounded vessel has changed her position from savaging the summit of a roller to plunging into the gulf on the other side of it? When this morning I had fought my way into the dining saloon—finding, by the way, nothing hot to drink there—I was unable for a while to fight my way out again. The door was jammed. I rattled the handle peevishly, tugged at it, then found myself hanging from it as she (the monstrous vessel has become "she" as a termagant mistress) she lurched. That in itself was not so bad but what followed might have killed me. For the door snapped open so that the handle flashed in a semicircle with a radius equal to the width of the opening! I saved myself from fatal or serious injury by the same instinct that drops a cat always on its feet. This alternate stiffness then too easy compliance with one's wishes by a door—one of those necessary objects in life on which I had never before bestowed much interest—seemed to me so animated a piece of impertinence on the part of a few planks of wood I could have believed the very genii, the dryads and hamadryads of the material from which our floating box is composed, had refused to leave their ancient dwelling and come to sea with us! But no—it was merely—"merely"—dear God what a world!—the good ship doing what Bates called "rendering like an old boot".

I was on all fours, the door having been caught neatly against the transverse or thwartships bulkhead (as Falconer would have it) by a metal springhook, when a figure came through the opening that set me laughing crazily. It was one of our lieutenants and he stumped along casually at such an angle to the deck—for the deck itself was my plane of reference—that he seemed to be (albeit unconsciously) clownish and he put me in a good humour at once for all my bruises. I climbed back to the smaller and possibly more exclusive of the two dining tables—that one I mean set directly under the great stern window—and sat once more. All is firmly fixed, of course. Shall I discourse to your lordship on "rigging screws"? I think not. Well then, observe me drinking ale at the table with this officer. He is one Mr Cumbershum, holding the King's Commission and therefore to be accounted a gentleman though he sucked in his ale with as nauseating an indifference to polite usage as you would find in a carter. He is forty, I suppose, with black hair cut short but growing nearly down to his eyebrows. He has been slashed over the head and is one of our heroes, however unformed his manners. Doubtless we shall hear *that* story before we have done! At least he was a source of information. He called the weather rough but not very. He thought those passengers who were staying in their bunks—this with a meaning glance at me—and taking light refreshment there, were wise, since we have no surgeon and a broken limb, as he phrased it, could be a nuisance to everyone! We have no surgeon, it appears, because even the most inept of young sawbones can do better for himself ashore. It is a mercenary consideration that gave me a new view of what I had always considered a profession with a degree of disinterestedness about it. I remarked that in that case we must expect an unusual incidence of mortality and it was fortunate we had a chaplain to perform all the other rites, from the first to the last. At this, Cumbershum choked, took his mouth away from the pot and addressed me in tones of profound astonishment.

"A chaplain, sir? We have no chaplain!"

"Believe me, I have seen him."

"No, sir."

"But law requires one aboard every ship of the line does it not?"

"Captain Anderson would wish to avoid it; and since parsons are in as short supply as surgeons it is as easy to avoid the one as it is difficult to procure the other."

"Come, come, Mr Cumbershum! Are not seamen notoriously superstitious? Do you not require the occasional invocation of Mumbo Jumbo?"

"Captain Anderson does not, sir. Nor did the great Captain Cook, I would have you know. He was a notable atheist and would as soon have taken the plague into his ship as a parson."

"Good God!"

"I assure you, sir."

"But how—my dear Mr Cumbershum! How is order to be maintained? You take away the keystone and the whole arch falls!"

Mr Cumbershum did not appear to take my point. I saw that my language must not be figurative with such a man and rephrased.

"Your crew is not all officers! Forward there, is a crowd of individuals on whose obedience the order of the whole depends, the success of the voyage depends!"

"They are well enough."

"But sir—just as in a state the supreme argument for the continuance of a national church is the whip it holds in one hand and the—dare I say—illusory prize in the other, so here—"

But Mr Cumbershum was wiping his lips with the brown back of his fist and getting to his feet.

"I don't know about all that," he said. "Captain Anderson would not have a chaplain in the ship if he could avoid it—even if one was on offer. The fellow you saw was a passenger and, I believe, a very new-hatched parson."

I remembered how the poor devil had clawed up the wrong side of the deck and spewed right in the eye of the wind.

"You must be right, sir. He is certainly a very new-hatched seaman!"

I then informed Mr Cumbershum that at a convenient time I must make myself known to the captain. When he looked surprised I told him who I am, mentioned your lordship's name and that of His Excellency your brother and outlined the position I should hold in the governor's entourage—or as much as it is politic to outline, since you know what other business I am charged with. I did not add what I then thought. This was that since the deputy-governor is a naval officer, if Mr Cumbershum was an average example of the breed I should give the entourage some tone it would stand in need of!

My information rendered Mr Cumbershum more expansive. He sat down again. He owned he had never been in such a ship or on such a voyage. It was all strange to him and he thought to the other officers too. We were a ship of war, store ship, a packet boat or passenger vessel, we were all things, which amounted to—and here I believe I detected a rigidity of mind that is to be expected in an officer at once junior and elderly—amounted to being nothing. He supposed that at the end of this voyage she would moor for good, send down her top masts and be a sop to the governor's dignity, firing nothing but salutes as he went to and fro.

"Which," he added darkly, "is just as well, Mr Talbot sir, just as well!"

"Take me with you, sir."

Mr Cumbershum waited until the tilted servant had supplied us again. Then he glanced through the door at the empty and streaming lobby.

"God knows what would happen to her Mr Talbot if we was to fire the few great guns left in her."

"The devil is in it then!"

"I beg you will not repeat my opinion to the common sort of passenger. We must not alarm them. I have said more than I should."

"I was prepared with some philosophy to risk the violence of the enemy; but that a spirited defence on our part should do no more than increase our danger is, is—"

"It is war, Mr Talbot; and peace or war, a ship is always in danger. The only other vessel of our rate to undertake this enormous voyage, a converted warship I mean, converted so to speak to general purposes—she was named the *Guardian*, I think—yes, the *Guardian*, did not complete the journey. But now I remember she ran on an iceberg in the Southern Ocean, so her rate and age was not material."

I got my breath again. I detected through the impassivity of the man's exterior a determination to roast me, precisely because I had made the importance of my position clear to him. I laughed good-humouredly and turned the thing off. I thought it a moment to try my prentice hand at the flattery which your lordship recommended to me as a possible *passe-partout*.

"With such devoted and skilful officers as we are provided with, sir, I am sure we need fear nothing."

Cumbershum stared at me as if he suspected my words of some hidden and perhaps sarcastic meaning.

"Devoted, sir? Devoted?"

It was time to "go about," as we nautical fellows say.

"Do you see this left hand of mine, sir? Yon door did it. See how scraped and bruised the palm is, you would call it my larboard hand I believe. I have a bruise on the larboard hand! Is that not perfectly nautical? But I shall follow your first advice. I shall take some food first with a glass of brandy, then turn in to keep my limbs entire. You will drink with me, sir?"

Cumbershum shook his head.

"I go on watch," he said. "But do you settle your stomach. However, there is one more thing. Have a care I beg you of Wheeler's paregoric. It is the very strongest stuff, and as the voyage goes on the price will increase out of all reason. Steward—what's your name—Bates! A glass of brandy for Mr Talbot!"

He left me then with as courteous an inclination of the head as you would expect from a man leaning like the pitch of a roof. It was a sight to make one bosky out of hand. Indeed, the warming properties of strong drink give it a more seductive appeal at sea than it ever has ashore, I think. So I determined with that glass to regulate my use of it. I turned warily in my fastened seat and inspected the world of furious water that stretched and slanted beyond our stern window. I must own that it afforded me the scantiest consolation; the more so as I reflected that in the happiest outcome of our voyage there was not a single billow, wave, swell, *comber* that I shall cross in one direction without having, in a few years time, to cross it in the other! I sat for a great while eyeing my brandy, staring into its aromatic and tiny pool of liquid. I found little comfort in sight at that time except the evident fact that our other passengers were even more lethargic than I was. The thought at once determined me to eat. I got down some nearly fresh bread and a little mild cheese. On top of this I swallowed my brandy and gave my stomach a *dare* to misbehave; and so frightened it with the threat of an addiction to small ale, thence to brandy, then to Wheeler's paregoric and after that to the ultimate destructiveness of an habitual recourse, Lord help us, to laudanum that the poor, misused organ lay as quiet as a mouse that hears a kitchenmaid rattle the fire in the morning! I *turned in* and *got my head down* and *turned out* and ate; then toiled at these very pages by the light of my candle—giving your lordship, I doubt it not, a queasy piece of "living through" me for which I am as heartily sorry as yourself could be! I believe the whole ship, from the farm animals up or down to your humble servant, is nauseated to one degree or another—always excepting of course the leaning and streaming tarpaulins.

(4)

And how is your lordship today? In the best of health and spirits, I trust, as I am! There is such a crowd of events at the back of my mind, tongue, pen, what you will, that my greatest difficulty is to know how to get them on the paper! In brief, all things about our wooden world have altered for the better. I do not mean that I have got my *sea legs*; for even now that I understand the physical laws of our motion they continue to exhaust me! But the motion itself is easier. It was some time in the hours of darkness that I woke—a shouted order perhaps—and feeling if anything even more stretched on the rack of our lumbering, bullying progress. For days, as I lay, there had come at irregular intervals a kind of impediment from our watery shoulderings that I cannot describe except to say it was as if our carriage wheels had caught for a moment on the drag, then released themselves. It was a movement that as I lay in my trough, my bunk, my feet to our stern, my head to our bows—a movement that would thrust my head more firmly into the pillow, which being made of granite transmitted the impulsion throughout the remainder of my person.

Even though I now understood the cause, the repetition was unutterably wearisome. But as I awoke there were loud movements on deck, the thundering of many feet, then shouted orders prolonged into what one might suppose to be the vociferations of the damned. I had not known (even when crossing the Channel) what an *aria* can be made of the simple injunction, "Ease the sheets!" then, "Let go and haul!" Precisely over my head, a voice—

Cumbershum's perhaps—roared, "Light to!" and there was even more commotion. The groaning of the yards would have made me grind my teeth in sympathy had I had the strength; but then, oh then! In our passage to date there has been no circumstance of like enjoyment, bliss! The movement of my body, of the bunk, of the whole ship changed in a moment, in the twinkling of an eye as if—but I do not need to elaborate the allusion. I knew directly what had brought the miracle about. We had altered course more towards the south and in Tarpaulin language—which I confess I speak with increasing pleasure—we had brought the wind from *forrard of the starboard beam* to *large on the starboard quarter*! Our motion, ample as ever, was and is more yielding, more feminine and suitable to the sex of our conveyance. I fell healthily asleep at once.

When I awoke there was no such folly as bounding out of my bunk or singing, but I did shout for Wheeler with a more cheerful noise than I had uttered, I believe, since the day when I was first acquainted with the splendid nature of my colonial employment—

But come! I cannot give, nor would you wish or expect, a moment by moment description of my journey! I begin to understand the limitations of such a journal as I have time to keep. I no longer credit Mistress *Pamela*'s pietistic accounts of every shift in her calculated resistance to the advances of her master! I will get myself up, relieved, shaved, breakfasted in a single sentence. Another shall see me on deck in my oilskin suit. Nor was I alone. For though the weather was in no way improved, we had it at our backs, or shoulders rather, and could stand comfortably in the shelter of our wall, that is, those *bulkheads* rising to the afterdeck and quarterdeck. I was reminded of convalescents at a spa, all up and about but wary in their new ability to walk or stagger.

Good God! Look at the time! If I am not more able to choose what I say I shall find myself describing the day before yesterday rather than writing about today for you tonight! For throughout the day I have walked, talked, eaten, drunk, explored—and here I am again, kept out of my bunk by the—I must confess—agreeable invitation of the page! I find that writing is like drinking. A man must learn to control it.

Well then. Early on, I found my oilskin suit too hot and returned to my cabin. There, since it would be in some sense an official visit, I dressed myself with care so as to make a proper impression on the captain. I was in great-coat and beaver, though I took the precaution of securing this last on my head by means of a scarf passed over the crown and tied under my chin. I debated the propriety of sending Wheeler to announce me but thought this too for-mal in the circumstances. I pulled on my gloves, therefore, shook out my capes, glanced down at my boots and found them adequate. I went to climb the *ladders*—though of course they are staircases and broad at that—to the quar-terdeck and poop. I passed Mr Cumbershum with an underling and gave him good day. But he ignored my greeting in a way that would have offended me had I not known from the previous day's exchanges that his manners are uncouth and his temper uncertain. I approached the captain therefore, who was to be recognized by his elabo-rate if shabby uniform. He stood on the starboard side of the quarterdeck, the wind at his back where his hands were clasped, and he was staring at me, his face raised, as if my appearance was a shock.

Now I have to acquaint your lordship with an unpleas-ant discovery. However gallant and indeed invincible our Navy may be, however heroic her officers and devoted her people, a ship of war is an ignoble despotism! Captain Anderson's first remark—if such a growl may be so described—and uttered at the very moment when having touched my glove to the brim of my beaver I was about to announce my name, was an unbelievably discourteous one.

"Who the devil is this, Cumbershum? Have they not read my orders?"

This remark so astonished me that I did not attend to Cumbershum's reply, if indeed he made any. My first thought was that in the course of some quite incomprehensible misunderstanding Captain Anderson was about to strike me. At once, and in a loud voice, I made myself known. The man began to bluster and my anger would have got the better of me had I not been more and more aware of the absurdity of our position. For standing as we did, I, the captain, Cumbershum and his satellite, we all had one leg stiff as a post while the other flexed regularly as the deck moved under us. It made me laugh in what must have seemed an unmannerly fashion but the fellow deserved the rebuke even if it was accidental. It stopped his blusters and heightened his colour, but gave me the opportunity of producing your name and that of His Excellency your brother, much as one might prevent the nearer approach of a highwayman by quickly presenting a brace of pistols. Our captain squinted first—you will forgive the figure—down your lordship's muzzle, decided you were loaded, cast a fearful eye at the ambassador in my other hand and reined back with his yellow teeth showing! I have seldom seen a face at once so daunted and so atrabilious. He is a complete argument for the sovranty of the humours. This exchange and the following served to move me into the fringes of his local despotism so that I felt much like an envoy at the Grande Porte who may regard himself as reasonably safe, if uncomfortable, while all round him heads topple. I swear Captain Anderson would have shot, hanged, keel-hauled, marooned me if prudence had not in that instant got the better of his inclination. Nevertheless, if today when the French clock in the Arras room chimed ten and our ship's bell here was struck four times—at that time, I say, if your lordship experienced a sudden access of well-being and a warming satisfaction, I cannot swear that it may not have been some distant notion of what a silver-mounted and murdering piece of ordnance a noble name was proving to be among persons of a middle station!

I waited for a moment or two while Captain Anderson swallowed his bile. He had much regard for your lordship and would not be thought remiss in any attention to his, his—He hoped I was comfortable and had not at first known—The rule was that passengers came to the quarterdeck by invitation though of course in my case—He hoped (and this with a glare that would have frightened a wolf-hound), he hoped to see more of me. So we stood for a few more moments, one leg stiff, one leg flexing like reeds in the wind while the shadow of the *driver* (thank you, Falconer!) moved back and forth across us. Then, I was amused to see, he did not stand his ground, but put his hand to his hat, disguised this involuntary homage to your lordship as an attempt to adjust the set of it and turned away. He stumped off to the stern rail and stood there, his hands clasped behind his back, where they opened and shut as an unconscious betrayal of his irritation. Indeed, I was half sorry for the man, confounded as I saw him to be in the imagined security of his little kingdom. But I judged it no good time for gentling him. In politics do we not attempt to use only just sufficient force to achieve a desired end? I decided to allow the influence of this interview to work for a while and only when he has got the true state of affairs thoroughly grounded in his malevolent head shall I move towards some easiness with him. We have the whole long passage before us and it is no part of my business to make life intolerable for him, nor would I if I could. Today, as you may suppose, I am all good humour. Instead of time crawling past with a snail's gait—now *if* a crab may be said to be drunk a snail may be said to have a gait—instead of time crawling, it hurries, not to say dashes past me. I cannot get one tenth of the day down! It is late; and I must continue tomorrow.

(5)

That fourth day, then—though indeed the fifth—but to continue.

After the captain had turned to the stern rail I remained for some time endeavouring to engage Mr Cumbershum in conversation. He answered me in the fewest possible words and I began to understand that he was uneasy in the captain's presence. However, I did not wish to leave the quarterdeck as if retreating from it.

"Cumbershum," said I, "the motion is easier. Show me more of our ship. Or if you feel it inadvisable to interrupt the management of her, lend me this young fellow to be my conductor."

The young fellow in question, Cumbershum's satellite, was a midshipman—not one of your ancients, stuck in his inferior position like a goat in a bush, but an example of the breed that brings a tear to every maternal eye—in a sentence, a pustular lad of fourteen or fifteen, addressed, as I soon found in pious hope, as a "Young Gentleman." It was some time before Cumbershum answered me, the lad looking from the one to the other of us meanwhile. At last Mr Cumbershum said the lad, Mr Willis by name, might go with me. So my object was gained. I left the Sacred Precincts with dignity and indeed had despoiled it of a votary. As we descended the ladder there was a *hail* from Mr Cumbershum.

"Mr Willis, Mr Willis! Do not omit to invite Mr Talbot to glance at the captain's Standing Orders. You may transmit to me any suggestions he has for their improvement."

I laughed heartily at this sally though Willis did not seem to be amused by it. He is not merely pustular but pale, and he commonly lets his mouth hang open. He asked me what I would choose to see and I had no idea, having used him to get me off the quarterdeck suitably attended. I nodded towards the forward part of the vessel.

"Let us stroll thither," said I, "and see how the people live."

Willis followed me with some hesitation in the shadow of the boats on the boom, across the white line at the main mast, then between the pens where our beasts are kept. He passed me then and led the way up a ladder to the front or *fo'castle*, where was the capstan, the belfry, some loungers and a woman plucking a chicken. I went towards the bowsprit and looked down. I became aware of the age of this old crone of a ship for she is positively *beaked* in the manner of the last century and flimsy, I should judge, about the bow withal. I looked over her monstrous figurehead, emblem of her name and which our people as is their custom have turned colloquially into an obscenity with which I will not trouble your lordship. But the sight of the men down there squatting in the heads at their business was distasteful and some of them looked up at me with what seemed like impertinence. I turned away and gazed along her vast length and to the vaster expanse of dark blue ocean that surrounded us.

"Well sir," said I to Willis, "we are certainly making way ἐπ' εὐρέα νῶτα θαλάσσης, are we not?"

Willis replied that he did not know French.

"What do you know then, lad?"

"The rigging sir, the parts of the ship, bends and hitches, the points of the compass, the marks of the leadline to take a bearing off a point of land or a mark and to shoot the sun."

"We are in good hands I see."

"There is more than that, sir," said he, "as for example

the parts of a gun, the composition of powder to sweeten the bilge and the Articles of War."

"You must not sweeten the Articles of War," said I solemnly. "We must not be kinder to each other than the French are to us! It seems to me that your education is piled all on top of itself like my lady mother's sewing closet! But what is the composition of the powder that enables you to shoot the sun and should you not be careful lest you damage the source of light and put the day out?"

Willis laughed noisily.

"You are roasting me, sir," he said. "Even a landlubber I ask your pardon knows what shooting the sun is."

"I forgive you that 'even', sir! When shall I see you do so?"

"Take an observation, sir? Why, at noon, in a few minutes. There will be Mr Smiles, the sailing master, Mr Davies and Mr Taylor, the other two midshipmen sir, though Mr Davies does not really know how to do it for all that he is so old and Mr Taylor my friend, I beg you will not mention it to the Captain, has a sextant that does not work owing to his having pawned the one that his father gave him. So we have agreed to take turn with mine and give altitudes that are two minutes different."

I put my hand to my forehead.

"And the safety of the whole hangs by such a spider's thread!"

"Sir?"

"Our position, my boy! Good God, we might as well be in the hands of my young brothers! Is our position to be decided by an antique midshipman and a sextant that does not work?"

"Lord, no, sir! In the first place Tommy Taylor and I believe we may persuade Mr Davies to swap his good one for Tommy's instrument. It would not really matter to Mr Davies you see. Besides, sir, Captain Anderson, Mr

Smiles and some other officers are also engaged in the navigation."

"I see. You do not merely shoot the sun. You subject him to a British Broadside! I shall watch with interest and perhaps take a hand in shooting the sun too as we roll round him."

"You could not do that, sir," said Willis in what seemed a kindly way. "We wait here for the sun to climb up the sky and we measure the angle when it is greatest and take the time too."

"Now look, lad," said I. "You are taking us back into the Middle Ages! You will be quoting Ptolemy at me next!"

"I do not know of him, sir. But we must wait while the sun climbs up."

"That is no more than an apparent movement," said I patiently. "Do you not know of Galileo and his 'Eppur si muove?' The earth goes round the sun! The motion was described by Copernicus and confirmed by Kepler!"

The lad answered me with the purest simplicity, ignorance and dignity.

"Sir, I do not know how the sun may behave among those gentlemen ashore but I know that he climbs up the sky in the Royal Navy."

I laughed again and laid my hand on the boy's shoulder.

"And so he shall! Let him move as he chooses! To tell you the truth, Mr Willis, I am so glad to see him up there with the snowy clouds about him that he may dance a jig for all I care! Look—your companions are gathering. Be off with you and aim your instrument!"

He thanked me and dived away. I stood on the aftermost part of the fo'castle and looked back at the ceremony which, I own, pleased me. There was a number of officers on the quarterdeck. They waited on the sun, the brass triangles held to their faces. Now here was a curious and moving circumstance. All those of the ship's people who were on deck and some of the emigrants too, turned and watched this *rite* with silent attention. They could not be expected to understand the mathematics of the operation. That I have some notion of it myself is owing to education, an inveterate curiosity and a facility in learning. Even the passengers, or those of them on deck, stood at gaze. I should not have been surprised to see the gentlemen lift their hats! But the people, I mean the common sort, whose lives as much as ours depended on an accuracy of measurement beyond their comprehension and the application of formulae that would be as opaque to them as Chinese writing, these people, I say, accorded the whole operation a respect such as they might have paid to the solemnest moment of a religious service. You might be inclined to think as I did that the glittering instruments were their Mumbo Jumbo. Indeed, Mr Davies's ignorance and Mr Taylor's defective instrument were feet of clay; but I felt they might have a justifiable faith in some of the older officers! And then—their attitudes! The woman watched, the half-plucked hen in her lap. Two fellows who were carrying a sick girl up from below— why, even *they* stood and watched as if someone had said *hist*, while their burden lay helplessly between them. Then the girl, too, turned her head and watched where they watched. There was a moving and endearing pathos about their attention, as in a dog that watches a conversation it cannot possibly understand. I am not, as your lordship must be aware, a friend to those who approve the outrageous follies of democracy in this and the last century. But at the moment when I saw a number of our sailors in a posture of such intense regard I came as near as ever I have done to seeing such concepts as "duty", "privilege", and "authority" in a new light. They moved out of books, out of the schoolroom and university into the broader scenes of daily life. Indeed, until I saw these fellows like Milton's hungry sheep that "look up", I had not considered the nature of my own ambitions nor looked for the justification of them that was here presented to me. Forgive me for boring your lordship with my discovery of what you yourself must know so well.

How noble was the prospect! Our vessel was urged forward under the force of sufficient but not excessive wind, the billows sparkled, the white clouds were diversedly mirrored in the deep—*et cetera*. The sun resisted without apparent effort our naval broadside! I went down the ladder and walked back towards where our navigators were breaking from their rank and descending from the quarterdeck. Mr Smiles, the sailing master, is old, but not as old as Mr Davies, our senior midshipman, who is nearly as old as the ship! He descended not merely the ladder to the level of the waist where I was but the next one down as well—going away with a slow and broken motion for all the world like a stage apparition returning to the tomb. After leave obtained, Mr Willis, my young acquaintance, brought his companion to me with some ceremony. Mr Tommy Taylor must be a clear two years younger than Mr Willis but has the spirit and well-knit frame that his elder lacks. Mr Taylor is from a naval family. He explained at once that Mr Willis was weak in his attic and needed retiling. I was to come to him, Mr Taylor, if I wished to find out about navigation, since Mr Willis would soon have me on the rocks. Only the day before, he had informed Mr Deverel that at the latitude of sixty degrees north, a degree of longitude would be reduced to half a nautical mile. On Mr Deverel asking him—evidently a wag, Mr Deverel—what it would be reduced to at sixty degrees south, Mr Willis had replied that he had not got as far as that in the book. The memory of these cataclysmic errors sent Mr Taylor into a long peal of laughter which Mr Willis did not appear to resent. He is devoted to his young friend evidently, admires him and shows him off to the best advantage. Behold me, then, pacing to and fro between the break of the afterdeck and the mainmast, a young acolyte on either side; the younger one on my *starboard hand*, full of excitement, information, opinion, gusto; the other, silent, but smiling with open mouth and nodding at his young friend's expressions of opinion on any subject under and, indeed, including the sun!

It was from these two young hopefuls that I learnt a little about our passengers—I mean of course those who have been accommodated aft. There is the Pike family, devoted to each other, all four. There is of *course*, one Mr Prettiman, known to us all. There is, I learn from precocious Mr Taylor, in the cabin between my own hutch and the dining saloon, a portrait-painter and his wife with their daughter—a young lady characterized by the aforesaid young gentleman as "a regular snorter"! I found this to be Mr Taylor's utmost in the description of female charm. Your lordship may imagine that this news of the presence on board of a fair *incognita* lent an added exhilaration to my animal spirits!

Mr Taylor might have conducted me through the whole list of passengers; but as we were returning from the mainmast for (it may be) the twentieth time, a—or rather, the—parson who had earlier spewed so copiously into his own face came out of the lobby of the passenger accommodation. He was turning to ascend the ladder to the afterdeck, but seeing me between my young friends, and perceiving me to be of some consequence I suppose, he paused and favoured me with a reverence. Observe I do not call it a bow or greeting. It was a sinuous deflection of the whole body, topped by a smile which was tempered by pallor and servility as his reverence was tempered by an uncertainty as to the movements of our vessel. As a gesture called forth by nothing more than the attire of a gentleman it could not but disgust. I acknowledged it by the briefest lifting of my hand towards the brim of my beaver and looked him through. He ascended the ladder. His calves were in thick, worsted stockings, his heavy shoes went up one after the other at an obtuse angle; so that I believe his knees, though his long, black coat covered them, must be by nature more than usually far apart. He wore a round wig and a shovel hat and seemed, I thought, a man who would not improve on acquaintance. He was hardly out of earshot when Mr Taylor gave it as his opinion that the *sky pilot* was on his way to interview Captain Anderson on the quarterdeck and that such an approach would result in his instant destruction.

"He has not read the captain's Standing Orders," said I, as one deeply versed in the ways of captains and their orders and warships. "He will be keel-hauled."

The thought of keel-hauling a parson overcame Mr Taylor completely. When Mr Willis had thumped him to a tear-stained and hiccupping recovery he declared it would be the best sport of all things and the thought set him off again. It was at this moment that a positive roar from the quarterdeck quenched him like a bucket of cold water. I believe—no, I am sure—the roar was directed at the parson but the two young gentlemen leapt as one, daunted, as it were, by no more than a ricochet or the splinters flying from where the captain's solid shot had landed. It appeared that Captain Anderson's ability to control his own officers, from Cumbershum down to these babes-in-arms, was not to be questioned. I must confess I did not desire more than the one engagement I had had with him as a ration *per diem*.

"Come lads," said I. "The transaction is private to

Captain Anderson and the parson. Let us get out of earshot and under cover."

We went with a kind of casual haste into the lobby. I was about to dismiss the lads when there came the sound of stumbling footsteps on the deck above our heads, then a clatter from the ladder outside the lobby—which turned at once to a speedier rattle as of iron-shod heels that had slipped out and deposited their wearer at the bottom with a jarring thump! Whatever my distaste for the fellow's— shall I call it—*extreme unction,* in common humanity I turned to see if he required assistance. But I had taken no more than a step in that direction when the man himself staggered in. He had his shovel hat in one hand and his wig in the other. His parsonical bands were twisted to one side. But what was of all things the most striking was— no, not the expression—but the disorder of his face. My pen falters. Imagine if you can a pale and drawn counte-nance to which nature has afforded no gift beyond the casual assemblage of features; a countenance moreover to which she has given little in the way of flesh but been prodigal of bone. Then open the mouth wide, furnish the hollows under the meagre forehead with staring eyes from which tears were on the point of starting—do all that, I say, and you will still come short of the comic humiliation that for a fleeting moment met me eye to eye! Then the man was fumbling at the door of his hutch, got through it, pulled it to and was scrabbling at the bolt on the other side.

Young Mr Taylor started to laugh again. I took him by the ear and twisted it until his laugh turned into a yelp.

"Allow me to tell you, Mr Taylor," said I, but quietly as the occasion demanded, "that one gentleman does not rejoice at the misfortune of another in public. You may make your bows and be off, the two of you. We shall take a constitutional again some day, I don't doubt."

"Oh lord yes, sir," said young Tommy, who seemed to think that having his ear twisted half off was a gesture of affection. "Whenever you choose, sir."

"Yes, sir," said Willis with his beautiful simplicity. "We have missed a lesson in navigation."

They retreated down a ladder to what I am told is the Gun Room and suppose to be some sort of noisome pit. The last words I heard from them that day were spoken by Mr Taylor to Mr Willis in tones of high animation—

"Don't he hate a parson above anything?"

I returned to my cabin, called Wheeler and bade him get off my boots. He responds so readily to the demands I make on him I wonder the other passengers do not make an equal use of his services. Their loss is my gain. Another fellow—Phillips, I think—serves the other side of the lobby as Wheeler serves this one.

"Tell me, Wheeler," said I as he fitted himself down in the narrow space, "why does Captain Anderson so dislike a parson?"

"A little higher if you please, sir. Thank you, sir. Now the other if you would be so good."

"Wheeler!"

"I'm sure I can't say, sir. Does he, sir? Did he say so, sir?"

"I know he does! I heard him as did the rest of the ship!"

"We do not commonly have parsons in the Navy, sir. There are not enough to go round. Or if there are, the reverend gentlemen do not choose the sea. I will give these a brush again, sir. Now the coat?"

"Not only did I hear him but one of the young gentlemen confirmed that Captain Anderson has a strong antipathy to the cloth, as did Lieutenant Cumbershum earlier, now I recollect it."

"Did he, sir? Thank you, sir."

"Is it not so?"

"I know nothing, Mr Talbot, sir. And now, sir, may I bring you another draught of the paregoric? I believe you found it very settling, sir."

"No thank you, Wheeler. As you see, I have eluded the demon."

"It *is* rather strong, sir, as Mr Cumbershum informed you. And of course as he has less left, the purser has to charge more for it. That's quite natural, sir. I believe there is a gentleman ashore as has wrote a book on it."

I bade him leave me and lay on my bunk for a while. I cast back in memory—could not remember what day of the voyage it was—took up this book, and it seemed to be the sixth, so I have confused your lordship and myself. I cannot keep pace with the events and shall not try. I have, at a moderate estimate, already written ten thousand words and must limit myself if I am to get our voyage between the luxurious covers of your gift. Can it be that I have evaded the demon opium only to fall victim to the *furor scribendi*? But if your lordship do but leaf through the book—

A knock at the door. It is Bates, who serves in the passengers' saloon.

"Mr Summers's compliments to Mr Talbot and will Mr Talbot take a glass of wine with him in the saloon?"

"Mr Summers?"

"The first lieutenant, sir."

"He is second in command to the captain, is he not? Tell Mr Summers I shall be happy to wait on him in ten minutes' time."

It is not the captain, of course—but the next best thing. Come! We are beginning to move in society!

(X)

I *think* it is the seventh—or the fifth—or the eighth per-haps—let "X" do its algebraic duty and represent the unknown quantity. Time has the habit of standing still so that as I write in the evening or night when sleep is hard to come by, my candle shortens imperceptibly as stalac-tites and stalagmites form in a grotto. Then all at once, time, this indefinable commodity, is in short supply and a sheaf of hours has fled I know not whither!

Where was I? Ah yes! Well then—

I proceeded to the passenger saloon to keep my *ren-dezvous* with the first lieutenant only to find that his invi-tation had been extended to every passenger in this part of the vessel and was no more than a kind of short prelimi-nary to dinner! I have found out since, that they have heard such gatherings are customary in packets and com-pany ships and indeed, wherever ladies and gentlemen take a sea voyage. The lieutenants have concluded to do the same in this vessel, to offset, I suspect, the peremp-tory and unmannerly prohibitions the captain has dis-played in his "Orders regarding the Behaviour of the Ladies and Gentlemen who have been afforded"—*afforded*, mark you, not *taken*—"Passage."

Properly announced, then, as the door was held open, I stepped into a scene of animation that resembled more than anything else what you might find in the parlour or dining room of a coaching inn. All that distinguished the present gathering from such a *job lot* was the blue horizon a little tilted and visible above the crowded heads through the panes of the great stern window. The announcement of my name caused a silence for a moment or two and I

41

peered at an array of pallid faces before me without being able to distinguish much between them. Then a well-built young man in uniform and two or three years my senior came forward. He introduced himself as Summers and declared I must meet Lieutenant Deverel. I did so, and thought him to be the most gentlemanlike officer I had yet found in the ship. He is slimmer than Summers, has chestnut hair and sidewhiskers but is cleanshaven about the chin and lips like all these fellows. We made an affable exchange of it and both determined, I don't doubt, to see more of each other. However, Summers said I must now meet the ladies and led me to the only one I could see. She was seated to the starboard side of the saloon on a sort of bench; and though surrounded or attended by some gentlemen was a severe-looking lady of uncertain years whose bonnet was designed as a covering for the head and as a genuine privacy for the face within it rather than as an ambush to excite the curiosity of the observer. I thought she had a Quakerish air about her, for her dress was grey. She sat, her hands folded in her lap, and talked directly up to the tall young army officer who smiled down at her. We waited on the conclusion of her present speech.

"—have always taught them such games. It is a harmless amusement for very young gentlemen and a knowledge of the various rules at least appropriate in the education of a young lady. A young lady with no gift for music may entertain her *parti* in that way as well as another might with the harp or other instrument."

The young officer beamed and drew his chin back to his collar.

"I am happy to hear you say so, ma'am. But I have seen cards played in some queer places, I can tell you!"

"As to that, sir, of course I have no knowledge. But surely games are not altered in themselves by the nature of the place in which they are played? I speak of it as I must, knowing no more of the games than as they are played in the houses of gentlefolk. But I would expect some knowledge of—let us say—whist, as necessary to a young lady, always provided—" and here I believe there must have been a change of expression on the invisible face, since a curiously ironic inflection entered the voice— "always provided she has the wit to lose prettily."

The tall young officer crowed in the way these fellows suppose to be *laughing* and Mr Summers took the opportunity of presenting me to the lady, Miss Granham. I declared I had overheard part of the conversation and felt inferior in not having a wide and deep knowledge of the games they spoke of. Miss Granham now turned her face on me and though I saw she could not be Mr Taylor's "regular snorter" her features were severely pleasant enough when lighted with the social smile. I praised the innocent hours of enjoyment afforded by cards and hoped that at some time in our long voyage I should have the benefit of Miss Granham's instruction.

Now there was the devil of it. The smile vanished. That word "instruction" had a *denotation* for me and a *connotation* for the lady!

"Yes, Mr Talbot," said she, and I saw a pink spot appear in either cheek. "As you have discovered, I am a governess."

Was this my fault? Had I been remiss? Her expectations in life must have been more exalted than their realization and this has rendered her tongue hair-triggered as a duelling pistol. I declare to your lordship that with such people there is nothing to be done and the only attitude to adopt with them is one of silent attention. That is how they are and one cannot detect their quality in advance any more than the poacher can see the gin. You take a step, and bang! goes the blunderbuss, or the teeth of the gin snap

round your ankle. It is easy for those whose rank and position in society put them beyond the vexation of such trivial social distinctions. But we poor fellows who must work
or, should I say operate, among these infinitesimal grada-
tions find their detection in advance as difficult as what the
papists call "the discernment of spirits".

But to return. No sooner had I heard the words "I am
a governess", or perhaps even while I was hearing them,
I saw that quite unintentionally I had ruffled the
lady.

"Why, ma'am," said I soothingly as Wheeler's paregoric, "yours is indeed the most necessary and genteel
profession open to a lady. I cannot tell you what a dear
friend Miss Dobson, Old Dobbie as we call her, has been
to me and my young brothers. I will swear you are as
secure as she in the affectionate friendship of your young
ladies and gentlemen!"

Was this not handsome? I lifted the glass that had been
put in my hand as if to salute the whole useful race,
though really I drank to my own dexterity in avoiding the
lanyard of the blunderbuss or the footplate of the gin.

But it would not do.

"If", said Miss Granham severely, "I am secure in the
affectionate friendship of my young ladies and gentlemen
it is the only thing I am secure in. A lady who is daughter
of a late canon of Exeter Cathedral and who is obliged by
her circumstances to take up the offer of employment
among a family in the Antipodes may well set the affectionate friendship of young ladies and gentlemen at a
lower value than you do."

There was I, trapped and blunderbussed—unjustly, I
think, when I remember what an effort I had made to
smooth the lady's feathers. I bowed and was her servant,
the army officer, Oldmeadow, drew his chin even further
into his neck; and here was Bates with sherry. I gulped

what I held and seized another glass in a way that it must have indicated my discomfiture, for Summers rescued me, saying he wished other people to have the pleasure of making my acquaintance. I declared I had not known there were so many of us. A large, florid and corpulent gentleman with a port-wine voice declared he would wish to *turn* a group portrait since with the exception of his good lady and his gal we were all present. A sallow young man, a Mr Weekes, who goes I believe to set up school, declared that the *emigrants* would form an admirable background to the composition.

"No, no," said the large gentleman, "I must not be patronized other than by the nobility and gentry."

"The emigrants," said I, happy to have the subject changed. "Why, I would as soon be pictured for posterity arm in arm with a common sailor!"

"You must not have me in your picture, then," said Summers, laughing loudly. "I was once a 'common sailor' as you put it."

"You, sir? I cannot believe it!"

"Indeed I was."

"But how—"

Summers looked round with an air of great cheerfulness.

"I have performed the naval operation known as 'coming aft through the hawsehole'. I was promoted from the lower deck, or, as you would say, from among the common sailors."

Your lordship can have little idea of my astonishment at his words and my irritation at finding the whole of our small society waiting in silence for my reply. I fancy it was as dextrous as the occasion demanded, though perhaps spoken with a too magisterial aplomb.

"Well, Summers," I said, "Allow me to congratulate you on imitating to perfection the manners and speech of a somewhat higher station in life than the one you was born to."

Summers thanked me with a possibly excessive gratitude. Then he addressed the assembly.

"Ladies and gentlemen, pray let us be seated. There must be no ceremony. Let us sit where we choose. There will, I hope, be many such occasions in the long passage before us. Bates, bid them strike up out there."

At this there came the somewhat embarrassing squeak of a fiddle and other instruments from the lobby. I did what I could to ease what might well be called *constraint*.

"Come Summers," I said, "if we are not to be portrayed together, let us take the opportunity and pleasure of seating Miss Granham between us. Pray, ma'am, allow me."

Was that not to risk another set-down? But I handed Miss Granham to her seat under the great window with more ceremony than I would have shown a peeress of the realm, and there we were. When I exclaimed at the excellent quality of the meat Lieutenant Deverel, who had seated himself on my left hand, explained that one of our cows had broken a leg in the late blow so we were taking what we could while it was still there though we should soon be short of milk. Miss Granham was now in animated conversation with Mr Summers on her right so Mr Deverel and I conversed for some time on the topic of seamen and their sentimentality over a cow with a broken leg, their ingenuity in all manner of crafts both good and bad, their addiction to liquor, their immorality, their furious courage and their devotion, only half-joking, to the ship's figurehead. We agreed there were few problems in society that would not yield to firm but perceptive government. It was so, he said, in a ship. I replied that I had seen the firmness but was yet to be convinced of the perception. By now the, shall I say, animation of the whole

party had risen to such a height that nothing could be
heard of the music in the lobby. One topic leading to
another, Deverel and I rapidly gained a degree of mutual
understanding. He opened himself to me. He had wished
for a proper ship of the line, not a superannuated third-
rate with a crew small in number and swept up together in
a day or two. What I had taken to be an established body
of officers and men had known each other for at most a
week or two since she came out of ordinary. It was a great
shame and his father might have done better for him.
This commission would do his own prospects no good at
all let alone that the war was running down and would
soon stop like an unwound clock. Deverel's speech and
manner, indeed everything about him, is elegant. He is an
ornament to the service.

The saloon was now as noisy as a public place can well
be. Something was overset amidst shouts of laughter and
some oaths. Already a mousey little pair, Mr and Mrs Pike
with the small twin daughters, had scurried away and now
at a particularly loud outburst, Miss Granham started to
her feet, though pressed to stay both by me and Summers.
He declared she must not mind the language of naval
officers which became habitual and unconscious among
the greater part of them. For my part I thought the
ill-behaviour came more from the passengers than the
ship's officers—Good God, said I to myself, if she is like
this at the after end, what is she like at the other? Miss
Granham had not yet moved from her seat when the door
was opened for a lady of a quite different appearance. She
appeared young yet richly and frivolously dressed. She
came in with such a sweep and flutter that the bonnet
fell to the back of her neck, revealing a quantity of
golden curls. We rose—or most of us, at least—but with
an admirable presence she seated us again at a gesture,
went straight to the florid gentleman, leaned over his

shoulder and murmured the following sentence in accents of exquisite, far, far too exquisite, beauty.

"Oh Mr Brocklebank, at last she has contrived to retain a mouthful of consom!"

Mr Brocklebank boomed us an explanation.

"My child, my little Zenobia!"

Miss Zenobia was at once offered a choice of places at the table. Miss Granham declared she was leaving so that her place at it was free if another cushion might be brought. But the young lady, as I must call her, replied with whimsical archness that she had relied on Miss Granham to protect her virtue among so many dangerous gentlemen.

"Stuff and nonsense, ma'am," said Miss Granham, even more severely than she had addressed your humble servant, "stuff and nonsense! Your virtue is as safe here as anywhere in the vessel!"

"Dear Miss Granham," cried the lady with a languishing air, "I am sure your virtue is safe anywhere!"

This was gross, was it not? Yet I am sorry to say that from at least one part of the saloon there came a shout of laughter, for we had reached that part of dinner where ladies are better out of the way and only such as the latest arrival was proving to be can keep in countenance. Deverel, I and Summers were on our feet in a trice but it was the army officer, Oldmeadow, who escorted Miss Granham from our midst. The voice of the port-wine gentleman boomed again. "Sit by me, Zenobia, child."

Miss Zenobia fluttered in the full afternoon sunlight that slanted across the great stern window. She held her pretty hands up to shield her face.

"It is too bright, Mr Brocklebank, pa!"

"Lord ma'am," said Deverel, "can you deprive us poor fellows in the shadows of the pleasure of looking at you?"

"I must," she said, "I positively must and will, take the seat vacated by Miss Granham."

She fluttered round the table like a butterfly, a painted lady perhaps. I fancy that Deverel would have been happy to have her by him but she sank into the seat between Summers and me. Her bonnet was still held loosely by a ribbon at the back of her neck so that a charming profusion of curls was visible by her cheek and ear. Yet it seemed to me even at the first sight that the very brightness of her eyes—or the one occasionally turned on me— owed a debt to the mysteries of her *toilette* and her lips were perhaps a trifle artificially coral. As for her perfume—

Does this appear tedious to your lordship? The many charmers whom I have seen to languish, perhaps in vain, near your lordship—devil take it, how am I to employ any flattery on my godfather when the simple truth—

To return. This bids fair to be a lengthy expatiation on the subject of a young woman's appearance. The danger here is to invent. I am, after all, no more than a young fellow! I might please myself with a rhapsody for she is the *only tolerable female object* in our company! There! Yet— and here I think the politician, the scurvy politician, as my favourite author would have it, is uppermost in my mind. I cannot get me glass eyes. I cannot rhapsodize. For Miss Zenobia is surely approaching her middle years and is defending indifferent charms before they disappear for ever by a continual animation which must surely exhaust her as much as they tire the beholder. A face that is never still cannot be subjected to detailed examination. May it not be that her parents are taking her to the Antipodes as a last resort? After all, among the convicts and Aborigines, among the emigrants and pensioned soldiers, the warders, the humbler clergy—but no. I do the lady an injustice for she is well enough. I do not doubt that the less continent of our people will find her an object of more than curiosity!

Let us have done with her for a moment. I will turn to her father and the gentleman opposite him, who became visible to me by leaping to his feet. Even in the resumed babble his voice was clearly to be heard.

"Mr Brocklebank, I would have you know that I am the inveterate foe of every superstition!"

This of course was Mr Prettiman. I have made a sad job of his introduction, have I not? You must blame Miss Zenobia. He is a short, thick, angry gentleman. You know of him. I know—it matters not how—that he takes a printing press with him to the Antipodes; and though it is a machine capable of little more than turning out handbills, yet the Lutheran Bible was produced from something not much bigger.

But Mr Brocklebank was booming back. He had not thought. It was a trifle. He would be the last person to offend the susceptibilities. Custom. Habit.

Mr Prettiman, still standing, vibrated with passion.

"I saw it distinctly, sir! You threw salt over your shoulder!"

"So I did, sir, I confess it. I will try not to spill the salt again."

This remark with its clear indication that Mr Brocklebank had no idea at all of what Mr Prettiman meant confounded the social philosopher. His mouth still open he sank slowly into his seat, thus almost passing from my sight. Miss Zenobia turned to me with a pretty seriousness round her wide eyes. She looked, as it were, under her eyebrows and up through lashes—but no. I will not believe that unassisted Nature—

"How angry Mr Prettiman is, Mr Talbot! I declare that when roused he is quite, quite terrifying!"

Anything less terrifying than the absurd philosopher

would be difficult to imagine. However, I saw that we were about to embark on a familiar set of steps in an ancient dance. She was to become more and more the unprotected female in the presence of gigantic male creatures such as Mr Prettiman and your godson. We, for our part, were to advance with a threatening good humour so that in terror she would have to throw herself on our mercy, appeal to our generosity, appeal to our chivalry perhaps: and all the time the animal spirits, the, as Dr Johnson called them, "amorous propensities" of both sexes would be excited to that state, that *ambiance*, in which such creatures as she is or has been, have their being.

This was a distancing thought and brought me to see something else. The size, the scale, was wrong. It was too large. The lady has been at least an *habituée* of the theatre if not a performer there! This was not a normal encounter—for now she was describing her terror in the late *blow*—but one, as it were, thrown outwards to where Summers at her side, Oldmeadow and a Mr Bowles across the table and indeed anyone in earshot could hear her. We were to perform. But before act one could be said to be well under weigh—and I must confess that I dallied with the thought that she might to some extent relieve the tedium of the voyage—when louder exclamations from Mr Prettiman and louder rumbles and even thunders from Mr Brocklebank turned her to seriousness again. She was accustomed to touch wood. I admitted to feeling more cheerful if a black cat should cross the road before me. Her lucky number was twenty-five. I said at once that her twenty-fifth birthday would prove to be most fortunate for her—a piece of nonsense which went unnoticed, for Mr Bowles (who is connected with the law in some very junior capacity and a thorough bore) explained that the custom of touching wood came from a papistical habit of adoring the crucifix and kissing it. I responded with my nurse's fear of crossed knives as indication of a quarrel and horror at a loaf turned upside-down as presage of a disaster at sea—whereat she shrieked and turned to Summers for protection. He assured her she need fear nothing from the French, who were quite beat down at this juncture; but the mere mention of the French was enough to set her off and we had another description of her trembling away the hours of darkness in her cabin. We were a single ship. We were, as she said in thrilling accents,

> "—*alone, alone,*
> *All, all alone,*
> *Alone on a wide, wide sea!*"

Anything more crowded than the teeming confines of this ship is not to be found, I believe, outside a debtor's gaol or a prison hulk. But yes she had met Mr Coleridge. Mr Brocklebank—pa—had painted his portrait and there had been talk of an illustrated volume but it came to nothing.

At about this point, Mr Brocklebank, having presumably caught his daughter's recitation, could be heard booming on metrically. It was more of the poem. I suppose he knew it well if he had intended to illustrate it. Then he and the philosopher set to again. Suddenly the whole saloon was silent and listening to them.

"No, sir, I would not," boomed the painter. "Not in any circumstances!"

"Then refrain from eating chicken, sir, or any other fowl!"

"No sir!"

"Refrain from eating that portion of cow before you! There are ten millions of Brahmans in the East who would cut your throat for eating it!"

"There are no Brahmans in this ship."

"Integrity—"

"Once and for all, sir, I would not shoot an albatross. I am a peaceable person, Mr Prettiman, and I would shoot *you* with as much pleasure!"

"Have you a gun, sir? For I will shoot an albatross, sir, and the sailors shall see what befalls—"

"I have a gun, sir, though I have never fired it. Are you a marksman, sir?"

"I have never fired a shot in my life!"

"Permit me then, sir. I have the weapon. You may use it."

"You, sir?"

"I, sir!"

Mr Prettiman bounced up into full view again. His eyes had a kind of icy brilliance about them.

"Thank you, sir, I will, sir, and you shall see, sir! And the common sailors shall see, sir—"

He got himself over the bench on which he had been sitting, then fairly *rushed* out of the saloon. There was some laughter and conversation resumed but at a lower level. Miss Zenobia turned to me.

"Pa is determined we shall be protected in the Antipodes!"

"He does not propose going among the natives, surely!"

"He has some thought of introducing the art of portraiture among them. He thinks it will lead to complacency among them which he says is next door to civilization. He owns, though, that a black face will present a special kind of difficulty."

"It would be dangerous, I think. Nor would the governor allow it."

"But Mr Brocklebank—pa—believes he may persuade the governor to employ him."

"Good God! I am not the governor, but—dear lady, think of the danger!"

"If clergymen may go—"

"Oh yes, where is he?"

Deverel touched my arm.

"The parson keeps his cabin. We shall see little of him, I think, and thank God and the captain for that. I do not miss him, nor do you I imagine."

I had momentarily forgotten Deverel, let alone the parson. I now endeavoured to draw him into the conversation but he stood up and spoke with a certain meaning.

"I go on watch. But you and Miss Brocklebank, I have no doubt, will be able to entertain each other."

He bowed to the lady and went off. I turned to her again and found her to be thoughtful. Not I mean that she was solemn—no, indeed! But beyond the artificial animation of her countenance there was some expression with which I confess I was not familiar. It was—do you not remember advising me to *read* faces?—it was a directed stillness of the orbs and eyelids as if while the outer woman was employing the common wiles and archnesses of her sex, beyond them was a different and watchful person! Was it Deverel's remark about entertainment that had made the difference? What was—what is—she thinking? Does she meditate an *affaire du coeur* as I am sure she would call it, *pour passer le temps*?

(12)

As your lordship can see by the number at the head of this section I have not been as attentive to the journal as I could wish—nor is the reason such as I could wish! We have had bad weather again and the motion of the vessel augmented a colic which I trace to the late and unlamented *Bessie*. However, the sea is now smoother. The weather and I have improved together and by dint of resting the book and inkstand on a tray I am able to write, though slowly. The one thing that consoles me for my indisposition is that during my long sufferings the ship has got on. We have been blown below the latitudes of the Mediterranean and our speed has been limited, according to Wheeler (that living *Falconer*), more by the ship's decrepitude than by the availability of wind. The people have been at the pumps. I had thought that pumps "clanked" and that I would hear the melancholy sound clearly but this was not so. In the worst of the weather I asked my visitor, Lieutenant Summers, fretfully enough why they did not pump, only to be assured the people were pumping all the time. He said it was a delusion caused by my sickness that made me feel the vessel to be low in the water. I believe I may be more than ordinarily susceptible to the movement of the vessel, that is the truth of it. Summers assures me that naval people accept the condition as nothing to be ashamed of and invariably adduce the example of Lord Nelson to bear them out. I cannot but think, though, that I have lost consequence. That Mr Brocklebank and La Belle Brocklebank were also reduced to the state in which the unfortunate Mrs Brocklebank has been ever since we left home is no kind of help. The condition of the two hutches in which that family lives must be one it is better not to contemplate.

There is something more to add. Just before the nauseating complaint struck me—I am nigh enough recovered, though weak—a *political* event convulsed our society. The captain, having through Mr Summers disappointed the parson's expectation that he would be allowed to conduct some services, has also forbidden him the quarterdeck for some infraction of the *Standing Orders*. What a little tyrant it is! Mr Prettiman, who parades the afterdeck (with a *blunderbuss!*), was our intelligencer. He, poor man, was caught between his detestation of any church at all and what he calls his *love of liberty!* The conflict between these attitudes and the emotions they roused in him was painful. He was soothed by, of all people, Miss Granham! When I heard this comical and extraordinary news I got out of my trough and shaved and dressed. I was aware that duty and inclination urged me forward together. The brooding captain should not dictate to me in this manner! What! Is *he* to tell *me* whether I should have a service to attend or not? I saw at once that the passenger saloon was suitable and no man unless his habit of command had become a mania could take it from our control.

The parson might easily hold a short evening service there for such of the passengers as chose to attend it. I walked as steadily as I could across the lobby and tapped on the door of the parson's hutch.

He opened the door to me and made his usual sinuous genuflection. My dislike of the man returned.

"Mr—ah—Mr—"

"James Colley, Mr Talbot, sir. The Reverend Robert James Colley at your service, sir."

"Service is the word, sir."

Now there was a mighty contortion! It was as if he

accepted the word as a tribute to himself and the Almighty together.

"Mr Colley, when is the Sabbath?"

"Why today, sir, Mr Talbot, sir!"

The eyes that looked up at me were so full of eagerness, of such obsequious and devoted humility you would have thought I had a brace of livings in my coat pocket! He irritated me and I came near to abandoning my purpose.

"I have been indisposed, Mr Colley, otherwise I would have made the suggestion sooner. A few ladies and gentlemen would welcome it if you was to conduct a service, a short service in the passenger saloon at seven bells in the afternoon watch or, if you prefer to remain a landsman, at half-past three o'clock."

He grew in stature before my eyes! His own filled with tears.

"Mr Talbot, sir, this is—is—it is like you!"

My irritation increased. It was on the tip of my tongue to ask him how the devil he knew what I was like. I nodded and walked away, to hear behind my back some mumbled remark about *visiting the sick*. Good God, thought I—if he tries that, he will go off with a flea in his ear! However, I managed to get to the passenger saloon, for irritation is in part a cure for weakness in the limbs, and found Summers there. I told him what I had arranged and he greeted the information with silence. Only when I suggested that he should invite the captain to attend did he smile wryly and reply that he should have to inform the captain anyway. He would make bold to suggest a later hour. I told him the hour was a matter of indifference to me and returned to my hutch and canvas chair in which I sat and felt myself exhausted but recovered. Later in the morning, Summers came to me and said that he had altered my message somewhat and hoped I did not mind. He had made it a general request from the passengers! He hastened to add that this was more comfortable to the customs of the sea service. Well. Someone who delights as I do in the strange but wholly expressive Tarpaulin language (I hope to produce some prize specimens for you) could not willingly allow the *customs of the sea service* to suffer. But when I heard that the little parson was to be allowed to address us I must own I began to regret my impulsive interference and understood how much I had enjoyed these few weeks of freedom from the whole paraphernalia of Established Religion!

However, in decency I could not back down now and I attended the service our little cleric was allowed to perform. I was disgusted by it. Just previous to the service I saw Miss Brocklebank and her face was fairly plastered with red and white! The Magdalene must have looked just so, it may be leaning against the outer wall of the temple precincts. Nor, I thought, was Colley one to bring her to a more decorous appearance. Yet later I found I had underestimated both her judgement and her experience. For when it was time for the service the candles of the saloon irradiated her face, took from it the damaging years, while what had been paint now appeared a magical youth and beauty! She looked at me. Scarcely had I recovered from the shock of having this battery play on me when I discovered what further improvement Mr Summers had made on my original proposal. He had allowed in, to share our devotions with us, a number of the more respectable emigrants—Grant, the farrier, Filton and Whitlock, who are clerks, I think, and old Mr Grainger with his old wife. He is a scrivener. Of *course* any village church will exhibit just such a mixture of the orders; but here the society of the passenger saloon is so *pinchbeck*—such a shoddy example to them! I was recovering from this invasion when there entered to us—we standing in respect—five feet nothing of parson complete with surplice, cap of maintenance perched on a round wig, long gown, boots with iron-shod heels—together with a mingled air of diffidence, piety, triumph and complacency. Your lordship will protest at once that some of these attributes cannot be got together under the same cap. I would agree that in the normal face there is seldom room for them all and that one in particular generally has the mastery. It is so in most cases. When we smile, do we not do so with mouth and cheeks and eyes, indeed, with the whole face from chin to hairline! But this Colley has been dealt with by Nature with the utmost economy. Nature has pitched—no, the verb is too active. Well then, on some corner of Time's beach, or on the muddy rim of one of her more insignificant rivulets, there have been washed together casually and indifferently a number of features that Nature had tossed away as of no use to any of her creations. Some vital spark that might have gone to the animation of a sheep assumed the collection. The result is this fledgling of the church.

Your lordship may detect in the foregoing, a tendency to *fine writing*: a not unsuccessful attempt, I flatter myself. Yet as I surveyed the scene the one thought uppermost in my mind was that Colley was a living proof of old Aristotle's dictum. There is after all an order to which the man belongs by nature though some mistaken quirk of patronage has elevated him beyond it. You will find that order displayed in crude medieval manuscripts where the colour has no shading and the drawing no perspective. Autumn will be illustrated by men, peasants, serfs, who are reaping in the fields and whose faces are limned with just such a skimped and jagged line under their hoods as Colley's is! His eyes were turned down in diffidence and possibly recollection. The corners of his mouth were turned up— and there was the triumph and complacency! Much bone was strewn about the rest of his countenance. Indeed, his schooling should have been the open fields, with stone-collecting and bird-scaring, his university the plough. *Then* all those features so irregularly scarred by the tropic sun might have been bronzed into a unity and one, modest expression animated the whole!

We are back with fine writing, are we not? But my restlessness and indignation are still hot within me. He knows of my consequence. At times it was difficult to determine whether he was addressing Edmund Talbot or the Almighty. He was theatrical as Miss Brocklebank. The habit of respect for the clerical office was all that prevented me from breaking into indignant laughter. Among the respectable emigrants that attended was the poor, pale girl, carried devotedly by strong arms and placed in a seat behind us. I have learned that she suffered a miscarriage in our first *blow* and her awful pallor was in contrast with the manufactured allure of La Brocklebank. The decent and respectful attention of her male companions was mocked by these creatures that were ostensibly her betters—the one in paint pretending devotion, the other with his book surely pretending sanctity! When the service began there also began the most ridiculous of all the circumstances of that ridiculous evening. I set aside the sound of pacing steps from above our heads where Mr Prettiman demonstrated his anticlericalism as noisily on the afterdeck as possible. I omit the trampings and shouts at the changing of the watch—all done surely at the captain's behest or with his encouragement or tacit consent with as much rowdiness as can be procured among skylarking sailors. I think only of the gently swaying saloon, the pale girl and the farce that was played out before her! For no sooner did Mr Colley catch sight of Miss Brocklebank than he could not take his eyes off her. She for her part—and "part" I am very sure it was—gave us such a picture of devotion as you might find in the hedge theatres of the country circuits. Her eyes never left his face but when they were turned to heaven. Her lips were always parted in breathless ecstasy except when they opened and closed swiftly with a passionate "Amen!" Indeed there was one moment when a sanctimonious remark in the course of his address from Mr Colley, followed by an "Amen!" from Miss Brocklebank was underlined, as it were (well, a *snail* has a *gait*!) by a resounding fart from that wind-machine Mr Brocklebank so as to set most of the congregation sniggering like schoolboys on their benches.

However much I attempted to detach myself from the performance I was made deeply ashamed by it and vexed at myself for my own feelings. Yet since that time I have discovered a sufficient reason for my discomfort and think my feelings in this instance wiser than my reason. For I repeat, we had a handful of the common people with us. It is possible they had entered the after part of the ship in much the same spirit as those visitors who declare they wish to view your lordship's Canalettos but who are really there to see if they can how the nobility live. But I think it more probable that they had come in a simple spirit of devotion. Certainly that poor, pale girl could have no other object than to find the comforts of religion. Who would deny them to such a helpless sufferer, however illusory they be? Indeed, the trashy show of the preacher and his painted Magdalene may not have come between her and the imagined object of her supplications, but what of the honest fellows who attended her? They may well have been stricken in the tenderest regions of loyalty and subordination.

Truly Captain Anderson detests the church! His attitude has been at work on the people. He had given no orders, it is said, but would know how to esteem those officers who did not agree with him in his obsession. Only Mr Summers and the gangling army officer,

Mr Oldmeadow, were present. You know why *I* was there! I do not choose to submit to tyranny!

Most of the fellow's address was over before I made the major discovery in my, as it were, diagnosis of the situation. I had thought when I first saw how the painted face of the *actrice* engaged the eye of the reverend gentleman, that he experienced disgust mingled perhaps with the involuntary excitement, the first movement of warmth—no, lust—that an evident wanton will call from the male body rather than mind, by her very pronouncement of availability. But I soon saw that this would not do. Mr Colley has never been to a theatre! Where, too, would he progress, in what must surely be one of our remoter dioceses, from a theatre to a *maison d'occasion*? His book told him of painted women and how their feet go down to hell but did not include advice on how to recognize one by candlelight! He took her to be what her performance suggested to him! A chain of tawdry linked them. There came a moment in his address when having used the word of all others "gentlemen", he swung to her and with a swooning archness exclaimed, "Or ladies, madam, however beautiful", before going on with his theme. I heard a positive hiss from within Miss Granham's bonnet and Summers crossed then uncrossed his knees.

It ended at last, and I returned to my hutch, to write this entry, in, I am sorry to say, increasing discomfort though the motion of the ship is easy enough. I do not know what is the matter with me. I have written sourly and feel sour, that is the fact of the matter.

(17)

I think it is seventeen. What does it matter. I have suffered again—the colic. Oh Nelson, Nelson, how did you manage to live so long and die at last not from this noisome series of convulsions but by the less painful violence of the enemy?

(?)

I am up and about, pale, frail, convalescent. It seems that after all I may live to reach our destination!

I wrote that yesterday. My entries are becoming short as some of Mr Sterne's chapters! But there is one amusing circumstance that I must acquaint your lordship with. At the height of my misery and just before I succumbed to a large dose of Wheeler's paregoric there came a timid knock at my hutch door. I cried "Who is there?" To which a faint voice replied, "It is I, Mr Talbot, sir. Mr Colley, sir. You remember, the Reverend Mr Colley, at your service." By some stroke of luck rather than wit I hit on the only reply that would protect me from his *visitation*.

"Leave me I beg you, Mr Colley—" a dreadful convulsion of the guts interrupted me for a moment; then—"I am at prayer!"

Either a decent respect for my privacy or Wheeler approaching with the good draught in his hand rid me of him. The paregoric—it was a stiff and justifiable dose that *knocked me out*. Yet I do have some indistinct memory of opening my eyes in stupor and seeing that curious assemblage of features, that oddity of nature, Colley, hanging over me. God knows when that happened—if it happened! But now I am *up*, if not *about*, the man surely will not have the impertinence to thrust himself on me.

The dreams of paregoric must owe something surely to its constituent opium. Many faces, after all, floated through them so it is possible his was no more than a figment of my drugged delirium. The poor, pale girl haunted me—I hope indeed she may make a good recovery. There was under her cheekbone a right-angled hollow and I do not recollect ever having seen anything so painful to behold. The hollow and the affecting darkness that lived there, and moved did she but turn her head, touched me in a way I cannot describe. Indeed I was filled with a weak kind of rage when I returned in thought to the occasion of the service and remembered how her husband had exposed her to such a miserable farce! However, today I am more myself. I have recovered from such morbid thoughts. Our progress has been as excellent as my recovery. Though the air has become humid and hot I am no longer fevered by the pacing of Mr Prettiman overhead. He walks the afterdeck with a weapon provided of all things by the sot Brocklebank and will discharge a positive shower from his antique blunderbuss to destroy an albatross in despite of Mr Brocklebank and Mr Coleridge and Superstition together! He demonstrates to the thoughtful eye how really irrational a rationalist philosopher can be!

(23)

I think it is the twenty-third day. Summers is to explain the main parts of the rigging to me. I intend to surprise him with a landsman's knowledge—most collected out of books he has never heard of! I also intend to please your lordship with some choice bits of Tarpaulin language for I begin, haltingly it is true, to *speak Tarpaulin*! What a pity this noble vehicle of expression has so small a literature!

(27)

Can a man always be counting? In this heat and humidity—

It was Zenobia. Has your lordship ever remarked—but of course you have! What am I thinking of? There is a known, true, tried and tested link between the perception of female charms and the employment of strong drink! After three glasses I have seen twenty years vanish from a face like snow in summer! A sea voyage added to that stimulant—and one which has set us to move gently through the tropics of all places—has an effect on the male constitution that *may* be noted in the more recondite volumes of the profession—I mean the medical profession—but had not come my way in the course of an ordinary education. Perhaps somewhere in Martial— but I have not got him with me—or that Theocritus—you remember, midday and summer's heat τὸν Πᾶνα δεδοίκαμες. Oh yes, we may well fear Pan here or his naval equivalent whoever it may be! But sea gods, sea nymphs were chill creatures. I have to admit that the woman is most damnably, most urgently attractive, *paint* and all! We have met and met again. How should we not? And again! It is all madness, tropical madness, a delirium, if not a transport! But now, standing by the bulwarks in the tropic night, stars caught among the sails and swaying very gently all together, I find that I deepen my voice so that her name vibrates and yet I know my own madness—she meanwhile, why she heaves her scarcely covered bosom with more motion than stirs the glossy deep. It is folly; but then, how to describe—

Noble godfather, if I do you wrong, rebuke me. Once ashore and I will be sane again, I will be that wise and impartial adviser, administrator, whose foot you have set on the first rung—but did you not say "Tell all"? You said, "Let me live again in you!"

I am but a young fellow after all.

Well then, the problem, devil take it, was a place of assignation. To meet the lady was easy enough and indeed unavoidable. But then so was meeting everyone else! Mr Prettiman paces the quarterdeck. The *Famille* Pike, father, mother and little daughters, hurry up and down the afterdeck and the waist peering on this side and that lest they should be accosted, I suppose, and subjected to some indignity or impropriety. Colley comes by in the waist; and every time nowadays he not only favours me with his *reverence* but tops it off with a smile of such understanding and sanctity he is a kind of walking invitation to *mal de mer*. What could I do? I could scarcely hand the lady into the foretop! You will ask what is wrong with my hutch or her hutch. I answer "Everything!" Does Mr Colley but cry "Hem!" on the other side of the lobby he wakes Miss Granham in the hutch just aft of him. Does that windbag Mr Brocklebank but break wind—as he does every morning just after seven bells—our timbers shudder clear through my hutch and into Mr Prettiman's just across from me. I have had to prospect farther for a place suitable to the conduct of our *amours*. I had thought of finding and introducing myself to the purser—but to my surprise I found that all the officers shied away from mention of him as if the man were holy, or indecent, I cannot tell which, and he never appears on deck. It is a subject I propose to get clear in my mind—when I have a mind again and this, this surely temporary madness—

(30)

In sheer desperation I have persuaded Mr Tommy Taylor to take me down to the gun room which, though it has only three midshipmen instead of the more usual complement, is nevertheless so roomy it is used for the warrant officers as well, because *their* mess—I cannot go into the politics of it all—is too far forrard and has been taken over for the better sort of emigrant. These elders, the gunner, the carpenter and the sailing master, sat in a row beyond a table and watched me in a silence that seemed more *knowing* than the regard of anyone else in the ship if we except the redoubtable Miss Granham. Yet I did not pay much attention to them at first because of the extraordinary object that Mr Willis revealed as he moved his bony length towards the ladder. It was, of all things, a plant, some kind of creeper, its roots buried in a pot and the stem roped to the bulkhead for a few feet. There was never a leaf; and wherever a tendril or branch was unsupported it hung straight down like a piece of seaweed—which indeed would have been more appropriate and useful. I exclaimed at the sight. Mr Taylor burst into his usual peal and pointed to Mr Willis as the not particularly proud owner. Mr Willis vanished up the ladder. I turned from the plant to Mr Taylor.

"What the devil is that for?"

"Ah," said the gunner. "Gentleman Jack."

"Always one for a joke, Mr Deverel," said the carpenter. "He put him up to it."

The sailing master smiled across at me with mysterious compassion.

"Mr Deverel told him it was the way to get on."

Tommy Taylor cried with laughter—literally cried, the tears falling from him. He choked and I beat his back more severely than he liked. But unalloyed high spirits are a nuisance anywhere. He stopped laughing.

"It's a creeper, you see!"

"Gentleman Jack," said the carpenter again. "I couldn't help laughing myself. God knows what sort of lark Mr Deverel will get up to in the badger bag."

"The what, sir?"

The gunner had reached below the table and brought up a bottle.

"You'll take an observation through a glass, Mr Talbot."

"In this heat—"

It was rum, fiery and sticky. It increased the heat in my blood and seemed to increase the oppressiveness of the air. I wished that I could shed my coat as the warrant officers had; but of course it would not do.

"This air is confoundedly close, gentlemen. I wonder you can endure it day after day."

"Ah," said the gunner. "It's a hard life Mr Talbot, sir. Here today and gone tomorrow."

"Here today and gone today," said the carpenter. "Do you mind that young fellow, Hawthorne I think, come aboard at the beginning of this commission? Boatswain gets him to tail on a rope with the others, only last man like and says, says he, 'Don't you go leaving go no matter what happens.' The boat begins to take charge on the yard and drops 'cause the rest jumps clear. Young Hawthorne, who don't know the crown of a block from its arse—he come off a farm, I shouldn't wonder—he holds on like he's been told."

The gunner nodded and drank.

"Obeys orders."

It seemed the story had come to an end.

"But what was wrong? What happened?"

"Why, see," said the carpenter, "the tail of the rope runs up to the block—swit!—just like that. Young Hawthorne he was on the end of it. He must have gone a mile."

"We never saw him again."

"Good God."

"Here today and gone today, like I said."

"I could tell you a story or two about guns if it comes to that," said the gunner. "Very nasty things, guns when they misbehave, which they can do so in ten thousand different ways. So if you take up to be a gunner, Mr Talbot, you need your head."

Mr Gibbs the carpenter nudged the sailing master.

"Why, even a gunner's mate needs a head, sir," he said. "Did you never hear the story of the gunner's mate who lost his head? It was off Alicante I believe—"

"Now then George!"

"This gunner, see, was walking up and down behind his battery with his pistol in his hand. They was swopping shot with a fort, a foolish thing to do in my view. A red hot shot come through a gun port and takes off the gunner's head clean as this gallantine the Frenchies make use of. Only see the shot was red hot and cauterizes the neck so the gunner goes on marching up and down and nobody notices nothing until they run out of orders. Laugh! They nigh on died until the first lieutenant wants to know why in the name of Christ the guns had fell silent in the after starboard maindeck battery, so they asks the gunner what to do but he had nothing with which to tell them."

"Really gentlemen! Oh come!"

"Another glass, Mr Talbot."

"It's getting so *stuffy* in here—"

71

The carpenter nodded and knocked on a timber with his knuckles.

"It's hard to tell whether the air sweats or her wood."

The gunner heaved once or twice with laughter inside him like a wave that does not break.

"We should open a winder," he said. "You remember the gals, Mr Gibbs? 'Couldn't we 'ave a winder open? I've come over queer like.' "

Mr Gibbs heaved like the gunner.

"Come over queer, have you? Along here, my little dear. It's the way for some nice fresh air."

" 'Oh what was that, Mr Gibbs? Was it a rat? I can't abide rats! I'm sure it was a rat—' "

"Just my little doggie, my dear. Here. Feel my little doggie."

I drank some of the fiery liquid.

"And commerce can be obtained even in such a vessel as this? Did no one see you?"

The sailing master smiled his beautiful smile.

"I saw them."

The gunner nudged him.

"Wake up, Shiner. You wasn't even in the ship. We hadn't hardly come out of ordinary."

"Ordinary," said Mr Gibbs. "That's the life that is. No nasty sea. Lying up a creek snug in a trot with your pick of the admirals' cabins and a woman on the books to do the galley work. That's the best berth there is in the Navy, Mr Talbot, sir. Seven years I was in her before they came aboard and tried to get her out of the mud. Then they didn't think they'd careen her what with one thing and another so they took what weed they could off her bottom with the drag rope. That's why she's so uncommon sluggish. It was sea water, you see. I hope this Sydney Cove or whatever they call it has berths in fresh water."

"If they took the weed off her," said the gunner, "they might take the bottom with it."

Clearly I was no nearer my original objective. I had but one possible resource left me.

"Does not the purser share this commodious apartment with you?"

Again there was that strange, uneasy silence. At last Mr Gibbs broke it.

"He has his own place up there on planks over the water casks among the cargo and dunnage."

"Which is?"

"Bales and boxes," said the gunner. "Shot, powder, slow match, fuse, grape and chain, and thirty twenty-four pounders, all of 'em tompioned, greased, plugged and bowsed down."

"Tubs," said the carpenter. "Tools, adzes and axes, hammers and chisels, saws and sledges, mauls, spikes, trenails and copper sheet, plugs, harness, gyves, wrought iron rails for the governor's new balcony, casks, barrels, tuns, firkins, pipkins, bottles and bins, seeds, samples, fodder, lamp oil, paper, linen."

"And a thousand other things," said the sailing master. "Ten thousand times ten thousand."

"Why don't you show the gentleman, Mr Taylor," said the carpenter. "Take the lantern. You can make believe as you're the captain going his rounds."

Mr Taylor obeyed and we went, or rather crept *forrard*. A voice called behind us.

"You may even glimpse the purser."

It was a strange and unpleasant journey where indeed rats scurried. Mr Taylor, being accustomed, I suppose, to this kind of journey, made short work of it. Until I ordered him back he got so far ahead of me that I was left in complete, and need I say, foetid, darkness. When he *did* return part way it was only to reveal with his lantern our narrow and irregular path between nameless bulks and shapes that seemed piled around us and indeed over us without order or any visible reason. Once I fell, and my boots trod that same noisome sand and gravel of her bilge that Wheeler had described to me on the *first day*: and it was while fumbling to extract myself from between two of her vast timbers that I had my one and only glimpse of our purser—or at least I suppose it was the purser. I glimpsed him up there through a kind of spyhole between, it may be, bales or whatnot; and since he of all people does not have to stint himself for light that hole, though it was far below deck, blazed like a sunny window. I saw a vast head with small spectacles bowed over a ledger—just that and nothing more. Yet *this* was the creature, mention of whom could produce a silence among these men so careless of life and death!

I scrambled out of the ballast and onto the planks over the *bowsed down* cannon and crawled after Mr Taylor till a quirk of our narrow passage hid the vision and we were alone with the lantern again. We reached the forepart of the ship. Mr Taylor led me up ladders, piping in his treble—"Gangway there!" You must not imagine he was ordering some mechanism to be lowered for my convenience. In Tarpaulin, a "gangway" is a space through which one may walk and he was acting as my usher, or lictor I suppose, and ensuring that the common people would not trouble me. So we rose from the depths, through decks crowded with people of all ages and sexes and smells and noises and smoke and emerged into the crowded fo'castle whence I positively fled out into the cool, sweet air of the waist! I thanked Mr Taylor for his convoy, then went to my hutch and had Wheeler take away my boots. I stripped and rubbed myself down with perhaps a pint of water and felt more or less clean. But clearly, however freely the warrant officers obtained the favours of young women in these shadowy depths, it was of no use for your humble servant. Sitting in my canvas chair and in a mood of near desperation I came close to confiding in Wheeler but retained just enough common sense to keep my wishes to myself.

I wonder what is meant by the expression "Badger Bag"? Falconer is silent.

(Y)

It has come to me in a flash! One's intelligence may march about and about a problem but the solution does not come gradually into view. One moment it is not. The next, and it is there. If you cannot alter the place all that is left to alter is the time! Therefore, when Summers announced that the people would provide us with an entertainment I brooded for a while, thinking nothing of it, then suddenly saw with a *political eye* that the ship was about to provide me not with a place but with an opportunity! I am happy to inform you—no, I do not think gaiety comes into it, rather a simple dignity; My lord, I have at sea emulated *one* of Lord Nelson's victories! Could the merely civil part of our country achieve more? Briefly, I let it be known that such trivial affairs as the seamen's entertainment held no attraction for me, that I had the headache and should pass the time in my cabin. I took care that Zenobia should hear me! I stood, therefore, gazing through the louvre as our passengers took their way to the afterdeck and quarter-deck, a clamorous crowd only too happy to find something out of the ordinary, and soon our lobby was empty and silent as—as it could well be. I waited, hearing the trampling of feet over my head; and soon, sure enough, Miss Zenobia came tripping down to find perhaps a shawl against the tropical night! I was out of my hutch, had her by the wrist and jerked her back in with me before she could even pretend a startled cry! But there was noise enough from other places and noise enough from the blood pounding in my ears so that I pressed my suit with positive ardour! We wrestled for a moment by the bunk, she with a nicely calculated exertion of strength that only just failed to resist me, I with mounting passion. My sword was in my hand and I boarded her! She retired in disorder to the end of the hutch where the canvas basin awaited her in its iron hoop. I attacked once more and the hoop collapsed. The bookshelf tilted. *Moll Flanders* lay open on the deck, *Gil Blas* fell on her and my aunt's parting gift to me, Hervey's *Meditations among the Tombs (MDCCLX) II vols London* covered them both. I struck them all aside and Zenobia's tops'ls too. I called on her to yield, yet she maintained a brave if useless resistance that fired me even more. I bent for the *main course*. We flamed against the ruins of the canvas basin and among the trampled pages of my little library. We flamed upright. Ah— she did yield at last to my conquering arms, was overcome, rendered up all the tender spoils of war!

However—if your lordship follows me—although it is our male privilege to *debellare* the *superbos*—the *superbas*, if you will—it is something of a duty I think to *parcere* the *subjectis*! In a sentence, having gained the favours of *Venus* I did not wish to inflict the pains of *Lucina*! Yet her abandonment was complete and passionate. I did not think female heat could increase—but as bad luck would have it, at that very critical moment there came from the deck above our heads the sound of a veritable explosion.

She clutched me frantically.

"Mr Talbot," she gasped, "Edmund! The French! Save me!"

Was there ever anything more mistimed and ridiculous? Like most handsome and passionate women she is a fool; and the explosion (which I at once identified) put her, if not me, in the peril from which it had been my generous intention to protect her. Well there it is. The fault was hers and she must bear the penalties of her follies as well as the pleasures. It was—and is all the same— confoundedly provoking. Moreover she is I believe too experienced a woman not to be aware of what she has done!

"Calm yourself, my dear," I muttered breathlessly, as my own too speedy paroxysm subsided—*confound* the woman—"It is Mr Prettiman who has at last seen an albatross. He has discharged your father's blunderbuss in its general direction. You will not be ravished by the French but by our common people if they find out what he is at."

(In fact I found that Mr Coleridge had been mistaken. Sailors are superstitious indeed, but careless of life in any direction. The only reason why they do not shoot seabirds is first because they are not allowed weapons and second because seabirds are not pleasant to eat.)

Above us, there was trampling on the deck and much noise about the ship in general. I could only suppose the entertainment was being rowdily successful, for such as like that sort of thing or have nothing better in view.

"Now my dear," said I, "we must get you back to the social scene. It will never do for us to appear together."

"Edmund!"

This with a great deal of heaving and—glowing, as it is called. Really, she was in a quite distasteful condition!

"Why—what is the matter?"

"You will not desert me?"

I paused and thought.

"Do you suppose I can step overboard into a ship of my own?"

"Cruel!"

We are now, as your lordship may observe, in about act three of an inferior drama. She was to be the deserted victim and I the heartless villain.

"Nonsense, my dear! Do not pretend that these are circumstances—even to our somewhat inelegant posture— that these are circumstances with which you are wholly unfamiliar!"

"What shall I do?"

"Fiddlesticks, woman! The danger is slight as you know very well. Or are you waiting for—"

I caught myself up. Even to pretend that there might be something about this commerce that was *commercial* seemed an unnecessary insult. To tell the truth I found there were a number of irritations combined with my natural sense of completion and victory and at the moment I wished nothing so much as that she would vanish like a soap bubble or anything evanescent.

"Waiting for what, Edmund?"

"For a reasonable moment to slip into your hutch— cabin I would say—and repair your, your toilette."

"Edmund!"

"We have very little time, Miss Brocklebank!"

"Yet if—*if* there should be—unhappy consequences—"

"Why, my dear, we must cross that bridge when you come to it! Now go, go! I will examine the lobby—yes the coast is clear!"

I favoured her with a light salute, then leapt back into my cabin. I restored the books to their shelves and did my best to wrench the iron support of the canvas basin back into shape. I lay at last in my bunk and felt, not the Aristotelian sadness but a continuance of my previous irritation. Really the woman is *such* a fool! The French! It was her sense of theatre that had betrayed her, I could not help thinking, at my expense. But the party was breaking up on deck. I thought that I would emerge later when the light in the lobby was a concealment rather than discovery. I would take the right moment to go to the passenger saloon and drink a glass with any gentleman who might be drinking late there. I did not care to light my candle but waited—and waited in vain! Nobody descended from the upper decks! I stole into the passenger saloon therefore and was disconcerted to find Deverel there already, seated at the table under the great stern window with a glass in one hand and of all things a carnival mask in the other! He was laughing to himself. He saw me at once and called out.

"Talbot my dear fellow! A glass for Mr Talbot, steward! What a sight it was!"

Deverel was elevated. His speech was not precise and there was a carelessness about his bearing. He drank to me with grace, however exaggerated. He laughed again.

"What famous sport!"

For a moment I thought he might refer to the passage between me and Miss Zenny. But his attitude was not exactly right for that. It was something else, then.

"Why yes," said I. "Famous, as you say, sir."

He returned nothing for a moment or two. Then—

"How he does hate a parson!"

I was, as we used to say in the nursery, getting warmer.

"You refer to our gallant captain."

"Old Rumble-guts."

"I must own, Mr Deverel, that I am no particular friend to the cloth myself; but the captain's dislike of it seems beyond anything. I have been told that he has forbidden Mr Colley the quarterdeck on account of some trivial oversight."

Deverel laughed again.

"The quarterdeck—the afterdeck, poop and all! So he is confined more or less to the waist."

"Such *passionate* detestation is mysterious. I myself found Colley to be a, a creature of—but I would not punish the man for his nature other than to ignore him."

Deverel rolled his empty glass on the table.

"Bates! Another brandy for Mr Deverel!"

"You are kindness itself, Talbot. I could tell you—"

He broke off, laughing.

"Tell me what, sir?"

The man, I saw too late, was deep in his cups. Only the habitual elegance of his behaviour and bearing had concealed the fact from me. He murmured.

"Our captain. Our damned captain."

His head fell forward on the saloon table, his glass dropped and broke. I tried to rouse him but could not. I called the steward who is accustomed enough to dealing with such situations. Now at last the audience were indeed returning from the upper decks, for I could hear feet on the ladder. I emerged from the saloon to be met by a crowd of them in the lobby. Miss Granham swept by me. Mr Prettiman hung at her shoulder and orated to what effect I know not. The Stocks were agreeing with Pike *père et mère* that the thing had gone too far. But here was Miss Zenobia, radiant among the officers as if she had made one of the audience from the beginning! She addressed me, laughing.

"Was it not diverting, Mr Talbot?"

I bowed, smiling.

"I have never been better entertained, Miss Brocklebank."

I returned to my cabin, where it seemed to me the woman's perfume yet lingered. To tell the truth, though irritation was still uppermost in my mind, as I sat down and began to make this entry—and as the entry has progressed—irritation has been subsumed into a kind of universal sadness—Good God! Is Aristotle right in this commerce of the sexes as he is in the orders of society? I must rouse myself from too dull a view of the farmyard transaction by which our wretched species is lugged into the daylight.

ZETA

It is the same night and I have recovered from what I now think a morbid view of practically everything! The truth is I am more concerned with what Wheeler may discover and pass on to his fellows than considerations of a kind of methodistical moralism! For one thing, I cannot get the iron ring back into precise shape and for another, that curst perfume lingers yet! Confound the fool of a woman! As I look back, it seems to me that what I shall ever remember is not the somewhat feverish and too brief pleasure of my *entertainment* but the occasional and astonishing recourse to the Stage which she employed whenever her feelings were more than usually roused—or perhaps when they were more than usually *definable*! Could an actress convey an emotion that is indefinable? And would she not therefore welcome with gratitude a situation where the emotion was direct and precise? And does this not account for *stagey* behaviour? In my very modest involvement with amateur theatricals at the university, those whom we had hired to be our professional advisers named for us some of the technicalities of the art, craft or *trade*. Thus, I should have said that after my remark "Why, my dear, we must cross that bridge when you come to it!" she did not reply in words; but being half-turned away she turned wholly away and started forward away from me—would have gone much further had the hutch allowed of it—would have performed the movement we were told constituted *a break down stage right*! I laughed to remember it and was somewhat more myself again. Good God, as the captain would agree, one parson in a ship is one too many, and the stage serves as an agree-

able alternative to moralism! Why, was there not a performance given us by the reverend gentleman and Miss
Brocklebank in the course of the one service we have had
to suffer? I am this very moment possessed by a positively
and literally Shakespearean concept. *He* had found her
attractive and *she* had shown herself, as women will,
anxious to kneel before a male officiant—they made a
pair! Should we not do them good—or, as an imp whispered to me, do us all three good? Should not this
unlikely Beatrice and Benedict be brought into a mountain of affection for each other? "I will do any modest
office to help my cousin to a good husband." I laughed
aloud as I wrote that—and can only hope that the other
passengers, lying in their bunks at *three bells of the middle
watch* think that like Beatrice I laughed in my sleep! I
shall for the future single out Mr Colley for the most,
shall I say, distinguished attentions on my part—or at
least until Miss Brocklebank proves to be no longer in
danger from *the French*!

(Z)

Zed, you see, zed, I do not know what the day is—but here was a to-do! What a thing!

I rose at the accustomed hour with a faint stricture about the brows, caused I think by my somewhat liberal potations with Mr Deverel of a rather inferior brandy. I dressed and went on deck to blow it away—when who should emerge from our lobby but the reverend gentleman for whom I planned to procure—the word is unfortunate—such a pleasant future. Mindful of my determination I raised my beaver to him and gave him good day. He bowed and smiled and raised his tricorn but with more dignity than I had thought he had in him. Come, thought I to myself, does Van Diemen's Land require a bishop? I watched him in some surprise as he walked steadily up the ladder to the afterdeck. I followed him to where Mr Prettiman still stood and cradled his ridiculous weapon. I saluted him; for if I have a personal need, now, of Mr Colley, as you know, Mr Prettiman must always be an object of interest to me.

"You hit the albatross, sir?"

Mr Prettiman bounced with indignation.

"I did not, sir! The whole episode—the weapon was snatched from my hands—the whole episode was grotesque and lamentable! Such a display of ignorance, of monstrous and savage superstition!"

"No doubt, no doubt," said I soothingly. "Such a thing could never happen in France."

I moved on towards the poop; climbed the ladder; and what was my astonishment to find Mr Colley there! In round wig, tricorn and black coat he stood before Captain Anderson on the very planks sacred to the tyrant! As I

came to the top of the ladder Captain Anderson turned
abruptly away, went to the rail and spat over the side. He
was red in the face and grim as a gargoyle. Mr Colley
lifted his hat gravely, then came towards the ladder. He
saw Lieutenant Summers and went across to him. They
saluted each other with equal gravity.

"Mr Summers, I believe it was you who discharged Mr
Prettiman's weapon?"

"It was, sir."

"I trust you injured no one?"

"I fired over the side."

"I must thank you for it."

"It was nothing, sir. Mr Colley—"

"Well, sir?"

"I beg of you, be advised by me."

"In what way, sir?"

"Do not go immediately. We have not known our
people long enough, sir. After yesterday—I am aware that
you are no friend to intoxicants of any sort—I beg you to
wait until the people have been issued with their rum.
After that there will ensue a period when they will, even if
they are no more than now open to reason, be at least
calmer and more amiable—"

"I have armour, sir."

"Believe me, I know of what I speak! I was once of their
condition—"

"I bear the shield of the Lord."

"Sir! Mr Colley! As a personal favour to me, since you
declare yourself indebted—I beg of you, wait for one
hour!"

There was a silence. Mr Colley saw me and bowed
gravely. He turned back to Mr Summers.

"Very well, sir. I accept your advice."

The gentlemen bowed once again, Mr Colley came
towards me so *we* bowed to each other! Versailles could

have done no better! Then the gentleman descended the ladder. It was too much! A new curiosity mingled with my *Shakespearean* purposes for him. Good God, thought I, the whole southern hemisphere has got itself an archbishop! I hurried after him and caught him as he was about to enter our lobby.

"Mr Colley!"

"Sir?"

"I have long wished to be better acquainted with you but owing to an unfortunate indisposition the occasion has not presented itself—"

His *mug* split with a grin. He swept off his hat, clasped it to his stomach and bowed, or sinuously reverenced over it. The archbishop diminished to a country curate—no, to a hedge priest. My contempt returned and quenched my curiosity. But I remembered how much Zenobia might stand in need of his services and that I should keep him *in reserve*—or as the Navy would say—*in ordinary*!

"Mr Colley. We have been too long unacquainted. Will you not take a turn with me on deck?"

It was extraordinary. His face, burned and blistered as it was by exposure to the tropic sun, reddened even more, then as suddenly paled. I swear that tears stood in his eyes! His Adam's apple positively *danced* up and down beneath and above his bands!

"Mr Talbot, sir—words cannot—I have long desired— but at such a moment—this is worthy of you and your noble patron—this is generous—this is Christian charity in its truest meaning—God bless you, Mr Talbot!"

Once more he performed his sinuous and ducking bow, retired a yard or two backwards, ducked again as if leaving the presence, then disappeared into his hutch.

I heard a contemptuous exclamation above me, glanced up and saw Mr Prettiman gazing down at us over the forrard rail of the quarterdeck. He bounced away again out of sight. But for the moment I spared him no attention. I was still confounded by the remarkable effect of my words on Colley. My appearance is that of a gentleman and I am suitably dressed. I have some height and perhaps—I say no more than perhaps—consciousness of my future employment may have added more dignity to my bearing than is customary in one of my years! In which case, sir, you are obliquely to be blamed for—but I wrote earlier did I not that I would not continue to trouble you with my gratitude? To resume then, there was nothing about me to warrant this foolish fellow treating me as a Royal! I paced between the break of the quarterdeck and the mainmast for half an hour, perhaps to rid myself of that same stricture of the brows, and pondered this ridiculous circumstance. Something had happened and I did not know what it was—something, I saw, during the ship's entertainment while I was so closely engaged with the Delicious Enemy! What it was, I could not tell, nor why it should make my recognition of Mr Colley more than ordinarily delightful to him. And Lieutenant Summers had discharged Mr Prettiman's blunderbuss without injuring anyone! That seemed like an extraordinary failure on the part of a *fighting seaman*! It was a great mystery and puzzle; yet the man's evident gratitude for my attentions—it was annoying that I could not demand a solution to the mystery from the gentlemen or officers, for it would not be politic to reveal an ignorance based on a pleasant preoccupation with a member of the Sex. I could not at once think how to go on. I returned to our lobby, proposing to go into the saloon and discover if I could by attending to casual conversations the source of Mr Colley's extreme gratitude and dignity. But as I entered the lobby Miss Brocklebank hurried out of her hutch and detained me with a hand on my arm.

"Mr Talbot—Edmund!"

"How may I serve you, ma'am?"

87

Then throatily, contralto but pianissimo—

"A letter—Oh God! What shall I do?"

"Zenobia! Tell me all!"

Does your lordship detect a theatricality in my response? It was so indeed. We were at once borne along on a tide of melodrama.

"Oh heavens—it, it is a *billet*—lost, lost!"

"But my dear," said I, leaving the stage at once, "I have written you nothing."

Her magnificent but foolish bosom heaved.

"It was from Another!"

"Well," I murmured to her, "I refuse to be responsible for every gentleman in the ship! You should employ his offices, not mine. And so—"

I turned to leave but she held me by the arm.

"The note is wholly innocent but may be—might be misconstrued—I may have dropped it—oh Edmund, you well know where!"

"I assure you," said I, "that while I rearranged my hutch where it had been disturbed by a certain exquisite occasion I should have noticed—"

"Please! Oh please!"

She gazed into my eyes with that look of absolute trust mingled with anguish which so improves a pair of orbs however lustrous. (But who am I to instruct your lordship, still surrounded as you are by adorers who gaze on what they would have but cannot obtain—by the way, is my flattery too gross? Remember you declared it most effective when seasoned with truth!)

Zenobia came close and murmured up at me.

"It must be in your cabin. Oh should Wheeler find it I am lost!"

The devil, thought I. If Wheeler finds it, *I* am lost or near enough—is she trying to implicate me?

"Say no more, Miss Brocklebank. I will go at once."

I exited right—or should it be left? I have never been certain, where the theatre is concerned. Say then that I moved towards my spacious apartment on the larboard side of the vessel, opened the door, went in, shut it and began to search. I do not know anything more irritating than to be forced to search for an object in a confined space. All at once I was aware that there were two feet by mine. I glanced up.

"Go away, Wheeler! Go *away*!"

He went. After that I found the paper but only when I had given up looking for it. I was about to pour water into my canvas basin when what should I see in the centre of it but a sheet of paper, folded. I seized it at once and was about to return it to Zenobia's hutch when I was stopped by a thought. In the first place I had performed my ablutions earlier in the morning. The canvas basin had been emptied and the bunk remade.

Wheeler!

At once, I unfolded the note, then breathed again. The hand was uneducated.

DEAREST MOST ADORABLE WOMAN I CAN WATE NO LONGER! I HAVE AT LAST DISCOVERED A PLACE AND NO ONE IS IN THE NO! MY HART THUNDERS IN MY BOSOM AS IT NEVER DID IN MY FREQUENT HOURS OF PERIL! ONLY ACQUAINT ME WITH THE TIME AND I WILL CONDUCT YOU TO OUR HEVEN!
                    YOUR SAILOR HERO

Good God, thought I, this is Lord Nelson raised to a higher power of the ridiculous! She is having an attack of the *Emmas* and has infected this Unknown Sailor Hero with her own style of it! I fell into a state of complete confusion. Mr Colley, all dignity—now this note—Summers with Prettiman's blunderbuss that was really Brocklebank's—I began to laugh, then shouted for Wheeler.

"Wheeler, you have been busy in my cabin. What should I do without you?"

He bowed but said nothing.

"I am pleased with your attentiveness. Here is a half-guinea for you. You are sometimes forgetful though, are you not?"

The man's eyes did not flicker towards the canvas bowl.

"Thank you, Mr Talbot, sir. You may rely on me in every way sir."

He withdrew. I examined the note again. It was not Deverel's, obviously, for the illiteracy was not that of a gentleman. I wondered what I should do.

Then—really, at some later date I must amuse myself by seeing how the thing would fit into a farce—I saw how the theatre would provide a means whereby I might rid myself of Zenobia and the parson together—I had but to drop the note in his cabin, pretend to discover it—Is not this note addressed to Miss Brocklebank sir? And you a minister of religion! Confess, you dog, and let us congratulate you on your success with your inamorata!

It was at this point that I caught myself up in astonishment and irritation. Here was I, who considered myself an honourable and responsible man, contemplating an action which was not merely criminal but despicable! How did that come about? You see I hide nothing. Sitting on the edge of my bunk I examined the train that had led me to such gross thoughts and found its original in the dramatic nature of Zenobia's appeal—straight back to farce and melodrama—in a word, to the theatre! Be it proclaimed in all the schools—

Plato was right!

I rose, went to her cabin, knocked. She opened, I handed her the note and came away.

(Ω)

Omega, omega, omega. The last scene surely! Nothing more can happen—unless it be fire, shipwreck, the violence of the enemy or a miracle! Even in this last case, I am sure the Almighty would appear theatrically as a *Deus ex Machina*! Even if I refuse to disgrace myself by it, I cannot, it seems, prevent the whole ship from indulging in theatricals! I myself should come before you now, wearing the cloak of a messenger in a play—why not your Racine—forgive me the "your" but I cannot think of him as otherwise—

Or may I stay with the Greeks? It is a play. Is it a farce or a tragedy? Does not a tragedy depend on the dignity of the protagonist? Must he not be great to fall greatly? A farce, then, for the man appears now a sort of Punchinello. His fall is in social terms. Death does not come into it. He will not put out his eyes or be pursued by the Furies—he has committed no crime, broken no law—unless our egregious tyrant has a few in reserve for the unwary.

After I had rid myself of the *billet* I went to the quarterdeck for air, then to the poop. Captain Anderson was not there, but Deverel had the watch together with our ancient midshipman Mr Davies, who in bright sunlight looks more decayed than ever. I saluted Deverel and returned to the quarterdeck, meaning to have some kind of exchange with Mr Prettiman who still patrols in all his madness. (I am becoming more and more convinced that the man cannot conceivably be any danger to the state. No one would heed him. Nevertheless, I thought it my duty to keep an acquaintance with him.) He paid no attention to my approach. He was staring down into the waist. My gaze followed his.

What was my astonishment to see the back view of Mr Colley appear from beneath the afterdeck and proceed towards the people's part of the vessel! This in itself was astonishing enough, for he crossed the white line at the mainmast which delimits their approach to us unless by invitation or for duty. But what was even more astonishing was that Colley was dressed in a positive delirium of ecclesiastical finery! That surplice, gown, hood, wig, cap looked quite simply silly under our vertical sun! He moved forward at a solemn pace as he might in a cathedral. The people who were lounging in the sun stood at once and, I thought, with a somewhat sheepish air. Mr Colley disappeared from my sight under the break of the fo'castle. This, then, was what he had spoken of with Summers. The people must have had their rum—and indeed now I recollected that I had heard the pipe and the cry of "Up Spirits!" earlier on without paying any attention to a sound that by now had become so familiar. The movement of the vessel was easy, the air hot. The people themselves were indulged with a holiday or what Summers calls a "Make and Mend". I stood on the afterdeck for a while, hardly attending to Mr Prettiman's diatribe on what he called this survival of barbaric finery, for I was waiting with some curiosity to see the parson come out again! I could not think that he proposed to conduct a full service! But the sight of a parson not so much walking into such a place as processing into it—for there had been about him that movement, that air, which would suppose a choir, a handful of canons and a dean at least—this sight I say at once amused and impressed me. I understood his mistake. He lacked the natural authority of a gentleman and had absurdly overdone the dignity of his calling. He was now advancing on the lower orders in all the majesty of the

Church Triumphant—or should it be the Church Militant? I was moved at this picture in little of one of the
elements that have brought English—and dare I say
British—Society to the state of perfection it now enjoys.
Here before me was the Church; there, *aft* of me and
seated in his cabin was the State in the person of Captain
Anderson. Which whip I wondered would prove to be the
more effective? The cat-o'-nine-tails, only too material in
its red serge bag and at the disposal of the captain, though
I have not known him order its use; or the notional, the
Platonic Idea of a whip, the threat of hell fire? For I had no
doubt (from the dignified and outraged appearance of the
man before the captain) that the people had subjected Mr
Colley to some slight, real or imagined. I should not have
been too surprised had I heard the fo'castle to resound
with wails of repentance or screams of terror. For a time—
I do not know how long—I waited to see what would happen and concluded that nothing would happen at all! I
returned to my cabin, where I continued with the *warm*
paragraphs which I trust you will have enjoyed. I broke off
from that employment at a noise.

Can your lordship guess what the noise was? No sir,
not even you! (I hope to come by practice to subtler forms
of flattery.)

The first sound I heard from the fo'castle was applause!
It was not the sort of applause that will follow an *aria* and
perhaps interrupt the business of an opera for whole minutes together. This was not hysteria, the audience was not
beside itself. Nor were the people throwing roses—or
guineas, as I once saw some young bloods try to into the
bosom of the Fantalini! They were, my *social* ears told
me, doing what was proper, the done thing. They
applauded much as I for my part have applauded in the
Sheldonian among my fellows when some respectable
foreigner has been awarded an honorary degree by the

93

university. I went out on deck quickly, but there was now silence after that first round of applause. I thought I could just hear the reverend gentleman speaking. I had half a mind to advance on the scene, conceal myself by the break of the fo'castle and listen. But then I reflected on the number of sermons I had heard in my life and the likely number to come. Our voyage, so wretched in many ways, has nevertheless been an almost complete holiday from them! I decided to wait, therefore, until our newly triumphant Colley should have persuaded our captain that our ancient vessel needed a sermon or, worse, a formal series of them. There even floated before my thoughtful eyes the image of, say, *Colley's Sermons* or even *Colley on Life's Voyage*, and I decided in advance not to be a subscriber.

I was about to return from where I stood in the gently moving shadow of some sail or other when I heard, incredulously, a burst of applause, warmer this time and spontaneous. I do not have to point out to your lordship the rarity of the occasions on which a parson is applauded in full fig or as what young Mr Taylor describes as "Dressed over all". Groans and tears, exclamations of remorse and pious ejaculations he may look for if his sermon be touched with any kind of *enthusiasm*: silence and covert yawns will be his reward if he is content to be a dull, respectable fellow! But the applause I was hearing from the fo'castle was more proper for an entertainment! It was as if Colley were an acrobat or juggler. This second round of applause sounded as if (having earned the first one by keeping six dinner plates in the air at once) he now had added a billiard cue stood on his forehead with a chamber pot revolving on the top of it!

Now my curiosity was really roused and I was about to go forrard when Deverel descended from his watch and at once, with what I can only call deliberate meaning, began to

discuss La Brocklebank! I felt myself detected and was at
once a little flattered as any young fellow might be and a
little apprehensive, when I imagined the possible consequences of my connection with her. She herself I saw
standing on the starboard side of the quarterdeck and being
lectured by Mr Prettiman. I drew Deverel with me into the
lobby, where we fenced a little. We spoke of the lady with
some freedom and it crossed my mind that during my
indisposition Deverel might have had more success than he
cared to admit, though he hinted at it. We may both be in
the same basket. Heavens above! But though a naval officer
he is a gentleman, and however things turn out we shall not
give each other away. We drank a *tot* in the passenger
saloon, he had gone about his business and I was returning
to my hutch when I was stopped in my tracks by a great
noise from the fo'castle and the most unexpected noise of
all—a positive crash of laughter! I was quite overcome
by the thought of Mr Colley as a wit and concluded at
once that he had left them to themselves and they were,
like schoolboys, amusing themselves with a mocking
pantomime of the master, who has rebuked then left them.
I went up to the afterdeck for a better view, then to the
quarterdeck, but could see no one on the fo'castle except
the man stationed there as a lookout. They were all inside,
all gathered. Colley had said something, I thought, and is
now in his hutch, changing out of his *barbaric finery*. But
word had flown round the ship. The afterdeck was
filling below me with ladies and gentlemen and officers.
Those who dared had stationed themselves by me at the
forrard rail of the quarterdeck. The theatrical image that
had haunted my mind and coloured my speculations in the
earlier events now seemed to embrace the whole vessel. For
one dizzy moment I wondered if our officers were out in the
expectation of mutiny! But Deverel would have known, and
he had said nothing. Yet everyone was looking forward to

the great, unknown part of the ship where the people were indulging in whatever sport was afoot. We were spectators and there, interruptedly seen beyond the boats on the boom and the huge cylinder of the mainmast, was the stage. The break of the fo'castle rose like the side of a house, yet furnished with two ladders and two entrances, one on either side, that were provokingly like a stage—provoking, since a performance could not be guaranteed and our strange expectations were likely to be disappointed. I was never made so aware of the distance between the disorder of real life in its multifarious action, partial exhibition, irritating concealments and the stage simulacra that I had once taken as a fair representation of it! I did not care to ask what was going on and could not think how to find out unless I was willing to show an unbecoming degree of curiosity. Of course your lordship's favourite would have brought forward the heroine and her confidante—mine would have added the stage instruction *Enter two sailors.* Yet all I could hear was amusement growing in the fo'castle and something the same among our passengers, not to say officers. I waited on the event, and unexpectedly it came! Two ship's boys—not Young Gentlemen—shot out of the larboard doorway of the fo'castle, crossed out of sight behind the mainmast, then shot as suddenly into the starboard entrance! I was reflecting on the abject nature of the sermon that could be the occasion of such general and prolonged hilarity when I became aware of Captain Anderson, who also stood by the forward rail of the quarterdeck and stared forward inscrutably. Mr Summers, the first lieutenant, came racing up the ladder, his every movement conveying anxiety and haste. He went straight to Captain Anderson.

"Well, Mr Summers?"

"I beg you will allow me to take charge, sir."

"We must not interfere with the church, Mr Summers."

"Sir—the men, sir!"

"Well, sir?"

"They are in drink, sir!"

"Then see they are punished for it, Mr Summers."

Captain Anderson turned away from Mr Summers and for the first time appeared to notice me. He called out across the deck.

"Good day, Mr Talbot! I trust you are enjoying our progress?"

I replied that I was, couching my rejoinder in words I have forgotten, for I was preoccupied by the extraordinary change in the captain. The face with which he is accustomed to await the approach of his fellow men may be said to be welcoming as the door of a gaol. He has, too, a way of projecting his under-jaw and lowering the sullen mass of his face on it, all the while staring up from under his brows, which I conceive to be positively terrifying to his inferiors. But today there was in his face and indeed in his speech a kind of gaiety!

But Lieutenant Summers had spoken again.

"At least allow me—look at that, sir!"

He was pointing. I turned.

Has your lordship ever reflected on the quaintness of the tradition that signalizes our attainment of learning by hanging a medieval hood round our necks and clapping a plasterer's board on our heads? (Should not the chancellor have a silver gilt hod carried before him? But I digress.) Two figures had appeared at the larboard entry. They were now *processing* across the deck to the starboard one. Perhaps the striking of the ship's bell and the surely sarcastic cry of "All's well!" persuaded me that these figures were those in some fantastic clock. The foremost of the figures wore a black hood edged with fur, and wore it not hung down his back but up and over his head as we see in illuminated manuscripts from the age of Chaucer.

It was up and round his face and held by one hand close under the chin in the fashion that I believe ladies would describe as a tippet. The other hand was on the hip with elbow akimbo. The creature crossed the deck with an exaggeratedly mincing parody of the female gait. The second figure wore—apart from the loose garments of canvas which are the people's common wear—a mortarboard of decidedly battered appearance. It followed the first figure in shambling pursuit. As the two of them disappeared into the fo'castle there was another crash of laughter, then a cheer.

Dare I say what from its subtlety your lordship may well consider to be retrospective wisdom? This play-acting was not directed only inwards towards the fo'castle. It was aimed *aft* at us! Have you not seen an actor consciously throw a soliloquy outwards and upwards to the gallery and even into one corner of it? These two figures that had paraded before us had cast their portrayal of human weakness and folly directly *aft* to where their betters were assembled! If your lordship has any concept of the speed with which scandal spreads in a ship you will the more readily credit the immediacy—no, the instantaneity—with which news of the business in the fo'castle, whatever it was, now flashed through the ship. The people, the men, the crew—they had purposes of their own! They were astir! We were united, I believe, in our awareness of the threat to social stability that might at any moment arise among the common sailors and emigrants! It was horseplay and insolence at liberty in the fo'castle. Mr Colley and Captain Anderson were at fault—the one for being the occasion of such insolence, the other for allowing it. During a whole generation (granted the glory attendant on our successful arms) the civilized world has had cause to lament the results of indiscipline among the Gallic Race. They will hardly recover, I believe. I began to descend from the quarterdeck in disgust with a bare acknowledgement of salutations on every side. Mr Prettiman now stood with Miss Granham on the afterdeck. He might well, I thought bitterly enough, have an ocular demonstration of the results of the liberty he advocated! Captain Anderson had left the quarterdeck to Summers, who still stared forward with a tense face as if he expected the appearance of the enemy or Leviathan or the sea serpent. I was about to descend to the waist when Mr Cumbershum appeared from our lobby. I paused, wondering whether to interrogate him; but while I did so, young Tommy Taylor positively burst out of the fo'castle of all places and came racing aft. Cumbershum grabbed him.

"More decorum about the deck, young fellow!"

"Sir—I must see the first lieutenant, sir—it's true as God's my judge!"

"Swearing are you again, you little sod?"

"It's the parson, sir, I told you it was!"

"Mr Colley to you, sir, and damn your impudence for a squeaking little bugger!"

"It's true, sir, it's true! Mr Colley's there in the fo'castle as drunk as the butcher's boots!"

"Get below, sir, or I'll masthead you!"

Mr Taylor disappeared. My own astonishment was complete at finding the parson had been present in the fo'castle during all the various noises that had resounded thence—had been there while yet there was play-acting and the clock-figures mountebanking for our instruction. I no longer thought of retiring to my hutch. For now not merely the afterdeck and quarterdeck were crowded. Those persons who were sufficiently active had climbed into the lower parts of the mizzen shrouds while below me, the waist—the pit, I suppose in theatrical terms—had yet more spectators. What was curious was that round me on the quarterdeck, the ladies no less than the gentlemen were in, or exhibited a condition of, shocked cheerfulness. They would, it seemed, have been glad to be assured the news was not true—would rather be assured—were desperately sorry if it *was* true—would not for the wide world have had such a thing happen—and if, against all probability, no, possibility, it *was* true, why never, never, never—Only Miss Granham descended with a set face from the afterdeck, turned and vanished into the lobby. Mr Prettiman with his gun stared from her to the fo'castle and back again. Then he hastened after her. But other than this severe pair the afterdeck was full of whispering and nodding animation fitted more for the retiring room at an assembly than the deck of a man-of-war. Below me Mr Brocklebank leaned heavily on his stick with the women nodding their bonnets at him on either side. Cumbershum stood by them, silent. It was at some point in this period of expectancy that the silence became general so that the gentle noises of the ship—sea noises against her planks, the soft touch of the wind fingering her rigging—became audible. In the silence, and as if produced by it, my ears—*our* ears—detected the distant sound of a man's voice. It sang. We knew at once it must be Mr Colley. He sang and his voice was meagre as his appearance. The tune and the words were well enough known. It might be heard in an alehouse or a drawing room. I cannot tell where Mr Colley learnt it.

"Where have you been all the day, Billy Boy?"

Then there followed a short silence, after which he broke into a different song which I did not know. The words must have been warm, I think, country matters perhaps, for there was laughter to back them. A peasant, born to stone-gathering and bird-scaring, might have picked them up under the hedge where the workers pause at noon.

When I go over the scene in my mind I am at a loss to account for our feeling that Colley's misdemeanour would be rounded out to the fullness of the event. I had been vexed earlier to see how little the stage of the fo'castle was to be relied on for conveying to us the shape and dimensions of this drama! Yet now I too waited. Your lordship might demand with reason, "Have you never heard of a drunken parson before?" I can only reply that I had indeed heard of one but had not yet seen one. Moreover, there are times and places.

The singing stopped. There began to be laughter again, applause, then a clamour of shouts and jeers. It seemed after a while that we were indeed to be cheated of the event—which was hardly to be borne, seeing how much in sickness, danger and boredom we had paid for our seats. However, it was at this critical juncture that Captain Anderson came out on the quarterdeck, took his place at the forrard rail of it and surveyed the theatre and audience. His face was as severe as Miss Granham's. He spoke sharply to Mr Deverel, who now had the watch, informing him (in a voice which seemed to make the fact directly attributable to some negligence on Mr Deverel's part) that *the parson was still there*. He then took a turn or two round his side of the quarterdeck, came back to the rail, stopped by it, and spoke to Mr Deverel more cheerfully.

"Mr Deverel. Be good enough to have the parson informed he must now return to his cabin."

I believe not another muscle stirred in the ship as Mr Deverel repeated the order to Mr Willis, who saluted and went forward with all eyes on his back. Our astonished ears heard Mr Colley address him with a string of endearments that would have—and perhaps *did*—make La Brocklebank blush like a paeony. The young gentleman came stumbling out of the fo'castle and ran back sniggering. But in truth none among us paid him much attention. For now, like some pigmy Polyphemus, like whatever is at once strange and disgusting, the parson appeared in the lefthand doorway of the fo'castle. His ecclesiastical garment had gone and the marks of his degree. His wig had gone—his very breeches, stockings and shoes had been taken from him. Some charitable soul had in pity, I supposed, supplied him with one of the loose canvas garments that the common people wear about the ship; and this because of his diminutive stature was sufficient to cover his loins. He was not alone. A young stalwart had him in charge. This fellow was supporting Mr Colley, whose head lay back on the man's breast. As the curious pair came uncertainly past the mainmast, Mr Colley pushed back so that they stopped. It was evident that his mind had become only lightly linked to his understanding. He appeared to be in a state of extreme and sunny enjoyment. His eyes moved indifferently, as if taking no print of what they saw. Surely his frame was not one that could afford him any pleasure! His skull now the wig no longer covered it was seen to be small and narrow. His legs had no calves; but dame Nature in a frivolous mood had furnished him with great feet and knots of knees that betrayed their peasant origin. He was muttering some nonsense of *fol de rol* or the like. Then, as if seeing his audience for the first time, he heaved himself away from his assistant, stood on splayed feet and flung out his arms as if to embrace us all.

"Joy! Joy! Joy!"

Then his face became thoughtful. He turned to his right, walked slowly and carefully to the bulwark and pissed against it. What a shrieking and covering of faces there was from the ladies, what growls from us! Mr Colley turned back to us and opened his mouth. Not even the captain could have caused a more immediate silence.

Mr Colley raised his right hand and spoke, though slurredly.

"The blessing of God the Father Almighty, God the Son and God the Holy Ghost be with you and remain with you always."

Then there was a commotion I can tell you! If the man's uncommonly public micturation had shocked the ladies, to be blessed by a drunk man in a canvas shirt caused screams, hasty retreats and, I am told, one *évanouissement*! It was no more than seconds after this that the servant, Phillips, and Mr Summers, the first lieutenant, lugged the poor fool out of sight while the seaman who had helped him aft stood and stared after them. When Colley was out of sight the man looked up at the quarterdeck, touched his forelock and went back to the fo'castle.

On the whole I think the audience was well enough satisfied. Next to the ladies Captain Anderson seemed to be the principal beneficiary of Colley's performance. He became positively sociable with the ladies, voluntarily breaking away from his sacred side of the quarterdeck and bidding them welcome. Though he firmly but courteously declined to discuss *l'affaire Colley*, there was a lightness about his step and indeed a light in his eye which I had supposed occasioned in a naval officer only by the imminence of battle! What animation had possessed the other officers passed away quickly enough. They must have seen enough drunkenness and been part of enough to see this as no more than an event in a long history. And what was the sight of Colley's urine to naval gentlemen who had perhaps seen decks smeared with the viscera and streaming with the blood of their late companions? I returned to my hutch, determined to give you as full and vivid an account of the episode as was in my power. Yet even while I was busy leading up to the events, the further events of his fall raced past me. While I was yet describing the strange noises from the fo'castle, I heard the sound of a door opened clumsily on the other side of the lobby. I jumped up and stared (by means of my *louvre* or spyhole) across it. Lo, Colley came out of his cabin! He held a sheet of paper in his hand and he still smiled that smile of aery contentment and joy. He went in this joyous distraction in the direction of the necessary offices on that side of the ship. Evidently he still dwelt in a land of faery which would vanish presently and leave him—

Well. Where will it leave him? He is quite unpractised in the management of spiritous liquors. I imagined his distress on coming to himself and I started to laugh—then changed my mind. The closeness of my cabin became a positive fetor.

(51)

This is the fifty-first day of our voyage, I think; and then again perhaps it is not. I have lost interest in the calendar and almost lost it in the voyage too. We have our shipboard calendar of events which are trivial enough. Nothing has happened since Colley entertained us. He is much condemned. Captain Anderson continues benign. Colley himself has not been out of his hutch in the four days which have passed since his drunkenness. No one but the servant has seen him if you except me on the occasion when he took his own paper to the loo! Enough of him.

What might amuse you more is the kind of *country dance* we young fellows have been performing round La Brocklebank. I have not yet identified her *Sailor Hero* but am sure that Deverel has had to do with her. I taxed him with it and drew an admission from him. We agreed that a man might well suffer shipwreck on *that* coast and have decided to stand shoulder to shoulder in mutual defence. A mixed metaphor, my lord, so you can see how dull I find myself. To resume. We both think that at the moment she is inclined to Cumbershum. I owned that this was a relief to me and Deverel agreed. We had feared, both of us, to be in the same difficulty over our common *inamorata*. You will remember that I had some harebrained scheme, since Colley was so clearly *épris* with her, of having a MUCH ADO ABOUT NOTHING and bringing this Beatrice and Benedict into a mountain of affection for each other! I told Deverel this, at which he was silent for a while, then burst out laughing. I was about to inform him plainly that I took exception to his conduct when he asked my pardon in the most graceful way. But, said he, the coincidence was past the wit of man to invent and he would share the jest with me if I would give him my word to say nothing of what he told me. We were interrupted at this point and I do not know what the jest is, but you shall have it when I do.

ALPHA

I have been remiss and let a few days go by without attention to the journal. I have felt a lethargy. There has been
little to do but walk the deck, drink with anyone who will,
walk the deck again, perhaps speaking to this passenger or
that. I believe I did not tell you that when "Mrs Brocklebank" issued from the cabin she proved to be if anything
younger than her daughter! I have avoided both her and
the fair Zenobia, who *glows* in this heat so as almost to
turn a man's stomach! Cumbershum is not so delicate.
The boredom of the voyage in these hot and next to windless latitudes has increased the consumption of strong
spirits among us. I had thought to give you a full list of
our passengers but have given up. They would not interest you. Let them remain κωφὰ πρόσωπα. What is of some
interest however is the behaviour—or the lack of it—of
Colley. The fact is that since the fellow's fall he has not
left his cabin. Phillips the servant goes in occasionally and
I believe that Mr Summers has visited him, I suppose
thinking it part of a first lieutenant's duty. A lustreless
fellow like Colley might well feel some diffidence at coming again among ladies and gentlemen. The ladies are
particularly strict on him. For my own part, the fact that
Captain Anderson *rode the man hard*, in Deverel's phrase,
is sufficient to temper any inclination I might have
absolutely to reject Colley as a human being!

Deverel and I agree that Brocklebank is or has been
the keeper of both the doxies. I had known that the world
of art is not to be judged by the accepted standards of
morality but would prefer him to set up his brothel in
another place. However, they have two hutches, one for

the "parents" and one for the "daughter", so he does at
least make a tiny gesture towards preserving appearances.
Appearances are preserved and everyone is happy, even
Miss Granham. As for Mr Prettiman, I suppose he
notices nothing. Long live illusion, say I. Let us export it
to our colonies with all the other benefits of civilization!

(60)

I have just come from the passenger saloon, where I have
sat for a long time with Summers. The conversation is
worth recording, though I have an uneasy feeling that it
tells against me. I am bound to say that Summers is the
person of all in this ship who does His Majesty's Service
the most credit. Deverel is naturally more the gentleman
but not assiduous in his duties. As for the others—they
may be dismissed *en masse*. The difference had been in
my mind and I did, in a way I now fear he may have
found offensive, discuss the desirability of men being elevated above their first station in life. It was thoughtless of
me and Summers replied with some bitterness.

"Mr Talbot, sir, I do not know how to say this or
indeed whether I should—but you yourself made it plain
in a way that put the matter beyond misunderstanding,
that a man's original is branded on his forehead, never to
be removed."

"Come, Mr Summers—I did not so!"

"Do you not remember?"

"Remember what?"

He was silent for a while. Then—

"I understand. It is plain when I see it from your point
of view. Why should you remember?"

"Remember *what*, sir?"

Again he was silent. Then he looked away and seemed
to be reading the words of the following sentence off the
bulkhead.

" 'Well, Summers, allow me to congratulate you on
imitating to perfection the manners and speech of a somewhat higher station in life than the one you was born to.' "

Now it was my turn to be silent. What he said was true. Your lordship may, if you choose, turn back in this very journal and find the words there. I have done so myself, and re-read the account of that first meeting. I believe Summers does not give me credit for the state of bewilderment and embarrassment in which I had then found myself, but the words, the very words, are there!

"I ask your pardon, Mr Summers. It was—insufferable."

"But true, sir," said Summers, bitterly. "In our country for all her greatness there is one thing she cannot do and that is translate a person wholly out of one class into another. Perfect translation from one language into another is impossible. Class is the British language."

"Come, sir," said I, "will you not believe me? Perfect translation from one language to another is possible and I could give you an example of it. So is perfect translation from class to class."

"*Imitating* to perfection—"

"Perfect in this, that you are a gentleman."

Summers flushed red and his face only slowly resumed its wonted bronze. It was high time we moved our ground.

"Yet you see, my dear fellow, we have at least one example among us where the translation is not a success!"

"I must suppose you to refer to Mr Colley. It was my purpose to raise that subject."

"The man has stepped out of his station without any merit to support the elevation."

"I do not see how his conduct can be traced to his original for we do not know what it was."

"Come. It appears in his physique, his speech and above all in what I can only call his habit of subordination. I swear he had got out of the peasantry by a kind of greasy obsequiousness. Now for example—Bates, the brandy, please!—I can myself drink brandy as long as you please and I issue a guarantee that no man and particularly no lady will see in me the kind of behaviour by which Mr Colley has amused us and affronted them. Colley, plied, as we must suppose, with spirits there in the fo'castle, had neither the strength to refuse it nor the breeding which would have enabled him to resist its more destructive effects."

"This wisdom should be put in a book."

"Laugh if you will, sir. Today I must not be offended with you."

"But there is another matter and I had intended to raise it. We have no physician and the man is mortally sick."

"How can that be? He is young and suffering from no more than over-indulgence in liquor."

"Still? I have talked with the servant. I have entered the cabin and seen for myself. In many years of service neither Phillips nor I have seen anything like it. The bed is filthy, yet the man, though he breathes every now and then, does not stir in it. His face is pressed down and hidden. He lies on his stomach, one hand above his head and clutched into the bolster, the other clutching an old eyebolt left in the timber."

"I marvel you can eat after it."

"Oh that! I tried to turn him over."

"Tried? You must have succeeded. You have three times his strength."

"Not in these circumstances."

"I own, Mr Summers, that I have not observed much intemperance in Colley's line of life. But the story goes that the Senior Tutor at my own college, having dined too well before a service, rose from his seat, staggered to the lectern, slumped, holding on to the brass eagle and was heard to mutter, 'I should have been down had it not been for this bleeding Dodo.' But I daresay you never heard the story."

Mr Summers shook his head.

"I have been much abroad," he replied gravely. "The

event made little noise in that part of the Service where I then was."

"A hit, a palpable hit! But depend on it, young Colley will lift up his head."

Summers stared into his untouched glass.

"He has a strange power. It is almost as if the Newtonian Force is affected. The hand that holds the eyebolt might be made of steel. He lies, dinted into his bunk, drawn down into it as if made of lead."

"There he must stay then."

"Is that all, Mr Talbot? Are you as indifferent to the man's fate as others are?"

"I am not an officer in this ship!"

"The more able to help, sir."

"How?"

"I may speak to you freely, may I not? Well then—how has the man been treated?"

"He was at first an object of one man's specific dislike, then an object of general indifference that was leading to contempt even before his latest—escapade."

Summers turned and stared out of the great stern window for a while. Then he looked back at me.

"What I say now could well ruin me if I have misjudged your character."

"Character? *My* character? You have examined my character? You set yourself up—"

"Forgive me—nothing is further from my mind than offending you and if I did not believe the case desperate—"

"What case, for God's sake?"

"We know your birth, your prospective position—why—men—and woman—will flatter you in the hope or expectation of gaining the governor's ear—"

"Good God—Mr Summers!"

"Wait, wait! Understand me, Mr Talbot—I do not complain!"

"You sound uncommonly like a man complaining, sir!"

I had half-risen from my seat; but Summers stretched out his hand in a gesture of such simple—"supplication" I suppose I must call it—that I sat down again.

"Proceed then, if you must!"

"I do not speak in my own behalf."

For a while we were both silent. Then Summers swallowed, deeply as if there had been a real drink in his mouth and that no small one.

"Sir, you have used your birth and your prospective position to get for yourself an unusual degree of attention and comfort—I do not complain—dare not! Who am I to question the customs of our society or indeed, the laws of nature? In a sentence, you have exercised the privileges of your position. I am asking you to shoulder its responsibilities."

During—it may be—half a minute; for what is time in a ship, or to revert to that strange metaphor of existence that came to me so strongly during Mr Colley's exhibition, what is time in a theatre? During that time, however long or short, I passed through numberless emotions—rage I think, confusion, irritation, amusement and an embarrassment for which I was most annoyed, seeing that I had only now discovered the seriousness of Mr Colley's condition.

"That was a notable impertinence, Mr Summers!"

As my vision cleared I saw that the man had a positive pallor under his brown skin.

"Let me think, man! Steward! Another brandy here!"

Bates brought it at the run for I must have ordered it in a more than usually peremptory voice. I did not drink at once but sat and stared into my glass.

The trouble was that in everything the man had said, he was right!

After a while, he spoke again.

"A visit from you, sir, to such a man—"

"I? Go in that stinking hole?"

"There is a phrase that suits your situation, sir. It is *Noblesse oblige.*"

"Oh be damned to your French, Summers! But I tell you this and make what you choose of it! I believe in fair play!"

"That I am prepared to accept."

"You? That is profoundly generous of you, sir!"

Then we were silent again. It must have been in a harsh enough voice that I spoke at last.

"Well, Mr Summers, you were right, were you not? I have been remiss. But those who administer correction out of school must not expect to be thanked for it."

"I fear not."

This was too much.

"Fear nothing, man! How mean, how vindictive, how small do you think I am? Your precious career is safe enough from me. I do not care to be lumped in with the enemy!"

At this moment, Deverel came in with Brocklebank and some others so that the conversation perforce became general. As soon as possible I took my brandy back to my hutch and sat there, thinking what to do. I called Wheeler and told him to send Phillips to me. He had the insolence to ask me what I wanted the man for and I sent him about his business in no uncertain terms. Phillips came soon enough.

"Phillips, I shall pay a call on Mr Colley. I do not wish to be offended by the sights and smells of a sick-room. Be good enough to clean up the place and, as far as you can, the bunk. Let me know when it is done."

I thought for a moment he would demur but he changed his mind and withdrew. Wheeler stuck his head in again but I had plenty of rage left over and told him if he was so idle he might as well go across and lend Phillips a hand. This removed him at once. It must have been a full hour before Phillips tapped on my door and said he had done *what he could*. I rewarded him, then fearing the worst went across the lobby attended by Phillips but with Wheeler hovering as if expecting a half-guinea for allowing Phillips the use of me. These fellows are as bad as parsons over fees for christenings, weddings and funerals! They were disposed to mount guard at the door of Mr Colley's cabin but I told them to be off and watched till they disappeared. I then went in.

Colley's hutch was a mirror image of mine. Phillips, if he had not rid it completely of stench, had done the next best thing by covering it with some pungent but not unpleasantly aromatic odour. Colley lay as Summers had said. One hand still clutched what both Falconer and Summers agreed was an eyebolt in the side of the ship. His scrubby head was pressed into the bolster, the face turned away. I stood by the bunk and was at a loss. I had little experience of visiting the sick.

"Mr Colley!"

There was no reply. I tried again.

"Mr Colley, sir. Some days ago I desired further acquaintance with you. But you have not appeared. This was too bad, sir. May I not expect your company on deck today?"

That was handsome enough, I thought in all conscience. I was so certain of success in raising the man's spirits that a fleeting awareness of the boredom I should experience in his company passed through my mind and took some edge off my determination to rouse him. I backed away.

"Well sir, if not today, then when you are ready! I will await you. Pray call on me!"

Was that not a foolish thing to say! It was an open

invitation to the man to pester me as much as he would. I backed to the door and turned in time to see Wheeler and Phillips vanish. I looked round the cabin. It contained even less than mine. The shelf held a Bible, a prayer book, and a dirty, dog-eared volume, purchased I imagine at third hand and clumsily rebound in brown paper, which proved to be *Classes Plantarum*. The others were works of devotion—Baxter's *Saints Everlasting Rest*, and the like. There was a pile of manuscript on the flap of the table. I closed the door and went back to my hutch again.

Scarce had I got my own door open when I found Summers following me close. He had, it appeared, watched my movements. I motioned him inside.

"Well Mr Talbot?"

"I got no response from him. However, I visited him as you saw and I did what I could. I have, I believe, discharged those responsibilities you were so kind as to bring to my notice. I can do no more."

To my astonishment he raised a glass of brandy to his lips. He had carried it concealed or at least unnoticed—for who would look for such a thing in the hands of so temperate a man?

"Summers—my dear Summers! You have taken to drink!"

That he had not indeed was seen only too clearly when he choked and coughed at the first taste of the liquid.

"You need more practice, man! Join Deverel and me some time!"

He drank again, then breathed deeply.

"Mr Talbot, you said that today you could not be angry with me. You jested but it was the word of a gentleman. Now I am to come at you again."

"I am weary of the whole subject."

"I assure you, Mr Talbot, this is my last."

I turned my canvas chair round and sank into it.

"Say what you have to say, then."

"Who is responsible for the man's state?"

"Colley? Devil take it! Himself! Let us not mince round the truth like a pair of church spinsters! You are going to spread the responsibility, are you not? You will include the captain and I agree—who else?—Cumbershum? Deverel? Yourself? The starboard watch? The world?"

"I will be plain, sir. The best medicine for Mr Colley would be a gentle visit from the captain of whom he stands in such awe. The only man among us with sufficient influence to bring the captain to such an action, is yourself."

"Then devil take it again, for I shall not!"

"You said I would 'Spread the responsibility'. Let me do so now. *You* are the man most responsible—"

"Christ in his heaven, Summers, you are the—"

"Wait! Wait!"

"Are you drunk?"

"I said I would be plain. I will stand shot, sir, though my career is now in far more danger from you than it ever was from the French! They, after all, could do no more than kill or maim me—but you—"

"You *are* drunk—you must be!"

"Had you not in a bold and thoughtless way outfaced our captain on his own quarterdeck—had you not made use of your rank and prospects and connections to strike a blow at the very foundations of his authority, all this might not have happened. He is brusque and he detests the clergy, he makes no secret of it. But had you not acted as you did at that time, he would never in the very next few minutes have crushed Colley with his anger and continued to humiliate *him* because he could not humiliate *you*."

"If Colley had had the sense to read Anderson's Standing Orders—"

"You are a passenger as he is. Did you read them?"

Through my anger I thought back. It was true to some extent—no, wholly true. On my first day Wheeler had murmured something about them—they were to be found outside my cabin and at a suitable opportunity I should—

"*Did* you read them, Mr Talbot?"

"No."

Has your lordship ever come across the odd fact that to be seated rather than erect induces or at least tends towards a state of calm? I cannot say that my anger was sinking away but it was stayed. As if he, too, wished us both to be calm, Summers sat on the edge of my bunk, thus looking slightly down at me. Our relative positions seemed to make the *didactic* inevitable.

"The captain's Standing Orders would seem to you as brusque as he is, sir. But the fact is they are wholly necessary. Those applying to passengers lie under the same necessity, the same urgency, as the rest."

"Very well, very well!"

"You have not seen a ship at a moment of crisis, sir. A ship may be taken flat aback and sunk all in a few moments. Ignorant passengers, stumbling in the way, delaying a necessary order or making it inaudible—"

"You have said enough."

"I hope so."

"You are certain I am responsible for nothing else that has gone awry? Perhaps Mrs East's miscarriage?"

"If our captain could be induced to befriend a sick man—"

"Tell me, Summers—why are you so curious about Colley?"

He finished his drink and stood up.

"Fair play, *noblesse oblige*. My education is not like yours, sir, it has been strictly practical. But I know a term under which both phrases might be—what is the word?—subsumed. I hope you will find it."

With that, he went quickly out of my hutch and away somewhere, leaving me in a fine mixture of emotions! Anger, yes, embarrassment, yes—but also a kind of rueful amusement at having been taught two lessons in one day by the same schoolmaster! I damned him for a busybody, then half undamned him again, for he is a likeable fellow, common or not. What the devil had he to do with *my* duty?

Was that the word? An odd fellow indeed! Truly as good a translation as yours, my lord! All those countless leagues from one end of a British ship to the other! To hear him give orders about the deck—and then to meet him over a glass—he can pass between one sentence and the next from all the jargoning of the Tarpaulin language to the plain exchanges which take place between gentlemen. Now the heat was out of my blood I could see how he had thought himself professionally at risk in speaking so to me and I laughed a little ruefully again. We may characterize him in our theatrical terms as—enter a Good Man!

Well, thought I to myself, there is this in common between Good Men and children—we must never disappoint them! Only half of the confounded business had been attended to. I had visited the sick—now I must try my influence in adjusting matters between Colley and our gloomy captain. I own the prospect daunted me a little. I returned to the passenger saloon and brandy and in the evening, to tell the truth, found myself in no condition to exercise judgement. I think this was deliberate and an endeavour to postpone what I knew must be a difficult interview. At last I went with what must have been a stately gait to my bunk and have some recollection of Wheeler assisting me into it. I was bosky indeed and fell into a profound sleep to wake later with the headache and some queasiness. When I tried my repeater I found it was yet early in the morning. Mr Brocklebank was snoring. There were noises coming from the hutch next to mine from which I inferred that the fair Zenobia was busy with yet another lover or, it may be, client. Had *she*, I wondered, also wanted to reach the governor's ear? Should I one day find myself approached by her to get an official portrait of the governor executed by Mr Brocklebank? It was a sour consideration for the early hours that stemmed straight from Summers's frankness. I damned him all over again. The air in my hutch was thick, so I threw on my greatcoat, scuffed my feet into slippers and felt my way out on deck. Here there was light enough to make out the difference between the ship, the sea, and the sky but no more. I remembered my resolution to speak with the captain on Colley's behalf with positive revulsion. What had seemed a boring duty when I was elevated with drink now presented itself as downright unpleasant. I called to mind that the captain was said to take a constitutional on the quarterdeck at dawn, but such a time and place was too early for our interview.

Nevertheless, the early morning air, unhealthy as it may have been, seemed in a curious way to alleviate the headache, the queasiness and even my slight uneasiness at the prospect of the interview. I therefore set myself to marching to and fro between the break of the quarterdeck and the mainmast. While I did so, I tried to see all round the situation. We had yet more months of sea travel before us in the captain's company. I neither liked nor esteemed Captain Anderson nor was able to think of him as anything but a petty tyrant. Endeavour—it could be no more—to assist the wretched Colley could not but exacerbate the dislike that lay just beyond the bounds of the unacknowledged truce between us. The captain accepted my position as your lordship's godson, *et cetera*. I accepted his as captain of one of His Majesty's ships. The limit of his powers in respect of passengers was obscure; and so was the limit of my possible influence with his superiors! Like dogs cautious of each other's strength we stepped high and round each other. And now I was to try to influence his behaviour towards a contemptible member of the profession he hated! I was thus, unless I was very careful, in danger of putting myself under an obligation to him. The thought was not to be borne. At one time and another in my long contemplation I believe I uttered a deal of oaths! Indeed, I had half a mind to abandon the whole project.

However, the damp but soft air of these latitudes, no matter what the subsequent effect on one's health, is certainly to be recommended as an antidote to an aching head and sour stomach! As I came more and more to myself I found it more and more in my power to exercise judgement and contemplate action. Those ambitious of attaining to statecraft or whose birth renders the exercise of it inevitable would do well to face the trials of a voyage such as ours! It was, I remember, very clearly in my mind how your lordship's benevolence had got for me not only some years of employment in a new and unformed society but had also ensured that the preliminary voyage should give me time for reflection and the exercise of my not inconsiderable powers of thought. I decided I must proceed on the principle of the use of *least force*. What would move Captain Anderson to do as I wished? Would there be anything more powerful with him than self-interest? That wretched little man, Mr Colley! But there was no doubt about it. Whether it was, as Summers said, *my* fault in part or not, there was no doubt he had been persecuted. That he was a fool and had made a cake of himself was neither here nor there. Deverel, little Tommy Taylor, Summers himself—they all implied that Captain Anderson for no matter what reason had deliberately made the man's life intolerable to him. The devil was in it if I could find any word to sum up both Summers's phrase of "*Noblesse Oblige*" and mine of "Fair Play" other than "Justice". There's a large and schoolbook word to run directly on like a rock in mid-ocean! There was a kind of terror in it too since it had moved out of school and the university onto the planks of a warship—which is to say the planks of a tyranny in little! What about *my* career?

Yet I was warmed by Summers's belief in my ability and more by his confident appeal to my sense of justice. What creatures we are! Here was I, who only a few weeks before had thought highly of myself because my mother wept to see me go, now warming my hands at the small fire of a lieutenant's approval!

However, at last I saw how to go on.

(61)

Well! I returned to my hutch, washed, shaved and dressed with care. I took my morning draught in the saloon and then drew myself up as before *a regular stitcher*. I did not enjoy the prospect of the interview, I can tell you! For if I had established my position in the ship, it was even more evident that the captain had established his! He was indeed our moghool. To remove my foreboding I went very briskly to the quarterdeck, positively bounding up the ladders. Captain Anderson, the wind now being on the starboard quarter, was standing there and facing into it. This is his privilege; and is said by seamen to rise from the arcane suggestion that "Danger lies to windward" though in the next breath they will assure you that the most dangerous thing in the world is "a lee shore". The first, I suppose, refers to a possible enemy ship, the second to reefs and suchlike natural hazards. Yet I have, I believe, a more penetrating suggestion to make as to the origin of the captain's privilege. Whatever sector of the ship is to windward is almost free from the stench she carries everywhere with her. I do not mean the stink of urine and ordure but that pervasive stench from the carcass of the ship herself and her rotten bilge of gravel and sand. Perhaps more modern ships with their iron ballast may smell more sweetly; but captains, I dare say, in this Noah's service will continue to walk the windward side even if ships should run clean out of wind and take to rowing. The tyrant must live as free of stink as possible.

I find that without conscious intention I have delayed this description as I had dallied over my draught. I live again those moments when I drew myself together for the jump!

Well then, I stationed myself on the opposite side of the quarterdeck, affecting to take no notice of the man other than to salute him casually with a lifted finger. My hope was that his recent gaiety and elevation of spirits would lead him to address me first. My judgement was correct. His new air of satisfaction was indeed apparent, for when he saw me he came across, his yellow teeth showing.

"A fine day for you, Mr Talbot!"

"Indeed it is, sir. Do we make as much progress as is common in these latitudes?"

"I doubt that we shall achieve more than an average of a knot over the next day or two."

"Twenty-four sea miles a day."

"Just so, sir. Warships are generally slower in their advance than most people suppose."

"Well sir, I must confess to finding these latitudes more agreeable than any I have experienced. Could we but tow the British Isles to this part of the world, how many of our social problems would be solved! The mango would fall in our mouths."

"You have a quaint fancy there, sir. Do you mean to include Ireland?"

"No sir. I would offer her to the United States of America, sir."

"Let them have the first refusal, eh, Mr Talbot?"

"Hibernia would lie snugly enough alongside New England. We should see what we should see!"

"It would remove half a watch of my crew at a blow."

"Well worth the loss, sir. What a noble prospect the ocean is under a low sun! Only when the sun is high does the sea seem to lack that indefinable air of Painted Art which we are able to observe at sunrise and sunset."

"I am so accustomed to the sight that I do not see it.

Indeed, I am grateful—if the phrase is not meaningless in the circumstances—to the oceans for another quality."

"And that is?"

"Their power of isolating a man from his fellows."

"Of isolating a captain, sir. The rest of humanity at sea must live only too much herded. The effect on them is not of the best. Circe's task must not have been hindered, to say the least, by the profession of her victims!"

Directly I had said this I realized how cutting it might sound. But I saw by the blankness of the captain's face, then its frown, that he was trying to remember what had happened to any ship of that name.

"Herded?"

"Packed together, I ought to have said. But how balmy the air is! I declare it seems almost insupportable that I must descend again and busy myself with my journal."

Captain Anderson checked at the word "journal" as if he had trodden on a stone. I affected not to notice but continued cheerfully.

"It is partly an amusement, captain, and partly a duty. It is, I suppose, what you would call a 'log'."

"You must find little to record in such a situation as this."

"Indeed, sir, you are mistaken. I have not time nor paper sufficient to record all the interesting events and personages of the voyage together with my own observations on them. Look—there is Mr Prettiman! A personage for you! His opinions are notorious, are they not?"

But Captain Anderson was still staring at me.

"Personages?"

"You must know," said I laughing, "that had I not his lordship's direct instructions to me I should still have been scribbling. It is my ambition to out-Gibbon Mr Gibbon and this gift to a godfather falls conveniently."

Our tyrant was pleased to smile, but quiveringly, like a

man who knows that to have a tooth pulled is less painful than to have the exquisite torturer left in.

"We may all be famous, then," said he. "I had not looked for it."

"That is for the future. You must know, sir, that to the unhappiness of us all, his lordship has found himself temporarily vexed by the gout. It is my hope that in such a disagreeable situation, a frank, though private account of my travels and of the society in which I find myself may afford him some diversion."

Captain Anderson took an abrupt turn up and down the deck, then stood directly before me.

"The officers of the ship in which you travel must bulk large in such an account."

"They are objects of a landsman's interest and curiosity."

"The captain particularly so?"

"You sir? I had not considered that. But you are, after all, the king or emperor of our floating society with prerogatives of justice and mercy. Yes. I suppose you do bulk large in my journal and will continue to do so."

Captain Anderson turned on his heel and marched away. He kept his back to me and stared up wind. I saw that his head was sunk again, his hands clasped behind his back. I supposed that his jaw must be projecting once more as a foundation on which to sink the sullenness of his face. There was no doubt at all of the effect of my words, either on him or on *me*! For I found myself quivering as the first lieutenant had quivered when he dared to beard Mr Edmund Talbot! I spoke, I know not what, to Cumbershum, who had the watch. He was discomforted, for it was clean against the tyrant's Standing Orders and I saw, out of the corner of my eye, how the captain's hands tightened on each other behind his back. It was not a situation that should be prolonged. I bade the lieutenant good day and descended from the quarterdeck. I was glad enough to get back into my hutch, where I found of all things that my hands still had a tendency to tremble! I sat, therefore, getting my breath back and allowing my pulse to slow.

At length I began to consider the captain once more and try to predict his possible course of action. Does not the operation of a *statist* lie wholly in his power to affect the future of other people; and is not that power founded directly on his ability to predict their behaviour? Here, thought I, was the chance to observe the success or failure of my prentice hand! How would the man respond to the hint I had given him! It was not a subtle one; but then, I thought, from the directness of his questions that he was a simple creature at bottom. It was possible that he had not noticed the suggestiveness of my mentioning Mr Pretti-man and his extreme beliefs! Yet I felt certain that men-tion of my journal would force him to look back over the whole length of the voyage and consider what sort of figure he might cut in an account of it. Sooner or later he would stub his toe over the Colley affair and remember how he had treated the man. He must see that however I myself had provoked him, nevertheless, by indulging his animosity against Colley, he had been cruel and unjust.

How would he behave then? How had I behaved when Summers had revealed to me my portion of responsibility in the affair? I tried out a scene or two for our floating the-atre. I pictured Anderson descending from the quarter-deck and walking in the lobby casually, so as not to seem interested in the man. He might well stand consulting his own fading Orders, written out in a fair and clerkly hand. Then at a convenient moment, no one being by—oh no! he would have to let it be seen so that I should record it in my journal!—he would march into the hutch where Colley lay, shut the door, sit by the bunk and chat till they were a couple of bosoms. Why, Anderson might well stand in for an archbishop or even His Majesty! How could Colley not be roused by such amiable condescension? The captain would confess that he himself had committed just such a folly a year or two before—

I could not imagine it, that is the plain truth. The conceit remained artificial. Such behaviour was beyond Anderson. He might, he might just come down and gentle Colley somewhat, admitting his own brusqueness but saying it was habitual in a captain of a ship. More likely he would come down but only to assure himself that Colley was lying in his bunk, prone and still and not to be roused by a jesting exordium. But then, he might not even come down. Who was I to dip into the nature of the man, cast the very waters of his soul and by that chirurgeonly experiment declare how his injustice would run its course? I sat before this journal, upbraiding myself for my folly in my attempt to play the politician and manipulator of his fellow men! I had to own that my knowledge of the springs of human action was still in the egg. Nor does a powerful intellect do more than assist in the matter. Something more there must be, some distillation of experience, before a man can judge the outcome in circumstances of such quantity, proliferation and confusion.

And then, *then* can your lordship guess? I have saved the sweet to the last! He did come down. Before my very eyes he came down as if my prediction had drawn him down like some fabulous spell! I am a wizard, am I not? Admit me to be a prentice-wizard at least! I had said he would come down and come down he did! Through my louvre I saw him come down, abrupt and grim, to take his stand in the centre of the lobby. He stared at one hutch after another, turning on his heel, and I was only just in time to pull my face away from the spyhole before his louring gaze swept over it with an effect I could almost swear like the heat from a burning coal! When I risked peeping again—for somehow it seemed positively danger-ous that the man should know I had seen him—he had his back to me. He stepped to the door of Colley's hutch and for a long minute stared through it. I saw how one fist beat into the palm of the other hand behind his back. Then he swung impatiently to his left with a movement that seemed to cry out—*I'll be damned if I will!* He stumped to the ladder and disappeared. A few seconds later I heard his firm step pass along the deck above my head.

This was a modified triumph, was it not? I had said he would come down and he had come down. But where I had pictured him endeavouring to comfort poor Colley he had shown himself either too heartless or too little politic to bring himself to do so. The nearer he had come to dis-simulating his bile the higher it had risen in his throat. Yet now I had some grounds for confidence. His knowl-edge of the existence of this very journal would not let him be. It will be like a splinter under the nail. He would come down again—

BETA

Wrong again, Talbot! Learn another lesson, my boy! You fell at that fence! Never again must you lose yourself in the complacent contemplation of a first success! Captain Anderson did not come down. He sent a messenger. I was just writing the sentence about the splinter when there came a knock at the door and who should appear but Mr Summers! I bade him enter, sanded my page—imperfectly as you can see—closed and locked my journal, stood up and indicated my chair. He declined it, perched himself on the edge of my bunk, laid his cocked hat on it and looked thoughtfully at my journal.

"Locked, too!"

I said nothing but looked him in the eye, smiling slightly. He nodded as if he understood—which indeed I think he did.

"Mr Talbot, it cannot be allowed to continue."

"My journal, you mean?"

He brushed the jest aside.

"I have looked in on the man by the captain's orders."

"Colley? I looked in on him myself. I agreed to, you remember."

"The man's reason is at stake."

"All for a little drink. Is there still no change?"

"Phillips swears he has not moved for three days."

I made a perhaps unnecessarily blasphemous rejoinder. Summers took no notice of it.

"I repeat, the man is losing his wits."

"It does indeed seem so."

"I am to do what I can, by the captain's orders, and you are to assist me."

"I?"

"Well. You are not ordered to assist me but I am ordered to invite your assistance and profit by your advice."

"Upon my soul, the man is flattering me! Do you know, Summers, I was advised myself to practise the art! I little thought to find myself the object of such an exercise!"

"Captain Anderson feels that you have a social experience and awareness that may make your advice of value."

I laughed heartily and Summers joined in.

"Come Summers! Captain Anderson never said that!"

"No, sir. Not precisely."

"Not precisely indeed! I tell you what, Summers—"

I stopped myself in time. There were many things I felt like saying. I could have told him that Captain Anderson's sudden concern for Mr Colley began not at any moment of appeal by me but at the moment when he heard that I kept a journal intended for influential eyes. I could have given my opinion that the captain cared nothing for Colley's wits but sought cunningly enough to involve me in the events and so obscure the issue or at the very least soften what might well be your lordship's acerbity and contempt. But I am learning, am I not? Before the words reached my tongue I understood how dangerous they might be to Summers—and even to me.

"Well, Mr Summers, I will do what I can."

"I was sure you would agree. You are co-opted among us ignorant tars as the civil power. What is to be done?"

"Here we have a parson who—but come, should we not have co-opted Miss Granham? She is the daughter of a canon and might be presumed to know best how to handle the clergy!"

"Be serious, sir and leave her to Mr Prettiman."

"No! It cannot be! Minerva herself?"

"Mr Colley must claim all our attention."

"Well then. Here we have a clergyman who—made too much of a beast of himself and refines desperately upon it."

Summers regarded me closely, and I may say curiously.

"You know what a beast he made of himself?"

"Man! I saw him! We all saw him, including the ladies! Indeed, I tell you Summers, I saw something more than the rest!"

"You interest me deeply."

"It is of little enough moment. But some few hours after his exhibition I saw him wander through the lobby towards the *bog*, a sheet of paper in his hand and for what it is worth a most extraordinary smile on that ugly mug of his."

"What did the smile suggest to you?"

"He was silly drunk."

Summers nodded towards the forward part of the vessel.

"And there? In the fo'castle?"

"How can we tell?"

"We might ask."

"Is that wise, Summers? Was not the play-acting of the common people—forgive me!—directed not to themselves but to those in authority over them? Should you not avoid reminding them of it?"

"It is the man's wits, sir. Something must be risked. Who set him on? Beside the common people there are the emigrants, decent as far as I have met them. *They* have no wish to mock at authority. Yet they must know as much as anyone."

Suddenly I remembered the poor girl and her emaciated face where a shadow lived and was, as it were, feeding where it inhabited. She must have had Colley's beastliness exhibited before her at a time when she had a right to expect a far different appearance from a clergyman!

"But this is terrible, Summers! The man should be—"

"What is past cannot be helped, sir. But I say again it is the man's wits that stand in danger. For God's sake, make one more effort to rouse him from his, his—lethargy!"

"Very well. For the second time, then. Come."

I went briskly and, followed by Summers across the lobby, opened the door of the hutch and stood inside. It was true enough. The man lay as he had lain before; and indeed seemed if anything even stiller. The hand that had clutched the eyebolt had relaxed and lay with the fingers hooked through it but without any evidence of muscular tension.

Behind me, Summers spoke gently.

"Here is Mr Talbot, Mr Colley, come to see you."

I must own to a mixture of confusion and strong distaste for the whole business which rendered me even more than usually incapable of finding the right kind of encouragement for the wretched man. His situation and the odour, the stench, emanating I suppose from his unwashed person was nauseous. It must have been, you will agree, pretty *strong* to contend with and overcome the general stench of the ship to which I was still not entirely habituated! However, Summers evidently credited me with an ability which I did not possess for he stood away from me, nodding at the same time as if to indicate that the affair was now in my hands.

I cleared my throat.

"Well Mr Colley, this is an unfortunate business but believe me, sir, you are refining too much on it. Uncontrolled drunkenness and its consequences is an experience every man ought to have at least once in his life or how is he to understand the experience of others? As for your relieving nature on the deck—do but consider what those

133

decks have seen! And in the peaceful counties of our own far-off land—Mr Colley I have been brought to see, by the good offices of Mr Summers, that I am in however distant a way partly responsible for your predicament. Had I not enraged our captain—but there! I shall confess, sir, that a number of young fellows, ranged at upper-storey windows, did once, at a given signal, make water on an unpopular and bosky tutor who was passing below! Now what was the upshot of that shocking affair? Why nothing, sir! The man held out his hand, stared frowning into the evening sky, then opened his umbrella! I swear to you, sir, that some of those same young fellows will one day be bishops! In a day or two we shall all laugh at your comical interlude together! You are bound for Sydney Cove I believe and thence to Van Diemen's Land. Good Lord, Mr Colley, from what I have heard they are more likely to greet you drunk than sober. What you need now is a dram, then as much ale as your stomach can hold. Depend upon it, you will soon see things differently."

There was no response. I glanced enquiringly at Summers but he was looking down at the blanket, his lips pressed together. I spread my hands in a gesture of defeat and left the cabin. Summers followed me.

"Well, Summers?"

"Mr Colley is willing himself to death."

"Come!"

"I have known it happen among savage peoples. They are able to lie down and die."

I gestured him into my hutch and we sat side by side on the bunk. A thought occurred to me.

"Was he perhaps an enthusiast? It may be that he is taking his religion too much to heart—come now, Mr Summers! There is nothing to laugh at in the matter! Or are you so disobliging as to find my remark itself a subject for your hilarity?"

Summers dropped his hands from his face, smiling.

"God forbid, sir! It is pain enough to have been shot at by an enemy without the additional hazard of presenting oneself as a mark to—dare I say—one's friends. Believe me properly sensible of my privilege in being admitted to a degree of intimacy with your noble godfather's genteel godson. But you are right in one thing. As far as poor Colley is concerned there is nothing to laugh at. Either his wits are gone or he knows nothing of his own religion."

"He is a parson!"

"The uniform does not make the man, sir. He is in despair I believe. Sir, I take it upon myself as a Christian—as a humble follower at however great a distance—to aver that a Christian *cannot* despair!"

"My words were trivial then."

"They were what you could say. But of course they never reached him."

"You felt that?"

"Did you not?"

I toyed with the thought that perhaps someone of Colley's own class, a man from among the ship's people but unspoilt by education or such modest preferment as had come his way, might well find a means to approach him. But after the words that Summers and I had exchanged on a previous occasion I felt a new delicacy in broaching such a subject with him. He broke the silence.

"We have neither priest nor doctor."

"Brocklebank owned to having been a medical student for the best part of a year."

"Did he so? Should we call him in?"

"God forbid—he does so prose! He described his turning from doctoring to painting as 'deserting Aesculapius for the Muse'."

"I shall enquire among our people forrard."

"For a doctor?"

"For some information as to what happened."

"Man, we *saw* what happened!"

"I mean in the fo'castle or below it, rather than on deck."

"He was made beastly drunk."

I found that Summers was peering at me closely.

"And that was all?"

"All?"

"I see. Well, sir, I shall report back to the captain."

"Tell him I shall continue to consider how we may devise some method of bringing the wretched fellow to his senses."

"I will do so; and must thank you for your assistance."

Summers left and I was alone with my thoughts and this journal. It was so strange to think that a young fellow not much above my years or Deverel's and certainly not as old as Cumbershum should have so strong an instinct for self-destruction! Why, Aristotle or no, half an hour of La Brocklebank—even Prettiman and Miss Granham—and *there*, thought I, is a situation I must get acquainted with for a number of reasons, the least of them entertainment: and then—

What do you suppose was the thought that came into my mind? It was of the pile of manuscript that had lain on the flap of Colley's table! I had not noticed the flap or the papers when Summers and I entered the cabin; but now, by the incomprehensible faculties of the human mind I, as it were, entered the cabin *again* and surveying the scene I had just left, I saw in my mind that the writing-flap was empty! There is a subject for a savant's investigation! How can a man's mind go back and see what he saw not? But so it was.

Well. Captain Anderson had co-opted me. He should find out, I thought, what sort of overseer he had brought into the business!

I went quickly to Colley's cabin. He lay as before. Only when I was inside the hutch did I return to a *kind* at least of apprehension. I intended the man nothing but good and I was acting on the captain's behalf; yet there was in my mind an unease. I felt it as the effect of the captain's rule. A tyrant turns the slightest departure from his will into a crime; and I was at the least contemplating bringing him to book for his mistreatment of Mr Colley. I looked quickly round the cabin. The ink and pens and sander were still there, as were the shelves with their books of devotion at the foot of the bed. It seemed there was a limit to their efficacy! I leaned over the man himself.

It was then that I perceived without seeing—I knew, but had no real means of knowing—

There had been a time when he had awakened in physical anguish which had quickly passed into a mental one. He lay like that in deepening pain, deepening consciousness, widening memory, his whole being turning more and more from the world till he could desire nothing but death. Phillips could not rouse him nor even Summers. Only I—my words after all had touched something. When I left him after that first visit, glad enough to be gone, he had leapt from his bunk in some *new* agony! Then, in a passion of self-disgust he had swept his papers from the table. Like a child he had seized the whole and had jammed them into a convenient crack as if it would stay unsearched till doom's day! Of course. There was, between the bunk and the side of the vessel a space, just as in my own hutch, into which a man might thrust his hand as I then did in Colley's. They encountered paper and I drew out a crumpled mass of sheets all written, some cross-written, and all, I was certain, material evidence against our tyrant in the case of Colley versus Anderson! I put the papers quickly into the bosom of my coat, came out—unseen I pray God!—and hurried to my cabin. There I thrust the mass of papers into my own writing-case and locked it as if I were concealing the spoils of a burglary! After that I sat and began to write all this in my journal as if seeking, in a familiar action, some legal security! Is that not comic?

Wheeler came to my cabin.

"Sir, I have a message, sir. The captain requests that you give him the pleasure of your company at dinner in an hour's time."

"My compliments to the captain and I accept with pleasure."

GAMMA

What a day this has been. I commenced it with some cheerfulness and I end it with—but you will wish to know all! It seems so long ago that the affair was misty and my own endeavours to pierce the mist so complacent, so self-satisfied—

Well. As Summers said, I am partly to blame. So are we all in one degree or another; but none of us, I think, in the same measure as our tyrant! Let me take you with me, my lord, step by step. I promise you—no, not entertainment but at the very least a kind of generous indignation and the exercise not of my, but *your* judgement.

I changed and dismissed Wheeler only to find his place taken by Summers, who looked positively elegant.

"Good God, Summers, you are also bidden to the feast?"

"I am to share that pleasure."

"It is an innovation, for sure."

"Oldmeadow makes a fourth."

I took out my repeater.

"It still wants more than ten minutes. What is etiquette for such a visit on shipboard?"

"Where the captain is concerned, on the last stroke of the bell."

"In that case I shall disappoint his expectations and arrive early. He anticipates, I believe, knowing me, that I shall arrive late."

My entry into Captain Anderson's stateroom was as ceremonious as an admiral could wish. The cabin, or room, rather, though not as large as the passengers' saloon or even the saloon where the lieutenants *messed*, was yet of palatial dimensions when compared with our meagre individual quarters. Some of the ship's full width was pared off on either side for the captain's own sleeping quarters, his closet, his personal galley, and another small cabin where I suppose an admiral would have conducted the business of a fleet. As in the lieutenants' wardroom and the passenger saloon, the rear wall, or in Tarpaulin language *the after bulkhead*, was one vast, leaded window by means of which something like a third of the horizon might be seen. Yet part of this window was obscured in a way that at first I could scarcely credit. Part of the obscuration was the captain, who called out as soon as I appeared in what I can only call a holiday voice.

"Come in, Mr Talbot, come in! I must apologize for not greeting you at the threshold! You have caught me in my garden."

It was so indeed. The obscuration to the great window was a row of climbing plants, each twisting itself round a bamboo that rose from the darkness near the deck where I divined the flower pots were. Standing a little to one side I could see that Captain Anderson was serving each plant into its flower pot with water from a small watering can with a long spout. The can was the sort of flimsy trifle you might find a lady using in the orangery— not indeed, to serve the trees in their enormous vats, but some quaintness of Dame Nature's own ingenuity. The morose captain might be thought to befit such a picture ill; but as he turned I saw to my astonishment that he was looking positively amiable, as if I were a lady come to visit him.

"I did not know that you had a private paradise, captain."

The captain smiled! Yes, positively, he smiled!

"Do but think, Mr Talbot, this flowering plant that I am tending, still innocent and unfallen, may have been one with which Eve garlanded herself on the first day of her creation."

"Would that not presuppose a loss of innocence, captain, precursor to the fig leaves?"

"It might be so. How acute you are, Mr Talbot."

"We were being fanciful, were we not?"

"I was speaking my mind. The plant is called the Garland Plant. The ancients, I am told, crowned themselves with it. The flower, when it appears, is agreeably perfumed and waxen white."

"We might be Grecians then and crown ourselves for the feast."

"I do not think the custom suited to the English. But do you see I have three of the plants? Two of them I actually raised from seed!"

"Is that a task as difficult as your triumphant tone would imply?"

Captain Anderson laughed happily. His chin was up, his cheeks creased, twin sparks in his little eyes.

"Sir Joseph Banks said it was impossible! 'Anderson,' he said, 'take cuttings man! You might as well throw the seeds overboard!' But I have persevered and in the end I had a box of them—seedlings, I mean—enough to supply a Lord Mayor's banquet, if—to follow your fancy—they should ever require their aldermen to be garlanded. But there! It is not to be imagined. Garlands would be as out of place as in the painted hall at Greenwich. Serve Mr Talbot. What will you drink, sir? There is much to hand, though I take no more than an occasional glass myself."

"Wine for me, sir."

"Hawkins, the claret if you please! This geranium you see, Mr Talbot, has some disease of the leaf. I have dusted it with flowers of sulphur but to no effect. I shall lose it no doubt. But then, sir, he who gardens at sea must accustom himself to loss. On my first voyage in command I lost my whole collection."

"Through the violence of the enemy?"

"No sir, through the uncommon nature of the weather which held us for whole weeks without either wind or rain. I could not have served water to my plants. There would have been mutiny. I see the loss of this one plant as no great matter."

"Besides, you may exchange it for another at Sydney Cove."

"Why must you—"

He turned away and stowed the waterpot in a box down by the plants. When he turned back I saw the creases in his cheeks again and the sparks in his eyes.

"We are a long way and a long time from our destination, Mr Talbot."

"You speak as though you do not anticipate our arrival there with pleasure."

The sparks and creases vanished.

"You are young, sir. You cannot understand the pleasures of, no, the necessity of solitude to some natures. I would not care if the voyage lasted for ever!"

"But surely a man is connected to the land, to society, to a family—"

"Family? Family?" said the captain with a kind of violence. "Why should a man not do without a family? What is there about a family, pray?"

"A man is not a, a garland plant, captain, to fertilize his own seed!"

There was a long pause in which Hawkins, the captain's servant, brought us the claret. Captain Anderson made a token gesture towards his face with half a glass of wine.

"At least I may remind myself how remarkable the flora will be at the Antipodes!"

"So you may replenish your stock."

His face was gay again.

"Many of Nature's inventions in that region have never been brought back to Europe."

I saw now there was a way, if not to Captain Anderson's heart, at least to his approval. I had a sudden thought, one worthy of a *romancier*, that perhaps the stormy or sullen face with which he was wont to leave his paradise was that of the expelled Adam. While I was considering this and my glass of claret, Summers and Oldmeadow entered the stateroom together.

"Come in, gentlemen," cried the captain. "What will you take, Mr Oldmeadow? As you see, Mr Talbot is content with wine—the same for you, sir?"

Oldmeadow cawed into his collar and declared he would be agreeable to a little dry sherry. Hawkins brought a broad-bottomed decanter and poured first for Summers, as knowing already what he would drink, then for Oldmeadow.

"Summers," said the captain, "I had meant to ask you. How does your patient?"

"Still the same, sir. Mr Talbot was good enough to comply with your request. But his words had no more effect than mine."

"It is a sad business," said the captain. He stared directly at me. "I shall enter in the ship's log that the patient—for such I believe we must consider him—has been visited by you, Mr Summers, and by you, Mr Talbot."

It was now that I began to understand Captain Anderson's purpose in getting us into his cabin and his clumsy way about the business of Colley. Instead of waiting till the wine and talk had worked on us he had introduced the subject at once and far too abruptly. It was time I thought of myself!

"You must remember, sir," said I, "that if the wretched man is to be considered a patient, my opinion is valueless. I have no medical knowledge whatsoever. Why, you would do better to consult Mr Brocklebank!"

"Brocklebank? Who is Brocklebank?"

"The artistic gentleman with the port-wine face and female entourage. But I jested. He told me he had begun to study medicine but had given it up."

"He has some medical experience, then?"

"No, no! I jested. The man is—what is the man, Summers? I doubt he could take a pulse!"

"Nevertheless—Brocklebank you said? Hawkins, find Mr Brocklebank and ask him to be good enough to come and see me at once."

I saw it all, saw in the entry in the log—*visited by a gentleman of some medical experience!* He was crude but cunning, was the captain! He was, as Deverel would say, "keeping his yardarm free". Observe how he is forcing me to report to your lordship in my journal that he has taken every care of the man, had him visited by his officers, by me, and by a gentleman *of some medical experience*!

No one said anything for a while. We three guests stared into our glasses as if rendered solemn by a reminder of the sick. But it could not have been more than two minutes before Hawkins returned to say that Mr Brocklebank would be happy to wait on the captain.

"We will sit down, then," said the captain. "Mr Talbot on my right—Mr Oldmeadow here, sir! Summers, will you take the bottom of the table? Why, this is delightfully domestic! Have you room enough, gentlemen? Summers has plenty of course. But we must allow him free passage to the door in case one of ten thousand affairs takes him from us about the ship's business."

Oldmeadow remarked that the soup was excellent. Summers, who was eating his with the dexterity acquired in a dozen fo'castles, remarked that much nonsense was talked about Navy food.

"You may depend upon it," he said, "where food has to be ordered, gathered, stored and served out by the thousands of ton there will be cause of complaint here and there. But in the main, British seamen eat better at sea than they do ashore."

"Bravo!" I cried. "Summers, you should be on the government benches!"

"A glass of wine with you, Mr Summers," said the captain. "What is the phrase? 'No heel taps'? A glass with all you gentlemen! But to return—Summers, what do you say to the story of the cheese clapped on the main as a mastcapping? What of the snuff-boxes carved out of beef?"

I saw out of the corner of my eye how the captain did no more than sniff the bouquet of his wine, then set the glass down. I determined to humour him if only to see round his schemes.

"Summers, I must hear you answer the captain. What of the snuff-boxes and mastcheeses—"

"Mastcappings—"

"What of the bones we hear are served to our gallant tars with no more than a dried shred of meat adhering?"

Summers smiled.

"I fancy you will sample the cheese, sir; and I believe the captain is about to surprise you with bones."

"Indeed I am," said the captain. "Hawkins, have them brought in."

"Good God," I cried, "marrow bones!"

"Bessie, I suppose," said Oldmeadow. "A very profitable beast."

I bowed to the captain.

"We are overwhelmed, sir. Lucullus could do no better."

"I am endeavouring to supply you with material for your journal, Mr Talbot."

"I give you my word, sir, the *menu* shall be preserved for the remotest posterity together with a memorial of the captain's hospitality!"

Hawkins bent to the captain.

"The gentleman is at the door, sir."

"Brocklebank? I will take him for a moment into the office if you will excuse me, gentlemen."

Now there occurred a scene of farce. Brocklebank had not remained at the door but was inside it and advancing. Either he had mistaken the captain's message for such an invitation as had been issued to me, or he was tipsy, or both. Summers had pushed back his chair and stood up. As if the first lieutenant had been a footman, Brocklebank sank into it.

"Thankee, thankee. Marrow bones! How the devil did you know, sir? I don't doubt one of my gals told you. Confusion to the French!"

He drained Summers's glass at a draught. He had a voice like some fruit which combines the qualities— if there be such a fruit—of peach and plum. He stuck his little finger in his ear, bored for a moment, inspected the result on the end of it while no one said anything. The servant was at a loss. Brocklebank caught a clearer sight of Summers and beamed at him.

"You too, Summers? Sit down, man!"

Captain Anderson, with what for him was rare tact, broke in.

"Yes, Summers, pull up that chair over there and dine with us."

Summers sat at a corner of the table. He was breathing quickly as if he had run a race. I wondered whether he was thinking what Deverel thought and had confided to me in his, or perhaps I ought to say *our*, cups—*No, Talbot, this is not a happy ship.*

Oldmeadow turned to me.

"There was mention of a journal, Talbot. There is a devil of a lot of writing among you government people."

"You have advanced me, sir. But it is true. The offices are paved with paper."

The captain pretended to drink, then set the glass down.

"You might well think a ship is ballasted with paper. We record almost everything somewhere or another, from the midshipmen's logs right up to the ship's log kept by myself."

"In my case, I find there is hardly time to record the events of a day before the next two or three are upon me."

"How do you select?"

"Salient facts, of course—such trifles as may amuse the leisure of my godfather."

"I hope," said the captain heavily, "that you will record our sense of obligation to his lordship for affording us your company."

"I shall do so."

Hawkins filled Brocklebank's glass. It was for the third time.

"Mr, er, Brocklebank," said the captain, "may we profit from your medical experience?"

"My what, sir?"

"Talbot—Mr Talbot here," said the captain in a vexed voice, "Mr Talbot—"

"What the devil is wrong with him? Good God! I assure you that Zenobia, dear, warm-hearted gal—"

"I myself," said I swiftly, "have nothing to do with the present matter. Our captain refers to Colley."

"The parson is it? Good God! I assure you it doesn't matter to me at my time of life. Let them enjoy themselves I said—on board I said it—or did I?"

Mr Brocklebank hiccupped. A thin streak of wine ran down his chin. His eyes wandered.

"We need your medical experience," said the captain, his growls only just below the surface, but in what for him was a conciliatory tone. "We have none ourselves and look to you—"

"I have none either," said Mr Brocklebank. "Garçon, another glass!"

"Mr Talbot said—"

"I looked round you see but I said, Wilmot, I said, this anatomy is not for you. No indeed, you have not the stomach for it. In fact as I said at the time, I abandoned Aesculapius for the Muse. Have I not said so to you, Mr Talbot?"

"You have so, sir. On at least two occasions. I have no doubt the captain will accept your excuses."

"No, no," said the captain irritably. "However little the gentleman's experience, we must profit by it."

"Profit," said Brocklebank. "There is more profit in the Muse than in the other thing. I should be a rich man now had not the warmth of my constitution, an attachment more than usually firm to the Sex and the opportunities for excess forced on my nature by the shocking corruption of English Society—"

"I could not abide doctoring," said Oldmeadow. "All those corpses, good God!"

"Just so, sir. I prefer to keep reminders of mortality at arm's length. Did you know I was first in the field after the death of Lord Nelson with a lithograph portraying the happy occasion?"

"You were not present!"

"Arm's length, sir. Neither was any other artist. I must

admit to you freely that I believed at the time that Lord
Nelson had expired on deck."

"Brocklebank," cried I, "I have seen it! There is a
copy on the wall in the tap of the Dog and Gun! How
the devil did that whole crowd of young officers
contrive to be kneeling round Lord Nelson in attitudes
of sorrow and devotion at the hottest moment of the
action?"

Another thin trickle of wine ran down the man's chin.

"You are confusing art with actuality, sir."

"It looked plain silly to me, sir."

"It has sold very well indeed, Mr Talbot. I cannot conceal from you that without the continued popularity of
that work I should be in Queer Street. It has at the very
least allowed me to take a passage to, to wherever we
are going, the name escapes me. And imagine, sir, Lord
Nelson died down below in some stinking part of the
bilges, I believe, with nothing to see him by but a ship's
lantern. Who in the devil is going to make a picture of
that?"

"Rembrandt perhaps."

"Ah. Rembrandt. Yes, well. At least Mr Talbot you
must admire the dexterity of my management of smoke."

"Take me with you, sir."

"Smoke is the very devil. Did you not see it when Summers fired my gun? With broadsides a naval battle is
nothing but a London Particular. So your true craftsman must tuck it away to where it does not obtrude—
obtrude—"

"Like a clown."

"Obtrude—"

"And interrupt some necessary business of the action."

"Obtrude—captain, you don't drink."

The captain made another gesture with his glass, then
looked round at the other three of his guests in angry

frustration. But Brocklebank, his elbows now on either side of the marrow bone intended for Summers, droned on.

"I have always maintained that smoke properly handled can be of ma-material assistance. You are approached by some captain who has had the good fortune to fall in with the enemy and get off again. He comes to me as they did, after my lithograph. He has, for example, in company with another frigate and a small sloop— encountered the French and a battle has ensued—I beg your pardon! As the epitaph says, 'Wherever you be let your wind go free for holding mine was the death of me.' Now I ask you to imagine what would happen—and indeed my good friend, Fuseli, you know, the Shield of Achilles, and—well. Imagine!"

I drank impatiently and turned to the captain.

"I think, sir, that Mr Brocklebank—"

It was of no avail and the man drooled again without noticing.

"Imagine—who pays me? If they *all* pay there can be no smoke at all! Yet they must all be seen to be hotly engaged, the devil take it! They come to blows, you know!"

"Mr Brocklebank," said the captain fretfully, "Mr Brocklebank—"

"Give me one single captain who has been successful and got his K! *Then* there will be no argument!"

"No," said Oldmeadow, cawing into his collar, "no indeed!"

Mr Brocklebank eyed him truculently.

"You doubt my word, sir? Do you, because if you do, sir—"

"I, sir? Good God no, sir!"

"He will say, 'Brocklebank,' he will say. 'I don't give a tuppenny damn for me own part, but me mother, me wife and me fifteen gals require a picture of me ship at the height of the action!' You follow? Now after I have been furnished with a copy of the gazette and had the battle described to me in minutest detail he goes off in the happy delusion that he knows what a naval battle looks like!"

The captain raised his glass. This time he emptied it at a gulp. He addressed Brocklebank in a voice which would have scared Mr Taylor from one end of the ship to the other if not farther.

"I for my part, sir, should be of his opinion!"

Mr Brocklebank, to indicate the degree of his own cleverness, tried to lay a finger cunningly on the side of his nose but missed it.

"You are wrong, sir. Were I to rely on verisimilitude— but no. Do you suppose that my client, who has paid a deposit—for you see he may be off and lose his head in a moment—"

Summers stood up.

"I am called for, sir."

The captain, with perhaps the only glimmer of wit I have found in him, laughed aloud.

"You are fortunate, Mr Summers!"

Brocklebank noticed nothing. Indeed, I believe if we had all left him he would have continued his monologue.

"Now do you suppose the accompanying frigate is to be portrayed with an equal degree of animation? She has paid nothing! That is where smoke comes in. By the time I have done my layout she will have just fired and the smoke will have risen up round her; and as for the sloop, which will have been in the hands of some obscure lieu-tenant, it will be lucky to appear at all. My client's ship on the other hand will be belching more fire than smoke and will be being attacked by all the enemy at once."

"I could almost wish," said I, "that the French would

afford us an opportunity for invoking the good offices of your brush."

"There's no hope of that," said the captain glumly, "no hope at all."

Perhaps his tone affected Mr Brocklebank, who went through one of those extraordinarily swift transitions which are common enough among the inebriated from cheerfulness to melancholy.

"But that is never the end of it. Your client will return and the first thing he will say is that *Corinna* or *Erato* never carried her foremast stepped as far forrard as that and what is that block doing on the main brace? Why, my most successful client—apart from the late Lord Nelson if I may so describe him—as a client I mean—was even foolish enough to object to some trifling injuries I had inflicted on the accompanying frigate. He swore she had never lost her topmast, her fore topmast I think he said, for she was scarcely in cannon shot. Then he said I had shown no damage in the region of the quarterdeck of his ship, which was not accurate. He forced me to beat two gunports into one there and carry away a great deal of the rail. Then he said, 'Could you not dash me in there, Brocklebank? I distinctly remember standin' just by the broken rail, encouragin' the crew and indicatin' the enemy by wavin' me sword towards them.' What could I do? The client is always right, it is the artist's first axiom. 'The figure will be very small, Sir Sammel,' said I. 'That is of no consequence,' said he. 'You may exaggerate me a little.' I bowed to him. 'If I do that, Sir Sammel,' said I, 'it will reduce your frigate to a sloop by contrast.' He took a turn or two up and down my studio for all the world like our captain here on the quarterdeck. 'Well,' said he at last, 'you must dash me in small, then. They will know me by me cocked hat and me epaulettes. It's of no consequence to me, Mr Brocklebank, but me good lady and me gals insist on it.' "

"Sir Sammel," said the captain. "You did say 'Sir Sammel'?"

"I did. Do we move on to brandy?"

"Sir Sammel. I know him. Knew him."

"Tell us all, Captain," said I, hoping to stem the flow. "A shipmate?"

"I was the lieutenant commanding the sloop," said the captain moodily, "but I have not seen the picture."

"Captain! I positively must have a description of this," said I. "We landsmen are avid, you know, for that sort of thing!"

"Good God, the shloop! I have met the sh—the other sh—the lieutenant. Captain, you must be portrayed. We will waft away the sh—the smoke and show you in the thick of it!"

"Why so he was," said I. "Can we believe him anywhere else? You were in the thick of it, were you not?"

Captain Anderson positively snarled.

"The thick of the battle? In a sloop? Against frigates? But Captain—Sir Sammel I suppose I must say—must have thought me in the thick of it for he bawled through his speaking trumpet, 'Get to hell out of this, you young fool, or I'll have you broke!' "

I raised my glass to the captain.

"I drink to you, sir. But no blind eye? No deaf ear?"

"Garçon, where is the brandy? I must limn you, Captain, at a much reduced fee. Your future career—"

Captain Anderson was crouched at the table's head as if to spring. Both fists were clenched on it and his glass had fallen and smashed. If he had snarled before, this time he positively roared.

"Career? Don't you understand, you damned fool? The

153

war is nigh over and done with and we are for the beach, every man jack of us!"

There was a prolonged silence in which even Brockle-bank seemed to find that something unusual had happened to him. His head sank, then jerked up and he looked round vacantly. Then his eyes focused. One by one, we turned.

Summers stood in the doorway.

"Sir. I have been with Mr Colley, sir. It is my belief the man is dead."

Slowly, each of us rose, coming, I suppose, from a moment of furious inhospitality to another realization. I looked at the captain's face. The red suffusion of his anger had sunk away. He was inscrutable. I saw in his face neither concern, relief, sorrow nor triumph. He might have been made of the same material as the figurehead.

He was the first to speak.

"Gentlemen. This sorry affair must end our, our meeting."

"Of course, sir."

"Hawkins. Have this gentleman escorted to his cabin. Mr Talbot. Mr Oldmeadow. Be good enough to view the body with Mr Summers to confirm his opinion. I myself will do so. I fear the man's intemperance has destroyed him."

"Intemperance, sir? A single, unlucky indulgence?"

"What do you mean, Mr Talbot?"

"You will enter it so in the log?"

Visibly, the captain controlled himself.

"That is something for me to consider in my own time, Mr Talbot."

I bowed and said nothing. Oldmeadow and I withdrew and Brocklebank was half-carried and half-dragged behind us. The captain followed the little group that surrounded the monstrous soak. It seemed that every passenger in the ship, or at least the after part of it, was congregated in the lobby and staring silently at the door of Colley's cabin. Many of the crew who were not on duty, and most of the emigrants, were gathered at the white line drawn across the deck and were staring at us in equal silence. I suppose there must have been some noise from the wind and the passage of the ship through the water but I, at least, was not conscious of it. The other passengers made way for us. Wheeler was standing on guard at the door of the cabin, his white puffs of hair, his bald pate and *lighted* face—I can find no other description for his expression of understanding all the ways and woes of the world—gave him an air of positive saintliness. When he saw the captain he bowed with the unction of an undertaker or indeed as if the mantle of poor, obsequious Colley had fallen on him. Though the work should have gone to Phillips, it was Wheeler who opened the door, then stood to one side. The captain went in. He stayed for no more than a moment, came out, motioned me to enter, then strode to the ladder and up to his own quarters. I went into the cabin with no great willingness, I can assure you! The poor man still clutched the eyebolt—still lay with his face pressed against the bolster, but the blanket had been turned back and revealed his cheek and neck. I put three hesitant fingers on his cheek and whipped them back as if they had been burned. I did not choose, indeed I did not need, to lean down and listen for the man's breathing. I came out to Colley's silent congregation and nodded to Mr Oldmeadow who went in, licking pale lips. He too came out quickly.

Summers turned to me.

"Well, Mr Talbot?"

"No living thing could be as cold."

Mr Oldmeadow turned up his eyes and slid gently down the bulkhead until he was sitting on the deck.

Wheeler, with an expression of holy understanding, thrust the gallant officer's head between his knees. But now, of all inappropriate beings, who should appear but Silenus? Brocklebank, perhaps a little recovered or perhaps in some extraordinary trance of drunkenness, reeled out of his cabin and shook off the two women who were trying to restrain him. The other ladies shrieked and then were silent, caught between the two sorts of occasion. The man wore nothing but a shirt. He thrust, weaving and staggering, into Colley's cabin and shoved Summers aside with a force that made the first lieutenant reel.

"I know you all," he shouted, "all, all! I am an artist! The man is not dead but shleepeth! He is in a low fever and may be recovered by drink—"

I grabbed the man and pulled him away. Summers was there, too. We were mixed with Wheeler and stumbling round Oldmeadow—but really, death is death and if *that* is not to be treated with some seriousness—somehow we got him out into the lobby, where the ladies and gentlemen were silent again. There are some situations for which no reaction is suitable—perhaps the only one would have been for them all to retire. Somehow we got him back to the door of his hutch, he meanwhile mouthing about *spirits* and *low fever*. His women waited, silent, appalled. I was muttering in my turn.

"Come now, my good fellow, back to your bunk!"

"A low fever—"

"What the devil is a low fever? Now go in—go *in*, I say! Mrs Brocklebank—Miss Brocklebank, I appeal to you—for heaven's sake—"

They did help and got the door shut on him. I turned away, just as Captain Anderson came down the ladder and into the lobby again.

"Well gentlemen?"

I answered both for Oldmeadow and myself.

"To the best of my belief, Captain Anderson, Mr Colley is dead."

He fixed me with his little eyes.

"I heard mention of 'a low fever', did I not?"

Summers came out, closing the door of Colley's cabin behind him. It was an act of curious decency. He stood, looking from the captain to me and back again. I spoke unwillingly—but what else could I say?

"It was a remark made by Mr Brocklebank who is, I fear, not wholly himself."

I swear the captain's cheeks creased and the twin sparks came back. He looked round the crowd of witnesses.

"Nevertheless, Mr Brocklebank has had some medical experience!"

Before I could expostulate he had spoken again and with the tyrannical accents of his service.

"Mr Summers. See that the customary arrangements are made."

"Aye, aye, sir."

The captain turned and retired briskly. Summers continued in much the same accents as his captain.

"Mr Willis!"

"Sir!"

"Bring aft the sailmaker and his mate and three or four able-bodied men. You may take what men of the off-duty watch are under punishment."

"Aye, aye, sir."

Here was none of the pretended melancholy our professional undertakers have as their stock-in-trade! Mr Willis departed *forrard* at a run. The first lieutenant then addressed the assembled passengers in his customary mild accents.

"Ladies and gentlemen, you will not wish to witness what follows. May I request that the lobby be cleared? The air of the quarterdeck is to be recommended."

Slowly the lobby cleared until Summers and I were left together with the servants. The door of Brocklebank's hutch opened and the man stood there grotesquely naked. He spoke with ludicrous solemnity.

"Gentlemen. A low fever is the opposite of a high fever. I bid you good day."

He was tugged backwards and reeled. The door was shut upon him. Summers then turned to me.

"You, Mr Talbot?"

"I have the captain's request still to comply with, have I not?"

"I fancy it has ended with the poor man's death."

"We talked of *noblesse oblige* and fair play. I found myself translating the words by a single one."

"Which is?"

"Justice."

Summers appeared to consider. "You have decided who is to appear at the bar?"

"Have not you?"

"I? The powers of a captain—besides, sir, *I* have no patron."

"Do not be so certain, Mr Summers."

He looked at me for a moment in bewilderment. Then he caught his breath. "I—?"

But men of the crew were trotting aft towards us. Summers glanced at them, then back at me.

"May I recommend the quarterdeck?"

"A glass of brandy is more appropriate."

I went into the passenger saloon and found Oldmeadow slumped there in a seat under the great stern window, an empty glass in his hand. He was breathing deeply and perspiring profusely. But the colour was back in his cheeks. He muttered to me.

"Damned silly thing to do. Don't know what came over me."

"Is this how you behave on a stricken field, Old-meadow? No, forgive me! I am not myself either. The dead, you see, lying in that attitude as I had so recently seen him—why even then he might have been—but now, stiff and hard as—where the devil is that steward? Steward! Brandy here and some more for Mr Old-meadow!"

"I know what you mean, Talbot. The truth is I have never seen a stricken field nor heard a shot fired in anger except once when my adversary missed me by a yard. How silent the ship has become!"

I glanced through the saloon door. The party of men was crowding into Colley's cabin. I shut the door and turned back to Oldmeadow.

"All will be done soon. Oldmeadow—are our feelings unnatural?"

"I wear the King's uniform yet I have never before seen a dead body except the occasional tarred object in chains. This has quite overcome me—touching it I mean. I am Cornish, you see."

"With such a name?"

"We are not all Tre, Pol and Pen. Lord, how her timbers grind. Is there a change in her motion?"

"It cannot be."

"Talbot, do you suppose—"

"What, sir?"

"Nothing."

We sat for a while and I attended more to the spreading warmth of the brandy through my veins than anything else. Presently Summers came in. Behind him I glimpsed a party of men bearing a covered object away along the deck. Summers himself had not yet recovered from a slight degree of pallor.

"Brandy for you, Summers?"

He shook his head. Oldmeadow got to his feet.

"The afterdeck and a breath of air for me, I think. Damned silly of me it was. Just damned silly."

Presently Summers and I were alone.

"Mr Talbot," he said, in a low tone, "you mentioned justice."

"Well, sir?"

"You have a journal."

"And——?"

"Just that."

He nodded meaningly at me, got up, and left. I stayed where I was, thinking to myself how little he understood me after all. He did not know that I had already used that same journal—nor that I planned this plain account to lie before one in whose judgement and integrity—

My lord, you was pleased to advise me to practise the art of flattery. But how can I continue to *try it on* a personage who will infallibly detect the endeavour? Let me be disobedient to you if only in this, and flatter you no more!

Well then, I have accused the captain of an abuse of power; and I have let stand on the page Summers's own suggestion that I myself was to some extent responsible for it. I do not know what more the name of justice can demand of me. The night is far advanced—and it is only *now* as I write these words that I remember the *Colley Manuscript* in which there may be even plainer evidence of your godson's culpability and our captain's cruelty! I will glance through what the poor devil wrote and then get me to bed.

* * *

I have done so oh God, and could almost wish I had not. Poor, poor Colley, poor Robert James Colley! Billy Rogers, Summers firing the gun, Deverel and

Cumbershum, Anderson, minatory, cruel Anderson! If there is justice in the world—but you may see by the state of my writing how the thing has worked on me—and I—I!

There is light filtering through my louvre. It is far advanced towards morning then. What am I to do? I cannot give Colley's letter, this unbegun, unfinished letter, cannot give this letter to the captain, though *that* for sure, legalistical as it might sound, is what I ought to do. But what then? It would go overboard, be suppressed, Colley would have died of a *low fever* and that would be all. My part would disappear with it. Do I refine too much? For Anderson is captain and will have chapter and verse, justifications for everything he has done. Nor can I take Summers into my confidence. His precious *career* is at stake. He would be bound to say that though I was perhaps right to appropriate the letter I have no business to suppress it.

Well. I do not suppress it. I take the only way towards justice—natural justice I mean, rather than that of the captain or the law courts—and lay the evidence in your lordship's hands. He says he is "For the beach". If you believe as I do that he went beyond discipline into tyranny then a word from you in the right quarter will keep him there.

And I? I am writ down plainer in this record than I intended, to be sure! What I thought was behaviour consonant with my position—

Very well, then. I, too.

Why Edmund, Edmund! This is methodistical folly! Did you not believe you were a man of less sensibility than intelligence? Did you not feel, no, *believe*, that your blithely accepted system of morality for men in general owed less to feeling than to the operations of the intellect? Here is more of what you will wish to tear and not exhibit! But I have read and written all night and may be forgiven for a little lightheadedness. Nothing is real and I am already in a half-dream. I will get glue and fix the letter in here. It shall become another part of the *Talbot Manuscript*.

His sister must never know. It is another reason for not showing the letter. He died of a low fever—why, that poor girl there forrard will die of one like enough before we are done. Did I say glue? There must be some about. A hoof of Bessie. Wheeler will know, omniscient, ubiquitous Wheeler. And I must keep all locked away. This journal has become deadly as a loaded gun.

The first page, or it may be two pages, are gone. I saw them, or it, in his hand when he walked, in a trance of drunkenness, walked, head up and with a smile as if already in heaven—

Then at some time after he had fallen into a drunken slumber, he woke—slowly perhaps. There was, it may be, a blank time when he knew not who or what he was—then the time of remembering the Reverend Robert James Colley.

No. I do not care to imagine it. I visited him that first time—Did my words bring to his mind all that he had lost? Self-esteem? His fellows' respect? *My* friendship? *My* patronage? Then, *then* in that agony he grabbed the letter, crumpled it, thrust it away as he would have thrust his memory away had it been possible—away, deep down beneath the bunk, unable to bear the thought of it—

My imagination is false. For sure he willed himself to death, but not for that, not for any of that, not for a casual, a single—

Had he committed murder—or being what he was—!

It is madness, absurdity. What women are there at *that* end of the ship for him?

And I? I might have saved him had I thought less of my own consequence and less of the danger of being bored!

Oh those judicious opinions, those interesting observations, those sparks of wit with which I once proposed to entertain your lordship! Here instead is a plain description of Anderson's *commissions* and my own—omissions.

Your lordship may now read:

COLLEY'S LETTER

so I have drawn a veil over what have been the most trying and unedifying of my experiences. My prolonged nausea has rendered those first hours and days a little less distinct in my memory, nor would I attempt to describe to you in any detail the foul air, lurching brutalities, the wantonness, the casual blasphemies to which a passenger in such a ship is exposed even if he is a clergyman! But now I am sufficiently recovered from my nausea to be able to hold a pen, I cannot refrain from harking back for a moment to my first appearance on the vessel. Having escaped the clutches of a horde of *nameless creatures* on the foreshore and having been conveyed out to our noble vessel in a most expensive manner; having then been lifted to the deck in a kind of sling—somewhat like but more elaborate than the swing hung from the beech beyond the styes—I found myself facing a young officer who carried a spyglass under his arm.

Instead of addressing me as one gentleman ought to address another he turned to one of his fellows and made the following observation.

"Oh G—, a parson! That will send old Rumble-guts flying into the foretop!"

This was but a sample of what I was to suffer. I will not detail the rest, for it is now many days, my dear sister, since we bade farewell to the shores of Old Albion. Though I am strong enough to sit at the little flap which serves me as *priedieu*, desk, table and lectern I am still not secure enough to venture further. My first duty must be, of course (after those of my calling) to make myself known to our gallant captain, who lives and has his being some two storeys, or decks as I must now call them, above us. I hope he will agree to have this letter put on a ship proceeding in a contrary direction so you may have the earliest news of me. As I write this, Phillips (my *servant!*) has been in my small cabin with a little broth and advised me against a premature visit to Captain Anderson. He says I should get up my strength a little, take some food in the passenger saloon as a change from having it here— what I could *retain* of it!—and exercise myself in the lobby or further out in that large space of deck which he calls the *waist* and which lies about the tallest of our masts.

Though unable to eat I *have* been out, and oh, my dear sister, how remiss I have been to repine at my lot! It is an earthly, nay, an oceanic paradise! The sunlight is warm and like a natural benediction. The sea is brilliant as the tails of Juno's birds (I mean the peacock) that parade the terraces of Manston Place! (Do not omit to show any little attention that may be possible in that quarter, I must remind you.) Enjoyment of such a scene is as good a medicine as a man could wish for when enhanced by that portion of the scriptures appointed for the day. There was a sail appeared briefly on the horizon and I offered up a brief prayer for our safety subject always to HIS Will. However, I took my temper from the behaviour of our officers and men, though of course in the love and care of OUR SAVIOUR I have a far securer *anchor* than any appertaining to the vessel! Dare I confess to you that as the strange sail sank below the horizon—she had never appeared wholly above it—I caught myself day-dreaming that she had attacked us and that I performed some deed of daring not, indeed, fitted for an ordained minister of the Church but even as when a boy, I dreamed sometimes of winning fame and fortune at the side of England's Hero! The sin was venial and quickly acknowledged and repented. Our heroes surrounded me on all sides and it is to them that I ought to minister!

Well, then, I could almost wish a battle for *their* sakes! They go about their tasks, their bronzed and manly forms unclothed to the waist, their abundant locks gathered in a queue, their nether garments closely fitted but flared about the ankles like the nostrils of a stallion. They disport themselves casually a hundred feet up in the air. Do not, I beg you, believe the tales spread by vicious and un-Christian men, of their brutal treatment! I have neither heard nor seen a flogging. Nothing more drastic has occurred than a judicious correction applied to the proper portion of a *young gentleman* who would have suffered as much and borne it as stoically at school.

I must give you some idea of the shape of the little society in which we must live together for I know not how many months. We, the gentry as it were, have our castle in the backward or after part of the vessel. At the other end of the waist, under a wall pierced by two entrances and furnished with stairs or, as they still call them, *ladders*, are the quarters of our Jolly Tars and the other inferior sort of passenger—the emigrants, and so forth. Above that again is the deck of the fo'castle and the quite astonishing world of the bowsprit! You will have been accustomed, as I was, to thinking of a bowsprit (remember Mr Wembury's ship-in-a-bottle!) as a stick projecting from the front end of a ship. Nay then, I must now inform you that a bowsprit is a whole mast, only laid more nearly to the horizontal than the others. It has *yards* and *mastcapping, sidestays* and even *halyards*! More than that, as the other masts may be likened to huge trees among the limbs and branches of which our fellows climb, so the bowsprit is a kind of road, steep in truth but one on which they run or walk. It is more than three feet in diameter. The masts, those other "sticks", are of such a thickness!

Not the greatest beech from Saker's Wood has enough mass to supply such monsters. When I remember that some action of the enemy, or, even more appalling, some act of Nature may break or twist them off as you might twist the leaves off a carrot, I fall into a kind of terror. Indeed it was not a terror for my own safety! It was, it is, a terror at the majesty of this huge engine of war, then by a curious extension of the feeling, a kind of awe at the nature of the beings whose joy and duty it is to control such an invention in the service of their GOD and their King. Does not Sophocles (a Greek Tragedian) have some such thought in the chorus to his Philoctetes? But I digress.

The air is warm and sometimes hot, the sun lays such a lively hand on us! We must be beware of him lest he strike us down! I am conscious even as I sit here at my *desk* of a warmness about my cheeks that has been occasioned by his rays! The sky this morning was of a dense blue, yet no brighter nor denser than the white-flecked blue of the broad ocean. I could almost rejoice in that powerful circling which the point of the bowsprit, *our* bowsprit, ceaselessly described above the sharp line of the horizon!

Next day.
I am indeed stronger and more able to eat. Phillips says that soon all will be well with me. Yet the weather is somewhat changed. Where yesterday there was a blueness and brightness, there is today little or no wind and the sea is covered with a white haze. The bowsprit—which in earlier days had brought on attack after attack of nausea if I was so rash as to fix my attention on it—stands still. Indeed, the aspect of our little world has changed at least three times since our Dear Country sank—nay, appeared to sink—into the waves! Where, I ask myself, are the woods and fertile fields, the flowers, the grey stone church

in which you and I have worshipped all our lives, that churchyard in which our dear parents—nay, the earthly remains of our dear parents, who have surely received their reward in heaven—where, I ask, are all the familiar scenes that were for both of us the substance of our lives? The human mind is inadequate to such a situation. I tell myself there is some material reality which joins the place where I am to the place where I was, even as a road joins Upper and Nether Compton. The intellect assents but the *heart* can find no certainty in it. In reproof I tell myself that OUR LORD is here as much as there; or rather that here and there may be the same place in HIS EYES!

I have been on deck again. The white mist seemed denser, yet hot. Our people are dimly to be seen. The ship is utterly stopped, her sails hanging down. My footsteps sounded unnaturally loud and I did not care to hear them. I saw no passengers about the deck. There is no creak from all our wood and when I ventured to look over the side I saw not a ripple, not a bubble in the water.

Well, I am myself again—but only just!

I had not been out in the hot vapour for more than a few minutes when a thunderbolt of blinding white dropped out of the mist on our right hand and struck into the sea. The clap came with the sight and left my ears ringing. Before I had time to turn and run, more claps came one on the other and rain fell—I had almost said in rivers! But truly it seemed they were the waters of the earth! Huge drops leapt back a yard off the deck. Between where I had stood by the rail and the lobby was but a few yards, yet I was drenched before I got under cover. I disrobed as far as decency permits, then sat at this letter but not a little shaken. For the last quarter of an hour—would that I had a timepiece!—the awful bolts have dropped and the rain cascaded.

Now the storm is grumbling away into the distance. The sun is lighting what it can reach of our lobby. A light breeze has set us groaning, washing and bubbling on our way. I say the sun has appeared; but only to set.

What has remained with me apart from a lively memory of my apprehensions is not only a sense of HIS AWFULNESS and a sense of the majesty of HIS creation. It is a sense of the splendour of our vessel rather than her triviality and minuteness! It is as if I think of her as a separate world, a universe in little in which we must pass our lives and receive our reward or punishment. I trust the thought is not impious! It is a strange thought and a strong one!

It is with me still for, the breeze dying away, I ventured forth again. It is night now. I cannot tell you how high against the stars her great masts seem, how huge yet airy her sails, nor how far down from her deck the night-glittering surface of the waters. I remained motionless by the rail for I know not how long. While I was yet there, the last disturbance left by the breeze passed away so that the glitter, that image of the starry heavens, gave place to a flatness and blackness, a nothing! All was mystery. It terrified me and I turned away to find myself staring into the half-seen face of Mr Smiles, the sailing master. Phillips tells me that Mr Smiles, under the captain, is responsible for the navigation of our vessel.

"Mr Smiles—tell me how deep these waters are!"

He is a strange man, as I know already. He is given to long thought, constant observation. He is aptly named, too, for he has a kind of smiling remoteness which sets him apart from his fellow men.

"Who can say, Mr Colley?"

I laughed uneasily. He came closer and peered into my face. He is smaller even than I, and you know I am by no means a tall man.

"These waters may be more than a mile deep—two miles—who can say? We might sound at such a depth but commonly we do not. There is not the necessity."

"More than a mile!"

I was almost overcome with faintness. Here we are, suspended between the land below the waters and the sky like a nut on a branch or a leaf on a pond! I cannot convey to you, my dear sister, my sense of horror, or shall I say, my sense of our being living souls in this place where surely, I thought, no man ought to be!

I wrote that last night by the light of a most expensive candle. You know how frugal I must be. Yet I am forced in on myself and must be indulged in a light if nothing else. It is in circumstances such as these present that a man (even if he make the fullest use of the consolations of religion that are available to his individual nature), that a man, I say, requires human companionship. Yet the ladies and gentlemen at this end of the ship do not respond with any cheerful alacrity to my greetings. I had thought at first that they were, as the saying is, "shy of a parson". I pressed Phillips again and again as to the meaning of this. Perhaps I should not have done so! He need not be privy to social divisions that are no concern of his. But he did mutter it was thought among the common people that a parson in a ship was like a woman in a fishing boat—a kind of natural bringer of bad luck. This low and reprehensible superstition cannot apply to our ladies and gentlemen. It is no kind of explanation. It seemed to me yesterday that I might have a clue as to their indefinable *indifference* to me. We have with us the celebrated, or let me say, the *notorious* free thinker, Mr Prettiman, that friend of Republicans and Jacobins! He is regarded by most, I think, with dislike. He is short and stocky. He has a bald head surrounded by a wild halo—

dear me, how unfortunate my choice of words has been—
a wild fringe of brown hair that grows from beneath his
ears and round the back of his neck. He is a man of violent
and eccentric movements that spring, we must suppose,
from some well of his indignations. Our young ladies
avoid him and the only one who will give him countenance is a Miss Granham, a lady of sufficient years and, I
am sure, firmness of principle to afford her security even
in the heat of his opinions. There is also a young lady, a
Miss Brocklebank, of outstanding beauty, of whom—I say
no more or you will think me arch. I believe she, at least,
does not look on your brother unkindly! But she is much
occupied with the indisposition of her mother, who suffers
even more than I from *mal de mer*.

I have left to the last a description of a young
gentleman whom I trust and pray will become my friend
as the voyage advances. He is a member of the aristo-
cracy, with all the consideration and nobility of bearing
that such birth implies. I have made so bold as to salute
him on a number of occasions and he has responded
graciously. His example may do much among the other
passengers.

This morning I have been out on deck again. A breeze
had sprung up during the night and helped us on our way
but now it has fallen calm again. Our sails hang down and
there is a vaporous dimness everywhere, even at noon.
Once more and with that same terrifying instantaneity
came flashes of lightning in the mist that were awful in
their fury! I fled to my cabin with such a sense of our peril
from these warring elements, such a return of my sense of
our suspension over this liquid profundity, that I could
scarce get my hands together in prayer. However, little by
little I came to myself and to peace though all outside was
turmoil. I reminded myself, as I should have done before,
that one good soul, one good deed, good thought, and

more, one touch of Heaven's Grace was greater than all these boundless miles of rolling vapour and wetness, this intimidating vastness, this louring majesty! Indeed, I thought, though with some hesitation, that perhaps bad men in their ignorant deaths may find here the awfulness in which they must dwell by reason of their depravity. You see, my dear sister, that the strangeness of our surroundings, the weakness consequent on my prolonged nausea and a natural diffidence that has led me too readily to *shrink into my shell* has produced in me something not unlike a temporary disordering of the intellects! I found myself thinking of a seabird crying as one of those lost souls to whom I have alluded! I thanked GOD humbly that I had been allowed to detect this fantasy in myself before it became a belief.

I have roused myself from my lethargy. I have seen at least one possible reason for the indifference with which I feel myself treated. I have not made myself known to our captain and this may well have been thought a slight upon him! I am determined to undo this misapprehension as soon as possible. I shall approach him and express my sincere regret for the lack of Sabbath observance that my indisposition has occasioned in the ship, for she carries no chaplain. I must and will eradicate from my mind the ungenerous suspicion that on reaching or *joining* the ship I received less courtesy from the officers than is due to my cloth. Our Stout-hearted Defenders cannot, I am sure, be of such a sort. I will walk a little on deck now in preparation before readying myself to visit the captain. You remember my old diffidence at approaching the face of Authority and will feel for me!

I have been into the waist again and spoken once more with our sailing master. He was standing on the left-hand side of the vessel and staring with his particular intentness at the horizon; or rather, where the horizon ought to have been.

"Good morning, Mr Smiles! I should be happier if this vapour were to clear away!"

He smiled at me with that same mysterious remoteness.

"Very well, sir. I will see what can be done."

I laughed at the quip. His good humour restored me completely to myself. So that I might *exorcise* those curious feelings of the strangeness of the world I went to the side of the vessel and leaned against the railings (the bulwarks as they are called) and looked down where the timbers of our enormous vessel bulge out past her closed gunports. Her slight progress made a tiny ripple in that sea which I made myself inspect coldly, as it were. My sense of its depth—but how am I to say this? I have seen many a millpond or corner of a river seem as deep! Nor was there a spot or speck in it where our ship divided it, a closing furrow in the poet Homer's "Unfurrowed ocean". Yet I found myself facing a new puzzle—and one that would not have presented itself to the poet! (You must know that Homer is commonly supposed to have been blind.) How then can water added to water reproduce an opacity? What impediment to the vision can colourlessness and transparency spread before us? Do we not see clear through glass or diamond or crystal? Do we not see the sun and moon and those fainter luminaries (I mean the stars) through unmeasured heights of pendant atmosphere? Yet here, what was glittering and black at night, grey under the racing clouds of awful tempest, now began little by little to turn blue and green under the sun that at last broke through the vapour!

Why should I, a cleric, a man of GOD, one acquainted with the robust if mistaken intellects of this and the preceding century and able to see them for what they are— why, I say, should the material nature of the globe so interest, so trouble and excite me? *They that go down to the sea in ships!* I cannot think of our Dear Country without finding myself looking not over the horizon (in my imagination, of course) but trying to calculate that segment of water and earth and *terrible deep rock* that I must suppose myself to stare through in order to look in your direction and that of our—let me say *our*—village! I must ask Mr Smiles, who will be well enough acquainted with the angles and appropriate mathematics of the case, as to the precise number of degrees it is necessary to look beneath the horizon! How immeasurably strange it will be at the Antipodes to stare (near enough I think) at the buckles of my shoes and suppose you—forgive me, I am off in a fantasy again! Do but think that there the very stars will be unfamiliar and the moon stood on her head!

Enough of fantasy! I will go now and make myself known to our captain! Perhaps I may have some opportunity of entertaining him with the idle fancies I have alluded to above.

I have approached Captain Anderson and will narrate the plain facts to you if I can. My fingers are almost nerveless and will scarcely allow me to hold the pen. You may deduce that from the quality of this handwriting.

Well then, I attended to my clothes with more than usual care, came out of my cabin and ascended the flights of stairs to that highest deck where the captain commonly stations himself. At the front end of this deck and rather below it are the wheel and compass. Captain Anderson and the first lieutenant, Mr Summers, were staring together at the compass. I saw the moment was unpropitious and waited for a while. At last the two gentlemen finished their conversation. The captain turned away and walked to the very back end of the vessel and I followed him, thinking this my opportunity. But no sooner had he reached the rail at the back than he turned round again. As I was following closely I had to leap sideways in what must have appeared a manner hardly consonant with the dignity of my sacred office. Scarcely had I recovered my balance when he *growled* at me as if I had been at fault rather than he. I uttered a word or two of introduction which he dismissed with a grunt. He then made a remark which he did not trouble to modify with any show of civility.

"Passengers come to the quarterdeck by invitation. I am not accustomed to these interruptions in my walk, sir. Go forrard if you please and keep to looard."

"Looard, captain?"

I found myself drawn forcibly sideways. A young gentleman was pulling me to the wheel whence he led me—I complying—to the opposite side of the ship to where Captain Anderson was. He positively hissed in my ear. That side of the deck, whichever it may be, from which the wind blows is reserved to the captain. I had therefore made a mistake but could not see how I was at fault but by an ignorance natural in a gentleman who had never been at sea before. Yet I am deeply suspicious that the surliness of the captain towards me is not to be explained so readily. Is it perhaps sectarianism? If so, as a humble servant of the Church of England—the Catholic Church of England—which spreads its arms so wide in the charitable embrace of sinners, I cannot but deplore such divisive stubbornness! Or if it is not sectarianism but a social contempt, the situation is as serious—nay, *almost* as serious! I am a clergyman, bound for an honourable if humble situation at the Antipodes. The captain has no more business to look big on me—and indeed less business—than the canons of the Close or those clergy I have met *twice* at my Lord Bishop's table! I have determined therefore to emerge more frequently from my obscurity and exhibit my cloth to this gentleman and the passengers in general so that even if they do not respect *me* they may respect *it*! I may surely hope for some support from the young gentleman, Mr Edmund Talbot, from Miss Brocklebank and Miss Granham—It is evident I must return to the captain, offer him my sincere apologies for my inadvertent trespass, then raise the question of Sabbath Observance. I would beg to offer Communion to the ladies and gentlemen—and of course to the common people who should desire it. There is, I fear, only too plainly room for much improvement in the conduct of affairs aboard the vessel. There is (for example) a daily ceremony of which I had heard and would now wish to prevent—for you know how paternally severe my Lord Bishop has been in his condemnation of drunkenness among the lower orders! Yet here it is only too true! The people are indeed given strong drink regularly! A further reason for instituting worship must be the opportunities it will afford for animadverting on the subject! I shall return to the captain and proceed by a process of mollification. I must indeed be all things to all men.

I have attempted to be so and have failed abjectly, humiliatingly. It was, as I wrote before, in my mind to ascend to the captain's deck, apologize for my previous trespass, beg his permission to use it and then raise the question of regular worship. I can scarcely bring myself to recount the truly awful scene that followed on my well-meant attempt to bring myself to the familiar notice of the officers and gentlemen. As soon as I had written the foregoing paragraph I went up to the lower part of the quarterdeck where one of the lieutenants stood by the two men at the wheel. I lifted my hat to him and made an amiable comment.

"We are now in finer weather, sir."

The lieutenant ignored me. But this was not the worst of it. There came a kind of growling roar from the back rail of the ship.

"Mr Colley! Mr Colley! Come here, sir!"

This was not the kind of invitation I had looked for. I liked neither the tone nor the words. But they were nothing to what followed as I approached the captain.

"Mr Colley! Do you wish to subvert all my officers?"

"Subvert, sir?"

"It was my word, sir!"

"There is some mistake—"

"It is yours then, sir. Are you aware of the powers of a captain in his own ship?"

"They are rightly extensive. But as an ordained minister—"

"You are a passenger, sir, neither more nor less. What is more, you are not behaving as decent as the rest—"

"Sir!"

"You are a nuisance, sir. You was put aboard this ship without a note to me. There is more courtesy shown me about a bale or a keg, sir. Then I did you the credit to suppose you could read—"

"Read, Captain Anderson? Of course I can read!"

"But despite my plainly written orders, no sooner had you recovered from your sickness than you have twice approached and exasperated my officers—"

"I know nothing of this, have read nothing—"

"They are my Standing Orders, sir, a paper prominently displayed near your quarters and those of the other passengers."

"My attention was not drawn—"

"Stuff and nonsense, sir. You have a servant and the orders are there."

"My attention—"

"Your ignorance is no excuse. If you wish to have the same freedom as the other passengers enjoy in the after part of the vessel—or do you wish not to live among ladies and gentlemen, sir? Go—examine the paper!"

"It is my right—"

"Read it, sir. And when you have read it, get it by heart."

"How, sir! Will you treat me like a schoolboy?"

"I will treat you like a schoolboy if I choose, sir, or I will put you in irons if I choose or have you flogged at the gratings if I choose or have you hanged at the yardarm if I choose—"

"Sir! Sir!"

"Do you doubt my authority?"

I saw it all now. Like my poor young friend Josh—you remember Josh—Captain Anderson was mad. Josh was always well enough in his wits except when frogs were in question. *Then* his mania was clear for all to hear, and later, alas, for all to see. Now here was Captain Anderson, well enough for the most part, but by some unfortunate chance fixing on me in his mania for an object to be humiliated—as indeed I was. I could do nothing but humour him for there was, mad or no, that in his enraged demeanour which convinced me he was capable of carrying out at least some of his threats. I answered him as lightly as possible but in a voice, I fear, sadly tremulous.

"I will indulge you in this, Captain Anderson."

"You will carry out my orders."

I turned away and withdrew silently. Directly I was out of his presence I found my body bathed in perspiration yet strangely cold, though my face, by some contrast, was as strangely hot. I discovered in myself a deep unwillingness to meet any eye, any face. As for my own eyes—I was weeping! I wish I could say they were tears of manly wrath but the truth is they were tears of shame. On shore a man is punished at the last by the Crown. At sea the man is punished by the captain who is visibly present as the Crown is not. At sea a person's manhood suffers. It is a kind of contest—is that not strange? So that men—but I wander in my narrative. Suffice it to say that I found, nay, groped my way back to the neighbourhood of my cabin. When my eyes had cleared and I had come to myself a little I searched for the captain's written Orders. They were indeed displayed on a wall near the cabins! Now I did remember too that during the convulsions of my sickness Phillips had talked to me about *Orders* and even *the captain's Orders*; but only those who have suffered as I can understand how slight an impression the words had made on my fainting spirits. But here they were. It was unfortunate, to say the least. I had, by the most severe standards, been remiss. The Orders were displayed in a case. The glass was somewhat blurred on the inside by a condensation of atmospheric water. But I was able to read the writing, the material part of which I copy here.

> Passengers are in no case to speak to officers who are executing some duty about the ship. In no case are they to address the officer of the watch during his hours of duty unless expressly enjoined to do so by him.

I saw now what a hideous situation I was in. The officer of the watch, I reasoned, must have been the first lieutenant, who had been with the captain, and at my *second* attempt the lieutenant who had stood by the men at the wheel. My fault was quite inadvertent but none the less real. Even though the manner of Captain Anderson to me had not been and perhaps never would be that of one gentleman to another, yet some form of apology was due to him and through him to those other officers whom I might have hindered in the execution of their duty. Then too, for-bearance must be in the very nature of my calling. I therefore easily and quickly committed the essential words to memory and returned at once to the raised decks which are included in the seaman's term "Quarterdeck". The wind was increased somewhat. Captain Anderson paced up and down the side, Lieutenant Summers talked to another lieutenant by the wheel, where two of the ship's people guided our huge vessel creaming over the billows. Mr Summers pointed to some rope or other in the vast complication of the rigging. A young gentleman who stood behind the lieutenants touched his hat and skipped nimbly down the stairs by which I had ascended. I approached the captain's back and waited for him to turn.

Captain Anderson walked through me!

I could almost wish that he had in truth done so—yet the hyperbole is not inapt. He must have been very deep in thought. He struck me on the shoulder with his swinging arm and then his chest struck me in the face so that I went reeling and ended by measuring my length on the whitescrubbed planking of the deck!

I got my breath back with difficulty. My head was resounding from a concussive encounter with the wood. Indeed, for a moment it appeared that not one but two captains were staring down at me. It was some time before I realized that I was being addressed.

"Get up, sir! Get up at once! Is there no end to your impertinent folly?"

I was scrabbling on the deck for my hat and wig. I had little enough breath for a rejoinder.

"Captain Anderson—you asked me—"

"I asked nothing of you, sir. I gave you an order."

"My apology—"

"I did not ask for an apology. We are not on land but at sea. Your apology is a matter of indifference to me—"

"Nevertheless—"

There was, I thought, and indeed was frighted by the thought, a kind of stare in his eyes, a suffusion of blood in all his countenance that made me believe he might well assault me physically. One of his fists was raised and I own that I crouched away a few steps without replying. But then he struck the fist into the other palm.

"Am I to be outfaced again and again on my own deck by every ignorant landsman who cares to walk there? Am I? Tell me, sir!"

"My apology—was intended—"

"I am more concerned with your person, sir, which is more apparent to me than your mind and which has formed the habit of being in the wrong place at the wrong time—repeat your lesson, sir!"

My face felt swollen. It must have been as deeply-suffused as his. I perspired more and more freely. My head still rang. The lieutenants were studiously and carefully examining the horizon. The two seamen at the wheel might have been cast in bronze. I believe I gave a shuddering sob. The words I had learned so recently and easily went clean out of my head. I could see but dimly through my tears. The captain grumbled, perhaps a thought—indeed I hope so—a thought less fiercely.

"Come, sir. Repeat your lesson!"

"A period for recollection. A period—"

"Very well. Come back when you can do it. Do you understand?"

I must have made some reply, for he concluded the interview with his hectoring roar.

"Well, sir—what are you waiting for?"

I did not so much go to my cabin as flee to it. As I approached the second flight of stairs I saw Mr Talbot and the two young gentlemen he had with him—three more witnesses to my humiliation!—hurry out of sight into the lobby. I fell down the stairs, the ladders as I suppose I must call them, hurried into my cabin and flung myself down by my bunk. I was shaking all over, my teeth were chattering. I could hardly breathe. Indeed I believe, nay, I confess that I should have fallen into a fit, a syncope, a seizure or the like—something at all events that would have ended my life, or reason at least, had I not heard young Mr Talbot outside the cabin speak in a firm voice to one of the young gentlemen. He said something like—Come, young midshipman, one *gentleman* does not take pleasure in the persecution of another! At that my tears burst forth freely but with what I may call a healing freedom! God bless Mr Talbot! There is one *true* gentleman in this ship and I pray that before we reach our destination I may call him *Friend* and tell him how much his true consideration has meant to me! Indeed, I now knelt, rather than crouched by my bunk and gave thanks for his consideration and understanding—for his noble charity! I prayed for us both. Only then was I able to sit at this table and consider my situation with something like a rational coolness.

However I turned the thing over and over, I saw one thing clearly enough. As soon as I saw it I came near to falling into a panic all over again. There was—there *is* no doubt—I am the object of a particular animosity on the part of the captain! It was with a thrill of something approaching terror that I re-created in my imagination that moment when he had, as I expressed it, "walked through me". For I saw now that it was not an accident. His arm, when it struck me, moved not after the common manner in walking but continued its swing with an unnatural momentum—augmented immediately after by the blow from his chest that ensured my fall. I knew, or my person knew, by some extraordinary faculty, that Captain Anderson had deliberately struck me down! He is an enemy to religion—it can only be that! Oh what a spotted soul!

My tears had cleansed my mind. They had exhausted but not defeated me. I thought first of my cloth. He had tried to dishonour that; but I told myself, *that* only I could do. Nor could he dishonour me as a common fellow-being since I had committed no fault, no sin but the venial one of omitting to read his Orders! For that, my sickness was more to blame than I! It is true I had been foolish and was perhaps an object of scorn and amusement to the officers and the other gentlemen with the exception of Mr Talbot. But then—and I said this in all humility—so would my Master have been! At that I began to understand that the situation, harsh and unjust as it might seem, was a lesson to me. He puts down the mighty and exalteth the humble and meek. Humble I was of necessity before all the brutal powers which are inherent in absolute command. Meek, therefore, it behoved me to be. My dear sister—

Yet this is strange. Already what I have written would be too painful for your—for her—eyes. It must be amended, altered, softened; and yet—

If not to my sister then to whom? To THEE? Can it be that like THY saints of old (particularly Saint Augustine) I am addressing THEE, OH MOST MERCIFUL SAVIOUR?

I have prayed long. That thought had flung me to my knees—was at once a pain and a consolation to me. Yet I was able to put it away at last as too high for me! To have—oh, indeed, not touched the hem of those garments—but to have glanced for a moment towards THOSE FEET—restored me to a clearer view of myself and of my situation. I sat, then, and reflected.

I concluded at last that it would be proper to do either of two things. Item: never to return to the quarterdeck, but for the remainder of our passage hold myself aloof from it with dignity; the other: to go to the quarterdeck, repeat Captain Anderson's Orders to him and to as many gentlemen as might be present, add some such cool remark as "And now, Captain Anderson, I will trouble you no further," then withdraw, absolutely declining to use that part of the vessel in any circumstances whatever—unless perhaps Captain Anderson himself should condescend (which I did not believe) to offer me an apology. I spent some time emending and refining my farewell speech to him. But at last I was driven to the consideration that he might not afford me the opportunity of uttering it. He is a master of the brutal and quelling rejoinder. Better then to pursue the first course and give him no further cause or opportunity to insult me.

I must own to a great feeling of relief at reaching this decision. With the aid of PROVIDENCE I might contrive to avoid him until the end of our voyage. However, my first duty, as a Christian, was to forgive him, monster as he was. I was able to do this but not without recourse to much prayer and some contemplation of the awful fate that awaited him when he should find himself at last before the THRONE. There, I knew him for my brother, was his keeper, and prayed for us both.

That done, to trifle for a moment with profane literature, like some Robinson Crusoe, I set to and considered what part of the vessel remained to me as my—as I expressed it—my *kingdom*! It comprised my cabin, the corridor or lobby outside it, the passenger saloon, where I might take such sustenance as I was bold enough to in the presence of the other ladies and gentlemen who had been all witnesses of my humiliation. There were too the necessary offices on this side of the vessel and the deck, or *waist* as Phillips calls it, as far as the white line at the main mast which separates us from the common people, be they either seamen or emigrants. That deck was to be for my airing in fine weather. There I might meet the better disposed of the gentlemen—and *ladies* too! There—for I knew he used it—I should further and deepen my friendship with Mr Talbot. Of course, in wet and windy weather I must be content with the lobby and my cabin. I saw that even if I were to be confined to these areas I might still pass the months ahead without too much discomfort and avoid what is most to be feared, a melancholy leading on to madness. All would be well.

This was a decision and a discovery that gave me more earthly pleasure, I believe, than anything I have experienced since parting from those scenes so dear to me. Immediately I went out and paced round my island—my *kingdom!*—in the meantime reflecting on all those who would have welcomed such an expansion of their territory as the attainment of liberty—I mean those who in the course of history have found themselves imprisoned for a just cause. Though I have, so to speak, abdicated from that part of the vessel which ought to be the prerogative of my cloth and consequent station in our society, the waist is in some ways to be preferred to the quarterdeck! Indeed I have seen Mr Talbot not merely walk to the white line, but cross it and go among the common people in a generous and democratic freedom!

Since writing those last words I have furthered my acquaintance with Mr Talbot! It was he of all people who did in fact search me out! He is a true friend to religion! He came to my cabin and begged me in the most friendly and open manner to favour the ship's people in the evening with a short address! I did so in the passenger saloon. I cannot pretend that many of the *gentry*, as I may call them, paid much attention to what they heard and only one of the officers was present. I therefore addressed myself particularly to those hearts I thought readily open to the message I have to give—to a young lady of great piety and beauty and to Mr Talbot himself, whose devotion does credit not only to him in person but through him to his whole order. Would that the gentry and Nobility of England were all imbued with a like spirit!

It must be the influence of Captain Anderson; or perhaps they ignore me from a refinement of manners, a delicacy of feeling—but though I salute our ladies and gentlemen from the waist when I see them up there on the quarter-deck, they seldom acknowledge the salutation! Yet now, truth to tell, and for the past three days there has been nothing to salute—no waist to walk on since it is awash with sea water. I find myself not sick as I was before—I am become a proper sailor! Mr Talbot, however, is sick indeed. I asked Phillips what was the matter and the man replied with an evident sarcasm—*belike it was summat he ate!* I did dare to cross the lobby softly and knock, but there was no reply. Daring still further I lifted the latch and entered. The young man lay asleep, a week's beard on his lips and chin and cheeks—I scarce dare put down here the impression his slumbering countenance made on me—it was the face of ONE who suffered for us all—and as I bent over him in some irresistible compulsion I do not deceive myself but there was the sweet aroma of holiness itself upon his breath! I did not think myself worthy of his lips but pressed my own reverently on the one hand that lay outside the coverlet. Such is the power of goodness that I withdrew as from an altar!

The weather has cleared again. Once more I take my walks in the waist and the ladies and gentlemen theirs on the quarterdeck. Yet I find myself a good sailor and was about in the open before other people!

The air in my cabin is hot and humid. Indeed, we are

approaching the hottest region of the world. Here I sit at my writing-flap in shirt and unmentionables and indite this letter, if letter it be, which is in some sort my only friend. I must confess to a shyness still before the ladies since the captain gave me my great *set-down*. Mr Talbot, I hear, improves and has been visible for some days, but with a diffidence before my cloth and indeed it may be with some desire to spare me embarrassment, he holds aloof.

Since writing that, I have walked again in the waist. It is now a mild and sheltered place. Walking there I have come to the opinion of our brave sailors which landsmen have ever held of them! I have observed these common people closely. These are the good fellows whose duty it is to steer our ship, to haul on the ropes and do strange things with our sails in positions which must surely be perilous, so high they go! Their service is a continual round and necessary, I must suppose, to the progress of the vessel. They are for ever cleaning and scraping and painting. They create marvellous structures from the very substance of rope itself! I had not known what can be done with rope! I had seen here and there on land ingenu-ities of wood-carving in imitation of rope; here I saw rope carved into the imitation of wood! Some of the people do indeed carve in wood or in the shells of coconuts or in bone or perhaps ivory. Some are making the models of ships such as we see displayed in the windows of shops or inns or alehouses near seaports. They seem to be people of infinite ingenuity.

All this I watch with complacency from far off in the shelter of the wooden wall with its stairways that lead up to where the *privileged* passengers live. Up there is silence, or the low murmur of conversation or the harsh sound of a shouted order. But forward, beyond the white line, the people work and sing and keep time to the fiddle when they play—for like children, they play, dancing innocently to the sound of the fiddle. It is as if the childhood of the world were upon them. All this has thrown me into some perplexity. The ship is crowded at the front end. There is a small group of soldiers in uniform, there are a few emigrants, the women seeming common as the men. But when I ignore all but the ship's people, I find *them* objects of astonishment to me. They cannot, for the most part, read or write. They know nothing of what our officers know. But these fine, manly fellows have a complete—what shall I call it? "Civilization" it is not, for they have no city. Society it might be, save that in some ways they are *joined* to the superior officers, and there are classes of men between the one and the other—warrant officers they are called!—and there appear to be grades of authority among the sailors themselves. What are they then, these beings at once so free and so dependent? They are *seamen*, and I begin to understand the word. You may observe them when they are released from duty to stand with arms linked or placed about each other's shoulders. They sleep sometimes on the scrubbed planking of the deck, one it may be, with his head pillowed on another's breast! The innocent pleasures of friendship—in which I, alas, have as *yet* so little experience—the joy of kindly association or even that bond between two persons which, Holy Writ directs us, passes the love of women, must be the cement that holds their company together. It has indeed seemed to me from what I have jestingly represented as "my kingdom" that the life of the front end of the vessel is sometimes to be preferred to the vicious system of control which obtains *aft of the mizzen* or even *aft of the main*! (The precision of these two phrases I owe to my servant Phillips.) Alas that my calling and the degree in society consequent on it should set me so firmly where I no longer desire to be!

We have had a spell of bad weather—not very bad, but sufficient to keep most of our ladies in their cabins. Mr Talbot keeps his. My servant assures me that the young man is not seasick, yet I have heard strange sounds emanating from behind his locked door. I had the temerity to offer my services and was both disconcerted and concerned to wring from the poor young gentleman the admission that he was wrestling with his soul in prayer! Far, far be it from me to blame him—no, no, I would not do so! But the sounds were those of *enthusiasm*! I much fear that the young man for all his rank has fallen victim to one of the extremer systems against which our Church has set her face! I must and will help him! But that can only be when he is himself again and moves among us with his customed ease. These attacks of a too passionate devotion are to be feared more than the fevers to which the inhabitants of these climes are subject. He is a layman; and it shall be my pleasant duty to bring him back to that decent moderation in religion which is, if I may coin a phrase, the genius of the Church of England!

He has reappeared; and avoids me, perhaps in an embarrassment at having been detected at his too protracted devotions; I will let him be for the moment and pray for him while we move day by day, I hope, towards a mutual understanding. I saluted him from far off this morning as he walked on the quarterdeck but he affected to take no notice. Noble young man! He who has been so ready to help others will not deign, on his own behalf, to ask for help!

This morning in the waist I have been spectator once again of that ceremony which moves me with a mixture of grief and admiration. A barrel is set on the deck. The seamen stand in line and each is given successively a mug of liquid from the barrel which he drains off after exclaiming, "The King! GOD bless him!" I would His

Majesty could have seen it. I know of course that the liquid is the devil's brew and I do not swerve one jot or tittle from my previous opinion that strong drink should be prohibited from use by the lower orders. For sure, ale is enough and too much—but let them have it!

Yes here, *here* on the bounding main, under the hot sun and with a whole company of bronzed young fellows bared to the waist—their hands and feet hard with honest and dangerous toil—their stern yet open faces weathered by the storms of every ocean, their luxuriant curls fluttering from their foreheads in the breeze—*here*, if there was no overthrowing of my opinion, there was at least a modification and mitigation of it. Watching one young fellow in particular, a narrow-waisted, slim-hipped yet broad-shouldered *Child of Neptune*, I felt that some of what was malignant in the potion was cancelled by where and who was concerned with it. For it was as if these beings, these young men, or some of them at least and one of them in particular, were of the giant breed. I called to mind the legend of Talos, the man of bronze whose artificial frame was filled with liquid fire. It seemed to me that such an evidently fiery liquid as the one (it is *rum*) which a mistaken benevolence and paternalism provides for the sea-service was the proper *ichor* (this was the blood of the Grecian Gods, supposedly) for beings of such semi-divinity, of such truly heroic proportions! Here and there among them the marks of the discipline were evident and they bore these parallel scars with indifference and even pride! Some, I verily believe, saw them as marks of distinction! Some, and that not a few, bore on their frames the scars of unquestioned honour—scars of the cutlass, pistol, grape or splinter. None were maimed; or if they were, it was in such a minor degree, a finger, eye or ear perhaps, that the blemish hung on them like a medal. There was one whom I called in my mind my own particular hero! He had nought but four or five white scratches on the left side of his open and amiable countenance as if like Hercules he had struggled with a wild beast! (Hercules, you know, was fabled to have wrestled with the Nemaean Lion.) His feet were bare and his nether limbs—*my* young hero I refer to, rather than the legendary one! His nether garments clung to his lower limbs as if moulded there. I was much taken with the manly grace with which he tossed off his mug of liquor and returned the empty vessel to the top of the barrel. I had an odd fancy. I remembered to have read somewhere in the history of the union that when Mary, Queen of Scots, first came into her kingdom she was entertained at a feast. It was recorded that her throat was so slender and her skin so white that as she swallowed wine the ruby richness of the liquid was visible through it to the onlookers! This scene had always exercised a powerful influence over my infant spirits! It was only now that I remembered with what childish pleasure I had supposed my future spouse would exhibit some such particular comeliness of person—in addition of course to the more necessary beauties of mind and spirit. But now, with Mr Talbot shy of me, I found myself, in my *kingdom* of lobby, cabin and waist, unexpectedly dethroned and a new monarch elevated there! For this young man of bronze with his flaming ichor—and as he drank the liquor down it seemed to me that I heard a furnace roar and with my inward eye saw the fire burst forth—it seemed to me with my *outer* eye that he could be no other than the king! I abdicated freely and yearned to kneel before him. My whole heart went out in a passionate longing to bring this young man to OUR SAVIOUR, first and surely richest fruit of the harvest I am sent forth to garner! After he retired from the barrel, my eye followed him without my volition. But he went where I, alas, could not go. He ran out along that fourth mast laid more nearly horizontal, the bowsprit I mean, with its complication of ropes and tackles and chains and booms and sails. I was reminded of the old oak in which you and I were wont to climb. But he (the king) ran out there or up there and stood at the tip of the very thinnest spar and looked down into the sea. His whole body moved easily to counter our slight motion. Only his shoulder leaned against a rope, so that he lounged as he might against a tree! Then he turned, ran back a few paces and *lay down* on the surface of the thicker part of the bowsprit as securely as I might in my bed! Surely there is nothing so splendidly free as a young fellow in the branches of one of His Majesty's *travelling trees*, as I may call them! Or forests, even! There lay the king, then, crowned with curls—but I grow fanciful.

We are in the doldrums. Mr Talbot still avoids me. He has been wandering round the ship and descending into her very bowels as if searching for some private place where, perhaps, he may continue his devotions without hindrance. I fear sadly that my approach was untimely and did more damage than good. I pray for him. What can I do more?

We are motionless. The sea is polished. There is no sky but only a hot whiteness that descends like a curtain on every side, dropping, as it were, even below the horizon and so diminishing the circle of the ocean that is visible to us. The circle itself is of a light and luminescent blue. Now and then some sea creature will shatter the surface and the silence by leaping through it. Yet even when nothing leaps there is a constant shuddering, random twitches and vibrations of the surface, as if the water were not only the home and haunt of all sea creatures but the skin of a living thing, a creature vaster than Leviathan. The heat and dampness combined would be quite inconceivable to one who had never left that pleasant valley which was our home. Our own motionlessness—and this I believe you will not find mentioned in the accounts of sea voyages—has increased the effluvias that rise from the waters immediately round us. Yesterday morning there was a slight breeze but we were soon still again. All our people are silent, so that the striking of the ship's bell is a loud and startling sound. Today the effluvias became intolerable from the necessary soiling of the water round us. The boats were hoisted out from the *boom* and the ship towed a little way from the odious place; but now if we do not get any wind it will all be to do again. In my cabin I sit or lie in shirt and breeches and even so find the air hardly to be borne. Our ladies and gentlemen keep their cabin in a like case, lying abed I think, in hope that the weather and the place may pass. Only Mr Talbot roams as if he can find no peace—poor young man! May GOD be with him and keep him! I have approached him once but he bowed slightly and distantly. The time is not yet.

How next to impossible is the exercise of virtue! It requires a constant watchfulness, constant guard—oh my dear sister, how much must you and I and every Christian soul rely at every moment on the operation of Grace! There has been an altercation! It was not, as you might expect, among the poor people in the front of the ship but here among the gentlemen, nay, among the very officers themselves!

It was thus. I was sitting at my writing-flap and recutting a quill when I heard a scuffle outside in the lobby, then voices, soft at first but raised later.

"You dog, Deverel! I saw you come from the cabin!"

"What are you about then, Cumbershum, for your part, you rogue!"

"Give it to me, sir! By G—I will have it!"

"And unopened at either end—You sly dog, Cumbershum, I'll read it, I swear I will!"

The scuffle became noisy. I was in shirt and breeches, my shoes under the bunk, my stockings hung over it, my wig on a convenient nail. The language became so much more blasphemous and filthy that I could not let the occasion pass. Not thinking of my appearance I got up quickly and rushed out of the cabin, to find the two officers struggling violently for possession of a missive. I cried out.

"Gentlemen! Gentlemen!"

I seized the nearest to me by the shoulder. They stopped the fight and turned to me.

"Who the devil is this, Cumbershum?"

"It's the parson, I think. Be off, sir, about your own business!"

"I am about my business, my friends, and exhort you in a spirit of Christian Charity to cease this unseemly behaviour, this unseemly language, and make up your quarrel!"

Lieutenant Deverel stood looking down at me with his mouth open.

"Well by thunder!"

The gentleman addressed as Cumbershum—another lieutenant—stuck his forefinger so violently towards my face that had I not recoiled, it would have entered my eye.

"Who in the name of all that's wonderful gave you permission to preach in this ship?"

"Yes, Cumbershum, you have a point."

"Leave this to me, Deverel. Now, parson, if that's what you are, show us your authority."

"Authority?"

"D—n it man, I mean your commission!"

"Commission!"

"Licence they call it, Cumbershum, old fellow, licence to preach. Right parson—show us your licence!"

I was taken aback, nay, confounded. The truth is, and I record it here for you to pass to any young clergyman about to embark on such a voyage, I had deposited the licence from my Lord Bishop with other private papers—not, as I supposed, needed on the voyage—in my trunk, which had been lowered somewhere into the bowels of the vessel. I attempted to explain this briefly to the officers but Mr Deverel interrupted me.

"Be off with you, sir, or I shall take you before the captain!"

I must confess that this threat sent me hurrying back into my cabin with some considerable trepidation. For a moment or two I wondered whether I had not after all succeeded in abating their mutual wrath, for I heard them both laughing loudly as they walked away. But I concluded that such heedless—I will not call them more—such heedless spirits were far more likely to be laughing at the *sartorial* mistake I had made and the result of the interview with which they had threatened me. It was clear that I had been at fault in allowing myself a public appearance less *explicit* than that sanctioned by custom and required by decorum. I began hurriedly to dress, not forgetting my bands, though my throat in the heat felt them as an unfortunate constriction. I regretted that my gown and hood were packed or, should I say, *stowed* away with my other impedimenta. At length, then, clothed in at least some of the visible marks of the dignity and authority of my calling, I issued forth from my cabin. But of course the two lieutenants were nowhere to be seen.

But already, in this equatorial part of the globe, after being fully dressed for no more than a moment or two I was bathed in perspiration. I walked out into the waist but felt no relief from the heat. I returned to the lobby and my cabin determined to be more comfortable yet not knowing what to do. I could be, without the sartorial adornment of my calling, mistaken for an emigrant! I was debarred from intercourse with the ladies and gentlemen and had been given no opportunity other than that first one of addressing the common people. Yet to endure the heat and moisture in a garb appropriate to the English countryside seemed impossible. On an impulse derived, I fear, less from Christian practice than from my reading of the classical authors, I opened the Sacred Book and before I was well aware of what I was doing I had employed the moment in a kind of *Sortes Virgilianae*, or consultation of the oracle, a process I had always thought to be questionable even when employed by the holiest servants of the Lord. The words my eyes fell on were II Chronicles viii. 7–8. "The Hittites, and the Amorites, and the Perizzites, and the Hivites, and the Jebusites which were not of Israel"—words which in the next moment I had applied to Captain Anderson and Lieutenants Deverel and Cumbershum, then flung myself on my knees and implored forgiveness!

I record this trivial offence merely to show the oddities of behaviour, the perplexities of the understanding, in a word, the *strangeness* of this life in this strange part of the world among strange people and in this strange construction of English oak which both transports and imprisons me! (I am aware, of course, of the amusing "paranomasia" in the word "transport" and hope the perusal of it will afford you some entertainment!)

To resume. After a period at my devotions I considered what I had better do in order to avoid any future mistake as to my *sanctified* identity. I divested myself once more of all but shirt and breeches, and thus divested, I employed the small mirror which I have for use when shaving to

examine my appearance. This was a process of some difficulty. Do you remember the knothole in the barn through
which in our childish way we were wont to keep watch for
Jonathan or our poor, sainted mother, or his lordship's
bailiff, Mr Jolly? Do you remember, moreover, how,
when we were tired of waiting, we would see by moving
our heads how much of the exterior world we could spy
through the knot? Then we would pretend to be seized of
all we saw, from Seven Acre right up to the top of the hill?
In such a manner did I contort myself before the mirror
and the mirror before me! But here I am—if indeed this
letter should ever be sent—instructing a member of the
Fair Sex in the employment of a mirror and the art of,
dare I call it, "Self-admiration"? In my own case, of
course, I use the word in its original sense of surprise and
wonder rather than self-satisfaction! There was much to
wonder at in what I saw but little to approve. I had not
fully understood before how harshly the sun can deal with
the male countenance that is exposed to its more nearly
vertical rays.

My hair, as you know, is of a light but indeterminate
hue. I now saw that your cropping of it on the day before
our parting—due surely to our mutual distress—had been
sadly uneven. This unevenness seems to have been accen-
tuated rather than diminished by the passage of time so
that my head presented an appearance not unlike a patch
of ill-reaped stubble. Since I had not been able to shave
during my first *nausea* (the word indeed derives from the
Greek word for a ship!) and had feared to do so in the later
period when the ship was in violent motion—and at last
have been dilatory, fearing the pain I should inflict on my
sunscorched skin, the lower part of my face was covered
with bristles. They were not long, since my beard is of
slow growth—but of varying hue. Between these two
cropyielding areas, as I may call them, of scalp and beard,

king Sol had exerted his full sway. What is sometimes called a widow's peak of rosy skin delineated the exact extent to which my wig had covered my forehead. Below that line the forehead was plum-coloured and in one place burst with the heat. Below that again, my nose and cheeks appeared red as on fire! I saw at once that I had deceived myself entirely if I supposed that appearing in shirt and breeches and in this *guise* I should exert the authority inhering in my profession. Nay—are these not of all people those who judge a man by his uniform? My "uniform", as I must in all humility call it, must be sober black with the pure whiteness of bleached linen and bleached hair, the adornments of the Spiritual Man. To the officers and people of this ship, a clergyman without his bands and wig would be of no more account than a beggar.

True, it was the sudden sound of an altercation and the desire to do good that had drawn me forth from my seclusion, but I was to blame. I drew in my breath with something like fear as I envisaged the appearance I must have presented to them—with a bare head, unshaven, sun-blotched, unclothed! It was with confusion and shame that I remembered the words addressed to me individually at my ordination—words I must ever hold sacred because of the occasion and the saintly divine who spake them—"Avoid scrupulosity, Colley, and always present a decent appearance." Was *this* that I now saw in the mirror of my imagination the figure of a labourer in that country where "the fields are white to harvest"? Among those with whom I now dwell, a respectable appearance is not merely a *desideratum* but a *sine qua non*. (I mean, my dear, not merely desirable but necessary.) I determined at once to take more care. When I walked in what I had thought of as my kingdom, I would not only be a man of GOD—I would be *seen* to be a man of GOD!

Things are a little better. Lieutenant Summers came

and begged the favour of a word with me. I answered him
through the door, begging him not to enter as I was not
yet prepared in clothes or visage for an interview. He
assented, but in a low voice as if afraid that others would
hear. He asked my pardon for the fact that there had been
no more services in the passenger saloon. He had repeatedly *sounded* the passengers and had met with indifference. I asked him if he had asked Mr Talbot and he
replied after a pause that Mr Talbot had been much occupied with his own affairs. But he, Mr Summers, thought
that there might be a chance of what he called a *small
gathering* on the next Sabbath. I found myself declaring
through the door with a passion quite unlike my usual
even temper—

"This is a Godless vessel!"

Mr Summers made no reply so I made a further
remark.

"It is the influence of a certain person!"

At this I heard Mr Summers change his position outside the door as if he had suddenly looked round him.
Then he whispered to me.

"Do not, I beg you, Mr Colley, entertain such
thoughts! A small gathering, sir—a hymn or two, a reading and a benediction—"

I took the opportunity to point out that a morning
service in the waist would be far more appropriate; but
Lieutenant Summers replied with what I believe to be a
degree of embarrassment that *it could not be*. He then
withdrew. However, it is a small victory for religion.
Nay—who knows when that heart of awful flint may be
brought to yield as yield at last it must?

I have discovered the name of my Young Hero. He is
one Billy Rogers, a sad scamp, I fear, whose boyish heart
has not yet been touched with Grace. I shall try to make
an opportunity of speaking with him.

I have passed the last hour in *shaving*! It was indeed painful and I cannot say that the result justifies the labour. However, it is done.

I heard an unwonted noise and went into the lobby. As I did so, I felt the deck tilt under me—though very slightly—but alas! The few days of almost total calm have unfitted me for the motion and I have lost the "sea legs" I thought I had acquired! I was forced to retire precipitately to my cabin and bunk. There I was better placed and could feel that we have some wind, favourable, light and easy. We are moving on our way again; and though I did not at once care to trust to my legs I felt that elevation of the spirits which must come to any traveller when after some let or hindrance he discovers himself to be on the move towards his destination.

A day's rest lies in that line I have drawn above these words! I have been out and about, though keeping as much as possible away from the passengers and the people. I must reintroduce myself to them, as it were, by degrees until they see not a bare-headed clown but a man of God. The people work about the ship, some hauling on this rope, others *casting off* or slackening that one with a more cheerful readiness than is their wont. The sound of our progress through the water is much more clearly audible! Even I, landsman that I am and must remain, am sensible of a kind of lightness in the vessel as if she too were not inanimate but a partaker in the general gaiety! The people earlier were everywhere to be seen climbing among her limbs and branches. I mean, of course, that vast paraphernalia which allows all the winds of heaven to advance us towards the desired haven. We steer south, ever south, with the continent of Africa on our left hand but hugely distant. Our people have added even more area to the sails by attaching small *yards* (poles, you would call them) from which is suspended lighter material beyond the outer edge of our usual *suit*! (You will detect the degree to which by a careful attention to the conversations going on round me I have become imbued with the language of navigation!) This new area of sail increases our speed, and, indeed, I have just heard one young gentleman cry to another—I omit an unfortunate expletive—"How the old lady lifts up her p-tt-c-ts and makes a run for it!" Perhaps these additional areas are to be called "p-tt-c-ts" in nautical parlance; for you cannot imagine with what impropriety the people and even the officers name the various pieces of equipment about the vessel! This continues even in the presence of a clergyman and the ladies, as if the seamen concerned were wholly unconscious of what they have said.

Once again a day has passed between two paragraphs! The wind has dropped and my trifling indisposition with it. I have dressed, nay, even shaved once more and moved for a while into the waist. I should endeavour, I think, to define for you the position in which I find myself vis-à-vis the other gentlemen, not to say ladies. Since the captain inflicted a public humiliation on me I have been only too aware that of all the passengers I am in the most peculiar position. I do not know how to describe it, for my opinion of how I am regarded alters from day to day and from hour to hour! Were it not for my servant Phillips and the first lieutenant Mr Summers, I believe I should speak to no one; for poor Mr Talbot has been either indisposed or restlessly moving towards what I can only suppose to be a crisis of faith, in which it would be my duty and profound pleasure to help him, but he avoids me. He will not inflict his troubles on any one! Now as for the rest of the passengers and officers, I do sometimes suspect that, influenced by the attitude of Captain Anderson, they disregard me and my sacred office with a frivolous indifference. Then in the next moment I suppose it to be a kind of delicacy of feeling not always to be found among our countrymen that prevents them forcing any attention on me. Perhaps—and I only say perhaps—there is an inclination among them to let me be and make belief that no one has noticed anything! The ladies, of course, I cannot expect to approach me and I should think the less of any one who did so. But this (since I have still limited my movements to the area that I called, jestingly, my *kingdom*) has by now resulted in a degree of isolation which I have suffered in more than I should have supposed. Yet all this must change! I am determined! If either indifference or delicacy prevents them from addressing me, then I must be bold and address *them*!

I have been again into the waist. The ladies and gentlemen, or those who were not in their cabins, were parading on the quarterdeck where I must not go. I did bow to them from far off to show how much I desire some familiar intercourse but the distance was too great and they did not notice me. It must have been the poor light and the distance. It could have been nothing else. The ship is motionless, her sails hanging vertically down and creased like aged cheeks. As I turned from surveying the strange parade on the quarterdeck—for here, in this field of water everything is strange—and faced the forward part of the ship I saw something strange and new. The people are fastening what I at first took to be an awning before the fo'castle—*before*, I mean, from where I stood below the stairs leading up to the quarterdeck—and at first I thought this must be a shelter to keep off the sun. But the sun is dropping low and, as we have eaten our animals, the pens had been broken up, so the shelter would protect nothing. Then again, the material of which the "awning" is composed seems unnecessarily heavy for such a purpose. It is stretched across the deck at the height of the bulwarks from which it is suspended, or stretched, rather, by ropes. The seamen call the material "tarpaulin" if I am not mistaken; so the phrase "Honest Tar" here finds its original.

After I had written those words I resumed my wig and coat (they shall never see me other than properly dressed again) and went back to the waist. Of all the strangeness of this place at the world's end surely the change in our ship at this moment is the strangest! There is silence, broken only by bursts of laughter. The people, with every indication of enjoyment, are lowering buckets over the side on ropes that run through pulleys or *blocks*, as we call them here. They heave up sea water—which must, I fear, be most impure since we have been stationary for some hours—and spill it into the tarpaulin, which is now bellied down by the weight. There seems no way in which this can help our progress; the more so as certain of the people (my Young Hero among them, I am afraid) have, so to say, relieved nature into what is none other than a container rather than awning. This, in a ship, where by the propinquity of the ocean, such arrangements are made as might well be thought preferable to those our fallen state makes necessary on land! I was disgusted by the sight and was returning to my cabin when I was involved in a strange occurrence! Phillips came towards me hastily and was about to speak when a voice spoke or rather shouted at him from a dim part of the lobby.

"Silence, Phillips, you dog!"

The man looked from me into the shadows from which none other than Mr Cumbershum emerged and stared him down. Phillips retired and Cumbershum stood looking at me. I did not and do not like the man. He is another Anderson I think, or will be should he ever attain to captaincy! I went hastily into my cabin. I took off my coat,

wig and bands and composed myself to prayer. Hardly
had I begun when there came a timid knocking at the
door. I opened it to find Phillips there again. He began to
whisper.

"Mr Colley, sir, I beg you—"

"Phillips, you dog! Get below or I'll have you at the
grating!"

I stared round in astonishment. It was Cumbershum
again and Deverel with him. Yet at first I only recognized
them by Cumbershum's voice and Deverel's air of
unquestioned elegance, for they too were without hat or
coat. They saw me, who had promised myself never to be
seen so, and they burst out laughing. Indeed, their laughter had something maniacal about it. I saw they were both
to some degree in drink. They concealed from me objects
which they held in their hands and they bowed to me as I
entered my cabin with a ceremony I could not think sincere. Deverel is a gentleman! He cannot, sure, intend to
harm me!

The ship is extraordinarily quiet. A few minutes ago I
heard the rustling steps of the remainder of our passengers go through the lobby, mount the stairs and pass over
my head. There is no doubt about it. The people at this
end of the ship are gathered on the quarterdeck. Only *I*
am excluded from them!

I have been out again, stole out into the strange light
for all my resolutions about dress. The lobby was silent.
Only a confused murmur came from Mr Talbot's cabin. I
had a great mind to go to him and beg his protection; but
knew that he was at private prayer. I stole out of the lobby
into the waist. What I saw as I stood, petrified as it were,
will be stamped on my mind till my dying day. *Our* end of
the ship—the two raised portions at the back—was
crowded with passengers and officers, all silent and all
staring forward over my head. Well might they stare!

There never was such a sight. No pen, no pencil, not that of the greatest artist in history could give any idea of it. Our huge ship was motionless and her sails still hung down. On her right hand the red sun was setting and on her left the full moon was rising, the one directly across from the other. The two vast luminaries seemed to stare at each other and each to modify the other's light. On land this spectacle could never be so evident because of the interposition of hills or trees or houses, but here we see down from our motionless vessel on all sides to the very edge of the world. Here plainly to be seen were the very scales of GOD.

The scales tilted, the double light faded and we were wrought of ivory and ebony by the moon. The people moved about forward and hung lanterns by the dozen from the rigging, so that I saw now that they had erected something like a bishop's *cathedra* beyond the ungainly paunch of tarpaulin. I began to understand. I began to tremble. I was alone! Yes, in that vast ship with her numberless souls I was alone in a place where on a sudden I feared the Justice of GOD unmitigated by HIS Mercy! On a sudden I dreaded both GOD and man! I stumbled back to my cabin and have endeavoured to pray.

NEXT DAY

I can scarcely hold this pen. I *must* and *will* recover my composure. What a man does defiles him, not what is done by others—My shame, though it burn, has been inflicted on me.

I had completed my devotions, but sadly out of a state of recollection. I had divested myself of my garments, all except my shirt, when there came a thunderous knocking at the cabin door. I was already, not to refine upon it, fearful. The thunderous blows on the door completed my confusion. Though I had speculated on the horrid ceremonies of which I might be the victim, I thought then of shipwreck, fire, collision or the violence of the enemy. I cried out, I believe.

"What is it? What is it?"

To this a voice answered, loud as the knocking.

"Open this door!"

I answered in great haste, nay, panic.

"No, no, I am unclothed—but what is it?"

There was a very brief pause, then the voice answered me dreadfully.

"Robert James Colley, you are come into judgement!"

These words, so unexpected and terrible, threw me into utter confusion. Even though I knew that the voice was a human voice I felt a positive contraction of the heart and know how violently I must have clutched my hands together in that region, for there is a contusion over my ribs and I have bled. I cried out in answer to the awful summons.

"No, no, I am not in any way ready, I mean I am unclothed—"

To this the same unearthly voice and in even more terrible accents uttered the following reply.

"Robert James Colley, you are called to appear before the throne."

These words—and yet *part* of my mind knew them for the foolery they were—nevertheless completely inhibited my breathing. I made for the door to shoot the bolt but as I did so the door burst open. Two huge figures with heads of nightmare, great eyes and mouths, black mouths full of a mess of fangs drove down at me. A cloth was thrust over my head. I was seized and hurried away by irresistible force, my feet not able to find the deck except every now and then. I am, I know, not a man of quick thought or instant apprehension. For a few moments I believe I was rendered totally insensible, only to be brought to myself again by the sound of yelling and jeering and positively demonic laughter. *Some* touch of presence of mind, however, as I was borne along all too securely muffled, made me cry out "Help! Help!" and briefly supplicate MY SAVIOUR.

The cloth was wrenched off and I could see clearly—all too clearly—in the light of the lanterns. The foredeck was full of the people and the edge of it lined with figures of nightmare akin to those who had hurried me away. He who sat on the throne was bearded and crowned with flame and bore a huge fork with three prongs in his right hand. Twisting my neck as the cloth came off I could see the after end of the ship, *my rightful place*, was thronged with *spectators!* But there were too few lanterns about the quarterdeck for me to see clearly, nor had I more than a moment to look for a friend, for I was absolutely at the disposal of my captors. Now I had more time to understand my situation and the cruelty of the "jest", some of my fear was swallowed up in shame at appearing before the ladies and gentlemen, not to refine upon it, half-naked. I, who had thought never to appear but in the ornaments of the Spiritual Man! I attempted to make a smiling appeal for some covering as if I consented to and took part in the jest but all went too fast. I was made to kneel before the "throne" with much wrenching and buffeting, which took away any breath I had contrived to retain. Before I could make myself heard, a question was put to me of such grossness that I will not remember it, much less write it down. Yet as I opened my mouth to protest, it was at once filled with such nauseous stuff I gag and am like to vomit remembering it. For some time, I cannot tell how long, this operation was repeated; and when I would not open my mouth the stuff was smeared over my face. The questions, one after another, were of such a nature that I cannot write any of them down. Nor could they have been contrived by any but the most depraved of souls. Yet each was greeted with a storm of cheering and that terrible British sound which has ever daunted the foe; and then it came to me, was forced in upon my soul the awful truth—*I was the foe!*

It could not be so, of course. They were, it may be, hot with the devil's brew—they were led astray—it could not be so! But in the confusion and—to me—horror of the situation the thought that froze the very blood in my veins was only this—*I was the foe!*

To such an excess may the common people be led by the example of those who should guide them to better things! At last the leader of their revels deigned to address me.

"You are a low, filthy fellow and must be shampoo'd."

Here was more pain and nausea and hindrance to my breathing, so that I was in desperate fear all the time that I should die there and then, victim of their cruel sport. Just when I thought my end was come I was projected backwards with extreme violence into the paunch of filthy

water. Now here was more of what was strange and terrible to me. I had not harmed them. They had had their
sport, their will with me. Yet now as I struggled each time
to get out of the wallowing, slippery paunch, I heard what
the poor victims of the French Terror must have heard in
their last moments and oh!—it is crueller than death, it
must be—it must be so, nothing, *nothing* that men can do
to each other can be compared with that snarling, lustful,
storming appetite—

By now I had abandoned hope of life and was endeavouring blindly to fit myself for my end—as it were *betwixt
the saddle and the ground*—when I was aware of repeated
shouts from the quarterdeck and then the sound of a
tremendous explosion. There was comparative silence
in which a voice shouted a command. The hands that
had been thrusting me down and in now lifted me up and
out. I fell upon the deck and lay there. There was a pause
in which I began to crawl away in a trail of filth. But
there came another shouted order. Hands lifted me up
and bore me to my cabin. Someone shut the door.
Later—I do not know how much later—the door opened
again and some Christian soul placed a bucket of hot
water by me. It may have been Phillips but I do not know.
I will not describe the contrivances by which I succeeded
in getting myself comparatively clean. Far off I could
hear that the devils—no, no, I will not call them that—the
people of the forward part of the ship had resumed their
sport with other victims. But the sounds of merriment
were jovial rather than bestial. It was a bitter draught to
swallow! I do not suppose that in any other ship they have
ever had a "parson" to play with. No, no, I will *not* be bitter, I will forgive. They are my brothers even if they feel
not so—even if *I* feel not so! As for the gentlemen—no, I
will not be bitter; and it is true that one among them, Mr
Summers perhaps, or Mr Talbot it may be, did intervene

and effect an interruption to their brutal sport even if late in it!

I fell into an exhausted sleep, only to experience most fearful nightmares of judgement and hell. They waked me, praise be to GOD! For had they continued, my reason would have been overthrown.

I have prayed since then and prayed long. After prayer and in a state of proper recollection I have thought.

I believe I have come some way to being myself again. I see without any disguise *what happened*. There is much health in that phrase *what happened*. To clear away the, as it were, undergrowth of my own feelings, my terror, my disgust, my indignation, clears a path by which I have come to exercise a proper judgement. I am a victim at several removes of the displeasure that Captain Anderson has evinced towards me since our first meeting. Such a *farce* as was enacted yesterday could not take place without his approval or at least his tacit consent. Deverel and Cumbershum were his agents. I see that my shame— except in the article of outraged modesty—is quite unreal and does my understanding little credit. Whatever I had *said*—and I have begged my SAVIOUR's forgiveness for it—what I *felt* more nearly was the opinion of the ladies and gentlemen in regard to me. I was indeed more sinned against than sinning but must put my own house in order, and learn all over again—but there is no end to that lesson!—to forgive! What, I remind myself, have the servants of the LORD been promised in this world? If it must be so, let persecution be my lot henceforward. I am not alone.

I have prayed again and with much fervour and risen from my knees at last, I am persuaded, a humbler and a better man. I have been brought to see that the insult to *me* was as nothing and no more than an invitation to turn the other cheek!

Yet there remains the insult offered not to me, but through me to ONE whose NAME is often in their mouths though seldom, I fear, in their thoughts! The true insult is to my cloth and through it to the Great Army of which I am the last and littlest soldier. MY MASTER HIMSELF has been insulted and though HE may—as I am persuaded HE will—forgive it, I have a duty to deliver a rebuke rather than suffer *that* in silence!

Not for ourselves, O LORD, but for THEE!

I slept again more peacefully after writing those words and woke to find the ship running easily before a moderate wind. The air, I thought, was a little cooler. With a start of fear which I had some difficulty in controlling I remembered the events of the previous evening. But then the *interior* events of my fervent prayer returned to me with great force and I got down from my bunk or I may say, leapt down from it, with joy as I felt my own renewed certainties of the Great Truths of the Christian Religion! My devotions were, you must believe, far, far more prolonged than usual!

After I rose from my knees I took my morning draught, then set myself once more to shave carefully. My hair would have benefited from your ministrations! (But you shall never read this! The situation becomes increasingly paradoxical—I may at some time *censor* what I have written!) I dressed with equal care, bands, wig, hat. I directed the servant to show me where my trunk was *stowed* and after some argument was able to descend to it in the gloomy interior parts of the ship. I took out my Hood and Square and extracted his lordship's licence which I put in the tail-pocket of my coat. Now I had—not *my* but MY MASTER's quarrel just, I was able to view a meeting with anyone in the ship as an encounter no more to be feared than—well, as you know, I once spoke with a highwayman! I climbed, therefore, to the upper portion of the quarterdeck with a firm step and beyond it to the raised platform at its back or after end, where Captain Anderson was commonly to be seen. I stood and looked about me. The wind was on the starboard quarter and brisk. Captain Anderson walked up and down. Mr Talbot with one or two other gentlemen stood by the rail and he touched the brim of his beaver and moved forward. I was gratified at this evidence of his wish to befriend me, but for the moment I merely bowed and passed on. I went across the deck and stood directly in Captain Anderson's path, taking off my hat as I did so. He did not *walk through me*, as I expressed it, on this occasion. He stopped and stared, opened his mouth, then shut it again.

The following exchange then took place.

"Captain Anderson, I desire to speak with you."

He paused for a moment or two. Then—

"Well, sir. You may do so."

I proceeded in calm and measured accents.

"Captain Anderson. Your people have done my office wrong. You yourself have done it wrong."

The hectic appeared in his cheek and passed away. He lifted his chin at me, then sank it again. He spoke, or rather muttered, in reply.

"I know it, Mr Colley."

"You confess as much, sir?"

He muttered again.

"It was never meant—the affair got out of hand. You have been ill-used, sir."

I answered him serenely.

"Captain Anderson, after this confession of your fault I forgive you freely. But there were, I believe, and I am content to suppose they were acting not so much under your orders as by force of your example, there were other officers involved and not merely the commoner sort of people. *Theirs* was perhaps the most outrageous insult to

my cloth! I believe I know them, sir, disguised as they
were. Not for my sake, but for their own, they must admit
the fault."

Captain Anderson took a rapid turn up and down the
deck. He came back and stood with his hands clasped
behind him. He stared down at me, I was astonished to
see, not merely with the highest colouring but with rage!
Is it not strange? He had confessed his fault yet mention
of his officers threw him back into a state which is, I fear,
only too customary with him. He spoke angrily.

"You will have it all, then."

"I defend MY MASTER's Honour as you would defend
the King's."

For a while neither of us said anything. The bell was
struck and the members of one watch changed places with
another. Mr Summers, together with Mr Willis, took
over from Mr Smiles and young Mr Taylor. The change
was, as usual, ceremonious. Then Captain Anderson
looked back at me.

"I will speak to the officers concerned. Are you now
satisfied?"

"Let them come to me, sir, and they shall receive my
forgiveness as freely as I have given it to you. But there is
another thing—"

Here I must tell you that the captain uttered an imprecation of a positively blasphemous nature. However, I
employed the wisdom of the serpent as well as the meek-
ness of the dove and affected at *this* time to take no notice!
It was not the moment to rebuke a naval officer for the use
of an imprecation. That, I already told myself, should
come later!

I proceeded.

"There are also the poor, ignorant people in the front
end of the ship. I must visit them and bring them to
repentance."

213

"Are you mad?"

"Indeed no, sir."

"Have you no care for what further mockery may be inflicted on you?"

"You have your uniform, Captain Anderson, and I have mine. I shall approach them in that garb, those *ornaments* of the Spiritual Man!"

"Uniform!"

"You do not understand, sir? I shall go to them in those garments which my long studies and ordination enjoin on me. I do not wear them here, sir. You know me for what I am."

"I do indeed, sir."

"I thank you, sir. Have I your permission then, to go forward and address them?"

Captain Anderson walked across the planking and expectorated into the sea. He answered me without turning.

"Do as you please."

I bowed to his back, then turned away myself. As I came to the first stair Lieutenant Summers laid a hand on my sleeve.

"Mr Colley!"

"Well, my friend?"

"Mr Colley, I beg you to consider what you are about!" Here his voice sank to a whisper. "Had I not discharged Mr Prettiman's weapon over the side and so startled them all, there is no knowing how far the affair might have gone. I beg you, sir—let me assemble them under the eyes of their officers! Some of them are violent men—one of the emigrants—"

"Come, Mr Summers. I shall appear to them in the raiment in which I might conduct a service. They will recognize that raiment, sir, and respect it."

"At least wait until after they have been given their

rum. Believe me, sir, I know whereof I speak! It will render them more amiable, calmer—more receptive, sir, to what you have to say to them—I beg you, sir! Otherwise, contempt, indifference—and who knows what else—?"

"And the lesson would go unheeded, you think, the opportunity lost?"

"Indeed, sir!"

I considered for a moment.

"Very well, Mr Summers. I will wait until later in the morning. I have some writing in the meantime which I wish to do."

I bowed to him and went on. Now Mr Talbot stepped forward again. He asked in the most agreeable manner to be admitted to a familiar degree of friendship with me. He is indeed a young man who does credit to his station! If privilege were always in the hands of such as he—indeed, it is not out of the question that at some future date—but I run on!

I had scarcely settled myself to this writing in my cabin when there came a knock at the door. It was the lieutenants, Mr Deverel and Mr Cumbershum, my two *devils* of the previous night! I looked my severest on them, for indeed they deserved a little chastisement before getting forgiveness. Mr Cumbershum said little but Mr Deverel much. He owned freely that they had been mistook and that he had been a little in drink, like his companion. He had not thought I would take the business so much to heart but the people were accustomed to such sport when crossing the equator, only he regretted that they had misinterpreted the captain's general permission. In fine, he requested me to treat the whole thing as a jest that had got out of hand. Had I then worn such apparel as I was now suited in, no one would have attempted—in fact the d-v-l was in it if they had meant any harm and now hoped I would forget the whole business.

I paused for a while as if cogitating, though I knew already what I would do. It was no moment at which to admit my own sense of unworthiness at having appeared before our people in a garb that was less than fitting. Indeed, these were the sort of men who needed a *uniform*—both one to wear, and one to look up to!

I spoke at last.

"I forgive you freely, gentlemen, as I am enjoined to do by MY MASTER. Go, and sin no more."

On that, I shut the cabin door. Outside it, I heard one of them, Mr Deverel, I think, give a low, but prolonged whistle. Then as their steps receded I heard Mr Cumbershum speak for the first time since the interview began.

"I wonder who the d-v-l his Master is? D'you think he's *in* with the d-mned Chaplain to the Fleet?"

Then they had departed. I own I felt at peace for the first time for many, many days. All was now to be well. I saw that little by little I might set about my work, not merely among the common people but later, among the officers and gentry who would not be, could not be now so insensible to the WORD as had appeared! Why—even the captain himself had shown some small signs—and the power of Grace is infinite. Before assuming my canonicals I went out into the waist and stood there, free at last— why, no doubt now the captain would revoke his first harsh prohibition to me of the quarterdeck! I gazed down into the water, the blue, the green, the purple, the snowy, sliding foam! I saw with a new feeling of security the long, green weed that wavers under the water from our wooden sides. There was, it seemed too, a peculiar richness in the columns of our rounded sails. Now is the time; and after due preparation I shall go forward and rebuke these unruly but truly lovable children of OUR MAKER! It seemed to me then—it still seems so—that I was and am consumed by a great love of all things, the sea, the ship, the sky, the gentlemen and the people and of course OUR REDEEMER above all! Here at last is the happiest outcome of all my distress and difficulty! ALL THINGS PRAISE HIM!

As your lordship knows, Colley wrote no more. After death—nothing. There must be nothing! The only consolation I have myself over the whole business is that I can ensure that his poor sister will never know the truth of it. Drunken Brocklebank may roar in his cabin, "Who killed cock Colley?" but *she* shall never know what weakness killed him, nor whose hands—mine among them—struck him down.

When I was roused by Wheeler from a too brief and uneasy sleep, I found that the first part of the morning was to be passed in an enquiry. I was to sit with Summers and the captain. Upon my objecting that the body should—in these hot latitudes—be buried first of all, Wheeler said nothing. It is plain that the captain means to cloak his and our persecutions of the man under a garment of proper, official proceedings! We sat, then, behind the table in the captain's cabin and the witnesses were paraded. The servant who had attended Colley told us no more than we knew. Young Mr Taylor, hardly subdued by the man's death but in a proper awe of the captain, repeated that he had seen Mr Colley agree to taste of the rum in a spirit of something or other, he could not recollect quite what—On my suggesting that the word might be "reconciliation" he accepted it. What was Mr Taylor doing there, forrard? (This from Mr Summers.) Mr Tommy Taylor was inspecting the stowage of the cables with a view to having the cable to the bower anchor rousted out and walked end-for-end. This splendid jargon satisfied the naval gentlemen, who nodded together as if they had been spoken to in plain English. But what was Mr Taylor doing, in that case, out of the cable tier? Mr Taylor had finished his inspection and was coming up to report and had stayed for a while, never having seen a parson in that state before. And then? (This from the captain.) Mr Taylor had "proceeded aft, sir, to inform Mr Summers" but had been "*given a bottle* by Mr Cumbershum before I could do so".

The captain nodded and Mr Taylor retired with what looked like relief. I turned to Summers.

"A bottle, Summers? What the devil did they want with a bottle?"

The captain growled.

"A bottle is a rebuke, sir. Let us get on."

The next witness was one East, a respectable emigrant, husband to the poor girl whose emaciated face had so struck me. He could read and write. Yes, he had seen Mr Colley and knew the reverend gentleman by sight. He had not seen him during the "badger bag", as the sailors called it, but he had heard tell. Perhaps we had been told how poorly his wife was and he was in near enough constant attendance on her, himself and Mrs Roustabout taking turns, though near her own time. He had only glimpsed Mr Colley among the seamen, did not think he had said much before taking a cup with them. The applause and laughter we had heard? That was after the few words the gentleman had spoken when he was being social with the sailors. The growls and anger? He knew nothing about that. He only knew the sailors took the gentleman away with them, down where the young gentleman had been among the ropes. He had had to look after his wife, knew nothing more. He hoped we gentlemen would think it no disrespect but that was all anyone knew except the sailors who had the reverend gentleman in charge.

He was allowed to withdraw. I gave it as my opinion that the only man who might enlighten us would be the fellow who had brought or carried him back to us in his drunken stupor. I said that he might know how much Colley drank and who had given it to him or forced it on him. Captain Anderson agreed and said that he had ordered the man to attend. He then addressed us in not much above a whisper:

"My *informant* advises me this is the witness we should press."

It was my turn.

"I believe", I said, and braced myself—"we are doing what you gentlemen would call 'making heavy weather of it'! The man was made drunk. There are some men, as we now know to our cost, whose timidity is such that they are wounded almost to death by another's anger and whose conscience is so tender they will die of what, let us say, Mr Brocklebank would accept as a peccadillo, if that! Come, gentlemen! Could we not confess that his intemperance killed him but that our general indifference to his welfare was likely enough the cause of it!"

This was bold, was it not? I was telling our tyrant that he and I together—But he was regarding me with astonishment.

"Indifference, sir?"

"Intemperance, sir," said Summers, quickly, "let us leave it at that."

"One moment, Summers. Mr Talbot. I pass over your odd phrase, 'our general indifference'. But do you not understand? Do you think that a single bout of drinking—"

"But you yourself said, sir—let us include all under a *low fever*!"

"That *was* yesterday! Sir, I tell you. It is likely enough that the man, helplessly drunk, suffered a criminal assault by one, or God knows how many men, and the absolute humiliation of it killed him!"

"Good God!"

This was a kind of convulsion of the understanding. I do not know that I thought anything at all for minutes together. I, as it were, *came to*, to hear the captain talking.

"No, Mr Summers. I will have no concealment. Nor will I tolerate frivolous accusations which touch me myself in my conduct of the ship and in my attitude to the passengers in her."

Summers was red in the face. "I have made a submission, sir. I beg your pardon if you find it beyond the line of my duty."

"Very well, Mr Summers. Let us get on."

"But captain," said I, "no man will admit to *that*!"

"You are young, Mr Talbot. You cannot guess what channels of information there are in a ship such as this, even though her present commission has been of such a short duration."

"Channels? Your informant?"

"I would prefer us to get on," said the captain heavily. "Let the man come in."

Summers himself went out and fetched Rogers. It was the man who had brought Colley back to us. I have seldom seen a more splendid young fellow. He was naked to the waist and of a build that one day might be overcorpulent. But now he could stand as a model to Michelangelo! His huge chest and columnar neck were of a deep brown hue, as was his broadly handsome face save where it was scarred by some parallel scratches of a lighter tone. Captain Anderson turned to me.

"Summers tells me you have claimed some skill in cross-examination."

"Did he? Did I?"

Your lordship will observe that I was by no means at my best in all this sorry episode. Captain Anderson positively beamed at me.

"Your witness, sir."

This I had not bargained for. However, there was no help for it.

"Now, my good man. Your name, if you please!"

"Billy Rogers, my lord. Foretop man."

I accepted the honorific. May it be an omen!

"We want information from you, Rogers. We want to know in precise detail what happened when the gentleman came among you the other day."

"What gentleman, my lord?"

"The parson. The reverend Mr Colley, who is now dead."

Rogers stood in the full light of the great window. I thought to myself that I had never seen a face of such wide-eyed candour.

"He took a drop too much, my lord, was overcome, like."

It was time to *go about*, as we nautical fellows say.

"How came you by those scars on your face?"

"A wench, my lord."

"She must have been a wild cat, then."

"Nigh on, my lord."

"You will have your way, whether or no?"

"My lord?"

"You would overcome her disinclination for her own good?"

"I don't know about all that, my lord. All I know is she had what was left of my pay in her other hand and would have been through the door like a pistol shot if I had not took a firm hold of her."

Captain Anderson beamed sideways at me.

"With your permission, my lord—"

Devil take it, the man was laughing at me!

"Now, Rogers. Never mind the women. What about the men?"

"Sir?"

"Mr Colley suffered an outrage there in the fo'castle. Who did it?"

The man's face was without any expression at all. The captain pressed him.

"Come, Rogers. Would it surprise you to know that you yourself are suspected of this particular kind of beastliness?"

The man's whole stance had altered. He was a little crouched now, one foot drawn a few inches behind the other. He had clenched his fists. He looked from one to the other of us quickly, as if trying to see in each face what degree of peril confronted him. I saw that he took us for *enemies*!

"I know nothing, Captain sir, nothing at all!"

"It may not have anything to do with you, my man. But you will know who it was."

"Who was who, sir?"

"Why, the one or many among you who inflicted a criminal assault on the gentleman so that he died of it!"

"I know nothing—nothing at all!"

I had got my wits back.

"Come, Rogers. You were the one man we saw with him. In default of any other evidence your name must head the list of suspects. What did you sailors do?"

I have never seen a face of more well-simulated astonishment.

"What did *we* do, my lord?"

"Doubtless you have witnesses to testify to your innocence. If you are innocent then help us to bring the criminals to book."

He said nothing, but still stood at bay. I took up the questioning again.

"I mean, my good man, you can either tell us who did it, or at the very least you can furnish us with a list of the people you suspect or know to be suspected of this particular form of, of interest, of assault."

Captain Anderson jerked up his chin.

"Buggery, Rogers, that's what he means. Buggery."

He looked down, shuffled some papers before him and dipped his pen in the ink. The silence prolonged itself into our expectancy. The captain himself broke it at last with a sound of angry impatience.

"Come along, man! We cannot sit here all day!"

There was another pause. Rogers turned his body rather than his head to us, one after the other. Then he looked straight at the captain.

"Aye aye, sir."

It was only then that there was a change in the man's face. He thrust his upper lip down, then as if in an experimental manner tried the texture of his lower lip judiciously with his white teeth.

"Shall I begin with the officers, sir?"

It was of the utmost importance that I should not move. The slightest flicker of my eye towards either Summers or the captain, the slightest contraction of a muscle would have seemed a fatal accusation. I had absolute faith in them both as far as this accusation of *beastliness* was concerned. As for the two officers themselves, doubtless they also had a mutual faith, yet they too did not dare risk any movement. We were waxworks. Rogers was waxworks too.

It had to be the captain who made the first move and he knew it. He laid his pen down beside the papers and spoke gravely.

"Very well, Rogers. That will be all. You may return to your duties."

The colour came and went in the man's face. He let out his breath in a prolonged gasp. He knuckled his forehead, began to smile, turned and went away out of the cabin. I cannot say how long the three of us sat without word or movement. For my part, it was something as simple and ordinary as the fear of doing or saying the wrong thing; yet the "wrong thing" would be, so to speak, raised to a higher power, to such a power as to be fearful and desperate. I felt in the long moments of our silence as if I could not allow myself to think at all, otherwise my face might redden and the perspiration begin to creep down my cheeks. I made by a most conscious effort my mind as nearly blank as might be and waited on the event. For surely of the three of us it was least my part to speak. Rogers had caught us in a mantrap. Can your lordship understand how already touches of suspicion came to life in my mind whether I would or no and flitted from the name of this gentleman to that?

Captain Anderson rescued us from our catalepsy. He did not move but spoke as if to himself.

"Witnesses, enquiries, accusations, lies, more lies, courts martial—the man has it in his power to ruin us all if he be brazen enough, as I doubt not he is, for it would be a hanging matter. Such accusations cannot be disproved. Whatever the upshot, something would stick."

He turned to Summers.

"And there, Mr Summers, ends our investigation. Have we other informants?"

"I believe no, sir. Touch pitch—"

"Just so. Mr Talbot?"

"I am all at sea, sir! But it is true enough. The man was at bay and brought out his last weapon; false witness, amounting to blackmail."

"In fact," said Summers, smiling at last, "Mr Talbot is the only one of us to have profited. He had at least a temporary elevation to the peerage!"

"I have returned to earth, sir—though since I was

addressed as 'my lord' by Captain Anderson, who can conduct marriages and funerals—"

"Ah yes. Funerals. You will drink, gentlemen? Call Hawkins in, Summers, will you? I must thank you, Mr Talbot, for your assistance."

"Of little use I fear, sir."

The captain was himself again. He beamed.

"A low fever then. Sherry?"

"Thank you, sir. But is everything concluded? We still do not know what happened. You mentioned informants—"

"This is good sherry," said the captain brusquely. "I believe, Mr Summers, you are averse to drinking at this time of the day and you will wish to oversee the various arrangements for the unfortunate man's committal to the deep. Your health, Mr Talbot. You will be willing to sign, or rather counter-sign, a report?"

I thought for a while.

"I have no official standing in this ship."

"Oh, come, Mr Talbot!"

I thought again.

"I will make a statement and sign that."

Captain Anderson looked sideways up at me from under his thick brows and nodded without saying anything. I drained my glass.

"You mentioned informants, Captain Anderson—"

But he was frowning at me.

"Did I, sir? I think not!"

"You asked Mr Summers—"

"Who replied there were none," said Captain Anderson loudly. "None at all, Mr Talbot, not a man jack among them! Do you understand, sir? No one has come sneaking to me—no one! You can go, Hawkins!"

I set down my glass and Hawkins took it away. The captain watched him leave the stateroom, then turned to me again.

"Servants have ears, Mr Talbot!"

"Why certainly, sir! I am very sure my fellow Wheeler has."

The captain smiled grimly.

"Wheeler! Oh yes indeed! *That* man must have ears and eyes all over him——"

"Well then, until the sad ceremony of this afternoon I shall return to my journal."

"Ah, the journal. Do not forget to include in it, Mr Talbot, that whatever may be said of the passengers, as far as the people and my officers are concerned this is a *happy* ship!"

At three o'clock we were all assembled in the waist. There was a guard, composed of Oldmeadow's soldiers, with flintlocks, or whatever their ungainly weapons are called. Oldmeadow himself was in full dress and unblooded sword, as were the ship's officers. Even our young gentlemen wore their dirks and expressions of piety. We passengers were dressed as sombrely as possible. The seamen were drawn up by watches, and were as presentable as their varied garments permit. Portly Mr Brocklebank was erect but yellow and drawn from potations that would have reduced Mr Colley to a ghost. As I inspected the man I thought that Brocklebank would have gone through the whole of Colley's ordeal and fall with no more than a bellyache and a sore head. Such are the varied fabrics of the human tapestry that surrounds me! Our ladies, who must surely have had such an occasion in their minds when they fitted themselves for the voyage, were in mourning—even Brocklebank's two doxies, who supported him on either side. Mr Prettiman was present at this *superstitious ritual* by the side of Miss Granham, who had led him there. What is all his militant Atheism and Republicanism when pitted against this daughter of a canon of Exeter Cathedral? I made a note as I saw him fretting and barely contained at her side, that *she* was the one of the two with whom I must speak and to whom I must convey the kind of delicate admonition I had intended for our notorious Freethinker!

You will observe that I have recovered somewhat from the effect of reading Colley's letter. A man cannot be forever brooding on what is past nor on the tenuous connection between his own unwitting conduct and someone else's deliberately criminal behaviour! Indeed, I have to own that this ceremonious naval occasion was one of great interest to me! One seldom attends a funeral in such, dare I call them, exotic surroundings! Not only was the ceremony strange, but all the time—or some of it at least—our actors conducted their dialogue in Tarpaulin language. You know how I delight in that! You will already have noted some particularly impenetrable specimens as, for instance, mention of a *badger bag*—does not Servius (I believe it was he) declare there are half a dozen cruxes in the *Aeneid* which will never be solved, either by emendation or inspiration or any method attempted by scholarship? Well then, I shall entertain you with a few more *naval cruxes*.

The ship's bell was struck, muffled. A party of sailors appeared, bearing the body on a plank and under the union flag. It was placed with its feet towards the starboard, or honourable side, by which admirals and bodies and suchlike rarities make their exits. It was a longer body than I had expected but have since been told that two of our few remaining cannon balls were attached to the feet. Captain Anderson, glittering with bullion, stood by it. I have also been told since, that he and all the other officers were much exercised as to the precise nature of the ceremonies to be observed when, as young Mr Taylor expressed it, "piping a sky pilot over the side".

Almost all our sails were *clewed up* and we were what the *Marine Dictionary* calls, technically speaking—and when does it not?—*hove to*, which ought to mean we were stationary in the water. Yet the spirit of farce (speaking perfectly exquisite Tarpaulin) attended Colley to his end. No sooner was the plank laid on the deck than I heard Mr Summers mutter to Mr Deverel:

"Depend upon it, Deverel, without you aft the driver a handspan she will make a sternboard."

Hardly had he said this when there came a heavy and rhythmical thudding from the ship's hull under water as if *Davey Jones* was serving notice or perhaps getting hungry. Deverel shouted orders of the *warrarroohoowasst!* variety, the seamen leapt, while Captain Anderson, a prayerbook clutched like a grenade, turned on Lieutenant Summers.

"Mr *Summers!* Will you have the sternpost out of her?"

Summers said nothing but the thudding ceased. Captain Anderson's tone sank to a grumble.

"The pintles are loose as a pensioner's teeth."

Summers nodded in reply.

"I know it, sir. But until she's rehung—"

"The sooner we're off the wind the better. God curse that drunken superintendant!"

He stared moodily down at the union flag, then up at the sails which, as if willing to debate with him, boomed back. They could have done no better than the preceding dialogue. Was it not superb?

At last the captain glanced round him and positively started, as if seeing us for the first time. I wish I could say that he *started like a guilty thing upon a fearful summons* but he did not. He started like a man in the smallest degree remiss who has absentmindedly forgotten that he has a body to get rid of. He opened the book and grunted a sour invitation to us to pray—and so on. Certainly he was anxious enough to get the thing over, for I have never heard a service read so fast. The ladies scarce had time to get out their handkerchiefs (tribute of a tear) and we gentlemen stared for a moment as usual into our beavers, but then, reminded that this unusual ceremony was too good to miss, all looked up again. I hoped that Oldmeadow's men would fire a volley but he has since told me that owing to some difference of opinion between the Admiralty and the War Office, they have neither flints nor powder. However, they presented arms in approximate unison and the officers flourished their swords. I wonder—was all this proper for a parson? I do not know, neither do they. A fife shrilled out and someone rattled on a muffled drum, a kind of overture, or postlude should I call it, or would *envoi* be a better word?

You will observe, my lord, that *Richard is himself again*—or shall we say that I have recovered from a period of fruitless and *perhaps* unwarranted regret?

And yet—at the last (when Captain Anderson's grumbling voice invited us to contemplate that time when there shall be no more sea) six men shrilled out a call on the bosun's pipe. Now, your lordship may never have heard these pipes so I must inform you that they have just as much music in them as the yowling of cats on heat! And yet and yet and *yet*! Their very harsh and shrill unmusicality, their burst of high sound leading to a long descent that died away through an uneasy and prolonged fluttering into silence, seemed to voice something beyond words, religion, philosophy. It was the simple voice of Life mourning Death.

I had scarcely time to feel a touch of complacency at the directness of my own emotions when the plank was lifted and tilted. The mortal remains of the Reverend Robert James Colley shot from under the union flag and entered the water with a single loud phut! as if he had been the most experienced of divers and had made a habit of rehearsing his own funeral, so expertly was it done. Of course the cannon balls assisted. This subsidiary use of their mass was after all in keeping with their general nature. So the remains of Colley dropping *deeper than did ever plummet sound* were to be thought of as now finding the solid base of all. (At these necessarily ritualistic moments of life, if you cannot use the prayer book, have recourse to Shakespeare! Nothing else will do.)

Now you might think that there was then a moment or two of silent tribute before the mourners left the church-yard. Not a bit of it! Captain Anderson shut his book, the pipes shrilled again, this time with a kind of temporal urgency. Captain Anderson nodded to Lieutenant Cumbershum, who touched his hat and *roared*:

> "*Leeeoonnawwll!*"

Our obedient vessel started to turn as she moved forward and lumbered clumsily towards her original course. The ceremonially ordered ranks broke up, the people climbed everywhere into the rigging to spread our full suit of sails and add the stun's'ls to them again. Captain Anderson marched off, grenade, I mean prayerbook in hand, back to his cabin, I suppose to make an entry in his journal. A young gentleman scrawled on the traverse board and all things were as they had been. I returned to my cabin to consider what statement I should write out and sign. It must be such as will cause his sister least pain. It shall be a *low fever*, as the captain wishes. I must conceal from him that I have already laid a trial of gunpowder to where your lordship may ignite it. God, what a world of conflict, of birth, death, procreation, betrothals, marriages for all I know, there is to be found in this extraordinary ship!

(&)

There! I think the ampersand gives a touch of eccentricity, does it not? None of your dates, or letters of the alphabet, or presumed *day of the voyage*! I might have headed this section "addenda" but that would have been dull—far too, too dull! For we have come to an end, there is nothing more to be said. I mean—there is, of course, there is the daily record, but my journal, I found on looking back through it, had insensibly turned to the record of a drama—Colley's drama. Now the poor man's drama is done and he stands there, how many miles down, on his cannon balls, alone, as Mr Coleridge says, all, all alone. It seems a different sort of *bathos* (your lordship, as Colley might say, will note the amusing "paranomasia") to return to the small change of day to day with no drama in it, but there are yet some pages left between the rich bindings of your lordship's gift to me, and I *have* tried to stretch the burial out, in the hope that what might be called *The Fall and Lamentable End of Robert James Colley together with a Brief Account of his Thalassian Obsequies* would extend right to the last page. All was of no avail. His was a real life and a real death and no more to be fitted into a given book than a misshapen foot into a given boot. Of course my journal will continue beyond this volume—but in a book obtained for me by Phillips from the purser and not to be locked. Which reminds me how trivial the explanation of men's fear and silence concerning the purser proved to be. Phillips told me, for he is more open than Wheeler. All the officers, including the captain, owe the purser money! Phillips calls him *the pusser*.

Which reminds me again—I employed Phillips because

no matter how I shouted, I could not rouse Wheeler. He is being sought now.

He *was* being sought. Summers has just told me. The man has disappeared. He has fallen overboard. Wheeler! He has gone like a dream, with his puffs of white hair, and his shining baldness, his *sanctified* smile, his complete knowledge of everything that goes on in a ship, his paregoric, and his willingness to obtain for a gentleman anything in the wide, wide world, provided the gentleman pays for it! Wheeler, as the captain put it, *all over ears and eyes*! I shall miss the man, for I cannot hope for as great a share in the services of Phillips. Already I have had to pull off my own boots, though Summers, who was present in my cabin at the time, was good enough to help. Two deaths in only a few days!

"At least", said I to Summers with meaning, "no one can accuse me of having a hand in *this* death, can they?"

He was too breathless to reply. He sat back on his heels, then stood up and watched me pull on my embroidered slippers.

"Life is a formless business, Summers. Literature is much amiss in forcing a form on it!"

"Not so, sir, for there are both death and birth aboard. Pat Roundabout—"

"Roundabout? I thought it was 'Roustabout'!"

"You may use either indifferently. But she is delivered of a daughter to be named after the ship."

"Poor, poor child! But that was the mooing I heard then, like Bessie when she broke her leg?"

"It was, sir. I go now to see how they do."

So he left me, these blank pages still unfilled. News, then, news! What news? There *is* more to be recorded but germane to the captain, not Colley. It should have been fitted in much earlier—at Act Four or even Three. Now it must come limping after the drama, like the satyr play

233

after the tragic trilogy. It is not a *dénouement* so much as a pale illumination. Captain Anderson's detestation of the clergy! You remember. Well now, perhaps, you and I *do* know all.

Hist, as they say—let me bolt my door!

Well then—Deverel told me. He has begun to drink heavily—heavily that is in comparison with what he did before, since he has always been intemperate. It seems that Captain Anderson—fearful not only of my journal but also of the other passengers who *now* with the exception of steely Miss Granham believe "Poor Colley" was mistreated—Anderson, I say, rebuked the two men, Cumbershum and Deverel, savagely for their part in the affair. This meant little to Cumbershum, who is made of wood. But Deverel, by the laws of the service, is denied the satisfaction of a gentleman. He broods and drinks. Then last night, deep in drink, he came to my cabin and in the dark hours and a muttered, slurred voice gave me what he called necessary observations on the captain's history for my journal. Yet he was not so drunk as to be unaware of danger. Picture us then, by the light of my candle, seated side by side on the bunk, Deverel whispering viciously into my ear as my head was inclined to his lips. There was, it appears, and there is, a noble family— not I believe more than distantly known to your lordship—and their land marches with the Deverels'. They, Summers would say, have used the privilege of their position and neglected its responsibilities. The father of the present young lord had in keeping a lady of great sweetness of disposition, much beauty, little understanding and, as it proved, some fertility. The use of privilege is sometimes expensive. Lord L——(this is perfect Richardson, is it not?) found himself in need of a fortune, and that instantly. The fortune was found but her family in a positively Wesleyan access of righteousness insisted on the dismissal of the sweet lady, against whom nothing could be urged save lack of a few words spoke over her by a parson. Catastrophe threatened. The dangers of her position struck some sparks from the sweet lady, the fortune hung in the balance! At this moment, as Deverel whispered in my ear, Providence intervened and the incumbent of one of the three livings that lay in the family's gift was killed in the hunting field! The heir's tutor, a dull sort of fellow, accepted of the living and the sweet lady and what Deverel called her curst cargo together. The lord got his fortune, the lady a husband and the Reverend Anderson a living, a wife and an heir *gratis*. In due course the boy was sent to sea, where the casual interest of his real father was sufficient to elevate him in the service. But now the old lord is dead and the young one has no cause to love his bastard half-brother!

All this by an unsteady candle light, querulous remarks in his sleep from Mr Prettiman, with snores and farts from Mr Brocklebank in the other direction. Oh that cry from the deck above us—

"Eight bells and all's well!"

Deverel, at this witching hour, put his arm about me with drunken familiarity and revealed why he had spoken so. This history was the *jest* he had meant to tell me. At Sydney Cove, or the Cape of Good Hope, should we put in there, Deverel intends—or the drink in him intends—to resign his commission, call the captain out and shoot him dead! "For", said he in a louder voice and with his shaking right hand lifted, "I can knock a crow off a steeple with one barker!" Hugging and patting me and calling me his *good Edmund* he informed me I was to act for him when the time came; and if, *if* by some luck of the devil, he himself was taken off, why the information was to be put fully in my famous journal—

I had much ado to get him taken to his cabin without rousing the whole ship. But here is news indeed! So *that* is why a certain captain so detests a parson! It would surely be more reasonable in him to detest a lord! Yet there is no doubt about it. Anderson has been wronged by a lord—or by a parson—or by life—Good God! I do not care to find excuses for Anderson!

Nor do I care as much for Deverel as I did. It was a misjudgement on my part to esteem him. He, perhaps, illustrates the last decline of a noble family as Mr Summers might illustrate the original of one! My wits are all to seek. I found myself thinking that had I been so much the victim of a lord's gallantry I would have become a *Jacobin!* I? Edmund Talbot?

It was then that I remembered my own half-formed intention to bring Zenobia and Robert James Colley together to rid myself of a possible embarrassment. It was so like Deverel's *jest* I came near to detesting myself. When I realized how he and I had talked, and how he must have thought me like-minded with the "Noble family" my face grew hot with shame. Where will all this end?

However, one birth does not equal two deaths. There is a general dullness among us, for say what you will, a burial at sea, however frivolously I treat it, cannot be called a laughing matter. Nor will Wheeler's disappearance lighten the air among the passengers.

Two days have passed since I diffidently forbore to ask Summers to help me on with my slippers! The officers have not been idle. Summers—as if this were a Company ship rather than a man of war—has determined we shall not have too much time left hanging on our hands. We have determined that the after end of the ship shall present the forrard end with a *play*! A *committee* has been formed *with the captain's sanction*! This has thrown me will-he, nill-he, into the company of Miss Granham! It has been an edifying experience. I found that this woman, this handsome, cultivated maiden lady, holds views which would freeze the blood of the average citizen in his veins! She does *literally* make no distinction between the uniform worn by our officers, the woad with which our unpolished ancestors were said to paint themselves and the tattooing rife in the South Seas and perhaps on the mainland of Australia! Worse—from the point of view of society—she, daughter of a canon, makes no distinction between the Indian's Medicine Man, the Siberian Shaman, and a Popish priest in his vestments! When I expostulated that she bid fair to include our own clergy she would only admit them to be less offensive because they made themselves less readily distinguishable from other gentlemen. I was so staggered by this conversation I could make no reply to her and only discovered the reason for the awful candour with which she spoke when (before dinner in the passenger saloon) it was announced that she and Mr Prettiman are *officially* engaged! In the unexpected security of her *fiançailles* the lady feels free to say anything! But with what an eye she has seen us! I blush to remember the many things I have said in her presence which must have seemed like the childishness of the schoolroom.

However, the announcement has cheered everyone up. You may imagine the public felicitations and the private comments! I myself sincerely hope that Captain Anderson, gloomiest of Hymens, will marry them aboard so that we may have a complete collection of all the ceremonies that accompany the forked creature from the cradle to the grave. The pair seem attached—they have fallen in love *after their fashion*! Deverel introduced the only solemn note. He declared it was a great shame the man Colley had died, otherwise the knot might be tied there and then by a parson. At this, there was a general silence.

Miss Granham, who had furnished your humble servant with her views on priests in general might, I felt, have said nothing. But instead, she came out with a quite astonishing statement.

"He was a truly degraded man."

"Come, ma'am," said I, "*de mortuis* and all that! A single unlucky indulgence—The man was harmless enough!"

"Harmless," cried Prettiman with a kind of bounce, "a priest harmless?"

"I was not referring to drink," said Miss Granham in her steeliest voice, "but to vice in another form."

"Come, ma'am—I cannot believe—as a lady you cannot—"

"*You*, sir," cried Mr Prettiman, "*you* to doubt a lady's word?"

"No, no! Of course not! Nothing—"

"Let it be, dear Mr Prettiman, I beg of you."

"No, ma'am, I cannot let it go. Mr Talbot has seen fit to doubt your word and I will have an apology—"

"Why," said I laughing, "you have it, ma'am, unreservedly! I never intended—"

"We learnt of his vicious habits accidentally," said Mr Prettiman. "A priest! It was two sailors who were descending one of the rope ladders from the mast to the side of the vessel. Miss Granham and I—it was dark—we had retired to the shelter of that confusion of ropes at the foot of the ladder—"

"Chain, ratlines—Summers, enlighten us!"

"It is no matter, sir. You will remember, Miss Granham, we were discussing the inevitability of the process by which true liberty must lead to true equality and thence to—but that is no matter, neither. The sailors were unaware of our presence so that without meaning to, we heard all!"

"Smoking is bad enough, Mr Talbot, but at least gentlemen go no further!"

"My dear Miss Granham!"

"It is as savage a custom, sir, as any known among coloured peoples!"

Oldmeadow addressed her in tones of complete incredulity. "By Jove, ma'am—you cannot mean the fellow chewed tobacco!"

There was a roar of laughter from passengers and officers alike. Summers, who is not given to idle laughter, joined in.

"It is true," said he, when there was less noise. "On one of my earlier visits I saw a large bunch of leaf tobacco hung from the deckhead. It was spoilt by mildew and I threw it overboard."

"But Summers," said I. "I saw no tobacco! And that kind of man—"

"I assure you, sir. It was before you visited him."

"Nevertheless, I find it almost impossible to believe!"

"You shall have the facts," said Prettiman with his usual choler. "Long study, a natural aptitude and a necessary habit of defence have made me expert in the recollection of casual speech, sir. You shall have the words the sailors spoke *as* they were spoken!"

Summers lifted both hands in expostulation.

"No, no—spare us, I beg you! It is of little moment after all!"

"Little moment, sir, when a lady's word—it cannot be allowed to pass, sir. One of these sailors said to the other as they descended side by side—'Billy Rogers was laughing like a bilge pump when he come away from the captain's cabin. He went into the heads and I sat by him. Billy said he'd knowed most things in his time but he had never thought to get a chew off a parson!' "

The triumphant but fierce look on Mr Prettiman's face,

his flying hair and instant decline of his educated voice into a precise imitation of a ruffian sort threw our audience into whoops. This disconcerted the philosopher even more and he stared round him wildly. Was anything ever more absurd? I believe it was this diverting circumstance which marked a change in our general feelings. Without the source of it being evident there strengthened among us the determination to get on with our play! Perhaps it was Mr Prettiman's genius for comedy—oh, unquestionably we must have him for our comic! But what might have been high words between the social philosopher and your humble servant passed off into the much pleasanter business of discussing *what* we should act and *who* should produce and *who* should do this and that!

Afterwards I went out to take my usual constitutional in the waist; and lo! there by the break of the fo'castle was "Miss Zenobia" in earnest conversation with Billy Rogers! Plainly, he is her *Sailor Hero* who can "*Wate no longer*". With what kindred spirit did he concoct his misspelt but elaborate billet-doux? Well, if he attempts to come aft and visit her in her hutch I will see him flogged for it.

Mr Prettiman and Miss Granham walked in the waist too but on the opposite side of the deck, talking with animation. Miss Granham said (I heard her and believe she intended me to hear) that *as he knew* they should aim first at supporting those parts of the administration that might be supposed still uncorrupted. Mr Prettiman trotted beside her—she is taller than he—nodding with vehemence at the austere yet penetrating power of her intellect. They will influence each other—for I believe they are as sincerely attached as such extraordinary characters can be. But oh yes, Miss Granham, I shall not keep an eye on him—I shall keep an eye on you! I watched them pass on over the white line that separates the social orders and stand right up in the bows, talking to East and that poor, pale girl, his wife. Then they returned and came straight to where I stood in the shade of an awning we have stretched from the starboard shrouds. To my astonishment, Miss Granham explained that they had been *consulting with Mr East*! He is, it seems, a craftsman and has to do with the setting of type! I do not doubt that they have in view his future employment. However, I did not allow them to see what an interest I took in the matter and turned the conversation back to the question of what play we should show the people. Mr Prettiman proved to be as indifferent to that as to so much of the common life he is allegedly concerned with in his philosophy! He dismissed Shakespeare as a writer who made too little comment on the evils of society! I asked, reasonably enough, what society consisted in other than human beings only to find that the man did not understand me—or rather, that there was a screen between his unquestionably powerful intellect and the perceptions of common sense. He began to orate but was deflected skilfully by Miss Granham, who declared that the play *Faust* by the German author Goethe would have been suitable—

"But," said she, "the genius of one language cannot be translated into another."

"I beg your pardon, ma'am?"

"I mean," said she, patiently, as to one of her *young gentlemen*, "you cannot translate a work of genius entirely from one language to another!"

"Come now, ma'am," said I, laughing, "here at least I may claim to speak with authority! My godfather has translated Racine entire into English verse; and in the opinion of connoisseurs it equals and at some points surpasses the original!"

The pair stopped, turned and stared at me as one. Mr Prettiman spoke with his usual febrile energy.

"Then I would have you know, sir, that it must be unique!"

I bowed to him.

"Sir," said I, "it is!"

With that and a bow to Miss Granham I took myself off. I *scored* did I not? But really—they are a provokingly opinionated pair! Yet if they are provoking and comic to *me* I doubt not that they are intimidating to others! While I was writing this I heard them pass my hutch on the way to the passenger saloon and listened as Miss Granham *cut up* some unfortunate character.

"Let us hope he learns in time, then!"

"Despite the disadvantage of his birth and upbringing, ma'am, he is not without wit."

"I grant you," said she, "he always tries to give a comic turn to the conversation and indeed one cannot help finding his laughter at his own jests infectious. But as for his opinions in general—Gothic is the only word to be applied to them!"

With that they passed out of earshot. They cannot mean Deverel, surely—for though he has some pretension to wit, his birth and upbringing are of the highest order, however little he may have profited from them. Summers is the more likely candidate.

I do not know how to write this. The chain would seem too thin, the links individually too weak—yet something within me insists they *are* links and all joined, so that I now understand what happened to pitiable, clownish Colley! It was night, I was heated and restless, yet my mind as in a fever—a *low* fever indeed!—went back over the whole affair and would not let me be. It seemed as if certain sentences, phrases, situations were brought successively before me—and these, as it were, glowed with a significance that was by turns farcical, gross and tragic.

Summers must have guessed. There *was* no leaf-tobacco! He was trying to protect the memory of the dead man!

Rogers in the enquiry with a face of well-simulated astonishment—"What did *we* do, my lord?" Was that astonishment well-simulated? Suppose the splendid animal was telling the naked, the physical truth! Then Colley in his letter—*what a man does defiles him, not what is done by others*—Colley in his letter, infatuated with the "king of my island" and longing to kneel before him—Colley in the cable tier, drunk for the first time in his life and not understanding his condition and in a state of mad exuberance—Rogers owning in the heads that he had knowed most things in his life but had never thought *to get a chew off a parson*! Oh, doubtless the man consented, jeeringly, and encouraged the ridiculous, schoolboy trick—even so, not Rogers but Colley committed the *fellatio* that the poor fool was to die of when he remembered it.

Poor, poor Colley! Forced back towards his own kind, made an equatorial fool of—deserted, abandoned by me who could have saved him—overcome by kindness and a gill or two of the intoxicant—

I cannot feel even a pharisaical complacency in being the only gentleman not to witness his ducking. Far better had I seen it so as to protest at that childish savagery! Then my offer of friendship might have been sincere rather than—

I shall write a letter to Miss Colley. It will be lies from beginning to end. I shall describe my growing friendship with her brother. I shall describe my admiration for him. I shall recount all the days of his *low fever* and my grief at his death.

A letter that contains everything but a shred of truth! How is that for a start to a career in the service of my King and Country?

I believe I may contrive to increase the small store of money that will be returned to her.

It is the last page of your journal, my lord, last page of the "ampersand"! I have just now turned over the pages, ruefully enough. Wit? Acute observations? Entertainment? Why—it has become, perhaps, some kind of sea-story but a sea-story with never a tempest, no shipwreck, no sinking, no rescue at sea, no sight nor sound of an enemy, no thundering broadsides, heroism, prizes, gallant defences and heroic attacks! Only one gun fired and that a blunderbuss!

What a thing he stumbled over in himself! Racine declares—but let me quote your own words to you.

> Lo! where toils Virtue up th'Olympian fteep—
> With like fmall fteps doth Vice t'wards Hades creep!

True indeed, and how should it be not? It is the smallness of those steps that enables the Brocklebanks of this world to survive, to attain a deboshed and saturated finality which disgusts everyone but themselves! Yet not so Colley. He was the exception. Just as his iron-shod heels shot him rattling down the steps of the ladder from the quarterdeck to the waist; even so a gill or two of the *fiery ichor* brought him from the heights of complacent austerity to what his sobering mind must have felt as the lowest hell of self-degradation. In the not too ample volume of man's knowledge of Man, let this sentence be inserted. Men can die of shame.

This book is filled all but a finger's breadth. I shall lock it, wrap it and sew it unhandily in sailcloth and thrust it away in the locked drawer. With lack of sleep and too much understanding I grow a little crazy, I think, like all men at sea who live too close to each other and too close thereby to all that is monstrous under the sun and moon.

TO THE ENDS OF THE EARTH

Close Quarters

(I)

I signalized my birthday by giving myself a present since no one else seemed inclined to! I bought it, of course, from Mr Jones, the purser. As I emerged on deck with some relief from the fetor of the ship's bowels I met Charles Summers, my friend and the ship's first lieutenant. He laughed when he saw the manuscript book in my hand.

"The ship was aware, Edmund, that you had finished, that is, filled the book which was a present from your noble godfather."

"But how?"

"Oh, do not be surprised! Nothing can be hidden in a ship. But have you still more news for him?"

"This is not a continuation, but a new venture. When this is filled with an account of our voyage I mean to keep it for myself and no one else."

"There must be little of enough note for recording."

"On the contrary, sir, on the contrary!"

"More reasons for self-satisfaction?"

"And how am I to take that?"

"Why—elevate your nose as usual. Dear Edmund, if you only knew how maddeningly superior you can be—and now a writer into the bargain!"

I did not much care for his mixture of familiarity and amused irritation. For indeed I thought I had cured myself of a certain lofty demeanour, a consciousness of my own worth which had perhaps been too carelessly displayed in the earlier days of the voyage. Had it not gained me, among the common seamen, the nickname of "Lord Talbot"? Of course, "mister" or "esquire" is all I am entitled to.

"I amuse myself. I pass the time. What else can a poor

devil of a landsman do to occupy himself in a voyage from the top of the world to the bottom?"

"That is called folio size, is it not? You will need a great deal of adventure to fill it. The first one, for your god-father—"

"Colley, Wheeler, Captain Anderson—"

"And others. I wish sincerely that you will have much more difficulty in filling your second volume!"

"Your wish is granted here and now, for my head is empty. By the way—today is my birthday!"

He nodded gravely but said nothing and went on his way towards the forward part of our vessel. I sighed. I believe it has been the first time my birthday has gone unnoticed by all but myself! At home things would be different, with good wishes and presents. Here in this lumbering ship such modest entertainment, such pleasant customs go by the board.

I went to my "hutch" or cabin, that "little ease" which must serve me for sleep and privacy until we reach the Antipodes. I sat down in my canvas chair before my "writing-flap", my only desk, and cracked the folio open on it. The area was immense. If I bowed my head and peered at the blank surface—as I must, since so little light filters into my cabin—it seemed to spread in every direction until it was the whole of my world. I watched it, therefore, in the expectation that some material fit for permanence would appear—but nothing! It was only after a prolonged pause that I discovered my present stratagem and the full result of it in recording my own, surely temporary inadequacy. That unhappy shrimp of a man, Parson Colley, had nevertheless in his letter to his sister, as far as I could remember, unconsciously used the massive instrument of the English tongue with a dexterity which called up our ship and her people—including me—as if by magic! He had set her there, lolloping in the weather.

Yes, the weather, Edmund, the weather, you fool! Why do you not start with that? We have escaped from the *doldrums* at least. We were there too long for comfort. We have moved at last out of the fair weather of the equatorial regions and are now pushing south, the wind over our larboard bow so that there is once more a certain unsteadiness in the deck, a constant canting to the right to which I am now so accustomed I accept it and my limbs accept it as normal to living. The present weather is sharply defining our horizon for us in a dense blue which obeys Lord Byron's famous injunction and continues to roll on endlessly—such is the power of verse! I must try it some time. Sufficient and perhaps increasing wind (not, I seem to remember, included by his lordship) moves us slanting, or ought to but seems to have less effect on our vessel than it should. So much for the weather. Colley would have *integrated* it. But as far as I can see, it has no other effect than to cool our air slightly and set the ink in the well at a slight slant. Edmund, I adjure you! Be a writer!

But how?

There is an inevitable difference between this journal, meant for, for, I do not know for whom, and the first one meant for the eyes of a godfather who is less indulgent than I pretended. In that volume I had all my work done for me. By a remarkable series of strokes of fortune, Colley "willed himself to death" and "my servant" Wheeler drowned and the result was to fill my book! I cannot consult it, for it lies, all wrapped in brown paper, sewn in sailcloth, sealed and stowed away, in my bottom drawer. But I do remember writing towards the end of it that it had become some sort of a sea story. It was a journal that became a story by accident. There is no story to tell now.

Yesterday we saw a whale. Or rather we saw the plume of spray which rose where the creature was snorting, but the beast itself remained hidden. Lieutenant Deverel, that crony from whom to tell the truth I remain anxious to detach myself, remarked that it looked for all the world like the strike of a cannon ball. At this Zenobia Brocklebank shrieked and besought him not to mention anything so frighteningly horrid, a display of proper female weakness—or the appearance of it—which enabled Deverel to move closer, take her unresisting hand and murmur some sort of comfort with a kind of echo of amatory matters in it. Miss Granham, I remember, looked, if not daggers, penknives at least, and moved away to where her fiancé, Mr Prettiman, was extolling the social benefits of revolution to our marine artist, sodden Mr Brocklebank. All that on the poop under the eyes of Lieutenant Cumbershum who with young Mr Taylor had the watch! What else? This is small beer!

Yesterday there was part of a cable laid out in the waist, then wormed, parcelled and served for some mysterious operation of seamanship. It was the only thing to record but a damned dull sight.

What the devil! I need a hero whose career I may follow in volume two. Might it be our gloomy Captain Anderson? I do not think so. There is, for all his uniform, something indomitably unheroic about him. Charles Summers, my friend the first lieutenant? He is our Good Man and therefore only to be tragic if he falls from that small eminence which I do not expect or wish. The others, Mr Smiles, the remote sailing master, Mr Askew, the gunner, Mr Gibbs, the carpenter—why not our tradesman, Mr Jones, the purser? Oldmeadow, the Army officer with his file of greenclad men? I cudgel my brains, call Smollett and Fielding into the ring, ask their advice and find they have none for me.

I should perhaps tell the story of a young gentleman of much intelligence and more feeling than he was aware of who takes a voyage to the Antipodes where he is to assist the governor of the new colony with his undoubted talents for, for something or other. He, he—what? There is a woman in the fo'castle among the emigrants. Might not she be our heroine, a princess in disguise? Might not *he*, our hero, rescue her—but from what? Then there is Miss Brocklebank of whom I do not desire to write and Mrs Brocklebank with whom I am at present almost entirely unacquainted and who is far too young and pretty to be tunbelly's wife.

Wanted! A hero for my new journal, a new heroine, a new villain and some comic relief to ameliorate my deep, deep boredom.

It will have to be Charles Summers after all. We at least talk and do so with some regularity. Since as first lieutenant he is generally in charge of the ship he does not keep a watch. He seems to move about the ship for something like eighteen hours in the twenty-four and now knows the ship's company, let alone the emigrants and the passengers individually by name. I believe he also knows the fabric of the ship inch by inch. His only break as far as I can see is for an hour in the forenoon—perhaps from eleven to twelve when he walks the deck like a man taking a constitutional. Some of the passengers do likewise and I am happy and really rather proud to say that Charles commonly chooses me as his walking companion! A pattern has settled into a custom. He and I walk back and forth the length of the waist on the larboard side of the ship, Mr Prettiman and his fiancée Miss Granham do the same on the starboard side. By common consent we do not walk as a group of four but in two pairs. Thus just as they are turning to come back from the break of the fo'castle so we are turning to come back from the break of the aftercastle! As we move towards the midpoint the bulk of the mainmast hides our two pairs from each other so we do not have to raise our hats or incline the head smilingly at each passing! Is that not trivially absurd? Only the interposition of a lumpish column of wood preserves us from having to employ all the actions of landlubberly conduct!

I said as much to Charles the other forenoon and he laughed.

"I had not considered the matter but I suppose it is so; and a piece of neat observation!"

"The 'proper study of man' and most necessary to one who intends to be a politician."

"You have your career charted?"

"Yes indeed. And more precisely than most men of my years."

"You excite my curiosity."

"Why—I shall spend a few years—a very few years—in the administration of the colony."

"May I be there to see!"

"Mark me, Mr Summers, in this century I am convinced the civilized nations will more and more take over the administration of the backward parts of the world."

"And then?"

"Parliament. My godfather has what is commonly called 'a rotten borough' in his pocket. It sends two members to the house and the only electors are a drunken shepherd and a cottager who spends the weeks after an election in a state of indescribable debauchery."

"Should you profit by such excess?"

"Well, there are difficulties. Our wretched estates are heavily encumbered and since a seat in the house is only tenable by a man of means I must pick up a plum or two."

Charles laughed aloud, then stopped himself abruptly.

"I ought not to find that amusing, Edmund, but I do. A plum or two! And then?"

"Why—government! The cabinet!"

"What ambition!"

"You dislike that side of my character?"

Charles was silent for a while, then spoke heavily.

"I have no right to. I am just such a creature myself."

"You? Oh no!"

"In any event, I find you profoundly interesting. I hope sincerely that your career may prosper to your own satisfaction and the benefit of your friends. But does not the country begin to frown on 'rotten boroughs'? For is it not against reason and equity that a handful of English people should elect the assembly which will govern all?"

"Now there, Charles, I believe I may enlighten you! That apparent defect is the true genius of our system—"

"Oh no! It cannot be!"

"But, my dear fellow, Democracy is never and cannot be representation by everyone. What, sir, are we to give the vote to children, to men of no property? To the insane? To criminals in the common gaols? To women?"

"You had best not let Miss Granham hear you!"

"Indeed, I would not for the world denigrate that respectable lady. I concede the exception. Denigration? I would not dare!"

"Nor I!"

We laughed together. Then I resumed my explanation.

"In the best days of Greece voting was limited to a fraction of the population. Barbarians may elect their chieftains by acclaim and the thundering of swords on shields. But the more civilized a country is, the smaller is the number of people fitted to understand the complexities of its society! A civilized community will always find ways of healthfully limiting the electorate to a body of highly born, highly educated, sophisticated professional and hereditary electors who come from a level of society which was born to govern, expects to govern, and will always do so!"

But Charles was making quelling gestures with both hands. I believe my voice had indeed risen. He interrupted me.

"Edmund! Gently! I am not Parliament! You are orating. That time before Mr Prettiman vanished beyond the mainmast he was turning red in the face!"

I lowered my voice.

"I will moderate my voice but not my language. He is a theorist—if nothing worse! It is the common mistake of theorists to suppose a perfect scheme of government may be fitted over the poor, imperfect face of humanity! Not so, Mr Summers. There are circumstances in which only the imperfections of a contradictory and cumberous system such as ours will serve. Rotten boroughs for ever! But in the right hands, of course."

"Do I detect some of the elements of a projected maiden speech in the house?"

I felt a sudden warmth mantle my cheeks.

"How did you guess?"

Charles turned away for a moment and gave an admonition to a seaman who was idling with some twine, some grease, and a marlingspike. Then—

"But your personal life, Edmund—all that part which is not dedicated so straightforwardly to the service of your country?"

"Why—I suppose I shall live the way one lives! I shall have one day—may it be far off—to do something about the estates unless one of my young brothers can be induced to. I must own that my loftier flights in the future have seen me freeing the estates from their heavy load by"— here I did indeed laugh at the thought—"a gift from a grateful country! But you will think me a dreamer!"

Charles laughed too.

"There is no harm in that provided they are dreams of the future and not of the past!"

254

"My practical proposal, however, is no dream. At a suitable point in my career I shall marry—"

"Ah! I was wondering. May I ask if the young lady is already chosen?"

"How can that be? Do you think I propose to be Romeo to someone's Juliet? Give me ten years, then some lady perhaps ten or twelve years younger than myself, a young lady of family, wealthy, beautiful—"

"And at present in the nursery."

"Just so."

"I wish you joy."

I laughed.

"You shall dance at my wedding!"

There was a pause. Charles smiled no longer.

"I do not dance."

With a brief nod he went off, vanishing into the fo'castle. I turned to greet Mr Prettiman and his fiancée but saw them vanishing into the break of the quarterdeck. I returned to my hutch and sat before my writing-flap, thinking that this was a conversation I might retain in my journal. I thought, too, how likeable and intimate a friend Charles Summers had become.

All that was yesterday. What then this morning? Nothing has happened. I ate dull food, refused to drink since I drink too much, talked, or rather monosyllabled with Oldmeadow who cannot find employment for his men, *cut* Zenobia Brocklebank since she has made a habit of parleying with the common seamen—and found myself sitting once more in front of this vast white area with an empty head. Come to think of it I have one tedious matter to report. I have just met again with Charles Summers on the deck. He said there was now more weight in the wind, to which I replied that I had not been able to detect any increase in our speed. He nodded.

"I know it," he said gravely. "There should be an

increase but it is cancelled by the increase in our weed. We were rather too long for comfort in the doldrums."

I walked to the side and looked over the rail. The weed was visible, green hair. When we rolled there appeared further down a kind of darkness which suggested weed as long but of a different colour. Then we rolled back and the green locks spread on the surface again to be washed about then inclined all one way by our slight forward movement.

"Can you not get rid of the stuff?"

"If we were at anchor we might use the dragrope. We might lie up in some tidal creek, careen her and scrub her down."

"Are all ships as weedy in these waters?"

"Not the modern ships, up-to-date nineteenth-century vessels. They have coppered bottoms on which marine growths are slower to take hold."

"It is a great bore."

"So anxious to reach the Antipodes?"

"Time hangs heavy."

He smiled and went away. I reminded myself of my new employment, and came back to my hutch. There is this to be said about writing a journal which may well be read by no one but myself. I can decide that for myself! If I choose, I can be downright irresponsible! I do not have to look round me for witticisms which might entertain a godfather, or make sure that I present, as it were, my better profile like a bride sitting for her marriage portrait. I was, perhaps, too honest in the journal for my godfather and I have sometimes thought that instead of persuading him to think what a noble fellow I am, he may well have agreed with the literal meaning of my words and decided that I have shown myself unworthy of his patronage! The devil is in it if I can see a way out of that, for I cannot destroy my writing without destroying my godfather's present to me with all its unnecessarily splendid binding. I have been a fool. No. I have miscalculated.

Cumbershum and Deverel have urged Summers to represent to Captain Anderson the advisability of altering course towards the river Plate where we may careen and rid us of weed. My informant was young Mr Taylor, the more than ebullient midshipman who sometimes attaches himself to me. Summers, however, will not do it. He knows that Anderson wishes to make the whole voyage without visiting a port of call. I have to own that Summers, good man though he be and fine seaman though I am sure he is, does not relish in any way differing from his captain. Mr Taylor says that he refused them by pointing out what this morning is unquestionably true—that the wind has increased considerably and our speed is a little increased in consequence. The wind is still on the larboard bow, the horizon is a little dulled from its former sharpness and we take spray aboard now and then. All the ship's people and the passengers are cheered by it. The ladies are positively glowing with health and

(2)

It is necessary to suppose a space of some three days between that word with which SECTION ONE so inscrutably finishes and these I write today. I was interrupted. Ye gods, how my head aches, do I but turn my neck! There's no doubt I have had the devil of a thump, all unlooked for. I contrive to write in my bunk, for Phillips has given me a board to rest across my knees and done what he calls "chocking off" my back with an extra granite pillow or two. Fortunately, or unfortunately, I suppose I should say, the ship has little movement as far as I am concerned tho' the wind is pushing her back towards the doldrums, the devil take it all, twenty thousand times over! At this rate we shall reach the Antipodes when they are having their winter down there, a prospect I do not care for and neither do the seamen who have heard too much about the horrors of the Southern Ocean at that season! Summers came to visit me directly I was well enough to curse and told me with a painful smile that Captain Anderson refused the suggestion of the river Plate but had now conceded the possibility of calling at the Cape of Good Hope if we can get there.

"We are in some danger then?"

For a while he did not answer.

"A little. As ever. Do not, I beg of you—"

"Spread despondency among the other passengers."

He laughed at that.

"Come, you are better."

"If only I could make some connection between my tongue and the inside of my skull—do you know, Charles, I speak with the outside of myself?"

"It is the effect of concussion. You will be better presently. Only do not, I beg of you, perform any more acts of selfless heroism."

"You are roasting me."

"At all events, your head will not take any more cracks over it, let alone your spinal column."

"It is very true that I have a headache always on call, or on *tap* if you like and have only to move my neck so—ah, devil take it!"

He went away, and I set myself to the task of recording our adventure. I had been sitting at my writing-flap and idling with my pen, when the angle of the deck beneath my chair began to change. Since for days together we had made a dreary series of zigzags, or legs or beats or whatever the appropriate Tarpaulin is, I thought nothing of this at first. But then my posteriors (which have become a perfected seaman in their own right) felt the movement to be speedier than usual. Nor were there the usual concomitants of the operation such as boatswains' pipes, adjurations to the duty watch, leathery flapping of feet and the shivering of sails. There was instead a sudden and positive thunder from our canvas which ceased on the instant and with that cessation my perfected seaman informed me that our deck was tilting more and more rapidly, more urgently. I have become a writer; and my first movement was to jam my pen in the holder and cork the ink bottle. By the time I had done this I was dropped against my bunk ... there was noise enough now—shouts, whistles, thumps and crashes—and screams from the next hutch where my onetime inamorata, Zenobia, was screaming in approximate unison with Mr Brocklebank's alleged wife. I scrambled up the deck, contrived to get my door open and went, spiderlike, towards the daylight of the waist.

As they say in practically every travel book I have ever read, what a sight now met my eyes, my blood froze, my hair—and so on. The whole scene was changed beyond recognition. What had been comparatively level planking was now sloped like the pitch of a roof and increasing fast towards the perpendicular. I saw, with the kind of cool reason which stemmed from my own helplessness, that we were lost. We were going over, capsizing. All our sails were bulging the wrong way, all the wrong ropes were taut and all the right ones flogging like the ties of a rick cover come apart in a gale. Our lee bulwarks were nearing the sea. Then there came—not so much from "up there" as "out there"— a slow grinding and tearing and splintering. Somewhere forrard, the huge beams that look so small and are called "topmasts" swung sideways and hung down in a positive knitting of ropes and torn canvas. On the windward bulwarks there were a few men struggling now with ropes. One, near the break of the fo'castle, I saw striking out with an axe. Above me I saw what I still find difficult to credit: the ship's wheel spun so that the two men holding it were flipped away like raindrops, the one farthest from me into the air and over the wheel to land somewhere on the other side of it, the nearer man flung down against the deck as if struck by lightning. With the spinning of the wheel there came a most dreadful thudding from the rudder. I saw Captain Anderson himself let a rope go from a belaying pin and fling himself recklessly to haul on another ... I got there myself and hauled too. I felt the rope move with our combined strength but—as I am told—the rope he had flung loose was flailing in that area, for I felt a terrible blow on the top of my head and back. I will not subscribe to the commonplace of "From that moment I knew no more" but certainly, what I did know was confused and hazy enough. It seems to me that somehow I became entangled on the deck with young Mr Willis. Apart from the devil of a pain in my back and a loud singing in my head I was almost comfortable. That was Mr Willis, of course, on whom I was lying.

In any other circumstances I would not have chosen or
endured Mr Willis as a mattress, but as it was I felt a positive anger at the ineffectual efforts the boy made to get out
from under me. Then someone pulled at him and in a trice
I had no pillow but a deck I now felt to be level once more.
I opened my eyes and stared up. There were white clouds
and blue sky. There was the mizzenmast, its sails not furled
but bunched up against the yards. Further forrard, part
of the mainmast still stood and with the lower sails also
bunched but with the topmast hanging down in the kind
of tangle for which seamen have a number of expressive
terms. The fore-topmast was down too, but that had fallen
free and lay partly outboard and partly on the fo'castle
across the capstan. I shut my eyes against the light and lay,
waiting for my various pains to subside. I could hear, but
distantly, Captain Anderson giving a continual stream of
orders. I have never understood him so little nor liked him
so well. His voice resounded with calmness and confidence.
Then, believe it or not, there came a moment among a
whole volley or broadside of orders when he paused and
remarked in a more localized and conversational tone of
voice: "Look to Mr Talbot there." What a tribute! Phillips
leaned over me but I was not to be outdone in nobility.

"Let me be, fellow. There must be others in a far worse
case than I."

I am thankful to say that this had no effect on Phillips,
who was endeavouring to insert some relatively soft material between my head and the deck. I felt a little better for
it. The scarlet pulsation behind my forehead faded to pink.

"What the devil happened?"

There was a pause. Then—

"I can't say, sir. Directly we was on an even keel I came
to look for you immediate."

I flexed one leg then the other. They seemed uninjured,
as did my arms. The rope had done no more than scorch

my palms a trifle. It seemed that I had got off from the catastrophe whatever it was with no more than a sore head and a shaking.

"You should be looking to the ladies, Phillips."

He made no reply but inserted yet another fold of material between my head and the deck. I opened my eyes again. The hanging topmast was already being lowered inch by inch. Sailors were crowded among what was left of our rigging. I lifted my head painfully and was just in time to see the broken fore-topmast brought inboard and freed from the capstan. It was splintered and projected a yard or two over the waist. Above me the gaff of the driver had been lowered on its boom. I remembered the towering sails that had bulged over me as she put her bulwarks down till the sea foamed over them.

"What happened?"

"A ship full of fucking soldiers if you don't mind me saying so, sir."

I felt a great disinclination to move my body and did no more than raise my head further to look round. The result was a stab of the most excruciating pain which I have ever experienced—a kind of bright dagger of it thrust through my head. I gave up any further attempt and lay still. Summers and the captain were speaking fluent Tarpaulin with much earnestness. If the gudgeons were not too badly drawn—if she was not too severely wrung. Experimentally I moved my eyes so that I could see the two officers and found the action not accompanied by much pain. I heard what they said. Mr Talbot had most handsomely endeavoured to help the captain at a maincourse buntline until rendered unconscious by a flying sheet. Mr Summers would have expected no less of me. Mr Summers begged to be allowed to continue his duties, which request was granted. I was about to try sitting up when the captain spoke again.

"Mr Willis."

Mr Willis was standing by the abandoned wheel which was turning gently, this way and that. I was about to point out this awful neglect to the captain when two seamen came bounding up the ladder and laid hands on the wheel from either side.

"Mr Willis!"

Normally Mr Willis, one of our midshipmen, is of a pale complexion. Either the blow to my head had confused my eyes or Willis had in reality turned bright green.

"How many times do I have to address you before I get an answer?"

Poor young Willis got his lips together, then opened them. His knees, I believe, were supporting each other.

"Sir."

"You were on watch."

"Sir, Mr, sir, he, Mr—"

"I know all about 'he', Mr Willis. You were on watch."

Nothing emerged from Mr Willis's mouth but a faint clucking. Captain Anderson's right arm swung round and his palm struck the boy's face with a loud crack! He seemed to leap into the air, travel sideways and collapse.

"Get up, sir, when I am talking to you! Do you see those topmasts, you damned young fool? Get up! Have you any idea at all how much canvas has flogged into ribbons, how much hemp there is now good for nothing but stuffing fenders? By God, sir, when we have a mizzen masthead again you shall spend the rest of the commission there!"

"Sir, Mr, Mr—"

"Get him, Willis, do you hear? I want him standing in front of me and I want him *now*!"

I had not thought that so much anger and menace could be expressed in a single syllable. It was Captain Anderson's famous roar, an awful sound, and I felt that to lie still with my new reputation for valour was best. I kept my eyes closed and it was for this reason that I heard the following conversation though I saw neither party to it. There were stumbling steps, then Deverel's voice at once slurred and breathless.

"Damme, what's the boy done now, curse him!"

Anderson answered him angrily but in a low voice as if he did not wish the conversation to be overheard.

"Mr Deverel, you were on watch."

Deverel replied in as low a voice.

"There was young Willis—"

"Young Willis, by God, you fool!"

"I'll not—"

"You'll listen. There's a standing order against leaving a midshipman on watch at sea."

Deverel's voice rose to a sudden shout.

"Everyone does it! How else are the brats to learn?"

"So the officer of the watch can sneak off and swill himself into a wardroom stupor! I got on deck while she was still shivering and by God you weren't there! You come stumbling, you, you sot—"

"I'll not be called that by you or any man! I'll see you—"

Anderson raised his voice.

"Lieutenant Deverel. Your absence from the deck when you were on duty was criminal neglect. You may consider yourself under open arrest."

"Then sod you, Anderson, you sodding by-blow!"

There was a pause in which I did not dare even to breathe. Anderson spoke coldly.

"And, Mr Deverel, you are forbidden drink."

Phillips and Hawkins, the captain's servant, got me back to my bunk. I feigned as much unconsciousness as I could from policy. There must now be, I thought, a court-martial and I wanted to be no part of it as witness or anything else. I allowed myself to be revived with brandy, then grasped Phillips's sleeve to detain him.

"Phillips. Does my back bleed?"

"Not as I've seen, sir—"

"I was struck over the head and shoulders with a flying rope and rendered wholly unconscious. I feel cut to the very bone."

"Oh," said he, with great cheerfulness, "you was struck with a rope's end—what we call a starter, sir. It's what the last man down gets across his back or his bum, begging your pardon, sir. That don't hardly more than bruise, sir."

"What happened to us?"

"When, sir?"

"The accident, man, our broken masts—my aching head!"

So Phillips told me.

Taken aback. I was taken aback, thou wast, he, she or it was taken aback. I remember my lady mother telling her woman—"but when I heard what the creature wanted for a yard of the stuff, exquisite though it was, I declare to you, Forbes, I was quite taken aback!" That, from my dear mother who allowed me to travel on the Continent during the late peace but cautioned me against going too near the fence round the vessel! What a language is ours, how diverse, how direct in indirection, how completely, and, as it were, unconsciously metaphorical! I was reminded of my years of turning English verse into Latin or Greek and the necessity of finding some plain statement which would convey the sense of what the English poet had wrapped in the brilliant obscuration of figures! Of all human activities how we have chosen time and again to turn to our experience of the sea! To be three sheets in the wind, to sail too near the wind, to recognize someone by the cut of his jib, to be brought up all standing, to be adrift, to be on the rocks, to be half-seas over, to be sunk without trace—good Lord, we might fill a book with the effect on our language of the sea affair! Now here was metaphor come across at its origin. We, our ship, had been taken flat aback! Lying in my bunk I pictured it all. Deverel had nipped below for a dram, leaving the half-witted Willis in charge of the ship. Good God, as I thought of it my head throbbed anew. My country, said I to myself as I tried to attain to a state of good humour—my country might have suffered a notable deprivation. I might have drowned! So, with Willis on watch there had come a change, a confusion of the waves on the leeward bow, some foam, a squall, the water cuffed rapidly with two invisible hands that came even more rapidly nearer—those two fellows at the wheel would glance from the shivering leach of the main to the compass—glance round perhaps for Deverel and find only Willis with his mouth hanging open—would look for authority and find none—had they borne down on the wheel and brought her bows round to meet the squall they might fear flogging for it—so they did nothing because Willis did nothing and the squall struck into the wrong side of our sails which being sheeted home stopped her dead, then bore her back and down, sails bellied the wrong way, bulwarks forced down till the sea lipped over them, our rudder working in reverse!

So, while the crew laboured to undo the work which Deverel and Willis had achieved between them by a few seconds' inattention, I lay and waited for the throbbing in my head to cease which it partly did at length but only when I had got to sleep. The last thing I remember thinking before I slept was what a wealth of unexpected experience had come to me through that simple phrase "taken aback!"

(3)

But strangely, once in my bunk I felt myself compelled to stay there and that not just for an hour or two but days and nights. Summers sometimes brought me news of our state. We were now being borne back with an awful inevitability into the doldrums again: for if our vessel when fully rigged could make little way against the wind, in her crippled state she was helpless. Nor could we hope to set the same full sails as before. Our foremast was found to be sprung, said Summers. And the reduction in sail area was more than equal to the improvement made by the scrubbing he was now able to give to that fringe of weed all round us at the waterline. It was another of those metaphors perhaps, a "set back". Three more days passed before I was able to get up for more than the most necessary of purposes. It was a tottering Edmund who at last made his way into the waist. We were, I found at once, back in a wilderness of heat, stillness and mist. Our very bowsprit was out of sight and if I was able to see the tops of our masts it was only because they were now lower than before. The setting up of new topmasts, as Summers assured me, was a business which was taxing the resources of the ship both in timber and muscle power. Meantime we were helpless.

The fourth day, however, saw me more nearly recovered, and we soon had affairs that put all thought of soreness out of my head. I was awakened by Phillips and grunted him away even after I had heard him pour the water into my canvas basin. The air was close and seemed as humid and tepid as the water. As I rose more nearly to the surface of awareness I sadly recalled the wettest and greyest days of winter—rain, hail, snow, sleet—anything but this idling and crowded monotony! I was, not to put too fine a point on it, searching in my mind for any good reason why I should get out of my bunk at all when I heard a distant cry. I could not distinguish the words but they did not seem to come from the level of the deck. Moreover, that cry was followed by a shouted hail from nearly over my head, and another distant reply to it. I heard a rumbling roar from the quarterdeck which could only be Anderson himself, in his customary mood of belligerent admonition. Clearly there was a change in our circumstances and it could only be for the better. Wind, perhaps! I got myself out of my bunk with some effort and I was already in shirt and pantaloons when I heard a most extraordinary hubbub from the passengers all crowding through the lobby. I had eased myself into my coat when, with only the most cursory of taps, Deverel flung the door of my hutch open. But this was no longer the stiff and remote man consumed inwardly by the fires of his own shame and resentment! His eyes sparkled, his face, his whole bearing bespoke pleasure and animation. I saw to my astonishment that he held his scabbarded sword in his left hand.

"Talbot, old fellow! By God, Talbot! I have a way out of my difficulties! Come with me!"

"I was about to go on deck. But what is it?"

"Why, man, did you not hear? A sail!"

"The devil! Let us hope she is one of ours!"

"Where is your spirit, man? They spied her royals and they are white as a lady's kerchief! She is an enemy, depend on it!"

"Summers promised us the French were quite beat down—"

"Oh, that! Why, did you expect a fleet action? But a single ship—Boney may have sent a flyer to intercept us—but Frog, damned Yankee, Dutchman is all one—a bloody battle pays all debts—lucky at women and war, that's your honourable John!"

"This may advance your career, Deverel, and I am happy for you—but as for me—the devil take all Frenchmen!"

Deverel had not waited for my last words and I must own they were not in the heroic vein. But freshly out of my bunk and hardly healed of a sore head—a man who could immediately act the hero at such a moment would be a veritable Nelson. However, I recollected myself and made my way into the waist. Our passengers were grouped, or I might say huddled, against the break of the quarterdeck. The emigrants were similarly huddled against the break of the fo'castle. The silence was complete in our universe which the mist reduced to no more than a portion of our ship. Summers stood on the quarterdeck with Cumbershum. Captain Anderson was leaning over the rail of the poop and listening to Cumbershum who was speaking in what for him were moderate tones.

"The man is a fool, sir, and cannot properly indicate a bearing. I have sent Mr Taylor aloft with instructions to say nothing but point at her if he should get a glimpse."

"She gave no indication of having seen us?"

"No, sir. But with two topmasts down there is some chance of us avoiding her."

"Avoiding her, Mr Cumbershum? I do not like that word 'avoiding'. I shall not avoid her, sir. If we should come together and she is an enemy, I shall fight."

"Of course, sir."

"Mr Summers—we have six great guns on either beam. Can we man them all with seasoned men?"

"No sir. Hardly one side, in fact, not with the boats in the water at stem and stern and parties on deck to repel boarders. I am having the nets brought up now, sir. But for the rest—Mr Taylor is signalling."

Mr Taylor was visible above us in the mist. He clung to

a quite indescribable jumble at the top of the mainmast. Captain Anderson peered into the binnacle.

"Southeast I think."

"With respect, sir, from here Mr Taylor appears to be pointing more to the east."

"Boats in the water, Mr Summers. Then bring her round. I think we might prolong our period of preparation by towing away nor'west."

"Debatable, sir."

"The merest cat's paw could throw all. No, Mr Summers. Bring her round."

"Aye aye, sir. Mr Deverel—"

The orders followed thick and fast. I could not follow the tenth of them. I heard the ladies instructed as to the way down to the orlop deck and told they must retire there immediately if so commanded. They seemed to be quite extraordinarily composed. Miss Granham looked capable of repelling boarders with her expression. Mr Prettiman, for an avowed Republican if not Jacobin, had an air of indignant truculence which might stem from sheer wonder as to what his attitude should be. Had I not been depressed and irritated by this possibly quick termination to the career of Edmund Talbot, I should have liked to put the question to him. But there was no talk among us. We stood dumb, then by common consent drifted back to the passenger saloon where there was, I observed with interest, some slight consumption of wine before the meal as well as during it. I endeavoured to put off my own weakness and recurrent pain in order to raise the spirits of the company by declaring that since two ships in such an ocean would have difficulty in finding each other intentionally there was absolutely no prospect of us coming together by accident. But if we did, said I, why then we must fight; and I hereby lift my glass in a toast to victory! But never was there a sadder and less martial gathering!

All that happened was that little Pike flung down his knife and fork and burst into tears.

"My children, oh, my children! Little Arabella! Poor Phoebe!"

His wife laid her hand on his shoulder to comfort him. I spoke to him bluffly, as man to man.

"Come, Pike, never fear, man! We are in this together and shall give a good account of ourselves! As for your little girls, be easy—they are far too young for the French!"

I must own that this last remark was unfortunate in its implication. Mrs Pike burst into noisy sobs. Zenobia and Mrs Brocklebank shrieked in unison. Miss Granham laid down her knife and fork and fixed me with eyes of stone.

"Mr Talbot," she said. "You have excelled yourself."

"I only mean—"

But Prettiman was speaking.

"Do not believe the stories that are so current concerning the behaviour of the French, sir. They are as civilized as we. We may expect to be treated with the same and indeed more generosity and liberality than we should treat them!"

"Are we to stand about and be herded like sheep? Mr Bowles, you have some experience in the law, I believe."

"A solicitor's clerk, sir."

"May we civilians not fight?"

"I had considered the matter. I believe we passengers may 'run up a gun', as it is called, which entails hauling on a rope. We could plead compulsion. But seen on deck with sword and pistol in hand and we are legally entitled to have our throats cut."

"You are matter-of-fact," said I. "You might even be called cold-blooded."

"There is a way out of it, sir. I have considered that too. Passengers could volunteer, be sworn in, be entered on the ship's books, as it is called. I am not certain what the situation would be over naval pay in that event."

Nevertheless, I observed that his hands were quivering slightly. "A glass of wine with you, Mr Bowles! You show us all where our duty lies."

Miss Granham was pleased to smile her Minerva's moonlit smile on me.

"A noble resolve, Mr Talbot. I am sure I speak for the ladies in saying that we are all much easier in our minds for it."

There were noises of agreement and some laughter. But then her fiancé, the comic Prettiman, cried out above it with the passionate voice which often rises from his involvement with the philosophy of government.

"No, no, no! With respect, Miss Granham—Mr Talbot, how can you volunteer before you know what enemy we face? Suppose that ship to be no cruel emissary of a tyrant but one that has thrown off his yoke and now serves the land of liberty itself? Suppose she is from the United States of America?"

"What does that matter?" said I. "We are at war with America!"

That stopped the philosopher with his mouth still open and there was a babble of argument.

"Will you volunteer, Mr Bowles?"

"On terms, Mr Talbot."

"I must own to finding the prospect of engaging with a Yankee ship less exhilarating than battle with the French. After all, the Yankees are our own men—what the devil! That confounded rascal Paul Jones had more British seamen in his ship than American!"

"And the Dutch?"

"Let them all come. We shall make a notable defence. You, Mr Bowles, will shed any blood provided the agreement is precise. Mr Prettiman will aid us against the French or Dutch or pirates or even slavers though he will spare any American who should be rash enough to come in his way."

There was, as I had hoped, renewed laughter at this. But it was interrupted from a most unexpected source. Little Pike leapt to his feet and positively bawled at me as if he had fallen into the hysterics.

"How can you joke so? What does it matter what ship is out there hidden in the mist except that she has guns and may shoot them at us? I will fight as well as any man here whatever his degree. But I will not fight for my country! I am leaving it! I will not fight for my ship or my king or my captain. But I will fight against any ship and any country in the world in defence of my, my family—"

He burst into noisy sobs which were only too audible in the silence which had fallen as he spoke. Miss Granham stretched out a hand to him, then took it back again. Mrs Pike pressed his hand against her cheek. He sat down and his sobs died away but slowly. I believe most people had their eyes fixed on their plates at this most un-English display of emotion. I thought it high time we came down from our flights of martial fancy and hysterics. Exhausted as I was, I felt it my duty to persevere.

"Come," said I. "Let us consider the situation. There may be a ship, her sails seen for a few seconds in the mist. Most likely she is not concerned with us. Most likely she has not seen us. After all, our topmasts are down. If she sees us—why, we are a Royal Navy ship of the line to all appearances, the most feared, the most fearful of all the engines of destruction in this modern century! Believe me, the chances of an engagement are remote. If I myself have seemed thoughtlessly exhilarated by the prospect of battle, I beg the pardon of those of our company who are responsible for more lives than their own. But depend upon it. A thousand to one we shall neither meet nor see that ship again."

"I fear it is not so."

I looked up, startled, my head again stabbed with a dagger of pain. Summers stood just inside the door, hat in hand.

"Ladies and gentlemen, for all Mr Talbot's laudable efforts to calm your natural apprehensions, I fear it is not so. That ship, whatever she is, is becalmed as we are. In a prolonged calm, I mean of days or even weeks, ships are drawn together by the mutual attraction of heavy objects when nothing holds them apart but a smooth and readily divided fluid. If the wind does not get up we shall be drawn together until we lie side by side."

Now the silence was deadly.

"Charles, I do not find this credible."

"It is true, nevertheless. Captain Anderson believes that you are better able to conduct yourselves with propriety if the plain facts are laid before you. We have as you know sighted, or rather glimpsed, a ship which may or may not have sighted us. She may be French, sent to intercept us—"

Brocklebank interrupted him.

"How the devil would they know?"

Summers looked at me.

"Depend upon it," said I, "their Ministry of Marine will know as much about us as we do!"

"The French then," said Bowles. "Boney must have designs of conquest on the Antipodes!"

"He's too busy in Russia for that," said I. "What about the Yankees, Charles?"

"All we are sure of is that those white sails cannot be British."

"What are we to do then? The gentlemen here have engaged themselves to help you in what way they can."

Summers smiled.

"I expected no less and will provide you all with suitable employment. Mr Askew, the gunner, is rigging some very pretty fireworks with quick match and small parcels of gunpowder. Together with our few great guns they may give the appearance of a full broadside from the engaged side of our ship provided the enemy sees us dimly through the mist. We must hope that one thump will make him tow off, for we must look ugly enough."

"But if she see us only dimly through the mist? And darkness is falling!"

"How will she know we are an enemy? She will burn recognition lights and wait for our answer. If her lights do not appear in our secret list we shall answer with our broadside."

"And then?"

"One broadside and Captain Anderson can never be accused of giving up the ship without a fight."

"The devil he cannot!"

"Be easy, Edmund. We are a ship of His Majesty's Navy and shall do what we may."

He smiled round at everyone, put on his hat and withdrew. Little Pike, his sobs assuaged, positively snarled across the table at me.

"So much for your attempt at heartening us, Mr Talbot!"

"Summers has gone a better way about it. I have no sword. Have you a sword, Bowles?"

"I? Good God no, sir. The ship will have a supply, I don't doubt. They will be cutlasses perhaps."

"Mr Brocklebank, you are, forgive me, of a full habit. Will you descend with the ladies?"

"I have an inclination to remain on deck, sir. After all, though I have on numerous occasions depicted the war at sea, I have never before had an opportunity of taking notes in the midst of a battle. You will see me, sir, when the shot is flying, seated on my camp stool and observing with a trained eye whatever is worthy of notice. To take an example, I have often enquired of military men—I include naval in the term military—have often enquired precisely how a cannon ball in flight is visible to the naked eye. Obviously the more nearly the ball is flying directly towards the observer the more slowly it will appear to move. We could not be better situated for the observation. I only hope darkness is not too far advanced before we are engaged."

"On your reckoning, sir, the most accurate idea of a cannon ball is to be formed by the man who has his head knocked off by it."

"If it comes, why it comes. 'Ripeness is all'—indeed if I may refer to my own case, overripeness is all. What is life, sir? A voyage where no one, despite all claims to the contrary—we know not what if you follow me—"

It was clear that Mr Brocklebank was approaching his customary state of inebriety. I stood up therefore and bowed to the company. The oddest thought had come to me. I might in actual fact be killed! I had only now realized it which may seem strange to anyone who has not been in a like case. Or say I had realized it and not realized it. But now the knowledge was—oppressive.

"I must ask the company to excuse me. I have letters to write."

(4)

It was a confusion of my mental state that led me to say
something as simple as that when in fact my abrupt
departure needed an elaborate explanation if I had hoped
to be understood. The truth was that all the excitement
attendant on our sighting of a strange ship had made my
head begin to ache even more than it had previously, from
the blow with that flying sheet. I had now foreseen a danger to my reputation and was confusedly determined to
forestall it. If this acute discomfort in my skull was
allowed to increase or even remain as it was I would be in
no state to face an enemy! Imagine me, among the gentlemen volunteers whining that I would like to take part in
our defence but was quite incapacitated by a migraine and
must join the ladies in the orlop! I got Phillips to bring me
something for an aching head and took it in my bunk
where to my astonishment I found it was yet more of the
purser's paregoric so that though mercifully I stopped
myself from swigging the lot when I found what it was,
my first sip was enough to put the ache in my head about
six inches outside it and up to the left as I should judge.
It produced in me too a desire and ability to dwell with
Fancy and in a few minutes I found myself composing
(but in my head and bunk) letters to my mother and
father and even to my young brothers which I still think
were pieces of prose with a noble ring about them. But the
most natural and at the same time most dangerous effect
of the drug was (with an enemy hovering ever nearer us in
the mist) to send me fast asleep! I woke with a start from
an unpleasant dream in which poor Colley in a supernat-
ural way only too familiar in that state had summoned the

enemy and was bringing it hourly nearer. I fell out of my
bunk rather than climbed out of it, my headache subdued
but my confusion complete. I rushed into the waist. At
first I thought the mist was enfolding us more closely but
then saw it was the swift approach of the tropic night. Our
ladies were grouped by the break of the quarterdeck
where I suppose they might most immediately descend to
the orlop. They were staring towards the larboard beam.
Above them, on the quarterdeck, some of Oldmeadow's
soldiers were mustered with the officer himself. Forrard,
I could make out in the gloom, parties mustered on the
fo'castle. The emigrant women were gathered at its break.
All was deep silence.

Deverel came striding aft at the head of a group of emigrants. His shoes made the only sound in the ship. He was
in a state of high if suppressed excitement. He carried his
scabbarded sword in his left hand. He was shivering
slightly.

"Why, Edmund! I thought you was mustered at the
guns!"

"Devil take it, I fell asleep."

He laughed aloud.

"That's cool! Well done, old fellow—but the others are
all gone down. Good luck to you!"

"To you too—"

"Oh, I—why just now I would give my right arm for a
bloody battle!"

He passed on, bounding up the ladder to the poop.
I made my way down the contrary one to the cluttered
gundeck.

Here at once a most unfortunate fact became plain. I was
too tall for the gundeck. It had been designed for a company
of dwarfs, miners perhaps, and I could not stand upright in
it. I waited therefore to be directed. The gundeck was not
much dimmer than the upper deck, for all the ports were

open. Our six great guns were in position but their tackles not yet run up. There was a crowd round them but facing inboard where our commissioned gunner, Mr Askew, was pacing up and down as he addressed the company. He wore a belt with two pistols stuck in it.

"Now pay attention," he said, "particularly those what have never seen this done before. You have now seen the guns loaded and primed. Should we need to have a reload you will leave it to them that knows the business. You gentlemen and emigrants will lay your hands to such ropes as the captains of guns may direct and when he says 'Haul!' "—and here Mr Askew's voice rose to what can only be called a suppressed roar—"you will haul till your guts fall out. I want to see your guts strung out there and there and there and there and there and there! And you will be silent the first time you run up the guns because Mr Summers has directed us to be as quiet as little mice so as the Frogs don't know we are coming. So"—and his voice sank to a whisper—"when you have run the guns out silent you will pick your guts up, put 'em back, and stand waiting. If we should open fire you will see them gun trucks run back so fast you can't see 'em move! I have seen gun trucks there and I have seen gun trucks back there but I have never seen 'em halfway, gentlemen, they moves so quick. So you better not be lounging behind them or the Frogs when they come aboard of us will think you are what they calls *confiture*. Jam, gentlemen. Jam."

Little Pike put up his hand as if he were still at school.

"Won't the enemy be firing by then?"

"How do I know, sir, and what do we care? When fire is opened things is different, oh, you have no idea, sir, how different things is! It's very queer how different things is once a gun has been fired as they say in anger. So then you have the full permission of His Majesty the King, God bless him, to shout and yell and swear and shit yourselves and do what you like so long as it's noisy and you haul your guts in and out when told to."

"Good God."

Mr Askew resumed in a conversational tone.

"It's all flannel, of course. The Frogs don't scare so easy as you gentlemen may think. Howsomever we must play our game as long as we can. So if we have to fight and if any volunteer should feel that the other side of the ship is cooler like and just a little farther off from the enemy, these two little fire irons in my belt are loaded. So now, my heroes, run up them guns!"

The next few moments for me were complicated and infuriating. The man whom I supposed to be the captain of the nearest gun pointed to the end of a rope which projected behind Bowles who was the hindmost of the four volunteers holding it. I had no sooner crouched close when the captain of the gun roared again, the volunteers leapt and Bowles struck me, cannoned into me so that I reeled two paces then fell, my head once more striking the deck so concussively that the whole world was obscured for a moment by a brilliant display of lights. I struggled to get up and heard, as far off, Mr Askew addressing me.

"Now, now, Mr Talbot, sir, where was you going? Had we been in action I might have been forced to put a pellet in your head, you come so close to the mid-point."

The pain and the sense of having made myself a common mock was too much to bear. I leapt to my feet—and struck my head a second and even more shattering blow on the underside of the upper deck. This time I saw no lights and knew nothing until through a dizzying sickness I heard roaring laughter being shouted down by Mr Askew.

"Now then, you buggers, belay that and stand to! That was a hard knock the poor gentleman took and as stout a heart and head as there is in the ship I don't doubt. God knows how much the beams is wounded on their underside.

Half the deck planking must be started. Silence I said! How is it with you now, sir?"

I am sorry to say my only reply was a rehearsal of all the imprecations I could muster. Blood was trickling down my face. I sat up and the gunner held my arm.

"Easy does it, Mr Talbot. The gundeck is no place for you. Why, with Billy Rogers and Mr Oldmeadow you must be the three tallest men in the ship. You'll do better on deck, sir, where the Frogs can get an eyeful of you all bloody and glaring. Keep low as you go, sir. Handsomely! A round of applause, my lads, for a gamecock of the afterguard!"

I did not know that fury could overcome dizziness and sickness so soon. I staggered up the ladder. The first person—by his voice—to notice me was Deverel.

"What the devil? Edmund old fellow! You are our first casualty!"

"I am too tall for the gundeck, God curse it! Where are the ladies?"

"Down in the orlop."

"Thank God for that at least. Deverel, give me a weapon—anything!"

"Have you not had enough? Where it isn't bloody, your face is corpse white."

"I am coming to. A weapon for the love of God! A meat axe—sledge hammer—anything. I will engage to carve and eat the first Frenchman I come across!"

Deverel laughed aloud, then caught himself up. He was shivering with excitement.

"Spoken like a true Briton! Will you board with me?"

"Anything."

"Mr Summers, sir, a weapon for my latest recruit!"

Someone put a cutlass in his free hand. He tossed it, caught the blade and presented the hilt to me.

"Here you are, sir. The plain seaman's guide to advancement. Can you use it?"

For answer I made the three sabre cuts then saluted him. He saluted back.

"Well enough, Edmund. But the point is queen, remember. Join the band of brothers!"

I followed him to the poop where Mr Brocklebank sat in the gloom on his camp stool, an unopened portfolio on his knees. His head was on his chest or perhaps I should say the upper part of his stomach. His hat was over his eyes. On the quarterdeck the captain was now addressing Summers in a low and furious tone.

"Is this the silence I ordered, Mr Summers? Did I give you directions at the top of my voice? I command silence and am answered by a gale, a positive hurricane of laughter, orders shouted, conversations—is this a ship, sir, or a bedlam?"

"I am sorry for it, sir."

Old Rumbleguts subsided a little.

"Very well, sir. You may proceed with your duties."

Summers put his hat on and turned away. Captain Anderson went to the rail and peered down at the lighted binnacle.

"Mr Summers, she has drifted off half a point to the norrard."

Summers ran to the after rail and spoke down to the boat idling under our stern.

"Williams, bring her stern across half a point to starboard and roundly!"

He turned back. My eyes were full of water. I was still dazed and my head ached confoundedly. A settled rage had converted me from any, dare I say, usual calculating attitude to one of wishing for nothing so much as the opportunity to vent it on someone physically! I glanced round and saw that the quarterdeck was full. Some of Oldmeadow's men knelt by the larboard rail with muskets at the ready. I could just see that the waist was lined with men holding pikes to jab off any fool so thick-witted as to climb into our netting. In fact the whole of the ship's length on the larboard side was in a state of defence. I had the ridiculous thought that perhaps the nameless ship drifting inexorably towards us would after all approach from our starboard and completely defenceless side so that Captain Anderson would have to fire his great guns at nothing if he wished to be credited with an attempt at defence.

But Deverel was speaking or rather, since we were so near the captain, muttering in my ear.

"Now, old fellow, you'll follow me close. You'll have to scramble, d'you see? Wait till Oldmeadow's men have fired though or you'll get lead through you. Don't forget your boots."

"My boots, Jack?"

"Kick 'em in the balls, it's as good as anything. Mind your own. Go low with the point! But it'll be all over in seconds one way or another. Nobody goes on fighting—that's only in books and the gazette."

"The devil."

"If you're alive after one minute you'll be a hero."

"The devil."

He turned from me as he spoke and whispered into the crowding men.

"Are you all ready?"

The answer was a kind of muted growl and with it there blew a thick waft of an aroma that came near to making me fall. It was rum and I made a mental note never to go into the commonest kind of danger without my hunting flask filled to the stopper. I was far, far too sober for this escapade, and the dullness of paregoric was fading.

"How d'you think it'll go, Jack?"

He breathed in my ear. "Death or victory."

I heard Summers speaking to the captain. "All is ready, sir."

"Very good, Mr Summers."

"Might I suggest that some heartening message should be passed among the various groups of men at their stations, sir?"

"Why, Mr Summers, they have had their rum!"

"Trafalgar, sir."

"Oh well, Mr Summers, if you think it proper, have them reminded of the unforgettable signal."

"Very good, sir."

"And, Mr Summers."

"Sir?"

"Remind them that with the way the war is going this may well be our last opportunity of prize money."

Mr Summers touched his hat. The men on the quarter-deck clearly being seized of his information, he stepped down the ladder and disappeared in the gloom. I heard a succession of noises, that same muted growl spreading from the waist and then forrard to the fo'castle. Heroics and rum! The thought of that combination made me a little less of a madman and more aware of the silly position I had got myself into. Deverel, I knew, was the proper careless, dashing kind of fellow for such an enterprise. Besides, he was driven by the unquestionable fact that a gallant exploit would get him out of his difficulties. Even Captain Anderson would not be so mean-spirited as to proceed with the trial and punishment of a young officer who had led a desperate boarding party—but I, what had I to gain? All I had was everything to lose!

Then all reflection was banished from my mind. From out there in the darkness of the night and the mist there came the sound of a kind of whispering and multiplying creak. This was followed at once by a series of dull thumps.

Deverel muttered in my ear. "She has run out her guns!"

Silence again—and surely, a faint washing and rippling and splashing, as if some heavy object was being moved bodily sideways through the water, two bodies, two ships, we and they—There had been in Deverel's voice the fierce anticipation of a beast of prey which hears its victim close! But I—all at once I was vividly aware that out there in the darkness the round muzzles of guns were pointed at me! I could not breathe. Then instantly I was blinded by a brilliant flash, not the dagger in my head, but out there in the darkness: and the flash was followed, no, surrounded, by the awful explosion of the gun—a kind of wide roar with a needle-point of instantaneity in it. The roar was like no peacetime salute. It rebounded awesomely from the very sky in a brazen replication which set me jerking and shuddering with excitement. The cutlass fell from my hand and must have clattered on the deck though I heard nothing through the sound of blood beating in my head. I scrabbled after the hilt but my right hand was frozen and would not open to pick it up or close on the grip. I had to use both hands, then staggered up again.

Captain Anderson was speaking and apparently addressing the sky.

"Aloft there!"

Young Mr Taylor answered from the rigging.

"All ready, sir. She missed us, sir."

"That was a signal gun, you young fool!"

"Signal gun," muttered Deverel, "that's just what the Frogs would do to make us show ourselves. There's still hope of a battle, my lads! Here she comes!"

Before my eyes the green after-image of the explosion was fading. I stared where Deverel was pointing with his sword. Like hills appearing through mists, or—but I cannot find a comparison. Like anything, the appearance of which is doubtful and gradual then suddenly and unquestionably *there*, the dark bulk of a huge vessel came into view. She was broadside on to us. Good God, I thought, and my knees trembled for all I could do—she is the same rate as *L'Orient*, 120 guns!

Then high up in her rigging, sparks appeared. Directly after, the sparks took fire, became three dazzling lights, two white lights with a red light between them. The lights danced and glared and smoked and spilled down drops and sparks that joined their own reflections in the water. I heard Taylor shouting something, then above my head but outboard there was an answering dazzle—two white lights and a blue one! A cascade of drops fell before me like blazing rain. I saw Deverel staring up from one set of lights to the other. His mouth was open, his eyes wide, face gaunt in the glare. Then with a shouted or perhaps screamed stream of imprecations, he struck his sword inches deep into our rail! Captain Anderson had been using a speaking trumpet but I had not heard what he said. A voice spoke from the other ship, a hollow voice through a speaking trumpet so that it seemed the man hung among the brilliant rain from all the lights.

"His Majesty's frigate *Alcyone*, Captain Sir Henry Somerset, twenty-seven days out of Plymouth."

Deverel's sword remained fast in the rail. The poor fellow himself stood by it, his face in his hands. The isolated voice through the speaking trumpet went on.

"News, Captain Anderson, for you and your whole ship's company. The war with the French is over. Boney is beat and abdicated. He is to be King of Elba. God save our gracious King and God save His Most Christian Majesty, King Lewis of France, the eighteenth of that name!"

(5)

The roar that followed these words was almost as extraordinary as the sound of the cannon shot! I saw Captain Anderson swing round and aim his speaking trumpet down into the waist but he might as well have had no voice.

Our ship was all filled with moving, and, yes, capering figures. Here and there lights were appearing as by magic though the signal flares had dropped one by one into the sea. Men were carrying lanterns up into the rigging of our ship. Someone was drawing the screens from our great stern lanterns. For the first time in my experience the poop and quarterdeck were irradiated by the powerful light of their oil lamps. *Alcyone* was moving closer and strangely enough was becoming smaller as she came. I saw that she was much of our length, though somewhat lower in the water. Summers was standing on our fo'castle and his mouth was opening and shutting but no sound could be heard. There was a petty officer or boatswain or the like roaring his head off with commands about ropes and fenders while an anonymous voice— could it be Billy Rogers?—was shouting for three times three so that huzzahs resounded endlessly to be answered from the deck of *Alcyone*! Now she was so close that I could distinguish beards and bald heads, black, brown, white faces, eyes and open mouths and grins by the hundred. It *was* a bedlam, and I, with light and noise and news near enough as mad as the others!

Then I knew that this was no conceit and I was mad indeed. Before ever a gangway was securely in place between the two ships, a man climbed up cleverly from her bulwark to ours. He was, he must be an hallucination!

For it was Wheeler, that sly servant who had been lost overboard and drowned many days before—Wheeler who knew so much and contrived so much! It was the man himself, his once pale face blotched with the wounds of too much salt and sun, those two puffs of white hair still standing out on either side of his baldness. Now he was speaking to Summers and now he was turning, walking towards the quarterdeck where I still stood.

"Wheeler! Curse it, you was drowned!"

A strong convulsion shook the man. He said nothing, however, but stared at the cutlass in my right hand.

"Drowned! What the devil!"

"Allow me, sir."

He took the cutlass out of my hand with a slight inclination of the head.

"But, Wheeler! This is—"

Once more, that convulsion.

"The life was too strong in me, sir. You are wounded, sir. I will bring water to your cabin."

I was suddenly aware that my feet had been stuck in the same place and position for an age. It seemed they were embedded in the deck. My right hand was creased with the imprint of a hilt. My head, I discovered, was in a fearful state of pain and confusion. I was suddenly aware of what a figure I must present before so many new people and I hurried away to make myself as neat as possible. Peering into my small mirror I saw my face was indeed bloody and my hair matted. Wheeler brought water.

"Wheeler! You are a ghost. You were drowned, I said!"

Wheeler turned from the canvas basin into which he had poured a can of cold water. His gaze reached my neck but came no further.

"Yes, sir. But only after three days, sir. I believe it was three days. But you are right, of course, sir. Then I drowned."

My hair prickled. His eyes rose now to meet mine. They never blinked.

"I drowned, sir. I did—and the life in me so strong!"

Really, it was disconcerting and disturbing to be talked at so. Besides, the man needed calming.

"Well, Wheeler, you are a lucky dog. You was picked up and there's an end to it. Tell Bates I shall no longer require his services."

Wheeler paused. He opened his mouth and for a moment I thought he had some more to say, but he closed it again, bowed slightly and withdrew. I stripped to my shirtsleeves and washed as much blood as possible from my face and hands. When I had done I collapsed in my canvas chair, exhausted. It was becoming evident that I must pass this strange time in a wounded state where all was like a dream. I tried to realize what the news meant and could not. The war—except for the brief and deceitful peace of the year '08—had been the only state I knew. Now the war was gone, the state changed and I could not fill emptiness with anything which had meaning. I tried to think of a Louis XVIII on the throne of France and could not. I tried to think of all the glories of the ancient regime—now surely to be called the modern regime!—and found that I could not believe they would ever come again; common sense, a *political awareness* would not suffer it! The state of the world was too changed by catastrophes—the state of France, the ruin of her great families, a generation exposed first to the seduction of an impossible liberty and equality, then to the hardships imposed by tyranny, poverty and the draining of her conscripted blood—it would be a sad world which our people were greeting so noisily, that was my unwilling thought. But my head still rang with noises of its own; and though no man could think of sleep at such a moment I did not know if my strength was sufficient for the ordeal of our rejoicing! I tried once more to realize the fact—a turning point in history, one of the world's great occasions, we stood on a watershed and so on—but it was no use. My head became the arena of confused images and thoughts. A full shot garland such as the one I had crouched by on the gundeck seemed emblem of all the millions of tons of old iron lying about in corners of the civilized world—now never to be used, rusting cannon which would do for rubbing posts, muskets and musket balls sold as curios, swords, my famous cutlass—there seemed in my head no end to iron and lead. Then the ships newly built but now never to be launched!

I must own to a most eccentric feeling in the circumstances. It was one of fear. For a moment the reality of the situation did at last penetrate to my confused awareness. The fear was not a gross, common fright such as had rooted my feet to the deck when I heard as I thought my first shot fired in anger, but wider, almost a universal fright at the prospect of peace! The peoples of Europe and our own country were now set free from the simple and understandable duty of fighting for their king and country. It was an extension of that liberty which had already turned ordered societies into pictures of chaos. I told myself that one of the "political branch" should welcome this since affairs were now no longer put to the mortal arbitrament of swords. It was the politician's turn, our turn, my turn! But the moment of realization had passed and my head was all confusion again. The fact is that, for a while, I believe I wept.

But I could hear our ladies laughing and chattering as they passed by my door and issued into the waist. I even heard Miss Granham exclaim in a high voice: "And the skirt quite, quite beyond cleaning or repair!" It was time I emerged. I went into the waist, which was now full of light and people busy rather than hysterical with rejoicing. Our two ships were now fastened together by cables and though

Alcyone was lower than we, it was no more than by the height of a deck. The whole area of our little world had expanded. There were so many new people! Good God, the Emperor of China had no more crowded and confused a country! But our "tumblehome" and theirs kept the people a few feet apart. Our officers were in a state of grave displeasure with the people: and the petty officers for the first time in my experience were using their "starters" in earnest. It was, of course, the prospect of a release from the discipline of the service coupled with those minutes of complete indiscipline which had done the damage! I reminded myself, selfishly enough I fear, that we could now hang up our arms and let common sense take charge. I climbed to the quarterdeck and then to the poop. Captain Anderson was standing by the larboard rail, hat in hand. Sir Henry Somerset, a gentleman of a full habit and a somewhat florid complexion, was perched in the mizzen shrouds of *Alcyone* so that he and our captain were at an equal height. Sir Henry had one foot on each of two rungs, sat on the third, held the fourth with his right hand and his hat in the left. He was speaking.

"—bound for India with utmost dispatch and may arrive there with the news just in time to prevent a very pretty battle! Devil take it, sir, if I succeed I shall be the most unpopular man east of Suez!"

"What of the Navy, sir?"

"Oh, Lord, sir, not a day passes but the order comes down to lay up another dozen ships or so. The streets are full of seamen waiting to be paid and begging. I never knew we had so many rascals in our ships! We are well out of it together, sir. But that's peace for you, curse it. Who is this gentleman?"

Captain Anderson, his hand on the rail where Deverel's sword had almost divided it, introduced me. He mentioned my godfather and his brother and my prospective employment. Sir Henry was affable. He hoped to further our acquaintance and to present me to Lady Somerset. Captain Anderson interrupted our exchange of courtesies with his customary lack of *savoir-faire*. He hoped until we got a wind to have the pleasure of Sir Henry and Lady Somerset's company. But now the people, or his people at least, should be brought up smartly with a round turn and a couple of half-hitches. Meanwhile—

Sir Henry agreed, letting himself down the shrouds with the casual dexterity of an old seaman, and went to address an officer on his deck.

Captain Anderson vented his roar. "Mr Summers!"

Poor Summers came running aft like a midshipman. In the glare of the lights from both ships I could see that his usually composed face was flushed and sweating. He thrust this man and that out of the way in his attempt to obey the captain's summons. I thought it undignified and unworthy of him.

"Mr Summers, the men are breaking ship!"

"I know it, sir, and am doing my best."

"You had best do better! Look at that—and that! Devil take it, man—we shall be robbed like a hen roost!"

"Their rejoicing, sir—"

"Rejoicing? This is plunder! You may say the last man out of *Alcyone* shall be strapped with a dozen and I promise the like from Sir Henry!"

Summers saluted and ran off again. Anderson aimed a grimace at me with a bit of tooth in the middle, then set himself to stump up and down the larboard side of the quarterdeck, hands behind his back, sour face staring this way and that. Once he stopped by the forrard rail and roared again. Summers answered him from the fo'castle but, unlike the captain, used a speaking trumpet.

"Mr Askew has taken in the packets of powder, sir, and had the quick match stowed. He is now drawing the shot."

Captain Anderson nodded and resumed his unaccustomedly swift stumping up and down. He ignored me and I thought it best to withdraw. By the time I got to the waist I understood some at least of our moody captain's concern. There was too free laughter among the people. It was evident that some of them by means unknown to me, or I think to their officers, had obtained strong drink. The operation of Newton's laws, if that is what it was—what else?—in bringing two ships together that had not intended the encounter was setting the Rigid Navy—my private phrase for the Royal Navy—some problems which were not in the book. For I saw a bottle fly from one ship to the other and disappear among a group of men who were engaged in securing the bridge, or should I say gangway, between the two ships; and though I watched as closely as my ringing head would allow I never saw it emerge from them. It vanished as completely and mysteriously as the cards in the hands of a stage magician. I could not but think that the gangway made the unlawful interchange of our crews even easier than before. But the confusion continued and the way was opened across the gap for social intercourse and thievery. My restlessness seemed endless. For all my buzzing head and the weariness of my limbs I could not endure the thought of my bunk. What, sleep when this hollow space in the hot mists of the tropics was lighted brilliantly as a fairground and as noisy? I remember that in my dazed state I felt it necessary to *do something*, but could not think *what to do*. I thought of drink and ducked into the lobby by my hutch but was almost knocked sprawling by a young fellow who rushed out. Phillips and Wheeler and another man came after him but gave up when they saw me. It did seem to me that a faint aroma, not of rum but of brandy, emanated from Phillips's person. He addressed me breathlessly.

"That bugger was an *Alcyone*, sir. You best keep all locked."

I nodded to him and went immediately to the passenger saloon. Here, who should be present but little Pike, his tears all dried and his chest out like the breast of a pouter pigeon! He trusted at once that I had recovered from my injury, though he believed I looked sadly. He left me no time to reply, however. I had noticed in him normally a marked modesty in the presence of other men, but now there was no quelling him.

"Only think, Mr Talbot, I have served at the guns! Then I stood by the tackle while the charge was drawn."

"My congratulations."

"Oh, it was nothing, of course. All the same—Mr Askew remarked before he dismissed us that a few days of gun drill and he would have turned us out as prime gunners!"

"He did?"

"Why, he said we would be fit to fight all the Frogs in the world let alone the damned Yankees!"

"That was gratifying. Yes, the brandy, Bates. Bates—would you consult Wheeler about leaving a bottle of brandy and a glass in my cabin?"

"Very good, sir."

"A glass of brandy for Mr Pike here."

"Oh no, sir, I could not! I am unaccustomed to brandy, Mr Talbot. It burns my mouth. Ale, if you please, sir."

"You hear, Bates? That will be all."

"Aye aye, sir."

"I was very sorry to see you struck down, Mr Talbot. At the time when you hit your head on the ceiling—I mean the deckhead, as we ought to call it—I had to laugh it seemed so comical though of course it must have been very painful."

"It is."

"But we were so, what shall I say, strung taut as a violin string and the least thing set us off like it used to be in the office, for we were sometimes in the utmost distress not to laugh at Mr Wilkins—and when Mr Askew said you had come so close to the mid-point that—well—"

"I remember, Mr Pike."

"Call me Dick, sir, will you not, though in the office I was called Dicky or even Dickybird—"

"Mr Pike!"

"Sir?"

"I wish to forget the whole lamentable episode. I should be obliged therefore—"

"Oh, of course, sir, if you wish. Why, we were all comical it seemed to Mr Askew. Once I was standing there at the gun with my mouth open I suppose, though I was not conscious of it, but Mr Askew said, 'Now you, Mr Pike, sir, have you swallowed the tompion?' How the others laughed! A tompion, you know, Mr Talbot, is the plug at the end of the—"

"Yes, I do know. The ale is for Mr Pike, Bates."

"Well then, Mr Talbot, confusion to the—oh, we should not say that now, should we? A health to King Louis, then. Dear me, I shall be nigh on half seas over."

"You are still excited, sir."

"Well, I was and I am. It was exciting and it is exciting. Will you not allow me to buy you some brandy?"

"Not now. Presently perhaps."

"Only to think I have stood at a gun! I served at a gun on the, the larboard beam, it would be, would it not?"

"God knows, Mr Pike. The guns as I recollect were about half-way along the left-hand side of the ship as one looks forrard—towards the bow, the front end."

"Mr Pike."

It was Miss Granham. We rose to our feet.

"Mrs Pike asked me to be kind enough to say that she would value your assistance with the twins. They are so excited."

"Of course, ma'am!"

Pike dashed off, carrying his excitement where it might well not be appreciated. As far as I could see, his ale was untasted.

"Pray be seated, ma'am. Allow me. This cushion—"

"I had expected to find my, Mr Prettiman. Phillips was to cut his hair."

It was faintly comical to hear how she shied at the word fiancé. It was faintly human, dare I say, and unexpected.

"I will find him for you, ma'am."

"No, please, no indeed. Be seated, Mr Talbot—I insist—there! Good heavens, your head is wounded indeed! You do not look at all the thing!"

I laughed and winced.

"My skull now contains a large fragment of the ship's deck."

"It is a lacerated contusion."

"Pray, ma'am—"

"But there will be a surgeon aboard Sir Henry's ship, I believe."

"I have taken harder knocks at fisticuffs, ma'am. I beg you pay no attention to it."

"The episode was made to seem a little comical but now I see the result I rebuke myself for being amused by it."

"It seems I covered myself with blood but not glory."

"Not as far as the ladies are concerned, sir. Our initial amusement was soon lost in a positively tearful admiration. It would appear that you came from the guns, your face covered in blood, and immediately volunteered for the most perilous enterprise the mind of man can imagine."

This, of course, was my cutlass—also my two feet that had adhered so firmly to the place they found themselves in when the signal gun went off in the fog! I wondered for a moment in what way to accept the unexpected tribute to my courage. Perhaps it was the equally unexpected and faintly human look in Miss Granham's severe face which determined me in this instance to tell the truth.

"Indeed, ma'am, it was only partly so," said I, laughing again. "For looking back I see that when the comical fellow staggered up from the guns he was so abroad in his wits that they volunteered him before he knew what he was doing!"

Miss Granham looked on me kindly! This lady I had thought composed of vinegar, gunpowder, salt and pepper looked on me kindly.

"I understand you, Mr Talbot, and my admiration is in no way lessened. As a lady, I must thank you for your protection."

"Oh, Lord, ma'am, say no more—any gentleman—and Englishman—indeed—good God! But it must have been distressing for you down in the orlop!"

"It was distressing," she said simply, "not because of danger but because it was disgusting."

The door sprang open and little Mrs Brocklebank fairly bounced in.

"Letitia—Mr Talbot—our play! The party!"

"I had forgotten."

"A play, ma'am? Party?"

"We are quite unready," said Miss Granham, with some return to her customary bleakness. "The weather will not hold for it."

"Oh fudge! We may do it immediately as the Italians do, we might do it tonight—"

"It is already 'tonight'."

"Tomorrow then."

"My dear Mrs Brocklebank—"

"Down in that horrid place you was pleased to call me 'Celia' as I asked and even held my hand, Mr Talbot, for I am the greatest coward imaginable and what with the odours and the darkness and the rumbling and the, the— I was within an ace of swooning away."

"I will continue to address you as 'Celia' if you wish," said Miss Granham distantly, "though what difference——"

"Well then that is settled. But the most exciting thing—our captains are agreed that if the weather, I will not repeat how Sir Henry described it but if we are held for another twenty-four hours without wind—what do you think, sir?"

"I cannot imagine, ma'am, except perhaps they may agree that we shall all whistle for a wind together."

"Oh, get along with you, Mr Talbot, do, you will always be funning. You are just like Mr Brocklebank."

There must have been some instant expression in my face which showed the ladies how this comparison appealed to me. It set Miss Granham smiling and even impeded Mrs Brocklebank for a moment.

"I mean, sir, in the article of funning. Why, hardly a day passes but Mr Brocklebank makes a joke which has me positively screaming with laughter. Indeed I sometimes fear I am so noisy that I irritate the other passengers."

My head was singing and opening and shutting. The ladies were a long way away.

"You said that you had news for us, ma'am."

"Oh yes! Why, if we are still detained tomorrow they are agreed we may have a ball! Only think of it! The officers in full dress, and the little band from *Alcyone* to play for us—why, it will be a most elegant occasion!"

The confusion of my head merged with incredulity.

"Captain Anderson agreed to a ball? Surely not!"

"No, not at first, sir, he is said to have been most upright. But then Lady Somerset managed Sir Henry who visited Captain Anderson—but is it not remarkable—oh heavenly! More!"

"More, ma'am? What can be more heavenly than the opportunity——"

"This was unexpected ... they say Sir Henry having gained Captain Anderson's agreement went on to assume that we had all had our boxes up on entering the tropics and was quite demolished when he found it was not so! Apparently all ships that carry passengers declare a day for airing and changing and arranging and—why, you will understand it all, Letitia, even if Mr Talbot does not! They say Captain Anderson had omitted this ceremony in sheer bad temper at being—what do you think he called it? I heard from Miss Chumley who heard from Lady Somerset who was told in the strictest confidence by Sir Henry that Captain Anderson had described his anger at being concerned to carry the emigrants, I suppose, as being loaded with a cargo of pigs! But the upshot of all is that we may have our trunks and boxes brought up at dawn and the ball is to open at five o'clock with dusk."

"If the weather holds. Suppose there is wind. We cannot sail together and dance at the same time!"

"Lady Somerset declares there will not be a wind—she feels there will not be! She is a sensitive. Sir Henry declares that he relies on his 'little witch' to make the weather behave. They are a charming and delightful couple. It is said they will entertain some of us to dinner or a luncheon."

A marked silence ensued. Neither Miss Granham nor I seemed disposed to break it. Finally Mrs Brocklebank broke it herself.

"Lady Somerset has a fortepiano but declares she is sadly out of practice. She presses Miss Chumley to play, who does so delightfully."

"How do you know all this, ma'am?"

"And who", said Miss Granham, "is Miss Chumley?"

"Miss Chumley is an orphan and Lady Somerset's prodigy."

"Good God, ma'am," said I. "Can she be as finished a musician as that?"

"They are taking her with them to India where she is to

live with a distant relative, for she is quite without fortune, except for her skill."

Have I reported that conversation in its right place? I cannot remember. Certainly at some point I found myself thinking—all this is absurd, cannot be happening—it is my head that is wrong. How did I get away? I remember being pressed by Miss Granham to try the effect of repose, but I walked instead past my hutch and out into the waist, then up by way of the stairs to the quarterdeck. I cannot tell how long I stayed there staring at the invisible horizon and trying to think! I have never known such a queer condition! I understand now that it was the effect of excitement, fear, and the repeated blows that had kept my head ringing like a bell. At one point Wheeler appeared and suggested that I should get some sleep but I drove him off testily. I heard a muted roar from below the poop and soon Bates came and begged me not to walk the quarterdeck, for the captain was trying to sleep. So away I drifted in a kind of dream.

Wheeler came to me.

"All the other ladies and gentlemen are turned in long ago, sir, and fast asleep."

"Do you know, Wheeler, what I think about Mrs Brocklebank?"

"You've had a thump, sir, they say. But don't worry, sir. I'll stay near you."

"Is this a dagger which I see inside me, its handle—"

"Now come along and lie down, sir, I'll stay—"

"Keep your hands off me, man! Who has the watch?"

"Mr Cumbershum, sir."

"We are safe enough then."

All this inconsequence! But Wheeler must have persuaded or forced me into the lobby. I was surprised to find how the lobby had altered. For one thing, it was lighted by no less than two powerful oil-lamps! Trunks, boxes and bags were piled outside the cabins, my own among them, including, I noticed, the box that held the remainder of my travelling library. Wheeler got me into my chair and pulled off my boots.

"That reminds me. You are a careless fellow, Wheeler. How did you come to fall overboard?"

There was a long pause.

"Wheeler?"

"I slipped, sir. My brass rag blew out of my hand and caught in the main chains. I had to climb outboard for it. Then I slipped, sir, like I said."

It came to me in the confusion of my head that I knew the truth of the matter. His death had been convenient. He had informed on Billy Rogers and paid for it in the fearful currency of criminals. Yet so strange was my state that I merely nodded and let him continue with his work about me.

"You are a ghost, Wheeler."

"No, sir."

"Go and get some sleep."

"I'll stay with you, sir, you aren't fit to be left. I'll get my head down here on the deck."

I shouted at him, I think, and he went. As for me, I fell into my bunk.

(6)

THE GREAT DAY

Indeed I can call it no other. That day, from my rising to my strange setting, I could wish to go with me in every detail to my grave. I have little enough skill to preserve it. Words, words, words! I would give them all and live dumb for one moment of—no, I would not. I am absurd.

Only just now I was remembering Colley's long, unfinished letter. I cannot think that he supposed himself adept in description and narration, yet this very innocence, his suffering and his need for a friend if only a piece of paper, gave his writing a force which I can admire but not imitate.

Now, as I write this, my legs locked into the structure of the chair while the deck heaves and sidles—I wear my greatcoat even in my cabin.

But to return. I woke, sweatily in that humid heat. When I dressed myself it was only that the noise from the lobby was intense and would have kept me from sleep even if I had been capable of it. Moreover the calls of nature pay no attention to such trifles as a cracked head! So after I had dressed, I picked a careful way through the lobby to the privies on the starboard quarter. I mean on the right side at the back of the ship—and returning was like the exploration of a bazaar! There were not only bales and boxes, trunks and bags, but all our female passengers busy among them! They handled a mixed exhibition of stuff fit for an Eastern market. Zenobia was there with little Mrs Pike. Miss Granham rose from among a rainbow of dresses and flashed her smile at me! I had intended to plead my head as a reason for avoiding the ball, but that smile, together with an archly kind look from Mrs Brocklebank—I confess all this freely—changed my mind for me. I told Wheeler to get out my tailed coat and knee-breeches, together with the light suiting, the material for which had been recommended to me by a man who had done a tour in India. By the time I had changed into this last, even the passenger saloon had been turned into a milliner's shop. There was Miss Granham, just where she had sat the day before and looking, I will not say pretty, but indefinably excited and good-humoured and handsome! She was wearing a dress of dark blue silk and had a large and complicated shawl of lighter blue crossed over her bosom. It seemed more *oncoming* than was appropriate for a governess. But then, good God, I remembered in time that she was no longer a governess but the fiancée of a man who, however outrageous his politics, was none the less of considerable substance and unquestionably a gentleman. In short this was Miss Granham come out of her chrysalis!

"Good morning, Miss Granham. Like it, you are radiant."

"A pretty speech from our gallant defender. It would be prettier if the sun shone."

"The mists are golden."

"That was almost poetical. How does your head, sir?"

"I know now what is meant by 'heart of oak'. I appear to be roofed with it."

"Your own costume is admirably suited to the climate."

"I am dressed for comfort. But you ladies are going out of your way to delight us."

"You do not think highly of the nature of ladies, sir. The melancholy truth is we are prepared for a whole day of festivity. We dine in *Alcyone*'s wardroom. There is a ball to be given on our own deck, and an entertainment presented to us by our own seamen!"

"Good heavens!"

"I believe it may do some good in this, this——"

"Not entirely happy ship?"

"You have said it, sir, not I."

"But a ball!"

"Our neighbour has a band."

"But an entertainment presented by the seamen!"

"I hope it may be edifying but fear it will not."

"The ball at any rate—Miss Granham, may I claim your hand for a dance?"

"I am flattered but should we not wait? To tell you the truth I am not entirely informed of Mr Prettiman's views on such activities and until then——"

"Of course, ma'am. I say no more but will hope."

The door opened and in flew pretty Mrs Brocklebank. Her arms were full of some foaming material. In a second our ladies were deep in a discussion of such technical mysteriousness that I withdrew without interrupting them. If I defined our sailor's speech as "Tarpaulin", then I must define what our ladies were saying (both speaking together) as perfect "Milliner". It confirmed what I had felt when Pike had talked about the "larboard beam". I saw my efforts to talk as the seamen did as a crass affectation. I might as well have talked of hems and gores and gussets! Let the rest of the passengers make free with Tarpaulin. I myself would stand out for a landsman's lingo! So farewell, Falconer and his *Marine Dictionary*, without a twinge of regret but indeed, with some relief.

I took my hat from my hutch and walked into the waist. The sun was faintly visible in the mist and not yet more than its own diameter above the horizon but already the preparations for our extraordinary day of festivities were well under weigh—I mean in process of being completed. Perhaps "under weigh" is permissible as a phrase which has lost its technical and precise reference and become general?

But the scene, though I am persuaded I shall never forget it, must none the less be described. At the height of our mainyard our ship was roofed with awnings—either sails used for the purpose or awnings proper. Though as yet the swiftly rising sun shone levelly under them, in later hours they would provide a grateful shade. *Alcyone* had her awnings at the same level, though of course higher up the masts. The effect was of two streets side by side—we were a small township, or a village at least, a village out here in this deserted wilderness. It was preposterous. The wild almost mutinous behaviour of our sailors when they heard the tidings of peace had subsided and they worked everywhere in silence and with an apparent goodwill. It was the prospect of an entertainment. Like small children they had entered the world of "let's pretend" and were, it seemed, satisfied there. Hand flags and larger bunting were being hung from the awnings. There were even flowers—not from the captain's cabin as I thought at first but most cleverly constructed from scraps of material. From *Alcyone* came the sounds of a small band at practice! I suppose our two fiddles and a serpent were among them. Yet with all this, the ceaseless business of the ships went on—two men stood at our motionless wheel and two others stood at *Alcyone*'s. Our odd sailing master paced the quarterdeck, a spyglass under his arm, while a midshipman did the like aboard our neighbour! I had no doubt that above the awnings work still went on at the stumps of our decapitated masts and that somewhere in the fore or the main or the mizzen the lookout stared at the horizon, whence the sun was already drawing up mist. It was all so unexpected and quaint that I forgot the ringing of my head and came near to being myself once again. I now saw that our two streets were kept apart by those huge bundles of wood which are let down the sides of quays to prevent ships damaging themselves with rubbing on stone. The steep gangway formed an alley joining our two ocean streets. It was wide enough to be negotiated even by ladies. Two red marines were stationed at *Alcyone*'s end of the alley and two plainly disgruntled members of Oldmeadow's troop in green guarded ours. I went to the rail and looked over. I was in time to see a gunport close, or rather the last furtive inch of its closing! So that was one of the ways the people of both ships could communicate whether their officers wanted them to or no—and, of course, across from mast to mast, yard to yard, the monkeys would swing as in a forest! Small chance of perfect discipline when ships lie together!

A midshipman from *Alcyone* came up the gangway, saluted and, after enquiring my name, offered me a white and slightly scented note. I unfolded it. Captain Sir Henry and Lady Somerset request the pleasure of the company of Mr Edmund FitzH. Talbot to dinner aboard *Alcyone*, twelve o'clock, wind and weather permitting. Dress informal, a verbal reply will suffice.

"I accept with pleasure, of course."

I returned to my hutch. I remember clearly telling myself that all this was not a dream not a phantasy brought on by the wounding of my head. Yet with this extraordinary hamlet or village built a thousand miles from anywhere and wrapped now in a humid mist which seemed to invade my intellect as much as it drifted across our decks, what had gone before and what was to come seemed unimportant, trivial even, so that England at our back and the Antipodes before us were no more than engraved lines on a map. And Wheeler was back, intercepted by a frigate's course as improbably as that a thread thrown at the eye of a needle should go through it! *Here* was all. The two streets side by side—and *Alcyone*'s bell rang, to be echoed immediately by our own, so that it was four bells in the forenoon watch with the cry from her of "Up spirits" duplicated a few yards from me on our deck—the crowds that thronged those decks and the decks below them, the busy yet only half-understood business that was carried on twenty-four hours a day in both ships to keep life supportable—the planking with its black and sometimes bubbling seams—the very parallel lines of them which sometimes would enforce a dreary and sickening substantiality in which their movement was malign—this was all that was real.

What bathos! I have tried to say what I mean and cannot. This tropical nowhere was the whole world—the whole *imaginable* world. This was a neck of history, the end of the greatest war, was the middle of the longest journey, a … a nothing! An all, an astonishment, a cold factuality. I bend the English language in an effort to say what I mean and fail.

"Edmund."

I swung around in my chair. Deverel was looking in at the door. I must confess to finding his visit unwelcome.

"What is it, Deverel? I am about to—"

"Good God! The man has his own supply of brandy! A glass if you please for the bad boy of the school."

"Help yourself. But are not you—?"

"Forbidden the drink like the parson's son? Damn him, it's peacetime and I'll not be shackled any longer. If he does not let me out of arrest I'll snap my sword in his face, go ashore and hey for the open road!"

"I don't know what you're talking about."

"Why, my good Edmund, what can he do? Obtain for me the Lord High Admiral's Displeasure on Vellum? Let him break me; it's no more than my sword they break, a piece of damned cutlery I've no use for now there's so much peace about!"

"A gentleman's sword—"

"A white man east of Suez may do well enough."

"We are not east of Suez."

Deverel emptied an extraordinary fraction of the tumbler of brandy down his throat. It made him gasp. Then—

"I cannot beg from the man. It would break me as well as my sword to do so. I must have my dignity."

"So must we all."

"This is my plan. You are to tell him what I propose."

"I tell him?"

"Who else? The rest are rabbits. Besides, what have you to lose?"

"The devil of a lot!"

"Tell him that I engage to cause no trouble till we make a port—"

"That's good."

"Wait. *There* I shall resign my commission."

"Or have it taken from you, Deverel."

"What's the odds? You're not drinking, Edmund, and you're cursed dull today. Tell him if you like that as soon as I've ceased to be an officer you'll bear him my challenge—"

"I?"

"Don't you see? Can you imagine old Rumble-guts faced with a challenge?"

"Yes."

"Why, when we thought *Alcyone* might be a Frog he was shivering like a tops'l."

"Are you serious?"

"Did you not see?"

"You underestimate the man."

"That's my affair. But you'll tell him?"

"Look—Deverel—Jack. This is madness."

"You'll tell him!"

I was silent for only the briefest moment in which I made up my mind.

"No."

"No? Just like that?"

"I am sorry."

"By God, you're not! I had thought better of you, Talbot!"

"Listen. Try to be sensible. Don't you understand that I cannot in any circumstances take to the captain what is neither more nor less than an open threat? If you were not in an overexcited state—"

"Do you think I'm drunk? Or in a blue funk?"

"Of course not. Calm down."

Deverel poured himself another drink, not as large as the first but large enough. The bottle and glass clattered together. It was essential to stop him getting really drunk. I allowed my hand to go out and take the glass from him.

"Thank you, old fellow."

For a moment I thought he was about to strike me. Then with an odd kind of laugh—

" 'Lord Talbot'. I must say you're a cool one."

"Was this for you? I'm sorry—"

"No, no. Have it."

"The first day of peace. So up spirits!"

I coughed mightily over it. Deverel watched in silence, then slowly seated himself on the further end of my bunk.

"Edmund—"

I looked at him over the glass.

"Edmund—what am I to do?"

Deverel was no longer looking fierce. It was strange but after all the devil-may-care actions of the past twenty-four hours it was as if a far less assured young man had appeared in the place of the one I knew. I saw now how although he was of more than average height he was of a slight build and lightly muscled. As for his face—I saw with astonishment that the forward-projecting sweep of his sidewhiskers was an attempt of which he was quite possibly unaware to compensate for a weak and slightly receding chin. Gentleman Jack, the honourable Dashing Jack! It was a paroxysm of rage and, yes, fright that had given his right arm the momentary strength to sink his blade so deeply in the rail. Comprehension became so complete that I felt as lost and

frightened as ever he had been. It is a dreadful thing to
know too much. I saw that had it not been for the support
of his family name and an air which stemmed more from
imitation than worth, he might have been an ostler, a footman, a gentleman's gentleman! It was confusing to look at
this man whom I had once thought the most gentlemanlike of the officers—which indeed—the question is such
a confusion—which indeed he was! His negligence and
intemperance had nothing to do with what I now saw and
understood. His latest wild scheme, depending as it did on
a physical cowardice in Captain Anderson for which there
was less than no evidence, was phantasy. Anderson would
treat a challenge from Deverel, civilian or no, with contempt and no one would blame him. Deverel must not be
allowed to continue in it!

"Do, Mr Deverel—Jack? Let me think."

He sat back and slumped a little as if some strain had
gone out of him. He seemed almost respectful as before a
Thinker! But the truth was—

"Look, Deverel—"

"It was Jack just now, let alone when we were about to
board."

"Aye! That was a moment we shall remember—eh?
Jack, then. But look. I've had the devil of a clout or three
clouts over the head—I'm really in no condition to think
at all. It aches still."

"A glass—"

I made an involuntary and impatient gesture with my
right hand.

"You know—I would like—I will—do what can be
done. The first thing is for me to speak to Summers."

"Good God! The man's a Methodist!"

"Is he so? I know him deeply concerned with moral
questions but had not thought—"

"Is that the best you can do?"

"It's the first step. I must know what the situation is, I mean in, in naval law. You are too personally involved and do not yet see the thing clearly."

"You were present!"

"In body, yes, but I was unconscious. The wits had been knocked out of me by a rope's end."

"And this is your offer of help?"

"The trouble with you, Deverel, is you want everything done at once."

"Thank you, *Mr* Talbot!"

"I am trying to help. You must not expect from me the instant action of a naval officer."

"By God, I do not!"

"Be easy again! You cannot go at this as if you was boarding an enemy. Haste will ruin all."

"What? With two post captains and half a dozen lieutenants senior to me in these ships? They can fix me with a court-martial as easy as kiss my arse! Devil take it and you!"

"Jack!"

The word was emollient. Strange again! Though he looked sullen and his breast heaved, nevertheless he spoke in a lower tone. "There is enough of them to fix up a court-martial here and now."

"When the wind may send us on our way at any moment? You know I am not instructed in naval matters but I would swear they cannot try you at sea. It is no longer wartime and not as if there was a mutiny. You have not offered the man violence! Besides, deuce take it, while the weather holds we are to have a ball and an entertainment and as if that was not enough I am to dine with Sir Henry! Confound it, man, can you not see that with the peace and abdication and this resolution of a great crisis in the affairs of the civilized world—"

Deverel jerked upright between his hands on the edge of the bunk.

"Dinner? Why, man, there's your opportunity! Anderson will be there, depend on it! A word with him in Sir Henry's hearing after the drinks have gone round—"

"He hardly drinks at all. Besides—"

All at once I was aware of how my wounded head was humming. No—singing!

"If you knew how my cursed head aches!"

"You'll do nothing then."

"I will find out how the land lies—if the expression means anything in this limbo of streaming water! There is much that may be done if we go about it carefully."

"You mean I must wait. Endure this humiliation from a man my father would not have at his table!"

"I will endeavour my best in your behalf, little though that best may be."

"There's no need to get your rag out!"

The cant expression amused me. I had indeed spoken with a degree of warmth. But somehow it made Deverel more likeable. He saw my involuntary smile, misinterpreted it and was about to fire up again, so that I spoke hurriedly and almost at random.

"I will lead the conversation to duelling if Anderson is there and try to find out what his reaction would be to a challenge."

"Why—he may have a positive horror of being shot at!"

I looked at him in sheer astonishment. Anderson, a post captain who by report had taken part in bloody engagements! Anderson who had *boarded* as a midshipman and later taken a fire ship into the Basque Roads under Cochrane! There was more here than I had foreseen. Deverel was now excited in a way that a single glass of my brandy could not account for. He was hectic and rubbing his hands and grinning! I tried to bring him down.

"What is more to the point, my dear sir, is that he may have the strength—what some people would call the strength of mind—to reject any challenge out of hand. There is a strong feeling about in the country that it is folly to set life itself at stake in a trivial matter. Not, of course, that your affair is trivial but others may think it so."

"They do, they do."

"I will sound him out."

"No more?"

"At the moment I *can* do no more."

"At the moment. It is a convenient phrase, sir."

I said nothing. Deverel eyed me critically. Then his expression changed to a veritable sneer. I spoke shortly.

"I repeat. I can do no more at the moment."

He said nothing for a while but looked towards the mirror above my canvas basin. Then—

"Like the others."

I made no comment. He went on.

"Oh, I know about Gentleman Jack and Dashing Jack, but do you not detect the sneer? Remember when Colley was slung overboard, Summers deliberately delayed telling me the driver should be afted until the rudder nigh on carried away? But I thought you who was a gentleman and not one of the cursed jumped-up lubbers, at least you would be on my side and not set out to ruin me—"

"You must be mad!"

He said nothing but after a few more moments stood up slowly. He looked at me sideways and began to smile unpleasantly, a kind of inward or withdrawn smile as of one who has infinite comprehension and wariness among enemies. He opened the cabin door, glanced quickly this way and that, then fairly darted out of sight. He left me in a state of great perplexity and confusion. The worst of it was I had committed myself to a degree of intimacy with the man and now felt little inclined to interfere with his punishment for what I could not but see as the just result of his neglect of duty. Above all I did not wish to injure in any way the degree of understanding and mutual tolerance which now existed between me and Captain Anderson. It was all most provoking. I had nothing to push me towards engaging in an advocacy in this instance and believed more and more, to use an abrupt phrase, that Deverel was simply not worth it.

I was called back to immediacy by the sound of the ship's bells. This was the very hour at which we were summoned to the feast! I glanced into the glass, settled my hair round my wound (hesitated for a moment—why go? why not turn in?). However, I settled my clothing and made my way through the new milliner's shop. As I did so I heard, among all the shuffling of naked feet, the sound of firm and familiar footsteps above my head. I followed the captain to the broad gangway down which he strode. He stood rigid at the bottom, his hat held across his chest. I, following close, had much ado to prevent myself from crashing into him. I had the wit, however, to seize a side rope with my left hand, snatch my hat off with my right, then stand nearly as rigid as the captain. The deck round the foot of the gangway was crowded and the ceremonial nearly as elaborate as that for Colley's funeral. Here were sideboys with white gloves, boatswains with calls, marines with muskets, more marines with drums and trumpets, some midshipmen, and a lieutenant or two—and glittering at the end of the lane of ceremonial stood Sir Henry Somerset, unkindly wearing full uniform, the ribbon of his order strained into creases across the white splendour of his embonpoint! The trumpets blared, the drums ruffled, the calls screeched, our working parties stood to attention staring into the mist. All this at a man's stepping from one plank to another! The ceremony came to an end. Captain Anderson was now properly aboard *Alcyone* and the two crews might go about their business which I myself thought astonishingly various and complex, in view of the state of the weather, for from the gangway we could hardly see either end of the ships. I stepped forward myself, to be greeted most affably by Sir Henry who had not the privilege of knowing my godfather, though he had, like all the world—and so on. He conducted us towards his own quarters, talking all the time to our captain. Naval warfare is a lottery! Sir Henry is large rather than impressive. His wealth showed everywhere. Any touches of moulding about the poop were gilded. We walked to the ladder—no, I refuse to be seduced—to the stairs, along a pathway of coir matting laid lest our feet should be soiled by the melting seams. There were canvas chimneys leading up from the quarterdeck and secured to the mizzen rigging—devil take it, I find my determination *not* to speak Tarpaulin almost impossible to sustain!—in an attempt to replace the fetor of a ship's interior with purer air. We reached the quarterdeck and the end of the coir matting. I looked down and began carefully and unsuccessfully to avoid the seams when Sir Henry took notice of my attempt.

"Do not trouble yourself, Mr Talbot, I beg. There is nothing here to foul your feet."

Captain Anderson had stopped too and was looking down.

"Splined, by God!"

It seemed my Tarpaulin was to increase just as I was abandoning it.

"Splined, Sir Henry?"

Sir Henry waved a hand in a dismissive way.

"There was a cargo of rare woods among my prizes. Very fortunate. It is ebony, you know."

"But *splined*, Sir Henry?"

"It means replacing the tar and oakum which is commonly used, and makes such a damned mess of our feet, by strips of hard wood. The narrow planks are mahogany. I took up the idea from what I saw aboard the royal yacht when I had the honour of being presented to His Royal Highness. Everything is Bristol Fashion there, I can tell you! After you, Captain Anderson, Mr Talbot."

"After you, sir."

"Pray, sir—"

We descended to the stateroom. The lady who came towards us did not so much walk, or even float, as swim. Lady Somerset had an immediate claim on any gentleman's attention. She was a fine and most handsome woman and dressed in the height of fashion—indeed her costume was more suitable, I thought, for the evening than the middle of the day! Was this "informal dress"? On her bosom there glittered a positive appanage of sapphires which matched those at her ears and wrists. Sir Henry must have intercepted the jeweller to the Porte! Her gown was girt high under her bosom in what—but I have not yet learned to talk Milliner. Nor had I more than a moment to take in her appearance, for she was leaning towards me and moaning. I cannot by any other word describe the way in which having acknowledged Anderson's abrupt attention, abrupt nod down up—she broke from him, insinuated herself in my direction, gazed earnestly up into my eyes as if we were present at an occasion of most moving importance, then insinuated herself back to our captain and murmured in a deep contralto voice, "Such pleasure!" Since she appeared to be about to swoon at the thought of the pleasure, it was perhaps fitting that she should hold out a hand to each of us as if appealing for support. She was, however, a little too fragrant for my taste. Now I was lifting my hand towards hers when with a movement like that of weed in water she swung both hands in the other direction and moaned again.

"Dearest, valuable Janet!"

There was little doubt about the nature of valuable Janet. She held an embroidery frame in one hand with its material—the needle and thread still stuck in the pattern—

together with a fan upside down: and in the other hand a book with one finger marking the page from which she had been reading. She held a cushion under her arm and, as if that load were not enough, a length of ribbon was clenched in her teeth. She appeared to me to be a female of extraordinary plainness. Busily sorting these new people according to what information I had, I at once put her in the compartment labelled "companion". As I did so she made a ducking curtsey, then bolted out of the stateroom.

"Miss Oates," murmured Lady Somerset, "a kinswoman."

"A distant kinswoman," amplified Sir Henry. "Lady Somerset will not be parted from her. It is her generous heart. She will keep her and how could I say no?"

"Dear Sir Henry, he refuses me nothing, but nothing!"

I was about to make the expected gallant reply when Sir Henry's face brightened and he spoke in a more energetic voice.

"Come in, Marion, come in! I was laying odds that you would be up and about!"

The lightning that struck the top of the mizzenmast ran down, and melted the conductor into white hot drops. The mast split and flinders shot every way into the mist. The deckhead burst open and the electrical fluid destroyed me. It surrounded the girl who stood before me with a white line of light.

(7)

"Captain Anderson, may I present you? Mr Talbot? Miss Chumley. You look delightfully, Marion, quite the belle—if it were not for, of course—This is Mr Edmund *FitzHenry* Talbot, my dear. Lady Talbot is a FitzHenry and Mr Talbot is proceeding—"

He must have continued to talk, I suppose. I came to as if from another concussion to find that the gentlemen were holding glasses and strangely there was one in my own hand. Since it is clear that I performed the act of taking a glass and continued to hold it in those first few moments of life I can only suppose that I had been talking as well but what my first words were I am quite unable to say. Oh, *thou*, Marion, rising from the meekest and deepest of curtsies, sum of all music, all poetry, distracted scraps of which with their newly irradiated meaning tumbled through my mind! But it was Sir Henry's words I heard when I first emerged from my destroyed state.

"Poor Marion has been positively prostrate! The slightest movement, good God, not just a lop but the least shudder at anchor, and up it all comes! Once she is in India, as I tell her, she must stay there for good, for the return journey would surely make an end of her!"

"*Alcyone* is lively then, Sir Henry?"

"So-so, Captain Anderson. She is long for her top hamper and 'utmost dispatch' is 'utmost dispatch', you know. How is your ship?"

"Steady as a rock, Sir Henry, and dead beat as a compass card. Why—even when that fool of a lieutenant allowed her to be taken aback she put her rail under for less than ten seconds by my reckoning and in a fresh breeze too!"

"Sir Henry, Captain Anderson, you are making the poor child quite pale! Come, Marion, the gentlemen will say no more about it. The floor is steady as a ballroom and I have seen you happy enough on that!"

"Why," said Captain Anderson, "I believe we are to hold a ball aboard my ship which is even steadier than this."

"*Alcyone*," moaned Lady Somerset, "*anything* is steadier than this beautiful, wild creature!"

I found my conscious voice at last.

"I am certain beyond a peradventure that Captain Anderson would offer his vessel as a refuge for the rest of your journey, Miss, Miss—Chumley!"

Miss Chumley smiled—Marion smiled! The corners of her mouth turned up—my very heart jumps at the memory—it is a sweet pleasure to try to record it. Yet even when Marion was not smiling nature had provided her with a mouth which made her look not merely good-humoured but as if she were enjoying a joke of such power it was a source of permanent pleasure. But I had no sooner begun to find that the only cure for staring impolitely at this mouth was to stare even more impolitely—and more helplessly—at the eyes above it, which ignores her little nose—says nothing of those eyebrows that implied astonishment which by reason of the smiling mouth meant that her whole expression was lively and interested—oh, Lord! The trouble is that since the days of Homer the greatest of poets have exercised the utmost of their art in the description of young women. There is no eloquence, not a figure of speech from understatement to hyperbole that has not been laid under contribution! Go outside the common rules of rhetoric—look for an inspired absurdity, the positively insolent magic of a Shakespeare or a Virgil—

I have got in a tangle and am going nowhere. How was she dressed? It did not seem to matter at the time, but now—

Her dress was white. Blue ribbon I *think* was threaded through the neckline from shoulder to shoulder and round the ruched sleeves just above the elbows. Her earrings were silver flowers and a chain of the same lay round her neck above the promise of her bosom. She was slight, would always be slight, always suggest, imply more than state—like the greatest of poets!

But Captain Anderson was speaking—had spoken. I recall the words I was not then conscious of hearing.

"No, no, Mr Talbot. We are not going to India but Sydney Cove! Besides, our ship is full of emigrants, passengers, cargo—"

"You see, my dear," said Sir Henry, laughing, "there is no help for it! To India you must go and in *Alcyone* too!"

"I cannot understand," said Lady Somerset, "why there should be such an absolute requirement from naval gentlemen of haste now that we have defeated the French. Surely Captain Anderson—"

Both naval gentlemen laughed. Yes, Anderson laughed! I found my voice again.

"Miss Chumley, if you will take passage with us I will abandon my cabin to you. I will sleep in the orlop or the bilges. I will guarantee to spend the nights pacing the deck on the side opposite to Captain Anderson—but come, sir— we *have* an empty cabin. I will move there instantly and Miss Chumley shall have mine!"

I believe all this was said in a sleepwalking voice. Men should be poets—I understand that now, Edmund, Edmund, thou scurvy politician!

Anderson was giving a brief account of Colley—how intemperate he had been and how at last after a shocking escapade he had succumbed to a *low fever*. But my determination to defend the memory of Mr Colley was a distant thing. My journal did that well enough and I put the thought aside. The lightning stroke, the *coup de foudre*, was all.

"The rumour went, Miss Chumley, that you was a prodigy which word I discounted but now I see it was no more than the truth."

"Prodigy, Mr Talbot?"

"Prodigy, Miss Chumley!"

Her answer was a peal of laughter silvery as the flowers round her neck.

"The word was wrongly reported to you, sir. Lady Somerset is sometimes kind enough to refer to me as her 'protégée'."

"For me, Miss Chumley, a prodigy, ever and always."

She still smiled but looked slightly puzzled—as well she might; for whatever the lightning had done to me, for her it had been no more than the experience of something— someone—unexpectedly and impossibly familiar; I mean familiar in the sense of recognized to be known, and per- haps also encroaching! Indeed, having guessed that this was so I immediately had proof of it.

"We have not met before, sir?"

"Indeed, Miss Chumley, I should remember if we had!"

"Of course. Then since we are unknown to each other—"

She paused, looking away, laughed uncertainly, then looked back and was silent. So was I; and we both exam- ined the other's face with a serious intentness. I was the first to speak.

"We have—and have not!"

She glanced down and I saw that my left hand held her right one. I was not conscious of taking it and let go with a gesture of apology which she dismissed with a shake of the head.

I was aware of Sir Henry speaking by no means in the voice with which he had greeted Miss Chumley.

"Oh, come straight in, for heaven's sake, Janet! You need not be scared nor say anything, for you was only brought in to make up the numbers."

"Dearest Janet! There, if you please, between Captain Anderson and Sir Henry."

I drew back a chair for Lady Somerset who insinuated herself. Sir Henry did the same for Miss Chumley and I suppose Anderson did the same for the invaluable and unfortunate Janet. I could not but be involved with my hostess for a while and made a sad business of it, for most of my attention was on Sir Henry who was telling Miss Chumley what a pity it was that she could not sing in the entertainment and let the people hear what was meant by real singing. Fortunately Lady Somerset had the social perceptions which seem natural to women of any race or clime. For she turned away and engaged Anderson in a trivial conversation which nevertheless must have been a relief to him. He had been staring glumly and silently at Janet whose eyes were deep in her plate. Satisfied, I think, that Anderson was being looked after, Sir Henry began to eat with an assiduity which fully explained the rotundity of his person. Miss Chumley was pushing a little food round her plate with a fork but I did not see any of it touch her mouth.

"You are not hungry?"

"No."

"Then neither am I."

"All the same, sir, you must trifle with your fork, so. Is that not elegant?"

"It is charming. But, Miss Chumley, if you persist in declining food you will become even more ethereal."

"You could not have said anything more flattering to a young person, sir, nor held out a happier prospect!"

"For you perhaps; but for me the happiest prospect would be—no, forgive me. I presume on—dare I say—oh, indeed I must! An immediate sympathy, a recognition—"

" 'We have—and have not'?"

"Oh, Miss Chumley! I am dazed—no—dazzled! Rescue me, for heaven's sake!"

"That is easily done, sir. If we are to entertain each other let me tell you quickly what you have in hand. I am an orphan, sir, learned my three R's, considerable French, some Italian and Geography at an establishment for the children of clergymen in Salisbury Close. I am also able to recite you the Kings of England, ending with 'George, the third of that name whom may God preserve'. I am, of course, pious, modest, clever with my detestable needle and can sing very nearly in tune."

"I beg you to eat at least a little, for all these accomplishments need to be sustained!"

The wondrous creature actually leaned a little towards me. Our heads came intoxicatingly close.

"Be easy, Mr Talbot. I am also a little devious and at the moment not at all hungry!"

"Miss Chumley, do not say it! Oh no! Biscuits in your cabin!"

The genuine and silvery laughter rang round the stateroom.

"Mr Talbot, I thought the secret would not disgust you!"

"You have bewitched me already. You must have done so before—when we last met, in—oh, Cathay, Tartary, Timbuctoo, where was it?"

Sir Henry interrupted his mastication for a moment.

"You have travelled, Talbot?"

"No, Sir Henry."

"Well I am sure Marion has not."

She laughed again.

"Mr Talbot and I are making up a fairy story, uncle. You must none of you listen, for it is great nonsense."

"Nonsense, Miss Chumley? You cut me to the quick."

Our heads drew together again.

"I would never do that, Mr Talbot. And fairy tales are not nonsense to some."

I still cannot tell why tears came to my eyes! A grown man, a sane, really rather calculating man, a political creature to have water spring up behind his eyelids so that he is hard put to it to keep them from falling out down his face!

"Miss Chumley, you make me—inexpressibly happy. I rejoice to be wholly defenceless."

There was a pause while I swallowed not food but tears. Oh yes, it was my wounded head, my sleeplessness, it must have been—it could not have been what I knew it was!

But she was murmuring.

"We go too fast. Forgive me, sir, I have said more than I should and you too, I believe." Then looking round: "We have silenced the table! Helen!"

But Lady Somerset, dear woman, came to my rescue.

"And what have we older ones to say that is more important? Enjoy yourselves, my dears, while you may!"

Anderson and Sir Henry talked. It was professional, of course—who had been made post and so on. Lady Helen smiled and nodded and, bless her, ignored us.

So there I was, wishing with a sudden urgency that my wounds were real—not injuries but wounds! I wished I had led a forlorn hope and come back heroically wounded, wounded so severely that I must be nursed and by whom but this discovered angel? I desired with as much urgency as the other that I might have a uniform with which to dazzle her, or an order; and cursed inwardly the world that hangs ornaments on old men who no longer have a use for them! Yet I felt even in those first minutes that she was a girl of wit and understanding and not to be won by a confection of blue broadcloth and gold braid—oh, God, what have I said? She would not—

What did we talk about? I cannot now remember because our words meant little compared with the tides of feeling that swept through that strange drawing-room! At times I swear there was a living silence between us which was infinitely sweet. Like Lady Somerset we had become, I suppose, or I had become, by the power and influence of my feelings, a sensitive! I did really feel the very being of Marion beside me, a new thing in life, a new knowledge, means of it, awareness; and she I swear again was in the same way aware of me. The voices growled on in the state-room but we were in a silver bubble of our own.

A bubble! I passed those blessed hours like a spendthrift heir who thinks that money grows on trees and he need do nothing but bid his man of business wave a wand to make guineas fall instead of leaves. How I squandered those two hours which should rather have been divided into one hundred and twenty minutes, seven thousand two hundred seconds, each second, each instant to have been valued, savoured—no, that is too gross a word—every instant should have been prized—precious is a good word and so is enchantment. Like some knight in an old tale Edmund FitzHenry Talbot, with his whole career to make, spent those hours asleep on his shield in the ruined chapel of love! Forgive a young man, a young fool, his ardours and ecstasies! I understand now that the world will only give ear to them in the mouth of genius.

So what do I remember? Nothing clearly of that magic time but only its ending when we were brought out of it by hearing Anderson growl something about "the confounded ball".

"The ball—Miss Chumley, we are forgetting! There is to be a ball! A ball, do you hear? We shall dance the night away. You must promise me your hand for—oh, for what? For every dance of course, well if not, for some of them— most of them—for the longest dance—what is the longest dance? There will be a cotillion! *Yes*! And an allemande— shall we be allowed to dance the valse?"

"I do not think so, Mr Talbot. Lady Somerset as a devotee of Lord Byron cannot possibly countenance a valse, can you, Helen?"

"Lady Somerset, I implore you! Byron is a nonsensical fellow and if he will not allow the valse it is because he is lame and eating sour grapes!"

The argument became general, Marion agreeing with me and declaring (with Shakespeare *hors concours*) that there was no poet in the English tongue to equal Pope, Sir Henry declaring that most of what was written was rubbish, Anderson grunting, Lady Somerset quoting—
"Roll on, thou deep and dark blue Ocean—roll!"

"Helen! No! Do you desire to send me straight back to my couch?"

The bubble had burst.

Lady Somerset broke off in the middle of "ten thousand fleets".

"Sir Henry," I cried. "Should we not proceed in company to the Cape at least? Captain Anderson will tell you how hard put to it we were to make even a show of defence!"

"I would do my best to oblige you, Mr Talbot, but it is not in my power. Besides you need fear nothing, for we are now good friends with the French!"

"I did not mean—"

Anderson turned to me.

"*Alcyone* is a flyer to have made such time out of Plymouth. She would be hull down within hours." Then turning to Sir Henry, "You must have judged what she would carry to a hair, sir!"

"Why, as far as Gib, Captain Anderson, she was positively snoring. I tell you, now and then I had to take a look aloft! My first lieutenant would have the main course off her at a catspaw. I have had to tell him; Bellamy, I have said, this is a frigate, curse it, not a damned company ship. How does your man?"

"Well enough. I have no complaints, Sir Henry, a happy ship, you know. He knocked some sense into the people while we were windbound at Spithead."

"Windbound, was it? You should have been with us back of Plymouth Sound, over across from Shit Creek. They took us out with a steam tug. Good God, I have never been so astonished in my life."

"The smoke," moaned Lady Somerset, "the smoke from that metal chimney. My coach cloak was soiled by it. Marion says her pillow was black."

"Helen!"

"You did, my dear. Cannot you remember what trouble we had with your scalp?"

"Come, Lady Somerset," I cried, "Miss Chumley is not a Red Indian! But what is a steam tug?"

"It is an extraordinary invention, Mr Talbot," said Sir Henry, "and I swear nothing but the inventive genius of our country could have brought it forth! It is a craft with a steam boiler, the force from which makes great paddle wheels rotate on either beam. It would throw up fountains of water were the wheels not cased."

"There is too much fire below," said Anderson. "I cannot like the things. If they should explode they might touch off a fleet like tinder."

"And if the paddles should carry away," said Sir Henry, "they have neither sail nor sweep. I tell you, Anderson, all the while I was in tow till we cast off on the starboard tack to pass east of the Eddystone I had anchors hanging fairly by the hawse with such a swing, crash and bangle we lost a man clean out of the heads on a fluke and the seat with him."

"They are building a larger one at Portsmouth," said Anderson. "They will be the ruin of real seamanship."

"They appear to have a limited application," said Miss Chumley. "Their appearance is quite horrid."

"They make a devil of a mess," said Sir Henry, "but there's no denying they towed us out against the wind in two hours when it would have taken all day kedging."

I gathered my wits.

"Might not a larger vessel operate on the High Seas?"

"I suppose it is possible, Mr Talbot, but there is not the necessity. Once given sea room a ship may do well enough for herself."

"Might we not have steam warships then, that paddle out of harbour and seek the enemy?"

Both naval gentlemen roared with laughter ... indeed, I have never seen Captain Anderson so animated. For a few moments we heard nothing from them but an exchange of fragmentary Tarpaulin. At last Sir Henry wiped his eyes.

"A glass of wine with you, Mr Talbot, and when you come into government I beg you to accept any post but that of the Admiralty!"

Miss Chumley (and it was so *moving* to hear how she sprang to my defence) spoke up like a little heroine.

"But you have not answered Mr Talbot's question, uncle! I am sure he would make a splendid admiral or whatever it is!"

"Mr Talbot shall not be laughed at," said Lady Somerset, "and I am most anxious, Sir Henry, to hear what you have to say to him."

"Well, Lady Somerset," said Sir Henry, "it is the first time I have heard you express an interest in the subject. I believed you was interested in nothing naval but yellow hair, heroics and poetry! Good God, if we was to have these steam tugs large enough to engage an enemy we should need double the crews to keep them clean, let alone feed them with coal!"

Miss Chumley's defence had fortified me.

"The mechanical genius of the British would overcome all difficulties, I am sure."

"Speak up, Captain," said Sir Henry. "You have as much brains as there is to be found in the service, I think."

Captain Anderson, I thought, looked a little indignant at being accused of intelligence. It was, after all, next door to *clever*!

"The real objection," he said, "if you will have an answer to a preposterous question, is this. We may stay at sea for months. A vessel propelled by steam would consume her coal as she moved. Since the possible length of a ship is limited by the possible length of timber suitable for her construction she can never move more than a distance fixed by the amount of coal she can carry in her hull. Then secondly, if she is to be a warship, a paddle wheel on either side will reduce her broadside, that is, the weight of metal she is able to throw. And thirdly, during an engagement, if a single ball should strike the flimsy members of her paddle wheel she will be rendered uncontrollable."

"We are answered, Mr Talbot," said Miss Chumley. "We are beaten from the field."

Oh, the sweetness of that "we"!

"For my part, I could not understand you, Captain Anderson," said Lady Somerset, "for I declare I was the greatest addle-pate in the schoolroom."

"Nothing," said Miss Chumley, the corners of her mouth rising and a delicious dimple appearing in what (with my exposure to Tarpaulin) I was about to call her *starboard cheek*, "positively nothing is so becoming in a young person as a proper degree of ignorance."

But after her last remark, Lady Somerset gave a significant glance at the other two ladies so that we three gentlemen rose at once. The ladies departed and Sir Henry showed us *where to go*. So there I was, an exile from paradise, standing by Captain Anderson and relieving nature into Lord Byron's "dark blue ocean". I found my deprivation from that upturned mouth insupportable and—oh,

Lord, how I do go on! It was what I had always thought a myth, a stage convention, love at first sight, the *coup de foudre*, a fairy tale—but as she said, some people believe them!

It may be so. Yes, it may be so.

I hastened back to the stateroom and brandy. The ladies had not appeared and I had a dreadful fear that we had seen the last of them. I talked inanely but remained since the other two gentlemen did. They were deep in Tarpaulin. I heard about our possibly drawn gudgeons, about *Alcyone*'s sweet run aft, about topmasts and a drunken lieutenant whose negligence enabled Sir Henry to turn a handsome compliment, since it was a fortunate circumstance which had enabled him to overtake us. Both gentlemen agreed that if we found a capful of wind during the day neither looked forward to people giving grudging service for being cheated of their fun. I found that Captain Anderson, though approached by a deputation, had refused to splice the main brace even though the news had been so tremendous. He would only do so at anchor, for two doses of rum in one day was the quickest way to indiscipline. So it went on. I was almost in despair when at last the ladies came back. The stateroom of a frigate naturally enough has to serve as both dining and drawing room. It was surely by Lady Somerset's contrivance that I found myself—against all protocol—seated *again* by Miss Chumley in what I would have called a window seat, since it was under the great stern window of the ship, but is probably called something quite different—a stern thwart perhaps, but what does it matter? God bless Lady Somerset!

My talk I fear was wild. It was not the brandy. It was not entirely the endless time I seemed to have been without sleep. It was the most tragic of all intoxications, the most ridiculous, the sweetest.

"Miss Chumley, I beg the allemande of you—and the quadrille—and the round dance—and the cotillion—"

"Which shall I choose?"

"All if you please! I cannot bear—"

"It would be improper, sir. You must know that surely!"

"Then I am an advocate of impropriety. We shall dance the allemande round the mainmast and the cotillion from one end of the waist to the other and the—"

"Mr Talbot! A poor helpless young person such as I—"

"Come! You are about as helpless as *Alcyone*! I have no doubt your path is strewn with more conquests than Sir Henry's. You have added me to the list."

"I am not so hardhearted. I will release you. Nor—"

"Nor what then?"

"Peace has been declared, sir. Let us share it."

"You will not be so cruel as to let me go!"

"The wind will do so. Oh, how I fear a recurrence of that dreadful motion! Believe me, sir, *mal de mer* is so disgusting and so infinitely lowering that a young person ceases even to care how unbecoming her situation is!"

"We may prevail on them yet."

"Orders are terrible things, sir. Even when I was utterly prostrated Sir Henry would not roll up a single one of our sails to ease the motion, for all Lady Somerset begged him. You see the close limits of that power you credited me with."

"Had you begged him yourself—"

"I was then a miserable object, hoping only for death. Though come to think of it when we heard we were being drawn inexorably towards your vessel and did not know if you was an enemy or a friend, I found the imminent prospect of the death I had longed for quite, quite terrifying!"

"Dare I whisper, Miss Chumley? I put a brave face on things—but so did I myself!"

We laughed together.

"I honour you for the admission, sir, and will not betray you!"

"Was Lady Somerset not disconcerted too?"

Miss Chumley leaned her dark ringlets close to me and spoke behind her fan.

"Only becomingly so, Mr Talbot. I believe she was in hope she was about to meet a Corsair!"

I laughed aloud.

"And then to find what sailors call 'our miserable load of rotten timber' sitting there with her ports agape and mostly toothless!"

"Mr Talbot!"

"Well after all! But we are determined, are we not? I may take your hand for as many and perhaps rather more than the number of dances thought proper?"

"If I am seized by the wrist, Mr Talbot, what can I do but submit? The fault will be yours."

"I will be brazen."

There was a pause. It was then that I made my one desperate attempt to deepen this airy conversation towards something of more worth. But even as I drew a breath to make my outrageous confessions—*ma'am, I have been struck by a thunderbolt*—I saw how fixed Lady Somerset's smile had become. Captain Anderson rose to his feet. With a positive collapse of the heart I understood that our visit was—*must*—be over. I cannot tell now how I got from that enchanted palace, went to my hutch, immediately thinking and with a lump in my throat—how comical!—of who was speaking to her at that very moment and—but what am I about? I am no poet, whose *job* I now see is to ease men over these moments. "The World Well Lost" or "All for Love"! Such indeed was my sudden and overwhelming passion. I had a sharp feeling of panic at the thought of my appearance, felt my head where there was indeed a disagreeable hardness of clotted blood lying among the hairs of my scalp so that my only thought was how thoroughly this "young person" must have been disgusted. She was all politeness and—but I was clean-shaven, still clean-shaven, and my clothing was—oh, poor fool, poor Edmund, what a fall, no, what a climb—no, not either, but what a translation was there! I felt I should suffer, did suffer already, yet would not have changed places with any other man in the world unless perhaps there might be some man, some other man—*Alcyone* was full of them! Oh, God!

And I had not discovered Anderson's attitude to duelling!

(8)

Thus it was. A fire burned the exhaustion out of me and supplied with its unseen flames a temporary resource of strength which kept me, though fallen on my bunk with—but my store of language had not been assembled for what I now felt had befallen me, a man of such superior intellects, of common sense! Oh, I was, I am, fallen so deeply and generously in love! It was excitement but it was fear too—fear of treading in a new world for which my character was by no means suited or adequate, a chancy, gambler's world—she bound for India, I for the Antipodes—my career—that advantageous alliance with—

Edmund Talbot lay fully clothed on his bunk, desiring nothing so much, able to think of nothing so much, burning for nothing so much as a parson's penniless daughter!

At length I remembered and called for Wheeler, louder and louder till he came.

"Devil take it, man, you stink of rum!"

"Just spliced the main brace, sir. And I was owed some sippers."

"Captain Anderson—"

"Sir Henry persuaded him, sir. A real gentleman Sir Henry is."

"Very well. I require all my gear taken across and put in the cabin Mr Colley used."

"I can't do that, sir!"

"What do you mean 'can't do it'?"

"I haven't an order, sir!"

"I am giving you an order."

"Captain Anderson—"

334

"I have just been with him. He raised no objection, so you need not."

Wheeler began to grumble but I cut him off.

"Come to think of it you can lay out my evening clothes here before you do anything else."

Knee-breeches, pumps, stockings, tails—the man needed little guidance and it was soon done. I changed my clothes, then went across to Colley's cabin. What was stranger than I had imagined was to find myself in a cabin on the starboard side of the vessel—the right-hand side looking forward towards the sharp end! It was a mirror image of the one I had just vacated and to be there after all these weeks was like suddenly finding oneself left-handed! There was much noise from forrard and indeed noise of one sort or another from most parts of the vessel. Where I was at the back end of the ship there was noise too, from some of the cabins, voices raised and laughter. There had been, there still was what I was told later was called ship-visiting. The penalties for a similar activity on the part of the people were severe, for the same activity if carried out by them was known as "breaking ship". But we had had such an exchange of passengers and two sets of junior officers from wardroom to wardroom and gunroom to gunroom the air of this end of the ship was far livelier than it had been in Sir Henry's stateroom.

There came a knock at the door.

"*Entrez!*"

It was Summers wearing his accustomed shabby uniform suit and a worried expression.

"Mr Talbot, what is this?"

"Why are you not dressed for the ball, man?"

He brushed my question aside.

"Your change of cabin!"

"Oh that. We may well have Miss Chumley aboard."

"Edmund! This is impossible!"

335

"I am a little abroad in my wits, Charles. May we not leave it for a while?"

"You have had some hard knocks, but Colley's cabin—"

"I could not think of asking Miss Chumley to use a bunk in which the poor devil willed himself to death!"

Summers shook his head. He was not smiling.

"But do you not see—"

"Oh fudge, man! Why are you not dressed for dancing?"

Summers went pink under his tan.

"I shall not attend the ball."

"Methodist!"

"As I once told you, I have never learned to dance, Mr Talbot," he said stiffly. "Quadrilles, allemandes, valses have not come in my way. Do you not remember that I was promoted from the lower deck?"

"The sailors dance!"

"Not as you do."

"Still bitter, Charles?"

"Every now and then. But I have volunteered to keep the watch during the hours of the ball—if it gets under weigh, that is."

"Fate could not be so brutal as to prevent it."

"I shall spend the time pacing the quarterdeck and meditating the suddenly changed future before us."

"The peace. Changed? No, Mr Summers. I have studied history as much as I may. There will be no change. The only thing to be learnt from history is that nobody learns from history!"

"Who said that?"

"I did. Doubtless it has been said by others, will be said again—and with as little effect."

"You are a cynic."

"Oh, I? If you only knew, dear Charles—I am excited, and"—the words "in love" trembled on my lips, but some remaining trace of reserve in my character kept me from uttering them—"in a state of slight intoxication owing partly to a small amount of brandy and the fact that I have not slept for several years, I believe!"

"The blows on your head—"

"Self-inflicted wounds."

"*Alcyone* carries a surgeon."

"Not a word, Charles! He would keep me from the ball, a prospect not to be entertained for an instant!"

Summers nodded and withdrew. I could hear from the noises around me that the hour of the "entertainment" had come. I shot my lace cuffs and settled a ruffle that had been sadly crushed in its long stowage. I opened the door of my new *hutch* and joined the throng which was now making its way from our lobby up the stairs whence we were to watch the entertainment offered us by the people. It was quite extraordinary to see Miss Granham sweep past me in blue and Mrs Brocklebank in green and Miss Zenobia in all the colours of the rainbow! But my amusement at seeing such a festive gathering was nothing to my utter amazement when we issued into the waist! To begin with, dusk had become a night even darker than usual because of the humid mist which still enclosed us. Islanded in this night was a space. Our space, our whole world was now so brilliantly illuminated that instead of being a minute speck in the midst of infinite extents it had enlarged to become the vastest of arenas. The sailors had hung lanterns everywhere, some of them with coloured glasses so that our streets and squares were not only lighter than by day but prismatical. There was much bunting. There were garlands, swags, crowns and sceptres of flowers far too large to be natural. Stir, as it were, into that the brilliance of our ladies, the glitter of uniform and the sawing, blowing and banging of Sir Henry's band which was now dispensing jollity from some concealed cavern in the front end of our vessel! The ladies and officers of

Alcyone had now emerged into their square and were coming in procession up the street that had formerly been a gangway to *our* larger square at the entrance to which young Mr Taylor, all dressed up, was doing the pretty and far too attentive to the ladies for one of his tender years! Indeed, I had to step forward and detach Miss Chumley from him, as he seemed inclined to detain her. I did so with much firmness, fended off a couple of lieutenants and set her without more ado on Captain Anderson's left with myself on her other side. If the ship's people called me "Lord Talbot" in jest I might as well take advantage of my reputation! I did all this with the determination and success which I hope would have attended our own boarding party, had it been put to the test. Lady Somerset was on Anderson's right.

Sir Henry rose, and the whole assembly, both fore and aft, rose with him. The band struck up and "God Save the King" was rendered with much solemnity. That being concluded, we were about to sit down again when a fellow stood forth and gave us "Rule Britannia" which all echoed lustily and with much joy. Indeed, at the conclusion the huzzahs for His Majesty the King, for the French King, for the Prince Regent, for the Emperor of Russia, then coming nearer home, for Sir Henry and his lady, for Captain Anderson—why God bless my soul, I believe had not Sir Henry said a few well-chosen words of thanks we would have gone on huzzahing all night! However, we were seated at last and the evening entertainment began. A fellow stood forward and gave a *loyal address* in what he thought was verse—the most one-legged set of couplets ever composed, I swear.

> *Sir Henry Somerset and Captain Anderson*
> *Now that most battles is over and done*
> *With many losses of life and horrible wrecks*

We ask leave to come forward, toe the line, and pay our
respects.

My immediate feeling was one of pity and embarrassment
for the man. However, looking back, I have to admit that
Miss Chumley's quiet but positively schoolgirlish giggle
had little of sympathy in it. The man could read and was
conning paper. That was the extraordinary thing about him.
He was small and wizened. Every now and then his bald
head would gleam at us in the light from the lanterns. He
had several papers and I began to understand that this
address was a corporate effort. He had not thought, or perhaps had not enough paper, or had no previous experience to
impress on him the importance of a fair copy! He was forced,
therefore, to look from one paper to another, then get at a
third which he held upside down and so was compelled to
look up at it under his arm and address us in that position.
One of his contributors had a stale poetical vocabulary, so at
one moment we were in the high style and the French had

> *...ploughed in vain*
> *The foamy billows of the bounding main.*

Then in a line or two we were back with

> *...now we have done all these*
> *There is nothing between us and home but the damned*
> *Yankees—*

I leaned towards her and was about to comment on the
embarrassment it all caused me when she whispered
behind her fan that she had not heard anything so diverting
since the bishop's address at her confirmation! I was overcome with delight at this evidence of wit in the enchanting
creature and was about to confide that she had bound me
more firmly than before when I was interrupted by a roar
of laughter from the fo'castle—

339

"What did he say, Miss Chumley?"

"Something about 'Billy Rogers'. Who is he?"

I was deeply shocked but of course did not allow her to see it.

"He is one of our sailors."

But no sooner had I turned back to the performance when I heard that

> *Mr Prettiman and his lady have put up the banns*
> *In order to get a party of little Republicans—*

This was sailing near the wind with a vengeance! But I am sorry to say that the laughter of the ship's people was mixed with a great deal of unlooked-for applause. It did, however, disconcert the social philosopher who looked down and blushed as did, for once in her life, his redoubtable bride to be. I began to understand that this was to be a period of licensed fooling and listened with mild amusement to references to Mr Brocklebank and even contrived to look indifferent (oh, what a roar there was from the fo'castle!) when the man said of the wind that it

> *Roared loud enough to wake the dead*
> *Or loud as "Lord Talbot" when 'e 'it 'is 'ead.*

But all was turned the other side out and a private sun shone on me and on Miss Chumley when she said severely—

"That was most unkind!"

"You are all consideration, my—"

Oh, I could not even use the simple, the gentle familiarity of "my dear" with this smiling girl I had known since God drew out that first rib from Adam!—"Miss Chumley."

So the address went on. He wound to a peroration which was concerned neither with loyalty nor duty but *food*! Was there ever anything at all as much like the *art of sinking*? The main suggestion was that we should now make for a port in South America where we might take in fresh meat and green vegetables. I had not myself noticed any great deficiency in our diet and was about to remark on this to my fair companion when I heard:

> *We find*
> *That the vittals we have on board caused so much wind*
> *That it is strange the ship is so still and steady*
> *And has not been blowed to Sydney Cove already.*

Sir Henry shouted with laughter at this and made some jocular sound in Anderson's direction. Little Mr Tommy Taylor laughed so much he fell off his seat. To my astonishment this was the end of the address. The man gave a kind of curtsey to us, then made his way back into the crowd of emigrants and sailors who thronged the fo'castle and the *stairs* up to it. He received much applause from them and there was some chanting of "Fresh food! Fresh food!" but it died away. Now the orator's place on the deck was taken by, of all people, Mrs East! She had evidently recovered if not completely from her miscarriage, at least sufficiently to allow her to walk; but she was painfully thin and there were still the shadows like a wasting disease in her cheeks.

"That is Mrs East."

"You know her, sir?"

"I know of her. She has been mortally sick. A—she has been near to death, poor creature."

Mrs East began to sing!

The effect was extraordinary. An absolute stillness descended on the city, there was not a movement, not a sound. She stood, clad in the simplest of dresses, her hands clasped before her; and that stance made her seem child-like—an appearance which was enhanced by her physical emaciation. The song rose from her mouth. She was accompanied by no instrument. Her unaided voice silenced or kept silent a whole crowd of sailors warmed with drink. It was a strange song—strange and simple! I had never heard it before. It was called "Bonnie at Morn" and it was simple as a hedge rose yet it haunts me still—oh, not for her, not for Mrs East, not for anything but itself, I think— as the sounds of the boatswain's call haunted me after the funeral of poor Colley. I was confused in my head, of course, I had forgotten what it was to sleep—yet like the boatswain's call it changed everything. It admitted us—it admitted *me* to halls, caverns, open spaces, new palaces of feeling—how foolish and impossible! Those tears which I had been able to restrain at my introduction to a new life now fell. I could not help it. They were neither tears of sorrow nor of joy. They were tears—and I do not know how this is possible—they were tears of *understanding*! When the song ended there was still silence, as if people heard some echo and were loath to believe that it had died away. Then there was a kind of grunt that led to prolonged and I am sure heartfelt applause. Miss Chumley shut her fan, allowed it to hang from her little finger by the ring at one end and laid her palms together three times.

"She sings well, Mr Talbot, does she not?"

"Oh yes."

"Our singing master, you know, would have wished more tremolo and of course a more practised presentation."

"Yes. I suppose so."

"Why, sir—you—"

"Forgive me, Miss Chumley. Remember I have been hit over the head and am not entirely—"

"It is I who should ask forgiveness! I applaud your sensibility. The song was indeed touching, well sung and in tune. A piece of nature! There! Does that go any way towards contenting you?"

"Anything you say contents me."

"You must recover slowly, sir, from such an injury! You are not to be exposed all at once to the profounder human emotions. See! They are about to dance a hornpipe, I believe. So I may talk without fear of interrupting the music. Do you know, sir, I once had to compose an essay on the subject of Art and Nature? Now would you believe it? Though I fear young persons are sadly docile—or should I say dutiful?—yet while the others were positively eloquent in their defence or advocacy of Nature—for it is fashionable nowadays to believe in Nature, you know—I discovered to my astonishment that I preferred Art! It was the moment at which I became an adult. For you see I believe I was the only young person in the school who saw that orphans are the victims of Nature and that Art is their resource and hope. I was dealt with very severely, I can tell you."

"They had not the heart!"

"Oh indeed!"

"I am recovered, Miss Chumley, and can only apologize once more."

"I am *so* happy to hear it! Indeed, sir, I sacrificed myself on your behalf in a reference to my unfortunate essay. Lady Somerset must never be allowed to know that I have said a word against Nature. It would shock her deeply. She is persuaded that India is a natural paradise. I believe she may be disappointed."

"And you?"

"Oh, I? What I expect is nothing to the purpose. Young persons are like ships, Mr Talbot. They do not decide their fate nor their destination."

"I am grieved to hear you say so."

"Oh, something may be done! Come, sir, I will not have you grieving!"

"What are we to do?"

"Why, enjoy the entertainment and the ball and the, the company! I cannot speak more plainly."

The hornpipe was much less expert than the one we see commonly danced in theatres. It was replaced by Morris Dancers! They were eight men in the usual smocks and straw hats. They carried wooden swords which they wove into a ring and held up for our languid applause. They also had the Hobby Horse! He committed as many improprieties as he could and chased the young women. He then circled forward to where the ladies sat but was told sharply enough to go off and return whence he came. He did so, but by some simple mechanism erected his tail in a way which would have earned John Coachman his discharge on the spot! Sir Henry then stood up and thanked the people for their entertainment and wished them joy of the peace. His band now took up a new station and our quadrille commenced. The people did not take Sir Henry's hint but crowded every vantage point with a good enough humour. I might here set down the conversation which ensued between Miss Chumley and me. But it was sufficiently banal, I think. Despite what is written in novels it is difficult to dance and talk when you have got out of the way of such a social activity. Having little help from me, Miss Chumley was silent and we moved together with a feeling of such community it was perhaps more satisfying than speech.

Nevertheless I was soon a little disturbed. Deverel, though under open arrest and forbidden drink, had most unadvisedly joined the company. Since the officers were not wearing swords there was nothing to distinguish him from the other gentlemen and he might have enjoyed the ball without being noticed. But it was plain to me, at least, that he had been drinking; and now, when glasses of wine and spirits were borne round, he took a glass and despite the captain's express prohibition boldly tossed it off. He then claimed Miss Chumley for the next dance which I had begged—without any inclination but with what I hope was a well-feigned eagerness—from Lady Somerset. What with my endeavours to recollect the pattern of the dance and the lady's practised conversation I was able only to give a glance now and then at how Deverel was conducting himself. He was, I saw, if not encroaching, at the very least ingratiating. Lady Somerset gave it as her opinion that the allemande with its steps and circling movement was a more natural dance—by which she meant I believe more according to *Nature*—than the formal quadrille. Deverel made play with Marion's hand, oh God. Lady Somerset commended the energies of our men who had so sanded the deck it was quite, quite the equal to a ballroom. Deverel made a positive *advance* to his partner! I missed two steps.

"No, no! The right foot, sir!"

Somehow we got back into time. I begged Lady Somerset to allow her protégée to exchange into our ship—there was room—to do otherwise was to inflict such suffering on a delicate person—But Lady Somerset ceased to sway and showed unexpected and what I now see to have been a clear-sighted common sense.

"Come, Mr Talbot. We know who is suffering and who will continue to!"

"I refuse to allow circumstances to thwart me!"

"A proper sentiment in a young man, sir. Why this is the stuff of poetry and here am I, a devotee of the muses, forced to be the one all poets deride!"

"No, ma'am!"

"Oh yes. If you were yourself, Mr Talbot, and not suffering from the effect of your injuries you would see it as I do. Marion is in my care. She must remain in *Alcyone*. Of course she must. Daylight will bring you to your, your—"

She said no more and we danced for a while in silence. It seemed to me that Miss Chumley was finding Deverel positively impertinent. There was nothing I could do. However—

"If the mountain will not come to Mahomet—"

The dance ended, for which I was heartily thankful and for the fact that Miss Chumley hardly allowed Deverel to see her back to her seat but frankly walked away from him. After returning Lady Somerset to her husband I went to Miss Chumley, only to find Deverel slumped by her in my chair.

"Ha, Mr Deverel—my chair, I think!"

"Edmund Lord Talbot. Congratulations on your elevation, my boy. That makes you the highest rank in the Atlantic and is one in the eye for Rumble-guts and Windbag!"

Miss Chumley, who was not yet *quite* seated, quickly begged that we might take the air, for, said she, fanning herself busily, the atmosphere was insupportable to one so lately arrived from England. I offered her my arm and we went up to the rail of the quarterdeck where there was relief from the crowded company at least. I would wish to fill in the background to our dialogue with all the scenery of a tropic night—stars, an inky sea streaked and spotted with phosphorescence, but alas! Chance had wasted all that beauty in using it as a kind of backdrop for the trifling with Miss Brocklebank of which I was now ashamed and which I now felt, ridiculous as it must appear, had soiled me! I felt in need of a tub so that, did she but know, this young and delicate creature would not endure the merest touch of my hand! Who was now the Methodist? The scene in reality was more suited to my awareness of my new condition. It was a close mist, rendered foetid by the sojourn in one place of two crowded ships! We faced each other by the rail. I looked down at her, she looked up at me. The fan moved more and more slowly. Her lips moved and she made the shape of words without saying them. It was more than flesh and blood could endure.

"Miss Chumley, I will find some way—we must not

part! Do you not feel, do you not understand? I offer you—oh, what do I offer you? Yes, the ruin of my career, the devotion of a lifetime, the—"

But she had half turned away from me. She looked down into the waist, then immediately swung round and faced the other way, breathing quickly. I glanced down. Deverel lowered the glass he had raised in her direction, then staggered three steps sideways to end by putting out his left hand and supporting himself against the mast. He crossed his left leg over his right one, snatched a drink from a tray Phillips was carrying past, lifted the glass with what I can only call an air of bravado and drank directly to Captain Anderson! Now it is to be remembered that this transaction took place in full view of all the people of the two ships—the whole population of our town! I saw Captain Anderson's head sink as he leaned forward in his chair and knew, though he was facing away from us, that he had lowered the upper part of his face and projected that minatory jaw beneath it! The next dance had not yet begun so there was no music. I heard and everyone else heard each harsh word that he said.

"Mr Deverel, you were placed under open arrest and forbidden drink. Return at once to your quarters and stay there!"

I have never seen so furious a gaze in a face as that with which Deverel received this order. He lifted his glass not as if to drink but as if to dash it at Anderson—but some glimmer of common sense must have prevented him, for instead he turned aside and hurled it into the scuppers.

"By Christ, Anderson!"

Cumbershum got to him and had him by the shoulder.

"Be quiet, you fool! Say nothing!"

He shook Deverel impatiently and half-led, half-dragged him away. They disappeared into the lobby under the poop. There was a great burst of talking and laughter. Then the music struck up.

347

"Miss Chumley, let us stay where we are!"

"I must not disappoint your Mr Taylor."

"Little Tommy Taylor? Good God, the impertinent scamp! I will have his ears for this—and see! There he goes, led off by our Mr Askew by one of those same ears for some misdemeanour or other! You have lost a partner, ma'am, so we may stay where we are in the lee of the poop until the dance after this when I claim again. Do you resist?"

"I am your prisoner."

"Would it were so! But you are merciful and lend an ear to my heartfelt prayer."

Below us, Sir Henry was standing up and Captain Anderson.

"I beg the favour of a few words, Sir Henry. The quarterdeck?"

The two captains came up the ladder to the quarterdeck. Miss Chumley murmured to me.

"Should we not return?"

I laid my finger on my lips. The gentlemen passed and climbed up the second stairs. They began to march back and forth so that as they approached the rail their voices were clear, then faded as they turned away again.

"—is one of *the* Deverels, is he not? Unfortunate!"

Then after a turn—

"No, no, Anderson. There is no time for a court-martial. You know I am under express orders."

And again—

"—hope you may find some way on such an occasion to reduce the charge to one on which you are empowered to award your own punishment—the young fool! And a Deverel too! No, no, Anderson. It is your ship and your man. I heard nothing, you understand, and was deep in conversation with Prettiman's fiancée, a most superior woman."

Miss Chumley whispered again.

"I do believe we should return, Mr Talbot!"

"We are plainly to be seen by at least half of our little world, Miss Chumley, and—good God, what are they about?"

It was the ship's people on the fo'castle. They were performing their own quadrille! It was, to put it baldly, a parody of ours! It was quite horridly skilful. I do not believe the people themselves knew what cleverly satirical dogs they were! They could not, of course, perform the actual figures but by moving about in a more-than-stately manner, by curtseying and bowing they accomplished much. That young fellow in a sailcloth skirt who swooned, positively swooned past anyone he met, could be no one but Lady Helen! There was also a stocky old man with one of the "ship's boys" sitting on his shoulders. Together they reached to a considerable height and the rest of the company deferred to them ridiculously. There was much noise, laughter and clapping so that the music of the dance of which young Mr Taylor had been deprived was hardly to be heard. Miss Chumley observed the dance on the fo'castle with sparkling eyes.

"Oh, how happy they are, how gay! If only I—"

She said nothing for a while but I waited and at last she spoke, shaking her head.

"You would not understand, sir."

"Teach me."

Once more she shook her head.

Now Sir Henry and Captain Anderson descended from the quarterdeck and resumed their places of honour at the side of the dance.

"We should return too, sir."

"A moment! I—"

"I beg you will say no more. Believe me, sir, I understand our situation even more clearly than you do! Say no more!"

349

"I cannot leave you with as little mark of favour as might be accorded to any man in either ship!"

"It is the cotillion!"

So we did descend and took our places for this last dance. As we did so the ship's bells rang out, the boatswain's calls, and after that the voices of authority now speaking in unison.

"D'you hear there? D'you hear there? Pipe down! Pipe down!"

It was remarkable with what docility (for all their parodies and double issue of rum) the people disappeared into their own places. Only Sir Henry's band and a few of the emigrants, Mrs East among them, stayed to watch our final entertainment. We said little or nothing though the dance, as everyone knows, is designed for conversation. For me, it was only just bearable.

At last it ended, or as I might say—since it was less a pleasure than a grief—at last the thing was done. Some of the passengers said their farewells to Captain Anderson and left, the officers of *Alcyone* too. Sir Henry *collected* his lady and looked round. But Lady Somerset bore him away firmly to the gangway. Lanterns were going out everywhere in both ships. Captain Anderson, now a shadowy figure, stood by the mainmast, contemplated what had but now been a ballroom as if to see in what way it had been injured. Miss Chumley moved towards the gangway. I dared to take her by the wrist.

"I repeat, I cannot let you go tonight without more than such a mark of favour as might have been bestowed on any gentleman in either ship! Stay if only for a moment—"

"I am Cinderella, you know, and must run back—"

"Say rather in your fairy coach."

"Oh, it would turn to a pumpkin!"

From the deck of *Alcyone* came the dulcet voice of Lady Somerset.

"Marion dear!"

"Then say you do not regard me as little as these other gentlemen—"

She turned to me and I saw how her eyes shone in the gloom; and the whisper reached me, as heartfelt as a whisper can be.

"Oh—no indeed!"

She was gone.

(9)

My tears came again. Good God, I was a leaky vessel, used to keep my waters to myself but now cracked from top to bottom! I stood, my feet rooted to the deck, but this time by happiness not fear. Will there ever be a moment for me to match it? I do not think so. Unless—Captain Anderson turned, grunted me a "Good night, Talbot," and was about to ascend the stairs when Deverel emerged, or rather staggered, from below them. He carried a paper in his hand, came towards Anderson, then stood in front of him. He thrust the paper into the captain's face.

"Resign commission—private gentleman—issue formal challenge—"

"Turn in, Deverel! You are drunk!"

Now there ensued the most extraordinary scene in that semi-darkness which only the distant lights from the great stern lantern modified. For as Deverel endeavoured to make the captain take the paper the captain retreated. It became a chase, a ludicrous but deadly parody of "Touch" or "Blindman's Buff", for the captain dodged round the mainmast and Deverel chased him. Not convinced that the captain did this to avoid being struck—possibly a capital offence—Deverel shouted "Coward! Coward!" and continued to pursue. Now Summers and Mr Askew with Mr Gibbs behind them came running. One of them cannoned into the captain so that Deverel, following close behind, reached him at last. I could not see if the collision was intentional but certainly Deverel thought it was and cried out in triumph, to disappear almost instantly beneath a heap of the other officers. The captain leaned against the mainmast. He was breathing heavily.

"Mr Summers."

Summers's voice came, muffled, from the flailing heap.

"Sir."

"Put him in irons."

At that there was a positively animal howl from Deverel and the heap convulsed. The howling went on except when it was interrupted as Deverel sank his teeth into Mr Gibbs who took up the howling and cursing in his place. The group of struggling men moved away towards the shelter of the aftercastle, then disappeared. Shocked, I saw a shadowy Sir Henry climb to *Alcyone*'s quarterdeck. He seemed to be peering across at our ship. But he said nothing.

Young Mr Willis came running in his shirt, then disappeared forward. Captain Anderson stood by the folded paper that lay on the deck. He was breathing heavily and quickly. He spoke to me.

"I did not receive it, Mr Talbot. Pray be a witness to that."

"Receive in what sense, Captain Anderson?"

"I did not agree to take it. I made no move to take it."

I said nothing. Young Mr Willis returned. One of the older seamen came behind him with something clanking in his hand.

"What the devil?"

"It is the blacksmith," said Captain Anderson with his usual abruptness. "He is needed to restrain the prisoner."

"Good God! Good God!"

Summers came running.

"Sir, he is motionless. He is collapsed. Do you think—"

I could *feel* the captain lowering at him.

"Carry out my orders, Mr Summers. Since you are so tender you shall have them confirmed later in writing."

"Aye aye, sir. Thank you, sir."

"Now that paper on the deck. It is material evidence.

Observe I do not touch it. Kindly pick it up and take charge of it. You will be required to produce it later."

"Aye aye, sir."

"Mr Talbot, you have noted everything?"

I said nothing.

"Mr Talbot!"

What was best for poor Deverel? My head, no longer concerned with anything but the overwhelming absence of Marion Chumley, my love, my saint, had no place left in it for the severities of the law nor for calculation!

"I do not wish to interfere in a service matter."

Captain Anderson uttered that double cachinnation which the novelist is accustomed to denote inadequately by the letters "Ha! Ha!" But in this case they are more than inadequate, they are misleading. For they conveyed, if anything, his opinion of me and my actions in a less than flattering manner. It was nothing so cheery as laughter. It might be what the Old Testament credits the war horse with when it utters a like sound "in the midst of the battle". He was expressing his opinion of me in a way which could not be committed to paper and produced in evidence. It was clear that his opinion was unflattering. But subduing everything in me was my enchantment, my overthrow, sweet as it had been, and my need to get away and lie in that sweetness until at last after how many days and years I slept.

It made me angry.

"Devil take it, what do you expect of me? I am as aware as you are of the circumstances and their implications—"

"I do not think so, sir."

"It is possible that everything said in these moments may be produced in evidence. I will *not* be hasty!"

Captain Anderson lowered up at me in the gloom. Then with an abrupt nod he turned away and marched up to the quarterdeck. I held my head. Somewhere below us there sounded the hideous blows of a hammer on iron. I went to the gangway where even now a marine stood at one end and a soldier at the other. I retraced my steps and tiptoed up to the quarterdeck, then leaned on the rail to see if I could judge the exact spot behind the wooden wall where Marion might be trying to sleep. Sir Henry came across the deck.

"Sir Henry!"

"That was the devil of a row! Is all well now?"

"Sir Henry, I must speak with you!"

"Oh, Lord! Well, never let it be said a Somerset was less than obliging to a FitzHenry. Come aboard, my boy—no, not here, devil take it! Do you want to fall in the drink? There, by the gangway!"

I made my way round and he met me at the break of *Alcyone*'s poop.

"Now then, it's about little Marion, is it not? A charming girl but if you wish to correspond, my dear boy, you must get permission from Lady Somerset—"

"No, no, Sir Henry, it is more than that—"

"Good God! The little minx!"

"She is all sweetness, sir. I beg you will let me take passage in *Alcyone*."

"Good God! Have you—"

"I am Mahomet."

"Good God! You've been drinking, curse it, that's what it is!"

"No, sir! I wish to take passage—"

"Your career, my boy, your godfather, your mother, devil take it, what is all this about?"

"I—"

But what was I? Where was I?

"I'd do most things to oblige you, lad, but this is beyond anything!"

"I beg you, sir!"

"Of course, I was forgetting. You've had a rare clout over the head, my boy! Now come along!"

"Let me go!"

"Lend us a hand here!"

I do not know even now how Charles Summers appeared and Cumbershum. The soldier at the gangway must have helped. All I remember clearly as they forced me back was thinking that if Marion heard what went on she would never forgive me—and then I was being pushed into my bunk, with Wheeler pulling my pumps and unmentionables off. There was the pungent odour of the paregoric.

It seems probable that without Colley's natural ability in the art of description there is no way in which I can convey the confusion of what happened. Nor do I know at what point I became delirious nor, what is stranger and more awful to contemplate, at what point previously I had become delirious! I am told that the surgeon, called out of his bunk, did indeed come across to our ship and examine me, though I have no recollection of it. Perhaps then it was a young man in the grips of a real, physical fever induced by triple blows who dreamed of a meal in *Alcyone* and all that followed thereon? But no. I have been assured these things happened and that I conducted myself with no more than the *élan* natural in a young man until, that is, I went aboard our neighbour ship in the dark and spoke with Sir Henry. Then, as if some hold or brake had given suddenly, I became temporarily disordered in my wits. Certainly I remember—not fighting—but struggling with the group which was trying to restrain me. I remember, too, how desperately I tried to explain the absolute necessity of my transfer to *Alcyone*, a declaration of nothing but the truth, but taken by my nurses or gaolers as further proof of the derangement consequent on my wounded head! Then, while they removed my clothes I found that I could not say what I meant at all but was forced to utter a string of absurdities. I was in Colley's bunk, for when they got me to what had been mine, of course it was empty, so I was bundled across the lobby and heaved not without more danger to my head into a bunk forever reminiscent of that unhappy man. *Alcyone*'s surgeon they tell me could only advise rest and promised a complete cure at the end of it since my skull was not cracked. So, busily gabbling of what neither they nor I understood, I lay held down, while somehow they got the paregoric into me in a dose that rapidly had me singing for joy among the angels. So singing and so weeping with joy I fell at last into what we must call a healing sleep.

If to be restored to a complete understanding of one's situation is to be healed let us all, all prefer sickness. I did swim now and then up towards consciousness; or since the effect of the opiate was to elevate me towards some seventh heaven, let us say that now and then I swam or dived down towards consciousness without ever getting there. I remember faces—Charles Summers as might be expected, Miss Granham, Mrs Brocklebank. I am told that I implored Miss Granham to sing. Oh, the humiliations of delirium! The sordid, the very humbling necessities of the sickroom! Nor was my cabined humiliation complete, for I was to set a positive fool's cap on it myself—though once again if I am to be blamed it is for being so physically clumsy as to do nothing but bang my head while all the other passengers were obediently contributing to our defence! Delirious or sane I must remain enraged with myself and with my fate.

Partial understanding did return. As it had departed at a bound so it came back. I was aware of movement, my head thrust against the pillow, then allowed to fall back. I lay as this happened numberless times; and then, like a blast of cold wind, the understanding was there—we were under weigh, the wind was up and the sea. These were no flat regions but waters furrowed and rolling. I remember crying out. I fell out of my bunk, scrabbled the door open on the streaming lobby. Then I was out on deck, up the stairs and climbing into the shrouds, climbing up and howling some senseless words or other.

Yes. I remember that; and yes, I have pieced the episode together in all its absurdity. The ship is making what way she can over a beam sea and with much wind. For all the wind her way is little because the stumps of masts will not allow of a full spread. Few people are on deck, thank God. But then a haggard young man, shaggy as to the hair, and bearded not a little, staggers out from under the aftercastle, his thin body plainly to be discerned beneath the nightshirt that beats against him in the wind! He crawls up the shrouds, then clings, staring forward at the empty horizon and screaming at it!

"Come back! Come back!"

They got me down. They say I did not resist but finally allowed myself to be carried like a corpse and laid once more in Colley's bunk. I remember how Summers removed the key from the lock and put it in again on the outside. After that, for a time, any visitor unlocked the door, then locked it behind him when he left. I had declined to the status of a madman and prisoner. I remember, too, how when Summers left the first time and I was alone how I lay on my back and began to weep.

(10)

No man can weep for ever. There came a time when my preoccupation with my sorrow was first mixed and then near enough swallowed up in an awareness that the movement of our ship was not such as it had been, but more nagging and restless, with moments which seemed not so much of petulance as of fierce anger. I felt too weak to understand or combat it and fell into a childish panic at the thought of being worn down and abandoned in a sinking ship. I remember at last, God help me, shouting for Charles Summers, then bawling at Wheeler when he appeared instead.

"I must see Mr Summers! Get him!"

After that there was a long interval while the ship did its best to fling me out of my bunk. At last Charles appeared. He stood in the doorway, holding it open and frowning down at me.

"Again? What is it this time, Edmund?"

The words "this time" brought me up short.

"I am sorry. I believe I have been delirious."

"That will be all, Wheeler! I am speaking to Mr Talbot. Look, Edmund, I am the ship's husband—"

"The what?"

"I am responsible for more things than you can imagine. With the greatest goodwill in the world I cannot spare more than a little time for you! Now what is it?"

"The movement. It is killing me."

"Good heavens, Edmund, you are far down. Listen. You have been injured. *Alcyone*'s surgeon said you are suffering from delayed concussion. Sleep and rest are what he recommended."

"Neither is possible with the ship moving so."

"The movement cannot be helped. Will you be easier if I explain it?"

"I might feel easier to know we aren't sinking."

He paused for a moment, then laughed.

"Well then—do you understand the mechanism of a clock?"

"What do you take me for? A clockmaker? I know how to wind up my repeater. That's enough."

"Come. That's more like the old Edmund."

His mouth was open to say more but he was interrupted by the sounds of a screaming fit from one of the cabins at a distance from us. Perhaps it was the Pike children, in a quarrel near to hysteria. Charles ignored the screams and spoke again.

"A ship is a pendulum. The shorter a pendulum is, the quicker its oscillation. Our rig is shortened, in other words we have shortened our pendulum, and accelerated our motion. A completely dismasted ship can have a period of roll so brief there is no living with it, people are so flung about and sick and exhausted. I suppose ships have been lost so."

"But not us!"

"Of course not. The most this additional movement will do is discomfort our passengers. They do indeed need all the comfort they can get. Some of the gentlemen are gathered in the saloon. They spoke of you and wished you one of their number."

I sat up laboriously in my bunk.

"Accept my apologies, Mr Summers. I shall pull myself together and do what I can to cheer the other ladies and gentlemen."

Charles laughed, but amiably enough this time.

"From the depths of despair to a noble resolve in less than ten seconds! You are more mercurial than I supposed."

"Nothing like that."

"Well. The gentlemen will welcome you though you would be better advised to stay where you are like the ladies."

"I have been too long in my bunk."

Charles removed the key from the outside of the door and put it in the lock inside.

"Whatever you do, Edmund, take great care. Remember, one hand for yourself and one for the ship! In your case I advise both hands for yourself—you have been beaten about the head more than enough already."

So saying, he withdrew.

I climbed out of my bunk as cautiously as I could and inspected my face in the mirror. The sight appalled me. Not only was I heavily unshaven, my face was so thin as to be positively bony. I passed a finger over the prominent ridges of my cheeks, touched my high, but now thin nose, pushed the hair off my forehead. It is surely impossible that a skull should shrink!

I shouted for Wheeler who came with an instantaneity which showed he had been standing just outside the door. I had him help me to dress, refused his offer to shave me and then did it myself in a cupful of water which was no more than lukewarm when I started and stone-cold when I had finished. However, I contrived to perform the whole with no more than a single nick on my left cheek which in view of the ship's movement was a considerable achievement. Wheeler stood by me the while. He begged my pardon for making the suggestion but said that even if I was about to join the gentlemen in the saloon I should wear my India rubber boots there was so much water washing about. So observe me at last stumping, legs wide apart, one hand on the rail which was fastened to the outside of the passenger hutches. The ship swung me about pettishly and sheets of water slid across the darkened wood of the lobby. I knew at once it was not merely my weakness which made movement difficult. What was only tedious before was now an evil tax on strength.

Whatever talk had been among them, there was a silence for a while when I appeared. They sat round one end of the long table immediately under the stern window. Mr Bowles, the solicitor's clerk, was at the end. Oldmeadow, the young officer, sat on his left with Mr Prettiman left again. Mr Pike faced them. I reached the table at a run and collapsed on the bench next to him. Oldmeadow looked across at me down his nose. He means no hauteur by this carriage of the head. It is only natural to him because the extraordinary helmet the officers of his regiment wear has increased the angle somewhat and habituated him to it. He himself is the mildest and least warlike of men.

"I trust you are feeling more the thing, Talbot? It is good of you to join us."

"I am perfectly recovered, thank you."

That was a lie but in a good cause. Nevertheless it failed, for Mr Bowles shook his head at me.

"You do not look recovered, Mr Talbot. But then, all of us are affected."

"Oh, surely not! The movement if anything is cheering."

"Not to me. And not to the women and children."

As if to emphasize his speech, outside the great stern window the horizon sloped the other way with particular speed, then vanished downwards. The wet deck beneath lifted us up, then left us suspended as it fell. I felt sweat start out on my forehead.

"I think, gentlemen, that—"

But Bowles, whose stomach seemed indifferent to these antics, was going on.

"Now you are here, sir, you had better be co-opted at once. The motion—"

"It is due to the shortening of our rig, gentlemen. A pendulum—which is what—"

Bowles raised his hand.

"Not that motion, Mr Talbot. I refer to the motion before the committee."

"My children must be considered, Mr Talbot. And Mrs Pike, of course. But the little children, my Phoebe and my Arabella—"

I braced myself and emitted what I hope was a convincing laugh.

"Well, gentlemen, you surprise me! Britannia rules the waves, we all know, but—"

"We believe there may be a remedy."

"How? I cannot think what remedy you have found for a difficulty which is inherent in our situation! Or have you some such scheme as poor Dryden must have had in his head? I remember reading in his *Annus Mirabilis* where he describes in our seafight against the Dutch how the sailors when the masts were shot away 'raised them higher than before'."

"Mr Talbot—"

"And you know, even to a young landsman as I was then, the concept seemed the height of absurdity! I do not think that—"

Mr Prettiman shouted.

"Mr Bowles was elected chairman of this meeting, sir! Do you wish it adjourned or will you leave it?"

"Allow me, Mr Prettiman. Mr Talbot may be forgiven for supposing this is no more than a social gathering. Now, sir. We have constituted ourselves an *ad hoc* committee and come to certain conclusions. We wish to bring to the captain's notice, not so much our opinions, for it is doubtful that we have any right to them, but our deep feelings. I have the heads jotted down here. One. A prolonged continuation of the ship's movement as she endeavours to make way against the wind in her present unsteady condition constitutes a real danger to life and limb—particularly where the women and children are concerned. Two. We suppose that relief might be found by an alteration of course away from the wind and towards a South American port where the ship might be repaired and our health restored."

I shook my head.

"If such an alteration was necessary our officers would have made it."

Oldmeadow cawed into his collar in the way these fellows have when affecting to laugh.

"No, by Jove, Talbot. They may think of the ship and the people there in the front end but we may go whistle for consideration—and the Army most of all!"

"It would tediously prolong the time we spend in our voyage."

"Little Phoebe and Arabella—"

Bowles raised his hand again.

"One moment, Mr Pike. We hoped that you would agree with us, Mr Talbot. But then, does your agreement signify?"

"I beg your pardon, sir!"

"Don't misunderstand me. I mean that in the event the decision is not mine or yours but the captain's. All we plan at the moment is to make our wishes known. In fact, Mr Talbot, I must break it to you that *in absentia* you have been elected to—how shall I say—bell the cat!"

"The devil!"

"There was no one more able, Mr Talbot, we knew that—and you could take poor little Phoebe along and pull up her smock and show him the rash which I do not think is to be borne, sir, and what will happen if—"

"Mr Pike, for the love of God!"

"Or if you think it beneath you I will take her along—"

"Damn your insolence, Pike! I will take her along or them along or anyone along! Oh, for God's sake, all of you, let me think! I have been——"

I put my head down in my wet palms. Sick to the stomach—in love with a girl gone over the reeling horizon, head split and aching inside and out—the taste in my mouth of vomit already.

Bowles spoke softly.

"It is a compliment to you, sir. We are in your hands. No one else is so likely to have influence with the captain. Your godfather——"

I shook my head and he fell silent. I thought for a while.

"You are going the wrong way about it. An approach to the captain must be your last resort. Personally, I do not agree that we should alter course. Children are liable to rashes. Why—my young brothers—we ought to endure—carry on across this wilderness until we reach our end. But you have touched my, my … I will try to persuade the first lieutenant that he should carry your wishes to the captain. If he will not, or if the captain refuses that first approach, then yes, I myself will go to him." At last I took my head out of my hands and blinked round at them.

"We must go with great care. The position of a passenger in a ship of war—the captain's power may well be absolute. Who would have thought when I said he was our moghool that this occasion was waiting round the corner? I will make your views known to the first lieutenant. He may even be on deck—and now——"

I stood up and bowed. I reeled to the door and took a clumsy run through the streaming lobby, got the door of the hutch open and collapsed on my bunk. When Wheeler entered, he having, I suspected, waited outside the saloon door and then my door—and was only happy it seemed within arm's length of me as if he were harnessed for my convenience—Wheeler helped me into my oilskins. I muttered a queasy dismissal and he replied that he would remain to clean the cabin and "do what he could" with the bunk. I gave little thought to his curious assiduity but slumped for a while in my canvas chair to get myself together. At last I hauled myself to my feet and opened the door as the sheet of water in the lobby splashed over the combing which is supposed to keep it out of our hutches. I went forward into the daylight of the waist, holding on where possible. There was wind on the left, a grey sky above, grey sea, dirty white foam, a wet ship drab as the skirts of a beggar woman. The water in the lobby was as nothing to the positive tides of it which made an intermittent hazard of the open deck. There were safety lines rigged everywhere. These daunted by implication rather than invited and seemed at best no more than ropes tying together the wet, belaboured box that was our ship. I saw a seaman working his way along a rope to the fo'castle. He held on with one hand while a wave washed over him as high as his waist and a torrent of foaming water fell on his head and shoulders from the fo'castle itself. I waited for a pause in our motion, then made a staggering run to the windward side of the ship and hung on to a belaying pin under the ship's rail. I opened my mouth wide and took great gulps of the wet air which at least served to quell the unease of my stomach. I felt as strong an irritation at this latest demand on my tact and ingenuity as ever I had done when asked by Charles Summers to do what I could for the wretched Colley! And success, a turning aside from our present course to redirect the ship towards the coast of South America, would do no more for me myself than delay my arrival in the Antipodes! It would put beyond all possibility those faint hopes—a delay at the Cape of Good Hope—even their ship delayed and rescued by us as she wallowed mastless on our course—of seeing Miss Chumley once more before the remotest of remote futures!

I cursed aloud. As if to torment me further our ship, struck by a seventh wave, bucked like a frightened horse and seemed to remain without forward movement, for all her straining sails. I stared round me trying to understand what I could of our situation and I was rendered very thoughtful by what I saw.

The last time I had watched the conduct of our ship in such weather had been in the English Channel. There, as if she were aware that she was under the eye of Old England, for all the boisterousness of the sea and sky she had seemed to take part and revel in the friendly contest. She did so no more. Like a horse which knows itself tired and moving further and further away from its stable, she jibbed and went slow. She was sullen and needed a touch of the whip—better still, a whiff of the manger! Although her bows were pointed up towards the wind she had next to no forward movement. The waves passed under her— or sometimes, it seemed, over her—but she did hardly more than heave up, then slide down into the same trough in the same place. I dared to haul myself upright and peer over the rail by me. I was rewarded by the sight of what looked like green hair swirling among foam as if those fabled and inimical sisters swam about us holding us back and pulling us down! Before I had recovered from the cold thrill of the sight the whole sea with its hair and foam rose at me, over me, drowned me, pulled at me with appalling strength so that my two hands clutched round the iron barrel of the belaying pin were no more than just enough to prevent me from being washed clean out of the ship and lost for ever.

Someone was shouting in my ear.

"This is no place for passengers! Get back while you may! Come now—make a run for it!"

It was a voice with extraordinary authority. I did run, splashing through a few inches of pouring water as the deck came momentarily up to the horizontal, then continued to swing over in the other direction. My feet slipped and I should have performed a glissade which would have smashed my bones in the opposite scuppers had not the man running beside me grabbed my arm and fairly lifted me onto the stairs leading up to the afterdecks. Here he pushed me against the rail, made sure I was attached, then stood back.

"You were nearly gone, sir. Mr Talbot, I believe."

He pulled off his sou'wester and shook out far more golden locks than a man ought to have. He was smaller than I. But then—so are most people! He smiled up at me with great cheerfulness as a volley of spray shot past us. I had an instant impression of blue eyes, pink cheeks and ruddy lips which seemed by their delicacy to have evaded the wildness of the weather and even the touch of the tropic sun.

"Thank you for your assistance. To tell the truth my strength has not yet come back. But you have the advantage of me."

"Benét, sir. Lieutenant Benét with one 'n', and an acute accent on the second 'e'."

I was lifting my free hand to take his politely but as I did so he raised his head and his face changed to one of anger. His eyes seemed to sparkle as he stared forward and up into the rigging.

"Francis, you careless bugger! If I see you slip out of the strop to save yourself trouble I'll have you at the grating!" He turned back to me. "They are worse than children, Mr Talbot, and will kill themselves heedlessly where you might well have done it through ignorance. You must allow me to conduct you to your cabin—no, no, Mr Talbot, it is no trouble—"

"But you are employed about the ship!"

For answer he glanced up at the rigging again.

"Mr Willis! Although you are mastheaded you may consider yourself in charge of the work there and the men employed about it. Contrive not to lose the mainmast. Now, Mr Talbot—run for it!"

To my surprise I found myself obeying this young man with an alacrity which even Captain Anderson could not have produced in me. What is more I jumped into the lobby with a sense of what a jest it all was!

"That will be all, Wheeler. Mr Benét, pray be seated."

"You are a sick man, sir. I am not sick in body, though perhaps in mind it is a different story. Grief fills my sails.

> *Fairest woman*
> *In form and feature really most uncommon.*

I worked that out and more of the like during the last dog. Oh, I remember now. It went

> *Fairest creature lovelier than a woman*
> *In form and feature really most uncommon.*

The lines were wrenched from me. They came all in one piece.

> *Nor would I lay*
> *A feather of regret upon thy soul.*

The feather is particularly felicitous, is it not?"

A painful suspicion grabbed at my heart.

"You are from *Alcyone*!"

"Where else in this waste of water?

> *A long, long exile now must be my lot.*

Do you approve the alliteration? We shall meet again of course. But I am summoned to a conference with the first lieutenant in the hold."

He withdrew briskly. I shouted for Wheeler who as usual was near my hutch. He got me out of my oilskins.

"That will be all, Wheeler."

A young man with golden locks, fair face and weeks of access to Miss Chumley! Now I experienced all that anguish which I had thought exaggerated by poets!

(11)

I came to myself again to hear unusual noises in the hutches on my side of the lobby. They came nearer and at last, with a knock on my door, revealed themselves to have been caused by the carpenter, Mr Gibbs, who had curious leather pads strapped to his knees.

"Sorry to trouble you, sir, but I have to follow the run of the planking."

"What on earth for?"

Mr Gibbs scratched in his sandy hair. At a distance of about a yard I caught a whiff of strong drink.

"The fact is, sir—pardon!—they say she's moving a bit which is what you'd expect seeing she's so long in the tooth—"

"She's 'rendering like an old boot'."

Mr Gibbs seemed gratified by my comprehension.

"Just so, sir. Just that and nothing more. Nothing to worry the passengers. It's surprising when a gentleman like you as has been at sea no more than a dog watch knows what's what. Mr Brocklebank when I did his cabin didn't hardly understand what I was on about though he did give me a drink for my trouble—"

Mr Gibbs paused and eyed my bottle of brandy but I did not respond. He knelt down therefore and began to extract my two drawers from beneath my bunk which was not easy to do in that confined space.

"What the devil are you doing, Gibbs? Careful! Those are my shirts!"

"I won't dirty your dunnage, sir, but I just has to get my hand—ah!"

"Can't you hear me under there?"

371

"I got to get my hand where they're butted—"

His speech turned instantly into a kind of squeal. He backed out, put his fingers in his mouth and sucked them, rocking from side to side and moaning.

"What have you done, Gibbs?"

He went on rocking and moaning, one hand holding the other to his mouth.

"Brandy!"

"Help yourself if you must. Good God, man, you've gone sallow!"

Mr Gibbs did not trouble himself with the nicety of my tumbler. He took the bottle out of its hole in the shelf above my canvas washbasin, pulled the cork with his teeth and stuck the neck in his mouth. I believe before he took another breath he had swallowed a quarter of the bottle.

"You'll be drunk as an alderman!"

He put the bottle back in its hole, flexed his fingers and blew on them.

"After all these years to be caught that way like a 'prentice! Oh yes, she's what you might call rendering. Some might call it that, sir, and some might call it something else but it don't matter, do it?"

"Is there danger?"

"Rendering. You know, sir, being took flat aback didn't do her no good at all. Yes, she's rendering. I wouldn't really like to say what's going on in her one way and another— though when a man has stuck a spike into every piece of timber in the ship and had his nose to the planking like a dog after a bitch, why he gets her in his head—"

"Her?"

"Her whole shape more than if she was his own wife and neater than was ever drawed out in the loft. All the movement and every bolt—"

"Our ship?"

Mr Gibbs sat back on his heels.

"Our ship as ever is. And after all that, a man can do with a bleeding drink or two."

"We're in danger then!"

Mr Gibbs focused his eyes on me, frowning as if it were a great effort. He scratched again in his short, sandy hair and seemed to come to himself. His face cleared and he smiled. The smile was not convincing, however.

"Danger, Mr Talbot? Now don't you go worrying! I've knowed ships you might think was falling apart and they come home to lie up snug as if they was all seasoned timber and twenty-one shillings to the guinea. Not but what—"

He paused and sucked his fingers again.

"Go on, man. Tell me!"

Mr Gibbs smiled in my direction but vaguely.

"She's seasoned all right, sir. There isn't a bit of wood where it matters as isn't older than any man in the ship unless it might be Martin Davies, poor sod. The real danger you see, sir, is when you get a mix, like—seasoned and unseasoned. When I was only *that* high I come across a bud sticking out of a knee—must have been dead, of course, but how was I to know that? I told the chippy's mate but he took no kind of notice of it beyond giving me a clip over the earhole."

Mr Gibbs gave my depleted bottle of brandy a thoughtful look.

"I would advise against more brandy, Mr Gibbs."

"Ah well. I wasn't more than a nipper but I had nightmares about that bud. Once I woke up hollering, having fell out of the hammock and felt about in the dark for the chippy's mate—Gilbert, he was called, had me calling him Mr Gilbert—I felt about in the dark and of course I could no more than reach the underside of the hammock to give it a prod. 'What the fuck?' shouts he. 'Mr Gilbert,' I hollers, 'that there bud, it's a twig!' He leans out of his hammock and gives me a clip where he thought I was, only I wasn't.

'I'll give you twig, you bit of grommet,' he says. 'I don't like it,' I says, 'it's putting out a leaf.' He gives me a clip and that one took me fair between wind and water. 'A leaf is it now,' he says. 'You can call me when it puts out a fucking flower.' "

Mr Gibbs seemed to find the memory pleasant, for he was shaking his head and smiling.

"There was a ship once, Mr Gibbs, put out so much greenery you could hardly see it for leaves."

"You're having a little joke, sir."

"There was a vine grew out of the mast and it made everybody drunk."

"The drunk part don't surprise me at all, sir. What port was she said to come from?"

"She was a Greek ship, I think. Mythological."

"That them lot used unseasoned timber don't surprise me; but in those parts they don't hardly drink at all! You'll excuse me, I know—"

The man helped himself to another drink from the bottle.

"Well really, Mr Gibbs!"

"A nice drop, sir. I don't think I'll be in any case to work when it bites. Ah! Here it comes!"

Mr Gibbs, still sitting back on his heels, shut his eyes and swayed against the movement of the ship. There was a pause while he said nothing and my new passion returned upon me.

"Mr Benét seems a very pleasant gentleman. I imagine he might well make himself very pleasant to a lady."

"Very pleasant all round, sir, though his parents is hemmy-grease. He wrote some poetry for the entertainment, though it was so high and mighty I couldn't understand a word of it. The brandy is really biting, sir. I'd be glad if you don't let on to the first lieutenant. Yes, very pleasant Mr Benét is and, Lord, he might be the other side of the Cape and making fifteen knots and a nigger if he hadn't been so sweet on the captain's lady!"

"Doubtless he—what did you say?"

"There I go again. Never did know when enough was enough. Everybody knows, only they didn't say it above a whisper seeing he's an officer. Caught them the captain did, him on his knees and she not trying to get away very hard."

"Lady Somerset! And I, I feared that—but how was this?"

Mr Gibbs scrambled unhandily to his feet. He lurched against this table-flap at which I am writing. His face that had been sallow was now red and sweating. This together with his sandy hair made it easy to imagine a spirituous conflagration inside him! He touched his forelock in a way which I am sure is unbecoming in an officer even though he be no more than warranted. He staggered again, opened the door and went flying *downhill*, if I can so express it, half-way across the lobby. He returned backwards, thumped the next cabin, then was to be heard diminishingly as he made his way below. Wheeler, who must have been *appliqué'd* against the plywood bulkhead which formed the wall of our hutches, shut the door for me, then opened it again and announced submissively that he would replace the drawers. There seemed no room for me in my own cabin.

"Wheeler. The ladies must have found the movement of *Alcyone* insupportable."

"Yes, sir. I dare say, sir."

"Miss—Miss Chumley must have spent the whole voyage out from England in her bunk."

Wheeler said nothing. I was uncomfortably conscious of the impropriety of making such a remark to a servant. I tried again.

"Mr Benét—"

The words stuck in my throat. I could by no means move towards the subject which was the source of such delight and anguish to me! Yet surely there was someone to whom I might confess—it seemed that "confess" was the word—that I was in love and desired nothing so much as to *talk* about the Beloved Object even though I could not talk *to* her!

"Wheeler—"

The man was looking submissively at a point below my chin. Now he lifted his eyes and seemed to examine each part of my face in turn curiously as if the face of a man was something new and strange to him.

"Very well, Wheeler. That will be all."

For a moment or two the man continued to stare into my face, then seemed to "come to" with a slight start.

"Yes, sir. Thank you, sir."

"And another thing, Wheeler. You was a lucky dog, you know. It must have been a chance in a million! It would be proper to give thanks, you know."

An extraordinary shudder shook the man from head to foot. He bent his head and got out of the door without looking at me again. Certainly there was no possibility of making a confidant of him—and somehow I could not feel that Charles Summers, so understanding in many ways, would be understanding in matters of the heart! It was Mr Benét or no one—Mr Benét who must surely know Miss Chumley—who was in love—who would sympathize—

How was I to follow him down into the hold?

Deverel! Deverel my one-time friend whom sickness and love to say nothing of circumspection and dislike had driven from my mind! Deverel in irons! I would descend looking for him and come across Mr Benét and Charles Summers as it were accidently. I would open in that privacy not just the committee's request but my opinion of it. I rebuked myself for my lack of consideration, my forgetfulness of a friend in need. Only my injuries and my "delayed concussion" could excuse it. Later, I would detach Benét from Charles and lead the conversation gently round to *Alcyone* and her ladies!

I made a lurching, zigzag progress down the ladders, rehearsing my various speeches as I went. The last time I had come that way I had been impelled, not to put too fine a point on it, by lust. Now that I was descending again through those shadowy, those heaving and creaking and dripping and trickling levels, I understood only too well the difference between that descent and this one. I felt the depth of my engagement! The penalty of a "level head", of a politic and cautious habit of mind, is that the day of our first and last passion is delayed and all the stronger for being unexpected!

Picture me then descending to the low level of the gun-room which was yet the lightest of all. Those who make themselves the snuggest in a ship are the warrant officers and here they were using more light than all the becandled passengers together. No less than three lanterns swung from the deckhead. These three—not the cut bottles which the seamen fill with tallow but heavy objects of brass—exhibited a movement which you can find nowhere but in a ship unless it might be, of all places, the ballet. They swung exactly in time and to the same angle. Or rather—this is difficult to describe, I need Colley's pen—they appeared to swing. It was the ship that moved, of course, while the lanterns by virtue of their loaded bases hung steady. It was unnatural and sickening. I looked away and found that by contrast with this brilliant illumination the corners of the gun-room were densely dark. Patches of shadow moved and changed as the lanterns performed their strange dance. As I came through the door the three presented me with their brass bottoms, then flipped back with a revealed glare of light, hovered for a moment or two, then swung back towards me again. It was enough to drive a man out of his wits, these lights dancing in a row. I had difficulty in keeping my head clear and the foul taste out of my mouth.

Mr Gibbs was nowhere to be seen. But opposite me on the other side of a fixed table sat Mr Askew, our gunner, with the ancient midshipman, Mr Davies, beside him. Mr Davies rested his wrinkled and veined hands on the table. His mouth was slightly open and he was staring at nothing. It was as if the constant inconstant lanterns with their flash then dark (huge shadows performing a similar movement over further parts of the great room) had kept him silent, and spellbound as one of M. Mesmer's subjects—kept him with an empty head, waiting for some order which might never come.

Mr Askew looked at me bleakly. He had a glass before him. He did not seem glad to see me.

"And what might you want down here, sir? He's turned in."

He jerked his head towards a particularly dark corner. A sluglike object was suspended there from the deckhead by both ends.

"Mr Deverel—"

"That there, Mr Talbot, is George Gibbs. He come down here all of a twist saying you'd made him drink brandy to which his constitution is unused. He fairly tossed down his rum and was that far gone I had to sling his hammock and heave him into it. If we see him again any time between now and the middle you can call me Lady Jane."

"I wish to visit Lieutenant Deverel."

Mr Askew eyed me closely. Then he put down his glass and took out a short clay pipe. He fumbled about under the table.

"Martin! What have you done with my prick?"

He nudged Mr Davies who rocked a little but did nothing otherwise. Mr Askew thrust his right hand into the midshipman's left pocket.

"You thieving bastard, Martin!"

He drew out a long object wrapped in canvas and proceeded to cut a slice from the end of it. He crammed the slice into the bowl of the pipe, took a piece of "slow match" from a "half-bottle" and laid the glowing end on the tobacco. He puffed out a quantity of stinking smoke so that I gagged. I became aware that I was swaying between the doorposts, one hand on each in a way which must appear positively silly.

"Kindly tell me where Lieutenant Deverel is, Mr Askew, and I will withdraw from these premises since I do not seem to be welcome in them."

Mr Askew continued to puff without saying anything. Suddenly the lights and shadows, the insane, balletic dance of the lanterns, which was a counter-image of the ship's uneasy motion in the sea, took me by the head and throat and stomach and knees.

"If you don't mind—"

I staggered forward, grabbed the table and fell onto the bench. The evil smoke curled round me and I felt the sweat start out on my brow.

"Not feeling quite the thing are you, Mr Talbot? Not quite so much the 'lord' these days?"

This was too much. I swallowed whatever was in my mouth.

"I may not be a peer, Mr Askew, but I am commissioned to serve His Majesty in ways you probably never heard of and would not understand. You will oblige me by paying my position the respect due to it from a warrant officer of the Navy, however senior."

Mr Askew continued to puff. Under the deckhead the

smoke now hung, bellying as if a chimney needed cleaning. His face had turned a dusky red, but not, I think, as
Mr Gibbs's had done from his potations. One puff of
smoke rolled insolently near my face. When he spoke his
voice was cracked and tremulous.

"It's 'ardly—hardly lovable, is it?"

"Lovable? *Lovable?*"

"The carry-on. The swaying about. The hoity-toity.
Since we have got so far and there is no one to hear."

I glanced significantly at Mr Davies, still silent, still
bound by the spell. Mr Askew removed his pipe and
wiped the stem with a yellow and horny thumb.

"You see I liked the way you took those blows to the
head and come up all set to be a hero. To do what you
could, I mean. He'll be a man one day, I said to myself, if
someone don't kill him. Only you don't know nothing, do
you? In the entertainment when Joss read that bit about
'Lord Talbot' if you'd stood up and bowed with your
hand on your heart and a smile on your face we'd have
took our corn from your hand as sweet as a miller's don-
key. Only you puckered up like. Oh, I know it's hard
when you're young—"

"I am more than—"

"You're young, you see. There's officers and warrant
officers and petty officers and seamen of this and that—
captains of tops and captains of heads and the poor bloody
seamen what don't know sugar from shit as they say in
Pompey—"

"I will not allow this to continue in front of a witness!
Make a private conversation of it, sir, and I shall know
how to answer you!"

"Witness? Who? Martin? Bless you, Martin won't give
trouble. Why—listen!"

He nudged the old man, then leaned sideways and
spoke close to his ear.

"Sing, Martin! Good Martin!"

He paused. The lanterns danced, there were water noises and the creak and stretch of timber.

"Sing, Martin."

With a reedy, quavering voice, the old man sang: "Down to the river in the time of the day—"

It was the beginning and the end of his song. It was the endless end, over and over again.

"He's the real bottom of the barrel, isn't he? I suppose he might have rose to be a lieutenant if he'd had luck or a shove up the bum from an admiral. But it don't matter to him now, does it? Not what he was or might have become. He's had it all and gone home, sir. He don't hear us, isn't here."

"I—I don't know what to say."

"Brings a man up against it, don't it? Less trouble to stop a round shot in the guts if you ask me, though now there's no war to speak of except this Yankee sideshow there'll be a sight too many people living a sight too long if you ask me—which you have not done. But he's no trouble. Hasn't dirtied himself yet as far as I know. All right, Martin lad. Stow it."

My jaw must have dropped. I gulped my own spittle.

"Does everybody—"

"Bless you, no, sir. It's living and dying in ships. He's gone home like I said. The likes of me, well we're hard as the ship's bitts never having known what it is to have parents and all that gear. But Martin, you see, he could remember his parents so he has in a manner of speaking a home to go home to, I don't really mean go home but when he's like this it's the same really."

To my own astonishment I fell into a spontaneous fit of swearing. When I had done I had my face in my hands and my elbows on the table.

"Well I never, Mr Talbot. And you living among lords

even if you wasn't one of them. I've heard of being drunk
as a lord but for really strong language—well there!"

"I ought to tell you, Mr Askew, that Mr Gibbs obtained
strong liquor from Mr Brocklebank, then more from me
without an offer on my part."

"Ah. I did wonder if he was at it again."

"As you know, Mr Askew, I have been—unwell. Now
I am on my feet again I have come down to offer Mr
Deverel such comfort and assistance as I may without
prejudice to the 'customs of the sea service'. Where is he?"

There was a long pause while Mr Askew continued to
add to the fog lying under the deckhead.

"A good question, sir. I know you've been keeping your
bunk but I'm surprised you never heard seeing he was
such a friend of yours."

" 'Was'? He cannot be dead!"

"I have to tell you, sir, that Mr Deverel is aboard of
Alcyone and like as not by this time he's the other side of
the Cape."

"But I thought—"

"You thought he'd put his head in a noose? It's what
comes of not knowing the rules where you are, sir. I don't
mean the articles of war. I mean what goes on. Ever since
that lieutenant got himself hanged by that captain—I forget the names—in the West Indies it was—captains, to
say nothing of their lordships, has been walking on tiptoe.
So there's the rules of the service and there's what goes on
in ships. It was an exchange, you see."

"Lieutenant Benét!"

"Now you see, don't you, sir?"

"It cannot be within the competence of mere captains
to decide such things!"

"Mere captains? The saying is, once a ship's out of
sight of land a captain can do anything he likes to you but
get you in the family way. Sir Henry wouldn't want to put

Mr Benét out of the ship just like that, seeing as he's a watch-keeping officer. No, sir, he arranged an exchange so nobody would have cause to complain. Very anxious to keep officers happy are their lordships. So Captain Anderson having an unhappy officer to dispose of and Sir Henry having an officer to get rid of as was too bleeding happy, we lost Dashing Jack who was very eager to go and we got Lieutenant Benét who knows far more about everything than a gentleman properly should. They say Captain Anderson can't do enough for him. It's Mr Benét's idea to bring the chronometers up one deck whatever Mr Summers thinks and damn the rating. Very popular Mr Benét is with officers, old ladies, children and midshipmen—let alone powder-burnt old horses in charge of the ship's artillery."

"Deverel! Dashing Jack Deverel! Handsome Jack!"

"Just so, sir. If you ask me, Sir Henry is out of the frying pan and into the fire."

"Ladies! He must have—oh no. Lady Somerset is a fine woman and it is true his inclination does lie that way—"

Mr Askew laughed.

"If you're thinking of Jack Deverel it's any port in a storm with him from a lord's lady to a little girl what still bowls her hoop."

"A girl! A young girl! Deverel!"

"He's a rare one is Jack."

I found I had got to my feet. A lantern was poised perilously near my head.

"So you see, sir, it isn't any use looking down here for Mr Deverel, or anywhere else unless you can swim faster than she can sail. Come to that, there's one or two of us aboard would be very glad to get news of Dashing Jack so as they might have some hope one day of being able to ask for their money back."

"Mr Benét!"

"You'll find him with Mr Summers forrard there, aft of the mainmast and the after pump. God knows what they'll do to poor George if they want advice on how much she is moving and send for the chippy. You done him proper, Mr Talbot."

"As I told you, Mr Askew, he did himself."

(12)

It was dark indeed. On my previous visit to these nether regions I had been afforded the services of young Mr Taylor as my conductor. Moreover in those days we had been gliding gently through the waters of the tropics. Now I was in a frantic ship, and feeling my way. Two yards beyond the lights of the gun-room and there might never have been in my world such things as light and direction. By the time I had gone five yards I was more thoroughly lost than I had ever been in a covert! All I knew was sound, much creaking and gritty straining, but there were sounds of water as if I were crouched on a gravel beach! I waited for a while in the hope that my eyes by habituation would adjust to the darkness and was thus only too able to listen to our predicament! Yet my assessment could not be professional and ignorance turned what had been a natural apprehension into something like terror. There were what might be called the subsidiary splashes, drips and trickles of the water in our hold but these were not the worst. There was more beyond and below these local suggestions. I put my hand in a wetness and water poured over my fingers from where I could not discover and fell where I knew not. My one hand laid hold of a wooden edge, the other, some fabric stuff. My walkway was no more than a plank wide, so I crouched and waited until the awful, cold fact that underscored our lumbering progress forced itself into my understanding. There was a rhythm down here which was not to be heard on deck or in my cabin among the wilder sounds of wind and sea. It was a pouring sound which commenced at some distance—somewhere towards the bow, for what that was worth and if I had the right direction. I stopped in my tracks and crouched, using ears instead of eyes. There approached me with increasing speed all the complicated sounds of a breaking wave! It passed by me yet without an increase in the local wetness. It went on, back the way I had come, diminishing in volume so that once more I could hear near me the dripping and trickling of random water. Then, as my right hand tightened instinctively on wood to take my weight, water poured across under me from one side of the ship to the other—and here, returning, was the first wave, surely travelling the ship's length! I began to claw round, fell over rope and knelt for a moment on what might be sacking. Then there was blessed light above me as if the deck had opened and the sky looked in.

A voice spoke. "Who is it?"

"It is I!"

But then I could see I was looking up at the purser's contrived office. He was standing in the opening and had pulled the canvas aside to look down.

"You cried out. Once again, who is it?"

"It is I, Mr Jones, Edmund Talbot."

"Mr Talbot! What are you doing down here? Pray come up."

I pulled myself over the massive knots which secured the ladder to some even more massive crossbeam.

"You have been poorly, Mr Talbot, since we last met. Pray take a seat. That box will do, I think. Now what can I do for you, sir? You surely have not filled the folio I was able to sell you!"

"No indeed. I was—"

"Lost?"

"Confused."

Mr Jones shook his head and smiled benignly.

"I could tell you exactly where you are in terms of the ship's construction but I believe that would not help. You have just felt or fumbled your way past the stalk of the after warping capstan."

"No, it does not help. I will get my breath back, if you please, then go on my way. I am looking for Mr—"

"Mr—?"

"Mr Summers—or Mr Benét."

Mr Jones peered at me over the half-moons of his steel spectacles. Then he took them off and laid them down on his desk.

"You will find both gentlemen through there, on this side of the pump, which is in turn on this side of the mainmast. They are in some sort of conference."

"Are they debating the question of the ship's safety?"

"They have not confided in me and I did not enquire."

"But surely you are as concerned as anyone!"

"I am insured." He shook his head and smiled, apparently in admiration—"I'm odd like that, you know."

"But however that may secure the comfort of your dependants—"

"I have no dependants, sir. You mistake my meaning. My personal safety I have put in the hands of those I take to be most useful in a crisis—powerful seamen, skilled in their trade."

"That applies to us all!"

"No, sir. Why should I concern myself with us all?"

"You cannot be so selfish and you cannot be so secure!"

"Words, Mr Talbot."

"If your security is more than imaginary we ought all to share in it!"

"That is impossible. How many of the people in this ship could lay their hands on one thousand pounds? You perhaps, sir. No one else."

"The devil!"

"You see? I have an agreement, properly signed. At least, they have made their marks. Should there be an unhappy end to the ship I am worth one thousand pounds to some of the strongest and most skilful seamen in the world. The Bank of England is no safer."

Now I did indeed laugh aloud.

"That a man of business, of affairs, should be so simple! Why, sir, in the event of a catastrophe, they—may I say we?—should preserve the lives of women and children before such as you were even considered!"

Mr Jones shook his head with what seemed like pity.

"You cannot suppose that with the ship sinking round us I should count out gold and give each man his portion? You do not understand credit, Mr Talbot. I do not have any dependants, but my seamen have. The money is there for them ashore when they get me there, no sooner. Good heavens, Mr Talbot, the boats we have would not hold a tenth of our people! Without some such arrangement as I am accustomed to make, the whole of our life at sea would be no more than a lottery!"

"I am dreaming, I think. There cannot be such—and even reckless men such as sailors are commonly supposed to be—they would not set your life at a higher rate than their own!"

"My boat is up there on the boom, Mr Talbot."

"But Captain Anderson—"

Mr Jones appeared to stifle a yawn, then once more he shook his head, and smiled as if at some remembered pleasure—his own oddness, perhaps.

"I will hold the canvas aside for a while after you have gone down. That should give you enough light until you see theirs."

This *congé* left me surprisingly without speech. I tried to infuse a degree of contempt into a slight bow as I edged past him, but cannot feel that he took any notice. He was right in one thing. Before I had passed into complete darkness again—and it was strange how the light seemed to diminish the pouring sounds of our internal wave, our tiny internal wave!—I caught the glimmer of another light beyond what might be the sacking-wrapped body of a coach.

"I say! I say! Hullo! Is anybody there?"

There was a pause and no sound but the glutinous cluckings of appetite from the water within us. Then through the intestinal wash of our wave I heard a familiar voice.

"Who's there?"

"Charles? It is I, Edmund."

There was a brief pause, then the glimmer brightened and became a lantern held aloft by young Mr Taylor. Its light fell on coach wheels, harness, a shaft, all packed round with full sacks, against which the ship deposited me as water poured from one side of the ship to the other. I was by what looked like a hut.

"Mr Talbot, this passes everything! You must leave at once!"

"With respect, Mr Summers, is that wise? Mr Talbot is an emissary—"

"If you please, Mr Benét. I am still first lieutenant of this ship and shall remain so until their lordships see fit to declare otherwise!"

"With respect again, sir, since he bears a message from the committee—"

There was a pause while the two pale faces peered at each other. It was Charles Summers who moved first, lifting his hand in what looked like a gesture of defeat.

"Roberts, Jessop, report back to your stations for duty. Mr Taylor, leave the lantern here and report back to Mr Cumbershum. Don't forget to thank him. Now, sir; oh, for heaven's sake, Edmund, sit down! On that bale. You have been sick and are in no case to stand about when she is moving."

"I will lean against this cabin—"

"Against the magazine, you mean. Now do not, I beg of you, continue to use that box as a rest for your feet. It is the bed in which our three chronometers are kept."

"With respect, sir, kept for the time being."

"How did you know about the committee and my message—my alleged message?"

"Do you suppose such affairs can be kept secret? As it happens, you have come upon the best place in the ship for a private conversation! Your precious committee should have foregathered down here."

"With respect, sir, I will walk a step to make sure that Roberts and Jessop are not hanging about."

"Do so, Mr Benét. Well, Edmund, shall I take your message as spoken?"

"They—'we', I suppose I should say, wish to make known their *opinion* that for the sake of the women and children the ship's course should be redirected to South America."

"Have you ever heard of a null point?"

"Not as far as I can remember."

Mr Benét's face reappeared, pale in the light of the lantern.

"All clear, sir."

Charles Summers nodded.

"The sea, Edmund, which earlier peoples, savage peoples and poets such as Mr Benét, have credited with thoughts and feelings does sometimes exhibit characteristics which would still make the mistake understandable. Those who go down to the sea in ships can sometimes find themselves in a combination of circumstances which produce an appearance of malevolence! I do not refer to storms and flat calms, dangerous as they can be, but to small events and minor characteristics, to odd exceptions and unstatistical behaviours—you are listening, Mr Benét?"

"Devoutly, sir."

"—which soulless and material as they are can none the less produce a position in which men are conscious, strong, adept—and forced helplessly to watch a quiet destruction moving inexorably upon them."

We were all three silent for a while as the hold dripped and trickled around us. Below me, it seemed, the wave passed once more.

"I was not prepared for this. What are these circumstances? Is this what I am to take back to the committee?"

"Understand the circumstances first."

"I will try. But you have set my head spinning."

"The null point. The term is sometimes used of a line where two tides meet and so produce motionless water where a current might be expected. I can find no better words for our situation. *Point non plus*, perhaps? You see it's not a question of whether we will or will not stand towards South America. I suppose you mean the river Plate. We cannot proceed in that direction. What is more, we are satisfied that we cannot touch anywhere at the Cape of Good Hope. We have got ourselves too far south—"

"He, confound him, has got us too far south!"

Charles turned to Mr Benét.

"Observe, Mr Benét, that I express total disagreement with Mr Talbot's remark about our captain."

"Observed, sir."

"But ships go further south than this! Good God, how do they—why, whalers spend years in the Southern Ocean!"

"You do not understand. Are you willing to—I will not say 'to lie'—but to play down the seriousness of our situation as far as the passengers and indeed the rest of the people are concerned?"

"You had better explain."

Charles Summers sat on a bale, Mr Benét sat on what looked like a bench end, I lay against my bale and the lantern stood on the bed of chronometers and lit us all three palely.

"It goes back to—oh, as far as the ship is concerned, as far as when she was built!"

"They say of these ships, Mr Talbot, that they were built by the mile and sawn off as required!"

"Defective building is only too common in warships, Mr Talbot. Copper through-bolts are sometimes no more than a dummy head outside and a pin on the inside. It saves all the copper in between, you see, and lines someone's pocket. Commonly, of course, these things are not discovered until the ship is broken up."

Mr Benét laughed sunnily.

"Or at sea, of course, sir, when the holes begin to squirt, but this is not often reported!"

"Can men do such things? Why—it is our—"

"We do not know if this ship has such defects. They have not revealed themselves in detail. But we feel she moves too much, has spewed too much oakum to be sound in her main frame; and she is old. Now add to that, Edmund, that the wind elected to change by no less than a dozen points at the very moment when an unworthy officer, your friend Deverel, had sneaked below for strong drink and left the con to a poor creature—a midshipman—"

"Willis."

"—who will never make a seaman if he lives to be a hundred."

"Would you care to continue, Mr Benét, or shall I—? That is not the half of it, Edmund. She was taken aback, when any competent officer could have prevented it. She was wrung and might have gone over if we had not lost our topmasts. Even so the foremast moved in the step and broke it. Watch the foremast, Edmund, and you will see the hounds—the top bit of what is left—describing a small circle. We cannot use the foremast and by reason of a balance of forces which will be immediately apparent to you, we cannot as a consequence use the mizzenmast either. Now observe. The same wind which lamed us drove us back, helpless as we were, into warmer water. We idled and weed grew. That makes us even more helpless. The upshot of all is that we have no choice, you see. We can only go more or less where we are driven."

"What is going to happen? All is lost then!"

"By no means. By submission, by obedience to the forces of nature we may just outwit them."

"Moreover as you know, sir, I propose we should take steps over the weed—"

"Shall I finish what I have to say, Mr Benét?"

"I beg pardon, sir."

"Very well. Now, Edmund. Have you ever seen an atlas inscribed with lines showing the advised course for a ship between one point and another?"

"No."

"You will find it curious, I think. For example a ship bound for India would not take the direct route from the Cape across the Indian Ocean but would make a great curve taking her nearly to Australia—"

"We might come across *Alcyone* again!"

Charles smiled but shook his head.

"I am sorry, Edmund, believe me! But we shall not. They will use the wind and bend with it as we must. The course we must take from our null point takes us south again in the great Southern Ocean. There the prevailing winds will alter and blow from the west. It will blow us to Australia. So you see, by consenting to what must be we may reach our destination."

"It will be like going downhill, Mr Talbot, when you cannot go up but in any case wish to go down. We shall go downhill all the way to the Antipodes!"

"I see. No, gentlemen, I believe I really do see."

"It will be a long voyage, Edmund."

"And we may sink?"

The two officers looked at each other. Then Charles turned to me.

"I can trust you? Then yes. We may sink."

I said nothing but tried to digest this naked information into a feeling and succeeded more quickly than I had anticipated. I froze as I had done when Jack Deverel had furnished me with a cutlass. But Summers laughed a little.

"Come, Edmund! It is not today or tomorrow and may be never—with God's help!"

"And the chronometers, sir. Do not forget the chronometers!"

Charles Summers ignored the young man in a way that persons unaccustomed to the sea service would have found offensive.

"We do not think that this information should be made widely known among the passengers and emigrants."

"But we behaved well enough when we set up a defence against what proved to be *Alcyone*!"

"That was sudden, desperate and soon over. This is a danger of a different degree. It will wear down all but the strongest spirits—as if the effect of this motion was not trial enough!"

"I agree, Charles. But this puts me in a fix. I am to report back to that idiotic committee, cannot ignore them—but now I know too much!"

"Perhaps, sir, Mr Talbot might adopt my metaphor and tell them we propose to go downhill all the way?"

Charles smiled at him pallidly in the light of the lantern.

"A degree of ignorance among the gentlemen is certainly desirable at the moment and Mr Talbot adequate to the task, I believe."

"But devil take it, what am I to say?"

"Why that we shall alter course to the south and they will feel easier—"

"I submit, sir, that Mr Talbot should mention the drag-rope."

"If I say that we cannot reach either Africa or South America they will rightly fear the worst. If I say that Captain Anderson simply will not, they might well believe me and blame him for arbitrarily submitting them to this trial and real danger!"

"It is a difficulty. Perhaps the task is beyond you—oh, do not lift your chin at me in that Roman way, Edmund! I trust you to do your best but believe me that best would be a description of your own ignorance—"

"What the first lieutenant means, Mr Talbot, is that you should darken counsel a little and rely only on assuring them that all will be well and that we do the best in the circumstances. I must own the prospect of the Southern Ocean daunts me! There we shall get on with a vengeance. The reports make awesome reading. They write of seas the like of which are known nowhere else in the world. Even in a well-found ship—"

"We are rendering like an old boot."

Charles actually laughed but it was not a merry sound.

"Their lordships made do with what they could find. By the inattention of your friend Mr Deverel, we have no tops'ls, a sprung foremast and a ship that has been badly wrung."

He held out his two hands and demonstrated a wringing movement.

"Captain Anderson should have refused to command her!"

Mr Benét shook his head.

"A captain who refuses a ship will not get another."

Charles turned to him.

"Observe, Mr Benét, that I have no criticism to make

395

of Captain Anderson. He is a fine seaman. You are fortunate, Mr Talbot, to find yourself in the hands of such an officer. If you wish to apportion blame, aim it rather at the clerks of the Admiralty who indifferently thrust you into this, this—"

"I heard Mr Talbot use the word 'hulk', sir."

"Just so, Mr Benét. Mr Talbot used the word."

"What must I do?"

"Explain that we shall turn away a little from the wind and make what speed we may to the south where we may get a steady wind on one quarter or the other."

"And the movement will be easier?"

Again the officers exchanged glances.

"The first lieutenant would agree that it will be different, Mr Talbot. He would agree you should use the word 'different'."

"Well, I am willing to do anything in this emergency. Do you wish me to keep the tone of the passenger saloon amiable and pleasant? Cheerful?"

"For heaven's sake, Mr Talbot, I can see you going round the ship with such an air of demented cheerfulness you would dreadfully disconcert the whole company!"

"What can I do? I cannot do nothing!"

"Let there be no alteration seen. Be as you were before your—injuries. The only result will be congratulations on your recovery."

"Be as I was? How was I?"

There was a pause and then suddenly Charles and Mr Benét were laughing, Charles, it seemed, with a touch of hysteria. I had never seen him so before. Tears flashed on his cheeks in the light of the lantern. Head on his knees, he reached out a hand and laid it on mine. I flinched at the unaccustomed contact so that he snatched his hand away again and smeared the water from his face with the back of it.

"I beg your pardon, sir. Your present mood of cooperation, or perhaps I should say complicity, had made me forget how prickly you can be. Mr Benét, how would you suggest that Mr Talbot should conduct himself in order that our other passengers should detect no change in his demeanour?"

Mr Benét's grin broadened. He pushed back his yellow hair with both hands.

"My acquaintance with the gentleman has been short, sir, but I have heard of 'Lord Talbot'. A lofty, not to say toplofty demeanour—"

"Well, gentlemen, I see you are determined to roast me. Indeed it is not easy for a man of my inches to hit off the right bearing in this world of deck beams and squabby tars. If he goes about concealing his height he is bent down like an ancient cripple whereas if he stands up straight as God meant him to and lives with his own eye level he is always cracking his skull and stumbling over—you damned squat creatures, confound you!"

"This voyage will be the making of you, Mr Talbot. At moments I even detect a strong streak of humanity in you as if you was a common fellow like the rest of us!"

"Since we are all common fellows, allow me to share more information. There was mention made of chronometers."

"Yes indeed. You know that the chronometers enable us to measure our movement east and west? Our longitude? With the ship in such a state we are discussing the advisability of bringing them up one deck. But—"

"The wave!"

"What wave?"

"Why the one we—she—has in her. The one I heard as I scrambled towards you!"

"There is no wave inside her, Edmund. Before we allowed her to reach such a state we should have the whole crew pumping—"

"And the passengers, sir, watch and watch—"

"We should have had sails fothered over her bottom and be busy throwing the guns overboard! That was no wave. We have been heavily rained on. Our decks spew oakum. Some of the rain has found its way through the deck—for all rainwater and spray does not run straight into the well. It will puddle at one level or another and wash about, making for discomfort but nothing more. It is a small matter compared with the real danger that faces us."

"There was the corn, sir."

"We ditched a few tons of it, Mr Talbot. It was wet and swelling. We have trouble enough without that."

"Mr Talbot could also mention the dragrope, sir. The prospect of an increase in speed will go some way towards making their discomfort tolerable."

I looked at Charles levelly.

"I was deceived in thinking she makes so much water that between pumpings a wave washes to and fro in her bilges?"

There was a long pause. Charles Summers put his hand to his mouth, then took it away again.

"There was no wave. Your ears deceived you."

Now it was my turn to pause. Then—

"And the dragrope?"

"Mr Benét has persuaded Captain Anderson that we may use the dragrope here in the open sea to get weed off her. In that respect I do as I am ordered. After that we shall see about my own proposal to frap her hull with what cables we can spare for it. Frapping, carefully adjusted, will diminish her rendering to the seas."

"I see. An interminable period of nagging danger—the prospect of a catastrophe, perhaps. Well, so much for a career! And heigh-ho, so much for—but is there really no more to be done?"

"You could pray."

"As Colley did! I will not be bullied to my knees!"

I got to my feet. Light appeared beyond the mainmast like a dawn.

"What is that light?"

"It is the change of watch. Men under punishment are come down to pump for fifteen minutes at the beginning of it."

The light brightened. The men ranged themselves at long handles projecting on either side of the mast. They began to move the handles up and down with a kind of bend-and-stretch movement.

"I thought pumps clanked."

"When they suck dry. These are lifting water."

"I must thank you gentlemen, for taking me into your confidence. It shall not be abused."

"With your permission, sir, I will light Mr Talbot as far as the gun-room."

"You are kind, Mr Benét."

"Not at all, sir. Anything I can do for you, Mr Talbot—"

"And anything I can do for you, Mr Benét—"

Mr Benét beckoned me to follow him with much politeness.

"Lord, Mr Talbot, she is hogging like a wounded stick."

"Hogging, Mr Benét?"

"Sagging, too, sir. The one after the other. Bent up amidships, then bent down amidships."

"Like trying to break a sappy stick."

"Just so, sir. Hogged on the crest and sagged in the trough."

"I had not noticed."

"Well, you would not. You must not expect to detect the movement as excessive unless you have made a study of it. It is like the movement of the moon, sir, which you probably suppose to be a simple curve across the heavens. But it is infinitely complex. I have sometimes had the fancy that the moon is a ship with all her timbers a-creak, hogging, sagging, rolling, pitching—wrung badly and therefore not even moving all of a piece—in fact like our present old load of trouble."

"So that was why George Gibbs downed about a tumbler of my brandy and topped it off with another of rum! Following the run of the planking indeed! It is my belief he pretended to work where he knew there was drink, having got himself a thorough scare from the feel in his limbs of how the hull was working! Will he report to you?"

"To the first lieutenant, and should have done so already. I am the merest underling."

"It is not obvious. Would you care to come to my— hutch, I was about to say—and take some of whatever brandy Mr Gibbs has left us?"

"I am on duty, sir, and must return to Mr Summers. But another time *avec beaucoup de plaisir!*"

He passed a hand through his locks, clapped on his hat, held his hand at the salute as if he were about to remove it—the lanterns of the gun-room as if imbued with the "customs of the sea service" all assumed the same angle as his hand—then turned away to clamber whence we had come. Mr Askew still sat against our wooden wall. He looked at me under his brows.

"I heard you let on to the officer about George Gibbs. George won't be happy about that."

I answered him as shortly as I have ever spoken, for the movement seemed to have increased.

"That's not all he'll be unhappy about!"

I made my way up the ladders which seemed so imbued with the spirit of the sea rather than the service, they had not so much to be climbed as wrestled with. The movement had indeed increased but I soon grasped the reason. Where we had held our conference in the bowels of the ship, we had sat round the chronometers which would be kept at the point of least movement. Now I was moving away from that point and subject to the wildness of wind, water and wood, being in my proper person by no means as precious an object as these delicately fashioned clocks! By the time I had reached my hutch my calves were aching and were only the most noticeable weakness in a body grown suddenly wearied by the stresses of the motion and of sickness and of a mind belaboured with too much event. As I approached the door I heard a sudden scrambling noise from inside. I flung open the door.

"Wheeler! What the devil? You are haunting me!"

"I was just cleaning, sir—"

"For the third time today? When I want you I'll call for you!"

"Sir—"

He paused, then spoke in what I can only call his other voice, a voice with a curious trace of some other society in it, other places and customs.

"I'm in hell, sir."

I sat down in my canvas chair.

"What is all this?"

Wheeler, unlike the other servants in the ship, had commonly a submissive not say ingratiating attitude. He had never before raised his eyes to stare directly into mine but he did so now.

"Good God, man, have you seen a ghost? No! Don't answer!"

All at once the pendulum's movement against which I had been fighting, so far from the still centre by the chronometers, overcame me. I fairly threw myself at the bucket under my canvas bowl and vomited into it. For a time after that, as every sufferer from the condition will know, I was not aware of my surroundings more than that they nauseated me. At last I lay face down in my bunk and wished for death. Wheeler must have taken my bucket away. I know he came back with it and know that he stayed. I think he was urging me to try the effect of the paregoric and I must suppose that at some point I gave way and allowed the dose with its usual magical effect. I believe that Wheeler spent all the time I was unconscious sitting in my chair, for I have a dreamy memory of him there. The first time I swam up from the swathing visions of the opiate I saw him there. He was slumped sideways in the chair, his head resting on the edge of my bunk, in an attitude of complete exhaustion.

(13)

Later still I came to myself with something of a headache and a foul taste in my mouth. Wheeler was still in my cabin but standing up. I muttered at him but he did not go. I sat up and found that I could deal more or less with the movement of the ship.

"I think, Wheeler, you had better explain yourself. But not now. Hot water, if you please. Get me out a clean shirt—what are you waiting for?"

He licked his lips. The ship lurched in a daunting interruption to the relentless movement of the pendulum. Wheeler reeled. He would have fallen had he not grabbed the edge of my bunk.

"What's the matter with you, man?"

"Sorry, sir. A clean shirt, sir. This drawer—here, sir. But the hot water—"

"Well?"

"The fires is damped down, sir. I doubt that water would come more than warm."

"Coffee, too. Hot."

His eyes had focused far away. Whatever it was he imagined, it would seem he did not like it.

"Wheeler!"

"Sir. I might ask Hawkins to put a pot on in the captain's galley."

"Very well."

What a world a ship is! A universe! This was the first time in our whole voyage that I had considered the simple fact that hot water, to say nothing of a hot meal, implies a fire; and a fire implies, oh, firebrick, metal, what have you, some sort of chimney or flue! All these weeks the crew had gone about their business in the knowledge of which I was innocent! Only today, or was it yesterday, parts of the ship had come into my view for the first time—and now and then almost upside down as in a tele-scope!—the chronometers in their beds, the magazine, pumps aft of the main and forrard of the main—I who had determined once long ago to become master of "the sea affair"! I was irritated with myself for allowing Wheeler to give me the paregoric, as a man might be irri-tated who has forsworn liquor and now finds himself suf-fering from the effects of a debauch. I felt that I needed cleaning! There in a ship which might be the death of me, I felt soiled by real dirt, by paregoric, by my inability to shape circumstances—and all because of the distant vision of Marion Chumley! We might sink; but my mind returned upon Marion Chumley!

Wheeler came back but empty-handed.

"What is it now?"

"The captain's fire is out, sir."

"What the devil—I mean, why is it out?"

"Seeing we're likely to be at sea longer than expected, the captain said to put the fire out and save fuel for the ship's galley, sir."

"Captain Anderson? Doing without fire for the sake of the passengers?"

"For the crew, Hawkins said, sir."

"I never would have thought it!"

"Captain Anderson is a good captain, sir, nobody denies it."

"You are going to say that his bark is worse than his bite."

"No, sir. His bite is a deal worse than his bark and that's bad enough. So no drink, sir. I came to tell you. I've asked Bates to get some from the ship's galley but it won't be more than lukewarm."

He withdrew but I am sure went no further off than the lobby. I sat in my chair and waited in a confusion of head and circumstances. There was my dirt, inside and out. There was the movement of the ship, the pendulum which if it did not still nauseate me was a wearisome trial, minute by minute. There was Dashing Jack Deverel now loose where I so desperately longed to be, in that other ship, that beautiful, wild creature—

There was a strange feeling in my naked feet. It was true, good God, the planking was alive! There was a creeping and almost muscular movement! It was a realization even more disconcerting than the brutally uneven movement of the whole ship as the waves passed under her.

Wheeler came in and presented me with a mug of coffee. It was hardly lukewarm but I drank it. He poured a little water into my canvas bowl and I abandoned the coffee in my haste to wash myself. Carried away by a veritable passion for cleanness I scrubbed myself all over in water that soon became at once dirty and stone-cold—as if by so doing I could get rid not merely of my soiling of one sort and another but of the ship's dirt and of the ship's confused and daunting circumstances. As I wrapped the clean apron and tail of my shirt between my naked legs I felt more nearly myself than I had done since first a "starter" struck me over the back and head. I dressed, then opened this book and looked briefly through what I had written there. I even took the parcel containing an account of the first part of our voyage from the drawer, and weighed it in my hands, debating whether I should open it and read critically all I had written. But the prospect of repacking it daunted me.

Oh, that self-confident young man who had come aboard, serenely determined to learn everything and control everything! In prospect he had treated this awful expedition, this adventure, as resembling that in a stagecoach, its end as surely to be predicted as that between London and Bath! He was to reach Sydney Cove moving at an even pace over a level sea in some masterpiece of naval construction. But the war had ended, the ship had proved to be rotten as an old apple, Deverel and Willis between them had allowed the apple—the ship—the coach—to lose a wheel, *Alcyone* had overhauled him and struck him with lightning so that he now knew the pangs of passion, of separation, of jealousy—

"Deverel! Handsome Jack!"

After some time, I do not know how long, I came to myself like a diver returning to the surface. I stared into my small mirror at a too much altered face. I thought to myself then, as I inspected the wan and haggard visage there, that my godfather would be at once amused and condemnatory of me. Edmund in love with the wrong girl—with the impossible girl—why, the old *cynic* would have preferred me to attempt Lady Somerset! Then, on top of that, Edmund quite likely sinking in the wrong ship—

As if the wrong ship knew that I had insulted her, the planking under my feet fairly bounced.

"Surely—"

I stopped. I said silently to myself that there was something I did not understand behind this half-uttered "surely" which had escaped my lips without my volition. It was not so much a thought as a feeling that "I" ought to be able to do something about "it" and that if "I" could not, then "somebody" ought to be able to! Believe it or not, my thoughts began to centre on our glum captain! And after all, a committee, however *ad hoc*, had wanted me to interview him! I had obeyed my own instructions and seen Charles Summers, now I would obey theirs! I shouted for Wheeler who opened the door almost before the word was out. He huddled and strapped me into my oilskins. I stepped in my rubber boots through the door, and the whole ship slid away. I stumped, tilted like a seaman towards the waist. I do not know if it was my imagination or not but I thought I heard someone sobbing in the last of the hutches on my side of the lobby. I stood in the waist, holding on to the break of the poop. Our ship was indeed quicker in her roll. Her movement was a constant fret, with now and then a jerk in it which seemed like impatience or furious anger rather. Rain and spray flying horizontally over the windward rail stung my face like birdshot. The ship heaved at each wave as if she might get forward but then came upright in much the same place as before. The sails, rain and spray streaming from the clew, spread as they were on the mainmast alone and huge, now seemed a pitiful response to the wind's impulsion. Yet despite all this wild weather there was much activity with ropes of various sizes on the fo'castle. They were trying, it seemed, to perform some operation with cables, though I was quite unable to understand what it was. They seemed to spend quite a deal of their time under water and I was glad to be a passenger and not an officer, let alone a seaman. I turned and began to climb towards the poop. Above and aft of the wheel with its two glistening quartermasters, partly visible over the forrard rail of his deck, stood Captain Anderson. He wore a shabby oilskin and sou'wester and as one indifferent to a *capful* of water was staring moodily into the eye of the wind. I was working my careful way round the men at the wheel when the captain noticed me. He smiled! It was a dreadful sight, a momentary glimpse of a few teeth, as if someone had thrown a yellow pebble into his glumness. I opened my mouth but he was already turning away. I followed, riskily running up the ladder to detain him, but by the time I had reached the deck he had *nipped* down his private companionway and disappeared. The message was plain. Keep off! Yet he had smiled at me, however briefly and artificially, a thing not known before.

As in a dream, I imagined yellow hair, a fresh complexion, and heard the voice of Mr Benét say: *I submit, sir, in this difficulty you should habitually greet the passengers with cheerfulness. Once they feel the captain himself has cause for concern they will be no end of trouble!*

Would he dare? Oh yes, I believe a young officer who would "attempt" handsome Lady Somerset while her husband was no more than walking his rounds must be bold to the point of foolhardiness!

Our little sailing master, Mr Smiles, had the watch. Now that the captain had gone below he moved over from the starboard side and stood facing the wind.

"Well, Mr Smiles, I am recovered as you see and would not be anywhere else for one thousand pounds!"

Mr Smiles examined my face in a distant way as if it had been at the horizon. His eyes were red-rimmed from the spray. He lifted one finger to his lips as if to command silence.

"What do you mean, Mr Smiles? A thousand pounds, I said. I tell you what, sir. After I had suffered a few bangs on the head I thought I must be out of my wits; but down below there is a real madman who thinks in all this salt turmoil that he can buy safety!"

Mr Smiles took his finger from his lips.

"There are ships, Mr Talbot, in which every man Jack is mad save one."

"To tell you the truth I am coming to believe that all men who choose this awful waste as an habitation and profession must be mad so you may well be right! How she rolls—devil take it, I spend my time clambering like an ape from one handhold to another. I marvel you can so keep your feet and treat the movement with such indifference."

The sailing master did not reply. He returned to watch the sea. He seemed to be inspecting what could be seen of that vastly furrowed prospect as if he were choosing a path over it. It came to me that my conversation with the man was not just a casual infringement of the captain's Standing Orders but a positive shattering of them. Perhaps that was why the man had laid his finger to his lips! Times and the weather had changed! But I did not wish to make our position any more complicated than it was. I nodded to Mr Smiles and made my way down to the lobby again, having had enough of the freshness of the open air.

I saw Wheeler slide into my hutch. I could not bear more to do with the man and used the rails on the walls of the hutches to get myself to the saloon. But the committee was not there, only little Mr Pike. I am sorry to say that I collapsed on the bench below the stern window and stayed so with my head on the table.

"You are sick as the rest of them, Mr Talbot."

I grunted in reply. The man went on.

"I should not have thought it of you, Mr Talbot. But then you have been injured. I trust your head is better. I struck my own on the lintel when the ship rolled but it is better now. Have you seen Mr Summers?"

"Where is the committee?"

"The movement is too much for them. Mr Prettiman has had a heavy fall. But I will go and call them if you wish." I shook my head.

"I will wait till they are recovered enough to appear. I believe Bowles to be a superior man. He has what the Romans would call '*gravitas*'. I am surprised."

"You need not be, sir. He has studied law."

It was quite extraordinary how quickly little Pike was able to bore one.

"You should be resting like the others, Mr Pike."

"Oh no. I do not get flung about much, you see. As I

am small and light, if I lose my footing I generally manage to scramble up. Not like poor Mr Brocklebank who dare not leave his bunk in this weather except to—You know, sir, I prefer sitting here, talking to you, rather than being with my family? That is dreadful, quite dreadful I know but after a while I simply cannot stand it no matter how anxious I am and no matter how much I love them."

"Anxious? What on earth for?"

"They do not really rest, Mr Talbot. Every now and then they play in the bed—the bunk, the upper bunk, Mr Talbot, one at each end. They play like I said but then it is tears and seems to get worse. They don't play for more than a moment but lie there—well, whining, I suppose, I had better say it though Mrs Pike does not like the word. She is not well herself, sir. What are we to do? Mrs Pike seems to believe I can do something which to tell the truth is why I am out here but I cannot. That hurts more than anything."

I recalled Charles's instructions to me.

"You should find her faith in you flattering, Mr Pike."

"Oh no."

"I must say, I would not be anywhere else for a thousand pounds!"

"Will you not call me Dicky, Mr Talbot? I know I have not, what you said the Romans would think of Mr Bowles—"

" '*Gravitas*'. You should not worry, sir, some people have it, others not and are none the worse for the lack. I have been thought to exhibit a measure of the quality myself but it is nature, not nurture. Well, Mr Pike, I will call you Richard if it will make you happier."

"Thank you, Mr Talbot. Do you prefer Ed or Eddy?"

"Mr Pike, you may address me as 'Edmund' in this emerg—in the situation which we find ourselves in. So cheer up, man!"

"I will try, Edmund. But the children do not seem to get any better for all we can do."

"Now there I can give you comfort. Good God, sir, my young brothers are for ever breaking their knees or elbows or both—all four I should say! They get colics, rashes, colds like puppies. It is growing up, Mr Pike, Richard, I should say, and a damned lengthy and painful business if you ask me!"

"They say the wind is not blowing from where it ought to be. The movement of the ship—"

"The wind may change, man! Before we know where we are we may find ourselves riding along as easy as in a postchaise! Come, you know that Britannia rules the waves! I would not be anywhere else for—"

"I am afraid, that is the truth of it."

"—a thousand pounds."

"It is this sinking—"

"Now come! The officers assured me—"

"They do really seem to be sinking, a little weaker today, then again tomorrow. Oh, Edmund, is there nothing to be done? I begged the surgeon to get us transferred to the other ship, though what we should do in India I do not know—but he would not. And that was when the weather was fine."

"A foul wind cannot last forever. When we get into the Southern Ocean—"

"But the ship is not getting along, is it?"

"She will get there little by little. The seamen will operate the dragrope and take off our weed and increase our speed. Oh—I should not have said—You see? We have nothing to worry about, sir, nothing at all."

"And another thing. Edmund, I cannot help feeling that the ship is lower in the water. I do not mention my suspicions to Mrs Pike but only this morning I caught her eye—and I knew, Edmund! She was thinking the same thing!"

I laughed aloud, not a little relieved at finding there was some positive comfort I could give the poor, irritating fellow.

"What a man you are, Pike! I confess that when I was feeling sick and particularly *low* I imagined the ship was too! But today the sailors have pumped no more than they did when she was anchored at Spithead!"

"I do know that, Edmund, and everything you say is true. But Bates says she has more water in her."

"Would it interest you to know that the first lieutenant told me himself that they pump no more than they did? She has more water in her because of the rain and spray. It lies about where the pumps cannot get at it—annoying but not in any way dangerous! Be warned—it sounds worse than it is because of our movement. Down below if you are not experienced you would mistake the sound of rainwater washing about for a positive wave rolling from one end of the ship to the other!"

"The first lieutenant would tell you that, wouldn't he? I mean he would wish to keep everyone calm so as to avoid trouble. But it is good of you to talk so to me, Edmund, and I believe you partly and I will tell Mrs Pike, making as much of it as I can."

"I think before you return to your hutch—cabin, I mean, good God, man, you're not a rabbit, are you? Well—I had better give you a good stiff drink."

"Oh no, Edmund. Like I told you it burns my throat and makes me go silly. Edmund, I have even prayed but nothing happened. I keep thinking about 'Suffer little children'. It doesn't do them any good being young and small, does it? I mean they are the less able to defend themselves. Like you said the other day when we thought the other ship might be French, they are too young for the French. But I can't keep out of my head that they aren't too young for Our Lord, Edmund, and if they slip through our hands in this devilish place, this desert, I couldn't leave them to sink, not here; I should jump in after them—"

"Pike! Pull yourself together! Richard! I said Richard! Stop blubbering, man! Anyone would think you was a girl, curse it!"

"Administering comfort, Mr Talbot?"

I got clumsily to my feet. It was Miss Granham. She had one hand out before her and the other holding her skirts up away from the streaming floor. I stumbled round the table but she got to the one nearest the door and sank on to the bench. A shift of the vessel fairly tossed me towards the other side and I sat opposite her.

"Miss Granham, you really should not! A lady—where is Mr Prettiman? He should—"

Miss Granham spoke in a weary voice.

"He is sick and I am sick. But he has had a fall. A severe one."

"What can I do? Shall I visit him?"

Mr Pike sniggered through his tears.

"Edmund visiting the sick!"

"It is comic, I admit, sir. But then anything comic in our situation is a gain."

The man came round the end of the aftermost table and huddled himself on my bench. As if she was as irritated with him as I was, the ship shrugged, the sawtoothed horizon took up a crazy angle in the stern window and little Pike shot along the bench and collided with me. He muttered an apology and backed off. Miss Granham looked at him compassionately.

"Do they improve, Mr Pike?"

"They are no better. Will you go to them?"

"Later, Mr Pike. I believe you should ask Mrs Pike to invite me. I make every allowance for her natural distress—but really!"

"She is very sorry indeed, Miss Granham, and so much

regrets her unfortunate outburst. She said so. I beg you!"
Miss Granham sighed.

"I will do what I can but later. Now Mr Prettiman is
injured—"

"I will tell her so. And what you said, Edmund."

Pike got more or less to his feet. He was like a man balancing on the slope of a roof and he waited till the roof
changed its infernal mind and sloped the other way. He
went reeling through the door and contrived to get it
shut behind him. Miss Granham was leaning back. Both
hands grasped the edge of the table. Her eyes were shut
and either tears or perspiration ran in drops down her
cheeks.

"I had hoped to ask for a little warm water but the truth
is my voice is so weak—"

"That is readily remedied, ma'am, for you may borrow
mine. Bates! Bates! Where are you, man? Come out of
that damned cuddy—I beg your pardon, not you, Bates,
you, ma'am—we want hot water and at once."

"There isn't any."

"Say 'sir' when you speak to me!"

"Like Wheeler told you, sir, there isn't any."

"We'll see about that! Wheeler! Wheeler! Wheeler, I
said! Oh, there you are. What do you mean by it, giving a
gentleman hot water without telling him that the ladies
were in need of it?"

"Miss Granham is not on my side of the lobby, sir."

"Well neither am I now I've changed over!"

"Yes, sir, but, sir—"

"Hot water, Wheeler, and quick about it! If necessary,
light the damned fire again and tell whomsoever should
be told it was at my, my—"

"You are more than kind, Mr Talbot, but please!"

"Be easy, ma'am. Bring it to Miss Granham's cabin,
Wheeler."

"Even hot water, the touch of it in one's mouth, the warming suffusion. I never thought in the days when I was so particular over the making of a pot of tea that I should come to value hot water without it!"

"No tea—good God, ma'am, I am the veriest, the most absolute the outside edge of enough, the most thoughtless—"

The deck was momentarily level. I leapt to my feet, ran through the lobby to my hutch, fell on my knees and scrabbled at my bottom drawer, fished out the packet and ran back to Miss Granham before the deck had a chance to change its mind. It was, if not an elegant, at least a very nimble feat and I was pleased to have outwitted our soaked old wooden box for once and avoided doing myself a mischief.

"Here, ma'am, with my apologies."

"Tea!"

"I had it stowed away the first day we came aboard and to tell you the truth have not had much cause to remember it since then. I only hope the air of this savage ocean may not have ruined it entirely. I have seen you ladies in calmer weather clustered round the teapot and the, what is it, 'the cup that cheers but not inebriates—' "

"I cannot take it."

"Miss Granham, for heaven's sake!"

Miss Granham's head was turned away. She held out the scrap of paper she had removed from beneath the string. I recognized the familiar writing. "For 'The Little Duke' from 'old Dobbie' with love, in the hope he will drink nothing stronger."

"Oh, Lord, ma'am, good God. I mean—believe me— what a fool! She might at least have folded the paper, curse it—and here am I swearing like a trooper. I beg your pardon, really, ma'am, I do not care for tea and only drink it out of politeness. Why, Miss Dobson would be most angry if she thought—a disciplinarian I can tell you! She would stand me in the corner for an hour by the clock if she thought that—I suppose here I should find myself mastheaded by her if we have a masthead which in fact I suppose we do since young Willis spends so much time up there. She is a dear friend as you can imagine but perhaps too much addicted to the sentimental school—"

"Mr Talbot."

"—only a fanatic would have a small boy taught to read out of *Sir Charles Grandison*! She thought, I suppose, that such a perfect exemplar of Christian behaviour would do me good but I assure you, ma'am, that tale, if tale it be in all those volumes, has marked me for life!"

I thought for a moment that Miss Granham was trying to stop herself from laughing. But it was worse than that. Her face was contorted with effort, yet despite that the tears fairly burst from her eyes. They were of the "boo-hoo" variety. It is the first and possibly last time I have seen a lady grit her teeth! But still the tears flowed. I do not know how to convey my astonishment not to say my embarrassment. She began to beat on the table with her fist.

"I will not! I will not allow myself—"

Her bonnet, her very shoulders shook. Never have I seen such an evident conflict in a lady!

"Oh, God! Oh, I say, ma'am! You really must not—I did not mean that I was forced to read the whole of *Sir Charles Grandison*! Then you might well pity me! I doubt the great Panjandrum himself read it all! Did he not say that he had never read a book to the end? I will lay my horse to a shilling that he was thinking of Richardson—"

Miss Granham began to laugh. It was hysteria, I suppose, for which of course the accepted remedy is a smartly smacked face. But the truth is I did not dare.

"I believe, ma'am, you should allow me to escort you to your hutch—cabin, I would say—"

"What a fool!"

"Not really—but she hoped to bring me along in the style of Sir Charles but failed as you see. Wheeler will bring you the water. Allow me. A lady is naturally less able to counteract the movement of a vessel and even her garments must render the attempt additionally difficult, not to say dangerous. Permit me, ma'am."

She was docile. I gave her my arm but that was clearly not enough. I took her hand therefore; but before we had got fairly into the lobby the frantic movement of the vessel forced me to put my right arm round her narrow waist and I was holding her up.

An unexpected fact became apparent with stunning force. Between thirty and forty years she might carry in her reticule but she was a woman! More than that and not to put too fine a point on it, Miss Granham was not wearing stays! There was no doubt about it. Good God, her waist, her bosom was that of a young woman! It put the final touch to my embarrassment and I was most anxious to have done with her as soon as possible. But it was not to be. That other female, jealous, I suppose a poet would say, of this newly revealed femininity, suddenly savaged us as a hound will savage a fox. The first movement sent me spinning across the lobby so that I was forced to use all my strength and an agility I did not know I possessed in keeping my—I should say "our"—feet. The next movement set us instantly on the slope of a mountain and in a mountain stream at that. I grabbed at one of the handrails to prevent us from falling towards what was at least temporarily down. We swung out. We fell, because the handrail came with us and, awful to relate, the whole bulkhead, or wall, in this instant of thin ply, came with us too. As we approached the wooden drum of the mizzen I contrived to turn so that my shoulder struck it and Miss Granham did not. The whole of the buff-coloured sheet—the plywood—

now impeded us. Forced to let go of the handrail and forced by the countermotion to dance like a clown carrying a puppet I sped towards the open, the violated cabin. We were in it just long enough to see that an old lady lay there, her grey hair matted with sweat, her mouth open, her eyes in their sunken discoloured sockets staring at us with terror! I cannot think how I contrived to bow and mutter an apology before the ship swept us away. I got a handhold on the rails at the opposite side of the lobby without knowing what process had taken us there and worked along it until I could deliver Miss Granham safely to her door.

"Allow me, ma'am. It was a seventh wave I believe. I must apologize for—you are quite safe now. Allow me, ma'am."

I managed to usher her into her cabin and shut the door with great thankfulness. I made my way to my own hutch, keeping my eyes averted from the violated cabin which, I now realized with almost as much terror as she, contained none other than my onetime inamorata, Zenobia Brocklebank!

I pass over the grumbling from the sailors when they were ordered to mend the bulkhead at once, the shrieks from Zenobia until she was hidden again, the soul-destroying hammering which was necessary before the business was done. I got myself back to the saloon in a rage and a determination not to be defeated by the ship and the weather. I yelled for the servant and ordered food and drink. It came and proved to be salt beef but pickles to go with it and ale to wash it down. Never believe the complaints of seamen about their food! To a man with all his teeth in his head this proved to be a feast for a king, however much I had to wrestle with it! Admittedly, once the plate got away from me and I saved the beef, to say nothing of a mess of pickles with my right hand! What is more, I licked that hand clean with positive gusto. I cannot tell how it came about but the absurd passage with Miss Granham restored me to a state of cheerfulness which I believe is natural to me and which *mal de mer* had temporarily defeated! When I thought of Miss Chumley with a throb of longing, even that transformed itself into a determination to conquer all! This was more than recovery. It was enhancement! Once back into my hutch, I dared adventures of balance to get into a nightshirt and nightcap, got into my bunk and determined to have a good night! Astonishingly enough, with no qualms to interrupt it, I sank almost at once into a deep sleep that neither of the aches of my body—one shoulder confoundedly tender from that damned mizzenmast—could hinder.

(14)

I woke with the faintest trace of light through my louvre and lay for a while in a state of surprise at my restoration. I supposed that I had, as they say of sickness, "turned the corner", and that my concussion had run its course. I felt full of energy and determination. I even sat, half-dressed, at this flap and wrote a whole candle's worth of record—of Mr Askew, Mr Benét, Charles, Miss Granham and Mr Gibbs! By that time there was as much daylight about as ever did reach our sordid quarters and I put out the guttering candle. The effect of my restoration was still with me; but I cannot say that when I got myself dressed and oilskinned and went cautiously out for a breath of the open that there was much in sight to please a man now heartily tired of salt water! Too much of it flew everywhere. I looked up to discover if Captain Anderson was stumping up and down the weather-side of the quarterdeck but he was not to be seen. Instead of that, an oil-clad figure waved to me from the forrard rail of it. A faint voice came through the wind.

"Hullo there!"

It was Lieutenant Benét.

"Why hullo! A nasty morning!"

"I will be with you directly."

Cumbershum emerged from the bowels of the ship. He grunted at me and I grunted back. It is all that is necessary with the man. He ascended to the quarterdeck and the ship's bell struck eight times. The ceremony was brief. The gentlemen made to raise their hats but wore sou'westers secured by what they call, of course, "chin stays". Their action was therefore purely symbolic, a raising of the right hand to the level of the eyebrow. The men at the wheel presented the course to the new quartermasters. Benét came down the ladder. He held the forrard rail with both hands and leaned over.

"Come up, sir."

"You are cheerful this morning, Mr Benét."

"It is an appearance perhaps."

"Separation as I am beginning to find out—"

"I understand you. Wilson! Keep your eye on the bloody luff! Well, Mr Talbot, I spent the whole watch occupied with the two lines I quoted to you and have improved them materially. '*Essential Beauty lovelier than a woman, too fair of form and feature to be human—*' Is that not a gain?"

"I am no poet."

"How do you know, sir? I am told you wept when Mrs East sang—"

"Good God! They were tears, idle tears and where in heaven or hell they came from—or what—besides, I had been cracked over the head!"

"My dear Mr Talbot. Once faced with the necessity of communicating with the most sensitive, most delicate of creatures—only poetry will make that connection. It is their language, sir. Theirs is the language of the future. Women have dawned. Once they have understood what syllables, rather than prose, should fall from those lips, women will rise in splendour like the sun!"

"You amaze me, Mr Benét."

"Prose? It is the speech of merchants to each other, sir, the language of war, commerce, husbandry."

"But poetry—"

"Prose will do for persuading men, sir. Why, only yesterday I was able to persuade the captain that a small alteration of course would be beneficial. Now had I represented in verse to the captain that he was wrong—"

"I am surprised you are still alive."

"No—no! Do you not see that our motion is easier?"

"I had thought my ability to keep my feet and in fact to be cheerful was the result of my complete recovery."

"We have come a point off the wind and the increase in our speed, however slight, compensates for the extra distance. But the absence of the Beloved Object—"

"You refer to Lady Somerset."

Lieutenant Benét took off his sou'wester and shook out the golden fleece.

"Who else?"

"I did suppose," said I, laughing, "that you might have had Another in mind—"

"There is no other!"

"In your eyes, no, but to mine—"

Lieutenant Benét shook his head, smiling kindly.

"There cannot be."

"It did occur to me that perhaps you had an opportunity of forming some opinion on the character of Miss Chumley."

"She has none."

"I beg your pardon?"

"She can have none. She is a schoolgirl, Mr Talbot."

"Miss Chumley—"

"I have no opinion of schoolgirls. It is useless to look to them for sympathy or understanding or anything. They are blown by every wind, sir. Why, my own sisters would follow any redcoat if dear Mama did not have an eye to them."

"Miss Chumley is no longer a schoolgirl!"

"She is pretty, I grant you, amiable with a trace of wit—"

"A trace!"

"Malleable—"

"Mr Benét!"

"Why—what is the matter?"

"Lieutenant Deverel is aboard *Alcyone*—he is notorious—"

"A cockerel, Mr Talbot. I did not like the man even the little I saw of him."

"Mr Askew told me, Mr Askew said that Handsome Jack—"

"At least I must thank him for allowing me to choose this melancholy exile!"

"But, Mr Benét—forgive me. Exile! You seem a happy man! Your accustomed attitude, your very facial expression—it is sunny, sir!"

Lieutenant Benét looked astonished and revolted. He put on his sou'wester again.

"You cannot be serious, Mr Talbot. I happy!"

"Forgive me!"

"Were I small-minded enough, Mr Talbot, I should at this very moment envy your condition! You love Miss Chumley, do you not?"

"Indeed."

Mr Benét's face was wet but it was with rain or seaspray not tears. His golden locks beat about his brow. The spyglass under his arm seemed so mechanically and professionally a part of his character that when he suddenly whipped it out and ran back up to the quarterdeck, it was as if he had extended another limb which until then had been folded in like the leg of an insect. He levelled it at the horizon. He spoke to Cumbershum and for a while the two gentlemen aimed their parallel glasses, all the while contriving to remain upright in a way I found admirable. Mr Benét shut up his glass and came back to me at the run.

"A whaler, Mr Talbot. She would avoid us even if we made signals of distress."

"But, Mr Benét—you said 'My condition'?"

"Why, the letter, sir. I was to put it into your hand but you were indisposed. I gave it to your servant."

"Wheeler!"

"No—no. The other one. You slab-sided son of a sea cook! Keep your eyes on the horizon or I'll have the skin off your back! You never reported that sail!"

This was with a roar much like Captain Anderson's but it issued from the throat of Lieutenant Bénet. He had his head back and was addressing the top of what was left of our mainmast. Then he turned and spoke to me in his ordinary voice.

"The man is a half-wit. We shall talk together again, I hope."

He raised his hand in salute and then was racing away down the ladder before I had time to return it. I myself fairly ran to the lobby and shouted for Phillips. He came and when I demanded the letter he struck his head with his open palm and rebuked that organ for being, as he said, a sieve. But I had been sick and he had been this and that—I heard him with impatience and finally sent him off to find the missive which he passed some considerable time in finding. This enabled me to anticipate what impossible treasures it might hold! There would be a long letter from Miss Chumley, written after the ball in a sleepless night! In a confession of attachment, franker than mine, she would have given me her journal. It would be franker also than mine—which had been limited by a sense of masculine decorum! Here was a most affecting account of the death of her dearest mama! A pressed flower from the gardens of Wilton House, an endearingly inadequate sketch of her music master, that old, old man! Oh, the optimism and phantasy of a young man in love! The state heats every faculty like water in a saucepan on a fire! But for all the time he took, Phillips brought the missive to me too soon and it was small, thin, expensive and so heavily scented I recognized it at once with a downward lurch of the heart for what it was. But then, how could I have been so foolish as to expect anything more than a note from Mr Benét's "most adorable of women"?

I hurried into my hutch.

"Get out, Wheeler! Get out!"

I unfolded the paper and a wave of scent took me by the throat. I had to blink water out of my eyes.

"Lady Somerset presents her compliments to Mr Edmund FitzH. Talbot. Lady Somerset consents to a correspondence between him and Miss Cholmondeley subject to Lady Somerset's supervision. She assumes, nor would Mr Talbot wish her to do more, that the exchange of missives is one between acquaintances and may be broken off or suspended at the wish of either party."

Did the woman think I would *not* write, permission or no? But it was something—and then! Before me on the bunk lay another smaller piece of paper. It had been, for sure, folded into the larger missive. It had no scent but what it had acquired by contact with the more expensive wrapping. With a folly and ardour of which I should never have suspected myself, I pressed it, unread, to my lips. I unfolded it with trembling fingers. What man or woman whose heart has ever beaten more quickly at the sight of such a communication will not understand my joy?

A young person will remember for the rest of her life the meeting of two ships and prays that one day they may put down their ankers in the same harbour.

Foolish rapture, even to tears! I will not repeat the generous and copious and spontaneous promises that sprang unbidden to my lips at the thought of that dear, distant Vision! Those who run may read. This must be the crown of life and I would not have it otherwise!

A young person will remember for the rest of her life—She had written—perhaps in tears—there were marks too on the back of the paper. It had lain on another while that was still wet and unsanded. The words were none of them plainly to be read for they were smudged and backwards at that. There were blots too. It gave me a most complete and devout sense of nearness to her. What would I have not given to kiss the ink from her slender fingers? I seized my mirror, angled it and peered at what had been written. The mind had to restore a whole word from one letter and a smudge, divine the sense with a passion rare in scholarship! At last I made out what was surely the first line. "*Her faults are legion and her virtues small.*" (I made the word "virtue" to be plural myself. I did not think that Miss Chumley would have written anything so improper for her sex and years as a comment on a lady's "virtue".)

> *Indeed 'twas rumoured she had none at all.*
> *When gentlemen appeared she straight begun*
> *To turn her face as sunflowers to the sun.*
> *And if—*

Here the manuscript became quite illegible. But it was an enchanting fragment from that hand. I swear my first opinion was that Pope himself could have done no better than these gently satiric lines! I could hear her very voice and see her smile! She, like Lieutenant Benét, was an addict of poetry. Had he not said that the Muse is the shortest way to the female heart—or words to that effect?

I do not know if I have the boldness to describe what now occurred. I have always, and alas rightly, thought myself to be a prose person! Yet now and with no more ado, but with an ear-tingling sense almost of shame I entered those lists myself! Or tried to! It was the nearest way to her heart and what else could I do in a ship lost amid this waste of miles, this ocean of time, this separation from all that makes life—tolerable I would say, had I not now this overwhelming reason for living! for living. I lay my hand on my heart and declare that the very movement of the planks beneath my feet, evidence of our slow peril, begot in me no more than an impatience with such trivialities as stood between me and what I desired.

But my only experience of the Muse as they would call it was in Latin and Greek, elegiacs, fivers and sixers as we used to say. However—I blush confoundedly at the memory but the truth will be out—and even now I had some confused sense that it was to you, my dear, my clever Angel, that this journal should be written! I got out of my oilskins, sat at my flap, kissed her missive a few times and set out—let me make the confession—to write an Ode to the Beloved! Oh, indeed, Mr Smiles is right! We are all madmen! It is true—I am a witness to it that not poetry but the attempt at poetry is a substitute however poor for the presence of the beloved. I was above myself and saw things plainly as from a mountain top. Whether it be Milton's God or Shakespeare's Dark Lady and even darker Gentleman—whether it be Lesbia or Amaryllis or devil take it, Corydon, the Object lifts the mind to a sphere where only the irrational in language makes any sense. So then I, half-ashamed, with feelings of utter folly yet real need, stared at the blank white paper as if I might find at once relief and achievement there. I examine it now with its poor traces of real passion—those blots and crossings-out, those emendations, alternatives, laborious markings-down of shorts and longs, suggestions to myself or to her—these in their incompetence for those who understand were my real poetry of passion!

Candida for "whiteness". Indeed, an air of whiteness surrounded her, enhaloed her, the fit surround for an innocent girl whose beauty is known to others but not yet to herself! *Candida*, oh, nothing whiter—*Candidior lunâ*, therefore, a light to me, *mea lux*—*vector* is a passenger no, no, nothing so dusty, so drear, *puella, nympha, virgo*, is there not *nymphe* too?

So suddenly from nowhere I had my hexameter!

Candidior lunâ mea lux O vagula nymphe!

But is not *nymphe* a bride? It makes no matter. Then—
Pelle mihî nimbos et mare mulce precor—the pentameter
came all with a rush but I did not like it, there was no
smoothness, all was rough and dull. *Marmora blanditiis*—
better; and so:

Marmora blanditiis fac moderare tuis!

No—*moderare mihî!*

So there I had a hexameter and a pentameter, what you
might call an elegiac couplet. The effort seemed temporarily to exhaust not so much my Latin as my invention. Having besought Miss Chumley to take care of the
seas for me there seemed little left for her to do except—

No. I would not touch that innocent image with the
furthest off intimation of physical desire!

If we should reach land; and if at some time in the
future I should reread this book—if we should reread it
together, oh, devoutly to be desired! Shall I believe what I
now set down as the plain truth? For it was only when I sat
back and relaxed the tension consequent on my poetic
endeavours that I remembered Latin was not in the list of
accomplishments with which Miss Chumley had favoured
me! It was English or nothing, for my French was certainly not up to verse!

Brighter than moonlight, wandering maid,
By thy charms be the white seas allayed!

Turned into English my first efforts at the lyric seemed
on the thin side. I had read much poetry in an endeavour
to understand a side of life which I thought closed to
me by the extreme rationality of my mind and coolness of
my temperament! I had heaped other men's verses up and

"struck them down below" as we Tarpaulins say, as if mere quantity of lines was anything to the purpose. Now, with my first glimmer of its real purpose and source, here I was, reduced by fate to puttying together the elements of a dead language, when only a living one had any use. The effect was plainly to be read in these Latin lines. Now indeed I understood those strictures on my tasks which I had accepted so carelessly and with no real intention of amendment—

"No no, Mr Talbot. The lines are constructed according to the rules but Propertius would never have written them!"

So much for the rules. With what a moved understanding did I now see that poetry is a matter of enchantment. It is folly but a divine folly.

O she doth teach the torches to burn bright!

That is impossible, that is nonsense, but that is what happens, is as the clear and inarticulate voice of every young fool who has been struck by lightning, had all his *previous convictions* cancelled, erased; and let us add at last in the tail of the number, Edmund FitzHenry Talbot, MAGISTER ARTIUM!

It was evident I had shot my poetic bolt. It was only then that I made another discovery which set me laughing like a jackass. I had asked Miss Chumley to flatten the seas for me when the poor girl was even less able to avoid *mal de mer* than I myself! She might in her turn have been more likely to address her lines to Sir Henry! I returned to her little paper and quickly knew the simple sentence by heart. I turned it over and reread the few words I had so laboriously made out there.

Another few words met my gaze. These were not of blotted ink. They had been—and as if to escape me they vanished again—they had been pressed into the page, pressed through a previous page by a lead or silver point, which was why they became visible only when the paper was held at a certain angle.

He has left the ship and I

Who had left the ship? The only people to have left the ship were Wheeler—and Benét! Was he—could he be—had he been—

Benét was personable. He was far more personable than I. He was a poet—his hair—his fair complexion—his agility—

An impressionable girl—malleable—and with no prospects but what lay in marriage!

I started to my feet. It was an infatuation! Nothing more! There was, however, and before I had abandoned and forgotten this lamentable episode, one person who might throw light on the situation. I went quickly to the waist. The clouds had lifted and Mr Benét's new course meant that the ship was labouring indeed but more regularly. The horizon was dense blue and clipped all round in little curves as by a pair of nail scissors. Mr Benét himself was now returned from his "bite to eat" and stood by the mainmast talking to a seaman. The ship seemed to be all festooned by ropes, cables, lanyards which lay mostly on the fo'castle but led down from it also. Mr Benét finished his colloquy, turned, saw me and came to the break of the quarterdeck with his usual agile run. He seemed beamingly happy.

"All goes well, Mr Talbot. Soon we shall be able to experiment with the dragrope and after that get on with Mr Summers's frapping."

"Mr Benét, I wish to speak to you on a serious matter."

"Well, sir, I am at your service."

"A schoolgirl, you said—"

"Did I? I'm sorry, Mr Talbot, but my mind is all tied

up in the dragrope if you see my drift. Were we talking of my sisters?"

"No no."

"Ah—now I remember! You were asking my opinion of young Marion, were you not? She is entirely undeveloped, sir, as they all are. She is a sporty girl though, I give you that. Why, as man to man"—and here Lieutenant Benét looked round briefly then back again—"had little Marion not detained her 'uncle', as they agree she calls Sir Henry, with some plea about the conduct of the ship—she wanted sail reduced, I think—I don't mind telling you I should have been a devil of a sight nearer being detected *in flagrante delicto* than I was!"

"She knew! She understood! A criminal connection!"

"She was accustomed to keep *cave* for us."

There was what might be called a *moderate roar* from the companionway to the captain's quarters. Lieutenant Benét answered it as cheerfully and promptly as he had answered me.

"Immediately, sir!"

He raised his hand towards his forehead, gave what is fast becoming a kind of "salute to be employed at sea", then with his usual cheerful agility raced away along the sloping deck.

My own hand was lifted too. The scrap of paper with Miss Chumley's message on it escaped from my fingers. It went whirling aloft to cling shuddering in the shrouds. With a savage passion I determined to let it go—go, go! But without an order given a seaman put aside his swab, scrambled aloft as quickly as Mr Benét might have done and brought the paper back to me. I nodded my thanks and stood there, paper in hand. How had I made a phantom out of thin air? How had that phantom become the most important thing in the whole world? It was driving me, a sane and calculating man, to acts of sheer folly—

versifying—dragging unwelcome truths out of such as Lieutenant Benét—why (and this was a new dash of poison in the mixture) she might well be devoted to the man himself and he not know it in his foolish obsession with a woman old enough to be his mother!

"Get out, Wheeler! Devil take it, man, are you to be always under my feet?"

"Sir."

"In any case, Phillips should be serving this side of the lobby!"

"No, sir, with respect. The first lieutenant said as we was agreed, Phillips and me, the arrangement could stand since you changed cabins, sir."

"You've become too devilish long-faced for me!"

I flung out of the cabin, nearly brained myself on the mizzen and shouted for Phillips. But it was unnecessary, for he was making a careful way along the lobby to the saloon with a broom.

"Phillips, you may return to serving me."

The man looked round the saloon for a moment.

"Can I speak private, sir? It's where he died, sir."

"Good God, man—men must have died everywhere in this old ship."

Phillips nodded slowly, considering.

"But then, sir, Mr Colley was a latiner."

With that he knuckled his forehead and took his broom out of the saloon. I sat confounded. It was more and more evident that Mr Smiles was right. Here was one more madman. Wheeler made another. The truth appeared to me that I myself might well make a third. The horizon snarled at me, then disappeared. I did indeed have a mad feeling! I too was a "latiner" and perhaps it was the unappeased "larva" of Colley creeping about the ship like a filthy smell which was the "motus" of our idiotic decline into phantasy!

I marched into the saloon and shouted for Bates and got a further supply of brandy. Later still I ate yet more cold beef; and once more, as it might be a labourer eating his midday crust under a hedge, saved the meat at the cost of smeared pickles even on my unmentionables. Oldmeadow, the young Army officer, came and shared that meal with me and I remember a confused conversation we had about the *meaning of life*. He became quite disguised, poor fellow, not having as hard a head as I. When at last I helped him to his hutch we both went sprawling. I nursed a bruised elbow in my own hutch for some time ("that will be all, Wheeler") and did not object when he first assisted me into my bunk. Being, however, a little flown with drink I engaged the man in conversation, during which he elucidated the mystery of his desire to haunt my cabin. He had not informed on Billy Rogers but the people forrard thought he had. They would "do" him if he did not stay close to the gentlemen. It was a misunderstanding, of course. No, they had not thrown him overboard. He had in fact slipped, lost his footing. He was accusing no one. And did the officers think that the ship would sink? One way and another he was fairly at a stand to know what to do—

I am very vexed to think that elevated as I was I did not behave with that degree of circumspection which should be employed in dealing with all but the most devoted and trustworthy of servants. I even entered into a kind of bargain—he might "haunt" me, provided he told me the true story of what had happened to Colley! He consented on the understanding that his information should be revealed to no one so long as he was in the ship. The information was of such a nature that I do not propose to commit it to this journal.

(15)

I got out early into the waist, having been roused by the shouts from the deck.

"Fairly the fall about! Hazard the handybilly Rogers!"

And then the answering cry came from forrard—

"Lie all down handsomely together!"

She was there plainly to be seen on our starboard bow! *Alcyone*! She was dismasted completely, the masts lying about her, white sails spread on the water, the sailors hauling away and singing. The chant came to us clear over the waters.

"Where have you been all the day, Billy Boy?"

We drew somehow alongside her. Our sailors were miraculously dextrous in shortening sail.

"Stun the royals there!"

Sir Henry had climbed the shrouds of what was left of their mizzen.

"Anderson, you see all this? My cursed first lieutenant has fairly fucked us. 'Bellamy,' I said to him. 'Eat the main course or you'll have the masts off us.' "

And She was there on the deck, her arms outstretched! Tears of joy streamed down her cheeks! She came towards me! We merged—

It was Miss Granham. She had no stays—I wrestled with her but could not get away. No wonder the two ships were laughing and I was unclothed—

* * *

It was morning and Wheeler stood by my bunk. He had a cup of coffee in his hands.

"I have got it quite warm, sir."

My head felt constricted and my stomach queasy. Wheeler had his gaze modestly lowered in a proper servant-like manner. I opened my mouth to tell him to get out and then changed my mind. He helped me to dress though I shaved myself. The motion was regular. I left him to clean the cabin and made my way to the passenger saloon. Mr Bowles was there. He apologized for the non-appearance of the committee though to tell the truth I had forgotten that such a gathering had ever been constituted. He said that Mr Prettiman was in great pain and Mr Pike preoccupied with the state of his children. I said little, but grunted merely where it seemed appropriate. I believe Mr Bowles (a man of some intelligence who will prove to be useful, I think, when we reach Sydney Cove) seemed to understand my disinclination for speech. It was from him that I discovered I had missed an interesting operation in seamanship. This was another reason why I regret having got, not to put too fine a point on it, confoundedly drunk. I should have liked to follow what Lieutenant Benét had accomplished or been instrumental in accomplishing! At the time when I and Oldmeadow had been at our potations he had caused to be rigged something never rigged before! The crew had operated a "fore-and-aft dragrope". Thus they had removed weed from the "shadow of the keel". Mr Benét had proposed and invented it. My information is that it was a most elaborate affair. It entailed a simultaneous "bowsing and binding in" of the cable and a "fretting fore and aft" which had necessitated a positive orchestration of the ship's company under the orders of my friend Lieutenant Summers. This information illuminated an observation I myself had made when Oldmeadow and I were *at it* in the saloon. For glancing now and then out of the stern window I had on at least two occasions seen a patch of dark weed (not like the green weed of our waterline) rolling over and over in what

435

wake we had. It occurred to me with something like envy that if Mr Benét continued as he had begun he would finish the voyage in command of us!

By the time I had assimilated all this information from Mr Bowles I was feeling more the thing but in need of fresh air. I went oilskinned, therefore, to the waist and then to my usual lookout by the rail of the poop. The ship seemed still festooned with rope but this time no more than the forepart of her. There were gangs of seamen and contingent officers by a single cable which was being laid out on the fo'castle and rigged with what I suppose were called lanyards. Mention of a rope calls to one's mind the kind of thing used to secure the cover of a hayrick or of a roof which is being rethatched. But this I saw was of a different nature altogether. It was of a knotted texture, curiously woven and twisted so as to present what I can only call a "toothed" appearance. There were the lanyards at frequent intervals, each, it appeared, in the charge of two men. The difficulty of the operation may be gauged when I saw that it entailed threading this cable from one side of the ship to the other but under the bowsprit and through freeing ports on either side of the waist. It was easy, apparently, to lower the rope but by no means easy to draw it along and this was what they were doing or trying to do. The ship's movement did not help them. I made my way along the windward rail to examine the operation more closely but Mr Benét, coming from aft, stopped and spoke to me.

"I believe you should not be here, sir!"

"I will go back when I have satisfied my curiosity, and let the wind blow last night's drink out of me. I propose never to drink again."

"*Qui a bu, boira.*"

"Devil take it, Mr Benét, you speak French like a Frog! It's un-English. But returning to the subject of school-girls—"

436

"Oh, lord, no. I beg you, Mr Talbot. We may hope for another couple of knots I think. Do you notice how removing the weed from the garboard strakes has made a difference? I say a clear knot though Mr Summers does not think so. We shall know at midday, of course. He is cautious, is he not? Captain Anderson agrees with me. 'A clear knot, Mr Benét,' he said. 'I shall enter it in the log.' "

"You are to be congratulated."

"Before I leave the service and devote myself to the pen I hope to show the Navy that intelligence is not to be despised, sir, nor all virtue confined to senior officers!"

"Talking of virtue—"

"I beg you will not, sir. I have suffered from a wearisome repetition of Sir Henry's opinion on that subject. My distance from him is the only consolation for my distance from Her!"

Mr Benét sighed. I continued: "Miss Chumley—"

Mr Benét interrupted me. "Have you sisters, Mr Talbot?"

"No, sir."

Mr Benét said nothing but nodded gravely as if confirming something to himself. This and the remark he had made was so cryptic that I could find nothing to say.

"And now, Mr Talbot, I believe you must return to the break of the quarterdeck. This will soon be no place for a passenger."

Charles Summers hailed from the fo'castle.

"Mr Benét! When you have concluded your conversation be good enough to return to your duties. We are waiting."

I clambered back and held on to the rail by the entry to the lobby. The scene before me was not so much entertaining as confused. It appeared that Cumbershum had the charge of one side of the fo'castle and Mr Benét of the other. Charles Summers was in overall charge. There

were seamen lining the rail in that part of the ship all leaning outward and facing away from me. I had the nonsensical impression that a good number of our tarry heroes
were being sick into the sea. They were, I supposed,
holding the cable which would serve as a dragrope. As I
took this in, Summers shouted an order.

"Let go!"

The men lining the rail stood up. Benét and
Cumbershum started to shout and their parties of seamen
to move rhythmically. I cannot describe what they were
doing more accurately because at the time I did not
understand it. Now, I think, being wise after the event,
they were moving the dragrope with a sawing motion.
Nothing much seemed to be happening. I turned and
looked up aft. The sailing master, Mr Smiles, had the
watch apparently, with young Mr Taylor as his doggie.
Mr Taylor seemed more subdued than usual and this may
have been because not more than a yard or two away the
captain stood by the forrard rail, his hands clasped behind
his back, his feet wide apart. He watched the operation
from the quarterdeck in silence.

There was a sudden commotion on the fo'castle.
Cumbershum's party appeared to fall in a heap and he
could be heard swearing at them as they sorted themselves
out. After that there was a long pause. Apparently one end
of a necessary rope had been lost so the operation was to be
done again from the start. Lieutenant Benét was arguing
with Charles Summers who did not appear to be happy.
It seemed to me that his customarily weather-beaten face
was paler than usual—with anger perhaps. The fo'castle
became a mess of ropes and blocks among which men did
what I am persuaded they understood. It was a long wait.
I turned and climbed to the quarterdeck where the captain
acknowledged my salutation if not with amiability at least
without an open expression of bad temper.

"Good morning, Captain. But it is no kind of good day I think! Tell me—what are the crew doing?"

For a moment or two I thought he would not answer me. But then he opened his mouth and whispered. This I found was not secrecy but phlegm consequent on his having held his morose tongue longer than the constitution of a man was designed for. He walked to the rail, spat over the side, came back and stood by me without looking at me.

"They are rigging a dragrope."

Well I knew that! But it seemed that the details of that interesting operation would have to be extracted from him one by one.

"How can you ensure that the rope clings enough to the hull? There must be many areas that are inaccessible."

Unwittingly I had opened his mouth!

"There are indeed, Mr Talbot, though the underwater part of a ship is near enough semicircular in section. But a careful officer will exercise his wits in finding a way round such difficulties. The dragrope may be held from several directions, not merely from side to side but fore and aft. Mr Benét has proposed a plan which we think will work. The use of a dragrope in the open sea and when under weigh is most unusual. Indeed I do not know how often it has been done before. But in our circumstances— Mr Benét has already succeeded in removing weed from near the keel, something I believe unique."

"You have profited by the exchange of officers."

Captain Anderson lowered at me for a moment. But then it seemed to me as if the invitation to continue talking about his favourite was irresistible.

"I believe Mr Benét is determined to have us scraped as clean as if we was newly commissioned, Mr Talbot. We shall have tackles 'thwart ships and fore and aft and lifts from the yardarms. Mr Benét is a real seaman, sir, all ropes and blocks and canvas, sir. There is no *steam* about Mr Benét, sir. No chain cable or wire rope!"

"He is certainly using enough rope at the moment. I did not know the ship held so much."

"What a captain cannot do with good officers, rope, canvas, spars and a willing crew cannot be done!"

"Well, Captain, I will not dispute with you. Mr Benét is a very energetic young man and I must take your opinion of his seamanship on trust."

The captain spoke with positive animation.

"He will go far!"

"His French at all events sounds much as they speak it in Paris."

"That is natural, Mr Talbot. His parents are émigrés."

"Certainly his general appearance and air are very pleasing. Golden hair and a complexion which seems wholly resistant to salt—he is a veritable marine Adonis!"

The captain looked at me sternly as he tried the word in his mouth.

"Adonis. You will excuse me now, Mr Talbot. I am busy."

Good God, the man thought he had given me my *congé*!

"Do not allow me to interrupt you, Captain Anderson. I am deeply interested to see what you do."

What Captain Anderson did was to utter a kind of subdued snarl, turn, take a step to the forrard rail and hold it with both hands as if he would like to pick it up and use it as a club. He glanced up at the luff, roared at Mr Taylor who squeaked at the quartermasters who glanced at the luff then into the binnacle, rolled their quids as one man and moved the wheel a "handspan" which as far as I could see affected the ship not at all. I continued to watch the operation on the fo'castle. It was very slow going and even the captain gave up after a time and began to stump up and down on the larboard side of the deck, ignoring our rolling and pitching—and I suppose our hogging and sagging—in a way which spoke of the years he has passed doing precisely that. It seemed to me that he was capable, if the ship should capsize—which God forbid—of marching moodily over the side as she rolled, following the movement, then stumping backwards and forwards along her keel. He would wait for Lieutenant Benét to devise some cat's cradle of ropes, blocks, spars and canvas to bring the ship upright again! He and his certainties were much like the movement of the starry heavens.

Little Pike was coming up the stairways. There were tears on his face. The wind tore them away and his eyes replaced them. He reeled as he came, fell against me, clutched me with both arms and wept against my midriff. He whispered.

"Phoebe! Oh, my little Phoebe—"

"Good God! Dead?"

The captain had stopped in his tracks. Now he came quickly across and stared down at Pike.

"Who is dead?"

"They say she is dying. Oh, my little Phoebe!"

"This is Mr Pike, Captain. Phoebe is his daughter. Pull yourself together, Pike!"

"Who says your daughter is dying, sir?"

Pike sniffed and hiccuped.

"Mrs Pike, Captain, and Miss Granham."

"Come, Pike," said I. "They are neither of them medical men, you know! I told you about my young brothers, did I not? Always in the wars and—"

"What do you expect me to do about your daughter, Mr Pike?"

Pike shook himself free from my grasp, reeled and clutched the rail.

"If you could only ease the motion, Captain! It wears them out, you see—"

441

Captain Anderson answered him in what for him was a kindly voice.

"It is impossible, Mr Pike. I cannot go into the reasons but you must believe me when I say that no power on earth could stop the ship's movement."

We were all three silent. Pike smeared his face with a sleeve and then slowly, drearily *drooped* away below.

It was then that the idea came to me.

"Captain!"

But once more he was staring forward.

"Captain! Captain! Nelson—"

The captain turned and with a positive hiss of breath hurried past me and disappeared down his own private and holy companionway beyond my reach!

"Devil take it!"

For the idea was good. I knew it! I clambered down the ladders after Pike, hurried to the door of their cabin—and hesitated! It was not like me to hesitate but I did. I raised my hand to knock—and then dropped it again. But this was a terrible crisis for the little girl! I opened the door stealthily.

Her sister lay at one end of the bunk, propped up on granite pillows. She was picking at the face of a rag doll and she looked curst sullen to me. Mrs Pike and Miss Granham were bent over the other end of the bunk. I opened my mouth to explain my idea but never got a word out, for Miss Granham must have heard, or sensed something. For she turned—I had almost said turned *on me* quickly and stared in my eyes. Her face seemed stripped of flesh and her eyes were deep in their sockets.

"Go away, Mr Talbot. Do not say anything."

It was a command uttered in a stony voice which would have daunted Anderson himself. I found I had closed the door as if that arm was no longer my own. I went cautiously to the passenger saloon. Mr Pike was there under

the stern window. He sniffed now and then but was calm.
I remembered the only man in the ship in whom I had
complete faith. I hurried away, ran perilously along the
heaving deck and seized Charles Summers by the arm.

"Charles, I must speak with you—"

"Edmund! Mr Talbot!"

"The Pike child—Nelson—"

"Mr Talbot, this passes everything! Return to your
cabin or I must have you conducted there!"

"Charles!"

He positively shook his arm free and pointedly began to
issue orders.

I made my way back, holding on to the windward rail.

My idea was good. Nelson, who was a sufferer from *mal
de mer*, used to sleep in a cot which was slung like a hammock. The little girl should have had a hammock rigged for
her, a doll-sized hammock, and she would have lain as snug
as ever drunken Mr Gibbs did down in the gun-room! It
might have given her the rest so necessary, allowed her to
sleep perhaps and so gather a little strength. I had a sudden
thought that if I approached Mr Benét—but he was now
enmeshed in ropes and orders. However I did not return to
my hutch as Charles had directed but waited once more by
the break to see how the operation went. But it was slow.
So at last I went to my hutch and found the inevitable
Wheeler scrabbling round on the deck with a deckcloth
and pretending to mop up the seawater which was immediately replaced by more from the lobby as he did so.

"Get out, Wheeler!"

I had forgotten my drunken agreement and the order
had become habitual. Instead of obeying it he rose from
his knees, floorcloth in hand, and came close to me.

He whispered. "She's moving more, isn't she, sir?"

"You're out of your mind, Wheeler. Now be off with
you!"

"I can't drown, sir. Not again, I can't."

The man seemed calm for all the nonsense of what he spoke. I could think of nothing to say and muttered I know not what. So we stood, he continuing to stare into my face as if in longing and perhaps even in hope. But what use was "Lord Talbot"?

The ship's bell rang and there were noises from all over the ship—shouts and the thumping of booted feet, where the watch was being changed. Wheeler turned with a deep sigh and went away. To be helpless before such an evident need; and on the other hand to have an idea of real value to which no one would listen; to find our ship not so much breaking up but decomposing; and to find men, Charles Summers, Wheeler, Mr Gibbs, seeming to change as if something of the same was operating in them—whatever I had foreseen or planned in those distant days in England when I was made acquainted with the nature of my employment seemed a childish "supposing" and was all now rendered conditional on our surmounting this present peril and was likely enough to be cancelled by it! That employment itself I now saw would be conditioned by a world at once harsher and more complicated than I had anticipated.

I remembered with a kind of chill that spread over me like a change in the weather what "frapping" was. Charles Summers proposed then actually to *tie* the ship together! He would use our great cables as a last resort in an attempt to prevent her timbers from falling apart! The officers had attempted to soothe me with their assurances! They had lied in what they thought was a good cause! We *were* in deadly peril! At last I let out my breath, mopped my forehead, then sat down at my writing-flap. After some thought, I took out this journal and leafed through it, reading here and there as if I might find in the recorded wisdom of Edmund Talbot a solution to our difficulties. Would the book one day be bound handsomely and lie on

444

some shelf or other, my descendants' shelves, *Talbot's Journal*? But this one lacked the accidental shape of narration which Colley and fate had forced on the other volume! I had thought it might, as it were, group itself round the adventures of Jack Deverel. But at the very moment when he bid fair to occupy the centre of the stage he had escaped from it! He had exchanged clean out of this theatre and into another one where, alas, I could not follow him. Then again, this journal had been a sweet yet painful account of how young Mr Talbot had fallen in love—but the dear Object of my passion had been snatched away from me as mercilessly as you please, leaving me to dreams and Latin verses! Any furtherance of that connection, any fruition of it must look to so far in the future that I had a moment of breathless panic lest the whole connection should wear itself out and prove to be the merest flirtation in the skirts of a dinner and a ball! But as the thought came to me I dismissed it as unworthy. In the very instant of this ungenerous thought, the face and figure, the very being of that most precious Object—that Prodigy!—flashed upon the tablets of my memory and restored all to its true position. That last look she had given me and her last whispered words—oh no, she was all I had dreamed! Yet, remembering not a poetical phantasy but a real, breathing and feeling and speaking young lady, a young lady of much intelligence and *esprit*, I could not doubt she would undertake a course of parallel consideration as to my advisability, suitability, possibility, probability—I had a fleeting vision of myself through her eyes, now, *that young man who was so plainly épris*, and whom she now saw back there, left in a wallowing and dismasted vessel bound for somewhere else! It was a desolating consideration.

Besides, Lady Somerset had said the exchange of letters could be broken off at the wish of either party! No one was committed.

What had I foreseen? My position at Sydney Cove, a handsome workroom in the residency. There, I should apply that habit of study, that methodical approach which would make me master of any subject however complex and new—or at least more master than anyone else would be! Then in the social life which surrounded His Excellency I would be careless master of a subject, never letting it be known that hours of devoted work had given me such assurance! I would be a Burghley to His Excellency's Queen Elizabeth—

(16)

It was an evident folly! I started to my feet but my hutch
was not designed for a man stumping to and fro to settle
the turmoil of his mind. I went as quickly and nimbly
as the ship would allow to the greater space of the passenger saloon. But hardly had I got the door opened when
Oldmeadow, the Army officer, coming close behind,
shared it with me. He flung himself into a seat at the
windward end of the main table. He was wearing civilian
clothes and looked the better for it, a young man of some
breeding and sense.

"Talbot, old fellow—"

But here a stormy thump of a wave and a bounce of our
stern together with a more rapid roll to starboard made
him thrust with both hands at the table before him.

"The devil take the sea and the Navy together!"

I, on the contrary, had to lay hold of the other end of
the table and cling to it.

"They do their best, Oldmeadow!"

"Well it's not enough, that's what I say. If I'd known
how long and hard this voyage would be I'd have thrown
up my commission!"

"We have to put up with it."

"That's all very well, Talbot. But you know we're sinking or going to sink or may sink—I tell you that in confidence. My men know all about it. In fact they knew all
about it before I did! It's always the way, you know."

"What did you tell them?"

"What do you imagine? I told them they were soldiers
and the ship was the business of the Navy and none of
theirs." He gave his sudden, cawing laugh, chin drawn

447

back. "I told them if they had to drown they'd do so with leather properly pipe-clayed and muskets clean. I also ordered Corporal Jackson if he found we were sinking to get them properly fell in and standing by for further orders."

"What good does that do?"

"Have you a better suggestion?"

"We are not supposed—Summers assures me we shall not sink."

I was about to elaborate on this when the door opened violently as usual in lumpy weather, and portly Mr Brocklebank came through, supported on one side by Mrs Brocklebank and on the other side by Phillips. They manoeuvred him to a seat half-way between me and Oldmeadow and went away. The poor man seemed to me to have lost half his substance. His fat cheeks were now pendulous as those of a certain Royal Personage though his extreme embonpoint was no longer comparable.

"Mr Brocklebank, sir! I was told you were forced to keep your bunk! May we both congratulate you on your recovery?"

"I am not recovered, Mr Talbot. It is supposed that a little movement may improve me. I am in a sad way. But so, Mrs Brocklebank tells me, is our ship. I am summoning up what little strength I have left to be on hand when we attempt the operation of the dragrope. The artist's eye—"

"I admire your devotion to art, sir, but the ship is not in a bad way! I have the word of the first lieutenant! Devil take it, do you suppose I myself would be so cheerful if we was about to sink?"

I attempted a light laugh but it was so unsuccessful that both Oldmeadow and Mr Brocklebank laughed heartily which in its turn made me laugh—so there we were, the sea slanting crazily outside the stern window, glimpses of new sun sliding over the saloon at the ship's movement, and all laughing as if the place were bedlam.

"Well," said Oldmeadow at last, "we soldiers are fortunate, for we know what to do!"

"I tell you we are not going to sink!"

Brocklebank ignored me.

"I have given much thought to the situation, gentlemen. Huddled as I was in my bunk, passing days without event, I have had ample time to consider the future. It was a question, you see. I was able to formulate the great question."

I glanced at Oldmeadow to see if he thought, as I did, that Mr Brocklebank was as usual showing the result of extreme and habitual potations. But Oldmeadow watched him, saying nothing. The old man went on.

"I mean, gentlemen, we know how ships are lost. They run on the rocks. There are attempts to get ashore, et cetera, et cetera. Or they are sunk in action. You will have seen a dozen pictures—the battle smoke conveniently placed, and in the foreground a smashed stump of mast with three small figures clinging to it. There is a ship's boat making towards them to pick them up, with Sir Henry Somerset as a midshipman in the stern sheets—far in the distance through an arrangement of convenient smoke HMS *Whatnot* is seen to be on fire—it has all been seen, all recorded."

"I am not sure, sir—"

"The question? It is this. How does a ship sink when it is not seen or recorded? Every year—you young gentlemen will not remember peace, but even in peacetime—ships will disappear. They do not strike on rocks or lie bilged in sand. They are not those which become hulks for prison or supply, their ribs do not decay in estuaries. They pass over a horizon and they enter a mystery, gentlemen. They become 'overdue'. No one paints a picture of the *Jean and Mary* alone in the sea, disappearing in the sea, swallowed—"

"Devil take it, Brocklebank, I said the first lieutenant—"

"Somewhere in a circle of sea not to be distinguished from any other part they come to their end—"

"Look, man, they may be taken aback as we were, over-set, but not lose their topmasts and therefore sink with a gurgle, I suppose—oh, with babbling prayers and curses, shrieks and screams, shouts for help where there is none—"

"But you see, Mr Talbot, the weather may be fair, the water stealthy. It creeps on them, over them. They pump until they are exhausted and the water wins. They say the water will always win."

I reeled because I had stood up.

"Once and for all, Mr Brocklebank, we are not going to sink! You must not speak so, and if you cannot think of a way to paint the event, well I am sorry but to tell you the truth not very—"

"You mistake me, sir. I am not thinking of paint. Oh yes, there is a great, terrible picture to be painted by someone of the ship foundering somewhere, anywhere, lost with all hands, overdue, the sea and the sky and the ship—but not I, sir. Besides, what client would ask me for such a canvas? How would such an engraving sell? No, sir. It is a question not of paint but of conduct."

Oldmeadow cawed again.

"By Jove, Talbot, he's put his finger on it!"

"Mr Oldmeadow understands. My meditation has been long. How does a man drown when he sees it coming? It is a question of dignity, Mr Talbot. I must have my dignity. How must I drown? Oblige me, Mr Talbot, by calling your servant."

"Wheeler! Wheeler, I say! Damn it, Wheeler, why aren't you—ah, there you are!"

"I beg pardon, sir? You called for me."

Brocklebank answered.

"We are interested, you see, Wheeler. You're about the only man alive who has had what must have been a deuced unpleasant experience. You'd oblige us by describing—"

I interrupted him.

"Brocklebank, you can't! I don't believe the man's recovered, if he ever will!"

Wheeler was looking at each of us in turn.

"No no, Wheeler! Mr Brocklebank had not thought—I am sure he spoke in jest!"

A goose walked over Oldmeadow's grave.

"God, Talbot! It would be like asking some poor devil what happened after he was turned off!"

A strong interior convulsion seemed to shake Wheeler from head to foot.

"Describe?"

Brocklebank waved his hand expansively.

"No matter, my man. I am in a minority."

Wheeler looked at me.

"That will be all, sir?"

"I—regret this. Yes. That will be all, thank you."

Wheeler bowed in a way I had never seen before. He went away.

I turned to Brocklebank.

"I am sorry to have interrupted you, sir, but really!"

"I am still at a loss to understand you, Mr Talbot. We had what might well be a unique opportunity to understand life—and what is even more important, understand death!"

I stood up.

"I believe, Mr Brocklebank, not being a devotee of the muse, as you are, that I am quite content to wait on the event."

I went away to find Wheeler and give him the *douceur* which I thought the artist's enquiry warranted.

But Wheeler was not in the lobby nor in my hutch. I stood there, looking down at this very book where it lay open on the writing-flap. The truth is Wheeler had frightened me into a cold perspiration. Whether it was my recent foray into the realms of poetry or his strong gaze at something which existed for him alone—but it might not be his alone! I might conceivably share it with him! Images of the latter end stormed through my mind. Mutiny—a fight for the last few places in the boats, Mr Jones's bodyguards clubbing down the opposition as his majesty moved calmly towards his private insurance!

These images evidently worked on me more strongly than I supposed, for I *came to* in the lobby. I was holding on to the rail which was placed alongside my door and I had not put on oilskins. I cannot remember opening the door. I simply found myself where I was. My heart was beating as if I had run a race.

Mr Jones himself stood in the doorway which gives on to the waist. He wore oilskins though for once they did not seem necessary. A dense blue sea surrounded us with white horses galloping across our course.

"Well, Mr Jones, have they taken any weed off yet?"

"I believe so, Mr Talbot. Some have averred they saw it go, but I cannot say I did so myself."

"I saw some weed in our wake the other day. I suppose that was owing to Mr Benét having 'cleaned the garboard strakes in the shadow of the keel'."

"That is far too nautical for a simple shopkeeper, sir."

"I mean his operations with the dragrope were unexpectedly successful."

"I must approve his care of my investments."

"You own the ship as well as everything else?"

I did not attempt to keep the irritation and dislike out of my voice. But the purser continued, placidly enough.

"No, no. That remains to the Crown. But there is a

matter of certain goods of mine which are stowed in the hold and will spoil if the water gains on us."

"The first lieutenant—"

"Assured you that the water was not gaining. Yes, I know. But in my important and shopkeeperly way I have wondered whether the weed which Mr Benét is so anxious to scrape off the ship's hull may not in fact be keeping the water out?"

"Mr Benét—"

"He is a persuasive young gentleman. I believe, sir, that he could sell anything, did he put his mind to it. Even damaged goods."

"They will have considered what the effect of removing the weed will be."

"I observe that the first lieutenant is co-operating in the business under protest."

"Yes. But then he is—"

I did not like to say the word. It would seem to credit Charles Summers with an almost feminine weakness. The purser turned his head on his thick neck and looked me in the eye. He spoke the words softly.

"He is?"

I said nothing. "Jealous" is a dangerous word. He returned to watching the fo'castle. I stood, not holding on now but with feet wide apart, for Mr Benét's change of course had had an evening effect on our movements. Together then, standing just beyond the opening to the waist, we watched the operation. The groups on either side of the ship were moving rhythmically and alternately. Then as we watched, at a shouted order both groups stood easy, the lanyards slack in their hands. I saw what the matter was. Since our rigging came down to the sides of the vessel there would come point after point at which the dragrope would have to be passed "outboard" and brought in again before the operation could continue.

Such a pause the men were now enjoying and one unexpectedly prolonged, for the ship's bell rang again and there came a pipe and the cry of "Up spirits!" It was, I thought, another example of the extraordinary ossification of Noah's Service that the vital operation which might increase our speed now had to be set on one side while the crew tossed down what Colley had called "the flaming ichor!" The groups were streaming down from the fo'castle, leaving the officers, Cumbershum, Benét, Summers waiting, doubtless impatiently, by the abandoned ropes. What had the carpenter said all those weeks ago when I had first heard the word "dragrope"? *They didn't think they'd careen her what with one thing and another so they took what weed they could off her bottom with the dragrope*—and Mr Askew, the gunner—*If they took the weed off her they might take the bottom with it.*

"It is an operation for harbour."

I was a little confused to find I had spoken aloud.

"It is not a case in which they can afford to make a mistake, Mr Talbot."

"No, indeed. I propose to obtain from you a watertight and buoyant container for my manuscripts, so that they, at least, may stand some chance of reaching a reader."

That was a joke, of course, but so weak that Mr Jones nodded seriously.

We turned to watch once more. Men were climbing back to the rope. All at once I saw that Charles Summers was gesticulating at Mr Benét with a fierceness which was unwonted in him. The two gentlemen fell into an animated argument. The purser stirred, I thought, uneasily.

"Is something really wrong, do you suppose, Mr Talbot?"

All at once it came upon me that Charles Summers had been—was—my friend and it was improper in me to discuss him. I shrugged lightly, turned away and climbed the stairway to the quarterdeck. Captain Anderson was standing again by the forrard rail and staring at his ship broodingly.

"An operation for harbour, Captain?"

He glanced across at me, opened his mouth, then shut it again. I turned too. From this elevation it was possible to see more clearly the plan of what was being executed. The dragrope was not a simple unadorned cable. From regular intervals at either end subsidiary ropes were stretched or coiled on the deck. But the intricacy is beyond my seamanship or my powers of description.

"Is that really weed, sir, that great patch at the waterline?"

The captain grunted. "Some has been cut away from under her now. There will be more yet."

"And our speed will increase again?"

"So it is hoped."

"How much, Captain?"

Captain Anderson gave the sign of his displeasure which many found so daunting. That is to say he projected his jaw and lowered the sullen mass of his face onto it.

"Oh, do not answer, Captain! It is, of course, none of my business—though come to think of it. I have as great a stake in the affair as anyone!"

"Stake, sir! What stake?"

"My life."

Now the captain did look at me. But it was from deep inside and loweringly. A seventh wave, which washed the fo'castle, filled the waist and made the quarterdeck shudder. It took my attention from anything but the need to keep my feet. Was it my imagination or did the quarterdeck move in a way which was not repeated by the rest of the ship? The wind felt very cold and I regretted not having my oilskins. Nevertheless I watched a whole series of waves and rolls but could not detect that peculiarly local movement again.

"I am told she has been badly wrung."

Captain Anderson drew in his breath sibilantly. His knuckles on the rail showed dirty white. He roared. "Mr Summers!"

Charles stopped and picked up a speaking trumpet. His voice came the length of the ship with that curious, otherworldly resonance which such an instrument imparts.

"Sir?"

"What is the delay?"

"A foul lead, sir. We are trying to clear it."

" 'Trying', Mr Summers?"

" 'Trying.' "

Charles turned aside his head. He spoke briefly to Mr Benét who saluted and came racing aft. He spoke up from the waist.

"We think it is old coral, sir. Her last commission was in the West Indies. We believe it is dead coral down there which may need more than pully-haully."

" 'We,' Mr Benét?"

"Mr Summers thinks it possible. I suggested taking a lead to the forrard warping capstan but he does not want to go as far as that for a number of reasons."

"And you, Mr Benét?"

"I believe we should try a tackle to begin with."

Captain Anderson said nothing for a while. He made small chewing movements. Other than that, all that moved was his right leg—his starboard leg which flexed and straightened without, I am sure, his being aware of it. After all, my own starboard leg, and Mr Benét's—no. As Mr Benét was facing aft was it not his port leg? It depends whether, et cetera. I am so deucedly tired of this nautical rigmarole! We all flexed and straightened our appropriate

456

legs and did so in the ship whenever we were not sitting or lying. It was a small piece of unconscious behaviour to have attached to us and no kind of compensation for the suffering surely implied in its acquirement.

Captain Anderson nodded. "Very well, Mr Benét. But—"

"Handsomely, sir?"

Captain Anderson smiled! He did! He shook his forefinger at the young man.

"Now now, Mr Benét! Wait for it! Yes. Handsomely."

"Aye aye, sir."

Good God—but this was *arch*!

Now there occurred one of those timeless pauses in a ship when men seem to do nothing but paw at ropes. Leads, it appeared, had to be rerun. Mr Summers, it seemed, was making use of a freeing port next to the break of the fo'castle and also the bitts—oh, lord! And a positive cat's cradle of ropes and blocks—there was argument. At last a party of men was mustered at the tail of a rope they were adjured to pull with a cry of "Gee up, horsies!" This producing no useful effect they were then adjured to "Walk away," then "Put your backs into it!", then "Sweat out your guts" which did indeed produce a result. There was a report like a pistol shot, I was about to say, but why not like a rope breaking? For that is what it was and they all fell down. The cat's cradle was a long time repairing. I myself went to the passenger saloon and ate some more cold beef, then came back. The cat's cradle was in place again and the men went through their motions. The lead to the dragrope stretched rigid and remained motionless.

Mr Benét cantered aft again.

"We believe we should use the capstan, sir."

Captain Anderson straightened up abruptly. He turned and began to stump up and down with his hands behind his back. Lieutenant Benét waited. Another big wave passed under us—

I was certain. Where the captain was walking away from me, his legs straddled apart, the deck had moved and moved in a way that the fo'castle had not, nor the waist either!

Now the captain came back.

"Mr Summers agrees?"

"He believes you yourself should give the order, sir."

"The man on the spot, Mr Benét. And can you not move the rope forrard?"

"I—we think that the rope has sawn its way into the coral and now cannot be moved forrard or aft."

"What does Mr Gibbs think?"

Mr Benét smiled.

"He says, 'Maybe it's coral and maybe it isn't,' sir."

"Very well. My compliments to the first lieutenant and ask him to be good enough to step up here."

Was it my imagination or had Captain Anderson shared with Lieutenant Benét some kind of reference, reminder, opinion, in the way he said "first lieutenant"? But I was versed enough now in the customs of the sea service to realize what a monstrous dereliction from duty that would be! No, it was my imagination; for Captain Anderson had lowered his face glumly again and Lieutenant Benét was cantering in his usual fashion towards the fo'castle. Summers came back quickly enough but walking. His face was expressionless. He and the captain walked away from me to the very stern of the vessel and stood there together. I heard nothing of their conversation but occasional words which flew from them like leaves on the wind. Forrard, I could see that Lieutenant Benét with the briskness I was coming to expect from him had gathered together some men from the other parties.

"Responsibility."

That word flew by. It had been said in a rather raised tone as if Charles Summers had said it before and now was repeating it with emphasis.

How could they be certain that when they dragged off or broke off the coral that they would not break off wood with it? And that word again and in the captain's voice this time!

"Responsibility."

Gone on the wind.

Mr Summers came back. He passed me without speaking. His face was stony, but his whole demeanour that of an anxious and angry man. How we were all changed! Charles who had been so equable, now as often in the sulks as out of them; Anderson once so aloof, now said to be eating out of Mr Benét's hand; and I—? Well, I have put down, it may be, more that I might regret about Edmund Talbot.

There were now lines stretching from the dragrope itself and a master rope which gathered all the subsidiaries together and led them, not to a warping capstan below deck, but to the huge drum of the capstan on the fo'castle. Some men were putting in the capstan bars. It came to me on the cold wind that this operation carried on along there at an angle to the sea, washed with salt water and spray-shot; that this work by those ear-ringed fellows with their pigtails and quiffs was employed about my life; was something which might well see the end of that precious career towards which my godfather had impelled me!

Without much thought I abandoned my station on the quarterdeck and went down to the waist, meaning to look along the ship's side and catch if I could a glimpse of the dragrope where it vanished under water. I do not know what impulse made me do it other than a new sense of urgency which made me want to "do something!" It was an impulse not peculiar to me. This ship resounded to rumour, scandal and nightmare as a stringed instrument resounds to the bow. Our passengers, or those of them who were at all capable of leaving their bunks, were now grouped, I might say crowded, at our entry to the waist. Bowles was there, wrapped in a greatcoat and peering forward I thought shortsightedly, his face screwed up, dark curls fluttering all over his hatless head. Mr Brocklebank of all people, our marine painter, was there, still out of his bunk, though for the first time since we had struck bad weather! But what a change! That belly which had once included his chest and seemed to descend to his knees had now contracted to a shelflike protuberance positioned between his navel and the upper part of the thigh. He and it were draped in a travelling shawl or blanket, a carriage rug perhaps which had seen far better days. His beaver was bound on his head by a length of material which passed over the crown and under his chin. I do not think I was mistaken in believing it to be a lady's stocking! The former owner of the stocking, Mrs Brocklebank, crouched under his lee. As I passed them she opened the carriage rug and huddled herself inside it against her husband and beneath his right armpit. Her pretty face was pale. No one said anything. All eyes were on the distant capstan.

And now, as if the rumour, the "buzz", had been too loud to be endured in those forrard parts of the ship where the emigrants lived as best they could, they began to issue into the waist, and then to swarm into it. There were angry shouts from the officers. Summers descended from the fo'castle and spoke with them. He gestured at the ropes. Behind me firm steps descended the stairs to the quarterdeck and poop. It was Captain Anderson, of course, and he made his majestic way forrard over the streaming deck. He spoke with Summers. He spoke with the emigrants. Like bees returning to their hive they retreated backwards into the entry to the fo'castle and the operation saw them no more. Captain Anderson picked his careful way round the cat's cradle and climbed to the fo'castle itself. He stationed himself forrard of the capstan and on our larboard side where the "foul lead" was occurring. I myself clambered to the raised rail of our larboard side, and held it, then looked over.

Colley said much of colour! I must remember the colour of things. Greyness had gone. The sky was dense blue and the sea a deeper blue over which white horses dragged their varying humps and hummocks and walls of water. The sea was covered with them to the sharp horizon, and the sun blazed down from a sky carved here and there with white and rounded clouds. The side of our ship was wasp-coloured as befits a warship, black and yellow and streaming. Certainly the first operation of the dragrope had been successful until it jammed. There was no doubt of that. A great carpet of weed floated many yards out from the side of the ship. As we rolled, the green weed along the waterline came up through the darker weed from lower down, a whole carpet of it, still attached to the ship but easy enough to cut away or be dragged away should our forward movement increase or the dragrope be moved further aft. The carpet was as nasty a sight I thought as there could well be. Now and then, at the outer edge of the carpet whole waggonloads of the pipy, bagged and leathery stuff together with a helping of small crabs and shellfish would detach itself and float away in a sloth which told only too clearly that for all her rolling, her hogging and sagging, her bucking, and her wringing, the ship was nearly stationary in the water. Yet the dragrope had worked and would continue to do so. Weed had come off her hull.

Someone sighed. It was Wheeler at my elbow and not staring into the water but into my face.

461

"It's true, isn't it, sir?"

I whispered back—in all that wind and spray, noise, commotion!

"What's true, man?"

"They're taking a chance, aren't they, sir? You've spoken to the officers, sir, haven't you?"

The man irritated me beyond bearing.

"For God's sake, Wheeler! You'll have to put up with whatever happens like the rest of us!"

Wheeler moved away.

On the fo'castle, Mr Gibbs knuckled his forehead in obedience before the captain and departed downwards. A detached load of weed drifted slowly by.

But Mr Brocklebank was approaching. He had shuffled over with much caution and now took up the position at my elbow which had been vacated by Wheeler.

"A scene fit for your brush, Mr Brocklebank."

"Are you offering to commission me, Mr Talbot?"

"I? Good God! The idea—"

Mrs Brocklebank who had come along with her husband peeped up at me out of the carriage rug.

"If only the motion were to be easier I'm sure Mr Brocklebank—Wilmot—would be happy to paint your portrait, Mr Talbot!"

Was there ever so silly and pointless an interruption? I did not answer it but stared forrard where our fate was being decided. This will indicate how wrought on I was, and indeed how tense and anxious all we passengers were. I cannot speak for the seamen but after all they are human and had each a life to lose. Indeed my own anxiety may be judged by the fact that I preferred to ignore Mrs Brocklebank, for she was, in good weather, a pretty little thing and I had enjoyed the few moments of conversation I had ever passed with her. Indeed, in those distant days before we lost our masts—but that is irrelevant.

The purser had reappeared and stood wedged between me and Mr Brocklebank.

"They are very slow about it, Mr Talbot, the lazy dogs."

"Perhaps they do not care for the possible outcome, Mr Jones, and are putting off the evil moment."

"Debt-ridden and dissolute. What should the outcome matter to such?"

"If you prick us do we not bleed?"

"I beg your pardon, sir!"

Mr Brocklebank edged in a trifle closer.

"Mr Talbot was quoting from *The Merchant of Venice*. No, no, Mr Talbot. You do not know the lower orders as I do who have been forced to live among them at one time and another. It is fashionable to talk about the corruption and vice of high society. That is nothing to the corruption and vice of low society, sir! We should never forget that the vicious we have always with us, as some poet or other may have said. Even aboard here—I have been robbed, sir. Lying on a bed of pain—"

Mrs Brocklebank emerged again.

"Now, Wilmot, we agreed to say nothing of the matter. As far as I am concerned I am glad to see the thing go!"

The men at the capstan began to walk around it.

"Handsomely!"

Charles Summers was leaning over the side and watching the dragrope.

"Roundly, now!"

The men went a little faster. What ropes on the deck had been slack now rose from it and their individual catenaries disappeared. There came a loud creaking and groaning from the ship or the rope or the capstan or all of them together. I looked over the side as the ship's side rose out of the water with all its streaming weed, then swung down again. The dragrope was visible from the deck down to the weed. It did not seem to be moving but water was spurting from it. There was a sudden confusion round the capstan. Men were falling over each other. The dragrope moved.

I have seen all this and much else which was to come in nightmare, not once but several times, and shall do so again. In nightmare the shape is bigger and rises wholly awesome and dreadful. My dreaming spirit fears as my waking spirit fears that one night the thing will emerge, bringing with it a load of weed that only half conceals a face. I do not know what face and do not care to dally longer with the thought. But then, that morning in the wind, the salt air, the rocking, heaving ship, I saw with waking eyes down by the crazily unstable waterline something like the crown of a head pushing up through the weed. Someone screamed by my shoulder, a horrible, male scream. The thing rose, a waggonload of weed festooned round and over it. It was a head or a fist or the forearm of something vast as Leviathan. It rolled in the weed with the ship, lifted, sank, lifted again—

"Vast heaving!"

I know now that this was a foolish order and unnecessary. For the men had first fallen with the sudden movement of the dragrope, then fled from the capstan as if their work had been unlawful. I am told that the petty officers used their starters and that the ship was in confusion from one end to the other. But I saw none of that. I could not look anywhere but at this awful creature which was rising from the unknown regions. Its appearance cancelled the insecure "facts" of the deep sea and seemed to illustrate instead the horribly unknown. Impossible as this is, but with a rolling and pitching ship the sea was where it could not be and the thing towered black and streaming above me. Then it slid sideways, showed a glimpse of weedy tar and timber massive as the king tree of a tythe barn, slid sideways and disappeared.

(17)

"Still!"

That was the captain's famous roar, late this time but to be obeyed on pain of death. It came from the waist. Somehow he had got himself there in the seconds during which I had been mesmerized by the apparition. Even we, the passengers, felt the compulsion of that roar and froze where we stood.

Captain Anderson now continued in a very loud voice.

"That was flotsam caught under the forefoot, Mr Summers."

"The dragrope had worked past the forefoot, sir. I believe that was a piece of the keel."

The captain snarled.

"It was flotsam, sir! Flotsam! Do you hear?"

"Aye aye, sir."

"Come with me."

The two officers stumped towards us. Captain Anderson ignored us but continued to issue orders.

"Let the men stand by. Check in the hold."

"Aye aye, sir. Mr Cumbershum—"

And then as they went up the stairway Summers continued in an angry voice. "It was indeed the keel, sir. I saw it. A scarfing must be rotted and the rope able to catch under it then work along."

"No, no, Mr Summers, it was not! *And do not talk so loud!*"

I believe that in circumstances such as ours were at that time there comes to an educated and thinking man something as strange and perhaps in its kind as awesome as the wooden monster itself. There is an ingrained habit of

465

dignity which asserts the positive necessity of proclaim-
ing to a world of blind force and material something
like—*I am a man. I am more than blind nature!* At this
imperative discovery or command I found I was searching my mind for some word or action which would make
this evident.

"I suppose the keel may still be called 'flotsam'."

Mr Jones at my shoulder cleared his throat ineffectu-
ally, then tried again. He did not turn his face towards me
but continued to watch the place where the ancient baulk
of timber had appeared and disappeared.

"How can it be flotsam, Mr Talbot? It has sunk."

I found myself nodding sagely. But as the import of his
words came home, my feet stuck to the deck as they had
done at the cannon shot, or only just now at the captain's
roar. Aware of this, I surveyed the scene before me as
if searching for something—a friend perhaps. The men
were standing idly but quietly now. The emigrants were
crowded back into the fo'castle, but visible by their pale
faces in the opening to it. Mr Benét emerged from the
depths below the fo'castle in company with Mr Gibbs.
They came down the deck towards us, Mr Benét accom-
modating his pace to that of his fellow. Round us the sun
was bright, the billows white and bounding as Mr Benét
had bounded on every other occasion when I had seen
him moving from one part of the ship to another. All
crests in that lively sea were exactly delineated and the
horizon was taut as a rope under strain. Mr Gibbs was
talking in an aggrieved tone of voice.

"What did you expect, Mr Benét, you and him?
Though there's but the one through-bolt drawn that's bad
enough."

"Well, plug it!"

"What do you think I was about down there? Water
may come in, but not that way from now on!"

Mr Jones shifted his feet as if they too had been stuck. He cleared his throat again.

"Well, Mr Talbot. At least I have taken every precaution I can." He shook his head admiringly. "I'm odd like that, you know. My boat on the boom is supplied with every necessity."

"I have no boat, sir! I do not see accommodation in boats even for the children and ladies!"

Mr Jones nodded slowly, as if he, too, had noticed that lack. Then, as slowly, he shook his head.

Mr Benét came down the stairs, bounding again, and went forward in the same fashion as if he were the very personification of this bright air and wind and sea. Mr Gibbs followed him like a dull after-thought. Then at the last came Charles Summers, pale and thoughtful. I spoke to him by name as he passed but he seemed deep in some consideration and did not hear me. Nor did Mr Brocklebank who now stood between me and the way back to my hutch.

"After all it was given back to me and I am positive I put it away in the lower drawer. You have not seen it by any chance, Mr Talbot?"

But Mrs Brocklebank was shaking him by the sleeve.

"Oh, let it go, Wilmot dear! I am sure I am very glad to see the back of the horrid thing!"

They walked their wet way together before me into the lobby. Mr Brocklebank was speaking with that painful clarity and emphasis which a man employs to make clear his own patience and understanding in difficult circumstances, particularly, I have noticed, when addressing his wife.

"It was *in* the *bottom drawer* under my *bed*. Bunk, I suppose I must call it, for never was bed so uncomfortable—and now it is gone. We have a thief and I shall tell Mr Summers."

Mrs Brocklebank, who all the while had been talking,

prattling rather, like a kind of descant on his base, fairly thrust him through the door of their hutch and pulled it to behind them.

I made my way towards my own hutch, the one that for some time had been used by the late Reverend James Colley.

Life should serve up its feast of experience in a series of courses. We should have time to assimilate, if not digest one before we attack another. We should have a pause, not so much for contemplation as for rest. However, life does not operate in such a reasonable fashion but huddles its courses together, sometimes two, three or what seems to be the whole meal on a single dish. Thus it was with me—with us. I will try to report what happened next as accurately as I can. That grim baulk of waterlogged timber was still, I suppose, sinking towards the ooze where Colley stood on his cannon balls when I approached my hutch—his hutch. I see it still and try to change what happened but cannot. I saw that Wheeler was inside. I could tell it was Wheeler though only his baldness and the two puffs of white hair on either side of it was visible through the louvre. Then as my mouth opened to dismiss him with a severe injunction against his haunting of my cabin beyond the necessity of cleaning it, his head tilted and lifted. His eyes were shut, his expression peaceful. He raised towards his lips a gold or brass goblet. Then his head exploded and disappeared after or with or before, for all I know, a flash of light. Then everything disappeared as a wave of acrid smoke burst out of the louvre. My left eye was, or had been, struck and filled with a wet substance.

I heard nothing. Is that not impossible? Though others heard the explosion of the blunderbuss I who saw it heard nothing.

I have tried again and again to put what I saw in logical order but come always to the fact that there was no order

468

but only instantaneity. The brass goblet which Wheeler held to his peaceful face was the bell of Mr Brocklebank's blunderbuss, but realization of that fact came to me later. What I experienced was the peaceful face, the head bursting, the flash, the smoke—and silence!

I staggered away from the door, fanned smoke, tried to smear my stuck left eye open—saw at once the colour of the mess in my hand and made a rush for the open deck, reached the rail by Mr Jones and vomited over it.

"Are you injured, Mr Talbot? Are you shot?"

For answer, I did no more than vomit again.

"You do not speak, Mr Talbot. Are you injured? What has happened?"

The voice of the lawyer's clerk, Mr Bowles, came to me.

"It is the steward Wheeler, Mr Jones. He has killed himself in the cabin which Mr Talbot is at present occupying."

Mr Jones's uncomprehending and calm voice answered him.

"What did he do that for, Mr Bowles? He had been rescued. He was a most fortunate man. You could say he was the object of a special providence."

My knees were loosed. I sank to the deck and voices faded far away as a wave of faintness engulfed me.

I came to lying on my back, my head supported in a lap. Someone was sponging my face with cold water. I opened the other eye and examined a dazzle of light reflected on a wooden ceiling. It was the passenger saloon and I was lying on a bench. Miss Granham's voice spoke above me!

"Poor boy. He has far more sensibility than he knows."

There was a long period of pendulum movement. I became aware that my coat had been removed, my stock undone and my shirt opened. I sat up slowly. The lap belonged to Mrs Brocklebank.

"I believe you should lie still for a while, sir."

I embarked on what would have had to be a lengthy expression of thanks and excuse, but Miss Granham had other ideas.

"You must lie still, sir. Celia will fetch a cushion."

I tried to get off the bench but she held me with surprising firmness.

"Thank you, Miss Granham, but believe me I am able to return now."

"Return, sir?"

"Why, to my hutch—cabin, I would say!"

"It would be most inadvisable. At least sit for a while."

What I remembered more than anything was the mess in my eye. I gulped and looked at my hand. It had been washed but there was an indefinable tinge of what I suppose was the remains of dried blood and brains on it. I gulped again. It now came to me that I was homeless! What still puzzles me is that I felt this strange "homelessness" more than anything else and had some difficulty in restraining my tears—tears for the seclusion of that cabin or one like it where I had spent such hours—what am I saying—such weeks and months of boredom! But Zenobia now lay in the bunk which once had been mine, and Colley's was not to be thought of.

"I have been in a faint I suppose and for no reason! Ladies, I do most sincerely—"

"Better, Mr Talbot?"

It was Charles Summers.

"I am quite recovered, thank you."

"He is not, Mr Summers!"

"I have questions to ask him, Miss Granham."

"No, sir!"

"Believe me, ma'am, I regret the necessity. But you must see that in a case like this the questions are official and not to be delayed. Now, Mr Talbot. Who did it?"

"Mr Summers, really!"

"Excuse me, Miss Granham. Well, sir? You heard the question. Shall I repeat it? The sooner you answer, the sooner Colley's—that is, your—cabin is able to be—tidied."

"Tidied, sir? That is landsman's talk. You should have said 'made all shipshape'."

"You see, ma'am, he is recovered. Well, Mr Talbot. As I said, 'Who did it?' "

"Good God. You know already. He did it himself!"

"You saw it happen?"

"Yes. Do not remind me!"

"Really, Mr Summers, he should be—"

"Please, Miss Granham. Only one more question. He had constituted himself your servant. He may have let fall some observation—have you any knowledge of why the wretched man did it?"

I thought for a while. But against the bloody fact my thoughts were trivial and wandering.

"No, sir. None whatever."

All at once and as it were on the rebound, the full fact of my homelessness came over me.

"Oh, God! What shall I do? Where shall I go?"

"He cannot use that cabin, Mr Summers! It is impossible!"

Charles Summers was staring down at me. With a dreary sense of loss and a foreboding that the feeling would grow to a real pain, I perceived a look of evident dislike on his face.

"I am supposed to make special arrangements for you again, Mr Talbot. We have kept the wardroom out of bounds to passengers. We lieutenants are, after all, entitled to our own place. But the circumstances are unusual as is your position. Come with me if you are able to withstand the movement of the ship. I will find you a cot."

"I beg you will be careful, Mr Talbot!"

Charles Summers led the way down, waiting for me now and then when the swift roll made the descent difficult. He opened the door of the wardroom and gestured me through. It was a large room with many doors leading off it, a long table and a variety of instruments and objects which I had neither the time nor the inclination to examine. The whole was lighted by what I suppose was the lowest register of our great stern windows.

"But this is big enough for every officer in the ship and you have only yourself, Cumbershum and Benét!"

He said nothing but opened one of the doors. The cot was empty, the folded blankets lying ready on the thin mattress.

"This is for me?"

"For the time being."

"It is small."

"What did you expect, Mr Talbot? It was good enough for your friend Mr Deverel and is good enough for your new friend, Mr Benét. It is designed, sir, for a mere lieutenant, some poor man with no prospects, no hope; designed perhaps for a man thrust out of his legitimate place by a, a—"

"My dear Mr Summers!"

"Do not protest, sir. At least I may say what I choose now you have found a new friend for your patronage!"

"My what?"

"That patronage which you once promised me but have now withdrawn as is evident from the—"

"What is all this? There is some dreadful mistake! I never promised you my patronage, for I have none to bestow!"

The first lieutenant laughed briefly and angrily.

"I understand. Well, it is as good a way of ending the affair as another. So. He has everything then."

I seized the door and hung on to the handle as a roll promised to throw me across the wardroom.

"Who has everything?"

"Mr Benét."

"You are talking in riddles. What has Mr Benét to do with us? Where on earth did you get the idea that I had the gift of a ship or a place in my pocket?"

"Do you not remember? Or is it more convenient for you to forget?"

"I think you had better explain. What have I said which promised you anything?"

"Since you have forgotten the words it would shame me to repeat them."

"Once and for all, before my brain bursts—no, not that!—once and for all will you not tell me what you think I have said?"

"It was in your old cabin when we were concerned with Colley. I said, 'I have no patron.' You answered immediately, 'Do not be so certain, Mr Summers!' Those were your very words! Deny it if you choose!"

"But that was not an offer of patronage! It was an expression of esteem, of my sincerely proffered friendship! I am as far beneath the possibility of exercising patronage as I thought you was above it!"

"Say no more. I have mistaken us both. I will wish you good day."

"Mr Summers! Come back!"

There was a long pause.

"To what end, sir?"

"You compel me—we are down among embarrassments. And the ship may sink, good God! Are we not laughable? But enough of that. The journal which I kept for my godfather and which you suppose to contain nothing but a description of our good captain's injustice—you may read it if you choose. It will lie before my godfather, a nobleman of much influence in our country's affairs. He will read every page. Take it away, sir, slit the canvas, read every word. I—you will find there a positive hymn in your praise. There can hardly be a page on which your name, your conduct and character is not set down in terms of admiration and dare I say—esteem and—affection. That was all I could do for you and it is what I have done."

There was now an even longer pause. I believe we did not look at one another. When at last his voice answered me, it was hoarse.

"Well, now you know better, Mr Talbot. I am not worthy of your admiration or regard."

"Do not say so!"

We were facing each other, each, as usual, with one leg straight, the other bending and stretching. Despite or perhaps *because* of the high seriousness of our exchange I could not but be aware of a certain comedy in the situation. But it was no time for pointing this out. Mr Summers was speaking. His voice vibrated with emotion.

"I have no family, Mr Talbot, and I do not believe myself inclined to marriage. Yet my attachments are deep and strong. Men, like cables, have each their breaking strain. To lose my place in your regard, to see a younger man, one with all the advantages which were denied me, achieve on every level what I could never hope for—"

"Wait, wait! If you were only aware of my meanness, my attempts at manipulation, let alone a self-esteem which I now perceive to be—I cannot explain myself. Measured against you I am a paltry fellow, that is the fact of the matter! But I would be honoured above all things if you would agree to continue my friend."

He took a sudden step forward.

"It is more than I could hope for or deserve. Oh, do not look so distressed, sir! These clouds will pass. You have been sorely tried of late on several counts and I am much to blame in adding to your cares."

"I am learning too much, that is the fact of the matter. Men and women—I beg you will not laugh but I had proposed myself a political and detached observation of the nature of both, yet in my association with you and her too and with poor Wheeler—these tears are involuntary and the result of my repeated blows to the head. I beg you will disregard them. Good God, a man of—"

"*How* old are you?"

When I repeated the figure, he cried out.

"No more than that?"

"Why so astonished? How old did you think I was?"

"Older. Much older."

The forbidding distance in his face disappeared, to be replaced by quite another expression. Hesitantly I held out my hand; and like the generous-hearted Englishman that he is, he seized it with both his own in a thrilling and manly grip.

"Edmund!"

"My dear fellow!"

Still conscious as I was of a certain comical element in our situation, it was a moment at which reserve was no longer possible and I returned the pressure.

Postscriptum

I must record here in this same folio an explanation and apology for the abrupt ending of my journal. A possible reader—a dear reader—might tease himself or herself endlessly in pursuit of that explanation without ever coming to the right one. The reason for my abandoning my pen was in a sense trivial and even vexing, yet at the same time the cause of much hilarity. Now I am safely ashore and have got back my landlegs I have begun to suspect—though it may seem unkind to say so—that our hilarity was a kind of madness throughout the ship as if the sailing master, Mr Smiles, had been right!

Briefly then.

While I and my dear friend Charles Summers were ridding ourselves of a foolish misunderstanding Cumbershum came off watch. I myself was not witness to what followed, for the suicide of poor Wheeler before my very eyes came to work on me strongly and I was forced to retire to the cabin Charles had found for me and lay there for a long time shuddering as if the blunderbuss had wounded me in addition to killing Wheeler. But I was given an exact account of what occurred.

Cumbershum was buttonholed in his descent by Mr Jones, the purser. Mr Jones, increasingly concerned for his property in the ship, begged for a few moments of Mr Cumbershum's time. Later Mr Cumbershum related the interview to Charles Summers and the other officers with every evidence of enjoyment.

"Mr Cumbershum, I beg of you. Will the ship sink?"

As luck would have it, Cumbershum was one of the

most heavily endebted officers. He shouted with laughter.

"Yes, the bloody ship will sink, you yellow-bellied bastard, and death pays all debts!"

The result was not what Cumbershum expected. Mr Jones, in the grip of his ruling passion, hurried away, then returned with a handful of IOUs for which he demanded payment on the spot. Cumbershum refused, suggesting a use for the papers which I do not feel called on to particularize. The effect of this refusal was to throw the man into a kind of subdued panic. He hurried about the ship, heedless of her movement which sometimes put him in peril of drowning as if his own safety were the last thing in the world he was considering. In another man it would have been folly or heroism or both. He tried to call in his IOUs throughout the whole ship and met everywhere with a refusal sometimes even blunter than Cumbershum's. I believe nothing, neither the arrival of King Neptune when we crossed the line, nor the entertainment given when we and *Alcyone* lay side by side, caused such general and on the whole beneficial amusement. For a while we were indeed a "happy ship"!

By the time I had recovered from my strange disability or sickness, whatever it was, it was my turn to be approached. Mr Jones presented me with an inflated account for candles and paregoric. I was inspired! I reduced the man to stillness and silence when I replied that I did not owe him anything. I owed money to Wheeler who was dead. I was prepared to pay Wheeler's heirs and assigns in due course.

After much anxious expostulation on his part Mr Jones recalled our previous conversation.

"At least, Mr Talbot, you will pay me for the container you spoke of!"

"Container?"

"For your journal—to float it off!"

"Ah, I remember. But why should I pay you? Is not an IOU sufficient?"

The man gave a kind of whinny.

"No cash, Mr Talbot, no container!"

I thought for a moment. As the reader may recollect, it was true I had asked for something in which to put my writings and commit them to the waves but the suggestion had been made more than half in jest. It was typical of Mr Jones to remember the remark, take it seriously and determine to profit therefrom. A way opened before me of revenging Humanity on Inhumanity!

"Very well, Mr Jones. I will buy a container from you—on one condition. That you find room for it in your boat!"

There now ensued a passionate argument. At last Mr Jones agreed to carry the thing ashore and see it forwarded to the appropriate address. The first container he produced he called a pipkin. When I saw how small it was and that it was made of pottery I would have none of it.

"Suppose you and your boat are dashed on the rocks, sir. Why you might burst like a dead sheep in the sun and the pipkin with you!"

Mr Jones's complexion took on a greenish hue. He would sell me a firkin.

"And what is a firkin?"

"A small wooden cask, sir."

"Very well."

The firkin when it came proved to be a barrel that had held eight gallons of some liquid or other.

"What the devil, man! This would go near to holding me myself!"

The price was exorbitant. I reduced it by more than half, using, I am compelled to say, some of that "hoity-toity" which had so displeased Mr Askew.

"And now, Mr Jones, you will swear to take this firkin ashore with you and forward it to the right address, remembering that at this solemn moment we are both near that eternal judgement which awaits all men—Good God!"

I must own that this last ejaculation was out of my part however much it was in character. The fact is, years of religious lessons, thousands of church services and the whole mighty engine of the Church rose up behind me and I found it come near to clouting me over the head like a flailing sheet. I did indeed experience a touch of that judgement I had mentioned so frivolously and I did not like it.

"Swear."

Mr Jones, touched possibly by the same feelings, answered tremulously,

"I swear."

Devil take it, this was Hamlet and I felt downright uneasy! I could not but feel that the ghost of Colley was roaming the ship. Well—we were in mortal danger, and the mind plays tricks.

"And Mr Jones, if we should survive you will buy the cask back for what I gave for it—I'm odd like that, you know!"

Now it has to be added that if the ship was in a perilous state and I in a strange one, her company were in even stranger case. As if Mr Jones and Cumbershum between them had released among us something until then bound in and confined, the happiness of our "happy ship" changed in quality and became what I can only call a communal hysteria. Nor was it womanish as the word suggests. At its worst and most severe it could be typified as a kind of uncontrollable laughter at the most trivial of causes. At its best it was a peculiarly British sense of fun, of play. There was a little coldness in it, a contempt for life, even a touch of savagery. It came to me that at its best it might be something like that humour said to prevail among the victims of the French Terror before their martyrdom. At its worst it had something of the blasphemy, wild humour, debauchery and fury which sometimes erupts in Newgate Gaol when the wretches confined there hear the last confirmation of their fate. I suppose, too, there were men and women who prayed. For by now there was not a man, woman or child who did not know in what a sad case we stood. The dragrope took off more weed and the business was finished but I do not believe many of the passengers or emigrants took much notice. By now we all saw too clearly.

So much, then, for the efforts at concealing the state of the ship from all but the naval officers! I thought my own joke was now over, but the truth is it got out of hand. Mr Gilland, the cooper, asking nothing for the service, loosened the bands of the firkin and knocked out the head. I placed the journal intended for my godfather inside and this same folio with it. But I had not realized how widely all was known. Good God, hardly a passenger or an emigrant but wished to have some message included, some small package, some object, a ring, a bauble, a book—a journal!—something, anything which whatever it was would seem by its survival to prolong a vestige of life. This is how people are, but if I had not had the experience I would never have believed it. Indeed so general was the demand for space in my firkin that Charles Summers was driven to protest, though amiably enough.

"My dear Edmund! You have so many clients that Webber who ought to be looking after the rest of the wardroom has become little more than your doorman!"

"What am I to do? The thing has become a bore and thoroughly out of hand."

"You are now the most popular man in the ship."

"If anything were needed to convince me of the volatility of the common people—"

"Speaking for us common people—"

"Charles, I will have no more of this modesty! I shall live to see you an admiral yet!"

"I will have it piped through the ship that papers may be brought to Mr Talbot but only during the first dog. The thing will die off in a day or two."

He went off to continue his preparations for the "frapping".

There was I, then, sitting like Matthew at the seat of custom for two hours a day. I do seriously believe that during one short period and before I had dressed him down, Webber was actually charging admission! Like the ghost of Colley, the spirit of Mr Jones was abroad. Nevertheless the great majority of those who came were simple souls. They divided sharply into two groups. There were those who giggled and hoped to share the jest against Mr Jones. There were those who were only too sadly in earnest. The white line which had been drawn across the deck at the mainmast was now, it seemed, washed clean away. I was to find this more than a simple fact—it was indeed a metaphor of our condition! But more of that at a later date. Suffice it to say my visitors were many and various. It might be a poor emigrant, his hat in one hand, his paper in the other, or a sniggering tar holding out an inch of his own queue or pigtail with the hope that I was "making the bugger sweat, sir". Indeed my cask soon began to resemble the "bran tub" which we children used to enjoy at Christmas. God knows, in that ship we could have done with any enjoyment we could get!

I must say also that among the other frivolities which rose so preposterously from our danger was a series of catch phrases. A part of watch ordered by a petty officer to pick up a rope or the like would reply as one man— "Aye aye. We're odd like that, you know!" There was even one occasion—and here I must implore the ladies, for after all poetry is their proper speech and prose means nothing to them—I must ask them to avert their eyes from the following paragraphs.

Mr Taylor appeared noisily with even more than his usual high spirits. He could not stop laughing until I shook him. Knowing Mr Taylor I was prepared to hear of some monstrous piece of misfortune which had befallen someone and which seemed to him the height of comedy— but no. When at last I got him quiet and he had recovered from my shaking I demanded to know the worst.

"It's a riddle, you see, sir!"

"A riddle?"

"Yes, sir! What—" but having got that far humour was too much for him and he had to be shaken again.

"Now then, my lad, finish what you have to say before I throw you overboard."

"Sir. The riddle is: 'What makes the ship roll so?' "

"Well, what makes the ship roll so?"

We had another convulsion before he got out the answer.

"Lord Talbot's firkin!"

I dropped the boy and returned to my hutch. If the result of peril was to lower the ship to that level, I thought, she has no need to sink but has done so already.

After I had sat for a dog watch without a "client" I asked for Mr Gilland, the cooper, and summoned Mr Jones. When they were together before me I had Mr Gilland replace the lid and put back the bands. They were, I said, witness to the security of the container. I had the bung left open though the rest of the cask was sealed. I explained to Mr Jones that I might want to insert some dying wish or prayer when we were foundering and before he himself left the vessel. I must confess the joke had become tedious. It even turned sour when I contemplated all that remained of Edmund Talbot bouncing round the Southern Ocean in circumstances where its chances of reaching the desired destination would be small beyond computation! More than that, I found myself suddenly deprived of my journals and with nothing to write or do except endure the antics and threat of our increasingly unseaworthy vessel.

The reader will have grasped that I, at least, survived the voyage. But like any possible reader, when I reread what I had written, the abrupt end of my journal—call it "book two"—troubled me and does so now. Indeed, to call it a journal is to stretch the term unduly. An attentive reader may well be able to identify the widely separated occasions on which I tried to describe what had happened during a period of days and so bring the thing up to date. I was often writing of the past when much was happening at the moment. A considerable length of time separates the ending of my journal proper and this *postscriptum*. I have been tempted to avoid the problem of the too abrupt ending by continuing the journal retrospectively so to speak, pretending to have written it in the ship. But the distance in time is too great. The attempt would be disingenuous. More—it would be plain dishonest. Worse than that if it were possible the attempt would be detected, for the style—I flatter myself I have a style, however threadbare—would change. Immediacy would be lost. When I reread "book one"—in the *next* volume you will find out when and why that was!—I found it had gained a great deal by the inclusion of Colley's affecting if unfinished letter. For though the poor fellow may not have been much of a priest there was a touch of genius in his vivid and fluent use of his native tongue: whereas "book two" must rely on my own unaided efforts except where I report the actual words of other people. It is true, however, that what I now think to have been an ingenuous opening of my heart to the page is not without a force which I did not suspect until I came to read it much later. But to return to the head of this paragraph. To add this *postscriptum* seemed the most reasonable solution to my difficulty.

Yet a properer and lengthier description of the remainder of our voyage still remains desirable. In my memory the voyage is a single thing, with a beginning, a middle and an end. Our further adventures were no less and perhaps more arduous than the preceding ones. Honesty compels me to promise a plain narrative at some later date which will see the voyage ended and which narrative shall be my "book three". I cannot pretend to Colley's talent and hope that the strangeness and hazard of the events will compensate for the plainness of the writing.

There is another consideration. I am in half a mind to publish! Perhaps then these words may be read not just by those dear to me but by a far wider audience. The desire of print has grown on me. What began at my godfather's behest proceeded by my own growing inclination and I now find myself no more or less than a common writer with all the ambitions if not all the failings of that breed. I put this very point to Mr Brocklebank during the highest days of our hilarity, confessing that I felt myself insufficiently dissolute for the profession, to which he replied in his voice rotten as a medlar—"My dear sir! Continue to drink as you do and you will carry all before you!" I need hardly say he was deeply in his cups on that occasion as on so many others. But may it not be that a man of breeding, education and intelligence will lend the profession a little of the dignity our hack-writers have taken from it?

Failings? I admit to ambitions. To be printed is the smallest of them! Come, my dear reader, who has ever written without the desire to communicate? We assume a reader of our words even when we use them to deny his existence. I will go further. Who has ever written extensively without finding himself lured little by little into the desire to captivate an audience? There is in me, as in all writers, what Milton called "that last infirmity of noble mind", the desire for a name more widely known, admiration more generously given, for a greater measure of interest in the author's character and person on the part of the Sex. So though I have sometimes said and often thought that I wrote only for myself I have more often wondered *to whom* I was writing—my Lady Mother, or Another, or an old school friend, his face remembered, his name forgotten. I have also found myself envisaging with gusto the three splendid volumes of *Talbot's Voyage* or *The Ends of the Earth!* All this then to apologize to a conjectural audience which may have been startled by the abruptly ended journal of "book two" but may be mollified and excited as much as I can contrive by this "puff" for a third volume!

TO THE ENDS OF THE EARTH

Fire Down Below

(1)

Captain Anderson turned away from me, cupped his hands round his mouth and roared.

"Masthead!"

The man who was straddled there next to the motionless figure of young Willis held up a hand as a sign that he had heard. Anderson lowered his hands from his mouth and "sang out" in what for him was more nearly a normal tone of voice.

"Is the boy dead?"

This time the man must have shouted back but his voice was not like the captain's and what with the wind and sea, let alone the ship's unsteady motion, I could not hear it. Thirty or more feet below him in the fighting top Lieutenant Benét—in a voice loud as the captain's but a tenor to his bass—repeated what the man had said.

"Can't rightly tell but he feels main cold."

"Get him down then!"

Now there was a long pause and what looked like a wrestling match going on at the masthead while yet another seaman ascended, taking a tackle up with him. Willis lurched, so that I gasped as he swung free. But he was made fast in a kind of seat. He was lowered down, turning and twisting on the end of the rope, now swinging out as we rolled and now coming in to thump the mast itself. Lieutenant Benét shouted.

"Bowse the man in there, you idle bugger!"

Willis was held and passed from one guiding hand to another. The duty watch or part of the watch who had stationed themselves in the rigging of the mainmast handled him as carefully as a woman with a baby.

Lieutenant Benét slid all sixty feet down a rope from the fighting top and landed lightly on the deck.

"Handsomely does it!"

He knelt by the boy. Captain Anderson spoke from the forrard rail of the quarterdeck.

"Is he dead, Mr Benét?"

Benét swept off his hat with an elegant gesture, revealing what I had come to regard as far too much yellow hair as he did so.

"Not quite, sir. All right, lads. Get him down to the gunroom and roundly now!"

The little group disappeared down the ladders—or stairs, as I was more and more determined to call them— with Lieutenant Benét after them as confidently as if he were expert in medicine as in all else.

I turned to Mr Smiles, the sailing master, who had the watch.

"He looked dead to me."

There was a fierce hiss from the captain. Once again I had violated his precious "standing orders" by speaking to the officer of the watch. But this time as if he was conscious that he was to blame in prolonging the boy's punishment to the point of danger he turned with a grimace, which on the stage would have had a snarl in it, and went to his private quarters.

Mr Smiles had looked all round the horizon. Now he examined the set of our few sails.

"It is a time for dying."

I was at once irritated and appalled. I believe myself to be wholly devoid of superstition but the words were— uncomfortable when spoken in a crippled and quite possibly sinking ship. I had been cheered by an improvement in the weather. For though we were now standing inexorably southward towards the polar seas, the weather seemed no worse than it might have been in the English

Channel. I was about to differ with the man but my friend the first lieutenant, Charles Summers, appeared from the passenger lobby and climbed to the quarterdeck.

"Edmund! I hear you rescued young Willis!"

"I, Charles? Never believe such a story! I am a passenger and would not for the world interfere with the running of the ship. I merely told Lieutenant Benét that I thought the young fellow looked deucedly comatose. Benét did the rest—as usual."

Charles looked round him. Then he drew me to the rail away from Smiles.

"You chose the one officer who could venture a difference of opinion with the captain and not be rebuked for it."

"That was diplomacy."

"You do not like Benét, do you? I too have differences with him. The foremast—"

"I admire Benét. But he is too perfect."

"His intentions are good."

"He is nimble in the rigging as a midshipman! But, Charles—do you realize that after all these months at sea I have never climbed a mast? Today, although the motion is unsteady it is slight compared with what it has been!"

"Is it? I am so habituated to the motion of a ship—"

"Oh, I am sure you could walk up the side of a house and not lose your balance. But the wind will get up, will it not? Now is perhaps my only chance of finding out what it is like to be a common sailor."

"I will take you as far as the fighting top."

"This will be a most valuable experience. Suppose me—as may befall—to be a Member of Parliament. 'Mr Speaker. To those of us who have actually climbed into the fighting top of a man of war at sea—' "

"The Honourable Member for Timbuctoo should pipe down, lay hold of the ropes and swing himself round.

Gently! You're not a midshipman playing tag through the rigging!"

"Oh my God, this is no place for seaboots!"

"Feel the rung with your boot before you put your weight on it. Don't look down. If you were to slip I should catch you."

" 'Safe in the arms of the Lord.' "

"Your casual blasphemy—"

"I beg your pardon, Bishop. The exclamation was forced from me. It was my seaboot swore, not I, as Euripides might have said but did not. It missed a rung."

"Now then. No nonsense about climbing out round. Up through the lubber's hole."

"If I must indeed choose the easier path—you insist?"

"Up with you!"

"Oh, God. It is commodious. Half a dozen good fellows might live up here provided they only used the vast hole I climbed through for purposes of necessity. 'For sale a villa. Luxuriously fitted, wooden construction, sea view—and a nautical gentleman with his eye sweeping the horizon!' "

"Fawcett. Now that Mr Willis has—vacated the masthead you may resume your lookout at that position."

The seaman knuckled his forehead, shifted his quid from one side of his mouth to the other and clambered out of sight.

"Well. How do you find it?"

"Now I dare to look down, I see that our ship, though she is a seventy-four, has shrunk. Really, Charles! Monstrous timbers such as this mast should not be stuck in such a rowboat! It is impossible that we should not be overset! I will not look—my eyes are shut."

"Inspect the horizon and you will feel more the thing."

"My hair is so erected it is pushing off my beaver."

"It is no more than sixty feet down to the deck."

" 'No more!' But our yellow-haired friend slid all that way down on a rope."

"Benét is an active young man, full of spirit and ideas. But how would you go on if you was mastheaded?"

"Like poor Willis? Die, I think. Smiles said it is a time for dying."

I sat up cautiously and held on with both hands to the comforting ropes which stayed the fighting top. The sensation was agreeable.

"That is better, Charles."

"You were worried by what Smiles said?"

"Did he mean the Pikes' little girls?"

"They are somewhat better in fact."

"Davies, that poor, senile midshipman? Mrs East? She must be better, for I have seen her with Mrs Pike. Does he mean Miss Brocklebank, I wonder?"

"Mr Brocklebank says she is very poorly. A decline."

A thought occurred to me which set me laughing.

"Does he mean Mr Prettiman, our testy political theorist? Miss Granham told me that her fiancé had suffered a severe fall."

"You find him comic?"

"Well. He cannot be entirely despicable or an estimable lady such as Miss Granham would not have consented to make him the happiest of men. But comic! He is wicked! Why—he is ill-disposed to the government of his own country, to the Crown, to our system of representation— in fact to everything which makes us the foremost country in the world."

"He is in a bad way none the less."

"No great loss if he leaves us. I am only sorry for Miss Granham, for though she has bitten my head off on several occasions, I repeat, she is an estimable lady and seems genuinely attached to the man. Women are very strange."

Someone else was climbing the rigging. It was Mr Tommy Taylor, who appeared with a monkeylike dexterity, swinging himself over the outer edge of the fighting top instead of coming the easier and safer way up through the hole in the middle.

"Mr Benét's compliments, sir, and Mr Willis seems comfortable. He is asleep and snoring."

"Very good, Mr Taylor. You are the watch?"

"Yes, sir. Mr Smiles, sir. His doggy, sir."

"You may return to the quarterdeck."

"Excuse me, sir. Watch changing now, sir."

Indeed the ship's bell was ringing out the time.

"Very well, you are off watch. Come and be a schoolmaster. Mr Talbot here is by way of thinking he would like to learn everything there is to know about a ship."

"No no, Charles! *Pax*!"

"For example, Mr Taylor, Mr Talbot would be interested to know what kind of a mast this is."

"It's a mainmast, sir."

"Are you trying to be witty, Mr Taylor? What is its construction?"

"It's a 'made' mast, sir. That means a mast which is all separate bits. Not 'bitts' of course. Bits."

Mr Taylor laughed so loudly I concluded he intended a witticism. Indeed, the boy was always in such high spirits I believe he found our desperate situation in a crippled and possibly sinking ship a joyous experience.

"Name those bits for Mr Talbot, Mr Taylor."

"Well, sir, the round bits on either side are the bolsters. Then there's the trestle trees which hold us up. Under them there's the round cheeks to keep the trestle from sliding down the mast. Mr Gibbs, the carpenter, he said—"

The boy broke into a loud laugh at the memory.

"He said, 'Every made mast has two lovely cheeks, young fellow, which is two less than what you've got, innit?' "

"After that sally, young man, you may take yourself off. You have a dirty mind."

"Aye aye, sir. Thank you, sir."

The boy departed with an offhand agility very suitable to his age and sex. The sight of him *diminishing* down the same rope which Mr Benét had used made me giddy. I looked up, fixing my eyes for security on the foremast which stood up between us and the bows.

"Charles! It is moving! There—see! No, it is still again. The top, I mean—there it goes, it is making a small circle, an uneven circle—"

"You knew that surely? We had thought it was sprung— a kind of greenstick fracture, but in fact the foot of the mast has broken the shoe and we have had to take measures. Come, Edmund! There is nothing to be done."

"It should not move like that!"

"Of course not. It is why we have spread no sail on the foremast or the mizzenmast since they are supposed to balance each other. Do you see the wedges where the foremast passes through the deck? No, you cannot—but they keep being forced out by the movement. We have made the mast as secure and motionless as we can."

"It makes me sick."

"Do not look then. I should have remembered how obvious the lurching is from up here. Oh no! Look! not at the mast but past it at the horizon! The wind, the south wind, the one we did not want!"

"What will it do?"

"Cold weather. We shall be able to haul round to the east, which of course is where we want to go, but we also want to get far south where the constant strong winds are. We must go down. Come. I will go first."

We climbed down to the deck and I stood in the lee of the starboard mainstays to watch as our old hulk lumbered round on the starboard tack when the south wind reached us. It had none of the softness which we associate with "south" in happier climes. Charles stayed on deck to watch Mr Cumbershum and Captain Anderson achieve the change of course. He was about to walk off forrard when I buttonholed him again.

"Can you spend another moment or two with me? I know how busy you are and do not want to interfere in your scanty time of leisure—"

"A first lieutenant is more at leisure in the middle of a voyage than at either end! But I must be seen about the ship and detect such awful crimes as a hammock left slung or a rope uncheesed—*that* is a properly cheesed rope, for your information. Well. Let us walk up and down in the waist as we used to."

"With all my heart."

Charles and I proceeded then to pace briskly back and forth in the waist. We stepped over the taut cables of his frapping, strode past the mainmast with its white line, its complication of wedges, ropes, blocks and bitts, on towards the break of the fo'castle before which the stripped foremast described its almost invisible circle in the sky. The first time we reached it I paused and looked. The complication was as great here as at the mainmast. The foremast was no less than three feet in diameter and where it passed through the deck it was surrounded by a collar made of great wedges. As I watched I saw them move, slightly and unevenly. A seaman stood by the mast and leaned on a huge maul. He saw the first lieutenant watching and shouldered the thing, waited for a few moments, then let it fall on a wedge which was standing a little *prouder* than its fellows.

Charles nodded. I felt his hand on my arm as he drew me away and we resumed our walk.

"Is he doing any good?"

"Possibly not. But the appearance of doing good is better than nothing. At least it comforts the passengers."

"That is *à propos*. Charles, I am deeply sensible of the courtesy you officers have extended to me in allowing me the use of one of your hutches—cabins, I would say! But all good things have an end and I must return to the passenger quarters, in short, to my cabin off the passenger lobby."

"Did you not know? Miss Brocklebank has appropriated it! I have said nothing, since the poor lady is so sick. Surely you have not the heart to displace her?"

"She has squatters' rights. I mean my other cabin."

"Where Colley willed himself to death and where Wheeler committed suicide? You must not sleep there! Is our company in the wardroom—my company—become tedious to you?"

"You know it is not!"

"Well then, my dear fellow! A roughcut piece of nautical timber like I—such as me—might reasonably sleep there! But you—the place is dirtied."

"I do not relish the idea, it is true."

"Why then?"

"It is a case where I think I may say I have considered more deeply than you—indeed more deeply than you need, for it is wholly my affair."

"I beg your pardon!"

"Oh no—I mean I alone am responsible. I do not in the least mind telling you everything. The fact is, you see, I shall be stuck for some time in the administration of the colony. What sort of reputation should I bring with me if it were known that I had been scared out of a cabin by fear of a haunting? You see? It is a form of service which I propose to myself just as you have promised yours to the King."

"That is a proper attitude and does you credit."

"I think so too."

Charles laughed.

"All the same, you must not return there for a day or two. I am having the interior of the cabin cleaned and repainted and so on."

"So on?"

"Come, Edmund—when a man has blown his head off in such a confined space—"

"Do not remind me!"

"You have a day or two to think it over. Well. This wind in the beam means the motion is easier, do you not feel? It also means the old tub takes in less water, which means less pumping."

"One thing I cannot understand. Why with this wind do we not simply go about and sail north to Africa and the Cape? We could replenish our food and drink and other stores—get our foremast fixed, land our sick—most of all, we could stretch our legs on lovely, dry land! How I long for it!"

"This wind will not hold. It is too light and unseasonable. To sail before it would be to do what is called 'chasing the wind'. A ship doing that may well go back and forth, round and round, and never get anywhere, like the *Flying Dutchman*. Take comfort in the three and a half knots we are making towards our goal. It is better than nothing—what is the matter?"

"Excuse me. It's this damned itching. As a matter of fact I have a rash between my legs."

"A rash. We all have them because of the salt."

"My clothes are gradually becoming impossible to wear. Phillips took my shirt away for a wash and though I was fierce with him in the end I had to put it on damp."

"Ah. That's rainwater."

"I thought rainwater was fresh."

"What do they teach young men nowadays? Of course it isn't. Well—rain may be fresh where you come from if you live far enough from the sea. Out here it is never less than brackish. Have you not been washing in it like the rest of us?"

"Of course I have, but the damned stuff will not lather. It gets covered in scum."

"What soap are you using?"

"My own, of course!"

"Has Webber not given you the ship's issue?"

"Good God, can that be soap? I thought it was a brick. I thought it was pumice or something for shaving in heavy weather like the ancients!"

"Trust you to know what the ancients used for shaving! But it is soap, my boy, saltwater soap!"

"I did not detect any scent."

The first lieutenant's laughter was almost as loud and prolonged as Mr Taylor's would have been. Then—

"I suppose you think soap is naturally scented."

"Well, is it not?"

But Charles was suddenly abstracted. He had his ear cocked. He wetted his thumb and held it up.

"What did I tell you? That wind has not even held for a dogwatch! Here we go again!"

(2)

I was still a guest of the wardroom when the next gale
arose in the middle of the night and it woke me with a
sense of the ship in ampler if not more violent motion. I
lay for some time calculating the direction of the wind
from the movement of the ship under me. She was over to
starboard mostly and never came over to the larboard
more than about to an even keel. Every now and then she
bucked like a horse. Now and then she jibbed like one
too—but not as she would have done with a wind over the
bow. I reasoned sleepily that the wind was on the larboard quarter and we were moving in a southerly direction with increased speed. In a ship there is nothing
which pleases so much as movement in the right direction! Our right direction was east, but southeast in search
of the westerlies which are said to circle the earth in
the high southern latitudes was a good second best. I lay
awake therefore, thinking of our crew, one part of the
watch pumping, one on deck with their eye on rigging
and canvas, a lieutenant and a midshipman standing as
officers of the watch—our moody captain emerging now
and then from his quarters to survey the whole—and our
blunt bows dividing the billows faster than a man could
walk! We were getting on. Life would have been more
than tolerable had it not been for the itch—and my hand
reached down hardly with my volition. At times the itch
seemed worse than our dangers.

The ship pitched heavily, a ninth wave perhaps. I sat up
in my bunk with a jerk, for the movement had been followed by a cry from above me—from one deck higher
towards the open air, up in the passenger lobby or from

one of the cabins ranged along either side. I waited for a repetition but it did not come, so I lay down once more. But the touch of cooler air outside my bedclothes now made the damp heat beneath them less tolerable. I was itching again.

I swung my legs out of the bunk and stood reeling in the near-complete darkness. A faint snore came from the cabin next to mine where Mr Cumbershum was sleeping after his turn at the middle watch. I felt round and got on my greatcoat—the one with three capes and now by no means the elegant garment in which I had begun this seemingly endless voyage. A nightshirt and a greatcoat! I pulled on woollen socks, then thrust my feet into seaboots. I got out into the wardroom. The dim horizon slanted across the great stern window at an angle. The dawn itself was not visible and a more diffused light allowed me to do no more than detect the line between sea and sky. We pitched again—a little more violently this time, as if our ship had come across a wave left from a wind in some other direction. It was followed again by the cry from above me—a cry of anguish, there was no doubt about that. Scarce knowing what I did—hardly awake—perhaps connecting the anguish with my own itch—yet one woke unwillingly and half one's mind was always tending bed-ward—I clambered up the stairs into the passenger lobby. But I had scarcely grabbed the rail outside our cabins when we pitched and the cry came again, and came from the cabin of our comic philosopher, Mr Prettiman!

Now the next door, Miss Granham's, his fiancée's, opened and the lady appeared. She held the rail, opened his door and disappeared inside. I hastened across the lobby—a feat helped by the ship which tipped to starboard again and set me for a moment or two positively tripping downhill! What had begun with a spontaneous attempt to offer help became a run at the end of which I thumped loudly into Mr Prettiman's cabin door and only just contrived to heave myself off before Miss Granham herself opened the door from inside. She stood there, looking at me. She wore a white nightdress. Her hair was decently concealed by a night-bonnet, or whatever it is called, and a large shawl hung over both shoulders. Her face was not welcoming.

"Mr Talbot?"

"I heard him cry out. Can I—that is—"

"Can you be of assistance? Thank you, no."

"A moment, ma'am. Paregoric—"

"The purser's laudanum? I have it."

She paused. I became conscious suddenly of my half-naked legs and of my nightshirt, which was showing between the open skirts of my greatcoat. Miss Granham smiled glacially and shut the door in my face. Another lurch sent me reeling along the rail and wincing as the cry burst again from the poor devil. Comic he might be—but the comic are able to suffer as much as the rest of us! I moved along the rail to the entry to the lobby and stood looking out at the waist in an effort to put some distance between me and his cries, but it was not far enough. I moved out into the cold dawn air and light and huddled under the larboard mainstays. Above me they were casting the log, for I heard a voice give the order.

"Turn!"

Then after a long pause:

"Five and a half knots, sir."

"Make it so."

There came the squeak of chalk on the traverse board. Five and a half knots! More than a hundred and thirty land miles to the southeast in twenty-four hours—and all from the sails on the one mast. Soon, surely, we should find those westerlies and be blown all the way to Sydney Cove!

Men were mustering forrard. There was a period of casual ritual as the watch changed. Mr Smiles and young Tommy Taylor handed over the watch on the quarterdeck to Mr Askew, the gunner. It was eight o'clock in the morning and the dawn bright all along the east. Then I saw my friend Lieutenant Summers, and Lieutenant Benét come to the top of the stairs from the quarterdeck and it was plain that there had been a disagreement between them. Charles, mildest of men, looked stormy. Mr Benét on the other hand seemed even more brisk and cheerful than usual. Behind them appeared Mr Gibbs, the carpenter, and Coombs, the blacksmith. This was something new! Benét stood back with what looked like courtesy to allow the first lieutenant precedence down the stair, but in his grin and in the moody face of my friend was neither friendship nor consideration. There was no doubt about it. Clever young Mr Benét was triumphing. He carried a small and rather complicated object in his hands. It appeared to be made of wood and metal. Charles strode into the lobby and down the stairs without looking at me. Mr Benét and the blacksmith stood in talk with Mr Gibbs, who knuckled his forehead, then followed the first lieutenant. Mr Benét thrust the model into the blacksmith's hand and waved him forward.

It was too much. I had to be informed: and besides—

"Good morning, Mr Benét. There is something afoot."

"There is indeed, Mr Talbot."

"May I be told? Shall you celebrate it in verse?"

"I am not sure that you should be told, Mr Talbot. After all, you are of the first lieutenant's party, are you not?"

"Party? Do you mean 'faction'? What is all this?"

"We are absurd, you know—but the thing has happened. Ever since my success in getting weed off her bottom with the dragrope and against the advice of the first lieutenant—"

"You pulled a baulk of timber off her keel!"

"And added more than a knot to her speed."

"Just one knot, the first lieutenant said."

"Whatever it is, we are now fated, he and I, to be on either side of the fence, backed by those who think I am saving our lives on one hand and those who think I took too big a risk on the other."

I was loath to quarrel with the man. He was, after all, in some sort the only connection I still had with a certain young lady.

"But 'faction', Mr Benét! As if the ship were a country in little!"

"Well, is it not?"

"He is your superior officer. What is more, these cables stretched across the deck—his frapping, as he calls it—are what stands between us and the ship's falling apart!"

"An idea old as St Paul, Mr Talbot. You credit the first lieutenant with too much invention."

"That object you gave to Coombs. Has it anything to do with the argument?"

"Everything. It is a model of the keelson, the shoe of the foremast and the lower part of the foremast itself. Seeing is believing. I have thought out a scheme not just for securing the mast—for you know it moves no matter what we do—but also for bringing it back to its former state. If I succeed we shall be able to spread sail on it again and therefore balance it with sails on the mizzen. Another two knots, Mr Talbot, in a moderate wind!"

"You showed the model to Captain Anderson!"

"Seeing is believing. He is convinced."

"But Charles not! I have faith in him, Mr Benét!"

"Oh yes. But he is a—well. He is a friend of yours and I say no more."

As if to indicate his resolve to be uncharacteristically silent Mr Benét clapped one hand over his mouth, sketched a naval salute with the other and then ran off, skipping over the cables of the frapping, and disappeared into the fo'castle. I hurried away down the ladders to the ward-room. Charles stood there, staring out of our stern window with his usual indifference to our movement. He turned when he heard me open the door.

"What is all this about, Charles?"

He did not pretend to misunderstand me.

"This time Benét wishes to give us back a couple of masts, that is all."

"And the captain agrees?"

"Oh yes. Mr Benét is a most persuasive young man. He will go far if he lives."

"If someone does not kill him first! But what is this risk?"

"Briefly, the foremast has split the shoe—the block of wood on which it stands. So the foot of the mast is able to move. We have stayed the mast below decks, rigged tackles, used chocks, wedges and props and reduced the movement a little. Benét wants to reduce it altogether."

"Where is the danger?"

"Any mistake and the foot of the mast may slip and go through the ship's bottom. That is all."

"He must be stopped!"

"More than that, his method involves the use of fire, red-hot metal—you understand my objections? It is the dragrope all over again. The thing may succeed but the risk is too great."

"Who else is of your faction?"

"Is it come to that?"

"I am of your faction, too!"

"You must not say so. Do you not understand? You have no business to use that word!"

"Benét did."

"He should not have done so. Most of all he should not have used it to you. You are a passenger with no right to an opinion in the matter."

I had no answer. He sank into the chair opposite me. He smiled bitterly.

"You would make it a matter of public discussion."

"A rebuke from you—"

"I did not mean a rebuke, only a warning. The captain has heard our arguments over a professional matter and given his decision. We must abide by it."

"I smell trouble."

"Stay out of it."

"We are friends, are we not? I must help you!"

He shook his head.

"I believe I may go so far as to make a formal protest at the appropriate time. Coombs is setting about the iron-work now. It is two vast plates—for which we have barely enough metal—four iron rods with screw ends and nuts to screw on them—"

"Do not tell me more, for I see it all! He will do what my father made them do to the old cottages down by the river: iron bars made red-hot which pulled some bulging walls together! I remember it well, for I saw it when I was a small boy—how the crosses on the ends of the rods pulled in the walls as the hot metal cooled. It was exciting as a Fair Day!"

"Was the building made of wood?"

"Brick."

"It will not have escaped your notice that we are made of wood. His bars will extend, red-hot, through four solid foot of timber—I almost heard your jaw drop! Of course, he will have holes bored wider than the rods and swears the heat will produce nothing inside the shoe but a thin layer of charcoal. His model worked, I allow him that. It produced plenty of smoke too."

"But only a while ago Captain Anderson was praising Benét for having no ironwork, no chain cable, no steam about him! A proper rope, blocks and canvas man!"

506

The first lieutenant struck the table with the flat of his hand.

"Listen to me, Edmund! We are still in mortal danger even if the mast should not go through the bottom! Have you watched a fireback as the fire dies down? How the sparks move through the layer of soot on the metal as if they were alive? Have you never seen a fire, apparently dead, brought to life again and flare up? It will be shut in there—in the shoe. We are to sail on gaily with that added to all the rest! Added to the cranky hull, the jury rig, the distance, the terrible weather towards which we are making our clumsy way and which we need because it is the only force which will get us to land and shelter before the fresh water and even the food run out—"

He paused for breath, and in that silence the sound of the water running and thumping on the outside of our hull was only too clearly audible.

"Forgive me, Edmund. That young man tries me beyond bearing. He thinks he can find our longitude by lunar distance—he thinks—oh, he thinks this and that! I should not have said so much. I have fallen into the error against which—"

"You can say what you like to me and I shall be honoured to guard your secrets with my life."

It made him smile.

"No, no. Just keep quiet, old fellow. Forget the whole business. That's all I ask."

"I will keep quiet. But I cannot forget it."

He rose to his feet and went to the stern window.

"Edmund!"

"What is the matter?"

"Do you trust me?"

"You sound excited—some more danger? Of course I do!"

He came back quickly to the table.

507

"Go and get into your daytime rig—no oilskins—then into the waist—stand there in the open—don't stir no matter what happens—hurry!"

I rushed into my borrowed cabin, tore off my greatcoat and nightshirt—huddled on my daytime clothing and was out again more quickly than I have ever changed in my life. I reached the waist thoroughly out of breath and had to hang on the mainstays to get it back. I saw Mr Brocklebank gathering his decayed coach cloak about him and lumbering back into the lobby. There seemed to be nothing about the waist to cause Charles's excitement. I leaned on the rail and stared astern.

"Well!"

What was astern of us and up wind was the blackest cloud I have ever seen in my life. Here and there it was touched with sour grey, giving it just the appearance of dirty water when you have done your worst with it and the steward has come to remove it from your disgusted sight. Moreover, this cloud was coming rapidly nearer and bringing its own wind with it—as I now saw it did! For our sails thundered, then filled again as our bows moved along the horizon from starboard to larboard. The cloud seemed to reach right down to the water and in a second, it seemed, it had enveloped us. The water was deadly cold, hissing, constant as the flow of a river which fell on me and took away my breath all over again. It soaked and resoaked my clothing, so that I loosed my hold on the mainstays and stumbled towards the lobby—only to remember Charles's prohibition and stumble back again, for I partly understood it though I cursed him for the first and last time in my life. The torrent continued to fall over me and my soaked clothes clung to me and the water rushed out of my unmentionables as if they had been drainpipes. Suddenly the cold increased as a fresh wind pushed my clothes even closer against me. Then as by magic the water ceased to thunder on the deck. I lifted my head. The wind was fierce in my face and the sea and sky were both alike dark. Webber, the wardroom steward, stood in the entry to the passenger lobby. He was grinning like a gargoyle.

"Mr Summers's compliments, sir. You may come in now you've had your bath!"

(3)

"Bath!"

I stumbled into the lobby, slopping water out of my clothes, then slid through what I was spilling. I fumbled, cursing, at the door of my old cabin, remembered sick and silent Zenobia, reeled across the lobby to Colley's cabin, then remembered that I was still using my borrowed cabin in the wardroom. I picked my way more cautiously down the ladder. Webber had the door open.

"I'll take your gear, sir."

Phillips was there too.

"Compliments of the first lieutenant, sir!"

It was a huge towel, rough as a rug and dry as a bone. Naked, I wrapped myself in it as I stepped out of the squelching pile of my clothes. I began to laugh, then whistle, towelling myself round, under, up and down, from hair to feet.

"What's this?"

"First lieutenant, sir."

"Good God!"

Item: a vest, apparently made of string. Item: a rough shirt such as a petty officer might wear. Item: a woollen overgarment of jersey worsted about an inch thick. Item: seaboot stockings almost as thick. Item: a pair of seaman's trowsers—not, I have to say, unmentionables—trowsers! Finally: a leathern belt.

"Does he expect me—"

Suddenly I was overcome with a great good humour and excitement! It looked very much like goodbye to my itching. It was like all those childish occasions of "dressing up", of wearing a paper cocked hat and carrying a wooden sword.

"Very well, Webber—Phillips—take this wet stuff away and dry it. I will dress this time for myself."

There was no doubt about it. A man had to get himself accustomed to the touch of this sort of material on the skin, but at least it was dry and, by contrast, warm. I had a suspicion that unless I regulated the number of layers I now wore, the warmth would turn into an uncomfortable heat. But by the time I was clothed in a complete costume I was wholly reconciled to the change. Of course, no man could be elegant in deportment when clad so! Such clothing would force on the wearer a decided casualness of behaviour. Indeed, I date my own escape from a certain unnatural stiffness and even loftiness of manner to that very day. I realized, too, why though Oldmeadow's soldiers always gathered in the straightest of lines and appeared to be held up by their own ramrods inserted in the spine, an assembly of our good seamen, though mustered regularly and standing in approximate rows, could never imitate the drilled and ceremonious appearance of the soldiers with their imposing uniforms! This was naval rig—in fact, "slops"! The curves and wrinkles defied a geometrical organization.

I went out into the wardroom. The first lieutenant was sitting at the long table with papers spread out before him.

"Charles!"

He looked up and grinned as he saw me.

"How do you find your rig?"

"Warm and dry—but good God, how do I look?"

"You'll do."

"A common seaman—What would a lady say? What *will* the ladies say? How did you do it? In this soaked ship! Why, there cannot be a dry corner anywhere or a dry inch of cloth!"

"Oh, there are ways—a drawer or box with bags of a suitable substance. But do not speak of that. The same cannot be done for the whole crew and the substance is not for casual handling."

"I have not been so moved by a man's kindness—it is exactly like the story of Glaucus and Diomede in Homer. You know they exchanged armour—gold armour on the one side for bronze armour on the other—my dear fellow—I have promised you the bronze armour of my godfather's patronage—and you have given me gold!"

"The story has not come my way. I am glad you are pleased, though."

"Bless you!"

He smiled a little uncertainly, I thought.

"It is nothing—or not much anyway."

"Will you not accompany me to the lobby and give me countenance for my first public appearance?"

"Oh, come! Do you see these papers? Water, biscuit, beef, pork, beans—we may have to—And after that I ought to take a look at Coombs and his ironwork—then there are my rounds—"

"Say no more. I am on my own. Well. Here goes!"

I left the wardroom, went as bold as brass up the stairs and into the passenger saloon. Our one Army officer, Oldmeadow, was there. He stared for a moment or two before he recognized me.

"Good God, Talbot! What have you done to yourself, man? Joined the Navy? What will the ladies say?"

" 'They say—what say they—let them say'!"

"They will say that 'tars' should stick to the front end and not take up the room set apart for their betters. You'd best stay in this part of the ship or a petty officer will lay his rope's end across your back for idling."

"Oh no, he will not, sir! Gentlemen do not need a uniform to be recognized as such. I am comfortable, decent and what is more I am dry, sir. Can you say the same?"

"No, I cannot. But then I ain't as thick as thieves with the ship's officers."

"I beg your pardon?"

"Spend too much of my time looking after my men to badger the Navy into dressing me up from the slop shop. Well, I must be off."

He made his way out of the saloon handily enough against the cant and reel. It did seem to me that he went in order to avoid an argument. He was, and perhaps is, a mild creature. There had been a note of asperity in what he said. But then, during the increasing decrepitude of our ship and more evident danger to our lives, there had been a corresponding change in the character of the passengers and change in the relationship between us. We, so to speak, *rubbed* on each other. Mr Brocklebank, who had once been an object of no more than amusement, had become an irritant as well. The Pikes—father, mother, little daughters— were, it seemed, divided among themselves. I and Oldmeadow—

"Edmund. Take hold of yourself."

I looked out of the great stern window. It was a different sea, starker now, right to the horizon but strewn with white horses which attempted to follow us but were outrun by their own waves and slid back out of sight. Gusts were whipping through the steadier wind, for sudden lines of spray crossed the direction of the waves which were being marshalled to follow and overtake us.

I gave an involuntary shiver. In the excitement of my shift into seaman's costume I had not noticed that the air, even in the saloon, was colder than it had been.

The door of the saloon opened. I looked round. Little Mrs Brocklebank stared, then bounced forward and stood with her arms akimbo.

"Where do you think you are?"

I rose to my feet. She gave a squeak.

"Mr Talbot! I did not know—I did not mean—"

"Who did you think it was, ma'am?"

For a moment or two she stood there, staring at me with her mouth open. Then she turned quickly and ran away. After a while I began to laugh. She was a pretty little thing and a man could do much worse—if it were not for, of course—Costume was proving to be a test of society.

I sat down again and returned to watching the sea. Rain lashed across the window and already the waves had taken up their new direction. The white horses were more numerous and galloped for a longer period on the waves which had engendered them. It seemed to me that our speed had increased. There came a tap! on the outside of the window. It was the log being lowered. The line stretched further and further astern of us. The saloon door opened and Bowles, the solicitor's clerk, came in. He shook the last traces of water from his greatcoat. He saw me but evinced no great surprise to see how I was dressed.

"Good morning, Mr Bowles."

"Good morning, sir. Have you heard the news?"

"What news?"

"The foremast. Mr Benét and the blacksmith are delayed in their preparation of the ironwork. So the perilous work of restoring the mast to its former efficiency must be put off."

"Believe me, I am thankful to hear that! But why?"

"Charcoal for heating the iron. The ship does not have a large enough supply. The first lieutenant happened to check that part of the stores and found more has been used than was thought."

"That might well be a good thing and give the captain time to think again. What will they do?"

"They are able to make more charcoal. I am told the shoe of the foremast is split and they wish to use the enormous power of metal shrinking as it cools to pull the wood together again."

"So Mr Summers told me."

"Ah yes. Well, you would know, would you not? Some people think that Mr Summers was not sorry to report how little charcoal was available. Mr Benét was not pleased and asked to be allowed to recheck the amount in case the first lieutenant had made a mistake. He was refused abruptly."

"Does Benét not realize how dangerous the attempt is? He is such a fool!"

"That is the trouble, Mr Talbot. He is not a fool—not precisely."

"He had best stick to his poetry which can harm no one except perhaps a sensitive critic. Good God, a cranky ship, a sullen captain—"

"Not so sullen, sir. Mr Benét, I think—speaking without prejudice—has brightened his life."

"Mr Bowles! Favouritism!"

"Without prejudice, sir. Cumbershum is not in favour of the red-hot iron."

"Nor is Mr Summers."

"Nor is our wrinkled old carpenter, Mr Gibbs. Naturally he is a man for wood and thinks red-hot iron should be kept as far away from it as possible. Mr Askew, the gunner, approves. He says, 'What's a bit of hot metal between friends?' "

"They speak each according to his humour as in an old comedy."

I was suddenly restless and stood up.

"Well, Mr Bowles, I must leave you."

I went away through the cold air of the saloon into the windy lobby outside it, then down the stairs again to the wardroom where the air was minimally warmer. Charles had left and Webber brought me a brandy. I stood, my legs apart, and stared out of the window. So soon one accepts as normal a state once desperately desired! I had forgotten what it was to itch!

There came a tap! on the glass. The log was being lifted out of the water.

"The man's a fool!"

It was Mr Benét speaking. He had entered the ward-room silently.

"The quartermaster?"

"He should pay the line out over the quarter. He will break every pane if he goes on like this."

"How is your charcoal?"

"So you have heard too! This ship reverberates like the belly of a cello! Coombs is seeing to it. I must wait. It is in his hands."

"Not yours?"

"I am in overall control. I am only thankful that Coombs knew exactly how much sheet iron he had before certain other people could measure the area."

"At all events you must be glad for a time of leisure with your many activities."

"Work enables me to forget my sorrow, Mr Talbot. I do not envy you, given twenty-four idle hours a day in which to feel the pangs of separation."

"It is good of you to remember my situation. But, Mr Benét, since we are companions in sorrow—you remember those too brief hours when *Alcyone* was compelled by the flat calm to lie alongside us—"

"Every moment, every instant is chiselled in my heart."

"In mine too. But you must remember that after the ball I was lying delirious in my cabin."

"I did not know."

"Not know? They did not tell you? I mean during that time when the wind returned and *Alcyone* was forced to leave us—"

" 'Utmost dispatch.' I did not know about you, sir. I had my own sorrows. Separation from Belovéd Object—"

"And Miss Chumley too! She must have known I was—lying on a Bed of Pain!"

"The fact is, what with my sudden—departure—from one ship and entry into another—my exchange with one of your lieutenants—"

"Jack Deverel."

"And what with my separation from One who is more to me than all the world—despite the warmth of your genial captain's welcome—"

"Genial! Are we thinking of the same man?"

"—I had no solace but my Art."

"You could not have known that there would be scope for your engineering proclivity!"

"My Muse. My poetry. The parting struck verses from me as quickly as the iron strikes a spark from the flint or vice versa."

Mr Benét put his left hand on the long table and leaned on it. He laid the other hand on that portion of the chest where I am assured the heart lies concealed. He then stretched that hand out towards the increasingly tormented sea.

> *The salutation which she cast*
> *From ship to ship had been our last!*
> *Her eye had dropped a winking tear*
> *Which I could see for she stood near—*
> *And standing did not smile nor frown*
> *As seamen drew the main course down,*
> *But 'twas a dagger at my heart*
> *To feel the two ships move apart!*
> *The tap of blocks, a loosened brail,*
> *A breath of air, a filling sail,*
> *A yard no more, of shadow'd sea—*
> *But oh, what leagues it was to me!*

"I am sure all the verses will seem very pretty, Mr Benét, when properly written down and corrected."

"Corrected? You find some fault?"

"I could detect little *enjambement* but that is by the way. She was with Miss Chumley. Did Miss Chumley not speak?"

"Lady Somerset and Miss Chumley were speaking together. They ran to Truscott, the surgeon, as soon as he came aboard from your ship."

"You could not hear what they said?"

"Directly *Alcyone* had cast off, Sir Henry left the deck and went below. Then Lady Somerset came to the taffrail and gestured thus."

Lieutenant Benét straightened up. He raised his cupped hand to his mouth and deposited something in it. Then with a female twist of the body he brought his right hand back over his shoulder and, opening the palm, appeared to throw something through our stern window.

"It seems an elaborate way of getting rid of her spittle, Mr Benét. Commonly people do what young Mr Tommy Taylor describes as 'dropping it in the drink'."

"You are facetious, sir. It was the Salutation!"

"But Miss Chumley—you could not hear what she said?"

"I had been below, stowing my gear. When I heard the pipes I knew the moment had come—thrust Webber out of the way—rushed up the ladder—it was too late. The springs and breast ropes were in. You, sir, I doubt you have the sensibility to understand the completeness of separation between two ships when the ropes are in—they might be two separate continents—familiar faces are those of strangers at once. Their future is different and unknown. It is like death!"

"I believe I have as much sensibility as the next man, sir!"

"That is what I said."

"But Miss Chumley did not speak?"

"She came to the rail, and stood there as *Alcyone* moved away. She looked woebegone. I daresay she was feeling seasick all over again, for you know, Mr Talbot, she was said to be a martyr to it."

"Oh, the poor child! I appeal to you, Mr Benét. I will not elaborate on the nights of tears, the yearnings, the fear that some other man, the need to communicate with her and the present impossibility of doing so! She is bound for India, I for New South Wales. I met her for no more than a few hours of that miraculous day when our two ships were becalmed side by side—I dined with her—later I danced with her at that ball aboard this ship—was ever such a ball held in mid-Atlantic? And then I collapsed—concussion—fell sick—was delirious—but we had parted—if only you could understand how precious to me would be some kind of description of her time in *Alcyone* when you were—wooing Lady Somerset—"

"Worshipping Lady Somerset."

"And she, Miss Chumley, I mean your acquaintance, even your ally in that reprehensible—what am I saying—that tender attachment—"

"The love of my life, sir."

"For you know, that one day thrust me into a new life! The instant I saw her I was struck by, destroyed by lightning, or if you are familiar with the phrase, it was the *coup de foudre*—"

"Say that again."

"*Coup de foudre.*"

"Yes, the phrase is familiar."

"And before we parted she did declare that she held me in higher regard than anyone else in the two ships. Later still I received a *billet doux*—"

"A *billet doux*, for God's sake!"

"Was that not encouragement?"

"How can I tell unless I know what was in it?"

"The words are chiselled in my heart. *A young person will always remember the time when two ships were side by side in the middle of the sea and hopes that one day they may put down their anchors in the same harbour.*"

Mr Benét shook his head.

"I find no encouragement for you there, sir."

"None? Oh, come! What—none?"

"Very little. In fact it sounds to me uncommonly like a *congé*, if you are familiar with the word. You would probably call it a 'congy' or something."

"A farewell!"

"With perhaps an undertone of relief—"

"I will not believe it!"

"A determination that the affair should end as painlessly as possible."

"No!"

"Be a man, Mr Talbot. Do I whine or repine? Yet I have no hope whatever of seeing the Belovéd Object again. All that consoles me is my genius."

With those words Mr Benét turned away and vanished into his own cabin. A tide of furious indignation overwhelmed me.

"I do not believe a word he said!"

For she was there, vividly—not the Idea of a young person, the lineaments of whose face I could never bring together no matter how I tried as I writhed in my bunk— but there, breathing lavender, her eyes shining in the darkness and her soft but passionate whisper—"*Oh no indeed!*"

Benét had not seen her so, heard her so.

"She felt as I do!"

(4)

So I stared out at the waters of separation until my anger subsided—but my grief remained! I heard a door open and close behind me, the brisk steps of Benét and another door open and close as he left the wardroom. I did not look round. Clearly the man was inclined to taunt me, and besides he was of the other faction. Even if Charles forbade the word he should not prevent me using it on his behalf to myself. He needed my support. With that thought I called for Webber and had him help me into my oilskins and seaboots. I then made a laborious way up to the waist and looked for Charles, who was nowhere to be seen. But what was immediately evident was that we had passed some invisible boundary in the open sea. There was a clear green tone in the water rather than blue or grey. The air had indeed become colder and a few drops of spray which struck my cheek felt as though they had frozen there. The wind was from the southwest now and we were reaching towards the southeast. It was no longer a gale but a strong wind marshalling the waves on our beam. Under the low clouds strands of mist were beginning to stream past us from the invisible western horizon. Our ship once again had begun that swift roll which was the result of our shortened masts and inadequate sail area. But at least she did not seem to pitch and the cables which Charles had passed round her belly remained taut and motionless. The crew were busy. I do not mean that part of the watch which stood by for sail changing and which supplied the lookouts and quartermasters for the wheel. I mean the other part, which was busily rigging lifelines from the break of the fo'castle to the bitts of the mainmast and then from there to the aftercastle and the stairs ascending to the quarterdeck. This was suggestive. As I watched, I saw Charles Summers come out of the fo'castle and stand talking with Mr Gibbs, who presently knuckled his forehead and went into the fo'castle again. Charles came aft to the foremast, examined the wedges and then talked with the petty officer who was directing the men at the lifelines. He then examined the lines, putting his weight on them here and there. There was an argument for a while about one point of attachment but finally Charles seemed satisfied. He climbed up and spoke to someone by the belfry on the fo'castle, saw me and raised his arm in greeting. I answered in a like manner but did not go forrard. Charles busied himself with some other people on the fo'castle. Then he turned away and came briskly along the waist to me.

"You are still dry?"

"As you see—and wearing oilskins as much for warmth as dryness. The air is much colder."

"The 'roaring forties'. We have found them at last but distinctly farther south than they ought to be!"

"The change was sudden."

"It always is, we are told. Waters have their own islands, continents, roadways. This is a continent."

"The lifelines are ominous."

"A precaution."

"You seem cheerful."

"I ought not to be but am. For—may I whisper?— forrard there, below decks, Coombs is making charcoal, which will take him days. Add to that the weather which as it gets rougher will render far too dangerous any tinkering with the foremast—"

"Our faction is in the ascendant!"

"Do not use that word!"

"I am sorry. I forgot."

"What sort of reputation would you carry to the governor if Captain Anderson told him that you had made trouble in the ship?"

"He will not do that so long as he remembers my journal which will lie before my godfather!"

"I had forgotten. How long ago all that affair seems! But to please me, avoid words which might suggest a division among us. All I meant was that I am happy because an unnecessary hazard has been postponed."

"I own I was looking forward to an increase in our speed. But that was before I understood the possible cost."

"May I advise you? Only wear oilskins for their proper purpose—keeping yourself dry. Inside them you heat up and sweat. Then before you know where you are all the good work of your rare bath will be undone."

He nodded meaningly, then strode back along the deck and into the fo'castle. I muttered to myself.

"A nod is as good as a wink. I used to stink."

I became aware that old Mr Brocklebank was standing within two yards of me. He was in the shelter (for what it was worth) of the starboard mainstays and had his right arm hooked through a bight of rope. Somewhere he had found or been given a large coach cloak which was ancient, worn and dirty. He had arranged this round his body so that it presented a kind of sculptural effect. His beaver was tied on by some material passed over the crown and fastened under his chin. I believe it was a lady's stocking! His plump face was melancholy as he gazed at nothing or perhaps into himself. I decided that I did not want any conversation with him, for he, at least, was unlikely to be able to add anything to what I knew of Miss Chumley. I went past him, therefore, with no more than a nod and into the passenger lobby. The door of the cabin to which I had planned so nobly to return was open. As I approached, Phillips came out with a brush and bucket and went to the larboard side of the waist.

I had not entered that cabin since Wheeler had chosen the place for his last, tragic and criminal act. With a sudden determination to get on with the business I opened the door and stepped inside. All seemed as before, except that the place was cleaner and brighter. For the bulkheads, the ship's side and the deckhead—or better, the walls and the ceiling—were now covered, not with the dull mustard-coloured paint which seemed to be the best the Navy could do for passenger accommodation, but with glossy white enamel. That was cheerful enough. I touched it here and there and found it dry. There was now no excuse for not returning. I sat down in the canvas chair and willed the place to be ordinary and not connected to its history. I could not succeed. No matter how hard I tried, my eye would return to that eyebolt in the ship's side so near the head of the bed. There the rigid hand of the dead man had hung, his body dinted as if leaden into the furnishings of his bed! My mind flinched away from Colley, only to imagine at once Wheeler standing by me, his head raised, the golden goblet of the blunderbuss only an inch or two from his face—there was no flinching from that! It was as if the man's misdirected courage in facing the shot of self-destruction held me too, chin up, staring up, his last sight of anything my last sight, nothing but the massive and worn timbers of the deckhead.

I went cold for all my seaman's clothing and oilskins—cold with more than the weather. White paint however carefully applied can conceal a corner but not the shape of a deformation. The beam most central to the deckhead was deeply pocked above the place where Wheeler's head had been. Some brains and a skull are little obstacle to a charge propelled by gunpowder at a range of an inch or two. In one of those pocks into which the brush had worked white paint it none the less could not conceal the point of a small, knife-like object which projected from the bottom of the hole. The seaman who had busily worked his brush into the hole had therefore painted the surface of this hideous *memento mori*. There were other traces I now saw and soon my eyes supplied a detailed knowledge which I could well have done without. I became *seized* of the explosion and the trajectories, knew intimately how the head had burst. This was no place to sleep. Yet sleep there I must, or be laughed at throughout the ship and later throughout New South Wales!

The deck moved under me, a sinewy motion lifting one seaboot and sliding away from the other. There came a moaning cry from Prettiman's cabin. Anguished as the sound was, I was almost glad to be reminded of the world outside this hutch. Fool Prettiman! Philosopher so called! Well, thought I, turning my attention away from dead men, he is paying for his folly. To which faction would he and his fiancée, Miss Granham, belong? My thoughts became mixed between the two cabins. If so strong-minded a lady consented to make Prettiman the happiest of men—But then again, he was a man of substance and such are always in danger of being married for their money. At all events, if *she* had to sleep here she would do so and stand no nonsense! The thought braced me in those morbid surroundings so that I got to my feet and out into the lobby. Through the opening to the waist I could see that at least part of the deck had a sheet of sea-water sluicing from one side to the other. We were beginning to get that weather we had looked for! This time I found myself walking splay-legged and glad of a hand on the safety rail of the lobby, let alone the rail of the stairs down to the wardroom.

"Webber, help me out of these oilskins if you please. After that you can get my gear back to the cabin among the other passengers."

"Sir, the first lieutenant said—"

"Never mind what the first lieutenant said. The paint is dry and I shall sleep there tonight."

There was a fierce slash of water across the panes of the stern window.

"Getting up, sir, an't it? Be rougher before it's done."

"Yes. Now do as I told you, Webber."

"It's the cabin where he done himself in, an't it? And afore him the parson?"

"Yes. Now get on."

Webber paused for a moment, then nodded more to himself I think than me.

"Ah."

He disappeared into the cabin which had been loaned to me. There was no doubt about it. All things were combining to make me uneasy. But relieved of my oilskins I decided to try the passenger saloon though the hour was early for eating. Who should I find there but little Pike slumped over the table? As the ship rolled, a shot glass clattered along the deck.

"Pike! Richard! What is this?"

He did not reply and his body rolled with the ship. I found his intoxication disgusting; for no one is as high-minded in the article of strong drink as a reformed drinker! But that is by the way.

"Richard! Bestir yourself!"

No sooner had I said that than I regretted it. The truth is that the job of intoxication once done, the poor devil was best left to the sad oblivion he had chosen. Who was I to decide whether he should sleep or wake? A clerk, somehow able to pay the passage for himself, his wife and two small daughters to the Antipodes—two daughters quite possibly dying and a wife who was turning, by all accounts, into a shrew if nothing worse! No. Let him be.

The door opened and Bowles came in.

"Well, Mr Bowles? What news of the foremast?"

"You should ask rather for news of the charcoal, sir. They can only distil or brew or reduce—or whatever one does to wood to make charcoal of it—in small parcels. The fo'castle resounds with argument for and against."

"You have been there, then."

"Believe it or not, I was asked to advise on the drawing up of a will. Then, I suppose as payment, I was taken down and shown the foot of the foremast in the broken shoe."

"The people are divided in their opinions?"

"Oh yes. The argument is high and not conducted with proper legal, or perhaps I should say parliamentary, propriety."

"Do you agree with the first lieutenant or Mr Benét?"

"With neither. I am astonished at the ease with which uninformed persons come to a settled, a passionate opinion when they have no grounds for judgement."

"I believe the attempt should not be made. It is far too dangerous."

"Yes. The first lieutenant does think so. You should see the shoe! It is gigantic. So, I am afraid, is the split, and frightening too. So is the groaning of the mast as it lurches and grinds into the wood with that small, irregular—unpreventable—circle. I do not know what they should do. The place, though, is a tangle of temporary measures. Some the layman can understand, some are quite inscrutable. There are beams jammed between the shaft of the mast and the thicker timbers of the ship's side. There are cables twisted about the mast so taut you would think them made of metal. Yet the mast moves, for all the beams and twisted cables, the blocks and tackles, crows, shores and battens. The sight is frightening. But then, when you see the small movement, the sight is more than frightening."

"Can there be more?"

"Dread."

He said no more but stared out of the stern window at the rising sea.

"Well, Mr Bowles, we have become a poor collection of mortals, I think. Here is Pike drunk and incapable. Oldmeadow is consumed with bad temper and chooses the company of his men rather than us. We have become—what?"

"Frightened out of our wits."

"Prettiman keeps his bunk—"

"He does not. He is helpless in it. The fall was of extraordinary force. Since we have no surgeon aboard and only the matron of the emigrants to minister to him—"

"I cannot imagine that doing him any kind of good!"

"Nor I. But the seamen and emigrants would have her do what she could, which was confined, I believe, to the muttering of spells and the hanging of garlic round the poor man's neck!"

"The seamen and emigrants sent her?"

"Prettiman is much respected among them."

"Have I dismissed him as a clown too readily? Oh, surely not!"

Bates, the steward, came to provide us with what food there was for those who still had a mind to eat—salt pork, cold since the fuel must be conserved for making charcoal, soaked beans also cold and the notorious ship's biscuit, which I herewith give my affidavit had no weevils in them, small beer or brackish water ameliorated by a dash of brandy. I ate and so did Bowles. Pike slumbered until Bates called Phillips in and the two men carried him to his cabin. Oldmeadow, I am told, ate a seaman's portion in the fo'castle with his men. The sea got up and our movement was more violent. The daily business of the ship which must go on whatever else happened—the changes of the watch, the bosun's calls, the bells, the tread above our heads of seabooted officers and the leathery slap of the seamen's naked feet on planking—this resounded about us, endless as the voyage, as time itself, while the anxious hours drew on. Bates—whether it was his duty or not, I cannot tell—took plates of food to the ladies in their bunks.

Bowles went to his cabin. Mr Brocklebank, wrapped in his coach cloak, came and sat by me. He gave me a description of the processes involved in engraving on stone, copper, zinc, together with the various difficulties attendant on these operations. I did not hear above the half and at last the old man heaved himself away. Every now and then a wave would strike the ship explosively.

At about nine o'clock of a dark night I got to my feet and walked with care to my newly painted cabin. Webber was there, pretending to straighten the coverlet but in reality waiting so that I should give him money for doing his duty.

"Thank you, Webber. That will be all."

To my surprise he did not go.

"This is where he done it then. I'm not surprised."

"What do you mean, Webber?"

"A place gets right greedy after the first taste and would have him, you see, once it knowed what he had in mind—"

"What are you talking about?"

"Wheeler. Joss, we called him. He was my oppo among the stewards."

"Be off with you!"

"Once they have it in mind there's no stopping them, is there? He told me it was like a kind of comfort. He was a queer one, Joss. I believe he must have lived among gentlemen before he came to sea. He had a way of saying things—said he had lived among collegers until he relinquished that employment."

"He never said anything to me! Now—"

"He said there's a hole kind of. 'It's always there, Webber,' he said. 'It's kind of a hole and you know that if the weather gets too rough you can use the hole, get into the hole, hide and sleep,' he said. 'It's always there. For I won't drown, not again.' "

"Good God! He said something like that—something—"

"But then, why here? The answer is the cabin drawed him. It knowed, you see."

"Get *out*, Webber!"

"I'm going, sir. I wouldn't stay here, not in the night, not if you paid me, sir—which you won't, of course."

He paused for a moment, still looking, but I gave him nothing and he left. Yet it was difficult after he had shut the door. I went out again and worked my way to the entry to the waist and peered round the edge. The waves were organized in lines that might have been ruled they were so straight. The light of a waxing moon lay along the completely marshalled crests and turned them to lines of steel.

(5)

"Mr Talbot, sir."

Phillips carried candles in one hand and a lighted lantern in the other.

"In there, Phillips."

"Will you be wanting a light now, sir?"

"Yes—no! Not yet. See here, Phillips. Never mind the candle. Leave the lantern."

"Oh, I couldn't do that, Mr Talbot, sir! You know the passengers isn't supposed to have lanterns but only candles because—"

"Because if candles are overset they douse themselves? Yes, I know. And you know me, don't you? Wait a moment. Now. This buys the lantern off you. I wish to keep a lantern as a memento of the voyage."

An expression of comprehension rearranged Phillips's customary wooden face.

"Sir."

"Hang the lantern on that hook. Turn down the wick."

Of course a ship never sleeps. There was always at least a part of the watch on duty, to say nothing of the officer of the watch and his doggy. I got into my oil-skins and made my way through the moonlight to the quarterdeck. Lieutenant Benét was leaning over the forrard rail.

"Come up, Mr Talbot! How do you like this wind? It is bustling us along capitally, is it not?"

"How does the ship like it?"

"She is making more water, of course. That is to be expected. I have been thinking. We ought to rig up some kind of windmill to pump her out."

"Oh no! Not again! Do not terrify us with some new contrivance! Dragropes, ironwork, red-hot rods—Have a care of us, Mr Benét. We are precious!"

Mr Benét tore off his oilskin headgear and spread his arms wide.

"Look about you, Mr Talbot! Is the view not magnificent? The moonlight on these moving waters, the silvered clouds, the unguessable distances up there—those brilliant bodies sparkling above us all! Where is your poetry? Does not the danger, the fear we all feel, give a keener edge to this intoxicating delight?"

"If it comes to that, where is *your* poetry? In days past you have been only too anxious to stuff it down my throat!"

"You are a severe critic. Then take a utilitarian view. This moonlight means that we may well have a clear horizon at dawn and take helpful star sights."

"I thought there was some difficulty over the navigation—erratic chronometers or something."

"You do pick about, sir, do you not? But at least we may find our latitude, which is nearly half the battle though not quite."

"Is that Mr Willis there? I hope you are recovered, lad. Mr Benét—cannot Mr Willis assist you in navigation?"

"I take that as a pleasantry, sir. Will you excuse me now? I am occupied with an Ode to Nature, a subject of such amplitude and depth I can scarcely get into it—or out of it!"

"Better that than sink us out of hand."

"I suppose you are talking about the foremast. We shall commence the operation when we have enough charcoal and when this sea has gone down."

At this point the odd young man shook his long locks about his face and orated:

"*Spirit of Nature—*"

"Are you sure, Mr Benét? The last time—no, the time before that—it was *Spirit of woman*—you are thrifty."

Mr Benét ignored me.

"*Spirit of Nature, warm or hot or cold. Solidity—*"

"No, no, Mr Benét! I am unworthy of the treat—as is Mr Willis! Allow me to detach Mr Willis from you. He speaks prose."

"Take him. Do what you like with him. Oblige me by returning to me what is left. One never knows what will prove useful."

Willis followed me sullenly enough, up to the poop.

"Well, Mr Willis. Are you quite recovered?"

"I'm deaf in me right earhole where the captain clouted me. And if anyone tries to get me up a mast he'll have to carry me up screaming."

"Good God, lad, your voice has broken! I suppose I should congratulate you. Not climb the mast again? Where's your spirit, lad?"

"What's that to you? It's my business not yours and I'm minding it."

"I'd be obliged for a little more courtesy from you, young man!"

"Why? You're a passenger. What in the Navy we calls a 'pig'. I don't have to take lip from you. Mr Askew, the gunner, said so. 'They're passengers,' he said, 'nothing more. This ain't a company ship,' he said, 'and you need pay no attention to them, not even when they're as high in the instep as Lord Talbot,' he said."

"I'll still require a little civility from you, Mr Willis, on the grounds that I'm older than you if nothing else. I'm sorry to hear that you were deafened but guess that the faculty will return to you. Good Heavens! Young Tommy was a bit lopsided after I cuffed him. Boys must be educated, you know! We all suffer! I doubt there's a schoolboy or midshipman in the world who has not some

533

temporary derangement of his faculties in one department or another. That's how we are made, young fellow, and you should be grateful!"

"Well, I'm not. I wish I was home. And I would be if Dad didn't have an account with one of the managers in the docks and wished to make a gentleman of me. I'd still be serving sugar and happy with the tally wenches in the storerooms. Now the war's over, they'll have to decommission this rotting old lump of wood and then you won't see my arse for dust."

The moon ducked into a cloud and by contrast the night seemed dark. Mr Benét sang out from the quarterdeck below us.

"Mr Willis, oblige me by having the quarter lanterns turned up. When you've done that, you can tell me what happens at a half hour before sunrise."

"Aye aye, sir. Bosun's mate—"

I twitched Willis by the sleeve and murmured to him.

"Half an hour before sunrise is the beginning of Nautical Twilight."

"Well, I know that! Did you think I was stupid?"

Clearly the boy was proof against the advances of social amiability. I was about to dismiss him, therefore, when a positive party of men came to the quarterdeck. Charles was with them. They brought a considerable quantity of gear up to the poop which seemed to include a sail triced up to a heavy yard, an enormous block of iron which needed three men to carry it, and coils of heavy rope.

"Edmund! You are not yet in your bunk!"

"Evidently. Do you never stop working? What is all this?"

"It is a sea anchor."

"This is new to me."

"In extremely heavy weather a ship may ride to such an anchor—"

534

"But this is our stern!"

"Our circumstances are unusual. That is all. We may need to stream the anchor over the stern to check her way and ensure that she does not drive herself under. Oh, of course, not in this weather—it is moderating! But farther south, where the really heavy weather is—it is a precaution."

The men were tricing the gear to the rails of the poop.

"The captain's orders?"

"No. I have sufficient authority for this myself. Mine is an ancient profession, you see, and the duties defined well enough. But the time is nigh on six bells in the first—Why are you not in your bunk?"

"I—explanations are tedious! I am happy in my dry clothes and there was moonlight, to say nothing of a slight decrease in our motion—and so forth."

Charles looked closely into my face.

"You have moved back to the passenger accommodation?"

"Yes."

Charles nodded and turned to his men. He went round, as I saw, and personally checked the security of the lashing that held all this heavy gear ready for use. If care and forethought could secure our survival he would provide it! I had a sudden awareness of the two of them, Benét and Charles, the one brilliantly putting us at risk, the other soberly and constantly taking *care*!

Charles spoke again.

"Very well, Robinson. Carry on."

He turned to me.

"Are you going down?"

"Are not you?"

"Oh, I have more work to do. I suppose it will be the middle before I turn in."

"Well then—yes, I will go down. Good night, Charles."

I made my reluctant way down to the lobby. There was now a lantern fixed to the mizzenmast just above the copy of the captain's standing orders, in its glassfronted case. Someone had left two huge piles of rope beneath it. I opened the door of my hutch and stepped inside. By holding it open I had enough light from the lantern in the lobby to allow me to find my way round. I fumbled in the top drawer, got out my tinderbox and contrived to light the lantern I had bought from Phillips. I shut the door and sat in my canvas chair. I have to confess that already I was feeling something like one feels when bracing oneself to leap into cold water—very cold water. I stripped off my oilskins and my seaboots more slowly than an ancient. I remember bending to my boots as if the effort were painful and the business impossibly long. But at last I was in my "slops". There was still a way of postponing the unpleasant moment. I went to our office of necessity on the starboard side, turned up the blue bud of the oil lamp fixed to the bulkhead, adjusted my trowsers and sat on the nearer of our two holes to the door. Scarcely had I settled myself when the door opened and a petty officer of huge dimensions edged himself in.

"Well, damn my soul!"

"Sorry, sir!"

"Get out!"

"First lieutenant's orders, sir."

The man inserted a rope's end into the farther hole and proceeded to pay it out. I pulled up my trowsers in a rage, buckled the belt and flung myself out. There were more seamen in the lobby. A rope was creeping from the pile past my feet. Another rope was creeping in a like manner into the "female" offices of necessity on the larboard quarter. The place had gone mad. A young seaman, clad as I was in nothing but slops, came quickly out of the larboard office and ran to Miss Granham's door! This was

the outside edge of enough! I got to him in a stride or two
and had him by the shoulder.

"No, you don't, my lad!"

I spun him round—good God! It was *Miss Granham*!
Her face, even in the dim light from the lantern, was scarlet.

"Let me go, sir, at once, sir!"

"Miss Granham!"

My hand had sprung from her thin shoulder as if it had
touched a snake. An unnoticed heave caught me off balance. Miss Granham grabbed the knob of her door
handle. I somersaulted backwards and was only saved
from mortal injury by those same coils of rope which
though diminished were still enough to break my fall. I
was on my knees and scrabbled back towards her.

"Pray, Miss Granham—pray, Miss Granham—forgive
me—I thought you was a seaman who intended you some
harm—allow me—I will close your—"

"I cannot close it myself, Mr Talbot, while you have
your hand on the sill. You have an uncommon knack of
falling about, sir! Far be it from me to offer advice—"

"I do not hurt myself on these occasions, ma'am. But I
should value your advice on anything."

She paused, her back to me, her door half-open.

"Sarcasm, Mr Talbot?"

The fall had warmed my temper.

"Why am I always misunderstood?"

She turned back. I continued.

"You do not comment, ma'am. During this voyage,
people's opinions of their associates and companions have
been modified—must have been—modified! That is as true
of me as of anyone. What I said was a simple expression of
the truth of—of my respect and for your—your—"

"My years, young man?"

She had swung round completely to face me. In the dim
light the ravages of time on her handsome face were not

visible. She was smiling and a lock of hair had escaped from the scarf in which the rest was confined and lay across her face. She put it up, and some trick of the half-light made her look as young as I, if not younger! My mouth opened and shut. I swallowed.

"No, ma'am."

"Let us be acquainted all over again then, Mr Talbot. Indeed, it falls pat. It would perhaps make you less indifferent to where and how you fall—Now, do not pucker up, sir! Hear me out! You may take more care of yourself if you see what the result of a fall can be. Mr Prettiman wishes to see you. I—the fact is, I recommended him to ask someone else. I see that perhaps I was wrong."

I believe I laughed.

"Mr Prettiman wishes to see me? Good God!"

"So, if you agree, I will call you to him tomorrow morning."

"I do agree, ma'am. Nothing would give me greater pleasure!"

The lock of hair had fallen once again. She put it up, frowning.

"Why do you say that, Mr Talbot? Is it the kind of remark you scatter among the members of my sex?"

I made a gesture of dissent. But quickly the smile returned.

"You do not answer, Mr Talbot. Nor should you. You find me minatory. I see the thought which is forming at the back of your mind, 'Once a governess, always a governess.' I was at fault, sir, and curtsey as you observe like the veriest milkmaid."

With that she closed the door. I stayed where I was, holding on to the rail, and I was bemused. There was no doubt about it. Miss Granham had the capacity to reduce a person to his constituent parts, apparently without trying! But we were—she had said so!—acquaintances once more. I do not believe myself quarrelsome and the change filled me with unusual relief and pleasure. I went to the entry to the waist and looked out. The deck was moon-drenched, white. Those stars that the moon had not quenched swung in great curves through the rigging like silver bees. I stared up at them until I was dizzy. I blinked and looked down. Men were coming aft, working their way along a bouncing lifeline, for they carried a heavy burden which seemed to make them unhandy. They laboured up to the quarterdeck with what appeared to be the body of some recently killed animal and large at that. Charles came hurrying along, unburdened, did not see me and went rapidly up the stairs after the men. I turned away and went into my hutch and shut the door behind me. I looked at the freshly made-up bunk with disfavour. There was no doubt about it. Coming back to this hutch was going to be a trial. It was like the time when I was a boy riding by the churchyard in the dusk on a pony which took me indifferently too near the graves. So now. However I had supposed the world and human life to be arranged, I found an air, an *atmosphere* in this hutch to which I had condemned myself! I seemed to breathe unease. True, compared with the light of the candle to which I was accustomed a degree of brilliance blazed from my oil lamp, which hung steady by the wall, while the wall moved and shadows drawn in black ink raced over me as the ship moved under us. I turned down the wick until only a glimmer of light was left. I told myself that I would not undress for a while but wait until familiarity had made the place a little more mine than—*theirs*. Is not a cure for a burnt finger to hold it next to a fire so that the heat is drawn out? Then Colley had sat here. His elbow, pen, inkwell, sander—here he had known the extremes of dread and sorrow, of humiliation, mortification—experience of a misery beyond the power of my imagination! If that misery, that whirlpool of human suffering had drained away without trace, as my reason told me, why suddenly was there a winter on my skin? Why was this cabin different from the last time I had slept here? I came up from that state, muttering something about a poor boy who had too much sensibility—or in other words too much blue funk! That made me grin but with what must have been little more than a grimace. To "share the common lot of the other passengers who would one day be part of my care"! That was a noble sentiment. I found myself speaking out loud.

"In future, my boy, avoid noble sentiments. They are like drawing a card blind. You may get anything from the joker to the—"

Nevertheless I am a rational man.

The day had been long. Sleep ought to have been easy. Yet I did not chuse to throw off my garments and get at once into the bunk. A naked man is defenceless. He cannot run naked out onto a moon-drenched deck. Not unless he is delirious. Well, thought I, I will do myself the kindness of going little by little. I lay down, fully dressed in my slops, on the coverlet of the bunk. I lay on my back. The eyebolt was inches from my face. I shut my eyes but was provoked by the slight intimations of light and shadow passing over them. I opened my eyes, therefore, and determining to ignore the eyebolt, focused my eyes on the white-painted deckhead. I found myself examining in detail the wounded underside of a deckbeam, a hole with a pointed thing in the bottom.

I turned over and lay on my face, but the roll of the ship and the occasional pitch made me lurch uncomfortably. I fumbled for the side of the bunk with one hand and at the side of the ship with the other. My fingers took hold. It was the eyebolt, of course. The hair of my head sprang erect. There was an instant in which I might have flung myself from the bunk and rushed away to find Charles or someone, anyone warm and living who breathed and spoke! Yet in that fearful instant I made up my mind and stayed where I was, the fierceness of my clutch making my whole body tremble. Eyes shut, I stayed there, in the very position of the dying man, and was as cold as he.

The change was gradual. The petrifaction of fear diminished into unease, then into a greyness of consent. Thus it had been. Thus it was.

There was a moan from somewhere, from Prettiman in his bunk. I let go the eyebolt and turned over on my back. The wounded deckbeam had less to say to me. I shut my eyes.

I did not experience the passage from waking to sleeping. But it seems that at some point before the coming of the light I must have fallen into a kind of sleep or trance or place.

He was saying something. His voice was far away. A familiar voice, choked with sobbing. I could not place the voice but knew I must. Who in the name of God? I was in a place lit by a savage light which leapt and sank, again and again. The voice drew nearer.

"You could have saved us."

The voice was my own voice. I was awake, the flame was leaping and sinking behind the glass of the lantern. I turned it out and lay back, waiting for the dawn.

(6)

When the dawn came I dressed thoughtfully enough. But life must go on and even the sadness of self-knowledge cannot come wholly between a man and his stomach!

The passenger saloon was deserted except for little Pike. He sat under the window, his arms folded on the table, his head on them. I thought he was drunk again but as I entered he looked up, smiled sleepily, then put his head down. So there was another cabin in which people found it difficult to be at ease! I got myself a mug of small ale from Bates—there was nothing else to have—and drank "breakfast" quite in the antique manner. I went back to my hutch and got into my oilskins and seaboots and was about to go into the waist but saw old Mr Brocklebank standing there in the shadow of the larboard main chains. He had usurped my place. I sat in my canvas chair then, all oilskinned as I was, and surveyed my few books on the shelf at the end of the bunk. I remembered Charles and his gift of the slops that I was wearing. I took down the *Iliad*, therefore, and read in book *zeta* the story of Glaucus and Diomede. They had exchanged armour recklessly, it seemed, trading bronze armour for gold. I could not decide whether my determination to see Charles promoted was gold or bronze—certainly his care of me, getting me bathed and changed as if he were my old nurse, was gold in the circumstances! I read on but soon found the words drifting apart. It had been a short and troubled night. I remembered that Charles had told me not to wear my oilskins except to keep myself dry so I put the book back and went out to the waist. Mr Brocklebank had gone. I stayed in the lee of the main chains to allow the wind to freshen me.

Mr Benét came briskly out of the lobby.

"Well, Mr Talbot, we get on!"

"This weather is still too lively to allow you to tamper—I should say to mend, the foremast?"

"For the time being. But the wind moderates. And fortunately the movement does not prevent Coombs from making charcoal."

"Stay, sir. A moment. I have heard that in an emergency masts may be cut away."

"You have been speaking to the first lieutenant!"

"Indeed I have, but he said nothing of that. It is my own idea—cut away the foremast and you save yourself the risk of mending the shoe! I do have occasional ideas, you know."

"I am sure you do, sir. But if we cut away the foremast we should probably have to cut away the mizzenmast to balance things. Nor do masts fall precisely where you mean them to. Imagine the foremast going over the side, still tethered to the ship, and dragging her round so she broached to! We might be overset and swamped in seconds. Bravo, Mr Talbot, but no, sir. That will not do. The moment it is possible we shall crimp the shoe and draw it together. Bite your nails a watch or two longer."

I did not like his tone but there seemed nothing I could do about that. However, we did have interests in common—

Benét was moving away. I hastened after him.

"I had meant to ask you, sir, to explain a certain episode in which you and Lady Somerset and Miss Chumley—"

"Later, Mr Talbot. Oh, this weather! It makes a man want to sing!"

He ran swiftly along the deck and vanished into the fo'castle between one roll and the next. Charles emerged from the lobby. A petty officer and two seamen came with him. He paused when he saw me.

"Well, Edmund?"

"A bad night, I am afraid."

"There is little colour in your face. Are you feeling the motion?"

"No. I have had a bad night, that is all."

"You could return to the wardroom."

I felt myself flushing, for it was evident that he understood something of my "bad night".

"And be laughed at? No."

"In discomfort and danger people are glad of something to laugh at."

"So we are still in danger?"

He turned to the petty officer and gave him an order. The man knuckled his forehead and the little party cantered—doubled, I suppose I should say—along the deck to the fo'castle.

"Yes, Edmund. We are in the same danger as before."

"At least the weather is improving."

"My dear fellow! This is a pause and will give Benét time to tamper with the foremast. I do not like the look of the weather. There is something big up there which will search us out. Well, I must get on."

"Let me come with you."

"No no. You cannot. My rounds are not for you."

He saluted in the naval manner and went forward along the deck. The lifelines were not so much bouncing now as vibrating gently. Charles ignored them.

"Mr Talbot."

I turned. Miss Granham, in slops and seaboots too big for her, was standing in the entry to the lobby.

"Good morning, ma'am. What can I do for you?"

"I wanted to call you to Mr Prettiman. Is the time convenient?"

"To visit him? Of course, ma'am, whenever you wish."

She opened his door a crack, looked in, then shut it again.

"He has fallen asleep again. It is the paregoric. Perhaps—"

She seemed doubtful. But I could see no reason for delay.

"May I not go in and wait?"

"If you wish."

I entered Prettiman's cabin and pulled the door to behind me. The cabin was like all the others, a bunk, a shelf for books, a canvas washbowl with a small mirror over it and, at the other end, a writing flap with the usual accountrements. There was a bucket under the washbowl and a canvas chair before the writing flap. Mr Prettiman had signalled his eccentricity by sleeping the wrong way round—his head was towards the stern, his feet towards the bow. His head was, in consequence, just above the bucket, which may have been his original intention in sleeping that way round. Certainly I had vivid and miserable memories of our first weeks in the ship and the nausea which had overcome me and the other passengers.

Prettiman was so deeply asleep that it was hard to believe he had been awake that morning. The air was thick, as must be the air of all sickrooms, I suppose, since fresh air is so deleterious to a troubled body. Though it was not to be thought that our ladies, accustomed as they must be to the treatment of childish ailments, would leave the sufferer unwashed, there was a distinct odour emanating from the man which made a close approach to him distasteful. I realized with a resigned determination that I was *in for* an unpleasant enough experience. However, I daresay that the hardly describable events of the night had made me a little more aware of my offhand ability to spread destruction! I sat down cautiously, therefore, with a vague feeling that as long as he slept I was doing what Miss Granham required by being present. The odour from his body strove with another which I had no difficulty in identifying as paregoric, or laudanum. No wonder he slept.

The bedclothes were pulled up to his neck. His bald head was dinted into a pillow far softer than the one which had been provided for me. His face above the tawny beard and scanty fringe of hair was very pale. It was a face I had seen often enough comically reddened by passionate anger. This mask of flesh and bone on which his emotions were so often played out for all to see was irregular enough. The tilted nose was as far from his long upper lip as that of a stage Irishman, a *Paddy*. His mouth was wide and firm, so that the lines of determination as well as anger were engraved there. Sickness had wasted his flesh and removed a great deal of the comedy. Those eyes which could glare in all the madness of social bigotry were veiled by dark lids and sunk deep under the frantic eyebrows. It was perhaps possible to laugh at the waking man. But this effigy, stretched as on the slab of a tomb, had nothing of the laughable. Where was ludicrous Prettiman, opinionated, sometimes frantic, indignant beside his unlikely fiancée? But she had suffered a like sea change without the trouble of a fall, a severe spinster, now seen to be handsome, dignified and sensible—and feminine! Why, the man himself—there came a ninth wave in our diminishing weather, for the cabin lurched. That same cry which I had heard when I was awake in the cabin off the wardroom—that cry which had drawn me forth—the anguish—woe—I sprang to my feet. It was not to be borne. I saw myself condemned to sit in this stink and be exacerbated time after time as the man woke and that cry burst out! I seized the door handle—

"Who is it?"

That was a feeble voice behind me. I turned.

"It is Edmund Talbot."

The man was sinking down in stupor again. I was exasperated. And I had said I would wait. Yet only that night I had known, found out what I bore in my hands! I sank down into the canvas chair again. The bedclothing was massed about his middle and hiding the lines of his body there. Lower down, his legs and feet lifted the blankets. The odour of paregoric was more perceptible since his cry. The spirit which had half-awakened in the tormented body had sunk away again into the depths. The eyelids fluttered and were still. The mouth fell open, but this time a sigh was all the sound he made.

I leaned back and surveyed him as he lay in the bunk. Under their lids his eyes moved rapidly from side to side. His breath came unevenly, he panted. I thought his eyes would open but they did not. He muttered in his sleep or swoon. The words dragged out.

"—John Laity for the term of his natural life. Hamilton Moulting Baronet as colonel light dragoons emoluments from clothing—expenses of the returning officer— Mungo FitzHenry master in Chancery for life four thousand and six pounds—"

Good God—it was my cousin and that superb *plum*! What the devil did this man mean by it? I leapt to my feet. I seized the door handle—and felt it turn from the outside. Miss Granham looked in. She whispered:

"Mr Talbot? Not yet awake?"

"No."

That same feeble voice again.

"Letitia? Is that you?"

"It is Mr Talbot come to see you, Aloysius."

"William Collier fourteen years for illegal assembly—"

"It is I, Mr Prettiman, Edmund Talbot. I am told you wish to see me. Well, I am here and waiting."

Behind me Miss Granham closed the door.

"Letitia?"

"Miss Granham has stepped outside. She supposed you wanted to speak to me, though what I have done to deserve such an unexpected honour—"

He was turning his head restlessly and gritting his teeth.
"I am not able to sit up."

"Do not incommode yourself. I am able to stand here and you are able to see me."

"Sit down, boy. Sit down!"

The man intended an order, there was no doubt about that. I wish I could say that I sat to humour a sick man but the truth is my body sat itself down before I was aware of what was happening! A slight movement of the cabin made him grit his teeth again and audibly. His face cleared little by little. I spoke abruptly, annoyed by my involuntary obedience.

"As I said. I am waiting to hear what you want."

"You are aware that Miss Granham and I—"

He was silent again. I did not know whether he was interrupted by some pain or whether he felt a natural embarrassment at raising the subject with a stranger. I thought it best to help the sick man where I could, otherwise this irritating interview would be more and more prolonged.

"I am aware as everyone else in the ship is that the lady has consented to make you the happiest of men. I have already felicitated the lady, I believe. Permit me to congratulate—"

"Don't smother the thing in nonsense!"

"I beg your pardon, sir!"

"She has agreed to marry me."

"That is what I said!"

"*Now, I mean.* Where are your wits?"

"We have no clergymen!"

"Captain Anderson will perform the ceremony. Do you know nothing?"

I was silent. Clearly the shortest way to the end was to listen and not interrupt. Mr Prettiman passed his tongue over his lips, then smacked them.

"Would you like a drink? This water—"

Now he turned his head and looked straight at me, examining my face as I had examined his. A trace of a smile, wintry enough, deepened the creases round his mouth and eyes.

"Unfair, amn't I?"

I grinned, however ruefully, at this sudden turn round.

"You're having a devilish bad time, that's what it is. Anyone—perhaps when the weather is better you could get out—"

"I am dying."

"But, Mr Prettiman! A fracture—"

He shouted aloud.

"Will you abstain from this foolish habit of contradiction? When I say I am dying I mean I am dying and I am going to die!"

The end of this shouted exordium was confused by another cry from the depth of his agony, which I am persuaded that time he inflicted on himself by some forbidden movement. The cry was not only the expression of despairing anguish but of furious resentment.

"Mr Prettiman, I beg of you!"

Once again he lay silent, but perspiration trickled down his face. Behind me the door opened and Miss Granham looked in again. She stepped over the sill, reached under his pillow, took out a handkerchief and wiped his face. A smile returned to it. In a far softer voice than he had used to me he murmured, "Thank you, thank you."

As Miss Granham was withdrawing he spoke again.

"Letty, there is no need for you to stand on guard. I am well enough and the dose still gives me some relief. Please return to your cabin and try to sleep. I am sure you need to. It frets me to think of you keeping yourself awake for my sake."

She glanced at me, then smiled at him, nodded and closed the door behind her.

"Mr Talbot, I wish you to be a witness."

"I?"

"You and Oldmeadow. To the ceremony—the marriage."

"That is ridiculous! We have no official standing in the ship! Charles Summers, on the other hand, or Mr Cumbershum—I will give the bride away if you wish or—why anything!"

"You are not needed to give the bride away. Mr East will do that."

"Mr *East*? The *printer*?"

"Will you listen? Or do you propose to prolong this interview indefinitely?"

There were many replies I could have made to that remark but in choosing the best I missed the opportunity. He had closed his eyes and now went on speaking.

"The officers of the ship will be distributed round the world. Who knows where they will go? In any case, they are at risk. Certainly this old ship will carry them no farther. You and Oldmeadow will remain at Sydney Cove. Do you not understand, Mr Talbot? Modest as it may be, Miss Granham will inherit my fortune. But without unimpeachable witnesses and at a distance of eighteen thousand miles from our courts, corrupt as they are—"

"No, they are not! That is outrageous! British justice—"

His eyes had snapped open.

"I say they are! Oh, in respect of money you may rely on them, but they are corrupt in all else by privilege, by land tenure, by a viciously inadequate system of representation—"

All this had been uttered on a rising note. But as if the man knew how close to him was the angel of the agony he lowered his voice suddenly in a way which might have seemed comic to me only a few minutes before.

"I need not go into all that, Talbot. After all, I am talking to a representative of—well, there. To resume: you and Oldmeadow will be guarantors of her inheritance by virtue of your position as witnesses of the marriage."

"I shall be happy to serve the lady in any way I am able—" It came to me, as I said that, that it was true! "Yes indeed, sir. But I trust it may be many years before—"

The trace of hectic had appeared in his cheeks.

"Do not talk nonsense! I have not many days or perhaps hours left."

"The banns—"

"They may be omitted in these circumstances. Let that be an end of the matter."

We were silent for a while. Then he stirred restlessly. I had half-risen from my seat but he held up his hand.

"I have not finished. I do not care to ask for favours. But now—"

"You may, sir. For the lady's sake."

"Mr Summers told me that you claimed at least to believe in 'fair play'. The phrase is juvenile—"

"The phrase is a good phrase, Mr Prettiman. What is 'fair play' in the slang of schoolboys is 'justice' among adults."

"You believe in justice."

There was another pause. I glanced at the shelf of books above his head. They were severe.

"I am an Englishman."

"Miss Granham has reported favourably on your progress—"

"My what?"

"I do not know how civilized the *mores* of a colony may be but I suspect the worst. I fear civilization may be sadly to seek. I ask you to see that the lady is treated as she should be in a civilized society."

"I would count her friendship a privilege, sir. I give you my word I will use every endeavour to protect her."

He smiled wearily, for his strength was ebbing.

"There are many ways in which she does not need protection. But in some things a lady by the unfairness of Nature will always be at a disadvantage. I believe the colony may not yet have accustomed itself to the proper attitude to the female nature."

"I do not know."

"One other matter."

I waited for some time but he was silent.

"Another matter, sir?"

He said nothing but seemed in some discomfort.

"May I not move you to a more comfortable position, sir? This mass of bedclothes round your waist—"

He was moving his head restlessly on the pillow.

"It is not a mass of bedclothing but a gross swelling of the lower abdomen and the upper part of the lower limbs."

"Good God! Good God!"

"Must every other sentence commence with an imprecation? You cannot move me. To move my body even for the most necessary purposes is a torture which is wearing me out and down, down and away."

He was silent again for a while. Then—

"This other matter. It is confidential. I have searched my conscience and believe that what I do is right. Come close."

I took my staying hand off the bulkhead and hitched the canvas chair to the bunk. I leaned my head down to his. The odour of the bunk and his body was quite plainly unpleasant. Was this the awful beginnings of decay? I was not well informed in the matter.

"I have a paper for you."

"Oh?"

"It is a paper signed by me. You see what a case I am in, helpless and dying. People will contest the will—there are always such, relatives so distant they have never before made themselves known. They might well bring a case that the marriage was not—could not—be consummated, that it was void and consequently the lady entitled to nothing."

There ensued a long pause.

"I do not follow what I am to do, Mr Prettiman."

He seemed in much discomfort.

"I have written a plain declaration that I have had carnal knowledge of the lady during the voyage and before the marriage."

"Good—"

"You were about to say, sir?"

"Nothing. Nothing."

His voice was a shout.

"Do you think, boy, that a superstitious rite such as a wedding ceremony means anything to such people as I and she are?"

My mouth was opened to speak, though I do not know what I should have said. For his anger was such that he had hurt himself all over again. He positively howled with pain, as if he were being punished for his blasphemy! I find the recollection amusing enough. For I did not believe in any of the superstitious rites myself and regarded them as serving to keep order. Christening, marrying and burying—they are the marks which distinguish men from beasts, that is all.

But the man was recovering.

"There is a green leather case in the upper drawer. Give it to me, if you please."

I did so. He held it to his chest, took out a folded and sealed paper which he held up close to his eyes.

"Yes. This is it."

"Why is the paper necessary? I could as easily stand before a court and swear that you had told me how matters stood between you and the lady."

"I do not trust them—that is all."

It was on the tip of my tongue to speak like a moralist! I felt like saying with all the force at the command of a member of the society which he despised—"You should have thought of that before!" Or—"The superstitious rites are then of some value, sir!" But I did not. This was all the odder, since I felt myself more and more out of sympathy with him and her—with her in particular. A lady, and one whom I had held in some esteem to behave so, like a drab! I did not know whether to laugh or what to do. She was provoking. It was very sad. Her—lapse made me sad and angry.

"I believe, Mr Prettiman, we have no more to say to each other. I presume I shall be told when the superstitious rite is to take place?"

He turned his head and looked at me in what seemed to be surprise.

"Of course!"

I put the green leather case back in the drawer and stood up.

"I agree to guard this paper and produce it in the circumstances which you envisage. I have no desire to read it."

"Thank you."

My bow was hampered. I had not got the door open when he spoke again.

"Mr Talbot."

"Sir?"

"Miss Granham is unaware of the existence of this paper. I wish her to remain so for as long as possible."

I bowed again and stumbled out of that fetid hutch.

(7)

I found myself standing by the entry to the waist and staring at the tattered garment which Mr Brocklebank had drawn round him. I could not tell how I came to be there. The wind was cold and searched me out even through my seaman's clothing.

There was something particularly disgusting about this furtive, middle-aged sexual congress! He might well be fifty years old, and she—

"Filthy, beastly, lecherous!"

Apparently the old man did not hear but was deep in some contemplation which must have been melancholy, to judge from his expression. I began to reason with myself. Why should I care? I looked at the sealed note in my hand. That, at least, contemptible as I thought it to be, was a duty. I took it to my cabin, wrenched the door open and slammed it behind me. I thrust the document into my bottom drawer, then flung myself into my canvas chair with a force which, had I any of Mr Brocklebank's substance, would have split it completely.

There was a knock at the door.

"Come in."

It was Charles Summers.

"Have you a moment to spare?"

"Of course. Will you sit here? On the bunk if you like. I am sorry Phillips has not yet put the clothes together. Everything is so dirty, so foul, so vile! Oh, I am so tired of this voyage! So much water! I wish I could walk on it. Oh, sorry, sorry! Well, what can I do for you?"

He sat down gingerly among the rumpled bed-clothes.

"I have a proposal to make. Should you care to be a midshipman?"

"Are you serious?"

"Half, shall we say. Let me explain. With only two other lieutenants, Cumbershum and Benét, and one warrant officer capable of discharging the same duties as they do—I mean Mr Smiles, the sailing master—"

"I have never understood his position."

"He is something of an—anomaly, would it be? He is the last of his kind, warranted by the Admiralty at a time when navigation was coming more and more into the hands of the King's officers. But he is only the third. Mr Askew will stand a watch occasionally. Now if I take a watch myself we can divide the watch-keeping between five and so benefit everyone—"

"Except you! Good Heavens, you spend all your time going about the ship! When do you sleep? I am sure your ceaseless activity cannot be necessary."

"You are wrong, you know. Is there not a saying among farmers that the best dung is the farmer's foot? But to resume: if I stand the middle, which by now you must know is—"

"—midnight until four o'clock in the morning."

"Just so. An officer of the watch has a doggy. Would you care to stand that watch with me as midshipman?"

"Should you leave me in charge?"

"You would do better than poor young Willis. Well. Do you agree?"

"Indeed I do. But you have added four hours to your duties! It is too much. For all that you have cheered me immensely!"

"Why do you need cheering? Is it our dangers?"

"Oh, that! No. I have—been told things. There is a young lady in whom I—It had seemed that she knew more of a criminal connection than she should and—Today someone said something which has raised the matter in my mind with much pain—so. When do we start?"

"I will get the quartermaster to give you a shake at a quarter to twelve."

"To stand a watch! Will you give me responsibilities?"

"I might put you in charge of the traverse board."

"Really, I have not felt so excited since I left home! 'Mr Speaker. To those of us who have actually stood the middle in one of His Majesty's ships of the line—' "

"Suppose when on watch you commit some awful error? 'Mr Speaker. To those of us who have actually been mastheaded in one of His Majesty's ships of the line—' "

"I can see you are an awful tyrant when roused."

"Indeed."

"By the way, how is Coombs getting on with the charcoal?"

"They have enough. Captain Anderson is only waiting for the sea to moderate a little more and he will give the order for the shoe to be mended."

"I must see this foremast with its shoe."

"Now you will go wandering where you should not. Do you want a direct order?"

"That would tempt me. But do you expect the weather to moderate even further?"

"Yes. Now. During the day I recommend that you get at least four hours' sleep to make up for what you are going to lose during the night. In fact, I believe I shall make that an order."

"Aye aye, sir!"

He nodded, and went away. I sat for a while and was ridiculously excited. The prospect was like that of childhood, when the idea of *staying up all night* has a mysterious attraction about it—the experiencing of how one day actually changes into another. There was something—

adult about it! There was an invitation to the world of men who are doing this strange thing not as a dare or discovery but because it is their duty. They are masters of the dark hours. It has about it something of the attraction of a secret society! Indeed, my main problem at the time seemed to be how to find occupation for myself between then and midnight. I ate a meal and heard from Bates all about the short commons to which we should soon be reduced. I smiled icily at Miss Granham in the lobby but she did not appear to notice. I "got my head down" since I was now a probationary seaman, as it were, with a prescriptive right to the language of the sea, and passed as much as two hours asleep of the four which Charles had stipulated. I settled down to write letters. I tried to compose one to Miss Chumley, the very sight of whom had turned my world and my future upside down, but could not say what I meant. For I could not say in so many words, "Are you corrupted?" Every time that lovely and innocent image came before the eyes of my heart, they refused to see what loathsome conjunction I tried to put before them. Besides, what was the use? There was no guarantee that the letter would ever be delivered. I abandoned the attempt, therefore, thought of writing verses instead, thought of Mr Benét's verses, thought of Glaucus and Diomede, looked through my books, found the spine of *Meditations among the Tombs* was cracked and wondered how it had happened. I read the *Iliad* until my eyes were heavy. Stretched out in my bunk, I fell asleep again, and woke only when a voice spoke in my ear and the quartermaster shook me. The lamp was low and I turned it down to the veriest bud—then went out.

The ship was a ghost, a spirit of silver and ivory. Before me the pool of the waist was full of light to be waded through. I went out, and as I turned to go up the ladders the waxing moon blazed in my face. The sails were unbearable, their whiteness seeming to invade the very apple of the eyes. I climbed up and was overtaken by men trotting aft to stand at the wheel or as messengers with the officers of the watch. Charles came up the ladder and took over formally from Mr Cumbershum. The ship's bell rang eight times.

"Mr Midshipman Talbot reporting for duty, sir."

"It is good to have you here, Edmund. We might read by this light, don't you think?"

"Easily. All the lanterns are out."

"The central lantern is out, the quarter lanterns turned down as far as possible. We must conserve oil, as we must conserve so many things."

I did not know what to say to this, for, as the illegal possessor and nominal purchaser of an oil lamp which at that moment was burning in my cabin, I felt the subject to be a delicate one.

"Where are we?"

"You mean our position? I wish I could tell you! We know our latitude if that is any comfort. It is all Columbus ever knew."

"The longitude?"

"The chronometers—I beg you will keep this to yourself—can no longer be trusted. After this length of time the accumulation of their rates is ridiculous. Besides, water has been clean over them."

"Did you not bring them up one deck?"

I thought Charles seemed a trifle uncomfortable at the memory.

"I—we—it might have been the thing to do. But it might have made matters worse. As far as the longitude is concerned we must consider it to be what you might call 'assisted dead reckoning'."

"With the accent on the 'dead'!"

He thrust out a hand and grasped the rail—then snatched his hand away as if the wood had been hot.

"I should not have done that! In a grown man it is a vile superstition!"

"My dear fellow, you are too scrupulous. If touching wood is any comfort, why not touch wood, say I!"

"Well, there it is. Navigation is still an inexact art, though it may be improved. I cannot think how, though."

"Could not the Admiralty co-opt Mr Benét? Or examine the works of Dean Swift a little more closely?"

"I do not know what Dean Swift has to do with navigation. As for Mr Benét, you are only too right. He believes he can find our longitude without relying on our three damp chronometers!"

"We are lost then!"

"No, no. We are somewhere in an area about ten miles broad and fifty miles long."

"I call that being lost!"

"Well, you would. You are just like me when I was first a midshipman and felt my foot was on the rung of however short a ladder—for to be a lieutenant at that time seemed to me a notable achievement—"

"So it is, so it is."

"My seamanship was learnt already, for there was little about the management of a ship I did not know. I am not boasting."

"It is what Mr Gibbs told me the other day. 'A son of a gun, every hair a rope yarn, every tooth a marline spike, every finger a fishhook and his blood Stockholm tar!' "

Charles laughed aloud.

"Hardly that! But I knew nothing of the theoretical and computational aspect of navigation. One morning the first lieutenant appeared with his own sextant. Mr Bellows, he was. We were in Plymouth Sound—this was before they built the breakwater, so we had a clear horizon to the south. Mr Bellows showed me how to handle the instrument. When he had done he said, 'Now, Mr Summers.

Oblige me by using this sextant to find out where we are by the time of local midday.' 'Why, Mr Bellows,' said I, thinking he was having a game with me, 'we are in Plymouth Sound.' 'Prove it,' he said. 'There's this sextant, chronometers in the hold and Mr Smith will be kind enough to lend you his pocket watch.' 'But, Mr Bellows, sir,' I said, 'we're at anchor!' 'You heard me,' he said and went away."

"You are remembering word for word!"

"Indeed it is written on my heart. You cannot think with what careful hands I held that precious instrument— no, Edmund, you cannot! It was not just a sextant. It was—I do not know how to say what I mean."

"Believe me, I understand you."

"I wonder. I am sure you try. But I took the height of the sun—oh, dozens of times, I think, both sides of midday. I am not a *tremulous* character, Edmund—"

"No indeed!"

"I believe I am rather stolid, in fact. But as the measurements increased then decreased, I really found it difficult to stop myself—crying, trembling, my teeth chattering or myself laughing out loud with whatever it was—No, you cannot possibly understand."

"You had found your vocation."

"There I was, picture me, taking the sun's height again and again and young Smith noting down the time of each shot by his pocket watch—seconds first, then minutes, then the hour: and after that, the angle—seconds, minutes, degrees. Then I—Why labour it? I searched through Norie's *Epitome of Navigation*. I revere that book next to the Bible, I believe."

"I am all at sea in every way."

"So I worked out our position, and yes, it was in Plymouth Sound! I laid it off on the chart—crossed lines, each about a tenth of an inch long and a circle drawn through them by means of the finest pencil in the ship. When Mr Bellows came aboard again I jumped out of the sailing master's cabin, stood to attention and saluted. 'If you please, Mr Bellows, I have worked out our position by means of the sextant, the chronometers and Norie.' 'Let me see,' said he, ducking into the cabin where the chart was spread out on the table. 'Lord, Mr Summers, have you a microscope? This is hardly visible to the naked eye. Spectacles will have to do, I suppose.' He put on his spectacles and had another look. 'That will be our quarter-deck,' he said. 'I shouldn't be surprised if you haven't nailed this cabin. Was you on the roof when you took the sight?' 'No, sir,' I said.

"Then he felt through his pockets and fished out a stub of pencil as thick as his thumb. He held it more like a dagger than anything. He scrawled a huge circle round my 'position'. 'Now,' he said, 'I think we can say we aren't up on Dartmoor nor more than five miles outside the Eddystone Rocks, but where we are inside that circle the Lord Himself only knows.' "

"He was unkind."

Charles laughed.

"Oh no. It was a lesson I did not like but I came to value it. I have passed the lesson on to young Tommy Taylor who stands in need of it and imagines we know latitude to the width of a plank, though otherwise he is your true 'Son of a Gun' and will do better than any of us in the service."

"The lesson stressed the necessity for caution, I suppose."

"Just so. And I have seldom found circumstances in the service where caution did not enable me to detect the correct line of duty."

"That is why you do not want the foremast restored to use?"

"But I do want it restored! And if the wind fell away little by little to a flat calm—"

"Why little by little?"

"A sudden fall leaves a wild sea with no means of managing a ship in it. That would be no time for tampering with the shoring and staying of the mast."

"This moonlight—one could bath in it—swim in it. Was there ever anything as beautiful? Nature is trying to seduce us into Belief in every possible way, into every possible philosophical anodyne."

"I do not know the word."

"When am I to learn celestial navigation?"

"That will have to wait, I am afraid."

"I will study it ashore. But then I should have no horizon. Well—I will ride down to the sea."

"You need not. You may take altitudes by measuring the angle between, let us say, the sun and its reflection in a bath of mercury."

"And halve the angle! How ingenious!"

"You saw all that at once?"

"Why, it is obvious."

"Young Willis does not find that sort of thing obvious, nor young Taylor, come to that."

"Mr Benét, of course, would hardly need a sextant. He would use dead reckoning or build a mercury bath into it."

"There is nothing wrong with dead reckoning if you know what you are doing. Mr Bellows could talk like a book when he wanted to and he had a sentence for that. He made me write it down in my log and learn it by heart. 'More seamen have been surprised by the accuracy of dead reckoning than have ever been disconcerted by its imprecision.' "

"He could indeed speak like a book!"

We were interrupted by the necessity of having the log cast. This was done every hour and it became my duty solemnly to lift the canvas cover of the traverse board and write in the result. But now I took great interest in the process, though it soon became so habitual as to be unnoticeable. It was followed this first time by a long silence while neither of us felt any need to speak. Occasionally wide clouds obscured the moon but they were fleecy round the edges and gave us almost as much light as from the round of moon itself. I climbed to the poop and stared at our gentle wake. That "body", which I had seen so laboriously carried up to the quarterdeck, now lay triced to the rail on the starboard quarter. A rope was attached to it—two ropes, in fact: and they led over the taffrail and down under the stern. Of course! One was the rope in the office of necessity—the other opposite—it was very mysterious. Suddenly our gentle wake burst into a splendour of diamonds. The moon was gliding out from the farther edge of a cloud. I turned back and went down to the quarterdeck where Charles stood by the stairs up to the poop. I was about to question him when I was interrupted.

"Charles—what was that?"

"It is the duty watch."

"Singing?"

They were visible, not sheltering now under the rail or to leeward of a mast but grouped at the capstan on the fo'castle. They were leaning against it. The music—for such it was, harmony and all—drifted about us, gentle as the wake and the wind, magic as the moonlight. I went forward to the rail of the quarterdeck and leaned over it, listening. As if they had seen and were glad of an audience they seemed to turn—or at least I had the impression of many moon-blanched faces looking my way—and the volume of sound increased.

"What is it, Edmund?"

Charles had come and stood beside me.

"The music!"

"Just the duty watch."

They were silent. Someone had emerged from the

fo'castle and was speaking to them. Evidently the concert was over. But there were still the moon and stars and the glitter of the sea.

"How awesome to think that we actually use all that up there—make use of the stars and refer to the sun as habitually as to a signpost!"

Charles spoke hesitantly and, it seemed, a little shyly.

"No man can contemplate it without being put in mind of his Maker."

A cloud was swallowing the moon again. The water and the ship were dulled.

"The concept is naïve surely. When I consult my repeater I do not *invariably* think of the man who made it!"

He looked round at me. He wore a mask of moonlight as I suppose I did. He spoke with due solemnity.

"When I consider the heavens the work of Thy fingers, the moon and stars which Thou hast ordained—"

"But that is poetry! Milton could do no better!"

"The psalms are prose, surely."

"Yet why should putting something into poetry make it truer than if it was in figures, as in your Mr Norie?"

"You are too clever for me, Edmund."

"I did not mean to be—oh, what a gross impertinence! Forgive me!"

"Was I insulted? I did not feel it. There is a difference between the sky and a pocket watch."

"Yes, yes. That is true. I was making a debating point which I suppose is one of the more detestable results of a gentleman's education. Poetry itself is a mystery—so is prose—so is everything—I used to think of poetry as an entertainment. It is more, far more. Oh, Charles, Charles, I am so deeply, so desperately, so deeply, deeply in love!"

(8)

Charles Summers was silent. The masks of moonlight which were hiding our faces made the night-time confession inevitable. It had burst from me without my volition.

"You say nothing, Charles. Have I annoyed you? I beg your pardon for mixing what must seem a trivial matter in all this going on round us—mixing it too into talk of the religion which is your deepest concern. In fact I do not know why you should be so kind as to listen to me. But so you are."

The first lieutenant went to the wheel and talked with the men there. He stared long into the binnacle. I wondered if anything was wrong, but after a few minutes he came back to me slowly.

"It is the young lady you met aboard *Alcyone*."

"Who else could it be?"

He seemed to brood. Then—

"Who else indeed? I have no doubt she is as virtuous as lovely—"

"Do not make virtue sound so elderly! But is it to be joy or wormwood?"

"I do not understand."

"A certain person engaged in, in fornication with a certain woman—She, Marion Chumley, stood guard, must have consented, must have seen, must have been a part of—Oh, it squeezes my heart to think of it!"

"You cannot mean—"

"If she took however passive a part she is wholly unlike the person I saw, met, talked with. And on top of that I am bound for Sydney Cove and she for Calcutta! The world could hardly thrust people farther apart. You cannot know what it is like."

"I know the young lady, at all events. I saw her. You remember how, since I do not dance, I elected to take the watch for the period of the entertainment and ball? I saw you dancing together."

"Well?"

"What do you expect me to say?"

"I do not know."

"I saw her next day too, early. She had come to the starboard quarter of *Alcyone* and was staring through the side of our ship as if she could see what was going on inside. You were inside, unconscious or delirious. She was wondering about you."

"How do you know?"

"Who else?"

"Benét?"

He made a dismissive gesture.

"Not in a thousand years."

"Who told you?"

"No one. I know, you see."

"Oh, you are making up speeches to comfort me!"

There was a smile, as it were, in Charles's voice.

"This, then, is the young lady 'perhaps ten or twelve years younger than myself, a lady of family, wealth—' "

"Did I say so? Before I met her it is certainly how I used to think in my nasty, calculating way. You must despise me."

"No."

He walked to the rail and stood for a while, looking over the side. At last he came back and leaned against the break of the poop.

"The moon is going down."

There was singing again from the fo'castle, very soft. I spoke too, but as softly.

"You know, however long I live I shall remember the middle watch. I shall think of it as a kind of—island—out of this world—made of moonlight—a time for confidences when men can say to a—transmuted face what they would never bring out in the daytime."

He was silent again.

"Think, Charles, had Deverel not slipped below for a drink we should not have lost our topmasts and she would have spent her life in ignorance of me!"

He laughed abruptly.

"You would have been ignorant of each other! There I saw a glimpse of the old 'Lord Talbot'."

"Are you puckering up there in the shadow of the poop? But it makes no sense. We might have met conveniently in a drawing room. Instead of which—Will she lapse once more into that dream of girlhood until some other—Oh no, it cannot be!"

"She will not forget you."

"It is good of you to say so."

"No. I understand women."

It made me laugh.

"Do you say so indeed? How can that be? You are a proper old tarry breeks, a son of a gun, a man master of an honourable profession and skilled in the way of a ship!"

"Ships are feminine, you know. But I understand women. I understand their passivity, gentleness, receiving impressions as in wax—most of all their passionate need to give—"

"Miss Granham, Mrs Brocklebank! And are there not bluestockings? This is no character of a female wit!"

He was silent for a while, then spoke heavily enough, as though I had defeated him in argument and dispirited him.

"I suppose not."

He walked away and presently the quarterdeck was concerned once more with casting the log.

"Five and a half knots, Edmund. Write it in."

"When I look back on this voyage—if I am alive to do so—I shall think that for all the danger there were compensations."

"Whatever they were, they have got you through the middle or nearly."

"Why so brusque?"

But he had turned away and was plainly more interested for the moment in the ship's affairs than mine. A pipe was shrilling and men were moving here and there. The next watch was falling in just aft of the break of the fo'castle. Mr Smiles, the sailing master, appeared with Mr Tommy Taylor who was yawning like a cat. Smiles and Charles performed their ritual exchange. The duty watch fell out and dispersed to the wheel, the quarterdeck and positions throughout the upper deck. The off-duty watch was now drifting away to disappear into the fo'castle. In the belfry on the fo'castle the ship's bell rang eight times in four groups of two.

Charles came back to me.

"Well, Mr Midshipman Talbot, you may go off duty until midnight tomorrow."

"Good night then, or good morning. I shall remember this watch for the rest of my life—fifty years or more!"

He laughed.

"Say that after you have stood a year or two of them!"

But I was right, not he.

So I went off watch, suddenly overcome with sleepiness at four o'clock in the morning and yawning like Mr Taylor. I opened the door of my hutch and found that the lantern had burned or blown out. But I seemed still to be in conversation with Charles. I got my oilskins and seaboots off somehow in the moonless hutch, tumbled into

my bunk, struck some eyebolt or other and cursed it sleepily. Nothing could keep me from falling into a dreamless
sleep.

* * *

It was many days before I in my ignorance realized what
had happened. Charles in his care of me had taken on the
burden of the middle watch partly, perhaps, to relieve the
other officers, but mainly, I am convinced, to spare me
the dark hours of that dreadful cabin! It was just like his
provision of dry clothing for me. The extraordinary fellow,
where he felt himself esteemed, responded with such generosity, such warm and manly thoughtfulness as I had not
experienced since the days of Old Dobbie or even earlier!
It was in him, so to say, a pedestrian care which contrived
much out of small things. It was a kind of science or study
of domestic donation, trifles set aside, saved, little schemes,
manoeuvres, which he would not for the world have known
to others but which must at last come to be understood by
the caring recipient. It was an odd trait in a fighting sailor,
I thought—yet not so strange when you think of the greater
part of his career as a ship's husband, who is a man either
shopkeeper and agent for the "domestic" care of a ship
in port, or the ship's officer most responsible for and
attending to her internal economy!

So I slept and the moon set and the sun came up, though
not in my dark hutch. I was positively shaken awake
by Phillips. He would not let me go back to sleep but
continued to shake me.

"Go away, man. Let me be."

"Sir! Wake up, sir!"

"What the devil is the matter with you?"

"You got to get up, sir. The captain wants you."

"What for?"

"They're getting married this morning."

A marriage at sea! For sure the idea does at once summon a variety of comments and did so in our ship, I believe. Comments! They had been varied enough at the engagement! But now—Had the reader himself received nothing but the merest intelligence of the fact, his first thought might be "Couldn't they wait?" His next would be the converse, "Oh, so they couldn't wait!" But the whole ship knew much more than the mere fact. They knew that a man (respected *forrard*!) was dying. His reason for marrying could not be one for jesting comment. But aft, opinions on the man I discovered to be neutral or a little on his side. Then again, the lady he was marrying had literally undergone a sea change. Miss Granham, brought up in circumstances which some would consider easy, had, by the death of Canon Granham, been forced to school herself into the behaviour and appearance of a governess, no more. Unexpectedly presented with the prospect of an alliance with a man of even easier circumstances than those of a canon of the Church of England, she had divested herself of both the appearance and the behaviour of a governess as quickly as she could. Or am I so certain where the behaviour is concerned? I believe she was by nature a woman of great dignity, intelligence and—austerity. She had also, as I was beginning to discover, a certain warmth, as unexpected as welcome. Given all this, that she had submitted to the man's astonishing advances wounded me more than I could understand! I believe she had been the first lady to present me with a proper view of the dignity possible to the sex and I was—disappointed. Oh, that young man! However, there could be little about the marriage for rejoicing. It might well call forth those tears which lesser females are ever ready to shed.

I will report what I can of the event. For sure it must be a report like Captain Cook's, though the participants were white people rather than black savages, and some of them were gentlefolk. It was as if the whole ship was determined to exhibit at least a little of human nature in the raw—its innate superstition, its ceremoniousness, its joy when forced by the necessity of procreation to celebrate the animal in man!

Let me be precise. There is rather more here of the woman than the man. Miss Granham was visited early by Mrs East, Mrs Pike and Mrs Brocklebank. I am told that she had had to be persuaded out of her seaman's rig, her slops. The whole female section of our company was determined that she should be properly dressed for the sacrifice! Yet this was make-believe! The man was dying and—though they did not know it—the sacrifice had already—but that is complicated. In any case there was an outbreak of the warm remark, the *risqué*, even the downright salacious, and some drinking to go with it, as is customary on these occasions. Inevitably it was young Mr Tommy Taylor who went far beyond what was proper, even at a wedding. For looking forward to an hypothetical, an impossible honeymoon, he remarked in a voice breathless and split with his usual hyaena laughter—I call it usual, but as the months passed it seemed to me that the boy began to disappear and the "hyaena" become customary—I have lost myself. He remarked, and in the presence of at least one lady, that Miss Granham was about to resemble an admiral's handrope. When rashly asked what the similarity was, he replied that the lady was about to be "wormed, parcelled and served". In sheer disgust I took it on myself to give him a clout over the head which must have made that organ ring and did, I was glad to see, leave him with his eyes crossed for as much as a minute.

The congregation which assembled in the lobby was gallant and pathetic. A procession of emigrants emerged the wrong, the way forbidden to them, up the ladder from the gundeck to the passenger lobby. They mixed, uninvited, with the passengers—Mr Brocklebank wearing a stock of pink material and divested of his coach cloak! The men wore favours, some, I thought, dating back to the "entertainment". The women had made efforts and were neat in costume if nothing more. Naturally enough, I changed into the appropriate costume. Bowles and Oldmeadow had never been out of it. Little Mr Pike was not to be seen. There was much chattering and laughter.

Now the most extraordinary change occurred, as if "Heaven smiled" on the ceremony! For there came a new noise altogether. The watch on deck was dragging the canvas cover and then the planking off the skylight. The gloom of the lobby was changed so that for a time we were in the same kind of modified daylight as you would find in some ancient village church. I am sure the change caused as many tears as smiles, this reminder of distant places.

Six bells rang in the forenoon watch. The canvas chair was bundled out of Prettiman's cabin. The noise of assembly diminished suddenly. Captain Anderson appeared, glum as ever, if not indeed more so. Benét followed him, carrying under his arm a large brown-covered volume which I supposed rightly to be the ship's log. The captain wore the rather splendid uniform in which he had dined in *Alcyone*. I had a mental picture of Mr Benét (the image of a flag lieutenant) murmuring to him, "*I think, sir, it would be appropriate if you was to wear your number ones.*" Well, for sure, Benét was wearing his and meditating, it might be, a polite, poetical tribute to the bride. The groom, of course, remained helplessly in his bed. Captain Anderson went into Prettiman's hutch.

Miss Granham appeared. There was a gasp and a murmur, then silence again. Miss Granham wore white! The dress may have been hers, of course I cannot tell. But the veil which concealed her was one which Mrs Brocklebank had worn to protect her complexion. Of that I am sure, for it had provided a provoking concealment. Behind Miss Granham and from her hutch—how had they managed to cram themselves in?—came Mrs East, Mrs Pike and Mrs Brocklebank. The bride moved the few feet from her hutch to the bridegroom's with a certain stately grace, not diminished by the fact that she kept a cautious hand near the rail. As she passed, the women curtsied or bobbed, the men bowed or knuckled their foreheads. Miss Granham stepped over the threshold and entered her fiancé's cabin. Benét stood outside. I and Oldmeadow pushed our way to the door. Benét was contemplating Miss Granham's back in a kind of trance. I plucked him by the sleeve.

"We are the witnesses. Oblige us by stepping back."

Benét obeyed at last and a murmur rose from the crowd and passed away. Miss Granham was standing by the bunk, level with Prettiman's shoulders, and all at once a simple idea occurred to me—so simple that it seemed no one had thought of it. Prettiman lay with his head to the stern!

Miss Granham put back her veil. It is, I think, unusual for the bride to face the congregation—but then, everything was unusual. Her face was pink—with embarrassment, I suppose. The colour did not look like fard.

I now have to report on a series of shocks which Edmund Talbot experienced. To begin with, after she had put back her veil, the bride shook her head. This set her earrings in motion. They were garnets. I had last seen them ornamenting the ears of Zenobia Brocklebank during that graceless episode when I had had to do with her. I remembered them distinctly, their little chains flying about Zenobia's ears in the extremity of her passion! This was disconcerting; but I have to own, and it may have been the influence of the general air of lawful lubricity, that I found the fact flattering.

Miss Granham carried a bouquet. She did not know

what to do with it, for she had no bridesmaids and the only publicly *plausible* recipient was Miss Brocklebank, now declining in her cabin. The bouquet was not made of cloth as were the favours which some of the congregation wore. It consisted of real flowers and greenery! I know that. For in the absence of a bridesmaid, the bride looked round her, then thrust out her arm at me and forced the bunch into my hands! All the world knows what will happen to the lucky girl who gets the bouquet, and there was an exclamation from Oldmeadow, then a howl of laughter from the congregation. At once my face was far redder than Miss Granham's. I clutched the thing and felt the softness and coolness of real leaves and flowers. They were, they must have been, from Captain Anderson's private paradise! Benét must have induced the sacrifice. "*I think, sir, the whole ship would be gratified if you was to honour the lady with a flower or two from your garden!*"

The next and last shock was delivered by the captain to everyone who heard it. He raised his prayer book, cleared his throat and began.

"Man that is born of woman—"

Good God, it was the burial service! Miss Granham, that intelligent lady, went from pink to white. I do not know what I did but the next time I looked at my bouquet it was sadly damaged. If any words followed this awful mistake I never heard them in the shrieks and giggles of hysteria which were followed by a rustle as our Irish contingent crossed themselves over and over again. Benét took a step past me and I had to haul him back. Captain Anderson fumbled with his book, which he had opened so thoughtlessly or which had opened itself at the fatal page, and now he dropped it, picked it up and fumbled again. Even his hands, accustomed to all emergencies and dangers, were trembling. The roots of our nature were exposed and we were afraid.

His voice was firm and furious.

"Dearly beloved—"

The service had been taken flat aback and was some time in returning to an even keel. Mr East, muttering what may have been an apology, pushed in past me and Anderson and placed the bride's hand in his. Benét was trying to get in and I held him back, but he hissed at me:

"I have the ring!"

So the thing was done. Did I detect a faint trace of scorn in the bride's face as she found herself literally being handed over? Perhaps I imagined it. Everyone held their peace as far as possible. No objections having been raised, this spinster and this bachelor were now both of them cleared for the business of the world and might do with each other what they would or could. Anderson neither congratulated the groom nor felicitated the bride. There was a sense, I suppose, in which such an omission was proper, seeing how little joy the two had to expect of the marriage. However, he leaned down over the writing flap and fiddled with documents. He opened the ship's log, signed papers on the opened page, then held the book open over the sick man. Prettiman had a sad job of signing his name upside down. Miss Granham, not according to custom, signed her new name, Letitia Prettiman, firmly and legibly. I signed, Oldmeadow signed. The captain presented her "lines" to the bride rather as if he had been giving a receipt. He grunted at Prettiman, nodded round, and left with the ship's log which I have no doubt he felt had been rendered a little ridiculous by the unusual entry.

We had now to complete our business. I felicitated Mrs Prettiman in a low voice and touched Prettiman's hand. It was cold. Rivulets of perspiration coursed past his closed eyes. When I remembered my great idea to improve his situation I opened my mouth to explain it. But a hearty shove from behind told me that I was in the way of Benét and Oldmeadow crowding forward. I turned resentfully, hoping for a quarrel, though it is difficult to understand why. The congregation were trying to crowd in and I had some difficulty in getting away from the bunk. The people had no knowledge of the proprieties and seemed to desire only to press the dying man's hand. Indeed, the first one tried to kiss it but was prevented by a faint rebuke from him.

"No, no, my good fellow! We are all equal!"

I squirmed away. I needed air. I had the crushed bunch of leaves and flowers in my hand. One flower was strangely foreign—what they call an orchid, I think. I got into the open air to throw the thing away but could not. Phillips, my servant, was coming from Prettiman's hutch.

"Phillips. Put these in water. Then leave them in Miss—Mrs Prettiman's cabin."

He opened his mouth, probably to object, but I went past him into my cabin and shut the door. I changed back into my seaman's rig, then sat at the writing flap. I could not think what I was doing there. I leaned my head on it for a while, then reached out for a book, leafed it and put it back. I lay on the bunk, fully dressed, thinking of nothing and doing nothing.

I have just looked at those last two words. How strange they are, how foreign! They might be Chinese or Hindoo—doing nothing, doing nothing. Nothing, nothing, nothing. I laughed aloud. It was a genuine "cachinnation" which sprang of its own accord from my lungs. Charles had assured me that Miss Chumley would not forget me. Miss Granham—Mrs Prettiman—had given me the real omen. She had thrown me her bouquet! I should be the next one to be married!

Nevertheless, as I lay there on my back, slow tears ran from the corners of my eyes and wetted my ears and pillow.

(9)

And then I fell asleep! The reason was the wholly unexpected behaviour of our world. We lived with noise of one sort or another. There was always the sound of the sea outside the hull, ship noises, feet on the deck, pipes, somewhere a loud and male voice cursing, squeaks and knocks from the rigging, groans from timber, sounds at that time all too frequently of a quarrel from one part of the ship or another—once, a fight. But what helped me into a deep sleep was nothing more than silence! Perhaps in our part of the ship people were exhausted by the wedding, but I cannot tell that. Charles gave the crew a "make and mend", keeping the very fewest number of the crew on watch. As seamen do in these cases, the rest slept, I as well.

What brought me back to the real world was the sound of Deverel being put in irons! I started up and then realized that this metallic banging came from right forrard in the eyes of the ship and must be Coombs, the blacksmith, at his forge! It was the moment! I was fully dressed and I leapt out of my bunk, pulled on seaboots and hastened into the waist. The sea was spread out like watered silk, light blue, and a faint haze reduced the sun to a white roundel much like the full moon. There was not a breath of wind. Benét and the captain had found their flat calm! I fetched my lantern from the cabin and lighted it, then turned the flame down. I descended the ladders—past the wardroom and down again to the gun-room. Here for the first time I found it was empty except for the ancient midshipman Martin Davies, who grinned emptily at me from his hammock. I smiled back, since it was impossible not to, and then proceeded to make my way forward. At once

I had to turn up the light. It was a dripping, a moist progress, but this time, mercifully steady. Why, even those balletic lanterns in the gun-room had hung still, and now what with my lantern and the flat calm I could have run along the narrow planking between the stacked stores. I saw things previously I had only felt or smelt or heard—a huge pillar which must have been the warping capstan, the dull gleam of twenty-four-pounder cannon, all "tompioned, greased and bowsed down" and beyond them again—for those were but iron barrels—the flat gleam of water and the gravel of our bilges. Two walls, wooden for the most part and irregular, packing cases, boxes, bags, sacks of every size, some seeming pendant above my head—but there is no way of describing that hold, half-seen, partly understood, with a narrow way of planking which led through it along the keelson! Here was a ladder on my right that Mr Jones had lashed in place as an entry to the kind of loft which he had taken over as his sleeping quarters, living quarters and office! I chose to ignore it and made my way onward to the vast bulk of the mainmast and the pumps—

"Stand! Who goes there?"

"What the devil?"

"Gawd, it's the Lord Talbot, Mr Talbot, I mean, sir. What are you doing, sir? You nigh on got a baggynet in the guts, sir, if you don't mind me saying so, sir."

"I'm making my way forrard—"

There came a thunderous banging from ahead of us. I had to shout.

"I'm going forrard!"

The corporal had to shout back.

"Orders, sir. Sorry, sir!"

The banging ceased for a moment or two.

"Look—the first lieutenant must be forrard there. You ask him!"

The petty officer seemed doubtful but the corporal with him had a little more sense and sent one of his two men to tell Charles that I had appeared. He came back with word that I was to wait, at which I was not a little crestfallen but leaned against a convenient support—I do not know what it was—and waited, looking as nonchalant as possible. Casually, I blew out my lamp. The little party ventured no comment.

Forward of us there was light and noise. Some of the light was daylight, as if hatches and skylights had been opened in view of the importance of the operation. Some of the light was smoky and flared redly now and then. I even saw a spark or two float across what I was able to see of the open space where the work was going on. The work became a steady beating with a hammer on iron as if the ship was being shod. What with the smoky light and the metal noises I was overcome with a sudden return to the world of stables and harness and horses and the heat of a smithy fire! But it passed quickly, for the work took on another sound—a dull thumping as of a maul on wood. Peering into the light, and foolishly holding up my extinguished lantern—it is impossible not to hold a lantern up when you look, if you are carrying one—I could now see some of the structures which had been erected to stop the mast from moving. Those huge ropes which led so stiffly from the mast to eyebolts in the side of the hold were *staying* it. The baulks of timber which spread out at an angle on either side were wedging it. As I watched, the dull thumping stopped suddenly, there was a shout and one of the baulks fell, with a thunderous reverberation. It frightened me and it frightened everyone who heard it, for there rose a sudden clamour round the mast, but it was simply overborne by the captain's famous "roar" which, to tell the truth, I was very glad to hear, for it suggested safety and awareness of what should be done. Presently—with a

brighter flaring and more banging on iron then wood—a
second baulk came down but was received this time on a
soft bed, for it did no more than thump. After that I
waited for a long time while the smoky light brightened,
then dimmed, then was extinguished.

There came the groan and scream of metal on metal.
This scream was repeated again and again. Then silence.
The light was beginning to die down.

Bang! It was metal contracting, I think. It was followed
by the shriek of metal again and then another bang!

There was a sudden clamour which was interrupted by
another "roar" from the captain. He was there—I could
see him, see his tricorned head! He was down at the foot,
the shoe, the heel, tenon, or whatever it was, and once
more as the last baulk fell his roar overbore the sound
of it.

"Still!"

Bang.

Bang.

Bang!

Silence.

The captain spoke in his normal voice.

"Carry on. Yes, Mr Benét, carry on."

Benét's voice.

"What do you think, Coombs?"

"Lat'un boide a whoile, zur."

Silence again. The wail of contracting metal and a vast
grinding and creaking from the mast.

Benét's voice.

"Water. Roundly now!"

A fierce and continuous hissing! Steam was rising in the
open space.

There was another pause, seeming interminable as the
steam rose and cleared. The mast creaked and groaned.

"All right, lads. Carry on."

One after another the dark shapes of men climbed the ladders. The captain's voice could now be heard. It was loud and *meant* to be heard by all.

"Well, Mr Benét, you may congratulate yourself. I believe you was the originator here. You too, Coombs."

"Thankee, zur."

"I shall enter your names in the log."

"Thank you, sir."

"Mr Summers. Come with me."

I saw their dark shapes ascend the ladder just forward of the foremast. A seaman came peering for me.

"Mr Benét says you may come forrard now, sir."

"Oh, he does, does he?"

I made my way towards the mast, then looked about me. Benét was there. Even in that light I saw he bore such an expression of rapturous triumph as I never had seen on the face of any other human being. I gazed about me with profound curiosity. Evidently the operation had been successful. I could only examine and try to understand the method of it. The huge cylinder of the foremast came down through the deckhead and appeared to enter a square block of wood. Since the mast was a yard in diameter, the size of the wooden block into which it was set may possibly be imagined. I suppose it was something like a six-foot cube. What a tree! I had never seen such a block of wood in my life. This in its turn rested on a member which ran the ship's length above the keel—the keelson. Facing me on the after side of the shoe was a sheet of iron with huge bolts projecting. These then were the bolts of iron which had been made red- or white-hot in the midst of all this *tinder*like wood at the risk of turning the whole ship into a bonfire! On the top surface of the wood the wide crack made by the leverage of the mast was no longer to be seen. It had, if anything, more than closed! Good God, the mere force of cooling iron had crushed the vast block of wood so that the surface had risen everywhere into parallel wrinkles! It was awesome. The words were jerked out of me.

"Good God! Good God!"

The expression on Mr Benét's face had not changed. He was staring at the iron. Only his lips moved.

> *Thy face is veiled, thou mighty form,*
> *The dry the chill the moist the warm,*
> *All modes—all modes—*

His voice died away. He appeared to see me at last and I do not think there had been any pretence about his abstraction. His face became that of a social man.

"Well, Mr Talbot. Do you understand what you see?"

"I suppose there is another plate like this one on the other side of the block—the shoe."

"And the bolts go through both."

"The wood must be on fire within!"

He waved a hand dismissively.

"For a little while, no more."

"Do you mean to burn us all before any of our other dangers finish us? Or do you propose that this one should be held in reserve in case our other perils are successfully surmounted?"

He was kind enough to laugh a little.

"Be easy, Mr Talbot. Captain Anderson was under the same misapprehension, but by means of a model Coombs and I were able to convince him. The channels are much larger than the bolts. Air cannot enter. When the air is depleted of its oxygen—its vital air, sir—it will start to cool and there will be no more than a layer of charcoal inside the channels. But do you see the degree of force we have at our disposal?"

"It is frightening."

"There is nothing to be afraid of. I have seldom seen

anything so majestically beautiful. The mast was moved upright in a matter of minutes!"

"So we may now use the mast. And the mizzen. Our speed will increase. We shall get there sooner."

He was smiling kindly.

"It is beginning to penetrate."

A testy reply was on the tip of my tongue, for I began to resent his condescension, but at that very moment there came a sharp report from inside the iron or wood which made me flinch.

"What was that?"

"Something taking up. It does not matter."

"Was to be expected, in fact!"

My sarcasm missed its mark.

"The sound was the expenditure of moderate force. *Thy face is veiled, thou mighty form—*"

It was evident that Mr Benét was no longer disposed for conversation. Idly I laid my hand on the iron plate and snatched it away at once.

"The thing must still be on fire inside!"

"No, no. There is ample area. My first line is a tetra-meter. How the devil did I come to think it was an iambic pentameter? We are lacking a foot! *Nature, thy face is veiled, thou mighty Form!* I shall have trouble with the rhyme now, because having personified Nature and mentioned 'Form' the whole thing becomes Platonic, which I did not desire."

"Mr Benét, I realize you are in the throes of seaman-ship, engineering and poetry but should be glad if you would kindly continue our previous conversation. I know that one should not pry into a gentleman's private affairs, but with regard to your time in *Alcyone* when you were acquainted with Miss Chumley—"

But the strange man was rapt again.

"Warm, swarm, corm. They would be an ear-rhyme. Or balm, calm, palm—cockney rhymes unendurably vulgar.

The dry the chill the moist the warm—why not the moist
the dry the warm the chill—"

It was no use. The ironwork *banged again*, to be echoed
dully from above. I set myself to climb the ladders into
modified daylight, then out onto the deck where the sun
was now completely obscured by clouds and the sea more
than ruffled. The forrard part of the waist was crowded.
Oldmeadow's soldiers were grouped there by the rail on the
larboard side. They had their Brown Besses. Oldmeadow
threw an empty bottle as far as he could into the water,
whereupon a fellow loosed off with a prodigious production
of smoke and noise and made a small fountain of seawater.
This drew shrieks of fear and admiration from the young
women who were in attendance while the bottle floated
very slowly away. So we were moving! I stared upward and
saw that the sails on the mainmast were rounded. Fellows
were swaying a yard up the foremast. Oldmeadow threw
another bottle, there was another explosion and fountain of
water as the second bottle followed the other one. I suggested to Oldmeadow then and there that he should attach
a string to the bottle and thus be able to make do with the
one but he ignored me. Companionship with the common
and ignorant soldiery was doing his wits and his manners
no good whatever. There were no passengers about. They
had evidently decided that the best way to spend that
upright and untroubled period was asleep in their bunks.

A little wind breathed on my cheek. I went back to the
lobby and looked into the saloon. There was no one at
either table—not even little Pike.

"Bates! Where is the first lieutenant usually at this time
of day?"

"Couldn't say, sir. He might have got his head down,
sir."

I went down to the wardroom.

"Webber. Where is Mr Summers?"

Webber nodded to Charles's cabin and spoke in a whisper.

"In there, sir."

I hurried to the cabin and knocked.

"Charles! It is I!"

There was no reply. But what is a friend? I knocked again, then opened the door. Charles was sitting on the edge of his bunk. His hands on either side grasped the wooden edge. He was staring at or through the opposite bulkhead. His eyes did not blink or turn towards me. His face under the tan of exposure was sallow and drawn.

"Good God! For Heaven's sake! What has happened?"

Now his head did turn, jerkily.

"Charles old fellow!"

His lips quivered. I sat by him quickly and set my hand down on the back of his. A drop of sweat rolled off his brow and fell on my fingers.

"It is I—Edmund!"

His other hand came up and he smeared it across his face, then put it down again.

"Tell me, for God's sake! Are you hurt?"

Still nothing.

"Look, Charles, the news is good! They are setting sails on all three masts!"

Now he spoke.

"Obstruction."

"What obstruction?"

"Obstruction. That's what he said. I am to cease my obstruction."

"Anderson!"

He shook as if with cold. I took my hand from him.

He muttered.

"I can feel her moving. He was lucky, wasn't he? A flat calm for the work and now—the wind again. An extra two knots, Anderson said. He gave me reasons. Coldly."

"What reasons?"

"For his words. Obstruction. I am—I did not know it was possible to be so brought down. The dragrope—but it tore away part of the keel. Who knows? And now—for a knot and a half, for two knots, Benét has stuck red-hot irons through wood and left them there!"

"He says they will no more than coat the inside of the channels with charcoal."

He stared into my eyes.

"You saw the man? You spoke with him?"

"I have—"

"I must not obstruct him, do you understand? A brilliant young officer—and I! Dull, superannuated—"

"He could not say so!"

"In defence of his favourite he would say anything! He will take no action yet but I am to watch my step—" He paused for a moment, then hissed with a fury of which I should never have thought him capable—"*Watch my step!*"

"I swear to you he shall be brought down! I will—I will raise the whole government of the colony against him! I will—"

He drew his breath in sharply, then whispered:

"Hold your tongue. It is mutiny."

"It is justice!"

There was a pause. He put his face in his hands. I could hardly hear what he said for the grief in the sound of it.

"I do not desire justice."

For a while neither of us said anything. Then—

"Charles—I know I am a passenger—but this monstrous—"

He laughed, bitterly.

"Oh yes, you are a passenger, but you may still put yourself in peril! And if it were possible to do what you have just said, do you suppose I should ever be employed again, let alone promoted?"

"Benét is a kind of meteor, a passing flash. Meteors always fall."

Charles sat up and hugged himself with both arms.

"Do you feel how she moves even in this light air? He will nigh on double our speed. And, mark my words, every knot he adds will double the intake of water!"

"He is writing an Ode to Nature."

"Is he so? Well, tell him Nature never gives something for nothing."

"I will tell him, though the statement will come oddly from me. I believe he would recognize the source."

A trace of colour had come into Charles's lips.

"Bless you, old fellow—may I still say that?"

"Heavens! Whatever you like."

"You are a true friend. It is like you to come looking for me with what comfort you could when no one else—Well. Forgive me. I have been less than a man."

"You are worth a hundred Benéts—two hundred Andersons!"

"Is that my lantern?"

The question disconcerted me. I followed his eyes, lifted my right hand with the lantern in it.

"No. In fact—"

I did not feel like going on. After a moment or two Charles shrugged.

"Dockyard issue. Well, what does it matter?"

Suddenly he struck one fist into the other palm.

"It was such a humbling, such a shaming rebuke! It was so unjust—for all I did was differ in opinion from my subordinate!"

"Did anyone hear him?"

He shook his head.

"He observed the forms. I am helpless therefore, you see. When we reached the quarterdeck he addressed me formally. 'Oblige me by stepping into my cabin, Mr

Summers.' There he faced me. He lowered up at me under his thick eyebrows and projected his jaw at me—"

"I know! I have seen!"

" 'Sticks and stones may break my bones but hard words won't hurt me.' A rhyme for children. What he said tore at me like hooks."

"You are better for talking about it. It has been searing for you, I can tell that. But I have sworn to see right done, justice—fair play! You remember?"

"Oh yes! A long way back, in Colley's time."

"Now what is to be done at the moment? I believe you are able to smile!"

"Did you feel that? The wind is increasing. Well, the captain and the officer of the watch—let them manage between them. Only think, Edmund, if this wind had come a couple of hours earlier—I can hardly believe in my own iniquity! I found myself wishing—no, no. The mast is repaired, our speed is increased and I am glad of it!"

"We must all be glad."

"But I tell you, Edmund, with that fire in the shoe—I will have a watch kept there as long as there is a trace of heat left in the iron. Other than that, there is nothing to be done. I must swallow everything and live out the commission— why are we such creatures that a few sentences from an angry man should matter more to me than the prospect of death?"

"At all costs no one must know—"

"What—in this ship? I have never been in one that so echoed and resounded with rumour!"

"The thing must be forgotten."

"The voyage will surely be remembered, for it bids fair to be the longest in history."

"Well, you, at any rate, must not go down as anything but the lieutenant who by and by was Captain Summers and, after that, a famous rear admiral!"

Charles had coloured deeply.

"That is a dream and I fear must remain so."

"When you saved my reason by providing me with dry clothes—did you know I itch no longer?—I spoke of Glaucus and Diomede. I doubt the story will have come your way any more than the parts of a mast or the niceties of stellar navigation have come mine. Well. There was a battle and in it these two enemies found they were related—"

"So you said. As I told you once, I have no relatives at all and prefer that to being related to Benét or Anderson!"

"Come! That is better. That is humanly bitter. What a turn up for the book it would be if you found you as well as Benét was a frog! But these two warriors I liken to you and me."

"Oh! I am sorry."

"They stopped fighting and exchanged armour for remembrance. The gods took away their wits so that they never noticed that bronze armour was being swopped for gold! I used to take that as no more than story for the sake of story—but do you know, Charles, I now understand it as a profound allegory of friendship! Friends will hand over anything that is needed and think nothing of it!"

"Yes indeed!"

"I *think* your gift of seaman's slops was golden armour! Now here is my bronze! The first ship that returns from Sydney Cove shall carry not just my journal in which you are described with such admiration but a letter to my godfather giving reasons and declaring that you deserve to be made 'post' on the spot!"

The colour came and went in his cheeks.

"I thank you with all my heart. Of course, it is impossible. Luck and promotion have passed me by. *Can* you do so?"

"Exactly as I have said."

"Well—I will try to believe it. I *will* believe it! You see, I am so unused to—what? To privilege—to—"

"To getting your desserts."

He stood up.

"It is like that time when Admiral Gambier had me made midshipman!"

He stretched out his hand to the shelf and touched a book—a prayer book by the look of it.

"I do not think I can face my fellows just yet."

"What will you do? Oh, I see! You wish to, to meditate."

"And you, Edmund—will you stand the middle?"

"Of course, I shall. Why, I have already slept in preparation!"

Suddenly I reeled and fell on the bunk. He laughed.

"We have the wind, you see! This will test his foremast!"

"I think—yes, I think I had better get out into the open."

(10)

I went cautiously out into the wardroom. Webber was polishing the corner of the long table with unwonted and indeed useless industry, for the wood was much too stained and hacked to take a polish. I clambered up to the lobby and was glad to get into the waist and hang on by the mainstays. We were indeed making way. Things must have been even more propitious while I had been down below with Charles, for stuns'ls were being struck on the mainmast in preparation for a further increase of wind. I could see quite a spread of light before our bow, but astern of us huge crenellated clouds seemed to be not so much sweeping forward towards us as towering upwards into preposterous castles of storm. I might have taken another bath but did not. I kept under shelter but looked out until I saw the first savage lash of rain beat along the decks and leap back from it. This was followed in what must have been less than a minute by hail, so that the duty part of the watch huddled in what shelter they could get or cowered with arms hiding their heads. One man I saw had climbed into the belfry and crouched there laughing at the others. The hail vanished even more quickly than it had come. It was followed—as if a curtain had been drawn back in some theatrical presentation—by wind, not rain. In only a few minutes the world was darkened and the sea dirty grey. Then, astonishingly, all this was wiped away and we were in wind and sun, bright sunlight, evening, sunset light, a hard, bright yellow sun shorn of its beams and lying down on the horizon like a golden guinea. But this faded as it dropt, thin clouds coming up between us and it, so that staring back along the ship's side at the break of the aftercastle I saw that the sun lay out to the north at an angle as it set. I was aware of thin cloud, high at the zenith and appearing to move forward slowly while the wind was moderate but constant, seeming made whole with a great deal more to come.

The bell rang for the end of the first dog. The ritual completed itself in the wind and newly rocked ship. Mr Smiles and Mr Taylor came down from the quarterdeck.

"Well, Mr Smiles. What have you to say about the weather?"

But apparently Mr Smiles had nothing to say at all. I went, as by habit, to the passenger saloon.

Bowles and Pike were sitting at the long table under the great stern window. Through long custom the central position looking *forrard* had become my own, I cannot tell why. I had sat there at the beginning and it had been so ever after that. Bowles in a somewhat similar way sat at the starboard end of the table and faced along the length. Pike, on the other hand, was a movable object and sat where he could. Just now he was sitting in *my* seat!

"Move up, Mr Pike."

He had his elbows on the table and his chin in his hands. His beaver was on the back of his head. When he heard me he began a kind of shuffle on the bench, his elbows still on the table. His whole body moved unhandily towards Bowles.

"What's the matter with you, Pike—Richard, I mean?"

Bowles answered for him.

"Mr Pike unfortunately indulged too freely last night, Mr Talbot."

"A thick head, eh? Good God, you was not used to drink at all! Well, we have taught you something! Bunk is the best place for a thick head, Richard—"

But Mr Bowles was shaking his.

"What is the matter, Bowles?"

"The moment is not propitious. What do you think of our weather, sir?"

"Mr Smiles, if you are able to believe me, had nothing portentous to say."

Mr Bowles shook his head moodily.

"I did not think I could be so hungry and yet accept the fact! I did not think I could come to terms with a settled state of dread!"

"Like Wheeler."

"I do not envy you your cabin, sir."

"I do not chuse to be separated from my charges by pandering to superstition."

"Insensitivity must be of assistance. What charges?"

"Insensitivity? Allow me to tell you, Mr Bowles—"

The ship heeled suddenly and as suddenly came back again. Mr Pike's beaver fell off the back of his head. He made no attempt to retrieve it.

"What charges, Mr Talbot?"

"That is my affair, Mr Bowles!"

After that we were all three silent. The only movement was made by little Pike. He closed his eyes.

Bates came in, splay-legged against what was now the constant movement of the vessel.

"What do you think of the weather, Bates?"

"It'll be worse before it's better, sir."

He collected the two lanterns and disappeared with them. There was a rattle of rain or spray across the wide window.

"That's what they all say."

" 'They', Bowles?"

"Everyone—Cumbershum, Billy Rogers, now Bates."

"So we are in for it."

There was a long pause. Bates came back with the two lanterns. One of them was lighted.

"Which side will you have it, gents?"

Bowles had one elbow on the table. He pointed upwards with a finger of that hand. Bates brought the lighted lantern to the starboard side and hung it up, then took the other and hung it opposite. Our shadows began their merciless movement on the unfestive board. It seemed as if the movement was amplified moment by moment.

"At least the masts——"

"——are firm. Yes, Mr Talbot. It was a brilliant concept and a brilliant piece of execution on the part of a young officer. I believe we passengers should ensure that it does not go unrewarded."

"Let us leave the Navy to look after itself, Mr Bowles."

"Has that always been your opinion, Mr Talbot?"

The ship bounced. Bates reappeared.

"I have to serve the ladies in their cabins, gents. Would you be having your pork and beans in the ordinary way?"

"What do you think, Bates? Bring it here!"

I turned in my seat, shielded my eyes from the lantern and tried to make out the shape of the sea. There was a great deal of white scattered over it. None of us had anything to say.

Bates came back with plates of pork and beans. Pike staggered up, went reeling and fell on the bench which was set aft of the smaller table. He put his elbows on it and sank back into the position he had previously endured. I examined my portion with disfavour.

"This is confoundedly small, Bates!"

Bates did a little dancing step which maintained him upright in the same place.

"Ah, but then, sir, it's very hard, sir, and will take you twice as long as the same quantity would at home, sir."

"Go to the devil!"

"Aye aye, sir. What is it, Mr Bowles?"

"You had better take the pork away again, Bates. I am not equal to it."

"Beg pardon, Mr Bowles, but you better, sir. It's what we got, sir, and so long as you can keep it down, you better."

"Brandy for me, Bates."

"The brandy is all right, sir. We have plenty of brandy. The ale is gone though and we have to make do with the small beer, sir. Would you want the brandy to improve the water, Mr Talbot?"

"Can anything?"

"Mr Cumbershum uses the brandy to improve the small beer, sir."

"I'll try that. Good God! This pig must have been made of iron!"

Bates, to my astonishment, ran backwards! At the end of his run, being now a little higher than those of us seated at table, he ran forward again. Bowles clapped his hands over his mouth, stood up, then sat down again with a thump.

"Are you all right, Bowles?"

Bowles snarled.

"What a damned silly thing to say!"

He stood up again and staggered away. Bates opened the door for him.

"I think, Bates—"

I too stood up, then worked my way carefully to the door. I managed to get to my cabin without vomiting but then changed my mind and staggered to the entry to the waist. I held on to the mainstays—I call them mainstays and sometimes I call them the chains, both terms being inaccurate though not contradictory. I never bothered to understand the complexity of that part of the rigging except to say that it held the mainmast up and to some extent could be adjusted to circumstances. I used to hold on to anything available. This time it was a huge wooden thing with a hole in it, called a *deadeye*, I think—or perhaps not. I hung there and saw a dim horizon ahead of us tilting now this way, now that. The wind had increased but not to any great extent. It had now been increasing for hours but slowly: and I began to feel in this inexorable approach the reason for the moody and apprehensive answer to that question we passengers were asking.

It'll be worse before it is better.

Once again it is a matter of Tarpaulin, that economical and expressive language! A man may say, "In for a bit of a blow!" or "It'll make her bounce a bit!" But in the foreboding phrase there is an admission of ignorance as though these salted creatures are admitting that the sea can always do more than you expect and is in train to do it.

I turned round, and squinted aft past the break of the fo'castle on the larboard side. What was to come lay there, over that already invisible horizon. The wind was steady as the flow of time itself and as inexorable. Suddenly I felt a great weariness. It was not hunger, not seasickness. It was a dreary awareness of our peril and the greater test which our crazy old vessel was about to face. I desired nothing so much as oblivion, and there was only one place to go. I reeled back, tottered *down* the lobby and fell into my bunk.

I woke with my nausea gone, but stayed where I was, for the movement was much increased. At last I gathered myself together, went to the passenger saloon and crammed down a meagre offering. I was alone. I did not venture into the waist, for I could see the water running on the deck. At a few minutes to midnight when I made my way up to the quarterdeck I had recovered from my threatened nausea. I suppose the very few hours of motionlessness or comparative motionlessness, if such a thing can be, had reminded my limbs too much of the land and they had to readjust to the melancholy facts of our situation. The night was not dark, for although the moon was hidden the clouds were thin enough for that luminary to shed her light dimly everywhere. This was not a white night such as had preceded it but a light night! That solid wind blowing endlessly from the west had increased in power and the successive waves were outlined at their crests with foam. Charles was before me and I stood aside while the little ritual of the changed watch was performed. When we were settled Charles hunched himself in the shadow of the poop. I went and leaned against the ladder up to the poop by him.

"Are you feeling more the thing?"

For a time he made no answer. He was looking in the direction of the bows, but I do not think he saw the ship at all.

"Be a good fellow, Edmund."

"Surely! But how?"

"Leave the subject alone. Entirely alone. It is painful to me and dangerous to us both."

"But how can I—"

"Leave it alone!"

"Oh, all right. If you wish."

The ladder was convenient to my feet. I went up slowly to the poop. That diffused brightness now lit our cloud of sails on all three masts. There was no doubt that our old ship was doing her best to get us to Sydney Cove. There was a wave thrown out from her bow and another from about level with her mizzen. Her wake was visible, smoothed and swirling water which blunted the top of each wave as it reached us. Below me Charles moved out from shelter and went to the forrard rail of the quarterdeck. He stood there, his hands driven deep into the great pockets of his tarpaulin, his legs wide apart. Evidently this middle watch was to differ from the one before in more than weather. It seemed to me that Charles needed cheering up.

"How fast is this, Charles?"

He had not heard me approach, for he started at the sound of my voice.

"I do not know. Seven knots. Perhaps seven and a half."

"About one hundred and eighty land miles in the twenty-four hours. Are we taking in more water?"

"The well fills in an hour. Nature is hurrying us along and presenting us with a bill for her assistance."

"Should we not reduce sail then?"

"Are you not hungry like everyone else?"

"I see. Of course. What a devil of a fix to be in."

"You have seen nothing yet, Edmund. There is something at the back of this wind."

"How can you tell?"

"I mean a matter of scale. The time the wind is taking to increase—and the quality of the wind."

"Now you are really worrying me."

I said that to give him a chance of forgetting his own troubles in cheering me up. But I was not successful. Still looking away from me at bows which as far as I could see stood in no need of his attention, he nodded merely. It was uncommonly like what Mr Benét would call a "*congé*". I went to the traverse board and examined the figures written there. Eight knots, seven and a half, eight and a half, seven and a half. Below decks they would be pumping, not on the watch but on the hour. As if reminded by my thought, the personnel of the quarterdeck performed the ritual of casting the log. Eight knots. The quartermaster reported his findings to me! I solemnly repeated the figure to Charles who must in fact have heard it as plainly as I did.

"Make it so, Mr Talbot."

"Aye aye, sir."

On the fo'castle the ship's bell rang out twice and once!

"Charles! He has it wrong! It should be one bell!"

"For Heaven's sake, man—have you never heard of 'easting'? We gain an hour for every fifteen degrees of longitude we make to the east. About once a week we miss out one bell in the middle but start the watch off at three bells instead."

"I suppose the people there in the fo'castle think they lose a piece of their life, just as when the Julian calendar was replaced by the modern one."

"I am not interested in what they think. Let them do their duty and think what they like!"

"Mr Summers! Charles! This is not like you! Oh, come! Do not disappoint me, old fellow! I think of you as the personification of equanimity!"

For a while we were both silent. Then he heaved himself away from the rail and stood upright.

"The ironwork is still hot."

It was my turn to fall silent, for it was plain that he could not get his mind away from the foremast and Benét. I did not know what to do and took to wandering round the quarterdeck aimlessly to pass the time. On the hour the log was cast again and everything repeated itself except that the ship was now making slightly more, the man said, than eight knots, but not enough to count! I chalked in eight knots and leaned against the poop ladder again. This watch was three hours long instead of four. Charles spent most of it without speaking and without even looking at me. So vexed and anxious was I at this that when we were coming off watch and descending from the quarterdeck I taxed him with it.

"Silence I can endure, Charles. But an averted face— what have I done?"

He paused at the top of the ladder down to the wardroom, face still averted.

"You have done nothing. I have been shamed, that is all."

He went away, down, heavily. As heavily as he, I made my way to my bunk, but sorrow could not keep me awake.

It was nearly midday when there came a tap at my door and I woke, to find myself in my bunk and fully dressed, oilskins and all! I had but put my head on the pillow!

"Come in!"

It was Charles—but a happier man, with a cheerful morning face.

"Rebuke me if you choose, Edmund! But I have been round the ship staring people in the face, looking them in the eye. Anderson, Cumbershum, even Benét! But you are only half awake! Come! I have something to show you."

I was about to express my surprise when we were interrupted by a terrible cry from Prettiman. Even Charles, inured as he must be to other men's suffering, winced as he heard it.

"Let us get on deck. Come, Edmund! You will need care. The weather has worsened, as I thought."

He led the way to the waist, where water foamed about my knees, then sank away.

"Good God!"

"Up with you!"

Now at last I did begin to understand about the Southern Ocean. We had no more than a scrap of sail set. Our roll seemed slower. I laboured up the stairs against the wind, and when we came into the open space of the quarterdeck I experienced what I should not have thought possible. The wind, which on other occasions I had thought severe enough in seeking to blow my mouth open, now did the same to my eyes, and no matter how I screwed up the lids the wind forced them open, a crack, through which I could see nothing but blurred light. I got into the lee of the poop and learned how to make a shade of my hands, which enabled me to see more or less clearly.

"Up on the poop. Are you man enough?"

He laboured up the stairs with me behind him. Now this was the open air. The very lanterns on their painted ironwork vibrated. We crept round the rail and then with eyes blasted open turned sideways and squinted for glimpses but could see nothing. It was not surprising. There seemed nothing to distinguish wind from water, spray from foam, cloud from light, small shot from rain! I bent my head and examined my body. I had a shadow. But this was not the absence or diminution of light, it was the absence of mist, of rain, of spray. Charles had the same shadow; and now as I looked sideways across the wind I saw that every element in the rail, the turned uprights, the rail itself, had the same shadow.

"Why are we here? There is nothing to see! Is not the middle enough!"

He did not turn nor reply but made a dismissive and perhaps irritable gesture. The seamen were dragging and lifting those same curious, wobbling sacks that had looked so much like bodies in the semi-darkness. Now I saw that they were full of liquid and attached to ropes. Charles had a large sailmaker's needle in his hand which he stabbed into the bags several times.

"Over with them!"

The men toppled the bags over the rail and into the sea. A wave rose up, a whole plateau of moving water. A secondary wave appeared on its surface, was torn off by the droning wind and hurled at us like a storm of shot.

"Belay!"

I turned and looked forward in time to see the bows slide back down from the plateau which had outsped us. I felt our stern rise. I turned to see other plateaux following us, the one partly hiding the next, a monstrous procession marching endlessly round the world and creating a place which surely was not for men!

"What have you done?"

"Look."

I followed his pointing finger. A plateau had heaved up slowly with every complication of tormented water on its surface as shot to strike us. Then, at the very farthest edge of what was visible, I saw a gleam of silver. It was spreading, drawing out into a kind of path astern of us not unlike that path of light which we see in water beneath the moon or sun. But this was very mild silver, glossy and unblemished. It was definite as a lane in chalk country. It shone beneath the fits and whirls of spray, the waves on waves which flew into the air like nightmare birds.

"Oil!"

A place for no man: for sea gods perhaps; for that great and ultimate power which surely must support the visible universe and before which men can do no more than mouth the life-defining and controlling words of the experience of living.

"Oil on troubled waters."

(11)

So it was. No matter how the waves pursued us and threatened to overwhelm us, when they reached that streak of silver it subdued them more thoroughly than a great rock or—if it were possible—some breakwater or quay. It is a marvel in the physical world how a vegetable oil, expressed from the tenderest and most ephemeral of Nature's inventions, can yet subdue the rage of a tempest as Orpheus put Hades to sleep! I am aware that the fact is thought to be a commonplace—but only by those whose lives have not been saved by this thinnest and most fragile of threads! The silver pathway reached now to within fifty yards of our stern and in that unoiled fifty yards of water the malicious sea had no time to organize its fury. We still rose up and sank. Still the water welled over our flanks and made a bath of the waist where the black lifelines twitched and vibrated above it, but there was a saving smoothness in our motion!

"Charles! I would not have believed it!"

He beckoned me down from the poop to the quarterdeck. I came down and he drew me aside into the lee of the bulkhead.

"I wanted you to see that I too have my ideas."

"I never doubted that!"

He laughed excitedly.

"Normally we should heave to and spill oil over the bows, you see? Then the ship would be more or less stationary and we should make a wide area of oil to windward, but now we cannot afford the time. We must get on. I have to tell you that our supply of vegetable oil is limited; but so long as it lasts we may run before a following sea in safety—comparative safety."

"As long as the oil lasts."

"Just so."

"And the pumping?"

"Pumping will increase, naturally. But not too much."

He nodded, laboured away across the quarterdeck, spoke to the quartermaster, then, pushed by the wind, made a rapid and irregular descent to the waist and disappeared from view. I followed in my turn, ignoring the officer of the watch for once in a rare obedience to the captain's standing orders! I entered the passenger saloon and yelled for Bates who brought me beans and a small portion of pork.

"Brandy too, Bates."

He went off to get a drink and I sat, guarding my food but slewed so that I could see our oil, our silver snail trail. Far off I heard again that terrible cry from the dying Prettiman. He should have had the paregoric as a wedding present I thought. We should all have it. Oil or not, the best thing for us all would be unconsciousness. I sat for hours, numbed by the sea, until at last darkness drove me to my bunk. It now seemed as if the very regularity of our motion, immense as it was, gave us time to brood! I cannot say I slept. I was conscious that the ship still swum, and that we were alive. That was all. I believe lack of sleep came near to unsettling my wits.

Of the middle watch that night I remember little, although for me it was short. When the call came I huddled my way through solid wind to the quarterdeck and crouched in the lee of the poop. I do remember the light, for it was a storm light and not to be described—which is one reason why people who have never seen it do not believe in it. It seemed to inhere in the very atmosphere!

Presently Charles worked his way to me and crouched down.

"Get back to your cabin, Edmund. You can do no good here."

"When will it stop?"

"How can I tell? But you must go down. Cumbershum has fallen."

"Oh, that is terrible! If even Cumbershum—"

"He is not hurt. I mean if a man so used to this sort of thing—you see? Come. I will go with you to the break of the quarterdeck. Your best place is in your bunk. Stay there!"

This conversation was not in the heroic vein. I can only plead that if I dared the deck at all during that twenty-four hours it was more than any other passenger did. I doubt that they were more frightened than I. Possibly they simply had more sense. In the passenger saloon Bates told me that the emigrants and the off-duty watch had received permission from Charles to keep their hammocks slung and turn into them. I cannot think what the state of that overcrowded deck was, for occasional seas seemed to sweep the waist and run down off the fo'castle like a waterfall. We rolled a little but other than that the ship seemed to lift up and down without pitching at all, as if she were held in a narrow channel which denied her any other movement.

I got to my cabin at length, fell on my bunk and lay there exhausted, though I had done nothing. I even slept at last and woke in a grey morning light while the wind still droned. How that waking to a merciless noise and movement clutched at my poor heart! What must it have done to the children? Or could their parents and friends persuade them that all was well? Oh no! The pallid face, the quivering mouth had a plainer language than mere words. The voice which attempts to whisper, then finds itself suddenly and unexpectedly loud, the flashes of anger, the tears, the hysteria—no, I do not think the children were unaware, poor things!

It was the afternoon, with no change in our situation, before I pulled myself together sufficiently to get out of my bunk. The basest necessity drove me: after which, oil-skins and all, I made my way to the saloon. Mr Bowles was there, sitting under the window and looking at nothing. I sat near him and looked at nothing too, but there was a touch of comradely suffering about this nothing. After a long time he spoke.

"Pumping."

"Yes."

"Soon they will need us too."

"Yes."

"Frankly—"

There was another long silence. Then Bowles cleared his throat and spoke again.

"Frankly I ask myself whether I should give up hope, crawl away and huddle into my bunk—"

"I have done so. It is no help."

The door of the saloon burst open. Oldmeadow, the young Army officer, reeled in and flung himself on the bench facing us. He was breathing in gasps. His face was smeared with dirt.

"I suppose—you expect the ship to be run for your convenience."

"Is that intended as an insult?"

"How like you, Talbot! Talk when you have hands like these!"

He spread them before us. The palms were blistered and bloody.

"Pumping did that. He took my men without so much as a by-your-leave! 'Your men must pump,' he said."

"Mr Summers!"

"Your crony, Lieutenant bloody Summers—"

"Take that word back!"

"Gentlemen! Gentlemen!"

"I'm tired of you, Oldmeadow! You'll answer me for this!"

"Do you think I'm going to shoot you, Talbot, just to save the sea trouble? I said to Summers, 'Why can't you take the passengers, Bowles, Pike, Talbot, Weekes, Brocklebank?' Even that sodden old wreck would last a minute or two. I am—"

Oldmeadow collapsed over the table. Bowles got up and laboured round to him. Oldmeadow snarled:

"Let me be, curse you!"

He hauled himself upright and staggered away to his hutch. Bowles made his way uphill, then downhill, to his seat and fell into it as the ship came up and hit him. So we sat, the two of us, saying nothing.

Late that afternoon I left Bowles there and went to the necessity and sat by the humming rope which helped to drag our bags of oil. For all the snail-trail the place seemed as much under the sea as on it. When I came back to the saloon through a wash of seawater Bowles had gone. I had scarce reached my seat when the door opened and Pike came in. He had little enough to recommend him to the society of other men but there was no doubt about it—his dwarfishness was a positive help in preserving him from injury. Now he came skating or perhaps levitating across the uneasy deck and landed on the bench opposite me like a bird on a twig. He was pale but seemed sober.

"Good afternoon, Edmund. This is a fearful storm."

"It will blow itself out, Mr Pike."

"You were going to call me Richard, Edmund."

"Oh, God. Bowles, Oldmeadow—and now you! Richard then."

"It sounds cosier, Edmund, do you not find?"

"No, I do not."

"Friendlier like."

"Oh, for—how is your family—Richard?"

"Mrs Pike—you may have heard, Edmund, we have

had words. It happens in every family, Edmund, between
married people—"

"I doubt it."

"Well, you are not married, are you?"

"What the devil do you mean by that?"

"Married people understand. Since Mr and Mrs East
took to helping Mrs Pike, our little girls have been better,
there is no doubt about that."

"It is time we had some good news."

"Oh yes. Do you know, I am convinced that weeks ago
when the dragrope pulled a piece off the keel—"

"You sound like a professional seaman, Mr Pike."

"—I was convinced that they were dying. But since we
adopted Mr Benét's idea they have improved immensely."

"Another of Mr Benét's ideas?"

"He said they were getting weaker because of seasickness and the continual motion. He said that Nelson was
the same."

"Oh no!"

"He said that Nelson had a cot rigged up for him so that
it swung freely while the ship moved about it. He said—"

I was standing on my feet and fell sideways.

"But that was *my* idea!"

"He said that if we rigged hammocks for them the
motion would be easier and they would think it a game—"

"But that was exactly *my* idea!"

"It doesn't matter whose idea it was, Edmund. It
worked and they have been getting better ever since."

"I went there. I went to the cabin. I knocked and
opened the door. Miss Granham was there. She looked at
me as I opened my mouth to tell her this same idea but
before I could get a word out, she—shut me up! Those
stony eyes!— 'Do not say anything, Mr Talbot. Just go!' "

"Like I say, Edmund, it doesn't matter whose idea it
was, does it? They're better, you see."

"I will strangle that woman!"

"Who, Edmund?"

"Just because he has yellow hair and a face like a girl's—God damn and blast my soul to eternal bloody perdition!"

"Edmund! Edmund!"

I sat down with a thump. I was hot inside my oilskins and jarred from the seat. I cursed and tore my oilskins open.

"She has set out deliberately to put me down from the very first moment we met!"

"Why are you angry? They are better!"

"I am glad, Pike—"

"Richard."

"Richard then. I am very glad. Your little girls are better and that is all that matters. I will—"

"Mrs East is very helpful. She sings to them and teaches them songs. I do not think Phoebe is very musical but Arabella sings like a lark. I have quite a good voice, you know."

"I suppose so."

"You are talking very peculiar, Edmund. Have you been drinking?"

I suppose he went on talking. I did not notice. He was an unnoticeable little man. When I came to myself I was alone.

"Bates! Where the devil is my brandy?"

"Here, sir. I got it from Webber, sir. We got to go easy with it."

"Bring me some more."

"Sir?"

I held out the empty glass and he took it away.

This was the beginning of it all. The period is one of which I am still ashamed and shall always be so, I think. Rage fed on rage. It was Mrs Prettiman's fault, of course—but he, Benét, with his plain theft of my idea for helping the little girls—she had taken from him, accepted from him what she would not accept from me. *Say nothing, Mr Talbot. Just go away.* The two of them colluded—

There came a point where I found myself standing in the dim lobby with seawater cornering in diagonals and triangles which consumed themselves against the doors and bulkheads. I had some idea of confronting them—but where was Benét? I went looking for him, therefore, unhandily out into the open where the black lifelines shook above water and under it; and there, as Fate willed it, came the man himself, out from the fo'castle where he had been about some employment with or for his iron-work perhaps! He seemed not to see me but swept off his hat, shook out his yellow hair in apparent joy at release from the stench of below decks—and, just as I was about to accost him, dashed past me as if I did not exist! I followed him at once into the lobby. Benét was gravely examining the captain's standing orders as he yielded to the motion of the ship while seawater washed over his boots.

"Are the captain's standing orders not familiar to you, Mr Benét? You had best be about your business—stealing ideas, pulling pieces off the ship or sticking a mast through the ship's bottom!"

Mr Benét "looked down his nose at me". He was able to do this despite my height, since I was hanging on to the rail outside my cabin.

"A hole or two in a ship's bottom is of no consequence, Talbot. Pull out the bung in a ship's boat, stick your knife blade through and, provided the boat is making enough way, all the bilgewater will run out."

"Where did you steal that idea?"

"I do not steal ideas!"

"I am not convinced of that."

"Your convictions are irrelevant."

"The little girls were in peril. We are all in peril, you fool!"

"I am not a fool! Leave my name alone, sir!"

"I say you are!"

"That I will not allow! You will answer to me for that!"

"Listen, Benét!"

It was at this point that as far as I was concerned the whole conversation became incoherent. I do not mean unintelligible, for each separate remark or sentence made clear sense. But they added up to confusion. Mr Benét appeared to be giving me his family history with increasing acerbity while I accused him of dishonesty. He replied that I was perfidious *like all my race*! I replied with a threat of violence and made it the precise suggestion of pistolling a young gentleman of French extraction. This he countered with a brief description—

"Ah, the English! When one first meets them one dislikes them—but when one gets to know them, dislike turns to genuine loathing!"

The door of Prettiman's cabin opened and Mrs Prettiman looked out. She had changed back into slops. She saw who were standing outside and quickly disappeared again. Mrs Prettiman's ample hair was wholly undone. There had been little of her visible but her face and the hair. In the silence between Benét and me that followed her appearance and swift disappearance we heard Mr Prettiman cry out. But the silence cleared our confusion and deepened the quarrel.

Briefly then, Benét and I had more words outside the door. I taxed him plainly with stealing my idea for the treatment of Pike's little girls—hammocks, à la Nelson. He denied it, saying that he had arrived at the same conclusion as I but independently. He was more inclined to believe that I had obtained the idea from him than the other way about! We reached a foolish state of pushing and shoving, during which I claimed to know how to help

Mr Prettiman; at which point I think he claimed the same knowledge and had come to the lobby with that in view. The brandy had much heated me. Perhaps I misunderstood him. At this point, Mrs Prettiman, her hair now decently concealed, appeared at the door and rebuked us in a way which would have sent us off had we not been mad. Talking and doing at the same time, quarrelling and thrusting, we entered the cabin. We told the man and woman what we intended, but both talking at once. Prettiman shouted:

"Anything, anything to stop the agony! Yes! Turn me if you will!"

Benét got his shoulders up, Mrs Prettiman expostulating. His legs were over the edge of the bunk and he was trying not to cry out. I got an arm under his swollen waist—the skin was disgusting to the touch, hard as a board and burning as a dinner plate. Benét thrust me, shouting something, and I fell on poor Prettiman's legs. Had the edge of the bunk not held him I should have pulled him to the deck. Before my eyes the man's face drained of blood, went paper white. He fainted. Benét and I, now crestfallen and ashamed, got the helpless body round, replaced the pillows, exercised the most delicate care in the adjustment of the bedclothes—Mrs Prettiman spoke in her stony, governess's voice.

"You have killed him."

Eyes really do flash. I saw them do so.

(12)

I was the first to leave the cabin. I stumbled out, not daring to confront those eyes or what words she might speak to me. As I left I did not see her face but only Benét's, appalled, white and anxious. I got to my cabin and climbed into my bunk as if it were a hole I could curl up in. I believe I had my hands over my ears. *You have killed him.* It is useless to try to describe the anguish I felt. During the voyage I had received a few shocks and found out a few things about myself which I did not much like. But this new event was like falling into the darkness of a measureless pit. The fact is that, in the end, somewhere in the darkness, I found myself articulating spontaneous prayers which I knew as they burst from my lips were useless, for they were made to a God in whom I did not believe. It was thus I suppose that gods were invented, for I found myself praying for a miracle—*Let it not have happened!* I do not think anything should be made of these "prayers" unless subjecting them to ridicule should be thought the adequate response. There was little consideration for Prettiman in them, some for Mrs Prettiman, widowed even earlier than she had expected; but in gross those "prayers" were for Edmund Talbot! He even went so far as to glance at the law as it applies to such concepts as murder, manslaughter, bodily harm and *intent*! Only slowly as the droning wind sounded an ever lower note did I see that legally none of these applied and the deepest of penalties I should suffer would be the disapproval of the passengers and officers and the implacable dislike, the vicious, female enmity of Mrs Prettiman! Let this be a full account of my folly—I even saw myself, after the man's death, offering my hand, the ultimate sacrifice of all I held dear, to the lady! But even in my despair that would not fadge. She would be a widow of substance and could pick and choose where she would and her choice would not be Edmund Talbot. It might—and with a flash of positive insight I felt myself assured that it would be—Benét! She would buy Benét with his yellow hair!

It was evening when I dared to venture forth from my cabin. I stole into the empty saloon and went to look for Bates, found him and asked for water in a whisper. On the way back, having drunk, I paused furtively outside Prettiman's cabin but heard nothing. I had heard nothing from him, no scream nor moan since the fatal occasion. I went to my cabin and sat in my canvas chair. Truly, I did not wish to hurt the lady. However much I might disapprove of her morals I still did not wish her to suffer. Indeed, I told myself that those who live in glass houses should not throw stones, but this is only an indication of the confusion of thought and feeling in which I found myself. If I had picked "the odd flower by the wayside" it was no more than might be expected of a young fellow, whereas Mrs Prettiman—oh, how different that was!

Late that evening, towards eleven o'clock, I dared once more to venture out. There was still no sound from Prettiman's cabin. I tapped very gently but Mrs Prettiman did not come to the door nor did Prettiman answer. I went to the saloon, thinking I might get a drink which would in its turn make me able to face a meal, for I knew that I had to eat, however I felt and whatever happened. I opened the door of the saloon and stood, unable to move. Mrs Prettiman sat in my accustomed place at the great stern window. Bates was taking a plate and a knife and fork from her. He glanced at me as he turned but said nothing. Neither did I.

"Come in, Mr Talbot."

Bates shut the door behind me. I advanced carefully to the nearer table and sat on the bench facing her. Of the two lanterns which swung in time from the deckhead only one was lighted on the larboard side. It lit the left side of her face. She waited.

"I am desperately sorry, ma'am."

She was silent still.

"Ma'am—what can I say?"

She was looking at me and still saying nothing.

"For God's sake, ma'am! Is he—has he—"

She was motionless as a judge.

"He is breathing."

"Oh, thank God!"

"He is still unconscious. The pulse is hardly to be felt."

Now it was my turn to be silent, imagining the heart fainting in its work, the chest hardly able to rise to take in stale, shipboard air. Mrs Prettiman put her small hands together on the table before her. It was a posture of judgement rather than prayer.

"Mrs East is with him. I shall return now. Mr East has taken the news through the ship."

"The news, ma'am?"

"Mr Prettiman is dying."

I believe I moaned or groaned. No words.

Mrs Prettiman spoke again. But her voice had altered. There was in it the vibration of extreme and hardly controlled anger.

"You do not know, do you? You never have, have you? This voyage, Mr Talbot, will be famous in history—not for you, nor for any of them, but for him. You thought it was a comedy, Mr Talbot. It is a tragedy—oh, not for you!—but for the world, for this new world which we are approaching and hope to reach. Your concerns will be forgotten and vanish as the wake of a ship vanishes. I saw you come aboard with your privileges about you like a cloud of, of pinchbeck glory! Now you have trodden with your clumsy feet into a place which you do not understand and where you are not welcome. He will regard you indifferently, not as a man but as an agent of his death, as it might be a spar fallen from the mast. He will be above forgiving you. But I am not above it, sir, and I will never, never forgive you!"

She stood up, swaying. I scrabbled round to stand but she stopped me with a gesture.

"Do not insult me by standing in my presence. Once, I remember, when the movement was too much for my weak limbs, you assisted me to my cabin. Do not stand up, Mr Talbot. Above all, do not touch me!"

This last was said with a positive venom which made my hair lift. She went away quickly. I heard the door open and close but did not look round. I sat huddled at the table—not even my usual one—crushed by humiliation and grief. All the things I might have said, the excuses, the pleas, even perhaps the bravado of carelessness, had fallen round my "clumsy feet".

I cannot tell how long it was before I felt a touch on my shoulder and a familiar voice in my ear.

"Here you are, sir. Brandy, sir. You need it."

The man's sympathy was too much for me. Hot tears fell on the table between my hands.

"Thank you, Bates—thank you—"

"Now don't you take on so, sir. She's a right terror, isn't she—I wouldn't like to be a nipper when she was around!"

That made me laugh, though I choked on it.

"Nor I, Bates. But she made me feel like a nipper, I can tell you!"

Bates answered me in tones of dark dislike.

"That's ladies for you, sir. Women is different. You can hit a woman if she gives you too much lip."

"You sound as if you know all about it."

"Married, sir."

"Thank you, Bates. You can go now."

Once more I was alone and cradling my glass. It seemed to me that the motion was if anything a little more noticeable but I did not care. I can honestly say it was a point at which I was indifferent to whether we sank or not.

Somewhere a bosun's mate was piping a call. It was my watch to muster, time for me to stand the middle with Charles in the islanding darkness. I took the glass to the shelf and put it in an appropriate hole, then went to the lobby. There were people about but not the duty watch. Four emigrants—three women and a man—were waiting outside Prettiman's cabin. I saw what it was. They had come, so soon after greeting him as a bridegroom, to say farewell to a dying man! It was too much. I felt my way into the waist, then burrowed up into the wind. There were others doing the same thing, Charles among them. He took over on the quarterdeck from Cumbershum. I stood against the bulkhead under the poop. Presently Charles came and leaned against it by me.

"We have a very slight decrease in the wind. It will lessen gradually, I think. But it may take a long time."

He heaved himself away from the bulkhead, went to the side of the ship and stared back at our wake. There was a little less storm light. He came back again.

"Our oil is holding up. Indeed, I think at this moment we hardly need it. But I daresay if we got the bags in, the wind would get up and we should have to put them out again. It is vexing. The great thing, other than keeping the crests of waves down, is to make sure the oil does not come aboard. That's why I insisted on this elaborate way of hanging the bags of oil under the stern rather than over the bow. If we had hung them over the bow every time we shipped green water—and even white, come to that—we

618

should have left a film of oil on the deck. Imagine in the weather we have had trying to keep your footing with oil to tread on!"

He was silent for a while, went to the other side of the ship, looked aft and forrard, then came back again.

"At least we are making famous way for a ship under bare poles. Nigh on five knots! I should be happy with that—but you know all this as well as I do. Well, let us be cheerful until something happens."

The bosun's mate approached.

"A message from Mr Cumbershum, sir. There's a lot of movement on the gundeck, sir. It's people trying to get aft to see Mr Prettiman and they can't hardly do it for the hammocks which is slung. Mr Cumbershum requests to forbid the waist to all but the duty watch in case these people take it into their heads to come that way, sir."

The man stopped talking and blew out his breath.

"You got that very well, bosun!"

"Yes, sir. Thank you, sir."

"Tell Mr Cumbershum I agree. We don't want any more men topsides than is necessary in this weather."

"Women too, sir."

"Even more so. Carry on."

The man hurried away with the message. For a while the waist foamed white and the safety lines were visible, blackly stretched along it.

"You are silent, Edmund."

I swallowed but did not speak.

"Come, Edmund. What is it?"

"I have killed Prettiman."

Charles said nothing for a while. He worked his way forward, stared into the binnacle, went to the side and stared back at our glistening wake, then came back to stand by me.

"You are talking of the quarrel between you and Benét."

"There is death in my hands. I kill people without knowing it."

"That is too much like the theatre."

"Colley, Wheeler and now the third—Prettiman."

"You have killed no one to my knowledge. If you had really killed someone the way a seaman does, you would not talk about it."

"Oh, God."

"Come. Do you know he is dead?"

"He is unconscious. His pulse and breathing are weak. The people are crowding to see him. She——"

"Were you drunk? Or 'disguised', as you call it?"

"I had had a couple of glasses of brandy. Nothing out of the way. I was turning him end for end——"

To my astonishment Charles burst out laughing. He quickly controlled himself.

"I beg your pardon, old fellow, but really, 'end for end'! Your grasp of the language of the sea is far firmer than a sailor's! Now be a little easier. You have killed no one and must not make a tragedy."

"They—the emigrants and, I think, the seamen—are flocking to bid him farewell."

"They are just as previous as you are. As far as my information goes you were trying to help——"

"How did you know that?"

"Good Heavens, do you suppose the news of your quarrel and its outcome were not immediately known throughout the ship? At least it took their minds off our situation."

"I fell on him."

"You do really find it difficult to know where your extremities are, old fellow. I daresay you will learn to control them when you are—older."

"How long will it be?"

"Before what?"

"Before he dies."

"I am moved by your faith in me, Edmund. We do not know he is going to die. The body is mysterious. Would it make you easier if I sent to find out how he is?"

"Please."

Charles called the bosun's mate and sent him below. We waited in silence. Charles stared critically into the rigging. Sails had appeared there since I had last been on deck. There was even a tops'l replacing the one I had seen blown out of its boltropes. There was also a difference in what I could discern of the water round us—the shapes of waves where, before, the surface had seemed to be planed off and blown flat.

The bosun's mate came trotting back, leaning into the wind.

"The lady says there is no change, sir."

"Very well."

The man went back to his station by the forrard rail of the quarterdeck. Charles turned to me.

"You heard? So we must not worry before we need to."

"I cannot help it."

"Now what have I done! My dear boy, you have been foolish, impulsive, clumsy. If he dies, or rather when he dies—"

"So he will die, then!"

"He was dying before you fell on him! Good Heavens, do you suppose a man can live in our circumstances with his body swoln like a melon and the colour of an overripe beetroot? He is smashed up inside where I doubt a surgeon could do anything. You may have hastened the process, that is all."

"It is bad enough. She hates me, despises me. How can I stay in the same ship!"

"You cannot do anything else. Be sensible. Good Heavens, I wish I had as little to be sorry for as you have."

"That is nonsense. I have never known so good a man."

"Do not say it!"

"I can do so and have. I have found that the middle is the time for confidences between man and man. I believe that when I look back on this voyage these middle watches will be precious memories, old fellow."

"For me too, Edmund."

For a time we said nothing after that. At last Charles broke the silence between us.

"All the same we have lived in such different worlds it is astonishing that we have anything to say to each other."

"I have recognized your quality, which is independent of 'worlds'—though why you for your part should be willing to make one in a conversation—"

"Oh, that. It is even more mysterious than the body, I think. Let us say no more about it. Besides"—there was a smile in his voice—" 'who would not be a friend with a young gentleman who promises him the moon and the stars?' "

"Promotion is much more down to earth."

"How would you define my promotion—for so it seemed and indeed was—from seaman to midshipman? It was all through getting into trouble."

"I cannot believe you were ever in trouble!"

"How dull you make me sound! Well, perhaps I am."

"Tell me."

His face glimmered towards me in the gloom.

"You will not laugh?"

"You know me better than that!"

"Do I? Well—you see in a fo'castle there must be live and let live, since there is hardly room to swing hammocks. No one minds a man reading a book, whatever it is. Are you listening?"

"I am all ears."

"We were at anchor. It was a make and mend but I was one of the anchor watch. There was no harm in my reading but the divisional officer caught me at it. He rebuked me at some length to show how strict he was, when suddenly he and everyone else was called to attention. It was Admiral Gambier."

"Dismal Jimmy?"

"Some people called him that. Now he *was* a good man. He asked me what I had done wrong and I told him I had been reading on duty. He told me to show him the book so I brought it out from behind my back and he looked at it.

" 'There's a time and a place for everything,' he said and went away. The divisional officer told the petty officer to give me some cleaning to do during the make and mend as a punishment. But before the day was out I was sent for by Captain Wentworth.

" 'Summers, that was very clever,' he said. 'Get your gear together, you're going to the flagship to be a midshipman. I'm disappointed in you, Summers. Don't come back.' "

"But what was the book? Oh, I see! The Bible!"

"Captain Wentworth was not a religious man."

"And that is how you got a footing on the ladder?"

"Just so."

I was confounded. Miles separated the two of us! I could think of nothing to say. It was my turn to work my way to the rail and stare at the wake. I came back and pretended to look critically at the set of our sails.

"You are right, Edmund. We can shake out a reef."

He called to the bosun's mate who piped the order from the forrard rail of the quarterdeck, then lumbered forrard by way of a safety line, the water washing round his knees, and did the same thing on the fo'castle. The black shapes of men moved up the ratlines and along the yards.

"Is it giving us more speed?"

"No more than we had before."

I was silent again.

"At least you did not laugh, Edmund."

"It does not match you. You do not do yourself justice!"

"Oh yes. I owe everything to that good man—after you, that is!"

"Gambier? Will you think me cynical, I wonder. But I believe the account of Captain Anderson's strictures and the story of why Gambier had you made midshipman had best be kept between us."

"The first yes. But why the second?"

"My dear fellow! Dismal Jimmy's recommendation might have helped you had you chosen the Church—what is the matter?"

"Nothing."

"But it will not see you very far in a fighting service! Good God! It would be about as much use as a testimonial to your courage from poor Byng."

"That is a sad comment on the service!"

"No, no!"

"Well, at least we have made you forget your miseries for the time being. Go off watch now, and sleep."

"I must see the watch out with you."

He seemed surprised at my serious and determined tone and even laughed a little. As I have said, I think, I had not then understood why he had got me an excuse to be out of my cabin for four hours of the night and I did really believe I was useful! Now I laugh a little as he did then. But in fact the watch changed soon after he had spoken. I went to my bunk, wading through water which coursed and *cornered* from side to side in the lobby. The wind howled but at least it did not drone. I cannot say I slept, for I lay listening for Prettiman who I thought must have been in a drugged sleep, for he did not cry out.

The rest of that night was a bad one for me. I went off to sleep at last but in what must have been broad daylight outside. I woke, nevertheless, with the determination to stay where I was and where it seemed I could at least do no harm to anyone else. I felt that I could have cried out now in a way which Prettiman did not.

(13)

When at last I tried my repeater I found it was already a quarter to ten! I took the instrument out from under my pillow and examined it with some incredulity, but sure enough, the hands confirmed the message of the chimes. I came to the conclusion that I had indeed slept but could not think how or when. Nor did I feel the benefit of sleep. I was fully clothed and reproached myself for this decline in my own standards. Once a man will turn into his bunk "all standing", as it were, there is no knowing where the thing will end! It is the next way to decline into Continental standards or lack of them. However, the omission was not to be repaired. I stood out of my bunk into the seaboots which were ready and made my way, first to the necessity, then to the passenger saloon. Early though it was in the forenoon, little Pike was there with a glass of brandy in his hand. Indeed, it soon became evident that as far as he was concerned the time was not early but late. I learnt later that he had been dismissed from his cabin by his unloving wife—though it seems far more likely that he had dismissed himself—and he had roused Bates to provide him with liquor at what was really an unsuitable hour. He was elevated indeed and careless of the booming wind and sea. He offered to "buy me a drink" which I declined with point, asking him at once how his family did.

"Family, Mus'Talbot? I 'ate families."

He peered at me, blinking the while.

"She 'ates me."

"I think, Mr Pike, you are not yourself and should not say things you will come to regret."

But Mr Pike had looked away and appeared to brood. Then as if he had come to a satisfactory conclusion he turned back to me, helped by a movement of the ship.

"Well, thass awri, innit? I 'ate 'er. I 'ate 'er. Sodder. Pardon my French."

"I think that—"

"I don' 'ate them. But they 'ate me, because she says— she says—"

I lost my temper and went blind. I say that advisedly. Then I saw, but it was red. I saw red. It was literally red. My mouth opened and I shouted at him. I heaped on him every contumely, every insult my tongue could find, and when I had done I could not remember what I had said. It left me weak though, for the time being. I could hardly cope with the ship's movement though I was sitting. Pike was leaning his elbows on the table and sniggering and laughing weakly. He pointed at me with his right forefinger, his elbow still resting on the table. His hand was slack as though it supported a heavy pistol but was only just able to do so. What with the motion of the ship and his drunkenness, let alone his silly, weak laughter, his finger circled like—like the hounds of a foremast broken in the step! I got my breath back. Far from feeling that I should apologize for my burst of rage I felt it was entirely justified.

"In fact, Pike, you are a disgusting little man."

But his sniggering, giggling laughter went on and on.

"Thass wha' she sez!"

More laughter. Bates, the steward, appeared loyally, my mug of small beer in his hand, a napkin over the other arm. He entered straddling, slipped in water, saved himself cleverly, then ran *down* the saloon under *"force majeur"* to end balancing the mug within my reach. I took it and drained it and would have had another but Bates had gone as cleverly as he had come. Pike was now screaming with laughter.

"Bates! Bates!"

Then as if he had changed his mind the silly little man laid his cheek on the table and appeared to go to sleep. His glass fell and went crosswise to the side of the saloon where it clattered for a while before shooting back. I tried to trap it with my foot but failed. It struck the other side of the saloon and at last shattered. The door opened. Bowles and the young Army officer, Oldmeadow, laboured in, followed by random wetness as a wave struck the outside of the chock in the doorway. Bates, as one having foreknowledge, came in with two mugs of beer in one hand and one in the other. He stood swaying and gesticulating by the table as if about to perform a conjuring trick. Perhaps, in effect, he did perform one, for he got all three of us served and went away again without breaking a glass or his neck. Pike slid against Oldmeadow.

"Is this fellow dead?"

"Dead drunk."

Oldmeadow shoved the man away who moved a foot or two then came back again.

"I wish I was myself, Talbot, that's a fact."

"Oh no! We have enough trouble as it is. Cumbershum has fallen and I believe we should treat ourselves as precious objects and help each other!"

Oldmeadow gave Pike a positively vicious shove. It moved him to a position where one arm fell off the end of the long table and held him from returning with the roll.

Bowles looked up at me over his mug.

"According to Mrs Prettiman, Mr Prettiman is in a bad way. His condition is dreadful and he cannot last. He does not even cry out."

"He is dying peacefully then, Bowles. I am glad of that at least."

"Mr Oldmeadow—have you seen Mrs Prettiman?"

"No, I have not, Bowles. I've avoided her since she rigged herself out as a common seaman. It's indecent."

"Bates! Bates! Where the devil are you? Take these mugs away!"

"Go easy, Talbot! I have not finished with mine yet! Good God—as if Summers ain't enough!"

Oldmeadow at normal times is so mild-mannered I found it easy to forgive him his irritation.

"Why, what has Charles done?"

"Taken my men for good, that's what he's done. I said I didn't think it was proper to use my men when there were so many emigrants about. Why shouldn't he sweat the lard off that idle lot? He would have none of it. 'Your men are disciplined,' he said. 'They are young and strong and you have often bemoaned to me the difficulty of finding them employment to keep them out of mischief! I promise you that a few hours a day at the pumps and they will be as gentle as lambs.' "

"Was that the end of the argument?"

"What do you think, Talbot? I wasn't going to have a damned navy man taking over my command! I told him that I'd see him further first and that I proposed to get the captain to enter my protest in the ship's log."

"That is an awful threat to a naval officer! It might jeopardize his whole career!"

"Well, I know that! But I got no further, for he said as cool as you like, 'If your men do not continue to help with the pumping, sir, no one will ever hear your protest.' So it is as bad as that."

Bowles grinned round at us both.

"We often hear that danger brings men together. I see no evidence of it."

"We are civilians, you and I. Why should the Navy bother with us? This is not a company ship and the officers do not know quite what their attitude should be.

Oldmeadow's men are not marines. Willis said to me—but I suppose I should tell you that I am a civilian no longer. Lord Talbot has been promoted to midshipman."

"You intend that as a pleasantry, sir."

"God, Bowles, a pleasantry! Colley, Wheeler and now Prettiman—oh well! To revert: the fact is, I act as the first lieutenant's midshipman during the middle watch. The middle watch is the one which—"

Astonishingly enough, Bowles, that quiet and composed man, positively shouted an interruption.

"Yes, sir, we do know what the middle is! God have mercy on us. Soldiers turned into sailors and now passengers put in charge of the ship!"

"After all, Bowles, he couldn't do much more damage to the ship than the new officer, what's 'is name—Benét. The man has lugged a lump off the ship's bottom and damned nearly set the front end on fire! Now he wants to find out where we are without using their clocks and things. I tell you what, Talbot. We should get all this raised in the House! My God, what a boat! There's that fool Smiles on the quarterdeck supposed to be in charge but simply grinning at the weather as if it were a friend of his, and that old fool Brocklebank standing outside the lobby door in the wind and rain, with seawater washing round his knees, and waiting for his morning fart to develop—"

"So that's why! I've wondered—Every day he stands out there in the waist, wind, rain or shine—"

"Well, that's what it is. The girls won't have him in the cabin until he's fired off a blank charge like a saluting gun!"

The very image set us all three laughing like jackasses.

"Did I hear someone mention my name?"

It was the man himself. The deck left us and he swung hard on the door handle. He was an old man after all. Oldmeadow and I got to him before he fell and lugged him to the table, while Bowles heaved the door shut against the inclinations of the sea. I believe that the old man recovered his breath before any of us.

"I could not stand it any longer, gentlemen, that is the truth of the matter. Soaked above the waist, buffeted, nigh on washed away, this good old coach cloak, which has protected me so well, now as wet inside as out—"

"Why, Mr Brocklebank, you should be in your cabin—in your bunk if possible!"

"The fact is, I need the company of men."

"Good God, sir, anyone privileged to be the companion of Mrs Brocklebank—"

"No, Mr Talbot, it is not so. She endeavours to cheer me but the truth is, already she regards me with a widow's eye."

"Oh, come, sir! I have often seen Mrs Brocklebank about the ship and never less than smiling—never less than merry!"

"That is what I mean, Mr Talbot, though you exaggerate a little. She may look merrily on you but not on me. I do not like widows, sir, and have taken care to avoid them in the only truly logical way. But despite that, Celia, in the privacy of our cabin, has just that air of sad triumph, that almost holy smile with which a widow contemplates a *job* well done, an account paid in full: and that"—here the old man did seem passionate—"and that she is not entitled to!"

"Mr Brocklebank!"

"Now you are going to accuse me of conduct unbecoming to a gentleman, Mr Talbot. Be that as it may, I say no more under that heading. But I could not endure to return, you know, even though I had fulfilled Celia's stipulation. Yes, Bates! Good Bates, it is I! Have you put the brandy in it?"

Bates delivered the mug but looked conscious at Mr Brocklebank's words.

"Just a lick, sir, no more than a smell of it, you might say."

"Bates, you dog, you've been giving him brandy from the wardroom whereas I—"

"Your'n was mine, sir, Mr Talbot!"

"I would share my mug with you, Mr Talbot, but I am a martyr to fears of contagion."

"Devil take it! I believe the contagion would be the other way about!"

The deck fell away from us monstrously. I clutched at the table but found I had hold of Bowles. He struggled free of me just as the deck came up again and hit him. He swore in a way I would not have thought possible in such a man.

"And the food," said Mr Brocklebank, following a train of thought to which he had given no voice, "the food is just as bad. Why, only the other day when I tried to bite, or rather I should say *effect an entry* like a felon, into a lump of cold pork, what should ensue but this?"

The disgusting old man fished round in the many folds that clung about him and produced from some recess of his garments or person a blackened tooth.

"Oh my God, this really is the outside edge of enough!"

I leapt to my feet and went to the door, and was deluged with spray from the block which was supposed to keep salt water out of the saloon. Benét was there. Like everyone else in the ship he was holding on but with two fingers to the rail between the cabin doors. He was staring at Mr Prettiman's cabin. His lips were moving and I suppose he was in what are called the throes of composition. The sight maddened me. I still do not know why.

"Mr Benét!"

He seemed to see me but as a vexation.

"Mr Benét, I wish to have some plain answers!"

He was frowning and perplexed.

"Have I accepted your apology?"

"*You* should apologize! The relationship between

you and a certain lady has caused a certain other lady—
that is, has caused me—my opinion of her—I called your
name—"

"Have you anything against my name, sir? Was that
derision?"

"I called out your name—"

"Twice! I am proud of my name, Mr Talbot, and if my
father used it ruefully as a reminder of his flight—"

"You are putting me off! I do not care about your name
which is French, I suppose. I want a plain answer. What
did she see? Was it a criminal connection?"

"Well really, Mr Talbot, after our late differences—"

"I wish to understand clearly the relationship between
you and a certain lady!"

"You mean Miss Chumley, I suppose. Oh dear. Well,
as I told you she kept *cave* for us, or if the Latin tongue is
unfamiliar to you—"

"It is not, I assure you!"

"Now you are going red in the face like poor Prettiman."

I fought down my rising irritation.

"I am more concerned with you and a lady of maturer
years!"

"So you have found me out! She is—oh, she is—"

Mr Benét seemed uniquely bereft of speech. He closed
his eyes and began to recite.

> *Since thou didst doff thy woman's weeds*
> *And loosed the glories of thy hair*
> *The eye that weeps, the heart that bleeds—*

"So you did have a criminal connection! Miss Chumley
did indeed understand! She did indeed see!"

"What connection?"

"Lady Somerset!"

"The heart grows with understanding. Profound though
my esteem for the lady is—"

I shouted. It was fortunate perhaps that the words were audible in that weather to no one but him.

"Did you have her? Did Miss Chumley *see*?"

A look of compassionate understanding came into his face.

"I might resent your words, Mr Talbot, on her behalf and my own. Your mind evidently cannot rise above the farmyard level."

"Do not talk to me about farmyards!"

"You are passionately moved and hardly responsible for what you say. I knelt before the lady. She offered me her right hand. I took it in mine and dared to imprint a kiss on it. Then—and I beg you will understand what passionate chastity was implied in the gesture—remembering my childhood and dearest mama coming to say good night to me in the nursery, with an irresistible flood of emotion I turned the white hand over, dropped a kiss in the dewy palm and closed the slender fingers over it!"

"And then? Then? You are silent, sir! That was all? That was all, Mr Benét?"

"Once again you are not amiable, Mr Talbot. This is the second time, like your jeering use of my name!"

"A plain answer, if you please, to a plain question!"

"That was 'all'. Though to a man of any sensibility—"

"Explain why she took her clothes off. Explain that!"

"Lady Somerset took nothing off!"

" 'Since thou didst doff thy woman's weeds'!"

There was an explosion of water. Spray drenched us. Benét dashed it from his face.

"I see it all. The coarseness of your mind has deceived you. The lady did indeed 'doff' her 'woman's weeds'—"

> *Since thou didst doff thy woman's weeds*
> *And loosed the glories of thy hair*
> *The eye that weeps, the heart that bleeds*

> *Has found a refuge in thy care,*
> *Letitia! Though thy hand be given*
> *The thought of thee is my delight,*
> *To dwell in the same ship is—*

"Miss Granham! Mrs Prettiman!"

"Who else? The lines are unpolished as yet."

"You are writing poetry to Mrs Prettiman!"

"Can you think of a worthier aim? She is all that the ages have looked forward to!"

"You wish to kiss her hand, sir, I have no doubt she would oblige. She has, after all, obliged gentlemen before—Mr Prettiman, her husband—but what has that word to do with poetry? He is in his bunk and cannot get out of it. I have no doubt that if you tapped on her door and asked nicely you might find yourself kissing her hand inside and out for a full watch by the sandglass!"

"You are nauseous."

I must have snarled.

"I believe I am, sir. But at least I do not drool round the oceans dropping kisses in the palms of women old enough to be my mother!"

That appeared to sting. He heaved himself away from the mast and stood rocking.

"You had best stick to schoolgirls, Mr Talbot."

"I resent the plural! For me there is only one lady!"

"You are loveless, Mr Talbot. It is your main defect."

"I loveless? I am saying 'ha ha', sir! Do you hear me?"

"You are not yourself. We will continue this conversation when you are sober. I bid you good day."

He vanished with what I might call an assisted celerity down the stairs to the wardroom, passing Mr Smiles as he did so. I shouted childishly after him.

"Mr Smiles, can you hear me? We are in love with our mothers!"

Mr Smiles came past me with a deft tread, neither look-ing at me nor speaking to me. He might have been a ghost with an appointment somewhere else.

I went to my cabin. Time, time itself was unendurable. I climbed into my oilskins and went out to stand on the deck. Immediately a wave lifted me up into the main chains and would have left me there had I not detached myself. It cooled my senseless rage. I stood holding on while the ocean performed. The crests of waves went past us, it seemed to me, at more than head height. Sometimes we bowed sideways into them so that the waist flooded deep, sometimes we leaned away and there was a gulf in which a solitary bird was suspended over darkness between hills of foaming green. Then horizontal rain and mist would blot out even the bird, and water would tumble down from the quarterdeck as from the guttering of a cathedral.

It cooled and calmed me. The ropes that bound us together and kept us from drowning were there before my eyes as a reminder of how and where we stood. I rebuked myself for my anger and for showing so much of my fear. It was not what I had expected of myself. I went to my cabin and at long last fell asleep.

(14)

What woke me from a dream of cliffs and slopes was a shattering blow. I was on the deck by my bunk from which I had fallen or been thrown, and as I scrabbled to get up, my canvas chair tipped over on me so that we went sliding together to thump the bulkhead beyond my writing flap. I got to my feet somehow and the angle at which my lantern with its loaded base now stood frightened me into a moment or two of near-immobility. I could only interpret the angle as information we were now sliding backwards— making a sternboard!—into the sea and should vanish there. My feet skidded from me and I was hanging from the bunk, the idiot lantern projecting above me as if the laws of Mr Benét's Nature had been suspended. From that moment, I believe, I did not know quite what I was doing. I had some idea that the ship was under water already and that at any moment all the orifices would start to squirt. Confused with this was the thought that it was now the middle watch, I was late for it and Charles without a midshipman. Nor, as I gathered my wits together, did things get any better, for it was plain that we were in some emergency. There were noises. The Pike children were screaming needle-sharp and so was another female—Celia Brocklebank probably. Men were shouting. There were other noises too, booming and banging of sails, batter of blocks—somewhere glass shattered and cascaded. I got out into the lobby and found myself hanging from the safety rail by both hands—literally hanging from it as though the ship had stood on its head. I took one hand off the rail and immediately a sudden tug tore my other hand from it. I went tumbling the length of the lobby head over heels and fetched up with a dizzying thud against the forrard bulkhead. Some force pinned me there for a while, so that I could see Oldmeadow fighting—and not succeeding—to get out of the passenger saloon. Then the pressure slackened a little bit and I used an interim to scramble into the waist and hang in my usual place—the larboard shrouds—as if for comfort in the familiar. But nothing was the same and what I could see held no comfort for me. Someone was cursing near me but I could not see who it was. Such sails as we had now glimmered into view as my eyes became accustomed to the dim light. It was that unearthly storm light again, which served not so much to light up the ship as illuminate what looked like solid walls of cloud surrounding us on every side and reaching up to a space in which stars swam erratically all together. The glimmering sails were empty! Below them the world of water made no sense, for there were dimly descriable mountains ahead and astern of us—black mountains. Then, in the first few moments of my gaze, the one astern changed shape, sank down and perhaps vanished. I say "perhaps", for I did not see it go! As the mountain sank away I felt a stronger and stronger pull on my limbs, so that once more I seemed to be hanging, this time from the shrouds. The whole length of the waist sloped away from me under another mountain which had grown up before the bows—grown up and bid fair to fall on us. The tops'ls filled with loud bangs and the main course followed suit with explosions like cannon shot. We were lifted to the top of the world. I made a run for the stairs and got there, clinging to the rail. While the ship was upright I reached the top of the stairs and thrust my head above the level of the deck. I could see no one!

Was that the most terrifying moment of my life? No— there were others to come. But this, which might have been the prime contender, was muted and qualified by my sheer inability to believe in it! The quarterdeck deserted—oh,

God, the wheel! I scrambled back down the stair which was suddenly flat and hauled myself—uphill? sideways?—into the steering space.

"Edmund! Oh, thank God! Help me!"

The need was plain enough. I trod on the body of a man, dead or unconscious. Charles hung from the starboard side of the wheel, bearing down on it.

"Starboard!"

That was the beginning of a period when I had no time to be frightened. For what was in fact minutes but seemed timeless, I put such strength as I had to aid and increase the efforts that Charles made to handle the wheel in that sea by himself. I did help. I felt the wheel move under my applications and often what Charles himself could only begin I helped him carry through to its conclusion. The beginning of a movement of the wheel is easy enough, the whipstaff sees to that! But then after your strength has been put into flexing it, there is always a moment at which nothing, it seems, but sheer blind determination to defeat some invisible monster will allow one's muscles to carry the thing through. I do not know how often the two of us moved the wheel. The movements were gross, for the ship was as near as nothing still since the puffs of air that filled her sails on the crests of these mountains were enough to give us only the merest token of steerage way. Presently Charles ceased to give me orders, for it was obvious that I could follow what he wanted without words. The requirements of the wheel spoke to me in their own language.

"All right, sir."

It was a seaman. There were two—taking the wheel from us. Someone was on his knees and shaking the unconscious body on which I had stepped. The captain was there in the waist. There was blood on his face and a pistol in his hand. He was hatless, staring up at the sails.

"Midships!"

And then in a calm voice:

"I have her, Mr Summers."

I crawled away from the wheel to the stairs. Mr Summers joined me on hands and knees.

"I was not called for the middle!"

He spoke exhaustedly.

"It is not the middle. It is the morning watch. I cannot talk."

"What in the name of God—"

He shook his head. I fell silent, glad of a rail to hold on to.

"Are you all right, Charles?"

He nodded. The sense of usefulness, of being able to do more than cower in my bunk, was strong upon me.

"I will see what is to be done. There may be—"

I made my way up to the quarterdeck. The captain and Lieutenant Cumbershum stood by the forrard rail. I worked along it and shouted unnecessarily at Cumbershum.

"Can I help?"

His snarled answer was still in the air when some force tore me from the rail, held me suspended in a moment of positive flight.

"Stay out of trouble!"

I fell *on* rather than against the stairs up to the poop. I crawled up and entwined myself in the rails at this loftiest part of the hull. There was a faint wind, but just enough to fill the sails when it had the opportunity. For the rest, the sight was enough to send a man scuttling down to the bilges so as not to see the end which was coming upon him. Those waves which had been hidden or even beaten down by the smother of the storm had now come forth. The dying wind had allowed them to form in their ranges. I saw that our world was limited to three waves, three ranges, one astern of us, one ahead, one supporting us for the moment between them. Then, as our stern sank, dimension and direction fell into confusion. The bows towered above us and then fell until we seemed to hang above them. The sight was unbearable and I shut my eyes. I became therefore, as they say in books, "all ears". As the stern sank under me I heard the successive flap and clatter as one course of sails after the other lost the wind. The thunder as of great guns was our sails filling as we were lifted up again into the faintest of airs—bows first, stern first? The con must take such movements into account, for they might make the rudder work in reverse, a contingency for which the men at the wheel would not be able to allow. Yet a small mistake in these vast seas would allow the ship to broach to, be overset and sunk—This then was why an officer must stand, hour after hour, exercising his judgement and minute by minute hazarding us all on it!

I opened my eyes and found it just possible to keep them open. The faintest trace of wind breathed on my cheek. We were, I saw, on a crest, though in the darkness behind my eyelids I had thought us in a trough. Now we slid back and it seemed a gulf opened under the stern—there was no light in that abyss towards which we sped and I *clenched* my eyes shut as that blackness of water moved the ship on to an even keel, then tilted her, pitched her the other way until she was standing on her bowsprit.

At last I got my eyes open once more. The snail-trail of our oil glistened astern of us over one mountain range which was all that could be seen there even when we were on the crest of the next. These ranges made no spray, had no foam on them. They were a welter of black flint.

Time and again.

There were gleams and glitters now and then, either moon on water or some curious quality of the water itself.

Time and again.

There was a noise to be detected. It was not a ship noise, sail noise, wind noise. It was a *thump*, then a prolonged but diminishing roar to follow. I could fit the noise to nothing in my experience for all the time we had spent, all those months with the limited repertoire of the sights and sounds of water—

Of course! It was solidity! It was one of those horrible ranges striking rock! I was on my feet, my mouth open to shout—but my seaboots shot from under me and in a moment I had skidded the short length of the poop and crashed into the after rail under the larboard lantern! My mouth had been open to shout something or scream, for the inference of solidity in all this water was very terrible, but the breath had all been knocked out of me. I do not know how near I came to breaking the rail and ending my career hopelessly in a streak of oily water, but at least the upright I struck was not rotten whatever was to be said of the rest of the ship. I scuttled back to my previous place as if that were safer. This was panic which now knocked out of me all the honour and heroics together with my breath.

I stared round me. We were rising at another range— they must have been a quarter of a mile apart—and saw nothing but black, horrible flint with a sullen dawn sky over it, dully shining flint, liquid flint—how to convey the sheer horror of *size*? For after all, the three moving mountains among which we were now living were nothing but ripples—yet magnified, multiplied in size past the huge, the colossal, to the point where they were overwhelmingly monstrous! They were a new dimension in the nature of water. This nature did seem to allow us to live—just; was not inimical, would not, so to say, go out of its way to harm us. For a mad moment I felt that could I but lay my ear close to the glistening, mobile blackness I should be able to hear into its very being, hear, it may be, the fricative movement of one particle against another. But then I remembered how we were literally tied together by the undergirdings and my soul became nothing but terror.

For I heard that same sudden *thump*, then grumbling diminution from somewhere over the larger horizon—that one which a man might see if he dared to climb the mast— a consideration which made me sick to think of—say then a horizon visible to some giant here who was made to the same measure as our watery ranges. Land, then, was within earshot?

The dawn was clouding over. Light lifted off the earth so that the sea itself collected blackness wherever there was allowed a temporary hollow. I will try to find the words which will describe what happened at this point of suspension between day and night. We were poised on one range when a new thing began to happen to the range which was pursuing us. I cannot tell even now what the cause was. We were not in shallow water, that is certain. Everywhere about us and for many hundreds of miles— perhaps thousands—the bottom, the solid globe was miles away down there under the majesty of the liquid element. Was there perhaps some confusion or even contrariety in that current with its endlessly marching billows, moving from one age to another round the bottom of the world? Whatever it was, the range pursuing us began to steepen and sharpen. Except for the trivial notch in which our oil lay, the whole wave—I call it "wave" having no better word—stood sheer. For a mile, it may be, on either hand it stood ready, then curved slowly and fell! I heard the hiss of the waters in the air even as they descended and then the strike of water on water, acres, miles of it, with a noise which went beyond noise. For that fall was a feeling, a stab in either ear, after which I could hear nothing. But I had my eyes still. At the moment of fall, as if the invisible air was a solid thing, a line of foam and spray flicked away across the sea. It *was* air, it was the air displaced by the fall of the mountain and thrust in every direction with the speed of a musket ball. But now on either hand the sea went mad, foaming past us higher than the waist, higher than the rail of the quarterdeck, the rail of the fo'castle. The poop, with my arms wound in the rail, was all that stood above the water. But then, as if the oil had slowed it, the water which had lain in our notch of safety, though it did not foam, stood up and washed clear over the poop as well. I suppose it was a moment at which a seabird gliding over these sunless gulfs would have seen nothing but foam and three masts projecting. I stared forward as soon as the water left me and saw our ship begin to labour up, water pouring off the fo'castle before the waist had reappeared. Two more sails were in tatters. Was it that fearsome gust of air?

To remain alone was no longer possible. I moved and slipped. It was a new hazard and a ridiculous one. For all Charles's care, his hanging of the bags of oil under the stern rather than the bows, our oil trail had come aboard at last. I crept to the ladder along the rail, or crawled rather, for most of the way I slipped and slid on my knees. High above me the sails "spoke".

Captain Anderson had the con. He stood just aft of the wheel. Cumbershum lolled by the starboard rail, one arm hooked through it, his legs stretched along the deck. He looked across at the captain. He was speaking, for I could see his lips move. It was only then that I understood I had been literally deafened by the fall of the wave. I stayed in the shelter of the poop until little by little my hearing came back to me. Forrard I could see Mr Benét had men working already in the rigging among torn sails, though I did not think there was anything to be done. Had we not suffered a mortal blow? I did, I suppose, credit our ship with feelings and supposed that at any moment she might decide to give up this unequal struggle with an ocean never intended for ships—and particularly not for a superannuated hulk rendering like an old boot.

I glanced up at the sails. Those that had escaped destruction were full and Benét's men were working the yards round. There was wind—enough for steerage way, enough even for security. The ranges themselves as though the monstrous billow which had broken round us like some marine cataclysm had been the peak of all, a seventh wave beyond all seventh waves, was being succeeded by smaller ones.

I could hear Charles speaking thickly, as though his mouth had been damaged.

"Wind's moving on to the quarter, sir. We could set stays'ls."

The captain stared over the quarter, then back at Charles.

"Are you fit?"

Charles laboured to his feet.

"Think so, sir."

"Stays'ls then—" The captain turned to me and seemed about to speak but changed his mind and stumped to the forrard rail.

(15)

It took that day which was dawning and the next one too for Captain Anderson and his officers to restore some order and routine to the vessel. For one thing, getting the pervasive film of oil off required the whole crew, the soldiers and the emigrants!

The stuff was everywhere. It even reached some fifteen feet up the mainmast, or so Bates assured us. In the lobby it was smeared to a height of three feet along the bulkheads and doors through which it had effected some degree of entry to the cabins. Of sheer necessity the panic among the people which had gone near to drowning us all was ignored tacitly, though I am sure the captain was enraged at the situation in which he found himself. To abandon the post of duty was of course a fault which should have been punished with the utmost severity. I do not say this in indignation but from a cool sense of what some other ship might expect of her people with such an example before them! I repeat, there is no doubt that men abandoned their duty and tried to hide from the sea. As Charles once said, "Men, like cables, have each their breaking strain." Next to open mutiny the crew had committed the blackest crime in a seaman's calendar.

Yet what was to be done about it? A minority, even one possessing the natural authority of office, cannot guarantee obedience in making the body politic punish itself! No one could deny they had been sorely tried. Apart from the weather, our outrageously lengthy voyage meant that the food was scanty and the drink almost gone. We had little firing left, so that hot water was a luxury no longer obtainable even for the ladies. The ship was labouring.

The pumping, though not constant as in the heaviest weather, was nevertheless a sore trial to men becoming weak through exposure, toil and inadequate nourishment.

However, the thing was done. The ship was scrubbed, squeegeed, mopped and dried until at least a man with a seaman's sense of balance could keep his footing. Those sails which could be mended were attended to and others spread. Whatever else the ship lacked she was well provided with rope and canvas. A great deal of fishing went on in the easier weather which we then experienced though nothing that was caught came my way. Fish do not appear to be tempted to the line from a large vessel. Perhaps rumour of that strangest of fish, Man, had descended among the finny tribes! We did, however, see whales often enough and Mr Benét was said to have suggested a number of ways of killing them. The crew, though most crafts and skills were represented among them—particularly after they had heard his mad idea for a harpoon with an explosive charge of gunpowder attached to it—were not eager.

My own suggestion of using our great guns and firing, as near as we could, a broadside at the monsters met with no better success. We settled therefore to our short commons and were only consoled by the thought—the fact—that we were *getting on*. The foremast had passed the severest of trials triumphantly. When the light wind was broad enough on the quarter we spread not just stuns'ls, but stays'ls too—large triangular areas of canvas stretched between the masts rather than on them. For days I believe we never made less than six knots.

The reader who is not a seaman must accept my apologies for these lengthy divergences into a detailed account of their craft and skill! The fact is that I miss continually the point I am trying to convey. When your life depends on it there is a pleasure like no other in the movement towards your goal, in the chuckle of cleft water at the forefoot, the swell of sails, the movement night and day of a mass of cleverly constructed timber which must come close to totalling two thousand tons! The very seamen themselves walked with a more cheerful gait and a readier response to orders. Everyone seemed happy, even the officers—except perhaps Charles. He, I have to say, clung to the idea of a spark of fire burrowing in the shoe under the foremast! During another of those middle watches which I so enjoyed I taxed him with it.

"Confess, Charles. The mast is safe. You are hugging to yourself the thought that Mr Benét might be wrong after all!"

"He cannot always be right. No man can. Since he is wrong in his proposed method of finding our longitude—"

"Wrong?"

"The theory is correct—but do you understand the difficulty, the near-impossibility of measuring the angular separation of two heavenly bodies—one of them at least changing shape all the time?"

"I asked the sailing master to explain Mr Benét's method to me but he would not."

"It is a question of parallax and so on. It seems to involve the moon, the sun, planets and even the moons of planets— a whole cobweb of measurements—the man is brilliantly mad!"

"Yet he was right before. Do not, I beg of you, Charles, let a habit of dislike blind you to the man's merits. I cannot endure to see you less than you are! Forgive me—I am now the one to preach."

"You may do so. My objection to Mr Benét's method of finding our latitude without reference to chronometers is based on reason not dislike. If the most learned and intellectual minds of our country have abandoned this method it is because the method is inaccurate. Is he mad or am I?"

"Not you, I beg—you are our prop and stay in informed common sense!"

"Well. We have a passage at least a hundred miles wide between the few islands of this ocean. Knowing the latitude is enough to keep us safely between them. We cannot yet be far enough advanced to risk running on our objective before we see it. That day must look after itself."

Mr Prettiman no longer screamed or roared when the vessel pitched. My simple plan of "turning him end for end" seemed successful. He might be dying but was doing so peacefully. I had tried to avoid Mrs Prettiman since the time when she had—oh, I felt it too deeply to play with the event in Tarpaulin!—when she had given her opinion of me in the measured tones of a judgement from the bench. Once, she came into the saloon when I was there but left before I had time even to get on my feet. Once, I detected her running *downhill* across the lobby at a roll of the ship, and after I had seen her arrive safely at the rail between the doors of the cabins I averted my face and passed on. She still kept to her "seaman's rig" and I could not but applaud her decision. Once you have accustomed yourself to a sight sufficiently shocking at first, there is little to disconcert you in the sight of a lady wearing "trowsers". Indeed, if you consider the possible inconveniences and *revelations* which the costume proper to a lady on shore might occasion in a pitching, tossing, reeling vessel, trowsers, or a cleverly made female form of them, might well be thought more appropriate than skirts. What is more, they are undoubtedly safer, since a lady has no longer to put propriety not to say decency at odds with safety and prefer death to immodesty like the girl in the French story.

All the same, I was fated to confront her again and in circumstances which were reminiscent—though she was devoting herself to the sick man—of high comedy. I had been walking, or rather staggering, in the waist, for the weather now seemed set so fair that where possible I had ceased to make use of the lifelines. At times the dark and soaked deck wore the dirty white of salt beneath which the ancient wood showed mouldy splinters and here and there oakum pushing through the tar of the seams like hair. It was not, one might have thought, a place in which the human mind could contemplate anything other than its latter end. Yet as far as I could see no one did so. We were inured to danger, some of us made indifferent to it, some of us—Bowles for example—in a state of constant dread, some of us coarsened by it and some finding in it a source of exhilaration, like young Mr Taylor who sang, whistled and laughed in a way that the more sullen of us, such as I myself, found positively demented. One, at least, appeared to be above such trivial matters as death. It was Mr Benét. As I staggered back from a brief word or two with Mr East at the break of the fo'castle I saw him coming off watch, down the ladder from the quarterdeck. He had a paper in his hand, his eyes which were wide open looked clean out of our dirty world, and there was an ecstatic smile on his face. He ignored me as I approached, and rushed into the lobby. The foremast being safe as far as anyone knew, I thought he had turned his attention to his next craze, the foolish scheme of finding our position without the use of a chronometer. It was a scheme I thought I might well understand and hurried after him. I reached the door of the lobby just as he had knocked on Mrs Prettiman's door and evidently been answered, for he opened the door wide, stepped into the cabin and *pulled the door to behind him!* This was too much. If *he* had no care for the lady's reputation, *I* had! Though it was "uphill" for the nonce, I was three-quarters of the way to that door and so careless through outrage that a buck of the ship flung me face down on the slippery deck. I was stunned, I think, for a moment, for I was no more than on my knees when the door of her cabin burst open and with a positive clatter of his tarpaulin garments, Benét came staggering out. He had no paper in his hand. The door slammed shut behind him. The next roll to the one which had floored me sent him flying downhill in a most unseamanlike manner across the lobby. He was no longer smiling. He struck the great cylinder of the mizzenmast and stood rocking above me. Then with speechless care he went to the ladder down to the wardroom and disappeared.

But I had seen! On his left cheek there was a white patch, and in the few moments during which he remained in view, with the deepest satisfaction and indignation I saw that patch turn to the pink shape of a lady's hand!

However, my duty was plain. Mr Prettiman was in no state to defend the lady. The offer must come from me. I went to the door and tapped. After a few moments it was— I will not say "pushed" but flung open.

The fact is I was intimidated by that lady! Was it perhaps her years? I do not think so. She stood there now and glared at me as if I had been Benét. As the voyage lengthened towards a year, her own years had become less and less obvious to the casual beholder. True, the sun and wind had darkened her features to a uniform brown which was more appropriate to the peasantry than a lady from the Close! Her hair, which she commonly bound up with a scarf instead of the bonnet she had once thought suitable to her condition, had a habit of escaping—for it was abundant. It tended to catch the eye irritatingly. It hung now about her face and shoulders. Her person was otherwise quite unexceptionable.

I had no time to offer my services. The crimson of indignation suffused her cheeks despite the attentions of the sun.

"Are all the young men in this ship stark, staring mad?"

My mouth was open to reply when we were both interrupted.

"Letitia!"

It was Mr Prettiman calling from his bed of pain—and now repeating the call in tones not much like those of an invalid.

"Letty!"

Mrs Prettiman closed the door behind her and opened that of her husband's cabin. She spoke over her shoulder.

"Please remain, Mr Talbot. I wish to speak with you."

She shut the door behind her. So there I stood, and just as a schoolboy who does not know whether he is to run an errand or be punished for a misdeed but fears the worst, and he cocks his ear to find (if he can) a clue to his fate but is not able to translate the sounds that come so faintly to him from an adult world, so nor could I! For the first human sound I heard was surely that of laughter! He—a dying man! She—his devoted wife! I—

His cabin door opened and she came out. I got the door of her cabin open and held it for her. She passed inside and stood by the canvas washbasin staring into her right hand. With an exclamation of distaste she seized a scrap of cambric and scrubbed the palm vigorously. She caught my eye, stopped, then flounced herself down in the canvas chair in a way which had she been a girl I would have called pettish. She put some of her hair back with her right hand but quite without effect, for it fell forward again.

"*Fudge!*"

She caught my eye again and had the grace to blush a little.

"Oh, come in, Mr Talbot. Kindly latch the door back against the stop. The proprieties must be observed. We must not sully your reputation—"

I suppose my jaw had dropped, for she seemed irritated.

"Sit on the bunk, for Heaven's sake! I cannot be for ever staring up at the ceiling."

I did so.

"If you please, Mrs Prettiman, I had wished to offer my services. Believing Mr Prettiman incapacitated by his injuries—"

"Oh, he is, he is!"

"By good fortune I saw Mr Benét force his attentions—"

"Say no more, sir."

"Force his ridiculous verses on you—"

Mrs Prettiman sighed.

"That is the trouble, Mr Talbot. They are not ridiculous except in the article of addressing me as 'Egeria'. He is a talented young man. Mr Prettiman and I desire that the affair should be forgotten. Yet I blame myself in part. I am not usually an unreasonable woman, but to be addressed in such terms, to have my hand seized in such a manner—and all from a man young enough to be—a younger brother, Mr Talbot."

"He deserves to be flogged!"

"There shall be no violence, sir. Once and for all, I will not have it!"

"He should be ashamed—"

"*I* am ashamed. I am not accustomed to such feelings. I am happy to say I have not merited them."

I opened my mouth to agree—then shut it again. She went on.

"The extraordinary events—the fearful weather—the queue of simple souls doing Mr Prettiman reverence—your well-meant but clumsy action—"

She paused for a while.

"Pray continue."

"You see, he is not dying! Since you stretched his poor torn leg the swelling has subsided. Perhaps he will not walk again. He is not out of danger. But the pain is becoming bearable. How can I be ashamed that he is recovering? I am delighted and ashamed! He too has owned that, in some ways, if it were not for the cessation of pain he would

himself be ashamed of his recovery! He and I, you see—we
are rendered *conscious* by the situation. This is all mad, you
see. But true!"

"I understand, indeed I do! Not dying! For there is a
kind of magical comedy about our situation. The intellect
disdains what the heart knows feelingly! I *know* that!"

"Mr Talbot! This from you whom I have thought
incapable—"

"Oh, I am, ma'am, wholly so. But, as you say, so much
has happened; and after all, the world is upside down, is it
not? We hang from it by our feet!"

"This is fanciful! We all change. It is danger, I suppose,
which shows us all in our true colours, our grim captain,
the right man to get us where we are going, our decayed
vessel contriving to float and Mr Prettiman's careful plans
all thrown into the melting pot."

"But he is recovering!"

"So he may be. But I cannot conceive of his leg ever
being as serviceable as it was. How can he get about to
examine the condition of the convicts? How can he endure
the hardship of exploration, of leading a crowd of reformed
criminals and settlers into the interior of this continent in
search of his promised land?"

"I see."

"Aloysius Prettiman—who was to be to the Southern
Ocean what Tom Paine was to the Atlantic—lamed and
having to be helped where he had hoped to lead!"

My immediate thought was, *This is phantasy*, but I did
not say so.

"I am sure our government will help, ma'am!"

She had been looking, as it were, through the bulkhead
as if at some more distant prospect. Now she glanced at
me and smiled—bitterly, I thought.

"To found the Ideal City? There a refreshing
innocence about you, sir. Mr Prettiman has revealed to

me the elaborations and knaveries of the government! Be sure they will have known of his intentions even before we sailed. There is no harm in your knowing now what we may have concealed from them, but he—we—carry a printing press with us."

The air about me and particularly about my ears seemed to burn, but I did not know what to say. It seemed as if my whole interior self was suddenly spread out for her inspection. I was once more in the high-ceilinged office before the huge desk.

By the bye, Talbot. You will be going out in the same ship as Prettiman and his printing press. Keep an eye on him.

"You were about to say, sir?"

"I shall be a part, however small, of that government."

"My dear Mr Talbot! I was not thinking of you! We believe now that they will have put a spy to sail with us."

"Spy!"

"An agent of the government if you prefer euphemisms. Indeed"—here she glanced through the open door, then back at me—"Mr Prettiman believes that the accident which crippled him may not have been a simple accident."

"That is impossible!"

"Lean your head a little closer, sir. I wish to whisper. He finds Mr Bowles's masquerade as a solicitor's clerk transparent."

"Bowles!"

"Your astonishment is natural. Well, there it is. What are we to do?"

"You should both go home, I believe."

"You think it is only in England—in Europe—he would find the medical attention which might restore him to some degree of mobility? He will not be so easily deflected from his purpose!"

"Even so, it is good news that he is better. Now for Mr

Benét. If he continues to plague you, you may call on me. I will take his verses and invite him to—"

"I wish things were as simple. As I said, his verses are not all ridiculous. This, though it addresses me as 'Egeria', is pompous but fluent and far above what might be expected from a naval officer. Put together with his two contrivances which are said to have saved our lives—"

"I would mention first the frapping invented by Lieutenant Summers! That above all has been the principal agent of our preservation. Why, even in the late tempest, it held the ship together! Believe me, Mr Summers—"

She held up her hand, smiling.

"I understand you. You need not continue. So believe *me* that at moments when your careless assumptions of privilege have been most provoking you have been rendered tolerable by your evident admiration for that worthy man!"

It was a backhander. But then, as I have said, Mrs Prettiman was an adept of the backhander. I was annoyed and should have said something like—"For a lady who indulges in premarital copulation", but I did not. As the words rang in my head I heard myself use other ones.

"Is it impossible that I should read the verses to Egeria?"

"Quite impossible. I am addressed in such terms as puts me to the blush."

Again the words in my head were pushed aside by others—

"I might agree with more of the verses than you think, Mrs Prettiman."

Oh, it was intolerable! She was looking at me with plain astonishment!

"One request, ma'am. May I visit the patient?"

"He is asleep, I think—I hope. Since we have no more laudanum sleep is precious and hard to come by."

"I would go in like a mouse and sit by him till he wakes."

She seemed doubtful. I pressed the point.

"Believe me, when I knew of him at first I made all the assumptions about your husband which could be drawn from gross political caricatures. But my first presence at his bedside—well. Now I remember my stumble against his leg—though I may be the unwitting agent of his recovery—as a moment which will haunt me for ever, the moment when I inflicted on him such agony that he fainted away with it."

"And so?"

"I should be less than human did I not wish to offer him my congratulations on his partial recovery, my commiserations on his disability and my profound sorrow for the agony I caused him."

"No man could say fairer than that, Mr Talbot. Had you by any chance evolved and put by you those ringing periods?"

I was silent. Suddenly she started to speak, I know not what, for now it was my turn to hold up a hand.

"Say no more, Mrs Prettiman. I am fated by my nature to talk like that sometimes. Generally it makes people believe me older than I am."

"So I suppose. But you will grow out of it."

I was silent for a moment. Who was she to be critical of me? A lady, a woman who had behaved like a common trollop!

"I do not desire to 'grow out of it'. And now, ma'am, may I visit the patient?"

Her face was quite without expression as she bowed in assent.

(16)

I left Mrs Prettiman's cabin and closed the door behind me without looking back. I stood for a few moments in the rocking lobby and thought. I had meant to be uniformly dignified and stern with her—but there it was!

I remembered the letter which the man had given me when he thought himself dying. Would he not wish to have it back now he was on the mend? But I had not pockets in my seaman's rig in which the letter might be carried without crumpling and I did not wish to carry it openly in my hand. She might look out, see, and ask and so set in train endless complications and confusions. I therefore opened Mr Prettiman's door as quietly as I had shut hers—there was a thump and hiss beyond the wall as some point of cornering water struck our hull—and brought it to behind me. He lay, as I have said, turned end for end. His head was now next to the writing flap. I moved forward cautiously and sat in the canvas chair by him. There was no longer a mound lifting the bedclothes at his waist. The blankets were gone as well. A cotton sheet and a shawl of woven material were all that covered his body. The air was not balmy. Such an adjective would be out of place for any sickroom! But the scanty bedclothes gave me a sudden awareness of the other change in our circumstances. Water might still swill about our feet and legs—condensation might lie on and stream down any wall, any bulkhead, but we were at last approaching, if we had not reached it, the southern spring! If this continued, I thought, we should find ourselves wearing "doldrums" rig again!

Mr Prettiman's eyes were closed and he breathed easily. His face was still wasted and lined but there was now the faintest trace of colour in his hollow cheeks where before there had been nothing but shadow. His hands lay outside the sheet, one of them on an open book. I leaned forward with a natural curiosity but must have disturbed him somehow. His head turned on the pillow, his breathing altered—became laboured. I kept deadly still in a state of apprehension that I had injured him all over again! But then his breathing eased, his hand moved from the book and a page stood up so that I could see what it was.

"Good God! Pindar!"

His eyes opened and he turned his head.

"You. Young Talbot."

"Mrs Prettiman said she thought you wouldn't mind if I sat by the bunk until you woke, sir."

"Had to move, didn't you? Had to speak? Had to wake me?"

"No, Mr Prettiman! The word was—involuntary."

A trace of a smile appeared.

"What else did you suppose I meant? But never mind. You said 'Pindar'."

"Yes, sir. There, by your hand."

"When you have to lie flat, holding up a book makes the whole thing a trial. I was looking for a quotation and drifted off. It's somewhere in the sixth Olympian. It goes—'φύονται δὲ καὶ νέοις ἐν ἀνδράσιν πολιαί—' "

The lines were very familiar to me.

" 'Grey hairs flourish even among young men'—and it goes on—'here and there before the right time of life for it'. But that's not the sixth Olympian. It's the fourth, right at the end. May I—? There!"

"So you know!"

"Well, sir, we are all having a rough time of it, aren't we? I daresay I could find a grey hair or two if I looked."

"Not that, boy! The Greek! You've kept it up—Why?"

"I just liked it, sir, I suppose. I read it now and then."

"No boy of your age who keeps up his Greek can be entirely witless—silly perhaps—but with some inkling of a wider view."

"I'm not precisely a boy, Mr Prettiman!"

"You're not precisely a mature man either! Now don't answer back. I must apologize for not looking you straight in the face all the time but I have to lie flat, you see. This leg. Have to hobble for the rest of my life, I suppose. How is a man to get round like that? I suppose the surgeons will strap me up. Do you think I shall be able to ride?"

"I can't say."

"Might be able to ride side-saddle. Mrs Prettiman would ride astride, of course, in her trowsers"—a laugh began in his chest but never reached the surface except to give it a heave or two—" 'Here come the Prettimans,' they'll say. 'Which is which?' "

"I came in to say, sir, that I congratulate you on your recovery, and apologize for my part in it."

The laugh was right there, loud and prolonged. Tears ran out of his eyes.

" 'Apologize for my part in it'! Oh, my hip!"

"I see what you mean, sir, and it is indeed amusing—or I would have thought it so had I not said it myself. But I am sincerely sorry for the terrible pain I caused you."

"You certainly gave me a twinge, Talbot. But without it I should still be in a sad case. Having your own thigh bone rammed up into your body is no joke, I can tell you. Well. So you know more Greek than was beaten into you. Latin, of course. But let us say nothing of Latin. It is a language for sergeants. Why do you read Greek then? Come along!"

"I don't know. Amusement perhaps. No, that won't do. Glaucus and Diomede—"

"Intellectual snobbery? Being better than your neighbour? Belonging to a select few?"

"Yes, to some extent. But there is more, sir, as well you know!"

"Ambitious to become a bishop?"

"No, sir. But you must not be plagued with me, Mr Prettiman. I have said how sincerely sorry I am for the pain I caused you. And now I will leave you."

Good God, this was in the very vein of Parson Colley! But the sick man was making fretful motions of denial with his right hand.

"Don't go!"

"I believe I am not an adequate conversationalist for you, sir. And so—"

"My dear Mr Talbot!—does that form of address content you?—if you had lain for days in the forced contemplation of a white-painted ceiling only eighteen inches above your head, I don't know what seamen call it—"

"The Tarpaulins would call it 'the deckhead', sir. Well, I am flattered to be regarded as a little more interesting than white paint!"

"Your opinions interest me profoundly. Some of them have been reported to me while others I must confess I have overheard, for you know you tend to speak in a loud not to say authoritative manner!"

"As I am clearly—"

"I said 'Don't go!' "

"That was certainly authoritative!"

"So it was. We must be gentle with each other. Sit down again—please! There. Now. What is the purpose of your voyage?"

"I would have said a few months ago that it was to fit me for a position of responsibility in the government of my country. Now my ambitions are somewhat different."

"Since *Alcyone* drifted alongside us with her ladies— Oh, sit down! Do you think that sort of thing can be private? Marriage is a public declaration! I should know!"

"I could only wish it had indeed been a question of marriage—but I do not suppose our conditions are similar."

"I should hope not indeed! The considered alliance of
two persons dedicated to the betterment of the human
condition is not lightly to be compared with—"

" 'Oh, she doth teach the torches to burn bright!' "

"You started your voyage with the objectivity of ignorance and are finishing it with the subjectivity of knowledge, pain, the hope of indulgence—"

"And you, sir, travelling with the avowed intention of
making trouble—of troubling this Antipodean society is
created wholly for its own betterment! It is a noble gesture
which offers freedom and rehabilitation even to the criminal elements of our own society at home!"

"Do you know 'our own society'?"

"I have lived in it!"

"School. University. A country house. Have you ever
visited a city slum?"

"Good God, no!"

"The cottages on your father's estates. Do the labour-
ers sleep in beds?"

"They are accustomed to the ground. They are happy
there. They would not know what to do with a bed stood
on legs!"

"You know nothing."

"You are clearly seized of universal truths, Mr Prettiman.
Some of us do not find them so easy to come by!"

"Some of us do not try to find them."

"The established order—"

"Is sick!"

This was a kind of cry which convulsed the man's
body. It was resumed—subsumed in one of those great
cries which had so disconcerted me. His body which had
jerked under the bedclothes now shook as with the
extremity of passion, but this was pain. His face had paled

again. Sweat coursed down it as he gritted his teeth. The door opened and Mrs Prettiman hastened in. She looked quickly from him to me. Then she pulled a large handkerchief from beneath his pillow and wiped his face with it. She murmured to him. I could catch no more than the word "Aloysius" and the word "calm". His anguish appeared to subside. I was rising from the chair again to withdraw from this private scene when his hand shot out and grasped my wrist firmly.

"Stay, Talbot. Letty. We have a specimen. What do you say? Shall we see if anything is to be done with it?"

The word "specimen" had a precise medical connotation as far as I was concerned. But to my surprise Mr Prettiman continued to hold my wrist instead of allowing my departure. Mrs Prettiman, on the other hand—and I noticed that her hair was now properly confined and hidden—said nothing but nodded solemnly, then withdrew. I feared that I might be about to be lured into some medical nastiness but the sick man simply continued our previous conversation.

"What *do* you know then, Mr Talbot?"

I thought.

"I know fear. I know a friendship which would exchange gold armour for bronze. Above all, I know love."

"Oh, do you? Do you not vaunt yourself? Are you sure you are not puffed up? Do you not seek your own?"

"Perhaps. But without it I am indeed become as sounding brass and tinkling cymbals. And long before St Paul, did not Plato claim that we may ascend from the one love to the other?"

"Well said, my boy! Well said indeed! There is a book above my head. The third along, I think. Please take it down. Thank you. Will you read it to me?"

"It is French."

"Do not speak so dismissively of the language just because you are acquainted with a greater one!"

"To tell you the truth, I have had such a dose of Racine from my godfather it has soured me with their whole literature."

"This is by a master who could stand with all but the very greatest of the ancients."

"Very well, sir. What do you want me to read?"

So, moving with roll and heave, with creak of timber and roar of wind, I found myself as we moved towards the unknown shore sitting by the bed of a man as strange and unknown; and reading aloud with an accent which appeared to satisfy Mr Prettiman, though it was little like Mr Benét's, from Voltaire's *Candide*! He had directed me as I now see was inevitable, to the passages concerning Eldorado. As I read, an astonishing change began to appear in Mr Prettiman. He nodded every now and then, his lips moved, his eyes, as if they did not merely receive light but could refashion it, seemed to shine with an interior source of their own. His face flushed, words moved towards his lips but were never given air, he listened so intently. When I read out the words of *le bon vieillard*: "We don't pray to God, he gives us what we need, we are eternally grateful—we do not need priests, we are all priests!" he interrupted at last, crying out, "Yes, yes, that's it!"

It was my turn to interrupt.

"But, Mr Prettiman! This is no more than an expansion of Pindar—the Fortunate Isles—you have it there under your hand—allow me!"

I took the book, found the place and read it out to him.

" 'ἀπονέστερον ἐσλοὶ δέκονται βίοτον, οὐ χθόνα ταράσσοντες ἐν χερὸς ἀκμᾷ—', and so on."

When I had done he took the book back, glanced at the text, smiling, and muttered a translation.

" 'The gift of easy life they get, not irritating earth with lusty hands, no, nor troubling salt water to scrape a bare living—' "

"And the rest, sir! They rejoice in the *presence* of the gods! There's the tower of Cronos—ocean breezes, flowers of gold blazing—"

"Yes, yes, I remember. I might as well tell you, Edmund, that I had to learn it all by heart as an imposition and even that did not entirely spoil it! It was—perceptive of you to bring it into the ring with Eldorado. You are well read, my boy—and you read well too! But don't forget the difference between Pindar and Voltaire. Pindar is talking about a mythological land—"

"So is Voltaire, surely!"

"No no! Oh, I have no doubt that literally speaking South America was much different from the country Candide discovered! How could it be otherwise in a country devastated by the Roman Catholic Church?"

"They had not reached it."

"But there was indeed an Eldorado, and there will be again."

"You are overexciting yourself, sir. Shall I—"

"It is what this voyage is about, you see. Do you understand? How can I—I am crippled. Not for me, not for me. I may see the promised land, glimpse a far peak of Eldorado, but the country itself will be for other men!"

"And *that* is what the voyage is about?"

"What else? We would have gone, a caravan of convicts released, our printing press with us, immigrants of goodwill, women convicts, or the poor young followers of their ignorant men—"

"You are feverish, sir. I will call Mrs Prettiman."

"Stay."

For a while he was silent. He lay quiet, then spoke with his head straight in the pillow and his eyes shut.

"It seems I shall—survive if we all do. A certain document which I entrusted to you—"

"I had wondered, sir. Shall I bring it to you?"

"Wait. Why will you always try to be one step ahead? I am confined to my couch. Mrs Prettiman devotes herself to me. She must not be troubled with the view of such a missive or *ever know* that I entrusted it to your hands."

"Of course not, sir."

"So do not bring it back to this cabin. Drop it in the sea."

"If that is your wish, sir."

"Wait again. This is—difficult. You must know, Edmund, that the lady is like the land we are approaching?"

"Sir?"

"Good God! Where are your wits, boy? Unpolluted, sir!"

"Oh, *that*! I—I rejoice to hear it, sir. Of course I—"

He cut me off, glaring at me with the anger which was so close to his heart and his lips.

"Rejoice? Rejoice? Why should you 'rejoice'? And there is no 'of course' about it, sir! Had I not had the misfortune to dislocate this hip the lady would not now be unpolluted—that is to say—"

"I understand, sir. You need say no more. I will do it immediately and with such a good will—"

"Not with a rush but casually, boy—man I should say, should I not?"

"I hope so, sir. But 'Edmund' would be better."

"We must not have a youth dashing through the lobby and waving a paper in the air as if he were, were—"

"Lieutenant Benét? I will be discreet."

"And, Edmund. You read well."

"Thank you, sir!"

"So does Mrs Prettiman. But of course she does not read Greek. It is too much for a woman's brain."

"I doubt that in the case of Mrs Prettiman, sir. There have been bluestockings! But I take the point. I shall be happy, indeed flattered, to read to you on your bed of pain. And now if you will excuse me—"

"Any time you feel like coming back—if I am not asleep—"

I went away with the most mixed feelings, happiness, strangely enough, being the uppermost. It was a feeling which I was, from that day forward, to associate with him and her. When the memory of Miss Chumley—most adorable and commonsensical of young persons!—returned upon me I felt no more than that she would have agreed that they were likeable but mistaken—whereas I—

What shall I say? No matter what nonsense Mr Prettiman talked—and I have never entirely convinced myself that it was nonsense—the listener came away with a sense of well-being, of enlightenment, of feeling that *yes* it was true, the universe was great and glorious and that these adventures of the mind and body were the crown of things—a feeling that drifted away naturally enough, of course, as other considerations supervened and hid them!

So this, then, was the beginning of what for me was the strangest adventure of our long voyage. Still battered but in weather that seemed never to rise above the level of a favourable gale we sped eastward towards our goal and life was *irradiated* by the nature of them both—for sometimes she would bring her canvas chair and sit by me while I read to him. They were quite unlike any people I had ever met before! He was donnish; but there was nothing laughable about him unless it was his capacity for explosive anger. Beyond that his mind ranged vastly through the universe of space and time as it did through the other universe of books! And she, following his lead but not scrupling to differ from him and sometimes leading us where we had not thought to go! The Crown, the principle of hereditary honours, the dangers of democracy, Christianity, the family, war—indeed there were times when it seemed to me that I threw off my upbringing as a man might let armour drop around him and stand naked, defenceless, but free!

Then after a doze in the evening I would spend the middle with Charles, bring ideas to him and test them against his absolute integrity. I found in truth that I had never examined an idea before! To have read Plato and not tested an idea! It sounds impossible, but it is not, for I had done it.

(17)

It could not have been more than a day or two after I had become acquainted with Mr Prettiman that I noticed a change in Charles. He was more silent than before. At first I thought that he was concerned with the state of the ship but it was not so. The fact was, he found my sudden esteem for the social philosopher strange, not to say incomprehensible. Charles did not generalize. He would not examine the ideas of liberty, equality and fraternity but dismissed that modern trio because of the way they had been applied among the Gallic Race by the medium of the guillotine and the splendid wickedness of the Corsican! Always his mind moved at once to the practical.

"You will do yourself no good with the governor of a penal colony, Edmund, by tossing such ideas about as if you approved of them!"

The truth is, Charles was well enough where he was. Unlike mine, his ideas had been tested in the fire of his religion, Prettiman's in the cruelties and torments of social condemnation, derision, dislike. It was not more than a very few days after I had begun to read and discuss with the Prettimans that I taxed Charles with his silences. His reply—if in unconscious sympathy with him I may revert to Tarpaulin—*brought me up, all standing.*

"You are moving away from me, Edmund. That is all."

I seized him by the arm.

"No! Never!"

But it was true nevertheless. I liked him as much, would do for him as much. But set in the foreground of the world which Prettiman was opening to me, Charles was—diminished. I understood his practical approach, his anxious grasp of his position in the ship, his battle with jealousy and spite, his devotion to the *customs of the sea service* which would not allow him to criticize his captain even when his captain was wrong! I saw, and admired, his simple goodness. Surely, I told myself, that is enough? I thought of the way he found me dry clothing at a time when it seemed a miracle in that soaked ship. Thinking thus, it was then I first realized how he had contrived to free me from my haunted hutch for four hours of every night. Then I would remember Glaucus and Diomede, the bronze armour Charles had given me and the gold armour I had sworn to give him! The only armour which Charles would find golden would be promotion to post captain.

Yet Charles? I had no doubt at all of his courage. His knowledge of the economy of a ship was complete. Yet *Charles*, a ship's husband, in command of a ship, a warship with the future of our world in his hands?

I did dare to put my problem before Mr and Mrs Prettiman. Prettiman bade me undertake the exercise of *untwisting* the affair back to where it had started, and I understood at last that I had simply promised more than I could or should promise or perform. Mr Prettiman declined to help.

"You must, of course, do what you think is right. If you do not believe he is worth making post you must tell him so."

Of course I could not tell him! Who was I to do so? The result was there were now periods of silence from me during the middle watch as well as silence from Charles. Oh that voyage towards which I had looked as a simple adventure! What ramifications it had, what effects on the mind, the nature, what excitement, what sad learning, what casual tragedies and painful comedies in our rendering old hulk! What shaming self-knowledge! For brooding on my problem I even imagined one saying in the future—when my naval client had at last demonstrated his inadequacy as a post captain—*that was one of Talbot's recommendations, you know*. Sometimes I thought, and bitterly enough, that the only human quality to the depths of which there could be no limit was my personal meanness!

My broodings were interrupted by another twist in our society. It was the question of our longitude. I had known that Benét and the captain were immersed in some high theory of navigation but had not thought much about it. A glum Bowles brought me up to date. He illustrated in water spilt on the saloon table the problem before the captain. Sooner or later we must approach the new continent. But though we knew where we were to larboard or starboard, so to speak, we could not define our position fore and aft! In a sentence, without an accurate knowledge of our longitude we might hit land before we saw it! The solution adopted by seamen in earlier days had been to heave to during the hours of darkness and only advance when there was light enough. Naturally, this was a luxury which our captain could not afford with a crew on half rations and only those with good teeth able to profit by what was left. Add to our uncertainty the circumpolar current which might or might not be helping us towards our destination and it will be seen what an added exacerbation was inflicted on me by Lieutenant Benét's confident assertion that he could find our longitude without a chronometer. I put aside my dislike of the man and, knowing the time of his watch, waylaid him from my usual position by the main chains.

"A word with you, sir."

"A challenge?"

"Not at the moment—"

"Ah! So we are back on conversational terms, are we?"

"This matter of the longitude and the chronometers—"

"I thought it was pistols. Good God, Mr Talbot! Do you suppose Captain Cook carried chronometers with him?"

"Of course!"

"Well, he did not!"

With that, he leapt away up the stairs as the duty watch set about its four-hourly dance during the minute or two before the bell rang out. I followed him but already he was deep in talk with Anderson. Even when the watch was changed and Mr Askew descended from the quarter-deck, Benét and Anderson talked on about the moons of Jupiter! They bandied astronomy as if it were a ball game—eclipses, parallax, perigee and apogee—I began to have an uneasy feeling that they were both aware of me and were deliberately keeping me out!

"Lunar distance, Mr Benét. Agreed. But the check—"

"The passage of Calypso. We shall present it to their lordships—the Anderson-Benét method!"

Anderson laughed aloud! He did!

"No no! It is all yours, my boy!"

"No, sir—I insist!"

"Well. You had better make it work first."

The message was plain. Even so, the contrast between this excited pair—whether their "method" was practicable or not—and poor dear, dutiful Charles was so clear as to be painful. I stood, ostensibly watching the waves, until I was heartily tired of it. But the two men continued to ignore me and at last there was nothing left for me to do but go away. It was one of those defeats which are so easy to describe in their outward event and so impossible to sum up in their total effect. I went below, knowing that I had been set aside in a matter which concerned not just the Navy but every man, woman and child in the ship. It would have needed more than all the assurance with which I had entered the ship to break in and interrupt them; but I could not think precisely why.

I went cautiously down the ladders, for the ship was moving more that day. Water was coming aboard even into the waist, which fact would once have seemed notable to me though now it was common enough. Clear water was running inches deep with every roll over the planking newly scoured from Charles's oil—planking from between which, as some unhandy configuration of the sea passed under us, the spewed oakum flopped this way and that like worms in a flooded field. I was making my moody way to the saloon when I saw old Mr Brocklebank open the door, his legs wide apart, his tall and portly figure wrapped in the dirty coach cloak, and I decided that I wanted no closer acquaintance with him. I went to Mr Prettiman's door therefore and asked if I might read to him. He was glad to see me, he said, for he had passed a wakeful night now that the paregoric or laudanum was exhausted. He was not in pain but ached, he said, which was wearisome. I thought he looked a little feverish, for there was colour now high on his cheekbones and his eyes seemed unnaturally bright. He would not have me read to him. He said he would be unable to fix his attention. He wanted instead to know what the state of the ship was. He said he could feel that the weather had worsened again. I told him that the water was indeed moving about a little more but that we were getting along capitally. I went on to say—and now Mrs Prettiman entered—that the great *political* point in the ship was Mr Benét's proposal to find the longitude without reference to the chronometers. I laughed as I said this and Mrs Prettiman agreed with me, saying that she understood the use of the globes, having had to instruct the young in their value. Without exact knowledge of the time at the Greenwich meridian no ingenuity on earth could discover our longitude.

"You are wrong, Letitia."

She was as disconcerted as I.

"Benét said that Captain Cook had no chronometer."

"He is right, Edmund. The angular distance between the

673

moon and the sun was used to find longitude before the invention or the perfecting, rather, of the chronometer. The defect of the method was the skill required in making use of it."

"So Benét is right again!"

"Anderson took his proposal seriously?"

"Very seriously, I thought—even excitedly. But then, anything which our naval Adonis proposes is certain of an enthusiastic reception from that quarter."

Mrs Prettiman opened her mouth to speak but shut it again. Prettiman frowned up at the deckhead a few inches above his face.

"Anderson is no fool. I am told he is a complete seaman."

"So is Mr Summers, sir. Mr Summers says—"

I heard my voice trail off into silence. It was broken presently by Mrs Prettiman.

"We are all indebted to Mr Summers, Mr Talbot. His care of us and the ship."

"He is brave, too, ma'am. Why, in the last dreadful storm among those mountains of water he managed the wheel with his own hands and alone in the greatest danger! It might have killed him!"

Mr Prettiman cleared his throat.

"No one doubts that the first lieutenant is everything you say. But, you see, I do not think you have experienced the difference between a man who has a natural aptitude for the mathematics and one who has not. The difference is absolute—a matter not of quantity but of quality."

I had nothing to say to that. Mrs Prettiman spoke:

"I am told that you helped Mr Summers at the wheel, sir. It seems I am always, as a lady, in the position of expressing my gratitude to you."

"Oh, Lord, ma'am! It was nothing! Nothing at all—"

"Since there have been times when I have had to express other feelings and opinions I am happy to tell you that I believe your conduct was admirable and most manly!"

But Mr Prettiman was turning his head from side to side on the pillow.

"I cannot envisage the method—will he use the passage of a satellite as a check? But how? It is not so easy—"

"Aloysius, my dear, should you not try to sleep? I am sure Mr Talbot—"

"Of course, ma'am, I will go at once—"

"Stay, Edmund. What is the hurry? I am well enough in my mind, Letty, and see their Heavens as clearly as I see you! A man is seldom better employed than in their contemplation!"

"I believe you should not excite yourself, sir."

" '*This majestical roof, fretted with golden fire*—' "

"If it comes to that, sir—'*The floor of heaven is thick inlaid with patens of bright gold.*' "

"Does Mr Benét see them so through his sextant?"

"The young man is a poet, Aloysius. Is that not so, Mr Talbot?"

"He writes verses, ma'am, as who does not?"

"You?"

"Only in Latin, ma'am. I dare not reveal my scanty thoughts in the nudity and plainness of English speech."

"I am really rather impressed, Mr Talbot."

"Since I have you at a temporary disadvantage, ma'am, may I beg you to follow Mr Prettiman's example and address me as 'Edmund'?"

I thought she looked disconcerted at the suggestion. I was bold enough to press her still further.

"After all, ma'am, it is not improper in view of your— that is to say, in view of my—your—"

She burst out laughing.

"In view of my age, you mean? Edmund, my dear boy, you are quite, quite inimitable!"

"We were having a rational discussion, Letitia. Where was I?"

"You and Edmund were exchanging quotations so as to get the universe on a proper literary footing."

"What could be better than ascending from the trivial matter of our exact position on this globe to a contemplation of the universe into which we have been born?"

"And which, sir, is more truly revealed by poetry than prose!"

"Aloysius may agree with you, Edmund, but I am a plain woman."

"You do yourself less than justice, Letty. But, Edmund—continue."

"It is only that—little by little during this voyage, for one reason and another, poetry—has become open to me not as entertainment, as mere beauty—but as a loftiness—man at full stretch—then at night, with the stars—with preposterous Nature—I am half-ashamed to admit it—"

"Oh, look, boy, look! Can the whole be less than good? If it cannot—why, then good is what it must be! Can you not see the gesture, the evidence, the plain statement there, the music—as they used to say, the cry, the absolute! To live in conformity with that, each man to take it to him and open himself to it—I tell you, Edmund, there is not a poor depraved criminal in the land towards which we are moving who could not, by lifting his head, gaze straight into the fire of that love, that χάρις of which we spoke!"

"Criminals?"

"Imagine our caravan, we, a fire down below here—sparks of the Absolute—matching the fire up there—out there! Moving by cool night through the deserts of this new land towards Eldorado with nothing between our eyes and the Absolute, our ears and that music!"

"Yes. I see. It would be—the adventure of adventures!"

"You could come too, you know, Edmund. Anyone could come. There is nothing to stop you!"

"Your leg, sir. You are forgetting it, I believe."

"I am not. It will heal. I know it will. The fire in me will heal me. I know it will! I *will* go!"

"But do as Mrs Prettiman wishes, sir, and keep your body still."

"But you will come!"

I said nothing. It was a silence that grew, lengthened until the very noise of the water hissing past our hull sounded like some wordless voice; and at last I knew that it did not need words and was something even closer to me than words themselves. It was the cold, plain awareness which we call common sense.

And yet I really had *seen*! For a time, in that increasingly fetid hutch, I had felt the power of the man, that attraction of his passion. I had even glimpsed, or thought I glimpsed, our universe as a bubble afloat in the uncommensurable golden sea of the Absolute, the myriad sparks of fire, each the jewel in the head of an animal which could "look up".

They were both watching me. My fists clenched themselves and the perspiration burst out on my forehead. It was an astonishing kind of shame, I think—shame at my inability to say quite simply, "Yes, I will come." There was, too, a degree of anger at finding myself so suddenly pushed up against a wall, held up as it were by some philosophical highwayman with poetry in one hand and astronomy in the other! At last I looked from his flushed face, his expectant eyes, to Mrs Prettiman. She lowered hers and looked at her hands—not the way a seaman does, inspecting his palms, but looking at the backs and the nails. She glanced at her husband.

"I believe you should try to sleep, Aloysius."

I stood up unhandily, swaying against the movement of the vessel.

"I will read to you tomorrow, sir."

He frowned as if the concept were strange to him.

"Read? Oh yes, of course!"

I tried to smile at Mrs Prettiman, but fear it was a sad grimace, and felt my way out of the cabin. I had not shut the door behind me before I heard her murmur to him. I cannot tell what she said.

I told myself that other occasions would occur in which we might renew the conversation, continue what felt like the rising curve of our intimacy. I wished with a spontaneous passion not unlike his that I might be their friend. Yet I saw already that the price was impossibly high. I am after all a political animal with my spark, my—if I may descend to the language fit for sergeants—my *scintillans Dei*, well hidden. I suppose the excuse to be presented to the Absolute is that I did and do sincerely wish to exercise power for the betterment of my country: which of course, and fortunately in the case of England, is for the benefit of the world in general. Let that never be forgotten.

That same night it was, the quartermaster shook me awake a little early. I went to the poop therefore, under a starry sky which was fleeced with moonlit clouds, and waited for Charles to appear. I have to confess that I did scan the sky and was, I think, alive to its transcendent beauty but could not elevate myself to see Mr Prettiman's Good, nor his Absolute. The truth is that while logic compels no belief passion does so quite easily, and it was Mr Prettiman's passion which convinced: so that when he was not there—but why labour the point? His painful presence was needed. Without it I could remember the occasion but not re-create the feeling, the—dare I say—perception. I felt a little rueful I must confess at not being the stuff of which followers are made—and a touch of pain when I felt that Mrs Prettiman had been disappointed in me. I was more than ever glad therefore when Charles appeared. He was cool however. For a time we were silent, standing side by side, each unable to begin. When we did, it was with such a collision that we both burst out laughing.

"After you, sir."

"No, First Lieutenant, after you. We cannot have midshipmen given right of way!"

"I insist."

"Well then—is that Jupiter? Where is the Southern Cross?"

"The Southern Cross will be behind that bank of cloud, I think. In any case it is not necessary to navigation."

"Not even to Mr Benét and his new method?"

"Do not remind me. It makes me—"

"Makes you what?"

"Never mind."

"Jealousy does not become you."

"*Jealousy*? How can I be jealous of a mountebank? That is not—not friendly of you, Edmund."

"I am sorry."

He nodded but was silent, then walked forward to look at the compass. I watched the bank of cloud move away but still could not identify the Southern Cross though Charles had pointed it out to me on other occasions. It is an insignificant constellation when you find it.

Charles came back.

"I am sorry, Edmund, too. I am in the dumps and do not seem able to get out of them."

"I tell you what, old fellow. You need a course of the strangest medicine! A course of the Prettimans!"

"They are witty no doubt. I have little sense of humour."

"Oh, *you*! They would pull you out of the dumps by sheer expansion. Before you knew where you were, you would be discussing things so lofty they make a man forget himself and his petty affairs wholly."

"That has happened to you?"

"While I was with them. Of course no man—except him—can expect to live at that heat, that height, that intensity!"

"What good is it, then?"

"Try but a single dose!"

"No thank you. We saw the result of that medicine, that concoction at Spithead and the Nore."

"But he is not like that! There is something about him—something which even I, a political creature compounded of equal quantities of ambition and common sense, *while I am there*—"

Charles lowered his voice.

"Do you know what you are saying? Do you know where you are? This is folly! You cannot consort with a Jacobin, an atheist—"

"That he is not!"

"I am glad to hear it."

"You do not sound glad!"

"Oh yes. There is, then, a limit to his infamy."

"That is not fair!"

"You do not understand. I have passed my life in ships, and shall pass the rest of it in them if I am lucky. This is the first ship I have sailed in which is loaded down with emigrants and passengers."

" 'Pigs' you call them."

"He received their adulation. He was clever and said nothing that could be construed as an invitation to—"

"To what, for God's sake?"

He muttered.

"I will not use the word."

"Oh, you exasperate me!"

Charles turned, stumped up the ladder to the poop. I

stayed where I was, annoyed and hurt at the sudden division between us. I could see Charles back there on the poop. He was grasping the taffrail with a hand on either side of him and staring back into our wake, above which the declining moon shone with an intermittent light. The log was cast and the man reported to Charles, not to me. There was a brief exchange between them. Then the man came down the ladder, went to the traverse board, lifted the canvas and scrawled in a figure seven. It was a repetition of that *snub*—another bit of Tarpaulin—which Benét and Anderson had given me.

So there we were, Charles hunched over the taffrail, I now facing in the other direction and leaning over the forrard rail of the quarterdeck. There was plenty to see, what with the roll of the ship, the rising wind, the mass of sails on our three masts, a whole world of ivory light—old ivory. Seven knots to the east! It was impossible to sulk. I went back, climbed to the poop and stood behind Charles. I spoke as lightly as I could.

"Am I dismissed then?"

To my surprise he did not answer either in the same tone or in anger, but bowed his head between his hands and spoke in tones of extraordinary grief.

"No. No."

"You see he does not talk like that. Why—he was talking, if I understand him aright, of a divine fire up there and down here—"

Charles jerked up his head.

"Here?"

"Well—a metaphor."

"The plates are still hot. There *is* fire down below there—"

"No, no, no! You mistake me. You mistake him."

"I mistake everyone it seems. Benét is preferred. Anderson addresses me as if I were a, a midshipman. Now you put yourself in danger. Do you not understand? I begin to see how strange a place a ship is. Men have been hanged, you know!"

"For Heaven's sake, Charles! Cheer up! Good God, we are making seven knots to the east, we have sails on all three masts, your frapping keeps us together, all things are well, old fellow!"

"I am confused. I am out of my depth. I believe you to be in danger."

"Don't be such an old woman! I am in no danger. I discuss philosophical matters with another gentleman and would never dream of involving the common seamen in such considerations."

"May I thank you on behalf of us common seamen?"

"Another snub! What is the matter with you? All these pinpricks! Cheer up, man. Look, there is the dawn in the east, there beyond the bows—"

He laughed aloud.

"That from the man who wished to become the perfect master of the sea affair!"

"What do you mean?"

"Dawn at this hour?"

"Why, there—no, it has gone, the clouds have covered it. But I tell you, Charles, we are standing eastwards at seven knots into the light! That should be cheering enough for any seaman, common or not, you sulky fellow!"

"Dawn!"

"There, just a little to starboard—one point on the starboard bow—"

He swung round and stared forward where I pointed.

"You can see it clearly, Charles, what is the matter with you? It is no ghost—look there and there—clearer now!"

He was silent for a moment while the grip of his right hand tightened on my arm.

"Heavens help us all!"
"Why, what is the matter?"
"It is ice!"

(18)

"Bosun's mate! Pipe all hands! Messenger, call the captain. Edmund, you must stand aside—"

I moved forward and down to the rail of the quarterdeck. The dull and fitful gleam from the ice which had deceived me into thinking I saw the dawn before us had now disappeared again. The blown spray and fog—perhaps begotten of the ice—the rain and low cloud which wove across our bows like the passes which might go with some sea spell clothed everything beyond the bows in thick opacity.

Captain Anderson's firm step resounded behind me.

"How far was it, Mr Summers?"

"Impossible to say, sir."

"The extent then?"

"Mr Talbot saw it first."

"Mr Talbot, what was the extent of the ice?"

"I saw no end to it, sir, in either direction. I saw ice broad on the larboard bow—at about that angle and ever broader to starboard. It seemed continuous."

"Was it low on the water?"

"No, sir. I think it was a continuous cliff."

My very feet were itching for the captain to order us away from our headlong eastward progress!

"You identified ice on a broader angle to starboard than to larboard?"

"Yes, sir. That may have been the—luck of the fog."

"Mr Summers, was there no call from the forrard lookout?"

"No, sir."

"Have the man arrested."

"Aye aye, sir."

It was unbearably near the tip of my tongue to shout "Alter course, for God's sake!" But Captain Anderson issued his orders in a calm voice as measured as his tread.

"Mr Summers. Bring her round on a broad reach to the larboard."

"Aye aye, sir."

I returned to the rail and held on to it as in an unconscious attempt to halt our violent approach. I even twisted that rail or tried to twist it as if it had been a wheel and I by myself able to turn the ship from her headlong course.

The pipes were shrilling along the deck, the order repeated again and again.

"All hands on deck! D'you hear there? All hands on deck!"

Someone was ringing the ship's bell, not striking out the requisite number for the passage of time and change of the watch but urgently, incessantly. The men came swarming out like bees at an unwonted season from some ill-judged or accidental blow on the skep. They swarm and fumble and tumble over each other on the step and rise in bands to confront the imagined danger. So men leapt into the rigging, some disdaining the ladders set for them—one I saw going hand over hand (his rigid legs held out at an angle) up some vertical rope until the main course hid him. Men were crowding the fo'castle, racing along the waist, sliding to a stop by every sheet and stay. Some came even to the quarterdeck. Few were tarpaulin'd even in that weather. Some were half naked or entirely naked just as they had tumbled out of their hammocks. Now among them and behind them appeared the emigrants, and below me in the waist, the passengers crowding out. Mr Brocklebank was shouting up at me but I could not summon the interest to listen to him. Captain Anderson was now staring into the binnacle. Throughout the ship larboard sheets were shrilling in the blocks and the starboard sheets groaning home.

"Mr Summers."

"Sir."

"Set every sail there is room for."

"The foremast, sir!"

"You heard me, Mr Summers. Every inch of canvas!"

Charles turned and began shouting down into the waist. I do not think seamen have ever moved more quickly. Indeed, they obeyed the captain's order rather than the first lieutenant's, for by the time he had begun shouting through his speaking trumpet the men were swarming up the shrouds as if the word "ice" had been instantly audible through every timber of our careering vessel! More sails billowed from the yards and took the wind with a gun's report. Now Charles was hurrying forward. I saw him gesticulating the emigrants out of his way. There were women among them—Mrs East wrapped over her trailing dress with an inadequate shawl she had snatched up in the general panic. The ice remained hidden. It had been the orange moonset in the west which had given us—given me—that deceiving vision of ice to the east through the fitfully opened passages in the smother. Now any passage was more often shut than open.

Anderson spoke again.

"Bring her round another point to larboard."

There were more pipes, orders *sung out* at each mast and repeated up among the glimmering mass of sails. The wheel was spun to starboard, the sheets screamed home! There was a confused shouting of "Light to!" and "Roundly now!" and "Check away!" and "Two blocks on the preventer!" Perhaps I have more than mixed what was mixed already, for I did nothing but will the ship round away from that ghastly cliff. She leaned hugely to starboard, the wind roared over the larboard beam and a mêlée of emigrants with a deal of seawater went cascading into the waist! Our speed increased. Here and there among the sails at their outer edges, the white stuns'ls, those fair-weather sails, began to appear. To wear them spread in this weather was desperate, like our situation, but the captain's order had been specific and peremptory.

He repeated it with his familiar roar.

"Every stitch of canvas there is room for!"

Once more, as in the days of the terrible storm, our masts were bending, but to starboard this time, and more than before, not because we had a storm wind but because we had set a monstrous deal of sail even on those makeshift topmasts! The spray which had deluged us from astern now flew across the ship along the whole length of the larboard side. The billows which had pursued us now struck along that same length. Each wave seemed to heave us bodily sideways towards the direction in which we did not wish to go.

Charles came, climbing hastily up from the waist.

"I caught a glimpse, sir. It seems like no ordinary berg. It lies squarely north and south and there seems no end to it. The cliff which Mr Talbot saw must be somewhere between a hundred and two hundred feet high."

As if to illustrate his words the clouds or fog parted along the starboard beam and bow and the ice glimmered little more than the sails in some strange light which, now the moon had set, seemed to have no source which was identifiable. Foam whiter than the ice climbed the cliff. Then, as we watched, the fog closed yellowly again. Captain Anderson leaned on the forrard rail of the quarterdeck and peered low as if he might be able to see under the smother. Neither he nor Charles, straightening up in defeat, remarked on what was obvious to us all—if we touched the hidden cliff, no man nor woman nor child would live to see daylight. I saw the danger, understood it in every particular and now began to feel it! The chill on my skin below my oilskins and warm clothing was not that of the Antarctic.

687

But all at once the chill itself turned to a definite and per-spiring heat, for a sudden and temporary parting of the fog on our starboard bow showed us that not only was the cliff nearer but it rubbed in the point with an appalling act of Nature, which, performed indifferently as it may have been, seemed a theatrical act made for the duration of our glimpse.

"Look!"

Was it I who cried out? It must have been. Before our eyes the face of that part of the cliff which had been revealed fell off, collapsed into a climbing billow. Two huge pieces which must have fallen just before we were permitted to see the action sprang upwards like leaping salmon! They were, I swear, ship-size fragments and falling again as the fog swept all from our sight.

How can a man react who has no service to offer, no counsel to give when he sees such monstrosities and knows that presently, unless there is a miracle, he will be smashed to pieces among them? That more than Antarctic chill became a settled *rigor* which sealed me in my place by the rail of the quarterdeck, careless of wind or spray or green water or anything but our peril. This was a horror of that neutral and indifferent but overwhelming power with which our own ridiculous wood and canvas had nothing to do. We might end as a child's toy, washed up, smashed—

No. The fact has to be experienced. Then, while the rigor still held me, I saw a wave coming at our starboard beam, but out of the fog, a contrary wave from where the unspeakable blocks of ice had fallen. It struck the side and washed clean over us. The bows came up into the wind, the sails thundered, then thumped open like a broadside as the men fought her at the wheel. She danced, losing headway among the contrary waters—

Was my voice among the others? I suppose so. I hope not but I shall never know. Certainly there were voices, shrieks of women and the anguished yelling of men, not merely emigrants and passengers but seamen, cries from aloft, wailing as though we were already lost. The waist below me was a pool of seawater not yet escaped through the scuppers. The black lifelines danced above it and black figures clung and bobbed as the water began to drain away.

Now, below me, a familiar figure in good oilskins waded into the waist! It was Mr Jones, our intelligent self-centred and honest purser. He was wading forward towards his boat on the boom. In his arms, cradled like a baby, he carried Lord Talbot's firkin, that mass of keepsakes and last wishes, last messages which he had sworn to preserve, not knowing that the whole ship had seen it as a joke! He waded forward and the mainmast hid him. The sight made me burst into hysterical laughter.

Charles who had gone somewhere to do something came racing back, splashing through the last inches of the green sea we had shipped. Captain Anderson spoke to him with a new urgency.

"Mr Summers. We must come up more into the wind."

"The foremast, sir!"

The captain roared:

"Mr Summers!"

Charles shouted back in his face.

"I wish to represent that the mast will take no more strain. If that goes—"

"Are you able to propose a better course of action? We are being moved towards the ice."

There was a long pause. Then Anderson spoke irritably.

"Are you *still* attempting to discredit Mr Benét's achievement?"

Charles stood stiffly and answered stiffly.

"No, sir."

"Carry out my orders."

Charles departed. There was more shrilling of pipes and shouting. The leeward sheets were tautened. The sails lost the roundness of canvas bellied by a wind on the beam and flattened. Wrinkles like splayed fingers stretched from every sheet. The sails drummed with tension. Young Mr Tommy Taylor came leaping up to the quarterdeck from below. He took off his hat ceremoniously to the captain.

"Well?"

"The carpenter, sir, Mr Gibbs, sir. He says she is taking much water. The pumping is continuous. The water is gaining."

"Very good."

The boy saluted again and turned away. The captain spoke again.

"Mr Taylor."

"Sir?"

"What the devil is that fool doing sitting in his boat on the boom?"

I spoke up, for the boy was plainly at a loss.

"It is Mr Jones, the purser, Captain. He is waiting in his own boat for a picked body of seamen to rescue him while the rest of us drown."

"The damned fool!"

"I agree, Captain."

"It is the worst of examples. Mr Taylor!"

"Sir?"

"Get the man down."

Mr Taylor saluted again and hurried away. I lost sight of him almost at once, for the attention was seized by the ice which appeared, perhaps a little nearer, then vanished again. It had been a projection high up and gleaming whiter than before in what must have been the real daylight. Anderson saw it too. He looked at me and smiled that same ghastly smile which he occasionally inflicted on persons near him at moments of extreme danger. I suppose it was brave. I have always been loath to credit him with admirable feelings but neither I nor anyone—except poor, silly, drunken Deverel—has ever doubted his courage.

"Captain—can we not come round a bit farther?"

Appalled, I heard myself, heard my own voice as if it had been that of another, make the presumptuous suggestion. Captain Anderson's smile *twitched*. His right fist, down by his waist, doubled itself and proclaimed to me as clearly as if it had had a mouth, *How I should like to be driven into the face of this insolent passenger!*

He cleared his throat.

"I was about to give the order, Mr Talbot."

He turned away and shouted to Charles.

"Try her another point to windward, Mr Summers."

There was renewed movement in the groups of the crew. Suddenly I remembered Mrs Prettiman and her helpless spouse. I ran quickly down to the lobby and made a rather brusque way through the little knot of passengers in the entry. Mrs Prettiman was standing between the doors of her and her husband's cabins. She was holding the rail lightly. She saw me at once and smiled. I went to her.

"Mrs Prettiman!"

"Mr Talbot—Edmund! How is it with us?"

I pulled myself together and explained the situation as briefly as possible. I believe she paled as she realized the nearness of shipwreck but her expression did not change.

"So you see, ma'am, it is a toss-up. Either we weather the ice or we do not. If we do not we have nothing left—"

"We shall have dignity left."

Her words confounded me.

"Ma'am! This is Roman!"

"I prefer to consider it British, Mr Talbot."

"Oh, of course, ma'am—but what of Mr Prettiman?"

"He is still asleep, I think. How long have we?"

"No one knows, not even the captain."

"Mr Prettiman must be told."

"I suppose so."

Mr Prettiman was awake after all. He greeted us with a great and, if the truth be told, unusual equanimity. I believe he had been awake for some time and with his degree of intellect it was not difficult for him to deduce from the noises and the ship's movement that we were at some crisis. In a word, he had had *time* to fortify himself. In fact his first thought was to get me out of the way so that Mrs Prettiman could attend to the intimate details of his toilet!

"For," said he, smiling into my face, "if they say Time and Tide wait for no man, how much more tyrannical is this mysterious physiology!"

I withdrew, therefore, but was buttonholed by Mr Brocklebank who had a flutter about his lips and who for the first time since the doldrums had appeared without his coach cloak. He was carrying on a quavery conversation with Celia Brocklebank careless of who might hear. As far as I could make out he was imploring her to share the *couch so that they might die in each other's arms*!

"No no, Wilmot, I cannot endure the thought—it is not congenial! Besides, you have not been there since Christmas when Mr Cumbershum lent you that salubrious book!"

Meanwhile a feeble voice was whimpering from Zenobia's cabin—

"Wilmot!! Wilmot! I am dying!"

"So are we all—I beg you, Celia!"

Has it not been said that in earthquakes and volcanic eruptions the same curious phenomenon of exacerbated sexuality occurs? But whatever the explanation, it gave me a higher opinion of my dear Mrs Prettiman's Roman stance. I spoke with Bowles, pulled the curls of Pike's little girls, suggested to him that a drink would be a good thing—was reminded by Mr Brocklebank there was none remaining, except, as he said, what he had obtained *under the counter* from Master Tommy Taylor. In fact, disappointed in his Celia he retired to the cabin to fortify himself with the bottle, abandoning Celia who showed a marked preference for my company quite suddenly, and I have no doubt that she was in train to find it *congenial* if I had—but Mrs Prettiman returned. I followed her. Mr Prettiman was a little propped up on pillows. He was still smiling with apparent cheerfulness.

"Edmund, we have a thing or two to settle. You will of course look after Letty."

"Of course, sir."

"It is impossible that I should survive in the state in which I find myself. It will be next to impossible for a man in full health. But I, with this leg—therefore, when the end is upon us you must get on deck, the two of you, wrapped in as much clothing as you can wear, and make your way to the boats."

"No, Aloysius. Edmund may do so—must do so. He is young and we are not in any way his responsibility. I shall stay with you."

"Now, Mrs Prettiman—I shall become testy!"

"You will not, sir. Edmund will go, not I. But I would like him to hear this, for I believe he stands in much need of an example—and you know, Edmund, I am a governess! So—now"—and here her voice sank both in pitch and volume and became warmer than I at least had ever heard it—"so now I must make a solemn declaration. In the short span of our married life I have never disobeyed you and would not have done so in the future had there been one, not because I am your wife but because of who and what you are! But we have no future, I think, and I shall stay with you here in this cabin. Goodbye, Edmund—"

"Goodbye, my boy. No woman—"

"I—"

My throat was choked. Somehow I got out of the cabin and closed the door behind me. As I did so the ship became upright, another and I guess contrary wave washed over the waist and burst into the lobby. I waded to the entrance, helped Bowles to his feet and saw him return silent and soaked to his cabin, suggested to the Pike children that it was all great *fun* and got myself into the waist.

"Charles! How is it?"

"I have not time, Edmund. But no one has ever seen a berg like this—like that!"

He nodded to the side, then pounded up to the quarterdeck. There was a little less fog—or rather it had seemed to retreat from us. We had perhaps a quarter of a mile—I should say a couple of cables of open water visible on all sides. Once more the ice was visible fitfully; and now in dim daylight looked harder, colder, more implacable. It seemed clear that we were moving parallel to the face of the cliff and at a great speed. The speed could not be due to our motion through the water but rather to our motion relative to the ice. If the fog cleared for a few moments we seemed to race by the white cliff, but as it thickened again so our speed seemed to slow to what was owing solely to the wind. There was, it was evident, a very fast current racing by the berg from south to north and taking us with it. The sea in fact was as savagely indifferent to us as the ice!

I turned to go up to the quarterdeck. Little Tommy Taylor came down it.

"How is the purser, Mr Taylor?"

"I couldn't persuade him to leave the boat, sir. The captain says I will have to tell him he's under arrest."

Tommy went forrard and I continued to the quarterdeck. Mr Benét had the watch with young Willis. The captain stood at the top of the ladder up to the poop, a hand on the rail at either side of the top. He was looking round constantly, at the fog, the glimpses of ice, the confused sea which resulted from the beating of the waves and their recoil from the cliff. As I reached the quarterdeck I heard thunderous explosions behind me where once more there was a cataclysmic fall of ice. Though it was veiled by the fog the noise of the fall was significantly louder.

"Well, Mr Benét, what do you think of Nature now?"

"We are privileged. How many people have seen anything like this?"

"Intolerable meiosis!"

"Understatement? Were you not some time ago the passenger who declared to all and sundry that he would not be anywhere else for a thousand pounds? Mr Willis, contrive to stand up straight and look useful even if you are not!"

"My declaration, Mr Benét, was made *pour encourager les autres*, as you would say."

"And you yourself would *fain die a dry death*, as you would say? Hazleton, you idle bugger, you should turn a rope after you've cheesed it! Captain, sir!"

"Yes, Mr Benét, I see the ice. Mr Summers! Have the longboat ready to drop on the starboard beam."

"Aye aye, sir."

More pipes, more hurry.

"Have you noticed, Mr Benét—"

"Just a moment, Mr Talbot. Mr Summers! Willis—go after Mr Summers and tell him that Mr Talbot suggests filling the longboat with hammocks."

"I did no such thing!"

The captain spoke behind us. It was the only time I ever heard Mr Benét receive even the shadow of a rebuke.

"It will keep some of them busy, Mr Benét, and is appropriate at this time. But you might inform the passengers in general terms that they are still advised not to interfere in the running of the ship!"

Having delivered this relatively mild rebuke to his favourite, the captain retired to the taffrail as if he was embarrassed by his own words. Benét turned to me.

"You heard that, Mr Talbot?"

"I said nothing about hammocks! Nor do I know why the longboat is to be got ready unless it is to ensure the escape of the more valuable persons, in which case—"

"There are no valuable persons, Mr Talbot. We shall all die together. The longboat is to persuade people that something is being done. It is to be a fender between us and the ice—"

"Will that do any good?"

"I think not."

Willis came back.

"Mr Summers says to thank Mr Talbot, sir."

"You are looking green, my lad. Cheer up! When it comes, it will be quick."

"Benét! The ice is nearer—look!"

"We have done what we can. Captain sir. Do we drop the boat?"

"Not yet."

Suddenly the ice was there, close. I could look at nothing else. To my eyes the cliff seemed monstrously high. It was uniformly undercut along the base and the water near it was full of huge fragments which had fallen and which were the immediate danger. I heard the captain shout some Tarpaulin order and saw the longboat drop over the starboard side—saw the thick painter snub as the pull of the water came on the boat. The ice, now gleaming dully white and green, was behaving preposterously. We had swung even farther to the north—I suppose an unordered and involuntary movement made by the men at the helm—and if our heading had been anything to go by should have

been moving markedly away from the cliff. But it was
evident even to my untutored eye that we were not doing
so. For the effect of the earth's rotation which is said to
cause that perpetual current round the Antarctic Ocean
should have moved the ice as much as it moved us. But
for whatever reason, it was not doing so. We were feelingly
approaching the ice as *Alcyone* had approached us, beam
on or even quarter on. Nor could our sails account for our
two movements—the one to the north, the other towards
the east and the ice.

I make all this sound too coldly rational! How many
times since those dreadful hours have I started up in my
bed and *willed* a change in our remembered circumstances! But then, as I clung to the windward side of the
vessel, I had no rational appreciation of what was happening, only the incomprehensible sight of it! How to explain
the disorganized fury of the sea, the towers, pinnacles, the
bursts of water that had replaced those steadily marching
billows which had swung under and past us for so many
days together? For now it seemed that those billows were
flung back at us. Columns of green water and spray
climbed the ice cliff and fell back from it. Wind against
wind, wave against wave, fury feeding on itself—I tried to
think of my parents, of my Belovéd Object, but it would
not do. I was a present panic, an animal in the article of
death. The ice was above us! Ice fell, leapt up monstrously
from beneath the foam, and still we swept in towards that
hideous, undercut and rotten wall. Some of our sails were
slack and beating, some filled the wrong way round and
yet we hurried towards and along the wall fast as horses
might have drawn us. If there was anything regular about
our situation it was in the explosive falls of ice from the
walls of this mortal and impregnable city! Then I recognized that Nature—the Nature which Miss Chumley so
rightly detested—had now finally gone mad. For hours we

had been thrust sideways towards the cliff of ice *downhill*, as Mr Benét had once said, and at a coaching speed. Now the ice, as if to demonstrate its own delirium, was performing the impossible. It was rotating round us. It appeared astern, then swung round past us and went by way of the bows where it had come from. It repeated the action, then drew in alongside to starboard. Among all the noises of that situation I heard the longboat crack like a nut. I do not know if the *coup de grâce* was given the boat by a floating block of ice or the cliff itself. There was a green road of smooth water close under the ice, only interrupted when the cliff above us spilled some incalculable weight. The blocks that had fallen into the road of green water were going with us at the same speed, crashing and crumbling where they jostled each other or the side of the cliff. A block fell and took a stuns'l off the outer edge of some sail on the mainmast and dropped, comfortably wrapped as it were, the stuns'l yard fluttering behind it like a feather. Another, the shape and more than the size of Lady Somerset's fortepiano, came sideways forward of the mainmast and took the front half of Mr Jones's boat with Mr Jones and Mr Tommy Taylor attached and shot with them through the larboard rail.

But we were now, it seemed, to be introduced even more intimately to the cliff, which arranged itself along our larboard side, careful, as it were, not to touch us.

We were, to use Tarpaulin once more, making a sternboard, or more intelligibly, we were going backwards faster than we had ever gone forwards! The cliff, dropping a few thousand tons of ice by our larboard bow, threw that off to starboard as a boy might thrust a model boat with his foot.

It was a crisis of helplessness beyond seamanship. My brain went. I saw a *mélange* of visions in the ice which swept past me—figures trapped in the ice, my father among them. A cave opened with an eye of verdure at the other end of it.

The last spasm of our ordeal came upon us. The ice moved violently and disappeared before our eyes and we raced *downhill*! It seemed the final sinking, the end of everything.

Only the sinking did not come. We were, it appeared, upright in a windless sea to the east of which a clear white day had spread. Around us in the water, blocks of ice lay still.

I straightened up from my crouched position, unstuck my hands from the rail. Along the decks, people were beginning to move again, but slowly as if they could never be too cautious. We were, after all, turning very slowly in the water. The sails were rustling.

Someone forrard shouted a sentence and there were bellows and screams of laughter and, after that, silence again. I never found out what the joke was or who had made it.

To the west of us lay the yellow fog with here and there a dull gleam of ice in it, some increasing distance away, courtesy, it seemed, of that same circumpolar current which for so many days had been bringing us to the east.

People began to talk.

(19)

It will save trouble if I insert here part of a communication made to me by a member of my old college who wishes to remain anonymous. However, the reader is assured that my old and learned acquaintance is the final court of appeal in matters of hydrology and associated -ologies.

Your description would be well enough for a fiction in the wild, modern manner! Was there not a demented woman screaming curses from the top of your "ice cliff"? Or was there perhaps an impassioned Druid imprecating your vessel before he threw himself down? I much fear it is all too highly coloured for a respectable geographer and if you *do* find someone rash enough to publish your descriptions I must insist on remaining unnamed! The effect of travel on the young, as I have only too often had to notice, is deplorable. It narrows the immature mind to a set of disjunct but gaudy impressions like the window of a print shop! Fortunately, as a man who has had the sense never to travel farther from his place of birth than the metropolis and who for many years has found a college a world in itself, I am able to lend an objective mind to the problems of terrestrial behaviour.

My good sir! If your ice cliff was a hundred feet high it extended seven hundred feet below the surface of the water. That may seem a great deal to you; but my information is that the waters at that latitude are far deeper. It is clear, then, that your cliff was aground and you have discovered a reef to which you should give your name at once if you care for that sort of exhibition. Granted (for a moment) a reef with your monstrous lump of ice on it, the following would be a plausible conjecture. Your ship was hurried towards it by wind and current, only to find as she approached that the current was deflected to the north along the face of the ice, then swirled round the northern end as a chip of wood might be whirled round a corner in the gutter. The constant falls of ice are *plausible* too, for your berg was far north and would be quite rotten.

I come to the major point. If your berg was so long, so vast that it even affected the weather, then it must have stretched so far south that it would be more like a floating continent than a patch of ice! You probably do not realize that an "ice cliff" of necessity implies land on which snow can accumulate, glaciers form and at last slide slowly into the sea where they may set off on such a voyage of destruction as you describe. In fact it implies a vast continent lying over and round the South Pole! As I have spent the greater part of my adult life perfecting a proof that such a continent is *geographically impossible* you will not expect me to accept your account as other than that of someone tried beyond endurance by a voyage as long as any in the memory of man. I would here (were you sufficient of a geographer to follow the argument) explain my "Principle of Orbital Balance and Reciprocity". Better I think to present you with an argument suited to a layman. I have shown by a simple calculation of the volume of ice contained in your cliff that its formation must date from several thousands of years previous to the creation of the world in the spring of the year four thousand and four B.C.! Pray, when next you write, offer my humble duty to your Lady Mother and her excellent spouse.

We in the ship, I think, could no more credit what we had been through than could my correspondent. Even copying out his letter has distanced me from the event. I believe my first conscious thought was to see if Charles had suffered in any way. He was on the quarterdeck, gripping to the forrard rail and staring down into the binnacle. This made me realize where I was. Somehow I had got out of the lobby and come to the main chains which I had clutched with both hands (an enormous deadeye affording the hold) and hung there like a leaf in a spider's web while all the madness performed itself round us. At my feet, where she had slipped from between my arms, lay Celia Brocklebank in a dead faint! Somehow we had clutched—now I remembered how she had leapt at me and I had seized her in some profound excess of human need and behaviour! But I picked her up again and bore her, wordlessly, back into the lobby while she sighed and rolled her head. I knocked on her hutch. A tremulous voice answered to my knock.

"Who is it? Who is it?"

"Mr Talbot with your wife. She has fainted."

"Pray take her somewhere else, Mr Talbot. I am not fit—I cannot—"

With one free hand I opened the door. The old man was sitting up in his bunk with a blanket covering him to the waist. He was naked, and mephitic. Carefully I laid the girl on him and steadied her head between his fat arm and shoulder. Then I went, shutting the door behind me.

"Mrs Prettiman? It is I—Edmund."

Her voice answered me.

"Come in."

She was sitting by the bunk. They were holding hands—she with her left hand holding his right. I supposed they had been like that ever since I had last seen them. They were both very pale, and the two locked hands lay beside the man in the bunk as if they had been indissolubly knit and then forgotten.

Mrs Prettiman looked up at me.

"We shall live a little longer?"

"It seems so."

She shuddered from head to foot.

"You are cold, Letty!"

"No."

She looked down at the hands and then, using her right hand, freed her left hand delicately from his. I do not know that he even noticed, for he was watching her face.

"Don't cry. It is unworthy of you."

"Come, sir! Mrs Prettiman is—"

"Quiet!"

"I need," said Mrs Prettiman with what I can only describe as rigid control, "a moment or two alone to collect myself."

"I will leave you, ma'am."

"No."

I opened the door for her and she disappeared.

"Tell me what happened, Edmund."

I gave him an account of our adventure as near as I could. I omitted, because I remembered it too little to be able to describe it, the strange way in which Celia Brocklebank and I had found ourselves together. I am sure she remembered it as little as I and I did not think such a passage was relevant to anything which Mr Prettiman would care to hear. I merely remarked that when the thing was over I picked up a woman who had fainted and restored her to her husband.

"Mrs Prettiman would not faint," said Mr Prettiman. "She might cry but she would not faint."

"I think, sir—"

"Well, don't. I will not have you interfering in her education!"

"*Mrs Prettiman?*"

"Do you suppose that if we ever contrive to lead a caravan to found the Ideal City that she can afford feminine weaknesses? I have rid myself of the ones too prevalent among men and she must do the same as a woman!"

"Allow me to tell you, Mr Prettiman, that I have met no woman—No. Yes. I have met no grown woman who has so impressed me with her lack of those same female weaknesses as you are trying to eradicate!"

"You know nothing about it!"

"I revere Mrs Prettiman, sir, and do not mind confessing it! I—value her highly!"

"What has that to say to anything? I am an educationist, sir, and will not have any judgement in that matter questioned. A man who has worked on his own character as long as I have may perhaps be credited with some knowledge of that of others!"

"And pray, sir, what have you done with your own character to so perfect it?"

"Is it not obvious?"

"No, sir."

"This is unendurable! To be lectured by a stubborn boy—it is endurance I have had to cultivate, sir, endurance and equanimity! Get out, before I—Of all the—"

"I am going, Mr Prettiman. But before I do, allow me to tell you—"

"No, Edmund."

It was Mrs Prettiman. She closed the door behind her and went to her seat. Perhaps I was deceived in thinking that her eyes were a little red.

"It is agreeable," she said, "after so much fuss to be able to sit quietly, do you not think so, Aloysius? But we have not invited Edmund to sit down and he stands there obediently. Pray be seated, Edmund. I have looked out of the lobby. We might be in a different world, you know. The sea is smooth and gentle. I would never have believed such a change possible. How do you suppose it happened?"

"I have no idea, ma'am. I have given up any intention of understanding Nature. I am now firmly on the side of those who confine their approach to the world to a wariness of it!"

There was a brisk rapping at the door.

"See who is there, Edmund, will you?"

I had not seen the man since the days of poor Colley! It was, of all people in the ship, Billy Rogers! He stood there, gigantic and smiling cheerfully. My firkin was cradled in his arms.

"Lord Talbot, sir? This here is yourn, I think, my lord, sir."

"Oh yes—please give it to me."

"Begging your pardon, my lord, sir, Mr Summers said I was to take it to your cabin but I dunno—"

"You don't know my cabin, Rogers?"

For a moment the man ignored me. His wide blue eyes were staring past me to where Mrs Prettiman sat in her canvas chair. There was, I thought, a trace of speculation in them. It irritated me and disgusted me. I stepped out into the lobby and pulled the cabin door to behind me.

"In here. Put it down by the bunk."

The man did as I told him, then straightened up and turned to me. He was tall as I and far broader—a giant.

"Will that be all, sir?"

"The men in the boat—Jones, the purser, and the little midshipman, Tommy Taylor—"

"Gone, sir. Davy Jones has them. Didn't have time to holler, as you saw, just took. There'll be many a man aboard this ship what will sleep more comfortable in his bunk or his hammock to know that Jones has made his last demand for payment. Thank you, Lord Talbot, sir."

He knuckled his forehead and rolled away.

Little Tommy Taylor! Gone. Had his last laugh. Aged what? Fourteen? Fifteen? I felt a great desire to speak with someone and express the fact of the complete and irreversible absence of Tommy and I turned to the Prettimans' door. But it occurred to me that Mrs Prettiman had never seemed as amused as I with Tommy's antics. In fact, if I had to hazard a guess I would say that dear Mrs Prettiman, perfect in so many ways and valuing all kinds of people, would make an exception and find herself able to contemplate if not the extinction at least the absence of a dirty-minded little boy with equanimity.

(20)

This, then, if not the end of our voyage, was the beginning of the end. There was a period of some days in which everyone came to believe that our troubles were over—and seldom has a popular belief been so triumphantly vindicated! The weather, though occasionally what we would once have called *rough*, was never uncomfortably so. Mr Summers and Mr Benét argued politely about the longitude. But no one could believe that it was still a matter of importance since the weather was so uniformly clear that it would have been impossible to miss seeing the land even from ten miles away. The middle watch, which I continued to keep with Charles, became a time of enchantment! The stars seemed near enough to touch. Night was a harmony of blue. The sailors seemed to sing the darkness away! During the day all those who could walked the deck, where the Pike children now played regularly and healthily. Mr Brocklebank was to be seen basking in the sun without his coach cloak. I continued to read to Mr Prettiman and once had the privilege of pacing the deck at the side of Mrs Prettiman and was proud of myself—that onetime gorgon now tamed! Indeed, I had hoped that Lieutenant Benét would observe our constitutional and be put in his place by it. But that afternoon when I read to Mr Prettiman, Mrs Prettiman did not stay to listen but excused herself and, I learnt afterwards, took an afternoon constitutional at the side of Lieutenant Benét. An encyclopaedia of behaviour could not have spoken plainer.

One morning Charles told me that I should see an operation worth watching. So it was. I came up on deck and looked round. There were no more than a very few white

clouds bulging up towards the meridian. Mrs Pike leaned
on the rail by the break of the fo'castle and talked with Billy
Rogers as Zenobia had done before she took to her bed. Mr
Gibbs with a couple of men was putting the last touches to
the repair of the rail where the ice had smashed it. Under
the main bitts and near it, Mrs East and the two small Pike
girls were holding a dolls' tea party! But now there was a
whole series of orders from Captain Anderson and the
dolls' party was interrupted by the need to use some ropes
made fast there as the ship was *hove to*. (Please consult
Falconer, for I shall not.) Men stationed themselves all
along the larboard side with sheaves of line in their hands.
There was a boom rigged outboard with a lead suspended
from it—a much heavier lead than the hand-lead which one
man can manage. Mr Benét in the waist shouted "Let go!";
down went the lead with a pfutt! The line was abandoned
all along the side of the vessel—another length lifted and at
once abandoned—another and another—

"Take up the slack!"

"Charles—what is this about? Will it tell us where we
are?"

"No indeed—" He paused for a moment, then smiled.
"You might say it tells us where we are not."

Now the line was no longer up and down but leading
out to an angle towards the northwest.

"There is your circumpolar current, Edmund. I suppose it is the only direct evidence anyone ever had."

"You are talking in riddles."

"Mr Summers, would you suspend your conversation
long enough to bring her over the lead?"

Charles smiled wryly. He went off and bade the parties of
men alter the strain on various sheets, easing some so that
their sails rounded their bellies a little, and a rustling and
tinkling of water now sounded from our travelling bows.
Captain Anderson smiled his brief yellow smile down at

me. Well, what captain would not be happy on such a day of sunlight and whispering, chuckling, delighted water?

"Hand over hand and roundly now!"

"Up and down!"

"A hundred and ten fathom, sir."

There was a pause while the vertical line was hauled in. At last the dripping lead itself broke the surface.

"Bear away, Mr Cumbershum. Northeast true."

Mr Benét hailed from the waist.

"The lead is inboard, sir. Sand and shell, sir!"

The captain nodded as though he had expected this information. I turned to the first lieutenant.

"That was all very interesting. What does it signify?"

"Why, that we are in soundings. Benét had his own ideas about our longitude and the captain too. So have I and so has Cumbershum. In this visibility it does not matter much."

He went off, about the ship's interminable business.

"Mr Talbot. A word with you."

I turned. Mr Brocklebank had emerged from the lobby. Once more he was massive in his wrapped coach cloak.

"What can I do for you, Mr Brocklebank?"

The old man drew close.

"I fear I did not appear at my best, sir, during the late emergency—"

"Well, you are old and cannot be expected—"

"It was not age, Mr Talbot, not decrepitude but sickness. I feared a syncope, a sudden failure of the vital organ."

"The ship seemed almost certain to sink and that was about to settle all our problems."

"Better without a syncope than with one. I fear the enemy within more than the sea without! You remember when *Alcyone* lay alongside us?"

"Indeed I do!"

"Oh, but now I remember—you was in your cabin, which was what she must have been crying about—"

"She?"

"The young lady. I was interrogating the surgeon from *Alcyone* when he came from your cabin but he brushed me aside! There's a medical man for you! He went back to his ship and the women crowded round him—I understand now! They wanted to know how you went on."

"Oh, it was Miss Chumley! It must have been!"

"Imagine that—a strong fellow like you monopolizing the surgeon, let alone the women—Good God, there never was such a consultation as I had then while two ships were parting! I halloed him and they implored him and orders were shouted and there was such a groaning and a creaking—and that silly young woman crying, '*Mr Truscott, Mr Truscott, will he live?*' and Lady Somerset crying, '*Marion, Marion, not before the sailors. Oh, this is so affecting*'—and so much '*Cheerily, my hearties, roundly now*'—so much noise from the sails and the surgeon—can you imagine it? Just bawling back at me, '*What do you want?*'—and I crying, '*I wish for a regimen*' and he—'*Less of the pipe, none of the bottle, less of the trencher and none of the couch, you fat old fool*'—and the young one flinging her arms round Lady Somerset's neck with a cry of '*Oh, Helen!*' And it sheered off, *Alcyone*, I mean, so I have had to do the best I could without proper medical advice, which accounts for my indifferent performance when—"

"She really cried out, '*Will he live*'?"

"The young woman? Yes, or words to that effect. It may have been '*I suppose he will live*' or '*He may live*'—"

"It must have been '*Will he live?*' She would not have cried out the surgeon's name twice had she not been distracted!"

"Yes. Well. She may have cried it twice, '*Truscott, Truscott*', or perhaps it was '*Oh, Truscott!*' or '*Mr Truscott*'!"

"Oh, God."

"I remember it clearly. Pipe, bottle, trencher, couch. I ask you!"

"Oh, if she did not cry his name twice I am the unhappiest of men!"

"Mr Talbot, this is unlike you! I was simply explaining my conduct during the late crisis. She may have cried, '*Truscott, Truscott, Truscott*'—or more. And the worst of it is, under his regime I let more wind than I did when I was eighteen stone of solid man!"

"But she did cry out!"

"How else could I have heard her?"

"Charles had seen her the night before staring through the side of the ship—"

"So did the surgeon cry out, '*No pipe, less trencher, no bottle and no couch*'? Or was it '*less couch*'? By which he would have implied an occasional healthy recourse to the connubial. He would not have said no bottle and no trencher—and here I have been living all these weeks chaster than a nun! Women are so cruel. '*You go right out on deck, Wilmot,*' she says. '*I cannot endure your horrid smells. Besides, I believe it is bad for my complexion.*' "

"And Miss Chumley expressed the deepest concern for my welfare!"

I waited for a reply, but the old man, one hand on the bulwarks, his feet spread wide, had lapsed into a state of concentration on his interior. I withdrew quickly.

So I added yet another atom of comfort and torment to the cobweb-thin collection of yearnings and surmises that bound me to her.

There is, I suppose, only one moment of drama towards which the reader is still looking. When, after this year-long or nearly year-long voyage, did we sight land? I sympathize with the reader's suspense. It has been, it still is, a difficulty to me too. The truth is that our first sight of land was about as undramatic as it could well be. I have thought now and then of ways round this dull patch. I had thought of introducing the slapstick, the low comedy of Nature making fools of everyone in sight. I pictured a misty morning, a slight air; and the moment at which someone on the ship, preferably a woman or child, realizes the ludicrous truth. There are gales of laughter from the crew and sheepish grins from our navigators. We are aground in still water, which sinks away slowly to leave us high and dry—and what is more, as the mist is drunk up by the sun, we see that we are able, by the use of ladders, to step ashore! But a certain *synaesthesia* with our noble vessel tells me that in such a case there would have been three dreadful reports as the weight came wholly on Charles's frapping and the hull subsided into its own weed and ballast and spread like— anything that melts in the sun!

Then again, I thought of preserving the truth but *sharpening* it a little. There was, for example, a hole in the bulwarks under the main chains, and examining this with Mr Askew, the gunner, I learnt about the dreadful art or craft of cannon-ball rolling. A disaffected sailor is able to lift a cannon ball out of a shot garland and allow it to decide for itself what damage it will do. Mr Askew—he muttered the information, for it is not to be spread throughout the lower deck of a ship—informed me that as a ship *works*, such a cannon ball, in an unfortunate case, is able to fly the full length of the vessel and take apart the random target as brutally as if it had been shot from a gun. But the hole had not been made by a cannon ball or there would have been damage to the main chains as well. Perhaps the ice did it, though I myself am inclined to rats. But build up the suggestion of disaffection, detect a mutter here and there, and you have your high drama to take the place of the low comedy. There is a confrontation. The crew and the emigrants inch out of the fo'castle threateningly. Captain Anderson is proud and defiant. The men move forward. One is about to strike a—

But the cry rings out from the crosstrees of the foremast.

"Deck there! Land ho! Land ahead and on the larboard bow! Deck there! Land ho!"

It will not do, of course. I do not mean because this is an autobiography, for I have come to think that men commonly invent their autobiographies like everything else. I mean it would be too stagey.

The truth in a way was subtler and more amusing. On a morning of perfect visibility, when Mr Summers handed the captain his folded paper with the computed latitude and longitude, the captain examined it with raised eyebrows and compared it with the other folded paper which had been given him by Mr Benét. His only comment was to order the ship's course to be maintained. We sighted land some hours later.

What a novelist could not have foreseen and the autobiographer must make as interesting as he may was the complete reversal of expected attitudes. The crew, which might have rolled cannon balls, or made protests, or grumbled and sent deputations *before* we sighted land, were quiet, good-humoured and obedient until the low-lying coast was there before them. Only then was there murmuring and the clear voice of dissent. They thought we should disembark at once on this land of milk and honey, pausing merely to select ourselves the slaves of our choice from the eager applicants!

It was at this time that Mr Prettiman had some kind of—revelation is the only word I can find for it. He confessed that he now believed there was a profound mystery (rather than secret) at the heart of the cosmos to which man would be admitted. He was made extraordinarily happy. I myself had a premonition of his death which like all the premonitions in my life proved to be mistaken. In brief, I learnt from a few words what I had no business to know. I have to own, it was moving and—confounding, even if he was, as he must have been, deluded.

On that day as I entered his cabin I saw that his eyes were closed and I paused, for in his pain, sleep was very precious to him. I wondered if I should go away again but as I stood there, he spoke, or rather muttered in what I can only describe as a tone of awed astonishment.

"I am able to bless—!"

Yes, I should have gone there is no doubt about that. But in a strange embarrassment I did nothing but utter an involuntary, and I fear silly, laugh. His eyes opened and looked straight into mine. A positive tide of crimson seemed to consume his face. I got out of the cabin, shut the door and only then was able to feel the extraordinary difference between these few humble words and the rarified concept of the Good which we were too often prone to discuss. My mind plunged back to that early interview when I had read to him from Voltaire's *Candide* the strange words of *le bon vieillard* "We have no need of priests—we are all priests"!

I went away confounded for a time and have thought since that it was one of several occasions in my life when I have felt myself to be on the brink of a mystery which through character, upbringing and education I am wholly unable to penetrate. But at the time, when I came to myself, I reflected that after all, the "good old man" had been one hundred and sixty five, and even *he* blushed as he spoke openly of the religious mysteries of El Dorado!

The day after that we sighted land, as I have said.

"Land ho!"

It was land indeed and visible at an astonishing distance. But the truth is that the diamond nature of the air in those climes has to be experienced to be believed so I will not labour the point. As for the longitude, it at once pleased and irritated all our navigators; for Charles and Benét had kept their workings to themselves like card players and revealed them only to the captain. He in his turn, with a sense of humour which I had not suspected, kept his own counsel—the longitudes were the same except for a mile or two! The Benét-Anderson method, therefore, might be good or bad. Nothing was proved or disproved. Charles, by rejecting the palpably wrong reading of one chronometer and relying on the other two, which were fairly close together—he added the readings and divided them by two—had achieved the same result. Luck must be considered to have favoured both parties. The land was where they said it was. So everyone and no one was satisfied.

Our adventure was now running down. We obtained fresh meat from one settlement and a quantity of vegetables from another. Beans we had always with us. It must be confessed that with the sight of land that common sense which is a useful though grey component of my nature gradually reasserted itself. There were changes among us all. Mr Prettiman returned to his customary state of excitement and anger. It rendered him more amusing than awesome. The emigrants, too, were a source of amusement to me. They appeared to think that we should steer straight for the nearest bit of land and disembark there! The rigid system of separation which had once obtained in our vessel had been so moderated by time and adventure that I could now walk among them without comment. They thought that one might walk round the coast to Sydney Cove, the weaker members riding in the wagons with which the aboriginals would provide them! Here, they thought, was a land of freedom, where crops and flocks grew themselves, black men and women were eager to learn and serve and every white man was a little king with a gang of chastened convicts to keep the blacks in order!

Winter had worn its worst away when we sighted the north point of Flinders Island and altered course to move up the east coast! We were held up by contrary winds for a while between there and Cape Howe. But we were cheered, I think, by moving among names which were familiar so that the bald points seemed to cry us a welcome in our own tongue. Despite all the increase to my reading and thinking which I got from the Prettimans, I cannot but be a patriot! I have been brought to see—and not only by them—the defects of England. I will not subscribe to the furious rubbish of "My country right or wrong!" But nevertheless, when I search my heart, among all the prejudices of my nature and upbringing, among all the new ideas, the acceptance of necessary change, the people, writers and artists, philosophers and politicians—even the wild-eyed *social philosophers*—the deepest note of my heart-strings sounds now as it will to my dying day—"England for ever!" So seeing those bald lumps of land and hearing their names, King Island, Flinders Island, Cape Howe, I felt, even if I did not cry, "England for ever!"

(21)

From Cape Howe, I believe it was, we had what Cumbershum irritated Oldmeadow by describing as a "soldier's
wind", meaning one so conveniently on the beam that even
a soldier could take the ship there and back. Oldmeadow
replied with some nonsense about "a sailor on a horse"
but by now I was bored to distraction by their service dislikes and rivalries. Oh, the restlessness in that ship! The
ladies! I have the word of both Mrs Prettiman and Mrs
Brocklebank that they were *dying to get their stuff out of the
hold and have everything clean*! Even the cleanest of us were
dirty, I believe. After all, it was now months since we had
been able to use anything better for washing than saltwater
soap! I had in fact wondered whether or no I should entitle
my three volumes nothing less than *Saltwater Soap* but
alas—owing to the pusillanimity of English book publish-
ers, the occasion has not arisen. So we came at last to
Sydney Cove and our little world burst wide open. We
were brought alongside the new quay and the ship was
invaded, for the articles we had brought in our hold were
long awaited. No one took much notice of the few passengers. Iron railings were of more account. Anderson left the
conduct of the ship to Mr Summers and hurried ashore
with Mr Benét (the *image* of a flag lieutenant).

I did not chuse to go with them, for it appeared that
the governor, Mr Macquarie, was absent, visiting an island
even more drearily penal than the Cove. Some of our passengers fought their way ashore through the agents, porters,
bales, boxes and noise. Miss Zenobia Brocklebank was carried on a stretcher, hustled on every side and with only the
tip of her nose showing. Mr Brocklebank stopped by me.

"Goodbye, Mr Talbot. I hear you propose to publish an unillustrated account of the voyage. I advise against it. Nothing you can ever write can match the success of your medical practice."

"I beg your pardon?"

"Have you not half cured our good friend Mr Prettiman? In fact, sir, I believe you should abandon the Muse for Aesculapius! Good day to you."

"Mrs Prettiman—Mrs Prettiman! I will not say goodbye but *au revoir*! Surely we shall meet again!"

I could not hear what she said for the noise, nor get near her because of the mob on deck and the opened hold. It was a distracted parting. Mr Prettiman was half sitting up on the stretcher and peering at the quay. Two or three men detached themselves from a crowd and pressed aboard. He was expected! He was borne off without a backward glance and Mrs Prettiman followed him docilely. I was about to run after her but the stretcher of the senile midshipman Martin Davies got in my way. The Pikes followed with the Easts in attendance, as if they were their servants! Mrs Brocklebank came running back—had she left her yellow shawl—oh no, she had been wearing it all the time—how silly! But she came very close to me and declared that she had quite forgotten what happened when we so nearly missed the ice—I could not tell what she meant then and cannot now.

"Farewell, dear Mr Talbot. Believe me, our secret is safe with me!"

Charles came up from the fo'castle.

"Edmund. You have not gone. I thought we had said farewell in the middle. This is insupportable."

"What sort of man do you suppose the governor is?"

"This gentleman seems to have business with you. God bless you!"

The gentleman had indeed. It was Markham, one of the

entourage! He welcom'd me, took me straight off to, as he said, "wet my whistle". The phrase was a mixture of the *knowing* and the *common* which I found fairly representative of the junior members at the Residency. An English inn does not transplant well, but I have to acknowledge that the settlers had done what they could. I was startled to find that a general air of piety was required in the governor's presence. However, Markham said we were "safe for the time being", though the governor's deputy was only marginally less pious than the governor himself.

"Captain Phillip is a naval man?"

"Oh, indeed. He and your captain will be discussing the fate of that old hulk of yours—not hard to settle, I should judge by the look of her!"

"We lost our topmasts and had the devil and all to do."

"You ain't a naval man, by any chance?"

"God forbid. Our captain does not carouse."

"Neither does Phillip. 'Goodbye, Mr Markham. I shall see you tomorrow at divine service.' "

"Good God!"

"It's tolerable here when you get used to it. The flies are the devil. Good riding and shooting. By the by, there's a pack of letters for you at the Residency."

"Letters!"

"Came in the bag."

"I must go."

"Hey, wait a minute! You have to report to Phillip, you know!"

The upshot was that we went back to the ship, the state of which was indescribable, for already they were unloading from her as much of her stores as were immediately required on shore. I changed into reasonable clothes.

My interview with Captain Phillip was not long. He accepted my credentials without comment, hoped I would be happy in what he was pleased to call "the family", hoped my godfather was well, then asked in a voice little above a whisper for a paper on Mr Prettiman. I had to reply that I had not committed anything to paper. The man was now a cripple and married. I was convinced that he represented no danger to the state. Phillip looked up at me under his brows but said nothing.

"Sir—there is another matter!"

"Yes?"

"The ship, sir. What will happen to her?"

"I am told she cannot go to sea again. She will become our guardship. The additional space for offices is very welcome."

"And her officers?"

"That scarcely concerns you, Mr Talbot."

"With respect, sir—"

"Mr Talbot, I make every allowance for the conduct of a young man in what amounts to the first few moments of an entirely new situation to any he has known hitherto, but you are a very junior officer and must be made aware of that fact at once!"

"I am aware of it, sir, and only the very deepest feelings of my heart could impel me to speak at such a moment. But, sir, as a naval officer you must have known many voyages, many commissions—must know how close friendships may become and how—passionately involved one may find oneself with the affairs and the future of a, a shipmate!"

The deputy governor regarded me for a moment or two in silence. Then his lips twitched into a smile.

"That is all true. I remember—but that is not to the purpose. Well. Captain Anderson is aware that continued command of a permanently moored guardship in this harbour is not possible for a post captain. He will return to England. Lieutenant Benét—a most unusual young man— goes with him."

"I was not thinking of the captain or Lieutenant Benét, sir."

Captain Phillip leaned back in his chair and regarded me solemnly.

"You interest me, Mr Talbot. Proceed."

"I was hoping to find, sir, that you would use your vast experience of things naval to reach down and promote a man who is not only my friend and a fine seaman but what is more a convinced and devout Christian!"

Captain Phillip leafed through the papers I had presented to him. Again the smile dawned round his lips.

"You not only interest me, Mr Talbot. You surprise me."

"Thank you, sir!"

"I offered command of the ship to Lieutenant Benét. But as I expected, after five minutes with him, he declined it. I hope the Navy does not lose him. He, with an address which seems natural to him but might be though impertinent in another youngster, pressed the claims of Lieutenant Summers."

"Good—Heavens!"

Captain Phillip smiled broadly.

"Captain Anderson had already done so. He said with emphasis that Lieutenant Summers was admirably suited to the charge of the ship."

"So Lieutenant Summers will be a captain!"

"Who said so?"

"I thought—"

"On the other hand, it is possible, of course. His duties would include King's Harbour Master with the emoluments from that position, for we have lost the one we had."

"I am sure emoluments are the last thing in Mr Summers's mind. He desires only to serve his God and his King."

"He said so, perhaps."

"Indeed. It was an injunction laid on him at the start of his career by Admiral Gambier in person and it has been his guiding star."

"Gambier is a good man. A pious man."

"It was my hope, sir, that my first letter to my godfather might contain a description of my joy at being able to represent to Governor Phillip the propriety of promoting a man of strict Christian principles—"

" 'Governor Phillip.' Yes. Well. Who knows? So you want Summers made a captain, eh? You know of course that Governor Macquarie will have to confirm? And then the promotion will have to be confirmed from Home? However, Yes. I'll do it."

"Thank you, Governor, a thousand times!"

"You'd better get him here as soon as possible. And now about your affairs, my boy. We won't work you too hard for a while. Take a week or two to settle in. Look round you. When you write to your godfather you might include—no. One doesn't want to seem to be—"

"It will give me great satisfaction to mention your kindness, Governor. I hardly like to ask—but would it be possible—could I take the good news to Captain Summers myself?"

"Handsomely, lad! I haven't even signed an acting commission! Good Heavens, we cannot go about a serious matter like promotion in such a scimble-scamble fashion!"

"I beg pardon, sir."

"No, no. By the by—isn't your mother a FitzHenry?"

"Yes, sir. My father—"

"We have the forms here, you know, printed quite in the modern manner. After all, it is only 'acting'. It isn't as if His Royal Highness's signature was required—*that* must wait to come out from England if it ever does."

"Yes, sir. A little more delayed, I suppose, in peacetime."

"Charles Summers, lieutenant—any middle name? No—of the ship—being—to acting—signed—deputy governor."

"I can't thank you enough, Governor!"

He was regarding me curiously.

"Anything for yourself?"

"For me? I—could I take the commission to him?"

The deputy governor looked a little startled. But then he burst into hearty laughter.

"It has indeed been a long voyage! Oh, I should not say that—but Benét and Summers, Cumbershum, is it? And Anderson—now you—I tell you what, my boy. That is—that must have been far and away the happiest ship in the service!"

"Do you have communication with India, Governor?"

"The Bag, of course. Anything you want sent, let Markham know. He oversees it."

"Thank you, Governor."

"And, Talbot—the entourage is expected to set a good example, you know."

"Yes, Governor."

"I'll see you at matins."

He lifted himself an inch or two off the seat and gestured in the direction of the door. It was all much unlike the rosy anticipations with which I had set off from England. But in my delight with the paper I held in my hand I could not be sorry. I went with winged feet towards the ship, a Glaucus with a gift of gold or bronze—and there was Charles, standing at the forrard rail of the quarterdeck. Two carts full of luggage were bumping away along the cobbles and Anderson and Benét were strolling by them! They had lost no time.

But the ship was in a turmoil. All the hatches had been broken up. Booms were swaying up burdens of every sort, casks were being rolled, bales piled, dust rising—

"Charles! Charles!"

I jumped the gap between the quay and the ship. Later, when I saw how wide it was, I took myself to task for attempting anything so silly.

"Here!"

He glanced at the paper, then back at the work in progress.

"Not now, Edmund! If I take my eye off the unloading there'll be a fight, before you blink!"

"Read it, man! You must read it!"

He glanced at the form, then back at the work in hand; then swung round and faced the paper squarely. He seemed prepared to look at it endlessly, his mouth open and his eyes anxious. I unrolled the paper and held it so he could read. The colour drained from his face, he put out a hand and sat down heavily. So that was my golden armour!

I found, when Charles had recovered and we were sitting by a bare cot in the captain's deserted quarters, that a junior captain's status is signified by one epaulette worn on the right shoulder. The dear old fellow was very bashful in his confession but finally told me that he did in fact have a single epaulette stored away—stowed away—which I thought a quite extraordinary and touching indication of what *had* been a modest yet hopeful character! He was changed by the voyage, as we all were, and I could only hope that time would restore to him the simplicity and amiability which had once been so evident in him. I begged him to come ashore but he would not.

"Before you know it they would be playing pranks or truant. The men would get careless and then somebody would have a bale dropped on him. There is more in this unloading than you dream of. I can only be thankful the voyage was so lengthened that we have no strong drink left in her."

I wondered for a moment whether to tell him that Benét and Anderson had both recommended him for his present position but dismissed the idea at once. Instead, I bullied him until he consented to put on his single epaulette for me. As far as I was concerned it was an anti-climax. The wretched ornament had been so long in store it was permanently crumpled and the gilting turned to something suspiciously like brass. It looked as if a large bird, an eagle or a vulture, had muted from a mast on his shoulder.

"I am most impressed, Charles! I may still call you

"It is ____ing from my lips now and then?"

"Well—let us c__

"No. I will see the governor here."

He fell silent and I wondered if the requirement of his religion had come before him. But then I saw that he was stroking the bare wood of the side of the bunk—the way, I thought suddenly, a man or woman might stroke the side of their onetime bridal bed! He stood up, went to the bulkhead and stroked it—stood by the great stern window and rubbed the mist of his breath from the glass—

"What is it?"

He came back, sat down by me on the bunk again.

"You will not understand me, Edmund. That time after I was made a midshipman and got my hands on a sextant. Then later when the board called me before them and told me I had passed for lieutenant—and now! Captain? Yes—but I have a ship, my ship!"

"Oh, come. You will do better than this! Captain!"

"You would not understand."

I left him at last, to take up residence in the spare bed-room which Markham had kindly loaned me. I went, with a sense I could not at first define, of disappointment. I did finally track it down to Charles's delight with a moored and superannuated vessel!

725

Markham had not returned from some assignation. I thought then that my sense of greyness and disinclination for anything but sleep was from short commons and nothing to drink. I went therefore to the only inn in the vicinity which looked respectable—and felt lonely. Then I remembered the letters—paid my shot and hurried to the Residency. My letters were in a tied bundle on Markham's desk. I sat there and opened one which I recognized by the straggling direction as from my father. In his usual rejoiced and indeed ungrammatical hand he told m... preamble that my godfather was de... and died of the at the fall of the Corsican Tyrrell in ruins round my feet. consequent apoplexy. My...

That was the b...ing of a strange time for me. I was given no work and was supposed to be "familiarizing" myself with the situation. In fact I was avoiding it and came slowly to recognize that I was missing *my friends!* Those friends, I now saw, were the people with whom I had passed the best part of a year and whom I knew as well if not better than I knew my own family! Oldmeadow, Brocklebank, Mrs East, Mrs Pike, Pike, Bowles, Smiles, Tommy Taylor, Prettiman, dear Mrs Prettiman—before I knew what I was doing I found myself moving in pursuit of them! But they had vanished! My friends had vanished! Charles was in the course of vanishing in his new obsession with that hulk!

The next morning I went to the Residency and tried to find out what had happened to them all. Prettiman was not in hospital, but they had taken rooms, it was thought. Oldmeadow had marched his men up river in pursuance of orders. It was not clear what had happened to the Brocklebanks—

And so on. Charles came to the Residency, epaulette and all, and was closeted with Captain Phillip for a time. He came out, burning with enthusiasm for the job of improving the buoyage system in the harbour! I walked back with him to the ship as if I had never left her, but once there found he was happily preoccupied with Mr Cumbershum in the business of ridding the ship of her guns and at the same time ensuring that the balance was kept as even as the eye could measure it. I wandered round, therefore, a revisiting ghost. I found my first cabin and my second cabin with the marks of suicide driven into the deckhead. I walked on the poop where I had dared those monstrous walls of black flint at the tail end of the tempest. My hand on the rail felt a roughness in the palm and I looked down. My hand had lain on the very place where Deverel's sword had nigh on cut the rail through!

There was a lump in my throat as if the memory had been happy. I could not understand what was happening. I stood with Charles and Cumbershum and they spoke of whips and timber-hitches, differed in some arcane detail of ropework, until Cumbershum stumped away muttering "Different ships, different long splices". Even then Charles seemed far away and regarding me as a speck on the horizon while he had himself his eye on a business of the utmost importance—though it was but the working of the decayed vessel alongside a sheerhulk where all her rigging but the stump of the mainmast was to be lifted out of her!

I found the Prettimans. Mr Prettiman was being fitted with a kind of harness or strapping which would enable him to walk with crutches and perhaps in time hobble on two sticks. Mrs Prettiman was already busy with papers and arrangements for meetings. She consented to give me half an hour. When I tried to describe my state she laid down her pen, put off her pince-nez and lectured me.

"You need employment, Mr Talbot. No. You cannot help here. In fact, you should not be here at all. It will do you no good up at the Residency. The voyage has been a considerable part of your whole life, sir. Do not refine upon its nature. As I told you, it was not an Odyssey. It is no type, emblem, metaphor of the human condition. It is, or rather it *was*, what it was. A series of events."

"I think there has been death in my hands."

"Stuff and nonsense. Goodbye, Mr Talbot. For your own good—do not come here again."

That was on the eve of the King's Birthday. I was still in a state bordering on the morbid. Mr Macquarie had not yet returned from his island; Markham and Roberts, the other two secretaries then resident, were kind but distant. The news of my godfather's death had reached them and Captain Phillip too.

Charles had our old ship towed out to the sheerhulk and moored alongside her. As far as I could see, he never moved out of her but was visible occasionally through the telescope which stood on the veranda of the Residency, his epaulette flashing in the eternal sun.

The King's Birthday intensified my loneliness if anything. There was a great dinner given by the deputy governor to those he thought deserved it, and this included, I am told, a number of discharged convicts, some of them wealthy. It began in the late morning and continued into the dusk. Captain Phillip had had some idea of controlling the number of healths drunk but he was unsuccessful. In fact, I believe that Edmund Talbot was the soberest man in Sydney Cove! I grieved for my friends the Prettimans, not really knowing which of the two meant the more to me—I grieved anew for Miss Chumley, that bright and unattainable star in the distant north—I grieved for Charles, who wore my golden armour and was so sure of my affection that he ignored me. Indeed, the fireworks had begun and the still waters of the cove redoubled them when I left that riotous company and went to stand by myself on the veranda, where I could stare at the sea and sky until they numbed me.

A little breeze brushed a shadow across the water. The myriad vessels—merchant, fishing, whaling, company or war—turned slowly to hang all one way on a single anchor. Our old hulk and the sheerhulk and the powder barge on the other side of her turned with them. There were red and blue and yellow stars over the water and the excited cry of children from beyond the hedges of the Residency garden.

I brooded on the disaster that had befallen me. Like Summers in the early years I should now have to *work my passage*. I should not be able to pass on a mention of the governor to my godfather, should not be able to press in high places for Charles's temporary promotion to be made permanent. No, indeed. It was no Odyssey, no paradigm, metaphor, analogue—it was the ridiculous sorrows of Edmund Talbot, whom life no longer spoiled as if he were its favoured child.

I went to the telescope and looked at the sheerhulk. Our—I have written our!—the foremast and mizzenmast of Charles's command lay on the sheerhulk's deck. All that remained standing of the mainmast was the lower portion as far as the fighting top. I found myself looking into the dark entry to the lobby and half expected to see Mr Brocklebank emerge with his so-called wife huddled next to him under the dirty coach cloak. But all was emptiness.

There was something strange about the forrard part of the vessel, something odd about the bows. The huge anchor hung motionlessly suspended above the water— fairly by the hawse, did not seamen call it?—so as to be let go at a moment's notice, the crown so near the surface I could see a reversed anchor hanging below the real one.

What was odd?

It was as if a mist was forming round her bows, rising, so faint a mist that only a man who had been examining the whole ship for so long—there was an acrid odour in my nostrils. It was the fireworks, of course, sheaves of them now ascending above the darkling water. The land breeze was beginning and the upside-down anchor had vanished.

Charles appeared on the quarterdeck—came stumbling out of the entry to the captain's quarters! He leapt down the ladders, ran full tilt along the deck and vanished into the fo'castle. Behind him, a column of mist rose through the hole in the deck where the foremast had been. Charles appeared on deck again. He rushed to the mainmast, worked at it, then came away with a great axe in his hands. He ran up to the fo'castle and began to hew at the ropes which held the hulls together. He raced aft through smoke which was beginning to rise now from the whole length of the ship, was on the quarterdeck striking out again! There was a gap of water—a yard, no more—between the two hulks—all along the side of the sheerhulk which had the powder barge nestling next to it! Suddenly the hole in the deck, where the foremast had been, turned red. A single flame stood up through the hole into the open air. Charles came racing back. He sprang to the belfry, beat the bell into a furious jangling. Slowly the burning ship, smoke billowing up from her everywhere, moved out under the impulsion of the breeze into the roadstead with its swarm of anchored craft. Still the bell, and again the bell! I turned the telescope on the nearest merchantman and saw men gathering in the fo'castle round the anchor cable. Beyond her a small schooner began to haul up her staysail—farther out, still another let her squaresail drop and swell on the topmast as she made a sternboard out of the path of the dreadful vessel. Charles dived into the fo'castle but came staggering out almost at once. He raced the

length of the deck, dived into the lobby and disappeared.
The entry to the lobby vibrated with a dim but furious
light. Over the harbour, but now no higher than a rising
column of smoke, the rockets banged and crackled.

Quite suddenly I understood that Charles was in deadly
danger! I did not know if he could swim, but most sailors
cannot. Without thinking I began to run, down through the
gardens, over cobbles, through an alley and came out pant-
ing between the godowns on this side of the quay. I ran in a
panic to the landing place where a gaggle of dinghies and
ships' boats lay to their painters, climbed down—saw one
had oars, cast off the painter, leapt in and set myself to row.
I am no oarsman and was unhandy. Nevertheless I kept on,
for all that the burning vessel seemed hopelessly beyond
my reach; and then it was apparent that I could catch her,
for she slewed to starboard and stopped, the tide running
past her as she lay, slightly canted and aground. Wherever
the ports had been open the smoke poured out of her sides,
and despite the smoke I could see how she glowed below
decks. I ran the dinghy hard against her, close by the aftermost of Charles's frapping—a huge cable that ran up her
side and vanished onto the deck. I clambered up her tumblehome, got myself over the bulwarks and fell on the deck
coughing out curses and smoke.

"Charles!"

He had gone into the lobby. I tore off my neckcloth and
bound it over my mouth and nose, then dived into the
smoke.

"Charles!"

One foot stepped on nothing and I fell—it was the hole
where the mizzenmast had been—and I was hanging half
over it. I got up and could not tell where the ladder was. I
found myself holding a rail, then a door handle. It was the
cabins. I felt along them, seemingly for ever. I could not
remember clearly why I had got out in the middle of the

night—and then thought, of course, that it was to stand the middle as usual.

"Charles! Midshipman Talbot—"

He was nowhere, it seemed. I pawed at doors and rails: and then my feet perhaps having a better memory than my head, I found myself at the entry to the waist; and after that my feet took me up the ladder to the quarterdeck where the watch was changing.

"Talbot!"

Charles was nowhere to be seen. My head cleared a little and I remembered how he had dived into the fo'castle. It was possible—I ran down the ladders.

"Talbot, you fool!"

There was a fearful explosion almost under my feet and the frapping burst, went flying in the air, and at once there were two other explosions, one after the other. I saw the deck split open from my feet right to the fo'castle itself. The whole ship opened and sent up a tower of bright flame in the midst of which what was left of the mainmast fell thunderously. A mighty tide of sparks rushed up to overtake the fire which hung above us.

"Jump, you silly bugger!"

My hair went in a burst of flame. I turned to climb the stairs but they had gone. I went to the bulwarks but they were on fire.

"The larboard side, for Christ's sake!"

That was downhill. There was enough left of the deck round the wheel for me to cross. It did not seem to matter. But my face was hurting and my hands. I reached a stretch of bulwark where there was no fire. I looked over into cool water which even the reflections of the burning world could not heat. I let myself fall into it.

Cumbershum got me by the collar, for I could not help myself. Somehow they lifted me into the boat; and it was there that I began to feel my pain; and until they got me to the hospital I had much ado to stop myself crying out. They stripped me and bound me with lamb's-wool and poured the sickly laudanum into my mouth.

I will not detail my sufferings. Did they pay for anything? I think not. But there came a time when my body was well enough to let me understand the situation. My godfather was dead. Charles was dead. All those people were gone from me as surely as if they had stayed and been consumed in the burning ship.

No trace of Charles was ever found. At low water the wreck had disintegrated and displayed her bowels for all to examine who would. He was gone. A service of remembrance was held and Charles praised as a devoted servant among those who have no memorial but have vanished away as though they had never been. I was praised far more than I deserved, but I knew grief feelingly. I dreamed of him and them and the dead ship. I woke with tears on my face to endure yet another day of harsh, intolerable sunlight. It was in the driest and emptiest of interior illuminations that I saw myself at last for what I was, and what were my scanty resources. I got up, as it were, and stood erect on naked feet. The future was hard and full. Nevertheless I girded myself and walked towards it. But I firmly believed that whatever might happen to me in the future, this was the unhappiest period of my life.

(22)

Truth, being stranger than fiction, is naturally less credible. An honest biographer, if such there be, will always reach a point where he would be happier if he could tone down the crude colours of a real life into the delicate tints of romance and legend! Such was my reflection only the other day when I reread some of the bald account which I have rendered of our antarctic adventures.

I have always been embarrassed for such authors as Fielding and Smollett, to say nothing of the moderns, Miss Austen, for example, who feel that despite all the evidence from the daily life around them, a story to be veridical should have a happy ending—or rather I *was* so embarrassed before my own life took a turn into regions of phantasy, of "faerie", of ridiculous happiness!

One day, still sorrowing, I was standing on the veranda of the Residency and wondering what interior power it is which keeps the majority of men from committing suicide, when a distant *thump* made me look up. A ship had come in through the heads, and as I saw her I jumped in good earnest, for our saluting gun answered from below the veranda with a bang and an immense cloud of white smoke. She was a warship, then. I went to our telescope and focused it on the stranger.

I believe even then something told me that a fairy story had begun! The ship was flying a signal—her number, I suppose—and other flags which might mean anything. Under her bowsprit there was a complicated glitter. I could make out a crown, a red centre surrounded by blue, and caught my breath as I saw it might well be what a dockyard would make of a crowned kingfisher, a blue bird, a halcyon, an *Alcyone*! I went quickly to the office and was very nearly hit by the wad from the next explosion of our answer to her salute. Daniels and Roberts were in the office and just abandoning the paper darts with which they had been conducting the affairs of the colony. Markham, coming through the other door, said it was His Majesty's Frigate *Alcyone* and now we should get some news we could believe instead of rumours from drunken merchant captains. I told myself that the most I could expect was a letter from Miss Chumley to answer the many I had sent to India by any ship going that way. But Sir Henry would have news of her. I remarked that I was acquainted with her captain and would stroll down. I went before anyone had the opportunity to offer me company and waited by the telescope until the small group that had gathered there had looked their fill. *Alcyone* was coming in quietly with all but her tops'ls clewed up, as was natural in such a crowded roadstead. But she was a warship and so we were signalling her into the new quay.

My turn came. I saw immediately Sir Henry Somerset on the quarterdeck and all aglitter in his full-dress uniform for a call on the governor. The reader may perhaps guess at the positive convulsion—no, I remember! My heart was all smashed as you might break an egg into a frying pan! What was my confused delight when I found myself gazing at the image of Miss Chumley! She stood by Lady Somerset on the quarterdeck, just *astern* of Sir Henry, who was busily issuing orders. The two ladies had their heads together, watching him, I think, and obediently silent as the ship turned in the channel. Now Sir Henry was examining the Residency with his telescope—we were eye to eye! He turned and said something laughingly to Miss Chumley. Now she was begging him for his telescope—a young officer was offering his own—he was holding it for her— she was making an adjustment—I took off my hat and waved—Miss Chumley abandoned the telescope and positively flung herself on Lady Helen's breast! They embraced, Miss Chumley stood away—seemed confused, distraught almost—she ran quickly to the companionway and disappeared! Suddenly I was aware of the unkempt appearance we were accustomed to present in the early morning—better than the positively *farouche* appearance of the generality of men in Sydney Cove but the difference was little—and hurried away to put myself straight. By the time I was shaved and dressed as I ought, *Alcyone* was tied up alongside. I raised my hat to Sir Henry, who was coming up the Residency steps as I went down them, but I believe he never noticed me. He was followed by a midshipman who carried a large *portefeuille*. Sir Henry was red in the face and puffing.

By the time I reached the quay, *Alcyone* had established her berth. Her after and forrard gangways were down, with sentries at them and quartermasters. Already she was taking in water and supplies. Despite the bustle on the quay, Lady Somerset was standing on it in a space which seemed sacred to her. Miss Chumley was not to be seen. As I approached Lady Somerset I took off my hat, but she instantly begged me to resume it. After India it was quite disconcerting to see a gentleman without his hat. I stammered a compliment on her appearance but she would have none of it.

"Mr Talbot, you have no idea the straits to which poor females are reduced in a frigate! But at least we did not suffer as this place appears to from flies—faugh!"

"One does not become accustomed to them. Lady Somerset, I beg you—"

"Now you are going to ask to see poor Marion."

"Poor Marion? Poor Marion?"

"She cannot abide the sea nor become habituated to it. She will even prefer the flies, I don't doubt."

"Lady Somerset—if you only knew how I have longed for this meeting!"

"I am a romantic at heart, Mr Talbot, but the care of a young female has gone some way towards curing me of what I begin to think an aberration. Your letters went far beyond what I proposed for you when I consented to a correspondence. Are you trifling, sir?"

"Lady Somerset!"

"Well, I suppose not. But a—what are you? Fourth secretary? And your godfather is dead, we hear."

"I fear so. Oh, it was so unfortunate!"

"For you, perhaps. Him too, we must believe. Though as far as the country is concerned—"

"She is coming!"

Indeed she was! Miss Chumley, in the time since we had been eye to eye through telescopes, had changed entirely! Where was the cloak of dull green which had hung from her shoulders? This radiant vision was dressed in white with a scarf of Indian gauze lying across her shoulders, then hanging from both arms. Her gloves buttoned to the elbows. A wide-brimmed straw hat was tied on lightly by another scarf which nestled under her chin. Her face glowed in the shelter of a rosy sunshade. Her other hand held a fan with which she attempted, not with entire success, to keep the flies away. I swept off my hat.

"Mr Talbot—your hair!"

"An accident, ma'am, a trifle."

"Marion dear, I believe we should invite Mr Talbot to come aboard, but tomorrow perhaps—"

"Oh, Helen! I beg of you! The land is unsteady but wonderful! It appears of such an extent, with trees and houses and things! Oh, Helen, they are English houses!"

"Well. You may stay for a while. I shall send Janet to you. Do not leave the quay. Mr Talbot will look after you."

"Indeed, ma'am, I ask nothing more than to be allowed——"

"And do not allow any of the natives, the aboriginals I believe they are called, to approach her."

"Of course not, ma'am."

"Nor convicts, naturally."

"No, ma'am. May I advise? We do not use that word here. They are 'government men'."

Lady Helen curtsied minutely, turned and went on board again. Miss Chumley and I continued to look at each other. She was smiling delightedly and shaking her head as if in disbelief and then fanning away flies—I suppose I was grinning like an idiot or laughing like one—behaving, in fact, very little as a secretary from the Residency should behave within ten yards of a surely amused audience! We spoke but as people in trances. By the magical properties of Mind so little understood, she and I could remember later what neither of us heard consciously at the time.

"Mr Talbot, you are quite, quite bronzed!"

"I apologize for it, Miss Chumley. It is not permanent."

"I fear I am weather-beaten."

"Oh, ma'am—an English rose! You have been in the rains, a monsoon or something."

"We have been at sea."

"Not all the time!"

"I did not know there was so much, Mr Talbot, that is the fact of the matter. One sees maps and globes but it is different!"

"It is indeed different!"

"Most of it you know, sir, is quite unnecessary."

"Quite, quite unnecessary! Away with it! There shall be no more sea! Let us have a modest strip between one country and another—a kind of canal——"

"The occasional ornamental lake in a prospect——"

"A fountain or two—"

"Oh yes! Fountains are of the utmost importance!"

It was at this moment, I believe, that we both became aware of the absurdity of our words and laughed, or rather giggled, at them. I began to reach out with my arms in a quite spontaneous gesture but I saw valuable Janet appear at the after gangway and dropped them again.

"Miss Chumley, we are both much put upon by the ocean—but surely you reached India?"

"Oh, yes. We were in Madras for a while and then Calcutta. But my cousin—after the death of poor Rosie Aylmer—all that talent, that goodness, her beauty—so tragic and so *frightening*, for she was little older than I am! My cousin thought me too *green* to last out the epidemic. Lady Somerset brought me away again and what must Sir Henry do but fall in with the admiral?"

"Kind fate has brought us together. I have maligned the universe!"

Miss Chumley laughed deliciously and—if I may so express it—more collectedly.

"The universe? Fate? Say rather that the Corsican Tyrant contrived our meeting! Well, it is no wonder, for many people and particularly the French have found it difficult to distinguish between him and Fate."

"Napoleon!"

"The wretched man has escaped from Elba and landed in France. We are at war again. The news came overland to the admiral in the Red Sea, so that when he met us off Cape Comorin he was able to order us here with *utmost despatch* and what is more, I suppose, we shall leave with the same desperate haste."

"I cannot endure it! You put me at once in the seventh heaven and in anguish!"

"Poor Mr Talbot! I believe any young person would do whatever—but I should not say such things!"

"Miss Chumley—oh, Miss Chumley—Miss Chumley!"

I became aware that Miss Oates, Lady Somerset's *valuable Janet*, was standing behind Miss Chumley. I took my hat off and bowed to her, she curtsied and we returned to our conversation but in less passionate tones.

"As you know, Mr Talbot, Lady Somerset has kindly taken me in charge."

"A precious responsibility that any—"

"There is a kind of agreement between us that I may not answer the question—that is—"

"Oh, Miss Chumley!"

"Young persons are generally thought to be too ignorant to be allowed to dispose of themselves in a proper direction and must have an elder to do it for them."

"I had thought her a devotee of Nature."

Miss Chumley fanned flies away from her face. Then, in a gesture which moved me inexpressibly, she leaned forward and fanned the flies away from mine.

"One should be a Shakespearean heroine, Mr Talbot, and take care always to be at Act Five. I mean the comedies, of course."

"Oh indeed! What have we to do with crookbacks and angry old men with wicked daughters?"

"Nothing, of course. But what was in my mind was that straightforward offering of the hand as if a young person were in fact a young man in disguise—"

"Miss Chumley! Like Juliet you would, I swear, teach the torches to burn bright! The air, the sun however bronzing—colour—forgive these tears—and flies—they are flies—tears, I mean, of joy!"

Impulsively I thrust out my hand. She allowed the fan to fall the length of its string from her wrist and laid her hand in mine, laughing.

"Dear Mr Talbot! You have quite swept me off my feet!"

At length—and how unwillingly!—I released her hand.

"Forgive me, Miss Chumley. I fear my nature is too ardent."

She flicked the fan back into her hand and busily cleared the flies from before me. In the space cleared momentarily her glowing face came near. Lady Somerset appeared beyond it. Miss Oates was nowhere to be seen. Miss Chumley turned quickly.

"Helen! Where is Janet?"

"She fled below when the sailors began to laugh. You should resume your hat, Mr Talbot."

"Sailors, ma'am? Laughing?"

"That went near to being *public*, Marion!"

"I am sorry for it, Helen. But as I told Mr Talbot he quite swept me off my feet, and what is a young person—"

"You should go below now."

"But, Helen—"

"Lady Somerset—"

"You shall see him tomorrow if we are still here—but on a lungeing rein, mind!"

She watched the girl out of sight.

"You have my sympathy, Mr Talbot, but nothing more. Your godfather's death will delay your rise to fame and fortune, I imagine."

"I have an allowance sufficient for a young man—too little I agree for any larger establishment. My father—"

"A junior secretary cannot marry even if he has private means. Until I came on deck—Mr Talbot, it was *too familiar*! Well. You are wholly eligible except in the article of fortune. I am vexed, Mr Talbot, caught between my care of a young female—"

"She is the most beautiful lady in the world!"

"A proper sentiment on your part, sir. She is also all wit, which will outlast beauty and is worth a lot more, though gentlemen can never be brought to think so. The remainder of her character, Mr Talbot, is compounded of determination and—until this episode I would have said—of common sense!"

"She was—we were—made for each other."

"In Calcutta she was besieged."

"I can believe it. Oh, God!"

"I am a romantic after all, it seems. You may see her tomorrow morning."

"I beg of you, ma'am, allow me to take her driving! Between now and sunset—"

"Tomorrow. Today we go to engage rooms in an hotel if there be one proper for us. Indeed the case is so desperate I believe we must make use of one even if it is not quite proper."

"Lady Somerset, I cannot believe you!"

Lady Somerset fixed me with a bold eye and spoke swooningly in her deep contralto.

"Since you expect to be a married man, Mr Talbot, you had better know the worst. Baths, sir, hot baths. It will be news to you, perhaps, but ladies require them just as much as you do!"

With that and the indication of a curtsey she returned to the ship. I hurried off and wrote a note requesting the privilege of driving Miss Chumley on the morrow. Back came an answer within an hour. Lady Somerset presented her compliments to Mr Talbot and consented to his driving Miss Chumley and *Miss Oates* on the morrow for an hour or two in the morning. Mr Talbot would be expected on the new quay by ten o'clock.

Lady Somerset may have expected a barouche. It was, however—and I was lucky to find it—an Indian buggy, with a rumble seat facing *aft* for Miss Oates and two seats facing *forrard*. This was brutal for poor Miss Oates—but love demands sacrifices from us all! I and the buggy were at the ship by a quarter to ten in the morning. It was already so hot that walking the horse was not merely unnecessary but inadvisable. I became once more an object of curiosity and—I think—amusement to the crew of the vessel.

Lady Somerset appeared first. She fanned disgustedly at the cloud of flies which surrounded both me and the horse.

"Good morning, Mr Talbot. That seat is dedicated to Miss Oates, I suppose. Your horse is small. At least he will not run away with you."

"The difficulty, ma'am, is to get him to move."

Lady Somerset signified her agreement. I had almost said "nodded"; but with her, the movement was as little of a nod as the bowed assent of Almighty Zeus.

"She will be here directly. You have no idea the number of times—ah! Here they come."

I cannot remember what I said or she said or they said—

(23)

And then?

I forgot so much these days, that is the trouble. Not that it matters, of course. None of these volumes is able to be published until we are all forgotten. In any case, journals tell so little. I leafed through these and found myself able to do no more than sample here and there. I shall not reread them. Letters too. Only the other day one reached me at the Foreign Office from—of all people—Lieutenant, or I should say Mr Oldmeadow. He has a grandson, of course, and wants this and that. He himself turned in his commission long ago and took up a land grant, then bought more. He is now lord, he swears, of a bigger estate than Cornwall! That, and the lanky boy with his strange way of speaking, had me dwelling on the glimpses I had of Australia. It was mostly a memory of the birds, green swarms of them, or white ones with a yellow crest. I suppose it all happened, the voyage too. Only the other day the Prime Minister himself said, "Talbot, you're becoming a deuced bore about that voyage of yours."

Oldmeadow's letter did afford me a glimpse of my friends the Prettimans. They came towards the interior by way of his estate. He gave a vivid picture of them—she leading in her trowsers astride a mettlesome steed, he just *astern* of her but riding side-saddle with his legs on the off-side as he had foreseen! A handful of immigrants and freed *government men* and one or two savages followed them.

Oldmeadow said—now what the devil did he say? Of course! He tried to persuade them that to go on was sheer insanity. But they rode off into the back of beyond, no matter what he could say to them. As he said in his letter, not a hair nor hide of any of them has been seen since. I hope they reached some sort of place. And then again, there was the letter years before that, from what's his name, Old Mr Brocklebank. He claimed to be prospering in his paint shop. Zenobia (his elder "daughter"!) had died only a month or two after leaving the ship. She had a message for me, he said. It was something like "Tell Edmund I am crossing the bridge." Devil take it, there were no bridges anywhere near Sydney in those days and our old tub wasn't a steamship!

But of course, I remember now. Miss Chumley appeared, followed by Miss Oates. I handed her up, Miss Oates fairly scuttled into the rumble seat. I do not know how she managed it. By the time I looked round she was seated and staring into the air, both hands gripping the handles on either side of her.

"Are you settled, Miss Oates? Miss Chumley?"

"I am very comfortable, sir. May I suggest?"

"Anything!"

"May we move away from the water? You know my aversion for the sea."

"Of course, ma'am. We shall drive inland."

We were off. I cannot say the drive was exhilarating as far as skill in driving is concerned. The small and sullen horse was perhaps more accustomed to funerals than to parties of pleasure. I did encourage him into a trot once, but it was not the "fast trot" and he soon gave up, clearly feeling that three passengers were more than enough. I thought so too, though for a different reason. Granted, however, that you are forced to be a threesome, Miss Oates was an ideal chaperon. I asked her if she was comfortable, Miss Chumley invited her to admire the extraordinary whiteness of a tree trunk and after that she might not have been with us at all!

"I divine that you are taking me to view a prospect, Mr Talbot. If I dare suggest—"

"Anything, of course!"

"Have you not a prospect of trees, woods, forests, fields at our disposal? An oak, now, or beech—"

"Our only proper road goes out to Paramatta. Our principal view or prospect is thought to be the harbour with its shipping. In the circumstances, I do understand your disinclination for it. What else? Our buildings, as you see, are not metropolitan. I might take you by way of the foundations of the new church past the place where services are sometimes held in the open air—"

Miss Chumley fanned the flies vigorously from before the small portion of her face which straw and gauze did not cover.

"I have had a great deal of religion, you know, sir," she said. "You can hardly conceive of the care which is lavished on the orphans of the clergy."

"You sound wistful, Miss Chumley. I suppose there was no chaplain in *Alcyone* nor no random parson such as we once had. I quite see that might be an additional hardship for a young lady."

"Yes. I suppose it was. Oh, what pretty birds!"

"We must go this way. There are savages down *there* and their appearance is not to be borne, the women in particular."

"It is a great thing that Helen has allowed you to take us off like this."

"It is a great compliment that Lady Somerset has confided you to my protection. No man ever had a more precious responsibility."

"Do not have too high an opinion of me!"

"It is impossible that I should—but why should I not?"

"Because, because it is my ambition never to—be a disappointment! I hope that was prettily said, but fear—"

"It was exquisite. It moves me to distraction—oh, Miss Chumley!"

"Janet—are you comfortable? You would not care to change places with me for a while?"

I mastered myself.

"Would you not care to sit by me here, Miss Oates?"

But it was plain that Miss Oates would not care to sit anywhere but where she was, facing backwards and petrified.

"Here is some country for you, Miss Chumley."

"Mr Talbot—those men! Are they—"

"Government men? Yes."

She spoke in a whisper.

"They are not restrained!"

"They will not harm us. As for restraining—to what end? That wild country, those blue distances, may extend for all we know for three thousand miles!"

"You are quite, quite sure?"

"I would not have brought you this way had I not been sure! Only the violent or hopelessly depraved ones are restrained. If they are really wicked, then they are sent off to an island and beaten too. I was beaten myself at school and thanked the master afterwards! It was the making of me, I believe. Of course, as the Greeks said, you know, 'Never too much.' Our country is very high-principled and we ought to be proud of the fact. These fellows have found this shore in no way fatal to them! Why, a few days ago, on the King's Birthday, I dined at the same table as a time-expired 'government man', a rich and successful one! Foreigners condemn us for what they call 'slavery'. This is not slavery, not the galleys, the dungeons, the gallows, the torture chamber! It is a civilized attempt at reformation and reclamation. Do not look to your left. There are some aboriginals in the bush."

Miss Oates squeaked. Miss Chumley spoke over her shoulder in a voice which I had not heard before.

"Do collect yourself, Janet! Mr Talbot assures me that the creatures will not harm us. But I am overcome with

the strangeness of things—the trees, the plants, the air—
Oh, what a butterfly! Look, look! And what flies!"

"One endures them, that is all, I am afraid."

"One should live in a city after all. This craze for Nature
must pass and society come to its senses!"

"Did you not have a great deal of Nature about in India,
Miss Chumley?"

"Calcutta is a city, of course. But we spent some days
ashore at Madras with the collector before proceeding to
Calcutta. Devoted as I am to dry land, I do not know that
the experience was valuable. There were so many directions in which the collector positively forbade us to go!"

"Because of the natives?"

"Oh no! They are harmless. He said he could not
permit us to approach a heathen temple—yet he himself,
I should have thought, was hardly a deeply religious man!
Have you ever seen an Hindoo temple, Mr Talbot?"

"I believe not. I have read about them though."

"I cannot see why buildings devoted to the practice of
another religion, or superstition, shall I call it, should be
out of bounds to a young person. In Salisbury, you know,
we have many buildings devoted to Nonconformity and
even a Quaker meeting house!"

It was too much for me.

"You are adorable!"

"I do not think I am, but am glad that you think so,
though you should not say so, I believe. In fact, I would
wish you to remain in that opinion for—I think our horse
is going to stop."

"This is agony, Miss Chumley—"

"Helen said we should take the collector's advice, though
I think myself that he meant it as an order! But then, Helen
is not at all intimidated by old gentlemen, you know!"

"Not even by beautiful young gentlemen like Lieutenant
Benét?"

Her answer was a peal of laughter.

"Oh, Mr Benét! He had such a *tendre* for Helen—the whole ship talked of nothing else!"

"And you, Miss Chumley—you?"

"We talked a great deal of French. I am always happy to talk French. Do you speak French, sir?"

"Not the way Mr Benét does."

"I think your ship saved his reason, for he was most unhappy at the end. He had begged for an *entretien*, a tête-à-tête—oh, I should not talk like this!"

"Please continue!"

"Janet, you are not to listen. Sir Henry was quite unreasonable. I was to stand outside the door *upwind*, because anyone who entered would naturally come that way. Mr Benét rushed through. He fell on his knees before her and seized her hand, all the time reciting his verses—then the ship rolled and there they were, positively *entangled*. Then, as luck would have it, Sir Henry, against all custom, did come in through the *downwind* door! It was like a play."

"And then?"

"He was so angry! Sir Henry, I mean! He was angry with me too. Can you understand that?"

"Perhaps. But I could never be angry with you myself."

"Even Mr Benét was angry with me for a while, though not long. I threatened to tell Lady Somerset that his name rendered him conscious even to blushing. Which is why he altered the—"

"I do not understand."

"It is complicated, is it not? You see, his father started the French Revolution but then had to flee from the guillotine, leaving their estates and everything—and took the new name in a kind of self-mockery, which is very French, I think."

"So *that*—is why our quarrel boiled over—why Mr Prettiman was—why Mrs Prettiman—she called me—"

"I suppose he will change his name back when the war is over."

I blurted it out.

"Miss Chumley—how old are you?"

Miss Oates squeaked again and Miss Chumley looked a little startled, as well she might.

"I am—I am seventeen, Mr Talbot. Nearly eighteen. You do not think that—"

"That what?"

We were looking at each other eye to eye. A positive tide of pink suffused what was visible of her face.

"You do not think me too young?"

"No, no. Time—"

"Come! I will not have you grieving!"

"I—"

"You are not to be sad, sir! Mr Benét will recover. Sir Henry is no longer angry with me. Does that satisfy you?"

"It does indeed. More than you can know."

Did I say so? Did she? Was she really as anxious, so innocent or ignorant, and was I ever so moved by her? It is the emotions of later life which are roused by these partial memories, memory of her extreme youth and beauty—and my youth too, lanky young fool with everything to learn and nothing to lose. We spoke something like that. I think we felt something like that.

"I believe, Mr Talbot, the episode is to be forgotten with no harm done. We shall treat it the way Mr Jesperson who instructed us in the Old Testament would sometimes tell us to go on. 'Young ladies, you need not examine verses 20 to 25 too closely and Chapter 7 is to be omitted altogether!'"

"It is sometimes advisable."

"India, you know, is not a biblical country. I am sure of that, because when we were in Calcutta I looked it up in

my cousin's copy of Cruden's *Compleat Concordance to
the Old and New Testament*. It goes straight from INDEED
to INDIGNATION, with nothing in between."

"A depressing thought!"

"I do not wish you to be sad!"

"Dear Miss Chumley, life is all sunshine and flowers.
Who cares if tomorrow the clouds come?"

"It is well enough for gentlemen to be bronzed, for they
are fortunate in not finding themselves hedged as we do.
But a young person—you see how high these gloves button
and I must hold a parasol every moment I am in the sun.
The brown natives of India—they sometimes look quite
elegant—the natives are positively awestrook like the angel
in *Comus* when they see an English lady! We must not be
bronzed, you know, or our influence for good among them
would quite disappear. My cousin says that by the end
of the century the whole of the Indian peninsula will be
Christian."

"All owing to the complexion of our English ladies."

"Now you are laughing at me!"

"Never!"

"Janet, you are not to listen. Mr Talbot, my little note
which I slipped into Lady Somerset's letter to you—you
discovered it?"

"I did indeed!"

"Believe me, the very moment it was sent off I would
have given anything to have it back, for I seemed then to
have presumed, to have made such a frank declaration—
you did not find it too—too—?"

"Oh, Miss Chumley! It kept me—restored me to sanity, I would say! I treasure the little paper and could
repeat the message to you word for word."

"You must not. But you did not find the words too—"

"They are sacred."

"Janet, you may unstop your ears now. Janet!"

I turned in the seat. Miss Oates had her bonnet pushed up and her hands pressed to her ears inside it. Her eyes stared back the way we had come. They were bolting like a hare's. An aboriginal was following us. He was stark naked and he carried a wicked-looking spear. I shouted at him repeatedly and at last he turned aside and vanished into the scrub. I do not think it was because I shouted. I think he had lost interest in us, as they do after a while.

"I believe we should turn here."

How the wretched horse pricked up his ears and trotted! He knew where he was going and went there for all I could do. He sketched out, as it were, the *mores* of his owner or the person accustomed to "drive" him. Who needs to stop by a particularly fine tree and then successively at two houses, a well and a boatyard? In the end, when my wrists were sore from unavailing persuasion, we came out to a slightly raised promontory with the harbour in full view. A wooden seat had been set there for weary travellers and I welcomed it, though an aboriginal stood by it, gazing out over the harbour as if he owned the place! The horse stopped by the seat. The native wandered off without a backward glance.

"My apologies for the wretched animal. Miss Oates, I will hitch him here and leave him in your charge."

Her answer was the expected squeak. I handed Miss Chumley down and led her along the verge, over the water. Presently I stopped and faced her.

"Miss Chumley—I have said that you and I have been the sport of Neptune as much as ever Ulysses was. The ordinary rules of behaviour cannot apply to us. The many letters I have written to you—"

"I treasure what I have received!"

All this conversation was breathless but in a strange way distracted. Something spoke which was not either of us.

"Miss Chumley—You must understand how instantly I knew my fate—how deeply I am attached to you? Tell me—what I cannot believe—that your affections are engaged elsewhere and I will retire to nurse a broken heart. But, oh, ma'am, if you should be free and disposed to receive my addresses not unkindly—in short, if you was to regard me in the light of more than a friend—"

Miss Chumley faced me with smiling lips and sparkling eyes.

"A young person, Mr Talbot, could not receive addresses more calculated to please her!"

"Oh, I could proclaim it to the whole world!"

"I promise you, Mr Talbot, the whole ship shall receive incontrovertible proof of our understanding before it leaves the harbour—Why, what is the matter?"

The tide was low. There, a mile or two away but clear as an etching in that diamond air, the black ribs of our poor old ship stood out of the water. I remember the impossibility of speaking about it to Miss Chumley. We stood there silent while the whole history of that voyage flooded me and started out under my eyelids so that I had to disguise the effort to wipe the water away as an attempt to rid myself of the eternal and infernal flies! For she knew nothing, none of the people, nothing of the terror, horror, savagery, devotion, boredom and mortality which yet seemed to cling round those distant baulks of timber.

"Miss Chumley—what happened to Lieutenant Deverel?"

"He left the ship and took service with a maharajah. He was made a colonel, though they did not call it that. He wears a turban and rides an elephant."

And then—

"Mr Talbot! That flag!"

I turned and looked to the right. Less than a mile away *Alcyone* lay alongside the quay.

"I very much fear, ma'am, it is the recall. The Blue Peter."

We turned and looked at each other.

I pass over the mutual declarations, the farewells and promises. They are able to be found in a thousand romances and why should I add to their number? In the end, of course, I had to take her—them—back to the ship. I hit the wretched beast harder, I imagine, than he had ever been hit before and was able with difficulty to prevent him running over the little cliff. At least he got us to the quay more quickly than we had left it. Miss Oates scurried to the gangway as if someone were chasing her. I handed Miss Chumley down. The ship's company was preparing for departure, there was no doubt about it. They showed considerable interest in us, there was no doubt about that either. I even heard the shouted order—"Eyes in the ship, curse you!" and the crack of a starter. But what was that to do with us? She turned to me with a smile.

"You have my word, sir, I will wait—if necessary for ever!"

"And I am yours for ever—there's my hand on it!"

Impulsively I thrust out my hand. Laughing now, she laid her hand in mine.

"Dear Mr Talbot! Once more you have quite swept me off my feet!"

Her glowing face came near. I snatched off my hat, and careless of propriety, and indifferent to the furtive glances of the seamen, seized her in a firm embrace. We kissed. I believe I have never, except when occasionally disguised by drink, made such a public exhibition of myself. It occurred to me even in that moment of delirium that the whole ship now knew exactly where we stood. Miss Chumley had done precisely what she knew had to be done.

Then the ship sailed, taking my heart with it.

* * *

My dear readers—for I am determined we shall have more than one descendant—may now imagine that they have the "fairy tale" to the end. They may suppose a steady rise in the ranks of the colonial administration—but no! The fairy tale was about to begin!

It was only the next day that Daniels remarked that the bag brought by *Alcyone* was a heavy one. He invited me to fetch my letters which were cluttering up his desk. I was too absorbed in my loss and my happiness to pay much attention. Letters from England at that time interested me but faintly. Indeed, it is a melancholy truth that letters commonly brought more bad news than good. It was therefore two days after *Alcyone* had left that I bothered to collect them. I read first a letter from my Lady Mother, who seemed, I thought, quite extraordinarily joyful for no detectable reason. Why was she "so comfortable"? Why did she refer to my dead godfather as a "dear, good man"? He had seldom merited such a description in public or private life! I turned to the letter from my father. My godfather's will had been read. He had left me nothing but had bought up the mortgages and left them to my Lady Mother! Though we could not be called wealthy or even rich, we were now in comfortable and what my father described as "suittable" circumstances!

More than this—dear readers, I beg you to suspend your disbelief as willingly as you can contrive—but concentrate rather on the well-known example of Mr Harrison, who was elected to Parliament without his knowledge and only discovered the pleasing intelligence when he chanced on an English news-sheet which was loaned him by a traveller in a Parisian brothel! By agreement one of the incumbents of my godfather's rotten borough had asked for the Chiltern Hundreds and I, Edmund FitzHenry Talbot, had been elected! Beat that, Goldsmith! Emulate me, Miss Austen, if you are able! The most striking expressions of astonishment are inadequate in the face of such a nearly unique experience! I read the joyful news over and over again—looked then at my mother's letter, which now made complete and indeed what I could only think of as "suittable" sense! My first impulse was to communicate the interesting facts to the Fair Object of my Passion! My second was to request an immediate interview with Mr Macquarie.

He was very understanding. I had scarcely told him the news and shown him the relevant portion of my father's letter when he besought me to regard him less as a governor than a friend.

What is there to add? Mr Macquarie pointed out the difficulties in the way of providing me with immediate transport. As soon as a ship should be available, of course— meanwhile, he thought that in view of this signal display of Divine Providence we should give thanks together. I humoured him. Indeed, good fortune and happiness seem to me much more compelling towards the Great Truths of the Christian Religion than their dreary opposites! Mr Macquarie, when we had risen from our knees, asked me humbly enough whether I would chuse to regard myself as entirely outside the ranks of government ("We are a happy family, Mr Talbot") or whether in the interim I would, as it were, loan the Colony my talents? I put myself at his disposal at once. He had, he said, many reasons for wishing a closer *liaison* with the government at home. He thought I would be interested to view what he had accomplished in the short time which had been available to him. Such knowledge would be of inestimable value to one of our legislators!

My letter to Miss Chumley grew to immense length. The sloop *Henrietta* put in but needed much attention to her rigging. There now occurred exasperating delays which were no one's fault in particular but endemic to the naval service in time of war. I transferred my gear to another ship, which incontinently left without me but with my gear and letter. *Henrietta*—but why should I elaborate? I followed hard on my letter but was delayed at Madras, which proved to be a fortunate circumstance since it gives me an opportunity of allowing the reader a glimpse of Miss Chumley's epistolary genius. I had, of course, in my own letter proposed matrimony formally. The words in which the Dear Object of my Passion consented to make me the happiest of men must be forever sacred to me. However, she consents to my copying some of the rest of that letter here.

The climate continues oppressive. Oh, for an English day! Well, I am busy counting my blessings, of which the greatest—but I shall not flatter you, for that would be the worst of beginnings, would it not? Let me turn rather to the "Draft of my Maiden Speech", which you was kind enough to include and invite me to criticize. Dear Mr Talbot, I found it truly admirable! When you declare "I accept election by the route of what has been called a 'Rotten Borough' solely that I may devote myself to the reform of an insane and unfair system!" my very heart cried out—*This was noble!* By the way, who is Mrs Prettiman?

Will you think me too oncoming if I refer to our proposed journey home together? My cousin (you know he is in the Church) has some reservations on the subject and I enclose a letter to you from him. I do so agree with you that we should attempt on the way to visit the great Centres of Civilization. The Pyramids! What excitement among all the others! But should we not get you to your important Parliamentary Duties as quickly as possible??

The Holy Land—you know of course how the Hallowed Places must shine in the heart of any young person! But I have always found it difficult to love the Israelites as I should! There! I have confessed it! I am sure they were a most estimable people, for they lived on manna, did they not, and a wholly vegetable diet is so lowering as to render a person young or old incapable of energetic wrong-doing. But when their diet changed—all that smiting hip and thigh, whatever that means—I am sure it is very violent! Of course, I would not dare to criticize the Great Founder of our Religion and do not mean to: but following that Sacred Career in the very Footsteps of the Master would be too painfully affecting for a young person to contemplate. In short, sir, may we not, as Mr Jesperson would say, "omit the Holy Land altogether"? But naturally I shall in all things be guided by you and my only wish is to stand by you in what you call "this momentous translation from Fourth Secretary to a Member of the most powerful Body of Legislators in the world"!

My readers may imagine with what joy I read and reread this tender missive! I turned at last to the letter from Miss Chumley's cousin. It was no lessened joy to find that he was a churchman indeed, for he was a bishop and signed himself "Calcutta +".

What more is there to say? So must end this account of Edmund Talbot's journey to the ends of the earth and his attempt to learn Tarpaulin! Yet I divine in my unborn readers an unease. Something is missing, is there not? The bishop could not consent to our journeying from India to England while still unmarried. It would be an extremely bad example set in a part of the world only too open to licence of every kind! He himself very cordially offered to perform the ceremony! So, my dear readers may rest contentedly assured: there did come a day when I leapt ashore in India from a pinnace. A "young person" under a rosy parasol stood, as it might be, twenty yards away. Valuable Janet was behind her and a group of dark servants. Above the rosy parasol a greater was held and spread. But she took no heed of the sun when she saw me. I swept off my hat—she broke into a run—and your great-great-great-great-great-grandmother fairly sprang into my arms!

(24)

After I read Oldmeadow's letter I went for a walk, remembering all those old acquaintances—enemies who in retrospect now seem to be friends. They came up one by one, some I had forgotten entirely—Jacobs, Manley, yes, Howell. I seemed to touch them all with my mind, one by one, Bowles, Celia Brocklebank, Zenobia, little Pike, Wheeler, Bates, Colley—and so on, from Captain Anderson down. It was a curious exercise. I found that I could remember them without much emotion—even Lieutenant Summers. Even Mr and Mrs Prettiman. That night I had a kind of dream. I hope it was a dream, for dreams in any event are mysterious enough. I do not mean their content but the very fact of them. I do not wish it to have been more than a dream: because if it was, then I have to start all over again in a universe quite unlike the one which is my sanity and security. This dream was me seeing them as it were from ground level, and I was seeing them from ground level because I was quite comfortably buried in the earth of Australia, all except my head. They rode past me a few yards away. They were laughing and chattering in a high excitement, the men and women following them with faces glowing as in a successful hunt for treasure. They were high on horses—she leading, astride with a wide hat, and he following, side-saddle, since his right leg was useless. You would have thought from the excitement and the honey light, from the crowd that followed them, from the laughter and, yes, the singing, you would have thought they were going to some great festival of joy, though where in the desert around them it might be found there was no telling. They were so happy! They were so excited!

I woke from my dream and wiped my face and stopped trembling and presently worked out that we could not all do that sort of thing. The world must be served, must it not? Only it did cross my mind before I had properly dealt with myself that she had said, or he had said, that I could come too, although I never countenanced the idea. Still, there it is.